BY THE

AUTHOR OF A FOOL'S ERRAND

Bricks Without Straw

A Novel

ALBION W. TOURGÉE

Edited with a New Introduction by Carolyn L. Karcher

DUKE UNIVERSITY PRESS

Durham & London 2009

Printed in the United States of America on acid-free paper ∞
Designed by Jennifer Hill
Typeset in Adobe Caslon by Keystone Typesetting, Inc.

Library of Congress Cataloging-in-Publication data appear
on the last printed page of this book.

Bricks Without Straw was originally published by
Fords, Howard, and Hulbert in 1880
and copyrighted by Albion W. Tourgée.

To

OTTO H. OLSEN,

who did so much to restore Tourgée's legacy,

and to

MY STUDENTS AT TEMPLE UNIVERSITY,

whose enthusiasm for *Bricks Without Straw* inspired me to

bring it back into print

CONTENTS

ACKNOWLEDGMENTS

IT GIVES ME ENORMOUS PLEASURE to thank everyone who has helped make this edition possible. My greatest debt, as always, is to my husband Martin, who has accompanied me throughout the intellectual odyssey of rediscovering Tourgée. H. Bruce Franklin not only introduced me to *Bricks Without Straw* and urged me many years ago to try teaching it, but supported this project at every stage, from the drafting of the proposal to the completion of the introduction. My students at Temple University, especially Hank Dallman, whose articulate letter I sent to publishers, deserve much of the credit for convincing two presses that the novel would find a ready course market. Mark Elliott shared his research on Tourgée with extraordinary generosity, providing numerous leads and professional contacts. The introduction has also benefited from the incisive criticism and valuable suggestions of Otto H. Olsen, Mark Elliott, Brook Thomas, H. Bruce Franklin, Jane Franklin, Jeannie Pfaelzer, and Thorell Tsomondo. Librarians have furnished me with crucial assistance. I particularly thank Charles E. Wright and Hubert Steward of the Interlibrary Loan Division at the University of Maryland's McKeldin Library; reference librarians Thomas Mann, David Kelly, and Sheridan Harvey of the Library of Congress; James O'Brien, president of the Chautauqua County Historical Society (CCHS), the repository of the Albion W. Tourgée Papers; and Ellen Schwanekamp, former assistant director of the CCHS's McClurg Museum. I am grateful to the Chautauqua County Historical Society for permission to quote from the Tourgée Papers. Finally, I thank Reynolds Smith for piloting the book through Duke University Press with such contagious enthusiasm.

NOTE ON THE TEXT

THIS TEXT is reprinted from the original 1880 edition of *Bricks Without Straw*. I have silently corrected obvious misprints but have let stand inconsistencies in spelling and in the rendering of dialect.

INTRODUCTION

Carolyn L. Karcher

ALBION W. TOURGÉE'S *Bricks Without Straw*, set in Reconstruction-era North Carolina, cries out to be rediscovered as one of the most powerful race novels ever written by a white American. The throngs of readers who rushed to purchase it when it came off the press in October 1880 certainly recognized its power. *Bricks Without Straw* sold 50,000 copies within a year—an extraordinary figure by today's standards—and Tourgée's publishers had to make a duplicate set of plates to keep pace with the demand, which averaged more than a thousand copies a day and seven thousand a week for the first six weeks.[1] Although Tourgée's better-known Reconstruction novel, *A Fool's Errand* (1879), sold three times as many copies, *Bricks Without Straw* in fact surpasses it both conceptually and artistically. Conceptually, *Bricks Without Straw* accomplishes the rare feat of envisioning Reconstruction from the black community's standpoint—a more ambitious undertaking than fictionalizing an author's own experience, as Tourgée does in *A Fool's Errand.* Artistically, *Bricks Without Straw* features an array of complex, fully rounded characters; a plot that successfully integrates the political action centered on African Americans with the love story centered on whites; a sophisticated narrative technique that relies on flashbacks rather than linear progression; a self-conscious use of dialogue and dialect to give voice to the voiceless; and an experimental open ending that calls attention to the problems history has left unresolved.

THE *UNCLE TOM'S CABIN* OF RECONSTRUCTION

The literary achievement modern readers will prize most highly in *Bricks Without Straw* is its revolutionary approach to depicting African Americans. Casting off the blinders that so drastically limited white perceptions of African Americans, Tourgée defies conventions of racial stereotyping ubiquitous in the writings of his predecessors and contemporaries, who either embraced these conventions uncritically or resorted to covert strategies for undermining them.[2] No other white writer of Tourgée's time—and few since then—portrayed African Americans with such realism, treated them as independent political agents instead of as menials attached to whites, and accorded them dominant roles in the plot.

Tourgée knew that the story he wished to tell demanded a new type of novel, as perfectly adapted to impelling the northern public to complete the work of Reconstruction as Harriet Beecher Stowe's *Uncle Tom's Cabin* (1852) had been to inspiring its antebellum readers to fight against slavery. Stowe's "literary marvel," Tourgée asserted in his tribute "The Literary Quality of 'Uncle Tom's Cabin'" (1896), had wrought its magic by painting "a slavery which the free man could understand and appreciate" and by embodying it in characters familiar to the northern mind because they were "essentially New Englanders" or "blacked Yankees." Curious to learn what the emancipated slaves themselves thought of the book that had so "vividly . . . impressed [his] own young mind," Tourgée had questioned many about it. Nearly all had found Stowe's sketches of blacks and master-slave relations untrue to life. "Seems like that Uncle Tom must have been raised up North!" Tourgée quoted "one of the shrewdest and most thoughtful" freedmen as commenting. Yet far from branding the "non-realistic" mode of *Uncle Tom's Cabin* a defect, Tourgée identified it as the secret of the influence the novel had exerted. An "absolutely 'realistic' . . . delineation of the master and the slave" would not only have failed to move readers, he argued, but would have gone over the heads of the majority "who did not, and do not yet, comprehend" the institution that had so fatally shaped southern society.[3]

If the crusade against slavery required an *Uncle Tom's Cabin,* Tourgée believed, the challenge the country faced in 1880 required a radically different fictional vehicle for mobilizing public opinion. Fifteen years after the war, the South remained engulfed in violence, white supremacy again reigned unchecked, and the freedpeople groaned under forms of bondage almost as oppressive as the one the country had abolished. These conditions persisted, according to Tourgée, because Northerners still viewed the South through the prism of *Uncle Tom's Cabin.* They had expected to regenerate the South through a mass religious conversion, and when it had not materialized, they had let the region work out its own salvation, confident that white and black Southerners would eventually reach an accommodation similar to that of Stowe's benevolent masters and lovable slaves.

To awaken the northern public from its slumber and summon it back to the unfinished task of liberating African Americans from white domination, Tourgée created a novel that combined the prime attribute of *Uncle Tom's Cabin*—its "power to touch the universal heart"[4]—with the social realism it conspicuously lacked. Through realism, *Bricks Without Straw* corrects readers' misconceptions and equips them for promoting effective policies in the South. Tourgée replaces Stowe's saintly Uncle Tom and comical Topsy with three-dimensional black characters endeavoring to forge new lives for themselves. He shows them interacting primarily not with whites but with each other, and he traces the development of a free, self-dependent African American community. Tourgée's realism illuminates the world of southern whites as well. *Bricks Without Straw* reveals the complexity of southern society, provides glimpses of the relations between poor whites and blacks, and probes the psychology of the former slaveholders.

Realism does not in itself arouse readers to action, however, as Tourgée's running quarrel with its literary proponents indicates that he discerned.[5] He therefore infuses the emotional appeal of *Uncle Tom's Cabin* into *Bricks Without Straw.* Speaking through a narrator appalled by the nation's moral torpor, he strives to ignite in his readers the same fervor Stowe had sparked in hers. Stowe's readers had gone to war to free the slaves. Tourgée wanted his readers to fulfill that war's promise by rededicating themselves to the forsaken goal of Reconstruction.

WHOSE RECONSTRUCTION?

Reconstruction, the turbulent twelve-year period stretching from 1865 to 1877, derives its name from the ideal of rebuilding the post–Civil War South on a foundation of freedom and equality rather than slavery. The government program implementing this ideal originated with the Radical wing of the Republican Party, whose roots lay in the prewar antislavery movement.[6]

Reconstruction has gone down in public memory, nonetheless, as a spree of vengeance against a defeated people, because the program's fiercest opponents—the South's former slaveholding aristocrats—overthrew it by violence and captured the national media. Through the mainstream northern press, and later through such works as Thomas Dixon's *The Clansman* (1905), D. W. Griffith's *The Birth of a Nation* (1915), Margaret Mitchell's *Gone with the Wind* (1936), and the multiple tomes produced by professors of the "Dunning School," the white South's propagandists fastened their version of history on the popular imagination. As a result, generations of Americans have supposed that after the Civil War, the "prostrate" South endured a gang rape by hordes of ignorant and brutish ex-slaves, unleashed by greedy "carpetbaggers" and abetted in their depredations by villainous "scalawags"—the epithets applied respectively to emigrant Northerners and renegade Southerners.[7] Only within the past few decades have these tenacious stereotypes begun to yield to the consensus of present-day historians, who now characterize Reconstruction, in Eric Foner's words, as "America's Unfinished Revolution."[8]

Published a mere three years after Reconstruction officially ended, and aimed at counteracting the very stereotypes historians have recently discredited, *Bricks Without Straw* offers an unparalleled inside view of this contentious epoch. As a Radical Republican, Tourgée had worked closely with African Americans and poor whites in the struggle to transform North Carolina's racial and class politics. He had also seen the ravages of the Ku Klux Klan at first-hand, braved death threats to bring the perpetrators of Klan atrocities to justice, and fought to the last against what he called the "counter-revolution" that destroyed Reconstruction (*Bricks* 394). Thus, *Bricks Without Straw* pulsates with the immediacy of lived history.

Tourgée places the newly freed slaves at the center of this history and presents the conflicts over Reconstruction primarily through their eyes—an enterprise that anticipates the African American scholar W. E. B. Du Bois's monumental revisionist study, *Black Reconstruction in America* (1935). Indeed, it is not too much to call *Bricks Without Straw* Tourgée's *Black Reconstruction.* The very words Du Bois uses to describe his project apply to Tourgée's. Both identify the "emancipated slave" as the "chief witness in Reconstruction," challenge a public record that had "almost barred" this crucial witness "from court," and emphasize the African American people's courageous striving for self-determination in the teeth of insuperable odds. Both also show how African Americans were driven "back toward slavery."[9]

Unlike Du Bois, however, Tourgée could exploit the mask of fiction and the authority he possessed as a white participant in Reconstruction to express his outrage at the nation's abandonment of African Americans. Grimly chronicling the "counter-revolution" that so swiftly eliminated the rights the freedpeople had won with the help of their white supporters, he excoriates the northern public for succumbing so credulously to the white supremacist propaganda campaign against Reconstruction. In the process, he articulates insights as relevant to the present as to the past.

Tourgée could assume his nineteenth-century readers' familiarity with the main contours of Reconstruction politics, as covered in the leading newspapers of the North. Hence, he concentrated on refuting myths about "Negro rule" and exploding the illusion that a new day of peace and harmony had dawned in the South since its ruling elites had been allowed to regulate race relations without federal interference. For twenty-first-century readers, on the other hand, an overview of Reconstruction history and of Tourgée's career, so inextricably intertwined with it, can enhance appreciation of his talents as a political novelist by revealing the factual basis of his gripping plot.

THE MAKING OF A RADICAL

Tourgée's life qualified him exceptionally well for setting the historical record straight so that the nation could undo its mistakes—the mission he undertook in *Bricks Without Straw.* Born in 1838 in Ohio's Western Reserve, a region burning with the abolitionist zeal its settlers credited to their New England heritage, he grew up exposed to many of the radical ideas he would later champion. Two of the nation's most committed antislavery politicians, Joshua R. Giddings and Benjamin F. Wade, both from Tourgée's native Ashtabula County, represented Ohio in the House and Senate. Though an "ardent disciple" of Giddings, as he afterward recalled, the youthful Tourgée did not act on his convictions that blacks were fellow human beings and slavery was "damnable." As late as February 1860, when his fiancée Emma Kilbourne announced that she had "become quite a rabid little petticoated Black Republican" (as members of the fledgling Republican party were labeled to associate them with African Americans), Tourgée made fun of her. "Will you require your Fiancée to swear fealty to your political views, and pledge himself, in black & white to vote for all Republican candidates and none others, as some others of your sex have done?" he demanded. In hindsight he berated himself as an "egregious ass" for having held himself aloof from the abolitionist movement he portrayed so admiringly in his mature writings.[10]

It was Tourgée's contact with fugitive slaves and black soldiers in Union army camps during his Civil War service that converted him into an impassioned advocate of racial equality. He enlisted as soon as the war broke out, driven like most early volunteers by a desire to prove his manhood and his patriotism. The battle of Bull Run left him paralyzed from the waist down after the wheel of a gun carriage struck him in the back during the Union army's frenzied rout. Regaining mobility nine months later by sheer force of will, he signed up as a recruiter and joined the regiment he had raised, the Ohio 105th Volunteer Infantry, made up of men who "carried the antislavery fervor of the Western Reserve with them to the warfront."[11] Hardly had the 105th arrived at its first destination in Lexington, Kentucky, than its members confronted the anomaly of an "'abolition regiment' in a loyal slave state," as Tourgée put it in his history of the 105th, *The Story of a Thousand* (1896). Along the march route, he reminisced, "colored men came, one by one, and offered to bring water, to carry guns or knapsacks,—anything, if they could only follow us" and thereby hasten their own liberation and the downfall of slavery. In their wake came irate masters seeking to reclaim their runaway property. Because Kentucky was siding with the Union, the Lincoln administration's policy obliged soldiers to surrender runaways to "loyal" claimants—orders "abhorrent" to men whose families in Ohio had been sheltering escaped slaves from the human bloodhounds on their trail. Tourgée cited several instances of soldiers and officers who defied their superiors by protecting the fugitives in their midst, provoking the Kentucky general commanding the 105th to shout, "You are all Abolition nigger-stealers."[12]

The opportunity to rub elbows with black men under wartime conditions taught Tourgée to respect a race he had hitherto considered inferior, as he subsequently admitted.[13] For example, while performing picket duty on a "dark and rainy night" in January 1863, shortly after Lincoln issued the Emancipation Proclamation, Tourgée was startled by the approach of a "trembling slave, who, when he had assured himself of kindly treatment, drew from secure concealment in his dusky bosom a paper containing a copy of [the president's] message, and asked—Please sir will you tell me—is this true."[14] (We do not know what Tourgée replied, but the Emancipation Proclamation did not in fact free slaves in loyal states, though it did enable thousands to win their freedom by enlisting in the Union Army.)[15] The encounter sharpened Tourgée's awareness of how attentively the slaves were following the war news. It also convinced him that despite draconian laws against allowing slaves access to literacy, some managed to learn to read and used that skill to free themselves and their fellows. On another occasion, Tourgée and a comrade attended a "meeting of the 'Cullud population' of the Brigade," as he recorded in his diary on 7 June 1863. What he saw there of African Americans as political agents apparently impressed Tourgée enough to prompt him to request a transfer two weeks later to a black regiment. "I know there is little hope of any mercy being shown" to a captured soldier "connected with the colored troops," he mused, but "it is certainly the place for men who would serve the country best."[16]

The requested transfer never materialized, yet Tourgée's racial views continued to evolve as he formed closer relations with the escaped slaves who served the 105th. His diary entry of 24 October 1863 furnishes a glimpse of that evolution. Describing the latest fugitive to arrive in the camp, a man who called himself William and did not know "his 'oder' name," Tourgée crossed out the word "colored" and substituted "an American citizen of African descent." He immediately took William into his "pay and employ" and rechristened him "*Nimbus*" [double underlining in original, meaning both "halo" and "storm cloud"], he reported, "by which ancient and honorable appellation he is hereafter to be known."[17] Living at close quarters, with time often hanging on their hands, the young officer and his body servant must have carried on long conversations, through which Tourgée gleaned insights he would weave into his portrayals of his African American characters. Chief among them, the militant hero of *Bricks Without Straw,* whom Tourgée likewise christened Nimbus, embodies the unforgettable image of black manhood that his real-life model imprinted on the future author's memory.

As the 105th fought its way through Kentucky, Tennessee, and Georgia, Tourgée met with more and more fugitives and saw slaves subjected to shocking brutality. "Oh! I am sick today—so sick! Not bodily sick—but *so* sick at heart!" he wrote Emma in November 1862 from a plantation in Danville, Kentucky, where he was recuperating from a shrapnel wound in his hip. "I have seen what would make a cynic heart-sore! My brain throbs—my blood boils!" His unwillingness to share the details with Emma hints at a sexual abuse—perhaps the stripping and flogging of a woman.[18]

Eight weeks later, Tourgée was captured in an ambush and spent four months in a series of Confederate prisons from January through April 1863. Prison completed his radicalization. As he told Emma, prison taught him the meaning of "bondage": "it is chagrin, humiliation—insult—fused in fierce flash of misery."[19] While his own experience of "bondage" led him to identify viscerally with the slaves fleeing in droves to Union army camps, prison threw him into the company of southern poor whites, kindling a sympathy that would help him forge ties with some of them during Reconstruction. "Never shall I forget . . . a prisoner in one of the Confederate Bastiles, a garulous soldier," he recalled in an 1868 speech. "Ah! sir, this is the rich man's [war] and the poor man's fight," he remembered his Confederate fellow inmate as telling him "with mournful emphasis." Tourgée added: "It was the whole matter in a nutshell, a volume in a sentence."[20]

Even before his capture, Tourgée had arrived at the conclusion that the war would serve no purpose if it did not instigate a "national revolution." In a letter to his fraternity brothers at the University of Rochester, he dedicated himself to a vision that he would promulgate for the rest of his life. Dismissing Lincoln's original goal of preserving the Union with slavery intact, Tourgée proclaimed: "I dont care a rag for '*the Union as it was.*' I want & fight for the *Union better* than '*it was.*' Before this is accomplished we must have a fundamental thorough and complete revolution & renovation. . . . For this I am willing to die—for this I expect to die" [underlining in original].[21] Tourgée's career during Reconstruction and its aftermath confirms that he took his pledge seriously.

To his lasting mortification, Tourgée's Civil War service ended in December 1863, when his commanders judged him unfit for active duty after he reinjured his back. Though he never won the military renown he wishfully bestowed on some of his fictional heroes, he led the vanguard of the social "revolution" in which he hoped the overthrow of slavery would culminate.

AN IDEALISTIC "CARPETBAGGER"

In the spring of 1865, Tourgée began exploring the idea of going south to aid in transmuting an oligarchy based on race and caste into a democratic republic. A vast tide of northern missionaries, teachers, and entrepreneurs, mostly of abolitionist background, had already embarked on this errand, setting up schools for the newly freed slaves and initiating experiments in "free labor," first in areas liberated by the Union army, such as Fortress Monroe, Virginia, and Port Royal, South Carolina, in 1861–62, then throughout the

South after the Confederacy's surrender in April 1865. They hoped to consummate the work of abolition by turning the South into a replica of New England and the Western Reserve. Tourgée shared their dream.

Like many carpetbaggers, Tourgée combined idealistic motives with a desire for economic gain. The notion that slavery caused economic backwardness while "free labor" (meaning free enterprise and uncoerced wage labor) furthered economic development had long buttressed the abolitionist creed, and Tourgée wholeheartedly subscribed to it. Still, his biographers agree that idealism outweighed self-interest in Tourgée's choice of Greensboro, Guilford County, North Carolina, as his new home. Though it lacked the opportunities for windfall profits available in the rice-growing and cotton-growing coastal regions, Greensboro attracted Tourgée because it boasted a large Quaker population that had opposed slavery before the war, backed the Union and campaigned for peace during the war, and was now energetically establishing freedmen's schools across the state.[22] Clearly, Tourgée was seeking a community of like-minded activists.

Accompanied by Emma's parents and sisters and two fraternity brothers from the University of Rochester whom he took as partners, Tourgée leased a 750-acre farm, the West Green Nursery, and started a law practice in October 1865. The nursery, specializing in fruit trees, enabled him to demonstrate the benefits of free labor by paying good wages to his black workers and earning their loyal service. His law practice entailed representing southern Unionists who were demanding compensation from the U.S. government for property destroyed by Sherman's troops. Through these twin pursuits, Tourgée linked himself with two of the constituencies he would soon weld into an interracial coalition.[23]

NORTH CAROLINA DURING PRESIDENT JOHNSON'S RECONSTRUCTION

Tourgée arrived in North Carolina at a critical juncture in national politics. Lincoln had not yet formulated a Reconstruction policy when he succumbed to an assassin's bullet in April 1865, but in his last speech, delivered to an audience that included John Wilkes Booth, he had indicated a limited willingness to award voting rights to some black men: "the very intelligent, and . . . those who serve our cause as soldiers."[24] Tourgée would always believe that Lincoln's endorsement of black suffrage, however tentative, sounded his death knell.[25]

The eight-month interval before Congress reconvened in December (an oddity of the nineteenth-century political calendar) left Reconstruction in the hands of Lincoln's successor, Andrew Johnson. A Tennessee Unionist of poor-white origin who harbored virulent anti-black prejudices, Johnson adamantly opposed black suffrage. Indeed, he opposed measures to *protect,* let alone empower, the ex-slaves. That stand led him to veto two key bills Republicans passed in February 1866: the first extended the life of the Freedmen's Bureau, the federal agency that mediated between whites and blacks during the transition from slavery to freedom; the second spelled out the basic civil rights to which freedpeople, like all other American citizens, were entitled. Johnson viewed such measures as infringements on states' rights. He wanted instead to readmit the defeated Confederate states into the Union as expeditiously as possible with minimal conditions—acceptance of the Thirteenth Amendment abolishing slavery and repudiation of both secession and Confederate war debts. Accordingly, he granted wholesale pardons to ex-Confederates and restored their property rights in plantations confiscated during the war, some of which had been turned over to the freedpeople on the understanding that by tilling the land, they could earn ownership of it. Johnson's lenient terms for "restoration" (the word he favored in lieu of "reconstruction"), his determination to allow the former rebel states "undisputed management of their own internal affairs," and his undisguised commitment to a "white man's government" emboldened the South's ruling elites to reassert their power.[26]

North Carolina followed the same pattern as other southern states. Conservatives swept the November 1865 elections, and the state assembly hastily enacted a Black Code designed to keep the freedpeople in subjection, so that despite the demise of slavery, employers could count on a captive black labor force. Its provisions labeled "vagrancy" (that is, unemployment) as a misdemeanor and allowed courts to fine or imprison offenders or sentence them to the workhouse; penalized employers for "enticing" or "harboring" workers who left exploitative bosses in quest of higher wages elsewhere; required convicted criminals to pay off their fines and court costs by laboring in ball and chain on road construction and other public works; forbade blacks to purchase "guns, swords, or knives" without a license obtained one year in advance; and imposed the death penalty for "insurrection, conspiracy, sedition or rebellion," as well as for "*intent* to rape a white woman" (italics added). As if the Black Code did not suffice, a Militia Law revived the antebellum slave patrol by establishing an "all-white militia . . . to be called out to quell any 'insurrection among free persons of color'" or any disturbances "*in any way* alarming the citizens of any county." Finally, taxes weighing unequally on black laborers and white landowners "compelled [blacks] to pay an unjust & extortionate share of the public expenses."[27]

The state's legislative assault on African American rights validated a drive already under way to terrorize the freedpeople into submission. By January 1866, agents of the Freedmen's Bureau in North Carolina were "so overwhelmed with cases of 'robberies, frauds, assaults, and even murders' committed against blacks that one reported hearing 'as many as a hundred and eighty complaints in one day' and lamented that 'no records of them could be kept.'" The bureau's records did nevertheless note "fifteen murders of blacks by white men in 1865 and 1866."[28]

Appalled by both the violence and the Black Codes, congressional Republicans sought to write into the Constitution guarantees that would prevent states from reintroducing slavery under new guises. The Fourteenth Amendment, passed in June 1866, defined "all persons born or naturalized in the United States" as "citizens of the United States and of the State wherein they reside" (terms that for the first time explicitly included African Americans); prohibited states from denying citizens "equal protection of the laws" or depriving them of "life, liberty or property, without due process of law"; and temporarily "barred from national and state office men who had taken an oath of allegiance to the Constitution and then aided the Confederacy."[29] Like most of the southern state legislatures elected in 1865 under President Johnson's restoration plan, North Carolina's General Assembly voted overwhelmingly against ratifying the Fourteenth Amendment.

While the dispossessed slaveholders were devising methods of securing a bonded labor force, their former chattels were exercising their new freedoms and organizing to protect them. In parades, demonstrations, and public meetings, the freedpeople celebrated their emancipation and "called for legal and political rights."[30] They also banded together in Union Leagues, which served simultaneously to impart "political education," provide a forum for airing grievances against employers, and arrange for self-defense. At typical league meetings, "Republican newspapers were read aloud, issues of the day debated, candidates nominated for office, and banners with slogans like 'Colored Troops Fought Nobly' prepared for rallies." Members additionally used league meetings to share information about "suing their employers, avoiding fines for attending political meetings, and ensuring a fair division of crops at harvest time." Some leagues even "engaged in strikes for higher wages" and held military drills.[31] Of the political activities in which North Carolina freedmen participated, the most impressive were two statewide conventions held in Raleigh at the African Methodist Church in 1865 and 1866. Both passed resolutions praising Radical Republican leaders for working to "secure to the colored citizen his rights." Both also addressed North Carolina white elites, at first in moderate, then in militant tones. The 1865 convention, as if anticipating and hoping to forestall the Black Codes, petitioned the state legislature to frame "some suitable measures . . . to prevent unscrupulous and avaricious employers from the practice of . . . acts of injustice towards our people." The 1866 convention protested against "outrages" local whites were committing, called on the African American community to publicize them in the national press, and organized a state Freedmen's Educational Association to "aid in the establishment of schools, from which none shall be excluded on account of color or poverty."[32]

AN AGITATOR FOR EQUAL RIGHTS

North Carolina's politically awakened black masses and intransigent white ruling class were poised for conflict when Tourgée inaugurated his model of free-labor farming in Greensboro. From the start, the relations he and Emma formed with the African American community constituted an affront to white mores and subjected the couple to ostracism so extreme that white women gathered back their skirts when Emma passed them in the streets.[33] Not only did the generous wages Tourgée offered undermine the planter class's strategy for maintaining a pool of cheap black labor, but his fraternization with his workers violated the racial hierarchy that upheld white hegemony. He and Emma founded Greensboro's first school for the freedpeople, situated on their premises, and the Tourgées and Emma's family members taught there until the school relocated in June 1867 (becoming Bennett Seminary in 1873, which remains extant today). Emma also "made a daily habit of reading the newspaper aloud" to the West Green Nursery's employees. Further grating on the sensibilities of the white gentry, the Tourgées interacted socially with their African American neighbors, sometimes attended black church services, and received African American guests in their home. Nor did they simply flout the racial caste system—Tourgée actually sapped its economic basis by helping African Americans to acquire land, in defiance of a ban by white planters. Like his autobiographical persona Comfort Servosse in *A Fool's Errand* (1879), Tourgée appears to have "cut up" a portion of his acreage into "little farms of ten and twenty acres," erected log houses on them, and sold them "to colored people on six or ten years' time."[34] He dreamed of launching a Freedmen Land Agency with branches in every state, which could enable African Americans to purchase land on easy terms through northern capitalists acting as intermediaries, but General Oliver O. Howard, head of the Freedmen's Bureau, never considered Tourgée's proposal.[35]

To be sure, Tourgée did not always escape the racial arrogance his culture bred in whites. His correspondence with local African American leaders reveals that he sometimes offended them. Responding to an unjust accusation of disloyalty, for example, Tourgée's political ally Harmon Unthank objected, "I understood that the principle of the republican party was liberty, Freedom of speech &c, but by the way you write, I do not think *freedom* of *speech* is *allowed*" [underlining in original].[36] Similarly, when Tourgée presumed to ask the African American candidate James E. O'Hara to withdraw from the ticket to prevent the defeat of the Republican slate, O'Hara shot back a "torrent of angry abuse," complaining that white Republicans were still treating their black colleagues as "masters" did their "servants."[37] These expressions of resentment nonetheless indicate that Tourgée's African American associates felt free to chastise him and expected him to listen to them. Far more representative of the local black community's assessment of him is a testimonial that appeared in an African American newspaper almost three decades later by a man who had known Tourgée since 1867. "He was then the same upright, brave, bold, courageous, outspoken friend of humanity" as he continued to be in the 1890s, wrote this admirer, adding: "In the hearts of the loyal people of [North Carolina] Judge Tourgee is idolized." Significantly, he cited as witnesses the "living" models on whom Tourgée had based the African American characters in his novels: "Unthank in 'Hot Plowshares,' Nimbus in 'Bricks Without Straw,' and Wilks, in the 'Fool's Errand.' "[38]

If Tourgée's efforts to promote racial equality foundered in the social and economic realms, they proved extremely effective in the political arena. Displaying a talent for coalition building, he unified Quakers, poor whites, upper-class converts to radicalism, and African Americans under the umbrella of the Republican party. His political career began in the local Union League and culminated in a judgeship.

Tourgée joined an interracial chapter of the Union League, perhaps at the invitation of a black member, as *A Fool's Errand* suggests. The association met in a schoolhouse furnished by the Freedmen's Bureau and brought together freedmen and a handful of white Union loyalists.[39] Tourgée served as corresponding secretary and apparently wrote the pledge members repeated at their councils, which reflects the group's radical egalitarianism. In language echoed again and again in his own political writings, it calls for "elective judges, equal justice to all men and an *everlasting* reconstruction" and vows not to "countenance any social or political aristocracy," to "aid in elevating and educating the people, to wrest power from the rich," and to "prevent the leaders of [the Confederate] rebellion from holding offices of trust and emolument."[40] Through his participation in the League and other interracial organizations, Tourgée soon won a reputation as an electrifying speaker and fearless champion of both the black and the white poor.

From local notability, Tourgée rose to national prominence when Unionists of Guilford County chose him as their delegate to the Southern Loyalists convention in Philadelphia, held on the heels of President Johnson's convention of his own supporters. The 1866 electoral campaign was shaping up as a referendum on the Fourteenth Amendment, which Johnsonites repudiated and Radical Republicans promoted. To refute the Johnsonites' claim that peaceful conditions in the South warranted swift readmittance of the ex-Confederate states with no further interference in their internal affairs, Radicals wanted first-hand testimony from southern loyalists on the violence raging in their home districts. Tourgée and the Louisiana carpetbagger Henry Clay Warmoth, who "emerge[d] as the two most influential men in the entire convention," presented a devastating report on the "Non-Reconstructed states." It charged that the old planter class had merely replaced slavery with "serfdom" and that Unionists of both races suffered "continual persecution" at the hands of the ex-Confederate "rebels" they had helped their country to defeat. The report also demanded that the "strong arm" of the federal government be "interposed" to protect its loyal citizens. In an extemporaneous speech, Tourgée elaborated on the reign of terror in the South, quoting a Quaker witness who had "seen the bodies of fifteen murdered negroes taken from one pond." He went on to prescribe a radical remedy: "*both* 'the disenfranchisement of all traitors' *and* 'the enfranchisement of *all* loyal men,'" black as well as white. "Two thousand North Carolinians had sent him to Philadelphia" to advocate these measures, Tourgée proclaimed. Despite the crowd's applause—and despite a powerful plea by Frederick Douglass—Tourgée could not muster a majority for black suffrage. But he could see that the tide was turning. Writing to Emma, he conveyed a message to one of his black associates: "Tell Clark that he will have a chance to vote and all other rights in less than two years."[41]

Unknown to Tourgée, Conservatives in North Carolina had been reading newspaper accounts of the Philadelphia convention. They seethed over the picture he had painted of the mayhem in their state—a picture they knew would impel congressional Republicans to prolong the Freedmen's Bureau's surveillance of North Carolina labor relations and possibly send back federal troops. The Conservative Governor Jonathan Worth denounced Tourgée as a "vile wretch," branded his speech "a tissue of lies from beginning to end," accused him of trying to "make the North hate the South," and unsuccessfully pressured Tourgée's Quaker supporters to disavow him. He also orchestrated a slander campaign against Tourgée in the Conservative Greensboro *Patriot,* which unleashed a flood of hate mail. "It is about time that your lying tong [*sic*] was stopped—and if you ever show your ugly face in Guilford County again, I will take care with some of my friends that you find the bottom of that *niger pond* you have been talking so much about," wrote one anonymous correspondent. "You have traduced and villified us at Philadelphia," charged another: "You *knew* that fifteen dead Negroes had not been taken from one pond. You *knew* that Southern loyalists and Negroes *are* safe here provided that they behave themselves." Contradicting himself, this correspondent warned in the next breath: "Your stay in North Carolina had better be short if you expect to breathe the vital air. It is settled that you cannot live here."[42]

Cut off from news of North Carolina during his whirlwind speaking tour after leaving Philadelphia, Tourgée did not realize that a "hurricane" was brewing over his household and that Emma was bearing the brunt of it in his absence. When he finally heard from her in mid-October, he learned that his business partners had dissociated themselves from him to avoid financial "ruin" and were menacing Emma and her family members with being "*turned out* of *doors*" [underlining in original]. The West Green Nursery had also stopped paying its workers. "The boys . . . look upon me as the only protector of their rights while you are away," Emma wrote. "They have had but half rations for some time and not a cent of money and some of them are getting barefoot and the cold weather coming on they need their winter clothing. . . . I have distributed ten dollars among them and fed them time and again." One "hungry and barefoot" man had told Emma, "We never would have known who was our friend here if Mr Tourgee had not gone away," revealing the true character of the firm's other owners.[43]

On his return, Tourgée bought out his partners, but he did not manage to prevent the firm from going under, leaving him penniless and in debt. Undaunted, he continued his political activism, starting a short-lived Republican newspaper, the *Union Register*, delivering speeches all over the state, and joining with other local Radicals to petition Congress in favor of a drastic Reconstruction plan that entailed long-term federal control of the South, the division of the region into territories rather than states, the enfranchisement of former slaves, and the disfranchisement of former Confederate office holders.[44]

In the Reconstruction Act of March 1867, Congress granted the Radicals' prayers for black suffrage in the South, but imposed only temporary disfranchisement on the leaders of the rebellion. Instead, the Reconstruction Act required the ex-Confederate states to hold new constitutional conventions, form new governments, and ratify the Fourteenth Amendment as conditions for readmittance into the Union. The changed suffrage rules meant that a very different electorate, consisting of 72,932 blacks and 106,721 whites, of whom a large segment had long resented the domination of slaveholding planters, would determine the outcome of that process in North Carolina.[45]

THE 1868 CONVENTION

Tourgée played a key role both in the 1867 election, during which he helped woo poor white voters to the Republican side with forceful appeals to their class interests, and in the 1868 state constitutional convention, where he served as one of 107 Republican delegates versus thirteen Conservatives. Though the youngest member of the convention, the twenty-nine-year-old Tourgée took the most conspicuous part in its deliberations and contributed more than anyone to shaping the constitution it produced. The newspapers covering the convention furnish a gauge of his visibility. Not only did the Republican North Carolina *Daily Standard* print long extracts from his speeches, but the Conservative *North Carolinian* caricatured them in detail. Tourgée obsessed white supremacists as a race traitor responsible for all the indignities they suffered at having their former slaves occupy fifteen seats in a once-exclusive forum where they themselves were now reduced to an impotent minority. Conservatives might dismiss the other Republican delegates as a "Troupe of Minstrels" performing in a "'Burnt Cork' Convention," but they could not ignore Tourgée. The *North Carolinian* dubbed him "the Tourgee" as if to indicate that it considered him sui generis—an unclassifiable anomaly, a "Nondescript animal" in a "Natural History" museum featuring "Baboons, Monkeys, Mules, Tourgee and other Jackasses."[46]

The epithets Conservatives slung at Tourgée show that they recognized him as a formidable adversary who too often carried the day. Tourgée's eloquent speech in favor of incorporating black suffrage into the state constitution, for example, shifted the debate from the "anatomical and physiological difference between white and black races" (the ground on which Conservatives argued against granting blacks the vote) to the debt the country owed African Americans for having helped defeat the Confederate rebellion. "The question of the colored man's right to vote . . . is a dead issue, a settled question, it has been forever fixed and decided, by the colored man himself" through the blood he shed in the war for freedom, Tourgée contended. Invoking the notorious Fort Pillow massacre in which scores of black soldiers had been murdered in cold blood after a fierce battle, he vowed: "If I forget that day and its lesson of noble manhood, and ever fail to give my voice and my strength for the equal, political, and Civil rights, to that race which gave one hundred and eighty thousand such heros in the darkest hour of the conflict to snatch the Banner of freedom from such foes, may God forget me and mine forever." The *North Carolinian*'s scorn testified involuntarily to the power of Tourgée's rhetoric: "In listening to his tribute to their valor and patriotism during the war, the uninformed hearer would have thought the nigger alone 'crushed the rebellion.'"[47] Clearly, Tourgée was challenging racist images of African Americans in ways that threatened to wean white voters away from Conservatives by promoting an alliance across lines of race.

Tourgée's leadership at the convention was so effective, writes his recent biographer Mark Elliott, that "nearly every article" of the state's 1868 constitution "bore the marks of [his] influence." Among the innovations he introduced were the division of counties into self-governing townships that elected their own commissioners, school boards, justices of the peace, and constables; the abolition of property qualifications for holding political office; the popular election of superior court judges, hitherto appointed by the state legislature; the abrogation of equity courts and the simplification of the judicial system; the banning of stocks, whipping posts, branding irons, and other methods of corporal punishment; the reduction in the number of crimes punishable by death from eighteen to four (unable to achieve his objective of abolishing the death penalty, which he called "Judicial murder,"

Tourgée privately lobbied Quakers to agitate for restricting it to cases of first-degree murder); the insertion of a clause affirming that the purpose of punishment was "not only to satisfy justice but also to reform the offender"; the elimination of court costs for defendants found innocent in criminal proceedings; and "the incorporation of a 'Homestead Clause' that protected debtors from having their land seized by creditors."[48] All these innovations served to democratize and humanize the political system, empower the common people, and alleviate the burdens of the poor.

The Conservatives made a last-ditch effort to defeat the proposed constitution in the April 1868 election. "WHITE MEN, ORGANIZE!" they exhorted poor voters: "Be true to your RACE" and "hand down to your children a white man's government."[49] Poor white voters did not rise to the bait, however, joining African Americans and carpetbaggers in ratifying the constitution by a healthy margin. This biracial coalition also elected William W. Holden, a Republican governor of poor-white origin, and sent a Republican majority to the state legislature. Tourgée himself won election as a state Superior Court judge, a position he would hold until 1874.

"THE REIGN OF TERROR"

The Conservative press began defaming Tourgée even before he assumed office. In "what became the standard method of creating the popular image of Republican debasement and villainy," newspapers circulated "irresponsible slanders" which they refused to retract when exposed as unfounded.[50] Although Tourgée's impartiality and competence eventually earned him tributes from fair-minded Conservatives, the public vilification of him never abated. Tourgée's commitment to upholding the rights of African Americans—whether by ensuring that they served on juries, by fining lawyers for using the epithet "nigger," or by setting aside guilty verdicts based on flimsy evidence—met with constant misrepresentation. Notwithstanding his stiff sentences of those he judged rightly convicted, white supremacists charged that his leniency toward black criminals provoked recourse to lynch law. In reply Tourgée vowed: "I shall continue to act on my own sense of justice, my own apprehension of the law, and my own conviction of duty entirely unmindful whether the same please friend or foe. . . . I prize my own self respect too highly to do otherwise, and believing as I do that justice should at least be 'color blind,' I shall know no man by the hue of his skin."[51]

Tourgée's judicial term coincided with the heyday of the Ku Klux Klan,

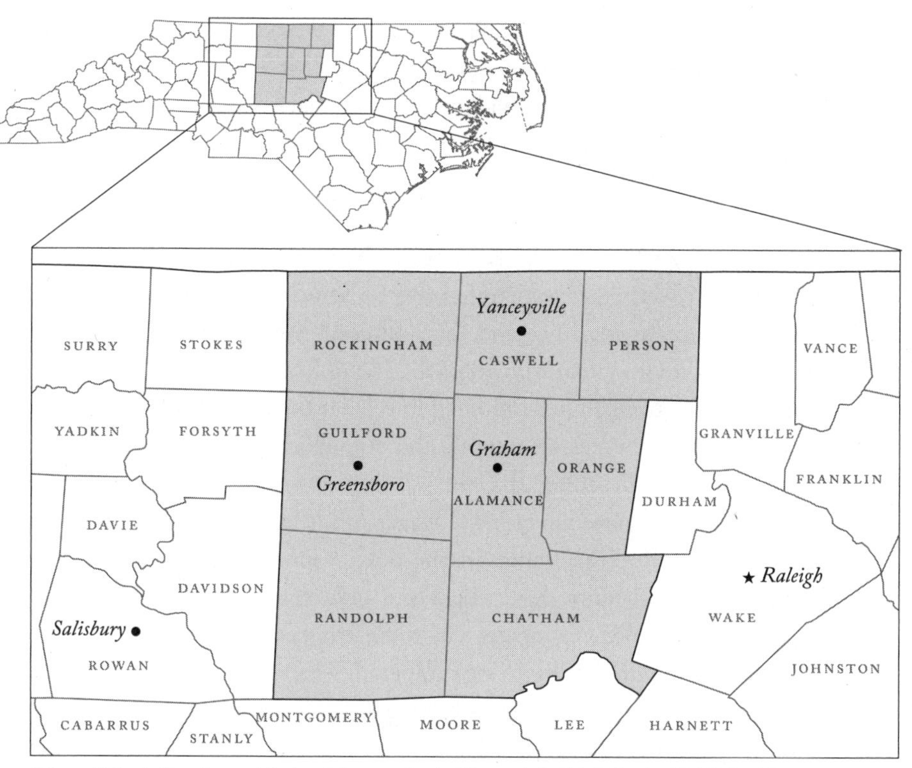

Map of North Carolina with the eight counties in Tourgée's judicial district highlighted in gray. Also indicated are Raleigh, the state capital and site of the North Carolina constitutional conventions Tourgée attended; Greensboro, the seat of Guilford ["Horsford"] County, where Tourgée resided during most of his stay in North Carolina; Graham, the county seat of Alamance, where Wyatt Outlaw was lynched; Yanceyville, the county seat of Caswell, where John W. Stephens was murdered; and Salisbury, the site of the Confederate prison whose graveyard Mollie visits before leaving North Carolina.

whose depredations centered in the piedmont counties of his own Seventh District circuit. Obtaining indictments and convictions of Klan members and persuading the U.S. Congress and President Grant to act against the organization represented the greatest challenges Tourgée faced as a judge.

What "precipitated the Ku Klux Klan's campaign of terror," as historians have shown, was "the strength of white Republicanism and biracial cooperation," and what dictated the form of that campaign was the Conservatives' "realization that appeals to race consciousness were not working" to deter low-to-middle-income whites from voting with blacks. Having failed to regain power through demagoguery, Conservatives turned to organized violence. They concentrated their attack on the piedmont counties where the "Republican party rested on a coalition of black and white voters," and "their strategy focused on intimidating enough blacks" and immobilizing or recapturing enough whites through scare tactics and racist manipulation to break the Republican coalition.[52]

Conservatives launched their campaign of intimidation and terror as early as mid-April 1868, when the Republican North Carolina *Daily Standard* reported that "outrages perpetrated by the atrocious Kuklux clans" were occurring in many localities and that landlords were threatening to "discharge every colored man who votes the Republican ticket."[53] By February 1869, Klan violence had mushroomed into what the *Daily Standard* called a "Reign of Terror." Week after week, this Republican organ tallied the victims. In March it described the case of "an industrious colored man" who, "to get his honest due, sued for the wages of his labor" and won. "A short time after, the Ku Klux came, in the dead hour of night, to his house, whipped him nigh unto death, beat and maltreated his wife, and nearly killed his little child, *five months old,* while lying in the cradle. Later they turned out, a hundred or more strong, paraded the streets and gave to such men as would assist this man in obtaining justice warning to 'beware.' "[54] In April the paper editorialized: "The murders and outrages committed by the bloody miscreants who call themselves the Ku Klux have become alarmingly frequent in this State. The houses of Union men have been broken into in the dead of night and themselves, and sometimes their families, murdered in cold blood. Union men have been driven from their homes because they dared to vote for the right. Hundreds of citizens have been prevented from voting at all by the threats of these midnight murderers."[55] In September after yet another "colored man [had] been hung, and several white men shot at and maltreated," the *Daily Standard* renounced its policy of advising victims to rely solely on the "protection of the law." The law did not afford adequate protection, concluded the paper's editor, because so many law officers belonged to or shielded the Klan: "We now tell those who are assailed to fight, to resist force with force, and murder with death," but not to "commit similar outrages in retaliation."[56]

The Republican organ's call for armed resistance triggered a barrage of self-righteous vituperation from the Conservative press, led by the Raleigh *Daily Sentinel.* Its editor, Josiah Turner Jr., "the man who did the most to promote the Ku Klux conspiracy in North Carolina," had himself been traveling around the state fomenting violence.[57]

Already totaling "at least fifteen murders and hundreds" of "beatings, cuttings, shootings," and other atrocities in 1869 alone, Klan terrorism in Tourgée's piedmont district reached its peak in the months before the 1870 elections. The two counties singled out for the brunt of the terror campaign, Alamance and Caswell, boasted "an able and moderate Negro-white Republican leadership, which Tourgée had helped to establish" and which had proved "instrumental" in "swinging" both counties to the Republican party in the fall 1868 elections.[58] The Klan thus targeted the leaders who had achieved these results—the black artisan Wyatt Outlaw in Alamance, town commissioner and president of a Union League chapter that brought together black and white workingmen, and the poor white artisan John W. Stephens in Caswell, a state senator and trusted champion of the black population, who had "incurred Conservative displeasure as a Freedmen's Bureau agent and as a magistrate handling controversies between Negro laborers and the tobacco planters of the county."[59]

On 26 February 1870, "a band of one hundred or more" masked night-riders took "military possession" of Alamance's county seat, dragged Outlaw from his home in front of his screaming child, "bludgeoned" him in the street, slashed his lips to advertise the fate all "mouthy" blacks could expect to meet, and hanged him from a tree limb "pointed in silent mockery toward Judge Tourgée's courthouse less than a hundred feet away." Tourgée knew Outlaw well and believed he was killed because he had been "ferretting out previous acts of violence which had been committed in the county," thereby discovering "the identity of some of the parties engaged in them." It is equally likely, as historians have argued, that Outlaw was killed because he had forged such successful cross-racial alliances, even organizing an "armed night patrol of five black and white men in response to Ku Klux attacks."[60]

On 21 May it was Stephens's turn to succumb to the assassins he had long expected. Tourgée felt especially close to the self-educated Stephens, whom he had tutored in the study of law, helped pass the bar exam, advised on political matters, and regularly stayed with while holding court in Caswell, once joining an interracial group of supporters in defending Stephens's home against an anticipated Klan attack that did not materialize. During his last visit with Stephens only a month before his murder, Tourgée had assisted him in drawing up his will. "Since you left," Stephens had written Tourgée in a letter completing arrangements to provide for his family, "the K.K.^s has still bin committing their helish deeds. They have taken out of his house another white man Mr W^m. I. Ward and tied him to a tree and severley beat him. & a col. man by the name of Young Richmond and in addition to there usual barbarianism they castrated him it is thought that he will die."[61]

Stephens's "murder sent a thrill of horror and alarm through the breast of every republican in the state—" commented Tourgée. "Each one saw that this was only the fate he himself might expect. . . . For the first time the conviction forced itself upon the mind of every reasoning man that the Conservative party in the state were bound to control it, if by no other means at least by the cord and dagger—If they could not outvote the republican party they were bound to out murder it—." The circumstances of Stephens's assassination particularly shocked his fellow Republicans, though their suspicions would not be verified until two years later, when a black servant woman testified in a sworn affidavit that she had overheard former sheriff Frank Wiley brag to her employer on the night of the crime: "I have done the best days work of my life today. We have put old Stephens out of they [*sic*] way and the negros will not have the sway here any longer." (Her testimony was confirmed long afterward by the deathbed confession of a participant in the murder.) Wiley, whom Stephens had ironically been wooing to run on a "compromise ticket" in the futile hope of placating Conservatives, took advantage of a political meeting in the courthouse to lure Stevens into a room where a "group of waiting assassins," including "leading citizens of the county," overpowered, strangled, and stabbed him to death.[62]

The Klan's campaign of terror worked. Republicans stayed away from the polls, and Conservatives recaptured the state legislature in 1870. The victors soon reinvigorated many of the Black Codes' provisions, but reframed them in race-neutral language to conform to the Fourteenth Amendment.[63] They also proceeded to consolidate their grip on power by devising methods of perpetuating one-party, one-race rule. These methods included gerrymandering districts, altering "voting procedures and requirements . . . in a manner hostile to black and lower-class voters," lengthening residence requirements, disfranchising voters for "petty crimes," "confus[ing] less literate voters" with a "multiplicity of ballot boxes," refusing to register black voters, stuffing ballot boxes, and throwing out returns from Republican-dominated precincts. Such tactics, replicated in other southern states, would last into modern times.[64]

"THE JURIES ARE ALL KU KLUX"

Throughout the Klan's ascendancy, Tourgée fought a losing battle against it. Though he held a special court session in the summer of 1869, at which he managed to secure indictments of twenty suspected Klan members, to his disgust "all the defendants 'proved a *perfect alibi* without a particle of trouble,'" necessitating a "Not Guilty" verdict.[65] Writing to Emma from Alamance, he fumed: "The juries are all Ku Klux or at least a controlling element of them are so. . . . Yesterday three men were tried for cutting a colored man in pieces almost—stabbing and beating and maltreating in every possible manner—but it was all of no avail—'Not Guilty' was the verdict—It is no crime for a white man to cut a colored man open in Alamance—" Tourgée would later tell President Ulysses S. Grant that he had tried "sixty-four times . . . to break into" the Klan's "impregnable fortress" so as to "secure testimony sufficient to enable [him] to demand from juries indictment and conviction." He had never obtained a conviction; at best, he had procured a few indictments where Republican jurors predominated.[66]

As Stephens's murder showed all too starkly, Tourgée was risking his own life by taking on the Klan. Indeed, after Stephens's mangled body was found in the courthouse basement, Governor Holden himself instructed Tourgée not to hold court in Alamance because he would be "in personal danger to do so"—a directive Tourgée characteristically disregarded, though he considered Alamance "decidedly the worst county in the district" and feared he might not "outlive" the session.[67] He later uncovered plots "to hang him in downtown Greensboro, to waylay him as he rode his circuit alone in his buggy, and to create a court row during which he was to be shot." In retrospect, he concluded that he escaped Stephens's fate mainly because Klan leaders feared they might provoke a clampdown by the federal government if they assassinated a nationally prominent figure. Meanwhile, Tourgée persisted in his defiance, "fortif[ying] his home against attack, and . . . [riding] to court heavily armed and via circuitous buggy routes."[68]

Besides continuing to stand up to the Klan in court, he lobbied for federal intervention. In a strong letter to Joseph C. Abbott, U.S. Senator from North Carolina and a fellow carpetbagger, Tourgée provided statistics on the atrocities that had culminated in Stephens's murder: four arsons, 400 or 500 houses broken into, eleven murders, and a total of at least a thousand outrages in his judicial district. By "outrages," he specified to correspondents who contested his figures, he meant "*all violations of the rights of the person, of property or of the domicil, by persons in disguise,*" including "the binding, gagging and beating of men and women, indiscriminate shooting," and "the wanton terrifying of pregnant females" [underlining in original]. He underscored that he based his statistics on complaints filed by parties who had "flocked to [him] from every county in the hope of legal redress," many of whom bore on their bodies "unmistakeable evidence" substantiating their allegations.[69] Abbott shared the letter with his Republican colleagues in the Senate and House, and Tourgée had the satisfaction of knowing he had "helped to speed the passage, ten days after Stephens' death, of the first Enforcement Act,"[70] a major step toward extending federal jurisdiction over state lawlessness.

Before Tourgée could savor this triumph, the *New York Tribune* published a leaked and garbled version of his letter to Abbott, which put his life in even greater danger, subjecting Emma to unbearable stress. Desperate to escape "this miniature Hell," Tourgée implored his friends in Washington to find him a foreign post. "I wouldn't mind yellow-fever, cholera, fleas, earthquakes, vertigo, small-pox, cannibalisms, icebergs, sharks or any other name or shape of horror—provided always there are no K.K.K.," he announced in one "Private and Confidential" appeal.[71] Nothing came of such pleas, but Klan violence in North Carolina abated once the victorious Conservatives took their seats in the state legislature. Now that they were back in power, they needed social stability rather than anarchy.

Meanwhile, Governor Holden had terribly "bungled" his own attempt to stamp out the Klan by forming a militia of white Unionist mountaineers, rounding up suspected Klansmen without adequate evidence, and suspending habeas corpus. Tourgée judged these measures ill-considered and illegal, and Holden paid dearly for them when the Conservative legislature impeached, convicted, and removed him from office.[72]

At the national level, however, Tourgée's tenacious lobbying yielded more promising results. A congressional investigating committee began holding hearings and taking testimony in 1871, with Tourgée supplying names of witnesses to summon from North Carolina, among them some "Alamance Kuklux who [were] willing to puke the thing up." Not only did the inquest produce a thirteen-volume *Report . . . [on] the Condition of Affairs in the Late Insurrectionary States* and a separate two-volume *Senate Report* on North Carolina that remain the best sources of information on the Klan, but it also led to passage of the April 1871 Ku Klux Klan Act. A departure from the prevailing understanding of federal versus state sovereignty, that act designated as federal crimes "conspiracies to deprive citizens of the right to vote, hold office, serve on juries, and enjoy the equal protection of the laws," and it provided for federal prosecution of such crimes and the possibility of military intervention and suspension of habeas corpus if states did not police themselves.[73]

His hands strengthened by legislation that confronted Klan members with the threat of being tried and convicted in federal courts, Tourgée doggedly pursued the murderers of Outlaw and Stephens. By December 1871 he had accumulated enough evidence to frighten two reluctant participants in Outlaw's hanging into confessing and naming their fellow murderers. Their revelations prompted others to turn themselves in or skip the country. "The waters are stirred and sinners are coming to step into the pool almost every hour," Tourgée wrote excitedly to Emma. "I have knocked a big hole in the bottom of the bucket and think the KKK milk will spill badly—"[74] Ten days later he exultantly informed President Grant that he had induced an Alamance grand jury made up largely of Klan members to indict "sixty-three members of the Klan for felony and eighteen for the murder of Wyatt Outlaw"—an achievement he credited to the "unflinching firmness" of the Grant administration's support. He added: "Many of those indicted are of the most respectable families of the county—The confessions now in my hands also reveal the perpetrators of similar crimes in other counties—"[75]

Tourgée's exultation proved premature, for Outlaw's assassins would never stand trial, and Stephens's would go to their graves undisturbed. Less "unflinching" than Tourgée believed and beleaguered by corruption charges, Grant sensed a shift in the public mood during the electoral campaign of 1872, when a group of Republicans bolted from the party and called for ending Reconstruction and cleaning up government. After winning reelection, Grant pardoned all convicted Klansmen. The North Carolina legislature followed suit with a blanket proclamation of amnesty that covered all crimes committed by Klansmen but did not extend either to blacks languishing in jail for lesser offenses or to the "unjustly impeached" Governor Holden.[76]

THE COLLAPSE OF RECONSTRUCTION

The bitterest defeats were yet to come. Alienated by Republican malfeasance and battered by a severe economic depression on the eve of the 1874 election, voters nationally delivered the Democrats a sixty-vote majority in the House of Representatives, awarded them the governorships of eight northern states, and drastically narrowed the Republican edge in the Senate. Tourgée took no consolation from the one accomplishment Republicans salvaged from their lashing at the polls—the passage by the lame duck Congress of the 1875 Civil Rights Act, authored by one of the chief architects of Radical Reconstruction, the late Massachusetts Senator Charles Sumner. Its outlawing of racial discrimination in public accommodations, theaters, transportation facilities, jury selection, and, in its original form, public schools, would affect white Southerners "like a blister-plaster put on a dozing man whom it is desirable to soothe to sleep"—it would generate a white supremacist firestorm, yet prove unenforceable, Tourgée prophesied.[77] North Carolina seemingly confirmed his forebodings. Fortified by the national mood registered in the election results, Conservatives there called another constitutional convention in 1875. This time they enjoyed the majority (having thrown out the votes in a Republican county), and Tourgée was reduced to a rearguard defense of the reforms he had fought so hard to institute in 1868. Reacting to one of his glum letters about the Conservatives' maneuvers, Emma agreed that she, too, could hardly "bear to think" about "how they are tearing up the Constitution . . . and all being done by *fraud* too" [underlining in original].[78] The "tearing up" nevertheless proceeded, and when the convention ended, the 1868 constitution so popular among North Carolina's common folk and so loathed by its elite was shorn of its most democratic feature: the system of local self-government Tourgée had introduced. Beginning in February 1877, the governor and the state legislature would appoint all officials, from judges down to supervisors of election, locking one-party rule into place. In addition, the constitution now mandated segregation and banned interracial marriage, thus giving legal sanction to African Americans' inferior status.[79]

The presidential election of 1876 completed the wreck of Reconstruction all over the country. A "tidal wave of fraud" and violence led to disputed returns in South Carolina, Louisiana, and Florida, and the results hung in the balance for months, until a fifteen-member electoral commission that included five Supreme Court Justices awarded the presidency to the Republican Rutherford B. Hayes. In what many contemporaries believed to be a quid pro quo, Hayes promptly initiated a "let alone" policy in the South, euphemistically called the New Departure, that entailed ending federal military intervention, abandoning the freedpeople, and conciliating the white supremacists who had returned to power throughout the former Confederate states.[80]

Tourgée would always blame northern Republicans for the debacle. Unable to think beyond the next election (in his judgment), they had been in too much of a hurry to readmit the ex-Confederate states to the Union and had sought a short-term panacea rather than a long-term solution to the problem of rebuilding the South on a democratic foundation. The congressional leaders who had formulated Reconstruction policy had assumed that if granted the ballot, the freedmen would be able to defend themselves

—an assumption that disregarded the gaping disparities of power, economic resources, education, and political experience between newly emancipated slaves and their erstwhile masters, as well as the lingering "effects of Slavery, upon every class of [the South's] inhabitants." Lacking first-hand insight into the "bitter scorn of a long dominant race for one they have held in bondage," they naively supposed that the dispossessed slaveholders would soon realize it was in their interest to woo the votes of their liberated chattels. Once the rise of the Klan revealed the intransigence and ferocity of the white supremacist opposition, northern Republicans simply walked away, betraying both the freedpeople and the white Unionists who had rallied to their side.[81]

The nationwide collapse of Reconstruction left Tourgée with no prospects for employment. Being reduced to penury for the second time in a decade all but destroyed the Tourgées' marriage, already strained by years of contending with social ostracism, public vilification, and Klan terrorism. "Your face has gathered a fixed patient look as if you were all the time carrying some burden—" Tourgée lamented to Emma, fearing he had "been so engrossed and careless" that he had paid scant attention to her feelings.[82] Emma's patience finally gave out, and in 1878 she returned to her family in Erie, Pennsylvania, taking their daughter with her, but Tourgée could not give up the struggle. Having lost his judgeship in the election of 1874, Tourgée ran for Congress in 1878 (against Emma's wishes) and met with a crushing defeat. "The feeling of hate to the North is growing so apparent here that I wonder I should not better have appreciated its strength," he admitted to Emma. Although Emma had held out hope of their starting a new life together in the North, Tourgée still could not make the break. "There is nothing for me here—and yet I hate to leave. . . . I have strung so many sweet hopes on bright dreams here that I seem almost to have knit my heart into the land," he wrote poignantly.[83] In the depths of his despair at being "dead politically," Tourgée found a new vocation. If he could no longer act in the political or judicial sphere, he could influence public opinion through literature and thus perhaps reverse the nation's catastrophic course.

A FOOL'S ERRAND

Tourgée had begun exercising his literary imagination toward the end of his judgeship. With the intention of demonstrating that despite its official demise, "*Slavery still lives and dominates*" through the "unconscious influences" it continues to exert, especially on the mentality of the "master race," he had started a novel titled *Toinette,* which he carried with him on his judicial circuit and wrote in off hours.[84] The plot, involving a slave concubine who renounces her illicit relationship with her master after he emancipates her and sends her to Oberlin College, illustrates two of Tourgée's principal ideas, which he would develop in many subsequent works, including *A Fool's Errand* and *Bricks Without Straw*: first, that education offers the key to regenerating the South by freeing the minds of whites and blacks alike from slavery's "unconscious influences"; and second, that the best hope for the region's future lies in an alliance between emancipated slaves and poor whites.[85] Published in 1874 under the pseudonym Henry Churton, *Toinette* sold modestly, to Tourgée's disappointment.

The novel that would at last gain Tourgée a national audience on the subject closest to his heart—Reconstruction and why it had failed—would be *A Fool's Errand. By One of the Fools* (1879). Its protagonist Comfort Servosse, whom the narrator refers to ironically throughout as "the Fool," follows a trajectory much like the author's. Tourgée portrays him as a political ingénue gradually radicalized by his exposure to southern intolerance, but he gives Servosse his own political opinions and shows him undergoing the same social ostracism, abuse in the local press, inundation of threatening letters, attempts on his life, and thwarted struggle with the Ku Klux Klan that he himself had undergone.[86] The thirteen chapters *A Fool's Errand* devotes to the Klan, drawn from Tourgée's voluminous files, overwhelm the reader by sheer accumulation. As if amassing evidence in the courtroom, Tourgée summons an array of witnesses brutalized by the masked marauders. The parade of grisly testimony climaxes with scenes faithfully rendering the murder of "John Walters" (aka Stephens) and the lynching of "Uncle Jerry Hunt" (aka Wyatt Outlaw).

A Fool's Errand provides not only a graphic eyewitness account of the terrorism that overthrew Reconstruction but a postmortem of the disaster. It is northern Republicans who turned Reconstruction into a fool's errand, he stresses, not the idealistic "fools" who dedicated their lives to implementing the Radicals' program of racial equality. The party's "cowardly, vacillating, and inconsistent" policy unleashed the Klan, and Republican leaders' "cowardly shirking of responsibility" and "snuffling whine about peace and conciliation" allowed it to triumph. Tourgée documents his charges with fictionalized versions of his exchanges with the northern politicians he sarcastically calls "the Wise Men." Cementing his case, a chilling letter from one of the Wise Men responds to the Fool's plea for decisive action against the Klan by arguing that the Constitution does not authorize the federal government to "interfere in the internal affairs" of the southern states: "If the colored people and the Union men of the South expect to receive the approval, respect, and moral support of the country, they must show themselves capable of self-government, able to take care of themselves. The government has done all it can be expected to do,—all it had power to do, in fact. It has given the colored man the ballot, armed him with the weapon of the freeman, and now he must show himself worthy to use it."[87] Only one remedy remains, concludes Tourgée at the end of *A Fool's Errand*: "Let the Nation educate the colored man and the poor-white man *because* the Nation held them in bondage, and is responsible for their education: educate the voter *because* the Nation can not afford that he should be ignorant."[88]

Published anonymously in November 1879, a few months after Tourgée left the South never to return, *A Fool's Errand* caused a sensation. The novel sold so fast that bookstores could not keep up with the demand, exceeding 5,000 copies in the first six weeks and nearly 150,000 before the year was out. Domestic sales would reputedly "[reach] the high water mark of 600,000" in Tourgée's lifetime, and translations into German, French, Italian, Swedish, and Russian would extend its fame beyond U.S. borders. Reviewers widely hailed *A Fool's Errand* as "The New 'Uncle Tom,'" predicting that it would prove "as serviceable in enlightening the North about the startling events of the reconstruction period" as Stowe's masterpiece had in exposing the evils of slavery. Even a North Carolina organ recognized the power of a novel "destined, we fear, to do as much harm in the world as 'Uncle Tom's Cabin.'" Tourgée must have been especially gratified by the reviews that urged statesmen to heed his message. "If every representative and senator in Congress, if the governors and state officers of every State in the Union, could read this volume," proclaimed one newspaper, " . . . we should be nearer a solution of the problem of reconstruction."[89]

Eager to capitalize on the success of *A Fool's Errand,* Tourgée's publishers persuaded him to drop his anonymity and furnish both a factual companion volume and a fictional sequel to his bestseller. *The Invisible Empire* (1880), bound together with *A Fool's Errand* as an appendix to the second edition, remains valuable as a contemporaneous documentary history of the Klan. Its fictional successor *Bricks Without Straw,* completed on the eve of the 1880 election, would become a popular hit in its own right and help bring to power a Republican president more sympathetic to African Americans.

BRICKS WITHOUT STRAW

Complementing *A Fool's Errand, Bricks Without Straw* shifts the focus from Tourgée's autobiographical persona to the freedpeople, whose story he had subordinated to his own in the earlier work. Elevating them from minor characters into central protagonists, and implicitly answering the Wise Man in *A Fool's Errand* who had questioned the capacity of the "colored people" for "self-government," Tourgée's second Reconstruction novel portrays the newly emancipated slaves not as pitiful victims of white violence but as active agents in a struggle for self-determination. *Bricks Without Straw* consequently restricts the Klan to a single, albeit devastating, episode in its dramatization of Black Reconstruction.

Tourgée explains the title in a satiric preface that purports to be a translation from an ancient Egyptian papyrus. Paralleling the Bible's Exodus story, it tells of how Pharaoh commands the laborers he holds in bondage to make bricks with stubble gathered from the fields instead of with straw furnished by the taskmaster. Pharaoh wants to build a palace that will advertise his "glory" to the world, but he wants his laborers to do it overnight without the necessary materials, just as the American nation wants the newly freed slaves to uplift themselves overnight by their own unaided efforts. Speaking through the "king's jester" Neoncapos, who undertakes the "fool's errand" of ridiculing Pharaoh's folly, Tourgée warns that the "palace" built with these ill-made bricks will eventually collapse. The rest of the novel illustrates how the nation has imperiled its own safety by condemning the slaves it has emancipated at such great cost to make bricks without straw.

COUNTERING STEREOTYPES, REPRESENTING AFRICAN AMERICANS

Tourgée carefully crafted the narrative strategies, characters, and plot of *Bricks Without Straw* to challenge the stereotypes that white supremacists had disseminated of Reconstruction as an era of rampant "Negro domination" and to present an alternative history of the brief interlude during which African Americans in the South had sought to exercise the rights the U.S. Congress had extended to them in the Thirteenth, Fourteenth, and Fifteenth Amendments awarding them freedom, citizenship, and (for men) qualified suffrage.[90] The novel proper opens with a fictional device that mirrors the legislative process of giving black men a voice in determining their own and the country's future—a chapter-long monologue in which the main protagonist Nimbus ponders the "strange queries which freedom had so recently propounded to him and his race." "I'm dod-dinged now ef I know who I be ennyhow," exclaims Nimbus as he reflects on the changes of identity he has undergone over the past few years and recalls how each step of his journey from slavery to citizenship has been marked by a white authority's forcing him to adopt an unwanted second name (89). Tourgée makes clear that Nimbus equates naming with establishing an identity and that he regards defining his identity for himself as the essence of freedom. Like Malcolm X a century later, Nimbus refuses to let white society "brand" him or his children with the "slave-mark" of his master's surname (119).

Nimbus speaks in dialect, as do all the uneducated characters in *Bricks Without Straw,* black and poor white alike, because Tourgée's commitment to giving the disempowered a voice requires transcribing their speech as authentically as he can. Indeed, he explicitly avows this aim in an 1894 letter to an editor at *McClure's.* "You know I am a realist, in a much broader sense than those who claim the name, and *my* realism compells me to represent men as talking as I find that they really do—" he specifies [underlining in original].[91] Reflecting the trend toward literary realism on which Tourgée comments, dialect appears in the fiction of most nineteenth-century American writers and even some British writers seeking to capture regional, ethnic, and class accents. Tourgée's rendering of southern black folk speech resembles Charles Chesnutt's, but falls short of the skill with which Mark Twain and Frances Ellen Watkins Harper convey their folk characters' accents to the ear rather than to the eye, minimizing demands on the reader. Of course white southern writers like Thomas Nelson Page and Joel Chandler Harris also pepper their fiction with dialect, but their black characters, inevitably stereotyped as faithful slaves, serve as mouthpieces through whom their creators lament the passing of the harmonious race relations that allegedly prevailed under slavery.

In striking contrast, Tourgée's description of Nimbus systematically reverses both the falsifications of racist ideology and the clichés of minstrelsy. Unlike the "burnt-cork" stage Negro, emphasizes Tourgée, Nimbus is no comic figure (100). "Earnest," "thoughtful," and "quiet," he does not shuffle or jump Jim Crow, but holds himself manfully erect. His head is not apelike, as caricatured in such proslavery texts as Josiah C. Nott's and George R. Gliddon's *Types of Mankind* (1854),[92] but "shapely" and "well-balanced." His "self-reliant character" gives the lie to claims that the Negro cannot manage without white supervision. While discrediting the stereotypes that "have come to represent the negro to the unfamiliar mind," Tourgée simultaneously draws attention to the racializing process that the white mind goes through on seeing a human being in a black skin. The white reader, he implies, cannot recognize a "fine figure of a man" in "ebon hue." Instead, the white mind automatically perceives the same traits differently under a different racial exterior, even resorting to a different vocabulary to register its impressions. Tourgée pointedly notes, for example, that "if [Nimbus] had been white," his face would be perceived as "grave," but because he is black, the appropriate word is "heavy." Similarly, the very person who "in a white skin would have been considered a man of great physical power and endurance" metamorphoses into a savage brute in the white imagination once the skin color changes to black (100).

Tourgée specifically dispels the image of the black man as a savage brute—a major ingredient of the white supremacist campaign against Reconstruction—in a scene that shows Nimbus demanding his rights and shielding himself against violence, but not retaliating in kind when his former master Potestatem Desmit brandishes a cane over his head. "I'se been a sojer sence I was a slave, an' ther don't no man hit me a lick jes cos I'm black enny mo'," warns Nimbus as he parries the blow and wrests away the cane (153). Loath to harm an "ole man," he leaves Desmit on the ground "where he had fallen or been thrown" in the tussle—an ambiguity that heightens Nimbus's self-restraint—and decides to lodge a complaint and "let de law take its course" (154). It is not the freed blacks who violate the rule of law, Tourgée indicates, contrary to white supremacist propaganda, but their disgruntled erstwhile masters.

Along with the stereotype of the lawless black savage, Tourgée counters allegations that Reconstruction had delivered the reins of government to ignorant ex-slaves who launched a carnival of misrule. Accordingly, he depicts Nimbus as unwilling to run for office on the grounds that he "hain't got no larnin'" and understands tobacco cultivation better than governance (207). Rather than aspiring to rule over whites, Nimbus acts as a leader of the African American community. Tourgée meticulously delineates the factors that have gained Nimbus his leadership: service in the Union army, which has "taught him to stand his ground, even against a white man," a crucial "lesson of liberty" (153); investment of his military bounty money in land, through which he has acquired economic independence; skill and hard work, which have helped him prosper as a tobacco farmer; community spirit, which he has demonstrated by donating a portion of his land and timber to establish a church and school for the freedpeople and by selling small parcels of his plantation to freedmen anxious to follow his example of home ownership and self-employment; and willingness to defend the rights of his fellow freedmen at great risk to his own safety, which encourages them to do likewise. In short, Tourgée characterizes Nimbus as a born leader whose illiteracy does not prevent him from exerting a beneficial influence over his peers, but does give him a sense of his limitations.

Tourgée's extensive interactions with African Americans enabled him to portray Nimbus with a realism unmatched by any other white writer of his day. Compared to Nimbus, for example, Mark Twain's Jim in *The Adventures of Huckleberry Finn* (1884), the best-known African American character of post–Civil War fiction, dwindles into a one-dimensional figure. Tourgée modeled Nimbus on several black men he had known during his stints as a Civil War soldier and Reconstruction politician and judge. His hero's first and most obvious real-life prototype, of course, is the fugitive slave Tourgée had renamed Nimbus, as recorded in his Civil War diary.[93] Perhaps commenting wryly on an actual altercation he had with this fugitive, Tourgée describes the fictional Nimbus as protesting vigorously against being christened "George Nimbus" by the Union army officer who musters him under that name into "Company C, of the — Massachusetts Volunteer Infantry" (105), paralleling Tourgée's Company E of the 105th Ohio Volunteer Infantry. A second model for Nimbus is Wyatt Outlaw. An ex-slave like Nimbus, he too had served in the Union army, contributed to building a church (in his case on land he had helped purchase), boldly resisted intimidation, and mobilized African American (and poor white) voters after the war, the transgression for which he had been lynched by the Klan.[94] A third model for Nimbus is Tourgée's Greensboro neighbor Harmon Unthank, who had cooperated with him during North Carolina's 1868 constitutional convention and the Republican and Union League campaigns the same year. A prosperous carpenter recognized as the "uncontested 'boss' of the black community," Unthank, like Nimbus, helped fellow African Americans to purchase property and thus start on the road toward economic independence.[95]

Yet no one-to-one correspondence links any historical figure to Tourgée's fictional hero.[96] As he explained to a reader who asked him to identify the historical originals of the characters in *A Fool's Errand,* his "characters were *all* creations pure and simple" [underlining in original], but "built upon actualities" that had come under his observation. In incorporating historical events into his novels and drawing on his "knowledge . . . of locality and incident to give verisimilitude, flavor and . . . interest," he sought to provide a "true picture of the time," not snapshots of recognizable people.[97]

Though Nimbus is the most memorable of the African American protagonists in *Bricks Without Straw* (or for that matter in Tourgée's entire corpus), the treatment of Nimbus's childhood friend and fellow community leader Eliab Hill also challenges stereotype. It invites comparison, for example, with such representations of mulattoes as Stowe's George Harris in *Uncle Tom's Cabin* and Rebecca Harding Davis's more complex, but problematic, Doctor Broderip in *Waiting for the Verdict* (1867). Unlike Stowe and Davis, Tourgée portrays Eliab not as a racial type but as an individual. He does not attribute Eliab's "erect," manly carriage, "thoughtful brow," and "nobility of expression" (118) to his white blood, as Stowe does George Harris's. Nor does he ascribe Eliab's "womanly" traits and physical weakness to the "taint" of black blood and the ill effects of miscegenation, as Davis does Broderip's.[98] Instead, Tourgée traces the "suffering" etched on Eliab's face to an "affliction" resulting from a childhood "cold . . . which settled in his legs . . . producing rheumatism" (apparently polio or rheumatic fever, as evidenced by his "shrunken and distorted" limbs [118, 127]). The severely impaired mobility this affliction has caused, Tourgée later specifies, accounts for Eliab's predisposition toward the passive, "womanly" courage of a martyr rather than the "aggressive," masculine courage of a soldier. Tourgée underscores, however, that Eliab is no Uncle Tom. Far from being religiously "averse to taking life in self-defense," Eliab reacts to a Klan incursion by wishing he had a good repeating rifle, so that "he might not only sell his life dearly, but even repel the attack" (272–73).

While eschewing the overt racial theorizing to which Stowe and Davis resort, Tourgée subtly controverts racist ideology. He depicts Eliab, like Nimbus, with a "broad, full forehead" and a "finely poised" head rather than the misshapen cranium imputed to the Negro in Nott's and Gliddon's *Types of Mankind* (a feature Davis reproduces in Broderip's "low, heavily marked forehead").[99] He offsets Eliab's "womanly eyes" with a masculine "directness of gaze" (118) that suggests pride in his identity rather than the sense of inferiority Broderip displays when he "cow[s] before the white skin and Saxon features" of a rival and assumes the "defeated, shrunken look" of a man who sees himself as "but a mulatto."[100] And once again countering the image of the Negro as a perpetual child, incapable of providing for his own needs, Tourgée accentuates the "self-helping" character Eliab shares with Nimbus, which the cripple exhibits by earning his living as a shoemaker (118).

Eliab represents an alternative route to African American empowerment —the acquisition of literacy—that historically complemented or substituted for the economic advancement Nimbus has attained through land ownership. Taught to read by his indulgent master and mistress, he has exerted a magnetic influence over his community as a preacher ever since his days as a slave. Eliab also personifies what Tourgée calls the "inseparable" fusion of religion and politics among African Americans, whose "religion is tinged with political thought, and their political thought shaped by religious conviction" (206).

Tourgée found Eliab's prototype, a crippled preacher from Clay Hill, South Carolina, named Elias Hill, in the thirteen-volume congressional report on Klan atrocities. Hill is there identified as "colored" (a term used either to designate a non-white or to connote mixed ancestry) and described as "crippled in both legs and arms, which are shriveled by rheumatism" dating from his seventh year, as in the case of Tourgée's Eliab. The real-life Elias Hill, though he boasted his fictional namesake's "finely developed intellectual head" and "unusual intelligence," was far more disabled. "He cannot . . . help himself," notes the transcriber of Hill's testimony before the congressional Select Committee, but "has to be fed and cared for personally by others." Foisted on his self-emancipated father as a "burden of which his master was glad to be rid," Hill had displayed his impulse toward independence by learning to read and write with the assistance of schoolchildren and by becoming, like the fictional Eliab, a teacher, preacher, and Union League organizer after the war.[101]

Tourgée suggestively revises his congressional source by changing Eliab's complexion from "colored" to "almost white" (118) and by making him dependent for physical aid not on his biological family but on a comrade from slavery days whose skin color, black as a "thunder-cloud" (98), contrasts strikingly with his. Through these revisions, Tourgée conveys the image of an African American community reliant for survival on the solidarity of mulatto and black, literate and illiterate, needy and prosperous. "The colored people must stand or fall together," preaches Eliab (218). His lifelong bond with Nimbus and the twin leadership roles the two play illustrate that message.[102]

The theme of racial unity aligns *Bricks Without Straw* more closely with such African American novels as Martin Delany's *Blake* (1859) and Frances Ellen Watkins Harper's *Iola Leroy* (1892)—though Tourgée never seems to have read either—than with any white-authored work of its era. Like Harper, Tourgée emphasizes his African American characters' relations with each other and correspondingly de-emphasizes their relations with whites—the subject that dominates *Uncle Tom's Cabin* and *Huckleberry Finn.* And like both Harper and Delany, he roots his black and mulatto protagonists firmly in the African American community and centers his novel on the collective fate of the African American people.[103]

Tourgée's departures from the white conventions of his time stand out even in the case of the one character in *Bricks Without Straw* who acts the part of a "jester" or minstrel: Berry Lawson, the cousin of Nimbus's wife Lugena. Unlike such minstrel figures as Stowe's Sam or Twain's Jim, Berry does not entertain the white reader with self-important posturing, malapropisms, superstitions, or slapstick as the butt of a white character's practical jokes.[104] Instead, he entertains his fellow blacks by "laughing to keep from crying" (as Langston Hughes would famously phrase it) over their white bosses' countless ways of cheating and exploiting them—a typical form of African American humor.[105] "When I went [to work sharecropping] dar I didn't hev a rag ter my back—nary a rag, an' now jes see how I'se covered wid 'em!" Berry jokes to roars of wry amusement (210). As Elliott points out, Berry's humor cuts not only against whites but against those blacks, like his kinsman Nimbus, who believe that through hard work they will be able to "compete with the planters" as "economic equal[s]." Berry's example suggests to the contrary that "however hard Nimbus works, the planters have the power to keep him in his place"—an admonition driven home by the lyrics of the "Poll Tax Song" Berry strikes up on Nimbus's approach. The song bitterly satirizes the contrivance of a levy "equivalent to at least one fourth of a month's pay" (223), through which the planters have shifted the burden of taxation onto the freedpeople. Most of the stanzas pertain especially to landless freedmen like Berry, who sink further into debt peonage because they owe interest to their employers for paying their poll taxes, but the opening lines also warn that because "De brack man's gittin' awful rich," whites perceive him as a threat (221). Tourgée had heard North Carolina freedmen sing the "Poll Tax Song" "with much gusto" during the 1867 electoral campaign, when he had sent the lyrics to the *National Anti-Slavery Standard.*[106] At the 1868 constitutional convention, he had fought unsuccessfully to abolish the poll tax. Thus, he merges his own voice with

Berry's as he highlights the "grim humor" (223) of the landowners' Machiavellian provisions for maintaining slavery after emancipation. Indeed, Berry's pose as a jester recalls the mask Tourgée himself assumes at the outset as the "king's jester" Neoncapos, who derides the folly of forcing laborers to make bricks without straw.

REWRITING RECONSTRUCTION

Just as Tourgée fashions his characters to counter the prevalent stereotypes of African Americans, he devises his plot to rewrite the history of Reconstruction. Instead of an orgy of misgovernment by black buffoons, he shows that Reconstruction can best be understood as a thwarted quest for self-determination. The first third of the novel highlights the freedpeople's progress toward economic self-sufficiency and political autonomy, the second third dramatizes their spirited resistance to the tactics white supremacists use to regain hegemony, and the last describes their relapse into semi-slavery once their resistance is crushed.

The initial phase of the action begins in 1867 but flashes back to the decades before the war and retraces the milestones on the road African Americans have traveled from slavery to citizenship. For Nimbus, who recapitulates his people's odyssey, the first of these milestones is his escape from Confederate army lines, where he has been sent to "work on fortifications," to the Union army encampment, where he enlists in the war for his people's freedom (102–104). Much as W. E. B. Du Bois would later characterize the slave's "withdrawal and bestowal of his labor" as a "general strike" that "decided the war" and would credit black soldiers with making "the slaveholders face the alternative of surrendering to the North, or to the Negroes," Tourgée underscores that "the South fell—stricken at last most fatally by the dark hands which she had manacled, and overcome by their aid whose manhood she had refused to acknowledge" (105).[107]

Tourgée hails the second milestone Nimbus passes—the registration of his marriage after he returns home from the war—as "the first act of freedom, the first step of legal recognition or manly responsibility!" (107). Once again exemplifying Tourgée's acuity as a historian, the understanding he reveals of this act of self-affirmation anticipates Herbert Gutman's groundbreaking analysis of North Carolina and Mississippi marriage registration records as proof of the ex-slaves' "commitment to legal marriage."[108] In Tourgée's words: "The race felt its importance as did no one else at that time. By hundreds and thousands they crowded the places appointed, to accept the honor offered to their posterity, and thereby unwittingly conferred undying honor upon themselves" (107).

To clarify the significance of the third milestone Nimbus crosses—his appeal to a Freedmen's Bureau officer to settle a dispute over wages owed his wife by her employer, their former master Potestatem Desmit—Tourgée must rehabilitate the reputation of the government agency so maligned by southern whites. The planters wanted a labor force that they could exploit and abuse at will. In their view, the Freedmen's Bureau indulged the native laziness of a race that needed to be driven to work with the lash and kept to the grindstone with draconian laws. Tourgée's nemesis, North Carolina's Conservative governor Jonathan Worth, expressed this opinion succinctly: "The race never did work voluntarily and never will," but "with the Freedmen's Bureau here the necessary discipline cannot be used."[109] Well before Reconstruction ended, southern planters had won their propaganda war against the Freedmen's Bureau, which was divested of its labor-regulating function in 1869 and dismantled in 1872.

As Tourgée observes, the credulous northern public believed the Freedmen's Bureau was a "terrible engine of oppression and terror and infamy, because of the denunciations which the former slave-owners heaped upon it" (154). He refutes this misrepresentation both by stressing that neither the freedmen themselves, nor white Unionists, nor the "teachers of colored schools" joined in the "torrent of detraction" (155) and by giving the reader a glimpse of a bureau officer mediating a typical dispute. In his rendition of the scene, Tourgée accentuates Nimbus's moderation, the bureau officer's low-key handling of the matter, and the ex-slaveholder's wounded pride, which led him to translate a minor altercation into "the most degrading ordeal he could by any possibility be called upon to pass through" because it put a "gentleman" on the same level as a "negro" (159). The real reason for the planter class's hostility to the Freedmen's Bureau, Tourgée indicates, is that by providing a mechanism through which laborers could seek redress for mistreatment, the agency schooled ex-slaves in the exercise of their rights as citizens entitled to equal protection under the law.

The mediation of the Freedmen's Bureau also helps Nimbus fulfill his dream of purchasing land—the fourth milestone he reaches. Tourgée thus arranges through fiction what he had failed to achieve in life—an expansion of the Freedmen's Bureau's mission that would enable the masses of ex-slaves to advance from the status of landless laborers to that of independent landowners. Nimbus's development into one of the most successful tobacco farmers in the county contradicts the propaganda of planters like Worth, who must surely have known as well as Tourgée did that tobacco cultivation required intensive year-round labor and that mastering the cultivation of the "fine tobacco for which the locality was already celebrated" (174) took "years of experience."[110] Nimbus's example, replicated by the growth around him of a black community made up of "thrifty" artisans and farmers to whom he has sold parcels of his land, likewise paints a picture of Black Reconstruction that Du Bois would amplify half a century later.

"These black folk wanted two things—" Du Bois would write: "first, land which they could own and work for their own crops," giving them "economic freedom"; and second, "schools," which could satisfy their thirst for knowledge and open the doorway to "political power."[111] The school and church Nimbus builds on his land at Eliab's suggestion, with the assistance of the Freedmen's Bureau, which additionally supplies a Yankee schoolteacher, constitute a fifth milestone for the community.

The last milestone on the road from slavery to citizenship was gaining the right to vote, the crowning legislative achievement of Reconstruction, introduced in the 1867 Reconstruction Act and written into the U.S. Constitution in the Fifteenth Amendment of 1870. Chapter 19, "The Shadow of the Flag," climaxes Tourgée's celebration of Black Reconstruction's successes as the "colored voters" of the vicinity, under Nimbus's leadership, "meet at the church on the morning of election and march in a body to the polls with music and banners, in order most appropriately and significantly to commemorate their first exercise of the electoral privilege" (183). This chapter also marks the transition to the next phase of the novel, which focuses on the conflict between the African American community and white supremacists.

To the dethroned white ruling class, the sight of black voters marching en masse to the polls can mean only that the racial order is being overturned. Convinced that the "niggers" are planning to "kill all the white men, burn the town, and then ravish the white women," "well-armed" whites block access to the polls, shoot into the procession, and almost precipitate a bloody clash (185, 186). Tourgée based the incident on an actual "massacre" that had taken place in the village of Camilla, Georgia, in September 1868, but he gave his fictionalized version a significantly different outcome. The Camilla procession was heading not toward the polls, but toward a political meeting at which the white (not black) Republicans in its vanguard were to address the crowd. Ignoring assurances of the parade's "peaceful intentions," a mob of "400 armed whites, led by the local sheriff, opened fire . . . and then scoured the countryside for those who had fled, eventually killing and wounding more than a score of blacks."[112] Tourgée instead allows the Yankee schoolteacher Mollie Ainslee to avert such a massacre by mediating between hostile whites and militant blacks. Galloping to the front on the black horse that symbolizes her power to tame the ex-slaves, Mollie asks Eliab to provide an eyewitness account of the outbreak and relegates Nimbus to the task of "keep[ing] order" among his brethren while she charges off under a flag of truce to negotiate with the white townsmen (188). "You provoked this affray by your foolish love of display," she scolds the hitherto dauntless Nimbus, from whom she metaphorically seizes the reins. Her "nerve" succeeds in disarming the enraged whites as well, and the sheriff himself gives Mollie three cheers, calls off the volley, and agrees to let the procession—and the voting—continue unimpeded. Does the scene hint at tensions between Tourgée and the African American leaders with whom he worked during Reconstruction? Is Tourgée implying that the mediation of a cool-headed northern white might have accomplished better results than African Americans' "display" of militancy, by preventing rather than unleashing the bloodshed that had occurred in Camilla? Is he paying homage to the courageous role that schoolteachers like Emma, on whom Mollie is partially modeled and to whom he dedicated *Bricks Without Straw,* played during the Klan's reign of terror? Or is he simply attempting to "sweeten the hellishness of that epoch" through a fictional device?[113] Whatever the reason for its departure from historical fact, the episode foreshadows the disempowerment Tourgée's African American characters undergo after the overthrow of Reconstruction, a development reflected in the plot's shift away from them and toward their white benefactors.

DRAMATIZING WHITE TERRORISM AND BLACK RESISTANCE

With the aborted celebration of black suffrage, Tourgée's revisionist history of Reconstruction moves from chronicling the ex-slaves' accomplishments since their emancipation to dramatizing the harassment, economic coercion, electoral fraud, and sheer terrorism through which white supremacists recaptured power, reversed black gains, and drove the freedpeople back into quasi-slavery. As in *A Fool's Errand,* Tourgée contests the era's dominant explanation of why Reconstruction failed. The blame should fall not on the ex-slaves, carpetbaggers, and scalawags scapegoated by white southern propagandists, he argues in *Bricks Without Straw,* but on "the Nation," which refuses to protect the ex-slaves it has enfranchised, yet expects them to uplift themselves in the face of unremitting opposition from an "unscrupulous, . . . aggressive, turbulent, arrogant, and scornful" ruling class (352).

While lashing out against the national government and exposing the viciousness of the white supremacist onslaught, Tourgée nonetheless highlights the black community's valiant resistance. When the freedpeople are confronted with threats of retaliation for their political activities, Nimbus and Eliab lead a mass meeting at which Nimbus advocates a general strike and vows to underwrite the striking plantation workers until their white employers back down, and Eliab urges "every man [to] do his duty and vote, and act as a citizen whenever called upon to do so, for the sake of his race in the future" (217). The two also organize the black community for self-defense after being sent a coffin-board painted with a "skull and cross-bones" and the letters K.K.K. (250). Even at the height of the Klan attack in which the white supremacist juggernaut culminates, Tourgée shows his black characters fighting back. Although the masked night riders succeed in brutalizing Nimbus's wife Lugena, bludgeoning the helpless Eliab almost to death, and burning down the church and schoolhouse that serve as the institutional vehicles of the freedpeople's uplift, they do not escape unscathed. Nimbus dispatches a Klansman with his army saber, "swung by a practiced hand" (276). Berry, who had earlier contended that it would be futile to fight against insurmountable odds, drives off the invaders with the "fierce angry challenge of [his] rifle" (277). Most memorably, Lugena, seeing a Klansman aim a pistol at Nimbus, seizes an axe and brings it crashing "down through mask and flesh and bone," cleaving the head of their foe (276).

As was his wont, Tourgée based this fictional episode on factual sources. Both the sources he selected and the ways he revised them confirm that he wanted to honor the militant struggle the freedpeople had waged before Klan terrorism finally subdued them. For the beating of Eliab, Tourgée drew on one of the most notorious Klan atrocities reported in the 1871 congressional investigations that he had helped initiate. The original testimony of Elias Hill describes his ordeal in much more graphic detail, however, and emphasizes the tortures to which he and his family members were subjected, not the gestures of self-assertion they made—an emphasis dictated by the purpose of the Congressional hearings. For example, the real-life Hill had asked his torturers to spare his life and was mockingly forced by them to "pray that God may forgive Ku-Klux," whereas the fictional Eliab masters his fear of suffering and death and deliberately confronts the "curses of his assailants" with the Christlike prayer "Forgive them, Father. . . . They know not [what they do]" (276). Similarly, the real-life Hill's sister-in-law had pointed the Klansmen to his house after they had struck her "five or six licks," but the fictional Eliab reveals himself to save Lugena from further abuse by the Klansmen who are pummeling her to make her divulge his whereabouts. Tourgée's account of Lugena's battering, on the other hand, is a far more graphic account. Lugena's shrieks of "Oh! don't! don't!" her agonized writhing, her torn garment, and her "fully exposed" body "roll-[ing] in the dust" all suggest rape in a scene that redefines the rape of the South as a trope more applicable to black women than to white (271–272). Still, Tourgée does not portray Lugena as a mere victim. Instead, he patterns her on a black wife in Alamance County who had "split [the] forehead" of a Klansman open and "severed his nose, while he and his party of K.K's were attempting to take her husband out of the house." This case of heroic self-defense had received wide publicity in the Republican North Carolina *Daily Standard,* which had cheered: "A few like her would be the best antidote for the K.K.K."[114]

PRESENTING BLACK PERSPECTIVES ON THE OVERTHROW OF RECONSTRUCTION

Despite the bravery and resourcefulness with which Tourgée credits his African American characters, he cannot sustain his vision of an autocentered black community. After the Klan attack, which ushers in the third and last phase of the novel, the black protagonists lose their agency, and white rescuers come to dominate the action. Perhaps Tourgée sought to spur his white readers to discharge their responsibility toward the freedpeople they had so shamefully abandoned, an explanation in keeping with his having timed the publication of *Bricks Without Straw* to intervene in the 1880 electoral campaign. Or perhaps he could no longer conceive of how the defeated freedpeople could help themselves in an era of unbridled white supremacy. In either case, through the device of letting his black characters tell their stories to sympathetic whites, Tourgée gives them a voice in exposing the realities of the unreconstructed South, if not in shaping the nation's future.

Nimbus bitterly recognizes that abstract rights mean nothing unless enforced, or, as he puts it, "dat de right ter du a ting an' de doin' on't is two mighty diff'rent tings, when it's a cullu'd man ez does it" (292). He doggedly keeps on fighting as he flees from one southern state to another—in fact, he even takes up arms against white supremacist troops in Louisiana during the Colfax massacre of 1873, which left an estimated 70 to 280 African Americans dead in "the bloodiest single act of carnage in all of Reconstruction."[115] Yet Nimbus's resistance only lands him in jail and subjects him to a new form of enslavement: fined for striking back at a white boss, he is "auctioned off" to pay the fine and repeatedly caught when he tries to escape (409). He resurfaces many years later completely "broken," with the look of "furtive wildness which characterizes the man long hunted by his enemies" (405). The intrepid defiance that served Nimbus so well during the Civil War and the early phase of Reconstruction, Tourgée indicates, turns into a dangerous liability under the draconian regime that has replaced slavery.

Admitting defeat more readily than her husband, Lugena concludes that "'tain't no use" to stand up to white supremacists because "dey'll hab dere will fust er last" (309). Metamorphosing with disconcerting suddenness into an abject dependent who kisses the hem of her benefactor, she entreats the schoolteacher Mollie Ainslee to take her and her children to safety before the Klan avenges the man she has axed. Only through Mollie does Lugena fulfill Nimbus's dream of landownership, this time in Kansas, where thousands of desperate freedpeople were embarking on a mass exodus as Tourgée was completing *Bricks Without Straw*.[116]

Berry, whose family Mollie has also rescued, makes his own way to Kansas after struggling in vain to escape from the cycle of debt in which sharecropping traps his class. No matter what he tries or how hard he works, he remarks with his usual pointed humor, he falls afoul of tactics the planters have invented to keep him down: a system of overcharging sharecroppers for supplies advanced on credit; a Landlord and Tenant Act that gives the landlord the power to seize the whole crop at his discretion; a "sunset" law that forces tenants to sell their crops only to the landlord rather than seeking the best price for their produce. Berry even sees election commissioners disposing of excess ballots and decides that it is "no use" risking his life to vote if the outcome is predetermined (413–418).

Of the African American protagonists, Eliab alone grows "more self-reliant" (405). Nursed back to health and spirited off to college in the North by his former master Hesden Le Moyne (unlike the historical Elias Hill, who opted to lead a party to Liberia because he had lost hope that African Americans would ever be permitted "to live in this country peaceably"),[117] Eliab illustrates Tourgée's belief that education will accomplish in the long run the racial uplift that Reconstruction failed to secure by legislative means. In a letter to Mollie, Eliab also articulates Tourgée's view that African Americans must not only free themselves "through the attainment of knowledge and the power which that gives," but strive to overcome the prejudice slavery has "created . . . in the hearts of the white people" (382). Eliab himself exemplifies the empowerment education confers and expresses the insights of a teacher who has shared his students' travails and who consequently understands their needs better than any outsider can. Still, he realizes that faced with such a monumental task and with so little prospect of regaining their stolen rights, all too many of his fellow freedpeople have sunk back into the "dull, plodding hopelessness of the old slave time" (381).

REVISING THE ROMANCE OF REUNION

Unwilling to invent a utopian solution to the problem of a thwarted Black Reconstruction—and not yet able to foresee a time when African American intellectuals would meet to debate solutions of their own to the race's continuing oppression, as they do in the "Friends in Council" chapter of Frances Harper's *Iola Leroy* (1892)—Tourgée reorients his plot from the quest for black self-determination toward the goal of unifying northern and southern whites around a common agenda of national regeneration. "Can the South and the North ever be made one people in thought, spirit, and purpose?" he asks through the aptly named Congressman Washington Goodspeed (419). This question had already given rise to a flourishing literary subgenre, dubbed by Nina Silber "the romance of reunion." Typically, the "romance of reunion" featured a plot culminating in a marriage between a Northerner and a Southerner, after one partner had come around to the other's political viewpoint. Thus, it is not surprising that Tourgée arranges a marriage between Mollie Ainslee and Hesden Le Moyne to show how "New England Puritanism and Southern Prejudice" can "be reconciled" (295).

Tourgée's version of the North-South marriage trope does not fit the "depoliticized" pattern of what Silber calls the "culture of conciliation," however.[118] On the contrary, both Mollie and Hesden experience a political awakening when they confront the meaning of the events that climax in the

Klan attack. Temporarily seduced by the charms of the Le Moyne household during a brief sojourn there—just as the northern public has been seduced by southern propagandists—Mollie returns to find her schoolhouse a smoldering ruin. Thereafter, she not only dissociates herself "with shame" from the policy of her "weak, vacillating nation" but consecrates herself anew to the freedpeople, whom she now feels "almost like calling . . . *her* people" (338, 352). Similarly, as Hesden gazes at the lacerated body of Eliab, he begins to doubt everything he has always believed about southern honor and black inferiority (291). The collapse of his worldview converts Hesden into a Radical Republican. Hitherto devoted to his invalid mother, who represents his sick motherland the South, for which he sacrificed an arm in the Civil War even though he disapproved of both secession and slavery, Hesden now transfers his allegiance to the wounded Eliab and to Mollie. In marrying Mollie, he marries the ideals she personifies, rebuilding her schoolhouse, hiring Eliab to take charge of it, and supporting her devotion to the freedpeople she has repatriated in Kansas. Genuine reconciliation between North and South must entail a joint commitment to equal justice for African Americans, Tourgée implies.

Tourgée reinforces the message of his revised "romance of reunion" with another popular fictional device—a plot involving a stolen inheritance. This plot device—variants of which appear in Rebecca Harding Davis's *Waiting for the Verdict* (1867), Frances Harper's *Iola Leroy*, Mark Twain's *Pudd'nhead Wilson* (1894), and Charles Chesnutt's *The Marrow of Tradition* (1901)—serves an allegorical purpose in novels that probe the legacy of slavery, allowing them to ask who is entitled to the wealth and status derived from theft, who bears responsibility for righting the wrongs of the past, and who can claim the mantle of political legitimacy when the nation's history has been tainted by fraud and violence.

In *Bricks Without Straw* the plot of stolen inheritance reveals the American nation to have been a house divided against itself from its very origins. The Le Moyne house, Hesden recalls, "was, in fact, two houses," whose "two parts were made into one" (333). The discovery within its walls of a will dated December 1789—the year after the ratification of the U.S. Constitution—and the account of how this will came to be violated suggest that the Constitution itself records the concealment of a crime in its many clauses protecting slavery under euphemistic guises, through which it papers over the fissure between two houses imperfectly "made into one."[119]

The family history that emerges further undermines the legitimacy of all hereditary aristocracies, southern and northern (a theme reiterated in many of Tourgée's political writings). Although Hesden's ancestor "Black Jim" has obtained his vast estates through murder and fraud, Mollie's ancestor "Red Jim," the rightful owner of the stolen property and the author of the will "Black Jim" has secreted within the walls of his house, has earned his own wealth through privateering and probably slave trading, occupations that also involve murder and theft. Thus, neither the southern cavalier nor the New England schoolteacher can boast an unblemished ancestry.[120] Both South and North share in the guilt of slavery, and consequently, in the obligation to uplift the freedpeople, Tourgée's inheritance plot allegorically affirms.

The story of how a portion of Hesden's family estate falls into the hands of Potestatem Desmit, who sells it to Nimbus knowing that his title to it will be worthless because of a neglected encumbrance, shows that the theft of African Americans' rightful inheritance continues. As a result of Desmit's fraud, the freedmen who have purchased land from Nimbus lose everything they have invested (337)—a tragedy reminiscent of a major Reconstruction-era scandal, the collapse of the maladministered Freedmen's Savings Bank during the Panic of 1873, sweeping away most of the depositors' earnings since their emancipation. Faced with "impoverishment and woe" on such a scale, Mollie and Hesden can at best "succor a few of the oppressed race" (340).

Notwithstanding their allegorical resonances and skillful linkage of the black and white characters' fates, the fictional formulas to which Tourgée resorts prove inadequate for envisioning the rescue of southern blacks from neo-slavery. Tourgée himself seems to have invited this judgment. His fourteen years in North Carolina had taught him that no one who publicly espoused the rights of African Americans could survive in the South, no matter how secure his social position. Besides suffering vilification and defeat himself, he had watched aristocratic white southern converts to Radical Republicanism like his friend Thomas Settle, a model for Hesden, undergo the "baptism of fire which every Southern man must face who presumes to differ from his fellows upon political questions" (359).[121] All too aware that the intransigence of the South's white supremacist ruling class would prevent any meaningful change in the racial and political status quo, Tourgée deliberately undercuts his fictional formulas by leaving his characters at an impasse and his plot at loose ends.

In the last two chapters, "What Shall the End Be?" and "How?," Tourgée abandons narrative for polemic. Speaking through Hesden and addressing northern politicians through Washington Goodspeed, he pleads for the measure he has come to consider "the *only* remedy" for the nation's ills: a federal education bill that circumvents state control and racial inequity, as well as conflict over integration, by donating funds directly to southern schools and tying the amounts to need and good management (428–430).

The novel's inconclusive ending disturbed even Tourgée's otherwise enthusiastic publishers. Complaining that it seemed "crude and unfinished" because "the story was not completed" and the conversation between Hesden and Goodspeed simply "stop[ped] short," they inserted a sentence to provide a sense of closure. Tourgée's insistence on retaining the "rough-hewn" aspect of his final scene confirms that he intended to deny his readers the gratification of their desire for a fictive closure at odds with historical reality.[122]

Modern readers accustomed to experimentation with literary form can better appreciate Tourgée's unresolved ending and subversion of fictional formulas. Compared with the farcical chapters climaxing *Huckleberry Finn,* for example, in which Tom Sawyer undertakes to "set a free nigger free" by subjecting Jim to ordeals that almost culminate in his lynching, the unsettling denouement of *Bricks Without Straw* works far more effectively to refocus readers' attention on the plight of African Americans in the post-Reconstruction South (the purpose some critics see in *Huckleberry Finn*'s much discussed "evasion").[123] Through its realistic depiction of the brute force and legal chicanery that drove the freedpeople back into slavery, *Bricks Without Straw* shows that the failure of Reconstruction can be attributed neither to the absurd pretense of freeing a people who are already free nor to the fantasies of a society enamored with romantic fiction, and that white Americans cannot escape their obligations to their black fellow citizens by "light[ing] out for the Territory," as *Huckleberry Finn* would have it. Reading and teaching *Bricks Without Straw* alongside classics like *Huckleberry Finn* and rediscovered masterpieces like Chesnutt's *The Marrow of Tradition* (whose searing dramatization of the 1898 Wilmington massacre owes much to *Bricks Without Straw,* though surpassing it in artistry) will eventually win Tourgée's powerful novel the reputation it deserves as one of American literature's best works of social protest, political critique, and race fiction.

"About the Negro as a man, with hopes, fears, and aspirations like other men, our literature is very nearly silent," yet "the life of the Negro as a slave, freedman, and racial outcast offers undoubtedly the richest mine of romantic material that has opened to the English-speaking novelist," Tourgée would note in a much-quoted essay, "The South as a Field for Fiction" (1888). While looking forward to the day when "the children . . . of slaves" themselves would "advance American literature to the very front rank" by exploiting that mine,[124] he pointed the way in *Bricks Without Straw.* His portrayal of African Americans as political agents is unprecedented for a white author of his time and has seldom been matched since.

Even more valuable are the insights Tourgée offers into a historical period that still shapes our political realities more than a century later. His eyewitness account of how a revolution that promised so much was suppressed; his chilling picture of terrorist violence against African Americans condoned, of civil rights abrogated, of constitutional amendments subverted, of electoral fraud institutionalized; and his scathing indictment of an American public too apathetic and gullible to challenge the propaganda that rationalized such outrages remain eerily relevant today.

A VOICE IN THE WILDERNESS

Bricks Without Straw at first sold even faster than *A Fool's Errand* had. Reviewers praised the book for its "caustic" irony reminiscent of Swift's, its "strongly drawn" characters (especially Nimbus and Eliab), its "thrilling" plot, its vivid picture of a representative black man's "unequal contest with the circumstances . . . which fettered . . . him after he became a freeman and a citizen almost as absolutely as when he was a slave," its truthful delineation of southern society, and its fair-minded criticism of both sections—the South for "the methods by which it has regained political control," the North for "the pusillanimity . . . by which the fruits of the war have been lost." They also quoted long extracts from the passages they pronounced most "striking": Nimbus's opening soliloquy, his argument with the clerk trying to register him with his master's surname, the scenes describing the black community's reactions to Klan terrorism, and Tourgée's analysis of southern psychology. Reviewers particularly commended Tourgée for prescribing a "remedy" for the "disease" he had diagnosed, "namely, education." Not even those who objected to the author's blatant "political sympathies" could "afford to disregard his suggestive and incisive treatment of a subject in which the whole country is profoundly interested," concluded *Harper's New Monthly Magazine.* Pervading all the reviews, however, was a sense that the mistakes of a botched Reconstruction could not be "undone"—a resigned acceptance of the status quo that boded ill for the commitment Tourgée hoped to inspire to a massive federal education program for the South. The review that most ominously reflected the national mood was the *Atlantic Monthly*'s. Once a bastion of abolitionism, this journal had so thoroughly imbibed the stereotypes Tourgée was vainly attempting to dislodge that its editor reproached him with having "left out of view . . . what history demands as a completion of the picture,—the scenes of negro political ascendency, and the disgraceful alliance with the baser Northern [carpetbagger] element."[125]

Despite these auguries of the marginalization Tourgée would shortly meet with, for the moment *Bricks Without Straw* and *A Fool's Errand* helped decide the 1880 election and won him more influence over the leaders of the Republican party than he had ever exerted. Both the party's platform and the inaugural address of Republican president-elect James G. Garfield, whom he had known since his childhood in the Western Reserve, echoed Tourgée's call for a nationally funded public education system to stamp out illiteracy in the South. Clearly, Tourgée had intervened in national politics at a pivotal moment, when a sizable segment of the Republican camp had come to recognize the bankruptcy of President Hayes's "let alone" policy and still hoped to rectify it. But Garfield's assassination four months later brutally ended Tourgée's fleeting access to political power, as well as the revival of the party's progressive wing. The new president, Chester A. Arthur, a member of the party's conservative faction, quickly indicated his intention to lay southern affairs to rest. Though Tourgée would seek to sway the next election by expanding his arguments for national aid to education into a full-length book, *An Appeal to Caesar* (1884)—"the most profound discussion of the American racial situation to appear in the 1880s" according to the historian George M. Fredrickson[126]—he could not overcome the public's weariness of the race problem.

Tourgée would spend the rest of his life championing African American rights in novels, articles, lectures, speeches, and letters to a total of six different presidents.[127] An increasingly lonely voice in the wilderness of white America, he would attract an immense black following in the late 1880s and 1890s after he launched the column "A Bystander's Notes" in the Chicago *Daily Inter Ocean*, a progressive Republican newspaper. Widely reprinted in the black press, Tourgée's "Bystander" column publicized the terrorism to which African Americans were still being subjected, berated the Republican party for ignoring the fraud and violence used to disfranchise African American voters throughout the South, attacked Jim Crow, and denounced lynching, denying that it was provoked by black men's rapes of white women and arguing rather that it served to cow blacks into abject submission. Tourgée's standing in the African American community reached its height when he founded an interracial civil rights organization in 1891, anticipating the National Association for the Advancement of Colored People (NAACP), and challenged segregation pro bono as the lawyer for the African American plaintiff in what became the *Plessy v. Ferguson* case of 1896.

Those who paid moving tributes to Tourgée as "a friend whose faith never wavered, whose courage never failed and whose loyalty was free from a 'shadow of turning' to his dying day" included Ida B. Wells, Charles W. Chesnutt, W. E. B. Du Bois, and Anna Julia Cooper. Wells confided to her diary her excitement at discovering *Bricks Without Straw* as a young woman in 1884, expressed appreciation in her newspaper for Tourgée's "inspiring and candidly critical" counsels to African Americans, lauded him repeatedly in her autobiography, and collaborated fruitfully with him in her crusade against lynching. Chesnutt sent Tourgée samples of his fiction, gratefully acknowledged Tourgée's encouragement of his talent, solicited new members for Tourgée's National Citizen's Rights Association, and hailed him as a "rare idealist who placed humanity above race, color, and artificial social distinctions." Du Bois not only honored Tourgée alongside those other "Friends of Freedom," William Lloyd Garrison and Frederick Douglass, when he inaugurated the Niagara Movement (the forerunner of the NAACP) after Tourgée's death in 1905, but drew on his predecessor's analysis of Reconstruction in his own magnum opus. And Cooper devoted six pages of *A Voice from the South* (1892) to eulogizing Tourgée's "life work," which she summed up with the remarkable assertion: "In presenting truth from the colored American's standpoint, Mr. Tourgee excels, we think, in fervency and frequency of utterance any living writer, white or colored" and "speaks with all the eloquence and passion of the aggrieved party himself."[128]

Yet African American accolades could not keep Tourgée's memory alive during the long reign of white supremacy. Indeed, nothing more starkly epitomized the triumph of the racist propaganda machine that Tourgée had fought so tenaciously than the bestseller status attained by Thomas Dixon's *The Leopard's Spots* (1902) and *The Clansman* (1905). Ironically, Dixon had sought Tourgée's literary advice, only to travesty his novels, and even more ironically, Tourgée himself had predicted the phenomenon Dixon represented. "Our literature has become not only Southern in type, but distinctly Confederate in sympathy," Tourgée had observed in "The South as a Field for Fiction."[129] Far outstripping the commercial success of *A Fool's Errand, The Clansman* even secured the imprimatur of President Woodrow Wilson after D. W. Griffith turned it into "the most successful and profitable film ever made," *The Birth of a Nation.*[130]

Not until *Brown v. Board of Education* (1954) marked the emergence of the modern Civil Rights Movement and the turn of the tide against white supremacist ideology did scholars rediscover Tourgée's writings. The 1960s and early 1970s brought Tourgée a flurry of attention from distinguished literary and cultural historians. With the publication of Otto H. Olsen's superb biography, the microfilming and indexing of the Albion W. Tourgée papers, and the reprinting of *A Fool's Errand* and *Bricks Without Straw,* Tourgée seemed poised for a comeback.[131] Instead, he underwent a second eclipse. Two factors perhaps accounted for his slide back into obscurity: the Civil Rights Movement had entered a separatist phase, and the scholarship and Black Studies programs springing out of the 1960s racial ferment concentrated on the study of slavery and the recovery of African American writers and activists. By the 1970s, white reformers, dismissed as fanatics during the high tide of political conservatism, began coming under attack as racists, or else disappeared from public view. Meanwhile, the modes of literary criticism that dominated the academy in the 1970s and 1980s devalued the genres Tourgée excelled in. The historical novel fell out of fashion, and fiction that preached a "message," whether political, social, racial, or religious, became an embarrassment.

Recent trends, however, have created a more propitious climate for reassessing Tourgée's literary achievements and political legacy. The rollback of civil rights and affirmative action over the past few decades has awakened new interest in Reconstruction, which likewise saw a tidal wave of reaction sweep away the gains of a long struggle for racial equality. A vast body of first-rate revisionist scholarship on Reconstruction now validates Tourgée's representations of the era in *Bricks Without Straw* and *A Fool's Errand* as extraordinarily true to life. The hundredth anniversary of *Plessy v. Ferguson* and the fiftieth anniversary of *Brown v. Board of Education,* paradoxically coinciding with a resurgence of de facto segregation, have also led scholars back to Tourgée. Further contributing to the revalorization of Tourgée's novels, historicist, ideological, and cultural approaches to literature have returned to prominence, sparking more insightful study of the very genres earlier critics had disparaged. The volume of scholarship Tourgée has generated since the late 1980s, crowned by Mark Elliott's prizewinning biography, suggests that conditions are finally ripe for the lasting revival of an unjustly neglected American hero.[132] In this reprint edition, *Bricks Without Straw,* Tourgée's magnificent novel of Black Reconstruction, can take its rightful place among the classics of American political fiction and restore to the public one of the nation's most trenchant writers.

NOTES

1 Editorial Notes, *New York Evangelist,* 21 Oct. 1880, APS Online; *Rochester American Rural Home,* excerpted in advertisement "Specimen Bricks," *Christian Union,* 8 Dec. 1880.

2 Herman Melville's "Benito Cereno" is perhaps the best example of a work that challenges racial stereotyping while purportedly conforming to it. Many critics have argued that Twain's Jim in *Huckleberry Finn* does so as well.

3 Albion W. Tourgée, "The Literary Quality of 'Uncle Tom's Cabin,'" *Independent* 48 (20 Aug. 1896), 3–4.

4 Ibid., 4.

5 In addition to "Literary Quality," see Tourgée's untitled editorial in his weekly magazine *The Continent,* 23 May 1883, 669; and his article "The Claims of Realism," *North American Review* 148 (March 1889): 386–88. For a cogent critique of realism, see Kenneth W. Warren, *Black and White Strangers: Race and American Literary Realism* (Chicago: University of Chicago Press, 1993), especially chap. 3.

6 For an account of the antislavery origins of the Republican party, see Eric Foner, *Free Soil, Free Labor, Free Men: The Ideology of the Republican Party before the Civil War* (New York: Oxford University Press, 1970).

7 See James S. Pike, *The Prostrate State: South Carolina under Negro Government* (1874), for one of the earliest and most influential formulations of this indictment. The historian William Dunning and his disciples perpetuated this view of Reconstruction in the academy until the 1960s.

8 Eric Foner, *Reconstruction: America's Unfinished Revolution, 1863–1877* (New York: Harper & Row, 1988).

9 W. E. B. Du Bois, *Black Reconstruction in America: An Essay Toward a History of the Part Which Black Folk Played in the Attempt to Reconstruct Democracy in America, 1860–1880* (1935; New York: Atheneum, 1977), 721, 708, and the chapter "Back Toward Slavery."

10 Albion W. Tourgée Papers (hereinafter AWTP) #765, AWT to W. M. Coleman, 4 Feb. 1868; AWTP #139, AWT to EK, 4 Feb. 1860.

11 Mark Elliott, *Color-Blind Justice: Albion Tourgée and the Quest for Racial Equality, from the Civil War to* Plessy v. Ferguson (New York: Oxford University

Press, 2006), 85. While relying heavily on the excellent biographical narrative Elliott provides, I have done my own research in the Tourgée papers and in Reconstruction-era newspapers. In cases where I am indebted to Elliott's analysis, I have cited both his book and the primary sources I have consulted; where my research has gone beyond Elliott's or led me to original insights, I have cited the primary sources alone. I have followed the same practice in using the work of other scholars.

12 Tourgée, *The Story of a Thousand: Being a history of the Service of the 105th Ohio Volunteer Infantry, in the War for the Union from August 21, 1862 to June 6, 1865* (Buffalo: S. McGerald & Son, 1896), 31–34, 83, 87–91, 106–107; Elliott, *Color-Blind Justice,* 85–88.

13 AWTP #801, "Speech on Elective Franchise Del[i]v[ere]d in Conv[entio]n of 1868," 1.

14 AWTP #1249, "*Emancipation—considered as an historical event*" [double underlining in original], speech delivered to African Americans in 1869, next-to-last page.

15 On military policy and the Emancipation Proclamation in Kentucky, see Ira Berlin, Joseph P. Reidy, and Leslie S. Rowland, eds., *Freedom: A Documentary History of Emancipation, 1861–1867,* Series II: *The Black Military Experience* (New York: Cambridge University Press, 1982), 183, 191–97; for the text of the Emancipation Proclamation, see www.archives.gov/exhibits/.

16 AWTP #577, Daily Pocket Remembrancer for 1863, 7, 22, and 23 June.

17 Elliott, *Color-Blind Justice,* 90; AWTP #577, 24 Oct. 1863. Though Tourgée refers to himself in the third person as the Commanding Officer of Company E in the entry describing his hiring and renaming of William/Nimbus, a letter to Emma of 29 Sept. 1863 confirms that he is now replacing a dead comrade who occupied that position before him (AWTP #556).

18 AWTP #446, AWT to EK, 23 Nov. 1862; Elliott, *Color-Blind Justice,* 88.

19 AWTP #455, J. R. Warner to Emma Kilbourne, 23 Jan. 1863; AWTP #467, AWT to EKT, 6 May 1863; Elliott mistranscribes the dash after "insult" as "and" (*Color-Blind Justice,* 97).

20 AWTP #801, "Speech on Elective Franchise Del[i]v[ere]d in Conv[entio]n of 1868," 13.

21 AWTP #454, AWT to Brothers of the Union [Jan. 1863, date illegible]; as Brook Thomas has pointed out in a personal communication, Tourgée is specifically repudiating the motto of Ohio Copperhead Clement Vallandigham, "The Constitution as it is, the Union as it was."

22 Elliott, *Color-Blind Justice,* 104–105; Richard Nelson Current, *Those Terrible Carpetbaggers* (New York: Oxford University Press, 1988), 51.

23 Olsen, *Carpetbagger's Crusade,* 28.

24 Foner, *Reconstruction,* 74.

25 AWTP #2392, "The Negro in America"; for a similar assessment by a leading modern historian, see James M. McPherson, *Battle Cry of Freedom: The Civil War Era* (1988; New York: Ballantine Books, 1989), 852.

26 Foner, *Reconstruction,* 189–90, 240.

27 Roberta Sue Alexander, *North Carolina Faces the Freedmen: Race Relations During Presidential Reconstruction, 1865–67* (Durham: Duke University Press, 1985), 45–47, 49, 51 (quoting a Freedmen's Bureau agent), 55–56. For further discussion of the North Carolina Black Code and African American resistance to it, see Laura F. Edwards, *Gendered Strife and Confusion: The Political Culture of Reconstruction* (Urbana: University of Illinois Press, 1997), 35–54.

28 Elliott, *Color-Blind Justice,* 106; Current, *Those Terrible Carpetbaggers,* 52.

29 Foner, *Reconstruction,* 254, 256; Fourteenth Amendment, section 1, www.nps.gov/archive. For an analysis of how the Fourteenth Amendment reversed the Supreme Court's 1857 *Dred Scott* decision, which held that African Americans could not be U.S. citizens, see Brook Thomas, ed., *Plessy v. Ferguson: A Brief History with Documents* (Boston: Bedford/St. Martin's, 1997), 14–16; as Thomas explains, *Dred Scott* itself was viewed by many as having taken away the U.S. citizenship that African Americans had enjoyed under earlier interpretations of the Constitution.

30 Alexander, *North Carolina Faces the Freedmen,* 16, 18.

31 Foner, *Reconstruction,* 283–85.

32 Alexander, *North Carolina Faces the Freedmen,* 26–27, 88–89. For other accounts of the 1865 and 1866 Freedmen's conventions, see Paul D. Escott, *Many Excellent People: Power and Privilege in North Carolina, 1850–1900* (Chapel Hill: University of North Carolina Press, 1985), 125–26, 134–35; and Edwards, *Gendered Strife and Confusion,* 25, 67.

33 Elliott, *Color-Blind Justice,* 134, based on a clipping from the *Cincinnati Commercial,* ca. 1880; see also Olsen, *Carpetbagger's Crusade,* 57.

34 Elliott, *Color-Blind Justice,* 106, 145: "It appears that Tourgée brokered land transfers and may have sold some of his own land" to the Quaker missionary Yardley Warner, whom he was assisting in "establishing a housing development" for Black refugees "on the southern edge of Tourgée's Greensboro property"; Albion W. Tourgée, *A Fool's Errand. By One of the Fools* (New York: Fords, Howard, and Hulbert, 1879), 47, 83.

35 Elliott, *Color-Blind Justice,* 145; Olsen, *Carpetbagger's Crusade,* 76–77. Tourgée details his plans for such a Freedmen's Land Agency in a letter to a Mr. Armstrong, perhaps General Samuel Chapman Armstrong, undated draft, AWTP #11028.

36 AWTP #845, Harmon Unthank to AWT, 27 July 1868, quoted, with slightly different capitalization and punctuation, in Deborah Patrice Hamlin, "'Friend of Freedom': Albion Winegar Tourgée and Reconstruction in North Carolina" (Ph.D. diss., Duke University, 2004), 175.

37 Quoted in Elliott, *Color-Blind Justice,* 147–48.

38 George Arnold, "In Tourgée's Defense," letter to the editor of the Detroit *Plaindealer,* 6 May 1892, clipping in AWTP #7614 (the documents sharing this item number take up almost three rolls of microfilm and are almost impossible to locate individually).

39 Tourgée, *A Fool's Errand,* 101–102, 105; Elliott, *Color-Blind Justice,* 106–107.

40 AWTP #699, "Institution of a Pioneer," 1867.

41 Current, *Those Terrible Carpetbaggers,* 56, 58–59; AWTP #687, "Notes for a speech in 1866"; Elliott, *Color-Blind Justice,* 108–109; AWTP #651, AWT to EKT, 16 Sept. 1866.

42 Elliott, *Color-Blind Justice,* 109–11; Current, *Those Terrible Carpetbaggers,* 62–64; AWTP #657, 24 Sept. 1866, #659, Sept. 1866.

43 AWTP #665, EKT to AWT, 7 Oct. 1866.

44 Elliott, *Color-Blind Justice,* 114.

45 Current, *Those Terrible Carpetbaggers,* 66; Otto H. Olsen, "North Carolina: *An Incongruous Presence,*" in *Reconstruction and Redemption in the South,* ed. Otto H. Olsen (Baton Rouge: Louisiana State University Press, 1980), 164; Elliott, *Color-Blind Justice,* 114–15; Paul D. Escott, "White Republicanism and Ku Klux Klan Terror: The North Carolina Piedmont during Reconstruction," in *Race, Class, and Politics in Southern History: Essays in Honor of Robert F. Durden,* ed. Jeffrey J. Crow, Paul D. Escott, and Charles L. Flynn Jr. (Baton Rouge: Louisiana State University Press, 1989), 8–10.

46 *North Carolinian,* 1 Feb., 6 Feb., 11 Feb., 26 Feb., 4 March, and 6 March 1868. See also the Raleigh *Sentinel,* which refers to the Republican delegates as "the mongrels."

47 AWTP #774, AWT to EKT, 19 Feb. 1868; AWTP #801, "Speech on Elective Franchise Del[i]v[ere]d in Conv[entio]n of 1868," 1, 3; *North Carolinian,* 22 Feb. 1868.

48 Quotations are from Elliott, *Color-Blind Justice,* 130–31; see also Tourgée, *Bricks Without Straw,* chaps. 57 and 61. For more details on Tourgée's role in the convention, see Olsen, *Carpetbagger's Crusade,* 97–102, 107–108, 113–14; and Current, *Those Terrible Carpetbaggers,* 104–106.

49 Broadside of a Guilford County meeting, quoted in Current, *Those Terrible Carpetbaggers,* 107–108.

50 Olsen, *Carpetbagger's Crusade,* 145.

51 Current, *Those Terrible Carpetbaggers,* 201–202; Olsen, *Carpetbagger's Crusade,* 152–55; AWT to Editor, Raleigh *Standard,* 1 Feb. 1870.

52 Escott, "White Republicanism and Ku Klux Klan Terror," 5, 28, 29; Otto H. Olsen, "The Ku Klux Klan: A Study in Reconstruction Politics and Propaganda," *North Carolina Historical Review,* 39 (July 1962): 354, 360; see also Escott, *Many Excellent People,* 152–60. For an overview covering the entire South, with several chapters on North Carolina, see Allen W. Trelease, *White Terror: The Ku Klux Klan Conspiracy and Southern Reconstruction* (Baton Rouge; Louisiana State University Press, 1971).

53 North Carolina *Daily Standard,* 11 April 1868.

54 North Carolina *Daily Standard,* "The Reign of Terror," 9 Feb. 1869; "The Fruits," 23 March 1869.

55 North Carolina *Daily Standard,* "Public Opinion Must Enforce Law," 17 April 1869.

56 North Carolina *Daily Standard,* "The Ku Klux Murders," 23 Sept. 1869; see also "Ku Klux in Guilford," 8 June 1869, in which a correspondent writing to the *Daily Standard* urges all citizens, "however humble, and of all colors, put your cabins in a state of defence. . . . Arm yourselves. Be sure and kill or maim as many as possible."

57 Current, *Those Terrible Carpetbaggers,* 201; see also Trelease, *White Terror,* 206–207. The *Sentinel* is quoted and answered in the North Carolina *Daily Standard,* 28 Sept. 1869. In "The Fruits," 23 March 1869, the *Standard* reports on Josiah Turner's travels, accuses him of "sowing the seed of discord, *rebellion,* and REVOLUTION," and cites a recent Klan attack as one of the "fruits of his work."

58 Olsen, *Carpetbagger's Crusade,* 147, 159, 161.

59 Ibid., 163.

60 Tourgée, AWTP #1366, "Ku Klux War in North Carolina," Aug. 1870, 13 (draft of article submitted to the abolitionist weekly *National Standard* but rejected because too long); Carole Watterson Troxler, " 'To look more closely at the man': Wyatt Outlaw, a Nexus of National, Local, and Personal History," *North Carolina Historical Review* 77 (October 2000): 404, 416, 417; Olsen, *Carpetbagger's Crusade,* 161.

61 AWTP #1270, John W. Stephens to AWT, 20 April 1870; Olsen, *Carpetbagger's Crusade,* 162–64; Current, *Those Terrible Carpetbaggers,* 204; Elliott, *Color-Blind Justice,* 136.

62 Tourgée, AWTP #1366, "Ku Klux War in North Carolina," 14–15; AWTP #1639, "Affidavit of Patsie Burton before J. G. Hester as to Murder of J. W. Stephens," 12 Dec. 1872; Olsen, *Carpetbagger's Crusade,* 164.

63 Foner, *Reconstruction,* 593–94.

64 Olsen, "North Carolina," 184–85; see also Edwards, *Gendered Strife,* 220–21.

65 Olsen, *Carpetbagger's Crusade,* 147.

66 AWTP #1131, AWT to EKT, 9 June 1869; AWTP #1572, AWT to Ulysses S. Grant, 28 Dec. 1871, and Ulysses S. Grant, *The Papers of Ulysses S. Grant,* ed. John Y. Simon (Carbondale: Southern Illinois University Press, 1967), 23: 370n.

67 AWTP #1472 (letterbook covering 1868–1870), William S. Ball to AWT, 8 June 1870; AWTP #1131, AWT to EKT, 9 June 1869; AWTP #1575 (letterbook covering Feb. 1869 through Feb. 1871), AWT to R. M. Tuttle, 26 May 1870.

68 Olsen, *Carpetbagger's Crusade,* 158, 162; AWTP #1612, AWT to EKT, 20 March 1872.

69 The original letter is no longer extant. Quotations are from drafts of letters to the *New York Tribune* and members of the Guilford Bar, AWTP #1331, n.d., and #1349, 16 Aug. 1870.

70 Current, *Those Terrible Carpetbaggers,* 205.

71 AWTP #1575 (letterbook for Feb. 1869-Feb. 1871), AWT to Jonathan R. French, 16 Aug. 1870; Olsen, *Carpetbagger's Crusade,* 168; Current, *Those Terrible Carpetbaggers,* 208.

72 Olsen, *Carpetbagger's Crusade,* 165–66, 168; Current, *Those Terrible Carpetbaggers,* 205–206; AWTP #1575 (letterbook for Feb. 1869-Feb. 1871), AWT to Joseph Abbott, 25 Aug. and 8 Sept. 1870.

73 AWTP #1575 (letterbook for Feb. 1869-Feb. 1871), AWT to Joseph Abbott, 27 Jan. 1871; Foner, *Reconstruction*, 454–55.
74 AWTP #1879 (1871–75 letterbook), AWT to EKT, 16 and 18 Dec. 1871. See also the affidavits of James M. Stockard and George Faucett on the hanging of Outlaw, AWTP #1551 and #1568.
75 AWTP #1572, AWT to Ulysses S. Grant, 28 Dec. 1871, and *Papers of Ulysses S. Grant*, 23: 370n.
76 Olsen, *Carpetbagger's Crusade*, 186–87.
77 AWTP #1739, AWT to Martin B. Anderson, 11 May 1874.
78 AWTP #1850, EKT to AWT, 14 Sept. 1875.
79 Tourgée, *Bricks Without Straw*, 392–96; Olsen, *Carpetbagger's Crusade*, 198–99, 203–205; Escott, *Many Excellent People*, 166–67, 170.
80 Elliott, *Color-Blind Justice*, 166–67; Foner, *Reconstruction*, 558, 573-82.
81 This summary of Tourgée's views is based on *A Fool's Errand*, 143–44, 146–48, 151–54, as well as on his article "Why Reconstruction Was a Failure," written under the pseudonym Henry Churton, AWTP #1797; and on his letter to the editor of the Wilmington (North Carolina) *Post*, AWTP #1813, 22 May 1875.
82 AWTP #1649, AWT to EKT, 5 June 1873.
83 AWTP #2269, AWT to EKT, 22 Dec. 1878; AWTP #2315, AWT to EKT, 13 April 1879. Tourgée declares himself "dead politically" in AWTP #2249, AWT to EKT, 9 Nov. 1878; see also #2250, AWT to EKT, 11 Nov. 1878.
84 Henry Churton (pseud.), *Toinette. A Novel* (New York: J. B. Ford, 1874); the quotation is from the preface to the 1881 edition, retitled *A Royal Gentleman* (reprint, Ridgewood, N.J.: Gregg Press, 1967), iv-v; AWTP #1648, AWT to EKT, 4 June 1873.
85 Tourgée spells out these implications of his plot in a self-written review, AWTP #1786, 13 Jan. 1875.
86 Tourgée, *A Fool's Errand*, 44–47, 82–84, 96–97.
87 Ibid., 152–53, 210–11.
88 Ibid., 346–47.
89 Quotations are from the extracts of press notices on the flyleaves of a later 1879 printing. For more extensive quotations from contemporary reviews, see Olsen, *Carpetbagger's Crusade*, 224; and Elliott, *Color-Blind Justice*, 170–71. For information on total sales figures and foreign translations, see the obituary from the Baltimore *American*, "Judge Tourgee, the Author Dead," in AWTP #9907.
90 As Foner points out, the Fifteenth Amendment, though it barred discrimination against voters based on "race, color, or previous condition of servitude," "did not forbid literacy, property, and educational tests that, while nonracial, might effectively exclude the majority of blacks from the polls"; see *Reconstruction*, 446–47, for his analysis of the reasons for the amendment's weak and narrow wording.
91 AWTP #7748, undated draft, replying to the editor's request that he cut a dialogue Tourgée considered essential to the story he had submitted to the magazine; also quoted in Elliott, *Color-Blind Justice*, 213. In AWTP #10766, an undated typed draft titled "Comments on J.C. Harris & W.D. Howells," Tourgée

further notes that during his years in North Carolina, his interest in his southern neighbors' speech was "constantly impelling [him] to write dialect on the side."

92 Josiah S. Nott and George R. Gliddon, *Types of Mankind: or, Ethnological Researches* . . . (1854; Miami: Mnemosyne, 1969); see the illustrations facing lviii and on 430–31.

93 AWTP #577, Daily Pocket Remembrancer for 1863, 24 Oct. 1863. Olsen, *Carpetbagger's Crusade,* 24, was the first to suggest this real-life model for the fictional Nimbus.

94 Outlaw participated in the 1866 North Carolina Freedmen's Convention. His woodworking and wagon-repairing shop "became a gathering place for blacks and for white and black workingmen" and consequently a hub for political strategizing; see Troxler, "'To look more closely at the man,'" 405–409, 411, 413–14, 416.

95 Like Outlaw, Unthank participated in the Freedmen's Convention of 1866. He differed from Nimbus in being highly literate (as his letters to Tourgée show) and in avoiding trouble with his white Conservative neighbors. Unthank's daughter claimed that Tourgée based Nimbus on her father. See Hamlin, "'Friend of Freedom,'" 166–67, 173, 177, 197–98.

96 Yet another real-life model historians have suggested for Nimbus is Jourdan Ware, a "renter-farmer living near Rome, Georgia," and a "prominent" and influential leader of the local African American community. Though Tourgée did not know him personally, he would have read about him in the thirteen-volume congressional *Report* on Klan atrocities that he cites elsewhere in *Bricks Without Straw.* The name "Ware" provides the most conspicuous link between the two men: when registering to vote, Nimbus takes the surname of his former overseer, Silas Ware, to avoid being assigned that of his master. See Edward Magdol, "A Note on Authenticity: Eliab Hill and Nimbus Ware in *Bricks Without Straw,*" *American Quarterly* 22 (winter 1970): 907–11.

97 AWTP #6688, undated draft to unknown correspondent, 1893.

98 The proud, handsome George Harris illustrates the racial theory Stowe puts in the mouth of Augustine St. Clare: "Sons of white fathers, with all our haughty feelings burning in their veins," are more prone to rebellion than full-blooded Africans; see *Uncle Tom's Cabin; or, Life Among the Lowly,* in *The Oxford Harriet Beecher Stowe Reader,* ed. Joan D. Hedrick (New York: Oxford University Press, 1999), 275–76. Davis depicts Broderip as undersized, sickly, and effeminate, but also "brutal" in temper; see *Waiting for the Verdict,* ed. Donald Dingledine (Albany: NCUP, 1995), 135–37, 140, 144–45, and the fine analysis in Dingledine's introduction of *Verdict*'s racial subtext.

99 Davis, *Waiting for the Verdict,* 161.

100 Ibid., 417.

101 United States Congress, *Report of the Joint Select Committee Appointed to Inquire into the Condition of Affairs in the Late Insurrectionary States* . . . (Washington: Government Printing Office, 1872), 1: 44, available at http://dns.hti.umich.edu/cgi/.

102 Tourgée also wove aspects of Harmon Unthank and Wyatt Outlaw into his portrait of Eliab. As Tourgée's liaison with the African American community of Greensboro, and as a leader in the Methodist Episcopal Church known for "maintain[ing] law and order at all times" in the congregation, Unthank may have helped flesh out the characterization of Eliab as a preacher on whom the Yankee schoolteacher relies to keep order among her charges. Coupled with his "unknown" paternity (127), Eliab's "almost white" (118) complexion, not mentioned in the congressional account of Elias Hill, may link him with Outlaw, who seems to have been the unacknowledged son of a white man. On Unthank, see Hamlin, "'Friend of Freedom,'" 186. Troxler, "'To look more closely at the man,'" 406, 408, suggests comparisons both with Outlaw and with a crippled white schoolteacher named Alonzo Corliss, who, like Elias Hill, was brutally beaten by the Klan despite his handicapped condition and, like Outlaw, was a "leader of the Loyal League in Alamance County."

103 Delany develops the idea of a partnership between Blacks and mulattoes in chapter 61, "The Grand Council," of *Blake; or, The Huts of America*, ed. Floyd J. Miller (1859; Boston: Beacon Press, 1970), where he puts it into the mouth of the mulatto poet Placido: "I hold that colored persons, whatever the complexion, can only obtain an equality with whites by the descendants of Africa of unmixed blood" (260). Harper embodies it in the friendship of the light-skinned Iola with the pure black Lucille Delany and in the marriage of Lucille with Iola's equally light-skinned brother Harry.

104 For a comparative view, see Stowe's portrayal of Sam in chaps. 6–8 of *Uncle Tom's Cabin* and Twain's portrayal of Jim in *The Adventures of Huckleberry Finn* (1884; Harmondsworth, UK: Penguin, 1985), chaps. 2, 14, 36–38. Although both Stowe and Twain use these minstrel figures to satirize whites, their satire is undercut by their concessions to white racism.

105 Langston Hughes, *Laughing to Keep from Crying* (1952); see also the chapter "Black Laughter" in Lawrence W. Levine, *Black Culture and Black Consciousness: Afro-American Folk Thought from Slavery to Freedom* (New York: Oxford University Press, 1977).

106 Elliott, *Color-Blind Justice*, 214–15; "Poll Tax. A Song of North Carolina Freedmen," *National Anti-Slavery Standard*, 9 Nov. 1867, 3. It is not clear whether Tourgée transcribed, adapted, or composed the lyrics. The *N.A.S.S.* subtitle and headnote give the impression that Tourgée has merely transcribed the song, but his letter three years later to the editor of the North Carolina *Daily Standard* implies that he composed it; see AWTP #1321, 19 July 1870; also Olsen, *Carpetbagger's Crusade*, 90.

107 Du Bois, *Black Reconstruction*, 57, 121.

108 Herbert G. Gutman, *The Black Family in Slavery and Freedom, 1750–1925* (New York: Random House, 1976), 429. For a more recent analysis of the different meanings that the former masters and the freedpeople attached to the legalization of slave marriages (mandated by the North Carolina Black Code), see Edwards, *Gendered Strife and Confusion*, 31–38, 45–47, 54–56.

109 Quoted in Elliott, *Color-Blind Justice*, 119–20.

110 On the difficulties of cultivating the "'bright' yellow tobacco that was the area's specialty," see Edwards, *Gendered Strife and Confusion,* 80–83.

111 Du Bois, *Black Reconstruction,* 122–23.

112 Foner, *Reconstruction,* 342; "Evidence in the Camilla Massacre," *National Anti-Slavery Standard,* 10 Oct. 1868, 1; "The Recent Riot at Camilla," *New York Times,* 23 Sept. 1868, 1.

113 Tourgée explained to an unidentified correspondent that such was the purpose of the "love incidents" in *A Fool's Errand;* see AWTP #6688, 1893. Tourgée himself had chosen to forgo a victory celebration after the 1868 election because he "did not think it right to expose" his African American allies, "who have always trusted me and relied upon my regard for their interest with unquestioning faith, to the danger of such persecution" as they would incur from local white supremacists; as he explained in a letter to the *National Republican,* "to me it seems infinitely better to forego a parade than to subject our friends to trouble—"; see AWTP #11042, undated draft.

114 For the case of Elias Hill, see U.S. Congress, *Report of the Joint Select Committee,* 1 (South Carolina): 45–47; for the case of the axe-wielding woman, see "A K.K. Come to Grief" (by Arcanum [pseud.]), "Young Steel," "The Joe Alston Case," and "The Alamance Outrages," North Carolina *Daily Standard,* 26 March and 2 April 1869. The case was also written up in the *Senate Report* of March 1871, lxvi, 33, 43; and in the *Report of the Joint Select Committee,* 2: 35–36.

115 Foner, *Reconstruction,* 437, 530–31; Foner is quoting the testimony of a contemporary witness, but one of the modern historians he cites estimates from sixty-nine to a hundred African Americans killed in the massacre. For a dramatic recent account of the Colfax massacre, see Nicholas Lemann, *Redemption: The Last Battle of the Civil War* (New York: Farrar, Straus and Giroux, 2006), 12–22.

116 For an account of the flight to Kansas, see Nell Irvin Painter, *Exodusters: Black Migration to Kansas after Reconstruction* (New York: Knopf, 1977).

117 U.S. Congress, *Report of the Joint Select Committee,* 1: 46; obviously Tourgée could not endorse this choice without betraying the struggle to obtain equal justice for African Americans in the United States, though he does give a nod to his historical source when he has Eliab say in his letter to Mollie: "If I were . . . whole and sound, I wouldn't stay in this country another day. I would go somewhere where my children would have a chance to learn what it is to be free" (382).

118 Nina Silber, *The Romance of Reunion: Northerners and the South, 1865–1900* (Chapel Hill: University of North Carolina Press, 1993), chap. 4.

119 For an analysis of how both the entire structure of the Constitution and many of its clauses protected slavery, see Paul Finkelman, *Slavery and the Founders: Race and Liberty in the Age of Jackson* (Armonk, N.Y.: M. E. Sharpe, 1996), chap. 1.

120 Tourgée once again based this on an actual case that he seems to have come across as a judge. His Pocket Calendar for 1872 notes the story of a dispute between "two George Ewbanks in Caswell [County]": "One was known as 'Black' George & the other 'Red' George. The children of Black George claimed property" that by right belonged to Red George. See AWTP #1784.

121 See Jeffrey L. Crow, "Thomas Settle Jr., Reconstruction, and the Memory of the Civil War," *Journal of Southern History* 62 (November 1966): 689–726.

122 AWTP #2380, John Raymond Howard to AWT, 29 Sept. 1880.

123 Twain, *Huckleberry Finn,* 318. See, for example, Charles H. Nilon, "The Ending of *Huckleberry Finn:* 'Freeing the Free Negro,'" in *Satire or Evasion? Black Perspectives on* Huckleberry Finn, ed. James S. Leonard, Thomas A. Tenney, and Thadious M. Davis (Durham, N.C.: Duke University Press, 1992), 62–76.

124 Albion W. Tourgée, "The South as a Field for Fiction," *Forum* 6 (December 1888): 409–10, 413.

125 Quotations are from the *San Francisco News Letter* and the *New York Examiner and Chronicle,* excerpted in "Specimen Bricks," an advertisement in the *Christian Union,* 8 Dec. 1880; "Bricks Without Straw," *Christian Union,* 13 Oct. 1880; "Editor's Literary Record," *Harper's New Monthly Magazine* 62 (Dec. 1880): 153–54; Leonard Bacon, "Bricks Without Straw," *Independent,* 7 Oct. 1880; "A Novel of Reconstruction," *New York Daily Tribune,* 26 Sept. 1880, 8; and "Some Political Novels," *Atlantic Monthly* 47 (Jan. 1881): 120. See also Joseph Kirkland, "A Partisan Romance," *The Dial* 1 (October 1880): 110; and "Redemption of the South," *New York Times,* 1 Oct. 1880, 3.

126 George M. Fredrickson, *The Black Image in the White Mind: The Debate on Afro-American Character and Destiny, 1817–1914* (New York: Harper & Row, 1971), 243, quoted in Elliott, *Color-Blind Justice,* 199.

127 Tourgée's letters to Presidents Ulysses S. Grant, Rutherford B. Hayes, James G. Garfield, Benjamin Harrison, William McKinley, and Theodore Roosevelt can be found in the papers of these presidents, housed at the Library of Congress.

128 [Ida B. Wells, representing the Illinois Division of the Niagara Movement and the Appomattox Club], *In Memoriam: Tributes of Respect by Colored Citizens of Chicago to the Memory of Judge Albion W. Tourgee,* AWTP #9838 (I am grateful to Mark Elliott for bringing this tribute to my attention); Wells, *The Memphis Diary of Ida B. Wells,* ed. Miriam DeCosta-Willis (Boston: Beacon Press, 1995), 52; Wells-Barnett, "Honor Well Won," Chicago *Conservator,* 15 May 1897, clipping in AWTP #9471; and Wells, *Crusade for Justice: The Autobiography of Ida B. Wells,* Wells, ed. Alfreda M. Duster (Chicago: University of Chicago Press, 1970), 120–21, 151, 156. See also Carolyn L. Karcher, "The White 'Bystander' and the Black Journalist 'Abroad': Albion W. Tourgée and Ida B. Wells as Allies Against Lynching," *Prospects* 29 (2005): 85–119; Charles W. Chesnutt to AWT, 26 Sept. 1889, AWTP #4026; Chesnutt, "Resolutions read at the funeral exercises of Hon. A.W. Tourgee at Mayville, New York, AWTP #9874; Du Bois, quoted in Elliott, *Color-Blind Justice,* 12; Anna Julia Cooper, *A Voice from the South* (1892; New York: Oxford University Press, 1988), 188–92, 199.

129 AWTP #3368, Thomas Dixon to AWT, 25 Feb. 1888; Elliott, *Color-Blind Justice,* 307; Tourgée, "The South as a Field for Fiction," 405.

130 Elliott, *Color-Blind Justice,* 308.

131 Dean H. Keller organized, microfilmed, and indexed the Albion W. Tourgée Papers, thus laying the foundations for further research; see Keller, "An Index to

the Albion W. Tourgée Papers in the Chautauqua County Historical Society, Westfield, New York," *Kent State University Bulletin Research Series* 7 (May 1964): v–59; also Keller, "A Checklist of the Writings of Albion W. Tourgée (1838–1905)," *Studies in Bibliography* 18 (1965): 169–279; Keller, ed., "A Civil War Diary of Albion W. Tourgée," *Ohio History* 74 (spring 1965): 99–131; and Keller, "Albion W. Tourgée as Editor of *The Basis,*" *Niagara Frontier* 12 (spring 1965: 24–28. Scholarly studies marking the revival of interest in Tourgée include Ted N. Weissbuch, "Albion W. Tourgee: Propagandist And Critic of Reconstruction," *Ohio Historical Quarterly* 70 (Jan. 1961): 27–44; Theodore L. Gross, "The Negro in the Literature of Reconstruction," *Phylon* 22, no. 1 (1961): 5-14; Otto H. Olsen, "The Ku Klux Klan: A Study in Reconstruction Politics and Propaganda," *North Carolina Historical Review* 39 (July 1962): 340-62; Edmund Wilson, *Patriotic Gore: Studies in the Literature of the American Civil War* (1962; New York: Oxford University Press, 1966), 529–48; Monte M. Olenick, "Albion W. Tourgée: Radical Republican Spokesman of the Civil War Crusade," *Phylon* 23, no. 4 (1962): 332–45; Theodore L. Gross, *Albion W. Tourgée* (New York: Twayne, 1963); Olsen, "Albion W. Tourgee: Carpetbagger," *North Carolina Historical Review* 40 (October 1963): 434-54; Theodore L. Gross, "The Fool's Errand of Albion W. Tourgee," *Phylon* 24, no. 3 (1963): 240-54; Otto H. Olsen, "Albion W. Tourgee and Negro Militants in the 1890's: A Documentary Selection," *Science and Society* 28 (2, 1964): 183-207; Sidney Kaplan, "Albion W. Tourgée: Attorney for the Segregated," *Journal of Negro History* 49 (April 1964): 128–33; C. Vann Woodward, "*Plessy v. Ferguson:* The Birth of Jim Crow," *American Heritage* 15 (April 1964): 52–55, 100–103; Olsen, *Carpetbagger's Crusade* (1965); Olsen, ed., *The Thin Disguise: Plessy V. Ferguson, A Documentary Presentation (1864–1896)* (New York: Humanities Press, 1967); Sylvia E. Bowman, "Judge Tourgée's Fictional Presentation of the Reconstruction," *Journal of Popular Culture* 3 (fall 1969): 307–23; Magdol, "A Note on Authenticity" (1970); Fredrickson, *The Black Image in the White Mind* (1971), 195–97, 236–37, 241–43; C. Vann Woodward, *American Counterpoint: Slavery and Racism in the North-South Dialogue* (Boston: Little, Brown, 1971), 217–33; Thomas Sancton, "The Creoles and Jim Crow," *The Crisis* 79 (Aug.-Sept. 1972): 222–25, 233; Daniel Aaron, *The Unwritten War: American Writers and the Civil War* (New York: Knopf, 1973), 193–205; David A. Gerber, "Lynching and Law and Order: Origin and Passage of the Ohio Anti-Lynching Law of 1896," *Ohio History* 83 (winter 1974): 33–50; Marguerite Ealy and Sanford E. Marovitz, "Albion Winegar Tourgee (1838–1905)," *American Literary Realism* 8 (winter 1975): 53–80; and L. Moody Simms Jr., "Albion Tourgée on the Fictional Use of the Post-Civil War South," *Southern Studies* 17 (winter 1978): 399–409. Both Fredrickson and John Hope Franklin wrote introductions to editions of *A Fool's Errand* (New York: Harper & Row, 1961; and Cambridge, Mass.: Belknap Press of Harvard University Press, 1961); and Olsen introduced the reprint of *Bricks Without Straw* (Baton Rouge: Louisiana State University Press, 1969). Studies before this initial revival include Roy F. Dibble, *Albion W. Tourgée* (New York: Lemeke

& Bucchner, 1921); Sterling Brown, *The Negro in American Fiction* (Washington D.C.: Howard University Press, 1937), 71–75; Russell B. Nye, "Judge Tourgée and Reconstruction," *Ohio State Archaeological and Historical Quarterly* 50 (April 1941): 101–14; George J. Becker, "Albion W. Tourgée: Pioneer in Social Criticism," *American Literature* 19 (March 1947): 59–72; Everett Carter, *Howells and the Age of Realism* (1950; Hamden, Conn.: Archon Books, 1966), 79–81; and Alexander Cowie, *The Rise of the American Novel* (New York: American Book Company, 1951), 521–35.

132 For recent scholarly studies referring to Tourgée, see Foner, *Reconstruction* (1988); Eric J. Sundquist, "Realism and Regionalism," in *Columbia Literary History of the United States,* ed. Emory Elliott (New York: Columbia University Press, 1988), 511–12; Andrew Kull, *The Color-Blind Constitution* (Cambridge, Mass.: Harvard University Press, 1992); Warren, *Black and White Strangers* (1993); Eric J. Sundquist, *To Wake the Nations: Race in the Making of American Literature* (Cambridge, Mass.: Belknap Press of Harvard University Press, 1993); Brook Thomas, ed. *Plessy v. Ferguson* (1997); Joseph R. McElrath Jr., "Why Charles W. Chesnutt Is Not a Realist," *American Literary Realism* 32 (winter 2000): 103–105; David W. Blight, *Race and Reunion: The Civil War in American Memory* (Cambridge, Mass.: Belknap Press of Harvard University Press, 2001); Rebecca J. Scott, "Public Rights, Social Equality and the Conceptual Roots of the Plessy Challenge," *Michigan Law Review* 106 (March 2008): 777–804; and Paula J. Giddings, *Ida: A Sword Among Lions: Ida B. Wells and the Campaign Against Lynching* (New York: HarperCollins-Amistad, 2008).

For more extended treatments, see Robert F. Sommer, "The Fools Errant in Albion W. Tourgée's Reconstruction Novels," *Mid-Hudson Language Studies* 5 (1982): 71–77; Ruth Currie McDaniel, "Courtship and Marriage in the Nineteenth Century: Albion and Emma Tourgée, a Case Study," *North Carolina Historical Review* 61 (July 1984): 285–310; Charles A. Lofgren, *The Plessy Case: A Legal-Historical Interpretation* (New York: Oxford University Press, 1987), chaps. 2, 3, 7, 8; Current, *Those Terrible Carpetbaggers* (1988), chaps. 3, 5, 10, 14, 18, 20; Robert O. Stephens, Tourgée's *Bricks Without Straw:* History, Fiction, Irony," *Southern Quarterly* 27 (summer 1989): 101–10; Brook Thomas, "Tragedies of Race, Training, Birth, and Communities of Competent Pudd'nheads," *American Literary History* 1 (winter 1989): 754–85; Ronald C. White Jr., *Liberty and Justice for All: Racial Reform and the Social Gospel (1877–1925)* (San Francisco: Harper & Row, 1990), chaps. 1, 3, 4; Ralph E. Luker, *The Social Gospel in Black and White: American Racial Reform, 1885–1912* (Chapel Hill: University of North Carolina Press, 1991), chaps. 1, 4, 5; Peter Caccavari, "Reconstructing Reconstruction: Region and Nation in the Work of Albion Tourgee," *Regionalism Reconsidered: New Approaches to the Field,* ed. David Jordan (New York: Garland, 1994), 119–38; Catherine Boeckmann, "The Invisible Color: Physical Description and Racial Liminality in the Novel of Passing," *The Historical and Political Turn in Literary Studies,* ed. Winfried Fluck, REAL 11 (1995): 255–82; Peter Caccavari, "A Trick of Mediation: Charles Chesnutt's Conflicted Literary

Relationship with Albion Tourgée," *Literary Influence and African-American Writers: Collected Essays,* ed. Tracy Mishkin (New York: Garland, 1996), 129–53; Michael Kent Curtis, "Albion Tourgée: Remembering Plessy's Lawyer on the 100th Anniversary of *Plessy v. Ferguson,*" *Constitutional Commentary* 13 (1996): 187–99; Brook Thomas, *American Literary Realism and the Failed Promise of Contract* (Berkeley: University of California Press, 1997), chap. 7; Brook Thomas, "*Plessy v. Ferguson* and the Literary Imagination," *Cardozo Studies in Law and Literature* 9 (spring/summer 1997): 45–65; Everett Carter, "Edmund Wilson Refights the Civil War: The Revision of Albion Tourgée's Novels," *American Literary Realism* 29 (winter 1997): 68–75; Jerzy Sobieraj, "Albion W. Tourgée and the Ku Klux Klan," *American Studies* [Poland] 17 (1999): 29–34; Troxler, " 'To look more closely at the man' " (2000); Mark Elliott, "Race, Color Blindness, and the Democratic Public: Albion W. Tourgée's Radical Principles in *Plessy v. Ferguson,*" *Journal of Southern History* 67 (May 2001): 287–330; Bill Hardwig, "Who Owns the Whip?: Chesnutt, Tourgée, and Reconstruction Justice," *African American Review* 36, no. 1 (2002): 5–20; Jeffrey W. Miller, "Redemption Through Violence: White Mobs and Black Citizenship in Albion Tourgée's *A Fool's Errand,*" *Southern Literary Journal* 35 (fall 2002): 14–27; J. Allen Douglas, "The 'Most Valuable Sort of Property': Constructing White Identity in American Law, 1880–1940," *San Diego Law Review* 40 (fall 2003): 881–946; Hamlin, " 'Friend of Freedom' " (2004); Harvey Fireside, *Separate and Unequal: Homer Plessy and the Supreme Court Decision that Legalized Racism* (New York: Carroll & Graf, 2004), chaps. 1, 3, 4, 5, 7, 8; Mark Golub, "Plessy as 'Passing': Judicial Responses to Ambiguously Raced Bodies in Plessy v. Ferguson," *Law and Society Review* 39 (Sept. 2005): 563–600; Karcher, "The White 'Bystander' and the Black Journalist 'Abroad' " (2005); Carolyn L. Karcher, "Ida B. Wells and Her Allies against Lynching: A Transnational Perspective," *Comparative American Studies* 3, no. 2 (2005): 131–51; Carolyn L. Karcher, " 'Men Are Burned at the Stake in Our Free Country': Albion W. Tourgée's Antilynching Journalism," *Resources for American Literary Study* 30 (2006): 178–215; Owen Fiss, *Troubled Beginnings of the Modern State: 1888–1910,* vol. 8 of *History of the Supreme Court* (Cambridge: Cambridge University Press, 2006), chap. 12; Elliott, *Color-Blind Justice* (2006); Brook Thomas, *Civic Myths: A Law-and-Literature Approach to Citizenship* (Chapel Hill: University of North Carolina Press, 2007), 158–67; Mark Elliott, "The Question of Color-Blind Citizenship: Albion Tourgée, W. E. B. Du Bois and the Principles of the Niagara Movement," *Afro-Americans in New York Life and History,* July 2008, 23–49; and Mark Elliott and John David Smith, eds., *Citizenship and the Race Problem: Selected Writings of Albion W. Tourgée* (Baton Rouge: Louisiana State University Press, forthcoming).

CHRONOLOGY

1838

May 2: Albion W. Tourgée born in Williamsfield, Ohio.

1854

Republican party organized, led by antislavery radicals and bringing together antislavery Whigs and Democrats; its platform calls for restricting slavery to existing states and opposing its extension into the territories.

1860

November: Republican presidential candidate Abraham Lincoln elected.
December 20: South Carolina secedes from the Union, followed within the next three months by Mississippi, Florida, Alabama, Georgia, Louisiana, Texas, Virginia, Arkansas, North Carolina, and Tennessee.

1861

April 12: Confederates fire on Fort Sumter, the opening shot in the Civil War.
April 15: Lincoln calls for 75,000 militiamen to put down the rebellion.
April 24: Tourgée leaves the University of Rochester and enlists in the 27th New York Infantry.
May 24: General Benjamin Butler initiates the policy of treating slaves

seeking refuge in Union army camps as "contraband of war," or confiscated enemy goods, on the grounds that they would otherwise be used directly or indirectly to aid the Confederate war effort; U.S. Congress legalizes this policy in the Confiscation Act of August 6.
July 21: Battle of Bull Run ends in the rout of Union troops; Tourgée suffers a paralyzing back injury.

1862

August 20: Tourgée reenlists in the 105th Ohio Volunteers.

1863

January 1: President Lincoln issues the Emancipation Proclamation; authorized under the president's war powers and framed as a "war measure" designed to hasten the defeat of the Confederacy, the Emancipation Proclamation applies only to states and areas still in rebellion against the United States and specifically exempts loyal states; nevertheless, it marks a turning point in the war by replacing the goal of preserving the Union with that of abolishing slavery; it also initiates the large-scale enrollment of African Americans into the Union army, enabling even slaves in the exempted states to win their freedom by enlisting.
January: Tourgée is captured; he spends most of the next four months in Richmond's Libby Prison and is released in a prisoner exchange.
May 14: Albion W. Tourgée and Emma L. Kilbourne marry in Columbus, Ohio.
May 25: Tourgée leaves to rejoin his regiment.
October 24: William, "an American citizen of African descent," arrives at the encampment of the 105 Ohio Volunteers; Tourgée hires him and renames him "Nimbus."
December 6: Tourgée resigns his commission after reinjuring his back and being judged unfit for active service.

1865

January 31: Congress passes the Thirteenth Amendment, abolishing slavery.
March: Bureau of Refugees, Freedmen, and Abandoned Lands (Freedmen's Bureau) created; its original mandate includes the distribution of confiscated Confederate land in forty-acre plots to freedmen and white refugees.
April 9: Confederate General Robert E. Lee surrenders to Union General Ulysses S. Grant at Appomattox Court House, ending the Civil War.

April 11: Lincoln delivers a speech suggesting that the vote be extended to literate African Americans and to Black veterans.
April 14: Lincoln assassinated on Good Friday by John Wilkes Booth, dies the following morning.
May 29: President Andrew Johnson initiates his "restoration" policy with a Proclamation of Amnesty that allows former rebels to reclaim confiscated property, thus preventing significant land redistribution; he also names William W. Holden Provisional Governor of North Carolina.
September 29–October 3: African Americans hold a convention in Raleigh.
October 15: Tourgée takes possession of the West Green Nursery in Guilford County, North Carolina.
November: Conservatives sweep North Carolina's elections; Holden loses the governorship to the Conservative Jonathan Worth; North Carolina General Assembly passes the Black Code.

1866

January: Violence rages against African Americans in the South; led by moderates, Senate Republicans respond to the Black Code by formulating the Freedmen's Bureau Bill (which extends the life of the agency, provides funding, and authorizes bureau agents to protect Black civil rights) and the Civil Rights Bill (which invalidates discriminatory laws throughout the nation and spells out the civil rights, short of the suffrage, that African Americans share with all other citizens).
February: Johnson vetoes the Freedmen's Bureau and Civil Rights Bill; the Senate fails by two votes to override Johnson's veto of the Freedmen's Bureau Bill but later extends the agency's life until 1870.
April: Senate overrides Johnson's veto of the Civil Rights Bill.
May or *June*: Ku Klux Klan founded as a social club in Tennessee but is transformed the following spring into an organization aimed at terrorizing African Americans and Republicans, as well as Freedmen's Bureau agents, schoolteachers, and others involved in advocacy or uplift for African Americans.
June 13: Congress passes the Fourteenth Amendment and sends it to the states for ratification. The Fourteenth Amendment defines "all persons born or naturalized in the United States," including African Americans, as "citizens of the United States and of the State wherein they reside" and further stipulates that no state can "deprive any person of life, liberty or property, without due process of law; nor deny to any person within its jurisdiction the equal protection of the laws."

August: Tourgée elected by Guilford County Unionists to represent them at the Southern Loyalist Convention in Philadelphia.
September: Tourgée attends the Southern Loyalist Convention in Philadelphia and goes on to campaign for the adoption of the Fourteenth Amendment; he receives death threats from North Carolinians.
October 2–5: North Carolina Equal Rights League of Freedmen holds a convention in Raleigh, in which Wyatt Outlaw and Harmon Unthank serve as delegates; the convention establishes the Freedmen's Educational Association of North Carolina, hails the passage by the U.S. Congress of the Freedmen's Bureau and Civil Rights Bills and the Fourteenth Amendment, protests against "outrages" occurring in the state, and demands the same voting rights that other citizens enjoy.
December 1: Tourgée issues the first number of the *Union Register*, a short-lived Republican newspaper.

1867

February: Tourgée signs a petition of Guilford and Randolph County Radicals urging Congress to divide the former Confederate states into territories under federal jurisdiction and to enfranchise loyalists and former slaves while disfranchising former Confederate office holders.
March: Congress passes the Reconstruction Act, which divides the South into five military districts, temporarily disfranchises former Confederate office holders and enfranchises African Americans, and requires the former Confederate states to hold new constitutional conventions, form new governments, and ratify the Fourteenth Amendment as conditions for readmittance to the Union.
June: *Union Register* ceases publication for lack of funding.
November: Republicans sweep elections in North Carolina under the new suffrage rules; Tourgée is among 107 Republicans out of 120 delegates elected to the constitutional convention.

1868

January 14–March 17: North Carolina constitutional convention meets in Raleigh; Tourgée is named one of three code commissioners charged with rationalizing North Carolina's legal procedures and law codes.
Spring: President Johnson is impeached in the House of Representatives and tried in the Senate.
April: Republicans sweep the North Carolina election, securing ratification of the new constitution and control of the state government; Republican

William W. Holden elected governor; Tourgée elected judge of the Seventh District Superior Court; Ku Klux Klan's campaign of terror in North Carolina begins.
May 16: Tourgée attends the U.S. Senate vote on President Johnson's impeachment, which falls one vote short of conviction.
July: North Carolina General Assembly ratifies the Fourteenth Amendment; North Carolina is readmitted to the Union.
July 9: Fourteenth Amendment ratified by the requisite three-fourths majority of states.
November: Republican Ulysses S. Grant elected to the presidency; during the preceding electoral campaign, Ku Klux Klan violence rages throughout the South; local Freedmen's Bureau agent reports that hundreds of African Americans who have voted for the Republican ticket are evicted from plantations in Alamance and Caswell counties.
December: Freedmen's Bureau ends operations in North Carolina; elsewhere Congress orders the Freedmen's Bureau to restrict itself, as of January 1869, to supervising education and helping Black veterans to obtain military bounties; inadequately funded, the Freedmen's Bureau's role in Black education declines, until the agency finally ceases all operations in June 1872.

1869

Reign of terror in Tourgée's seventh judicial district.
February 26: Congress passes the Fifteenth Amendment, declaring that the "right of citizens of the United States to vote shall not be denied or abridged by the United States or by any state on account of race, color, or previous condition of servitude" and sends it to the states for ratification; as worded, the Fifteenth Amendment leaves loopholes for literacy and education tests, property requirements, and other legal means of disfranchising voters.

1870

February 3: Fifteenth Amendment ratified by the states.
February 26: Wyatt Outlaw lynched in front of the Alamance County courthouse.
May 21: John W. Stephens murdered in the basement of Caswell County's courthouse.
May 24: Tourgée writes to North Carolina Senator Joseph C. Abbott providing statistics on Klan atrocities in his district and imploring Congress to pass a law enabling federal prosecution of the perpetrators.

May 31: Congress passes the first Enforcement Act, authorizing the president to appoint election supervisors with the power to bring state violators of voting rights to federal court.
June–August: Governor Holden declares martial law and suspends habeas corpus in Alamance and Caswell counties; his militia arrest approximately a hundred suspected Klansmen, but a federal judge orders them released on grounds of violated due process.
August 3: Garbled version of Tourgée's letter to Abbott published in the *New-York Daily Tribune*, having apparently been leaked by Governor Holden.
August 4: Conservatives win control of the North Carolina General Assembly, as intimidated Republican voters stay home on election day; Alamance and Caswell, still under protection of the militia, remain in Republican hands, but the new Conservative legislature invalidates their returns and mandates a special election in December, which results in Conservative victories.

1871

January: Congress begins holding hearings on Klan atrocities; Tourgée supplies names of North Carolina Klansmen willing to testify.
April: Congress passes the Ku Klux Klan Act, designating as federal crimes and providing for federal prosecution of conspiracies to deprive citizens of their civil and political rights.
December: Conservative-dominated General Assembly begins impeachment trial of Governor Holden, which culminates in his expulsion from office on March 22; Tourgée records confessions of Klan members involved in Outlaw's lynching and informs President Grant of his success.

1872

January–March: Tourgée continues to record confessions of Klan members and to seek indictments of them in court.
February: Conservative-dominated North Carolina General Assembly repeals the law making it a misdemeanor to go disguised with intent to terrorize and a felony to commit crimes while in disguise; the repeal retroactively invalidates indictments of Outlaw's murderers.
July: Tourgée campaigns for Grant's reelection.
November: Grant reelected.
December: Tourgée records an affidavit naming Stephens's murderers.

1873

Grant pardons all Klansmen imprisoned by the federal government; the Conservative-dominated North Carolina General Assembly votes amnesty for all crimes committed by Klansmen; Tourgée delivers a speech against the amnesty proclamation.

April: Colfax massacre occurs in Louisiana; "the bloodiest single instance of racial carnage in the Reconstruction era," it leaves 70 to 280 African Americans dead, according to different estimates made by recent historians and by contemporary witnesses.

June: Tourgée completes *Toinette* while on his judicial circuit.

September: Panic of 1873 ushers in a severe economic depression.

1874

June: Freedmen's Savings Bank collapses.

September: *Toinette* published.

November: Democrats recapture the U.S. House of Representatives; Tourgée loses his judgeship in North Carolina election.

1875

March 1: Civil Rights Act of 1875, first proposed by Massachusetts Senator Charles Sumner and Massachusetts Representative Benjamin Butler in 1870, is passed in diluted form by the lame duck Congress after Sumner's death and signed into law by President Grant; it outlaws racial discrimination in public accommodations, theaters, transportation facilities, and jury selection, but not in schools and churches as Sumner had originally advocated. Tourgée privately opposes the Civil Rights Act, especially its original school provision, on the grounds that it will merely fuel white supremacist propaganda and will prove unenforceable.

September: Conservatives (now renamed Democrats) call a convention to amend the 1868 constitution; Tourgée unsuccessfully fights against abolition of the township system providing for local self-government.

1876

March 27: Supreme Court verdict in *United States v. Cruikshank* invalidates indictments brought against leaders of the Colfax massacre under the 1870 Enforcement Act, holding that only the states, not the federal government, have the power to punish crimes by individuals; this verdict undermines the Enforcement Act to the point of rendering it virtually useless.

November: Disputed returns in South Carolina, Louisiana, and Florida leave presidential election results unresolved for several months. In North Carolina white supremacy dominates the campaign, as voters ratify the amended state constitution and elect a Democratic governor and majority in the legislature.

1877

February: North Carolina legislature abolishes elected county government in favor of government by appointed officials.
March: Republican Rutherford B. Hayes assumes office.
April: Hayes orders federal troops protecting the South Carolina and Louisiana state houses back to their barracks, in effect ending federal military intervention in the South.
North Carolina General Assembly passes a Landlord and Tenant Act that places the entire crop in the planter's hands until the rent has been paid and leaves it up to the planter to decide when a tenant has fulfilled his contract.

1878

August–November: Emma moves to Erie, Pennsylvania; Tourgée runs for election to Congress and is disastrously defeated; after his defeat, he devotes himself to preparing a digest of the North Carolina law code.

1879

January: Tourgée completes his digest of the North Carolina law code and begins working on the index to it.
March: Tourgée visits Emma in Erie, agrees to wind up his affairs in North Carolina.
September 2: Tourgée leaves North Carolina.
October: Publication of *Figs and Thistles: A Romance of the Western Reserve*; Tourgée's second novel is based on his youthful experiences but mistaken by many for a fictionalized campaign biography of future Republican presidential candidate James A. Garfield.
November: *A Fool's Errand* published anonymously.

1880

May: *The Invisible Empire*, a documentary history of the Klan, published as an appendix to a new edition of *A Fool's Errand*.
June: Tourgée attends the Republican national convention in Chicago, where his friend Garfield is selected as the presidential candidate; the party

platform incorporates the national education plank for which Tourgée has been campaigning.
October: *Bricks Without Straw* published; Tourgée campaigns for Garfield, who wins election by a narrow margin and credits his victory in part to the impact of Tourgée's novels.
December: Tourgée sends Garfield a fourteen-page letter advising him on southern policy; over the next few months, he frequently corresponds and meets with Garfield.

1881

March 4: Garfield's inaugural address emphasizes African American civil rights and national support for public education, apparently reflecting Tourgée's influence.
July 2: Garfield shot by an assassin.
September 19: Garfield dies; Chester A. Arthur replaces him as president and turns away from both the race problem and education.

1882–1884

Tourgée founds and edits an illustrated weekly literary magazine, *Our Continent*, in which he publishes many selections related to race issues and the Civil War, including his serialized novel *Hot Plowshares*; an overambitious venture, the magazine collapses, consuming all the money Tourgée had invested in it and leaving him deeply in debt.

1883

October 15: In the *Civil Rights Cases*, the U.S. Supreme Court declares the Civil Rights Act of 1875 unconstitutional.
Tourgée publishes *Hot Plowshares*, a novel about the antislavery movement in the Western Reserve.

1884

October: Timed to influence the 1884 election, Tourgée publishes *An Appeal to Caesar*, his most complete analysis of the race problem, together with a detailed plan for solving it through federal aid to public education in the South.

1886

Tourgée publishes *The Veteran and His Pipe*, a collected edition of his newspaper columns by that title in the Chicago *Daily Inter Ocean*; in it, assuming the persona of a Civil War veteran addressing his pipe, he laments the country's willingness to pursue reconciliation with the South at the price of abandoning the ideals of freedom and equal rights, for which so many Union soldiers sacrificed life and limb.

1888

April 21: In the Chicago *Daily Inter Ocean* Tourgée inaugurates his column, "A Bystander's Notes," which runs until October 1898, with gaps in 1893–94 and 1895–96; it addresses a wide range of social and political issues, including class struggle, workers' rights, free trade, tariffs, prohibition, Civil Service reform, and political corruption, but devotes special attention to the disfranchisement of African Americans in the South and to lynching and other forms of violence used to keep them in subjection.

1890

Tourgée publishes *Pactolus Prime*, a novel set on Christmas day; its title character, a Civil War veteran who once passed for white and now works as a boot black at an exclusive Washington hotel, exposes white America's racism and hypocrisy, arguing that the nation owes African Americans more than ten billion dollars in reparations for slavery and still more for the continuing theft of their civil rights.
Tourgée publishes *Murvale Eastman, Christian Socialist*; its title character, a minister, induces his congregation to explore the responsibility of Christian churches for helping end poverty and injustice by raising public consciousness and pushing for effective legal reform.

1891

October 17: Through his "Bystander" column, Tourgée launches the National Citizens' Rights Association, an interracial organization he conceives as a vehicle for publicizing and agitating against all violations of citizens' civil rights and as a pressure group for influencing elections; the same column announces that African Americans in New Orleans have raised money to challenge the constitutionality of Jim Crow car laws—the case that will become *Plessy v. Ferguson*, in which Tourgée will serve pro bono as the African American community's lawyer.

1894

Harry C. Smith, African American editor of the *Cleveland Gazette* and newly elected to the Ohio House of Representatives, solicits legal advice from Tourgée on framing a state anti-lynching bill; Tourgée testifies in favor of the bill and lobbies for its passage.

1896

Governor William McKinley signs Ohio's anti-lynching bill, which becomes a model for laws passed in nine other states.

Tourgée publishes *The Story of a Thousand. Being a history of the Service of the 105th Ohio Volunteer Infantry, in the War for the Union from August 21, 1862 to June 6, 1865*.

April 13: Tourgée presents oral arguments to the Supreme Court in the *Plessy* case.

May 18: Supreme Court rules 7 to 1 that segregation laws are constitutional; Judge John Marshall Harlan, the lone dissenter, argues that "our Constitution is color-blind"—an argument borrowed from Tourgée's brief to the Court, which had asserted: "Justice is pictured blind and her daughter, the Law, ought at least to be color-blind."

Fall: Tourgée campaigns for Republican presidential candidate William McKinley.

1897

May: Tourgée is appointed U.S. consul to Bordeaux.

1905

May 21: Tourgée dies in Bordeaux.

November 14: More than thirty African Americans attend a memorial service for Tourgée in his hometown of Mayville, New York, at which Charles Chesnutt and Ida B. Wells deliver major eulogies.

November 30: Founders of the Niagara Movement hold memorial services on Thanksgiving Day in honor of three "Friends of Freedom": Frederick Douglass, William Lloyd Garrison, and Tourgée.

1909

National Association for the Advancement of Colored People (NAACP) founded, fulfilling Tourgée's hopes for his short-lived NCRA.

1954

Brown v. Board of Education overturns *Plessy v. Ferguson*; Tourgée's arguments, rediscovered by Justice Robert H. Jackson, play a role in influencing *Brown*.

SATAN CAME ALSO

"You have not asked about Satan," said Mr. La Moyne suddenly one day.
"Why should I?" she replied. "If that personage will be equally forgetful of me, I am sure I shall be very glad."—p. 282

BRICKS WITHOUT STRAW

A Novel

by

ALBION W. TOURGÉE, LL.D.

LATE JUDGE OF THE SUPERIOR COURT OF NORTH CAROLINA,

Author of "A Fool's Errand," "Figs and Thistles," "The Code, with Notes," etc.

"Go therefore now, and work; for there shall no straw be given you, yet shall ye deliver the tale of bricks."—EXODUS V. 18.

NEW YORK:
FORDS, HOWARD, & HULBERT

LONDON: SAMPSON LOW & CO. MONTREAL: DAWSON BROS.

THIS VOLUME

I GRATEFULLY DEDICATE

TO

My Wife;

TO WHOSE UNFLINCHING COURAGE,

UNFALTERING FAITH, UNFAILING CHEER,

AND STEADFAST LOVE,

I OWE MORE THAN MANY VOLUMES

MIGHT DECLARE.

TRANSLATION:

[*From an ancient Egyptian Papyrus-Roll, recently discovered.*]

IT CAME TO PASS that when Pharaoh had made an end of giving commandment that the children of Israel should deliver the daily tale of bricks, but should not be furnished with any straw wherewith to make them, but should instead go into the fields and gather such stubble as might be left therein, that Neoncapos, the king's jester, laughed.*

And when he was asked whereat he laughed, he answered, At the king's order.

And thereupon he laughed the more.

Then was Pharaoh, the king, exceeding wroth, and he gave commandment that an owl be given to Neoncapos, the king's jester, and that he be set forth without the gate of the king's palace, and that he be forbidden to return, or to speak to any in all the land, save only unto the owl which had been given him, until such time as the bird should answer and tell him what he should say.

Then they that stood about the king, and all who saw Neoncapos, cried

* *Editor's note:* Tourgée is adapting Exodus 5, which tells of how Moses conveys God's message to Pharaoh, "Let my people go," and how Pharaoh responds by instead intensifying his oppression of the Israelites, through the command that they make the same quantity of bricks without the straw needed to temper them. Neoncapos does not appear in the biblical story.

out, What a fool's errand is this! So that the saying remains even unto this day.

Nevertheless, upon the next day came Neoncapos again into the presence of Pharaoh, the king.

Then was Pharaoh greatly astonished, and he said, How is this? Hath the bird spoken?

And Neoncapos, the king's jester, bowed himself unto the earth, and said, He hath, my lord.

Then was Pharaoh, the king, filled with amazement, and said, Tell me what he hath said unto thee.

And Neoncapos raised himself before the king, and answered him, and said:

As I went out upon the errand whereunto thou hadst sent me forth, I remembered thy commandment to obey it. And I spake only unto the bird which thou gavest me, and said unto him:

There was a certain great king which held a people in bondage, and set over them taskmasters, and required of them all the bricks that they could make, man for man, and day by day;

For the king was in great haste seeking to build a palace which should be greater and nobler than any in the world, and should remain to himself and his children a testimony of his glory forever.

And it came to pass, at length, that the king gave commandment that no more straw should be given unto them that made the bricks, but that they should still deliver the tale which had been aforetime required of them.

And thereupon the king's jester laughed.

Because he said to himself, If the laborers have not straw wherewith to attemper the clay, but only stubble and chaff gathered from the fields, will not the bricks be ill-made and lack strength and symmetry of form, so that the wall made thereof will not be true and strong, or fitly joined together?

For the lack of a little straw it may be that the palace of the great king will fall upon him and all his people that dwell therein. Thereupon the king was wroth with his fool, and his countenance was changed, and he spake harshly unto him, and—

It matters not what thou saidst unto the bird, said the king. What did the bird say unto thee?

The bird, said Neoncapos, bowing himself low before the king, the bird, my lord, looked at me in great amaze, and cried again and again, in an exceeding loud voice: *Who! Who-o! Who-o-o!*

Then was Pharaoh exceeding wroth, and his anger burned within him, and he commanded that the fool should be taken and bound with cords, and cast into prison, while he should consider of a fit punishment for his impudent words.

NOTE.—A script attached to this manuscript, evidently of later date, informs us that the fool escaped the penalty of his folly by the disaster at the Red Sea.

CONTENTS.

BRICKS WITHOUT STRAW.

CHAPTER I.

TRI-NOMINATE.[1]

"WAL, I 'CLAR, now, jes de quarest ting ob all 'bout dis matter o' freedom is de way dat it sloshes roun' de names 'mong us cullud folks. H'yer I lib ober on de Hyco twenty year er mo'—nobody but ole Marse Potem an' de Lor', an' p'raps de Debble beside, know 'zackly how long it mout hev been—an' didn't hev but one name in all dat yer time. An' I didn't hev no use for no mo' neither, kase dat wuz de one ole Mahs'r gib me hisself, an' nobody on de libbin' yairth nebber hed no sech name afo' an' nebber like to agin. Dat wuz allers de way ub ole Mahs'r's names. Dey used ter say dat he an' de Debble made 'em up togedder while he wuz dribin' roun' in dat ole gig 'twixt de diff'ent plantations—on de Dan an' de Ro'noke, an' all 'bout whar de ole cuss could fine a piece o' cheap lan', dat would do ter raise niggers on an' pay for bringin' up, at de same time. He was a powerful smart man in his day, wuz ole Kunnel Potem Desmit; but he speshully did beat anythin' a findin' names fer niggers. I reckon now, ef he'd 'a hed forty thousan' cullud folks, men an' wimmen, dar wouldn't ha' been no two on 'em hevin' de same name. Dat's what folks used ter say 'bout him, ennyhow. Dey sed he used ter say ez how he wasn't gwine ter hev his niggers mixed up wid nobody else's namin', an' he wouldn't no mo' 'low ob one black feller callin' ob anudder by enny nickname ner nothin' ub dat kine, on one o' his plantations, dan he would ob his takin' a mule, nary bit. Dey du say dat when he used ter buy a boy er gal de berry fust ting he wuz gwine ter du wuz jes ter hev 'em up an' gib 'em a new name, out 'n out, an' a clean suit ob close ter 'member it by; an' den, jes by way ob a little 'freshment, he used ter make de oberseer gib 'em ten er twenty good licks, jes ter make sure ob der fergittin' de ole un dat dey'd hed afo'. Dat's what my mammy sed, an' she allers 'clar'd dat tow'rd de las' she nebber could 'member what she was at de fus' no more'n ef she hedn't been de same gal.

"All he wanted ter know 'bout a nigger wuz jes his name, an' dey say he could tell straight away when an' whar he wuz born, whar he'd done lived, an' all 'bout him. He war a powerful man in der way ob names, shore. Some on 'em wuz right quare, but den agin mos' all on 'em wuz right good, an' it war powerful handy hevin' no two on 'em alike. I've heard tell dat a heap o' folks wuz a takin' up wid his notion, an' I reckon dat ef de s'rrender hed only stood off long 'nuff dar wouldn't 'a been nary two niggers in de whole State hevin' de same names. Dat *would* hev been handy, all roun'!

"When dat come, though, old Mahs'r's plan warn't nowhar. Lor' bress my soul, how de names did come a-brilin' roun'! I'd done got kinder used ter mine, hevin' hed it so long an' nebber knowin' myself by any udder, so't I didn't like ter change. 'Sides dat, I couldn't see no use. I'd allers got 'long well 'nuff wid it—all on'y jes once, an' dat ar wuz so long ago I'd nigh about forgot it. Dat showed what a debblish cute plan dat uv ole Mahs'r's was, though.

"Lemme see, dat er wuz de fus er secon' year atter I wuz a plow-boy. Hit wuz right in de height ob de season, an' Marse War'—dat was de oberseer—he sent me to der Cou't House ob an ebenin' to do some sort ob arrant for him. When I was a comin' home, jes about an hour ob sun, I rides up wid a sort o' hard-favored man in a gig, an' he looks at me an' at de hoss, when I goes ter ride by, mighty sharp like; an' fust I knows he axes me my name; an' I tole him. An' den he axes whar I lib; an' I tole him, "On de Knapp-o'-Reeds plantation." Den he say,

" 'Who you b'long to, ennyhow, boy?'

"An' I tole him 'Ole Marse Potem Desmit, sah'—jes so like.

"Den he sez 'Who's a oberseein' dar now?'

"An' I sez, 'Marse Si War', sah?'

"Den he sez, 'An' how do all de han's on Knapp-o-Reeds git 'long wid ole Marse Potem an' Marse Si War'?'

"An' I sez, 'Oh, we gits 'long tol'able well wid Marse War', sah.'

"An' he sez, 'How yer likes old Marse Potem?'

"An' I sez, jes fool like, 'We don't like him at all, sah.'

"An' he sez, 'Why?'

"An' I sez, 'Dunno sah.'

"An' he sez, 'Don't he feed?'

"An' I sez, 'Tol'able, I spose.'

"An' he sez, 'Whip much?'

"An' I sez, 'Mighty little, sah.'

"An' he sez, 'Work hard?'

"An' I sez, 'Yes, moderate, sah.'

"An' he sez, 'Eber seed him?'

"An' I sez, 'Not ez I knows on, sah.'

"An' he sez, 'What for don't yer like him, den?'

"An' I sez, 'Dunno, on'y jes' kase he's sech a gran' rascal.'

"Den he larf fit ter kill, an' say, 'Dat's so, dat's so, boy.' Den he take out his pencil an' write a word er two on a slip o' paper an' say,

" 'H'yer, boy, yer gibs dat ter Marse Si War', soon ez yer gits home. D'yer heah?'

"I tole him, 'Yes, sah,' an' comes on home an' gibs dat ter Marse Si. Quick ez he look at it he say, 'Whar you git dat, boy?' An' when I tole him he sez, 'You know who dat is? Dat's old Potem Desmit! What you say to him, you little fool?'

"Den I tell Marse War' all 'bout it, an' he lay down in de yard an' larf fit ter kill. All de same he gib me twenty licks 'cordin' ter de orders on dat little dam bit o' paper. An' I nebber tink o' dat widout cussin', sence.

"Dat ar now am de only time I ebber fault my name. Now what I want ter change it fer, er what I want ob enny mo'? I don't want 'em. An' I tell 'em so, ebbery time too, but dey 'jes fo'ce em on me like, an' what'll I do 'bout it, I dunno. H'yer I'se got—lemme see—one—two—tree! Fo' God, I don' know how many names I hez got! I'm dod-dinged now ef I know who I be ennyhow. Ef ennybody ax me I'd jes hev ter go back ter ole Mahs'r's name an' stop, kase I swar I wouldn't know which ob de udders ter pick an' chuse from.

"I specs its all 'long o' freedom, though I can't see why a free nigger needs enny mo' name dan the same one hed in ole slave times. Mus' be, though. I mind now dat all de pore white folks hez got some two tree names, but I allus thought dat wuz 'coz dey hedn't nuffin' else ter call dere own. Must be a free feller needs mo' name, somehow. Ef I keep on I reckon I'll git enuff atter a while. H'yer it's gwine on two year only sence de s'rrender, an' I'se got tree ob 'em sartain!"

The speaker was a colored man, standing before his log-house in the evening of a day in June. His wife was the only listener to the monologue. He had been examining a paper which was sealed and stamped with official formality, and which had started him upon the train of thought he had pursued. The question he was trying in vain to answer was only the simplest and easiest of the thousand strange queries which freedom had so recently propounded to him and his race.

CHAPTER II.

THE FONT.

KNAPP-OF-REEDS was the name of a plantation which was one of the numerous possessions of P. Desmit, Colonel and Esquire, of the county of Horsford, in the northernmost of those States which good Queen Caroline was fortunate enough to have designated as memorials of her existence. The plantation was just upon that wavy line which separates the cotton region of the east from the tobacco belt that sweeps down the pleasant ranges of the Piedmont region, east of the Blue Appalachians. Or, to speak more correctly, the plantation was in that indeterminate belt which neither of the great staples could claim exclusively as its own—that delectable land where every conceivable product of the temperate zone grows, if not in its rankest luxuriance, at least in perfection and abundance. Tobacco on the hillsides, corn upon the wide bottoms, cotton on the gray uplands, and wheat, oats, fruits, and grasses everywhere. Five hundred acres of hill and bottom, forest and field, with what was termed the Island, consisting of a hundred more, which had never been overflowed in the century of cultivation it had known, constituted a snug and valuable plantation. It had been the seat of an old family once, but extravagant living and neglect of its resources had compelled its sale, and it had passed into the hands of its present owner, of whose vast possessions it formed an insignificant part.

Colonel Desmit was one of the men who applied purely business principles to the opportunities which the South afforded in the olden time, following everything to its logical conclusion, and measuring every opportunity by its money value. He was not of an ancient family. Indeed, the paternal line stopped short with his own father, and the maternal one could only show one more link, and then became lost in malodorous tradition which hung about an old mud-daubed log-cabin on the most poverty-stricken portion of Nubbin Ridge.

There was a rumor that the father had a left-handed kinship with the Brutons,[2] a family of great note in the public annals of the State. He certainly showed qualities which tended to confirm this tradition, and abilities which entitled him to be considered the peer of the best of that family, whose later generations were by no means the equals of former ones. Untiring and unscrupulous, Mr. Peter Smith rose from the position of a nameless son of an unknown father, to be as overseer for one of the wealthiest proprietors of that region, and finally, by a not unusual turn of fortune's wheel, became the owner of a large part of his employer's estates. Thrifty in all things, he married in middle life, so well as nearly to double the fortune then acquired, and before his death had become one of the wealthiest men in his county. He was always hampered by a lack of education. He could read little and write less. In his later days he was appointed a Justice of the Peace, and was chosen one of the County Court, or "Court of Pleas and Quarter Sessions," as it was technically called. These honors were so pleasant to him that he determined to give his only son a name which should commemorate this event. The boy was, therefore, christened after the opening words of his commission of the peace, and grew to manhood bearing the name *Potestatem Dedimus* Smith.* This son was educated with care—the shrewd father feeling his own need—but was early instilled with his father's greed for gain, and the necessity for unusual exertion if he would achieve equal position with the old families who were to be his rivals.

The young man proved a worthy disciple of his father. He married, it is true, without enhancing his fortune; but he secured what was worth almost as much for the promotion of his purposes as if he had doubled his belongings. Aware of the ill-effects of so recent a bar sinister in his armorial bearings, he sought in marriage Miss Bertha Bellamy, of Belleville, in the State of Virginia, who united in her azure veins at least a few drops of the blood of all the first families of that fine-bred aristocracy, from Pocahontas's days until her own. The *rôle* of the gentleman had been too much for the male line of the Bellamys to sustain. Horses and hounds and cards and high living had gradually eaten down their once magnificent patrimony, until pride and good blood and poverty were the only dowry that the females could command. Miss Bertha, having already arrived at the age

* *Potestatem dedimus*: "We give thee power, etc." The initial words of the clause conferring jurisdiction upon officers, in the old forms of judicial commissions. This name is fact, not fancy.

of discretion, found that to match this against the wealth of young Potestatem Dedimus Smith was as well as she could hope to do, and accepted him upon condition that the vulgar *Smith* should be changed to some less democratic name.

The one paternal and two maternal ancestors had not made the very common surname peculiarly sacred to the young man, so the point was yielded; and by considerable persistency on the part of the young wife, "P. D. SMITH" was transformed without much trouble into "P. DESMIT," before the administrator had concluded the settlement of his father's estate.

The vigor with which the young man devoted himself to affairs and the remarkable success which soon began to attend his exertions diverted attention from the name, and before he had reached middle life he was known over almost half the State as "Colonel Desmit," "Old Desmit," or "Potem Desmit," according to the degree of familiarity or respect desired to be displayed. Hardly anybody remembered and none alluded to the fact that the millionaire of Horsford was only two removes from old Sal Smith of Nubbin Ridge. On the other hand the rumor that he was in some mysterious manner remotely akin to the Brutons was industriously circulated by the younger members of that high-bred house, and even "the Judge," who was of about the same age as Colonel Desmit, had been heard more than once to call him "Cousin." These things affected Colonel Desmit but little. He had set himself to improve his father's teachings and grow rich. He seemed to have the true Midas touch. He added acre to acre, slave to slave, business to business, until his possessions were scattered from the mountains to the sea, and especially extended on both sides the border line in the Piedmont region where he had been bred. It embraced every form of business known to the community of which he was a part, from the cattle ranges of the extreme west to the fisheries of the farthest east. He made his possessions a sort of self-supporting commonwealth in themselves. The cotton which he grew on his eastern farms was manufactured at his own factory, and distributed to his various plantations to be made into clothing for his slaves. Wheat and corn and meat, raised upon some of his plantations, supplied others devoted to non-edible staples. The tobacco grown on the Hyco and other plantations in that belt was manufactured at his own establishment, supplied his eastern laborers and those which wrought in the pine woods to the southward at the production of naval supplies. He had realized the dream of his own life and the aspiration of his father, the overseer, and had become one of the wealthiest men in the State. But he attended to all this himself. Every overseer knew that he was liable any day or night to receive a visit from the untiring owner of all this wealth, who would require an instant accounting for every bit of the property under his charge. Not only the presence and condition of every slave, mule, horse or other piece of stock must be accounted for, but the manner of its employment stated. He was an inflexible disciplinarian, who gave few orders, hated instructions, and only asked results. It was his custom to place an agent in charge of a business without directions, except to make it pay. His only care was to see that his property did not depreciate, and that the course adopted by the agent was one likely to produce good results. So long as this was the case, he was satisfied. He never interfered, made no suggestions, found no fault. As soon as he became dissatisfied the agent was removed and another substituted. This was done without words or controversy, and it was a well-known rule that a man once discharged from such a trust could never enter his employ again. For an overseer to be dismissed by Colonel Desmit was to forfeit all chance for employment in that region, since it was looked upon as a certificate either of incapacity or untrustworthiness.

Colonel Desmit was especially careful in regard to his slaves. His father had early shown him that no branch of business was, or could be, half so profitable as the rearing of slaves for market.

"A healthy slave woman," the thrifty father had been accustomed to say, "will yield a thousand per cent upon her value, while she needs less care and involves less risk than any other species of property." The son, with a broader knowledge, had carried his father's instructions to more accurate and scientific results. He found that the segregation of large numbers of slaves upon a single plantation was not favorable either to the most rapid multiplication or economy of sustenance. He had carefully determined the fact that plantations of moderate extent, upon the high, well-watered uplands of the Piedmont belt, were the most advantageous locations that could be found for the rearing of slaves. Such plantations, largely worked by female slaves, could be made to return a small profit on the entire investment, without at all taking into account the increase of the human stock. This was, therefore, so much added profit. From careful study and observation he had deduced a specific formulary by which he measured the rate of gain. With a well-selected force, two thirds of which should be females, he calculated that with proper care such plantations could be made to pay, year by year, an interest of five per cent on the first cost, and, in addition, double the value of the working force every eight years. This conclusion he had arrived at from scientific study of the rates of mortality and increase, and in settling upon it he had cautiously left a large margin for contingencies. He was not accustomed to talk about his business, but when questioned as to his uniform success and remarkable prosperity, always attributed it to a system which he had inexorably followed, and which had never failed to return to him at least twenty per cent per annum upon every dollar he had invested.

So confident was he in regard to the success of this plan that he became a large but systematic borrower of money at the legal rate of six per cent, taking care that his maturing liabilities should, at no time, exceed a certain proportion of his available estate. By this means his wealth increased with marvelous rapidity.

The success of his system depended, however, entirely upon the care bestowed upon his slaves. They were never neglected. Though he had so many that of hundreds of them he did not know even the faces, he gave the closest attention to their hygienic condition, especially that of the women, who were encouraged by every means to bear children. It was a sure passport to favor with the master and the overseer: tasks were lightened; more abundant food provided; greater liberty enjoyed; and on the birth of a child a present of some sort was certain to be given the mother.

The one book which Colonel Desmit never permitted anybody else to keep or see was the register of his slaves. He had invented for himself an elaborate system by which in a moment he could ascertain every element of the value of each of his more than a thousand slaves at the date of his last visitation or report. When an overseer was put in charge of a plantation he was given a list of the slaves assigned to it, by name and number, and was required to report every month the condition of each slave during the month previous, as to health and temper, and also the labor in which the same had been employed each day. It was only as to the condition of the slaves that the owner gave explicit directions to his head-men. "Mighty few people know how to take care of a nigger," he was wont to say; and as he made the race a study and looked to them for his profits, he was attentive to their condition.

Among the requirements of his system was one that each slave born upon his plantations should be named only by himself; and this was done only on personal inspection. Upon a visit to a plantation, therefore, one of his special duties always was to inspect, name, and register all slave children who had been born to his estate since his previous visitation.

It was in the summer of 1840 that a traveler drove into the grove in front of the house at Knapp-of-Reeds, in the middle of a June afternoon, and uttered the usual halloo. He was answered after a moment's delay by a colored woman, who came out from the kitchen and exclaimed,

"Who's dah?"

It was evident at once that visitors were not frequent at Knapp-of-Reeds.

"Where's Mr. Ware?" asked the stranger.

"He's done gone out in de new-ground terbacker, 'long wid de han's," answered the woman.

"Where is the new-ground this year?" repeated the questioner.

"Jes' down on the p'int 'twixt de branch an' de Hyco," she replied.

"Anybody you can send for him?"

"Wal, thar mout be some shaver dat's big enough to go, but Marse War's dat keerful ter please Marse Desmit dat he takes 'em all outen de field afore dey can well toddle," said the woman doubtfully.

"Well, come and take my horse," said he, as he began to descend from his gig, "and send for Mr. Ware to come up at once."

The woman came forward doubtfully and took the horse by the bit, while the traveler alighted. No sooner did he turn fully toward her than her face lighted up with a smile, and she said,

"Wal, dar, ef dat a'n't Marse Desmit hisself, I do believe! How d'ye do, Mahs'r?" and the woman dropped a courtesy.

"I'm very well, thank ye, Lorency, an' glad to see you looking so peart," he responded pleasantly. "How's Mr. Ware and the people? All well, I hope."

"All tol'able, Mahs'r, thank ye."

"Well, tie the horse, and get me some dinner, gal. I haven't eaten since I left home."

"La sakes!" said the woman in a tone of commiseration, though she had no idea whether it was twenty or forty miles he had driven since his breakfast.

The man who sat upon the porch and waited for the coming of Mr. Silas Ware, his overseer, was in the prime of life, of florid complexion, rugged habit, short stubbly hair—thick and bristling, that stood close and even on his round, heavy head from a little way above the beetling brows well down upon the bull-like neck which joined but hardly separated the massive head and herculean trunk. This hair, now almost white, had been a yellowish red, a hue which still showed in the eyebrows and in the stiff beard which was allowed to grow beneath the angle of his massive jaw, the rest of his face being clean shaven. The eyes were deep-sunk and of a clear, cold blue. His mouth broad, with firm, solid lips. Dogged resolution, unconquerable will, cold-blooded selfishness, and a keen hog-cunning showed in his face, while his short, stout form—massive but not fleshy—betrayed a capacity to endure fatigue which few men could rival.

"How d'ye, Mr. Ware?" he said as that worthy came striding in from the new-ground nervously chewing a mouthful of home-made twist, which he had replenished several times since leaving the field, without taking the precaution to provide stowage for the quantity he was taking aboard.

"How d'ye, Colonel?" said Ware uneasily.

"Reckon you hardly expected me to day?" continued Desmit, watching him closely. "No, I dare say not. They hardly ever do. Fact is, I rarely ever know myself long enough before to send word."

He laughed heartily, for his propensity for dropping in unawares upon his agents was so well known that he enjoyed their confusion almost as much as he valued the surprise as a means of ascertaining their attention to his interests. Ware was one of his most trusted lieutenants, however, and everything that he had ever seen or heard satisfied him of the man's faithfulness. So he made haste to relieve him from embarrassment, for the tall, awkward, shambling fellow was perfectly overwhelmed.

"It's a long time since I've been to see you, Mr. Ware—almost a year. There's mighty few men I'd let run a plantation that long without looking after them. Your reports have been very correct, and the returns of your work very satisfactory. I hope the stock and hands are in good condition?"

"I must say, Colonel Desmit," responded Ware, gathering confidence, "though perhaps I oughtn't ter say it myself, that I've never seen 'em lookin' better. 'Pears like everything hez been jest about ez favorable fer hands an' stock ez one could wish. The spring's work didn't seem ter worry the stock a mite, an' when the new feed come on there was plenty on't, an' the very best quality. So they shed off ez fine ez ever you see ennything in yer life, an' hev jest been a doin' the work in the crop without turnin' a hair."

"Glad to hear it, Mr. Ware," said Desmit encouragingly.

"And the hands," continued Ware, "have jest been in prime condition. We lost Horion, as I reported to you in—lemme see, February, I reckon—along o' rheumatism which he done cotch a runnin' away from that Navigation Company that you told me to send him to work for."

"Yes, I know. You told him to come home if they took him into Virginia, as I directed, I suppose."

"Certainly, sir," said Ware; "an' ez near ez I can learn they took him off way down below Weldon somewheres, an' he lit out to come home jest at the time of the February 'fresh.' He had to steal his way afoot, and was might'ly used up when he got here, and died some little time afterward."

"Yes. The company will have to pay a good price for him. Wasn't a better nor sounder nigger on the river," said Desmit.

"That ther warn't," replied Ware. "The rest has all been well. Lorency had a bad time over her baby, but she's 'round again as peart as ever."

"So I see. And the crops?"

"The best I've ever seed sence I've been here, Colonel. Never had such a stand of terbacker, and the corn looks prime. Knapp-of-Reeds has been doin' better 'n' better ever sence I've knowed it; but she's jest outdoin' herself this year."

"Haven't you got anything to drink, Ware?"

"I beg your *parding,* Colonel; I was that flustered I done forgot my manners altogether," said Ware apologetically. "I hev got a drap of apple that they say is right good for this region, and a trifle of corn that ain't nothing to brag on, though it does for the country right well."

Ware set out the liquor with a bowl of sugar from his sideboard as he spoke, and called to the kitchen for a glass and water.

"That makes me think," said Desmit. "Here, you Lorency, bring me that portmanty from the gig."

When it was brought he unlocked it and took out a bottle, which he first held up to the light and gazed tenderly through, then drew the cork and smelled of its contents, shook his head knowingly, and then handed it to Ware, who went through the same performance very solemnly.

"Here, gal," said Desmit sharply, "bring us another tumbler. Now, Mr. Ware," said he unctuously when it had been brought, "allow me, sir, to offer you some brandy which is thirty-five years old—pure French brandy, sir. Put it in my portmanty specially for you, and like to have forgot it at the last. Just try it, man."

Ware poured himself a dram, and swallowed it with a gravity which would have done honor to a more solemn occasion, after bowing low to his principal and saying earnestly,

"Colonel, your very good health."

"And now," said Desmit, "have the hands and stock brought up while I eat my dinner, if you please. I have a smart bit of travel before me yet to-day."

The overseer's horn was at Ware's lips in a moment, and before the master had finished his dinner every man, woman, and child on the plantation was in the yard, and every mule and horse was in the barn-lot ready to be brought out for his inspection.

The great man sat on the back porch, and, calling up the slaves one by one, addressed some remark to each, gave every elder a quarter and every youngster a dime, until he came to the women. The first of these was Lorency, the strapping cook, who had improved the time since her master's coming to make herself gay with her newest gown and a flaming new turban. She came forward pertly, with a young babe upon her arm.

"Well, Lorency, Mr. Ware says you have made me a present since I was here?"

"Yah! yah! Marse Desmit, dat I hab! Jes' de finest little nigger boy yer ebber sot eyes on. Jes' you look at him now," she continued, holding up her bright-eyed pickaninny. "Ebber you see de beat ub dat? Reg'lar ten pound, an' wuff two hundred dollars dis bressed minnit."

"Is that it, Lorency?" said Desmit, pointing to the child. "Who ever saw such a thunder-cloud?"

There was a boisterous laugh at the master's joke from the assembled crowd. Nothing abashed, the good-natured mother replied, with ready wit,

"Dat so, Marse Kunnel. He's *brack,* he is. None ob yer bleached out yaller sort of coffee-cullud nigger 'bout *him.* De rale ole giniwine kind, dat a coal make a white mark on. Yah! yah! what yer gwine ter name him, Mahs'r? Gib him a good name, now, none o' yer common mean ones, but jes' der bes' one yer got in yer book;" for Colonel Desmit was writing in a heavy clasped book which rested on a light stand beside him.

"What is it, Mahs'r?"

"Nimbus," replied the master.

"Wh—what?" asked the mother. "Say dat agin', won't yer, Mahs'r?"

"Nimbus—*Nimbus,*" repeated Desmit.

"Wal, I swan ter gracious!" exclaimed the mother. "Ef dat don't beat! H'yer! little—what's yer name? Jes' ax yer Mahs'r fer a silver dollar ter pay yer fer hevin' ter tote dat er name 'roun' ez long ez yer lives."

She held the child toward its godfather and owner as she spoke, amid a roar of laughter from her fellow-servants. Desmit good-naturedly threw a dollar into the child's lap, for which Lorency courtesied, and then held out her hand.

"What do you want now, gal?" asked Desmit.

"Yer a'n't a gwine ter take sech a present ez dis from a pore cullud gal an' not so much ez giv' her someting ter remember hit by, is yer?" she asked with arch persistency.

"There, there," said he laughing, as he gave her another dollar. "Go on, or I shan't have a cent left."

"All right, Marse Kunnel. Thank ye, Mahs'r," she said, as she walked off in triumph.

"Oh, hold on," said Desmit; "how old is it, Lorency?"

"Jes' sebben weeks ole dis bressed day, Mahs'r," said the proud mother as she vanished into the kitchen to boast of her good-fortune in getting two silver dollars out of Marse Desmit instead of the one customarily given by him on such occasions.

And so the record was made up in the brass-clasped book of Colonel Potestatem Desmit, the only baptismal register of the colored man who twenty-six years afterward was wondering at the names which were seeking him against his will.

No. 697—Nimbus—of Lorency—Male—April 24th, 1840—Sound—Knapp-of-Reeds.

It was a queer baptismal entry, but a slave needed no more—indeed did not need that. It was not given for his sake, but only for the convenience of his godfather should the chattel ever seek to run away, or should it become desirable to exchange him for some other form of value. There was nothing harsh or brutal or degraded about it. Mr. Desmit was doing, in a business way, what the law not only allowed but encouraged him to do, and doing it because it paid.

CHAPTER III.

THE JUNONIAN RITE.[3]

"MARSE DESMIT?"

"Well?"

"Ef yer please, Mahs'r, I wants ter marry?"

"The devil you do!"

"Yes, sah, if you please, sah."

"What's your name?"

"Nimbus."

"So: you're the curer at Knapp-of-Reeds, I believe?"

"Yes, sah."

"That last crop was well done. Mr. Ware says you're one of the best hands he has ever known."

"Thank ye, Mahs'r," with a bow and scrape.

"What's the gal's name?"

"Lugena, sah."

"Yes, Vicey's gal—smart gal, too. Well, as I've about concluded to keep you both—if you behave yourselves, that is, as well as you've been doing—I don't know as there's any reason why you shouldn't take up with her."

"Thank ye, Mahs'r," very humbly, but very joyfully.

The speakers were the black baby whom Desmit had christened Nimbus, grown straight and strong, and just turning his first score on the scale of life, and Colonel Desmit, grown a little older, a little grayer, a little fuller, and a great deal richer—if only the small cloud of war just rising on the horizon would blow over and leave his possessions intact. He believed it would, but he was a wise man and a cautious one, and he did not mean to be caught napping if it did not.

Nimbus had come from Knapp-of-Reeds to a plantation twenty miles away, upon a pass from Mr. Ware, on the errand his conversation disclosed. He was a fine figure of a man despite his ebon hue, and the master, looking at him, very naturally noted his straight, strong back, square shoulders, full, round neck, and shapely, well-balanced head. His face was rather heavy—grave, it would have been called if he had been white—and his whole figure and appearance showed an earnest and thoughtful temperament. He was as far from that volatile type which, through the mimicry of burnt-cork minstrels and the exaggerations of caricaturists, as well as the works of less disinterested portrayers of the race, have come to represent the negro to the unfamiliar mind, as the typical Englishman is from the Punch-and-Judy figures which amuse him. The slave Nimbus in a white skin would have been considered a man of great physical power and endurance, earnest purpose, and quiet, self-reliant character. Such, in truth, he was. Except the whipping he had received when but a lad, by his master's orders, no blow had ever been struck him. Indeed, blows were rarely stricken on the plantations of Colonel Desmit; for while he required work, obedience, and discipline, he also fed well and clothed warmly, and allowed no overseer to use the lash for his own gratification, or except for good cause. It was well known that nothing would more surely secure dismissal from his service than the free use of the whip. Not that he thought there was anything wrong or inhuman about the whipping-post, but it was entirely contrary to his policy. To keep a slave comfortable, healthy, and good-natured, according to Colonel Desmit's notion, was to increase his value, and thereby add to his owner's wealth. He knew that Nimbus was a very valuable slave. He had always been attentive to his tasks, was a prime favorite with his overseer, and had already acquired the reputation of being one of the most expert and trusty men that the whole region could furnish, for a tobacco crop. Every step in the process of growing and curing—from the preparation of the seed-bed to the burning of the coal-pit, and gauging the heat required in the mud-daubed barn for different kinds of leaf and in every stage of cure—was perfectly familiar to him, and he could always be trusted to see that it was properly and opportunely done. This fact, together with his quiet and contented disposition, added very greatly to his value. The master regarded him, therefore, with great satisfaction. He was willing to gratify him in any reasonable way, and so, after some rough jokes at his expense, wrote out his marriage-license in these words, in pencil, on the blank leaf of a notebook:

MR. WARE: Nimbus and Lugena want to take up with each other. You have a pretty full force now, but I have decided to keep them and sell some of the old ones—say Vicey and Lorency. Neither have had any children for several years, and are yet strong, healthy women, who will bring nearly as much as the girl Lugena. I shall make up a gang to go South in charge of Winburn next week. You may send them over to Louisburg on Monday. You had better give Nimbus the empty house near the tobacco-barn. We need a trusty man there.

Respectfully,

P. DESMIT.

So Nimbus went home happy, and on the Saturday night following, in accordance with this authority, with much mirth and clamor, and with the half-barbarous and half-Christian ceremony—which the law did not recognize; which bound neither parties, nor master nor stranger; which gave Nimbus no rights and Lugena no privileges; which neither sanctified the union nor protected its offspring—the slave "boy" and "gal" "took up with each other," and began that farce which the victims of slavery were allowed to call "marriage." The sole purpose of permitting it was to raise children. The offspring were sometimes called "families," even in grave legal works; but there was no more of the family right of protection, duty of sustenance and care, or any other of the sacred elements which make the family a type of heaven, than attends the propagation of any other species of animate property. When its purpose had been served, the voice of the master effected instant divorce. So, on the Monday morning thereafter the mothers of the so-called bride and groom, widowed by the inexorable demands of the master's interests, left husband and children, and those fair fields which represented all that they knew of the paradise which we call home, and with tears and groans started for that living tomb, the ever-devouring and insatiable "far South."

CHAPTER IV.

MARS MEDDLES.

Louisburg, January 10, 1864.

MR. SILAS WARE:

DEAR SIR: In ten days I have to furnish twenty hands to work on fortifications for the Confederate Government. I have tried every plan I could devise to avoid doing so, but can put it off no longer. I anticipated this long ago, and exchanged all the men I could possibly spare for women, thinking that would relieve me, but it makes no difference. They apportion the levy upon the number of slaves. I shall have to furnish more pretty soon. The trouble is to know who to send. I am afraid every devil of them will run away, but have concluded that if I send Nimbus as a sort of headman of the gang, he may be able to bring them through. He is a very faithful fellow, with none of the fool-notions niggers sometimes get, I think. In fact, he is too dull to have such notions. At the same time he has a good deal of influence over the others. If you agree with this idea, send him to me at once.

Respectfully,

P. DESMIT.

In accordance with this order Nimbus was sent on to have another interview with his master. The latter's wishes were explained, and he was asked if he could fulfil them.

"Dunno," he answered stolidly.

"Are you willing to try?"

"S'pect I hev ter, ennyhow, ef yer say so."

"Now, Nimbus, haven't I always been a good master to you?" reproachfully.

No answer.

"Haven't I been kind to you always?"

"Yer made Marse War' gib me twenty licks once."

"Well, weren't you saucy, Nimbus? Wouldn't you have done that to a nigger that called you a 'grand rascal' to your face?"

"S'pecs I would, Mahs'r."

"Of course you would. You know that very well. You've too much sense to remember that against me now. Besides, if you are not willing to do this I shall have to sell you South to keep you out of the hands of the Yanks."

Mr. Desmit knew how to manage "niggers," and full well understood the terrors of being "sold South." He saw his advantage in the flush of apprehension which, before he had ceased speaking, made the jetty face before him absolutely ashen with terror.

"Don't do dat, Marse Desmit, ef *you* please! Don't do dat er wid Nimbus! Mind now, Mahs'r, I'se got a wife an' babies."

"So you have, and I know you don't want to leave them."

"No more I don't, Mahs'r," earnestly.

"And you need not if you'll do as I want you to. See here, Nimbus, if you'll do this I will promise that you and your family never shall be separated, and I'll give you fifty dollars now and a hundred dollars when you come back, if you'll just keep those other fool-niggers from trying—mind I say *trying*—to run away and so getting shot. There's no such thing as getting to the Yankees, and it would be a heap worse for them if they did, but you know they *are* such fools they might try it and get killed—which would serve them right, only I should have to bear the loss."

"All right, Mahs'r, I do the best I can," said Nimbus.

"That's right," said the master.

"Here are fifty dollars," and he handed him a Confederate bill of that denomination (gold value at that time, $3.21).

Mr. Desmit did not feel entirely satisfied when Nimbus and his twenty fellow-servants went off upon the train to work for the Confederacy. However, he had done all he could except to warn the guards to be very careful, which he did not neglect to do.

Just forty days afterward a ragged, splashed and torn young ebony Samson lifted the flap of a Federal officer's tent upon one of the coast islands, stole silently in, and when he saw the officer's eyes fixed upon him, asked,

"Want ary boy, Mahs'r?"

The tone, as well as the form of speech, showed a new-comer. The officer knew that none of the colored men who had been upon the island any length of time would have ventured into his presence unannounced, or have made such an inquiry.

"Where did you come from?" he asked.

"Ober to der mainlan'," was the composed answer.

"How did you get here?"

"Come in a boat."

"Run away?"

"S'pose so."

"Where did you live?"

"Up de kentry—Horsford County."

"How did you come down here?"

"Ben wukkin' on de bres'wuks."

"The dickens you have!"

"Yes, sah."

"How did you get a boat, then?"

"Jes' tuk it—dry so."

"Anybody with you?"

"No, Mahs'r."

"And you came across the Sound alone in an open boat?"

"Yes, Mahs'r; an' fru' de swamp widout any boat."

"I should say so," laughed the officer, glancing at his clothes. "What did you come here for?"

"Jes'—*kase.*"

"Didn't they tell you you'd be worse off with the Yankees than you were with them?"

"Yes, sah."

"Didn't you believe them?"

"Dunno, sah."

"What do you want to do?"

"Anything."

"Fight the rebs?"

"Wal, I kin du it."

"What's your name?"

"Nimbus."

"Nimbus? Good name—ha! ha! what else?"

"Nuffin' else."

"Nothing else? What was your old master's name?"

"Desmit—Potem Desmit."

"Well, then, that's yours, ain't it—your surname—Nimbus Desmit?"

"Reckon not, Mahs'r."

"No? Why not?"

"Same reason his name ain't Nimbus, I s'pose."

"Well," said the officer, laughing, "there may be something in that; but a soldier must have two names. Suppose I call you George Nimbus?"

"Yer kin call me jes' what yer choose, sah; but my name's Nimbus all the same. No Gawge Nimbus, nor ennything Nimbus, nor Nimbus ennything —jes' Nimbus; so. Nigger got no use fer two names, nohow."

The officer, perceiving that it was useless to argue the matter further, added his name to the muster-roll of a regiment, and he was duly sworn into the service of the United States as George Nimbus, of Company C, of the — Massachusetts Volunteer Infantry, and was counted one of the quota which the town of Great Barringham, in the valley of the Housatuck, was required to furnish to complete the pending call for troops to put down rebellion. By virtue of this fact, the said George Nimbus became entitled to the sum of four hundred dollars bounty money offered by said town to such as should give themselves to complete its quota of "the boys in blue," in addition to his pay and bounty from the Government. So, if it forced on him a new name, the service of freedom was not altogether without compensatory advantages.

Thus the slave Nimbus was transformed into the "contraband"[4] George Nimbus, and became not only a soldier of fortune, but also the representative of a patriotic citizen of Great Barringham, who served his country by proxy, in the person of said contraband, faithfully and well until the end of the war, when the South fell—stricken at last most fatally by the dark hands which she had manacled, and overcome by their aid whose manhood she had refused to acknowledge.

CHAPTER V.

NUNC PRO TUNC.[5]

THE FIRST STEP in the progress from the prison-house of bondage to the citadel of liberty was a strange one. The war was over. The struggle for autonomy and the inviolability of slavery, on the part of the South, was ended, and fate had decided against them. With this arbitrament of war fell also the institution which had been its cause. Slavery was abolished—by proclamation, by national enactment, by constitutional amendment—ay, by the sterner logic which forbade a nation to place shackles again upon hands which had been raised in her defence, which had fought for her life and at her request. So the slave was a slave no more. No other man could claim his service or restrain his volition. He might go or come, work or play, so far as his late master was concerned.

But that was all. He could not contract, testify, marry or give in marriage. He had neither property, knowledge, right, or power. The whole four millions did not possess that number of dollars or of dollars' worth. Whatever they had acquired in slavery was the master's, unless he had expressly made himself a trustee for their benefit. Regarded from the legal standpoint it was, indeed, a strange position in which they were. A race despised, degraded, penniless, ignorant, houseless, homeless, fatherless, childless, nameless. Husband or wife there was not one in four millions. Not a child might call upon a father for aid, and no man of them all might lift his hand in a daughter's defence. Uncle and aunt and cousin, home, family—none of these words had any place in the freedman's vocabulary. Right he had, in the abstract; in the concrete, none. Justice would not hear his voice. The law was still color-blinded[6] by the past.

The fruit of slavery—its first ripe harvest, gathered with swords and bloody bayonets, was before the nation which looked ignorantly on the fruits of the deliverance it had wrought. The North did not comprehend its work; the South could not comprehend its fate. The unbound slave looked to the future in dull, wondering hope.

The first step in advance was taken neither by the nation nor by the freedmen. It was prompted by the voice of conscience, long hushed and hidden in the master's breast. It was the protest of Christianity and morality against that which it had witnessed with complacency for many a generation. All at once it was perceived to be a great enormity that four millions of Christian people, in a Christian land, should dwell together without marriage rite or family tie. While they were slaves, the fact that they might be bought and sold had hidden this evil from the eye of morality, which had looked unabashed upon the unlicensed freedom of the quarters and the enormities of the barracoon. Now all at once it was shocked beyond expression at the domestic relations of the freedmen.

So they made haste in the first legislative assemblies that met in the various States, after the turmoil of war had ceased, to provide and enact:

1 That all those who had sustained to each other the relation of husband and wife in the days of slavery, might, upon application to an officer named in each county, be registered as such husband and wife.
2 That all who did not so register within a certain time should be liable to indictment, if the relation continued thereafter.
3 That the effect of such registration should be to constitute such parties husband and wife, as of the date of their first assumption of marital relations.
4 That for every such couple registered the officer should be entitled to receive the sum of one half-dollar from the parties registered.

There was a grim humor about this marriage of a race by wholesale, millions at a time, and *nunc pro tunc;* but especially quaint was the idea of requiring each freedman, who had just been torn, as it were naked, from the master's arms, to pay a snug fee for the simple privilege of entering upon that relation which the law had rigorously withheld from him until that moment. It was a strange remedy for a long-hidden and stubbornly denied disease, and many strange scenes were enacted in accordance with the provisions of this statute. Many an aged couple, whose children had been lost in the obscure abysses of slavery, or had gone before them into the spirit land, old and feeble and gray-haired, wrought with patience day after day to earn at once their living and the money for this fee, and when they had procured it walked a score of miles in order that they might be "registered," and, for the brief period that remained to them of life, know that the law had sanctioned the relation which years of love and suffering had sanctified. It was the first act of freedom, the first step of legal recognition or manly responsibility! It was a proud hour and a proud fact for the race which had so long been bowed in thralldom and forbidden even the most common though the holiest of God's ordinances. What the law had taken little by little, as the science of Christian slavery grew up under the brutality of our legal progress, the law returned in bulk. It was the first seal which was put on the slave's manhood—the first step upward from the brutishness of another's possession to the glory of independence. The race felt its importance as did no one else at that time. By hundreds and thousands they crowded the places appointed, to accept the honor offered to their posterity, and thereby unwittingly conferred undying honor upon themselves. Few indeed were the unworthy ones who evaded the sacred responsibility thus laid upon them, and left their offspring to remain under the badge of shame. When carefully looked at it was but a scant cure, and threw the responsibility of illegitimacy where it did not belong, but it was a mighty step nevertheless. The distance from zero to unity is always infinity.

The county clerk in and for the county of Horsford sat behind the low wooden railing which he had been compelled to put across his office to protect him from the too near approach of those who crowded to this fountain of rehabilitating honor that had recently been opened therein. Unused to anything beyond the plantation on which they had been reared, the temple of justice was as strange to their feet, and the ways and forms of ordinary business as marvelous to their minds as the etiquette of the king's palace to a peasant who has only looked from afar upon its pinnacled roof. The recent statute had imposed upon the clerk a labor of no little difficulty because of this very ignorance on the part of those whom he was required to serve; but he was well rewarded. The clerk was a man of portly presence, given to his ease, who smoked a long-stemmed pipe as he sat beside a table which, in addition to his papers and writing materials, held a bucket of water on which floated a clean gourd, in easy reach of his hand.

"Be you the clerk, sah?" said a straight young colored man, whose clothing had a hint of the soldier in it, as well as his respectful but unusually collected bearing.

"Yes," said the clerk, just glancing up, but not intermitting his work; "what do you want?"

"If you please, sah, we wants to be married, Lugena and me."

"*Registered,* you mean, I suppose?"

"No, we don't, sah; we means *married.*"

"I can't marry you. You'll have to get a license and be married by a magistrate or a minister."

"But I heard der was a law—"

"Have you been living together as man and wife?"

"Oh, yes, sah; dat we hab, dis smart while."

"Then you want to be registered. This is the place. Got a half-dollar?"

"Yes, sah?"

"Let's have it."

The colored man took out some bills, and with much difficulty endeavored to make a selection; finally, handing one doubtfully toward the clerk, he asked,

"Is dat a one-dollah, sah?"

"No, that is a five, but I can change it."

"No, I'se got it h'yer," said the other hastily, as he dove again into his pockets, brought out some pieces of fractional currency and handed them one by one to the officer until he said he had enough.

"Well," said the clerk as he took up his pen and prepared to fill out the blank, "what is your name?"

"My name's Nimbus, sah."

"Nimbus what?"

"Nimbus nuffin', sah; jes' Nimbus."

"But you must have another name?"

"No I hain't. Jes' wore dat fer twenty-odd years, an' nebber hed no udder."

"Who do you work for?"

"Wuk for myself, sah."

"Well, on whose land do you work?"

"Wuks on my own, sah. Oh, I libs at home an' boa'ds at de same place, I does. An' my name's Nimbus, jes' straight along, widout any tail ner handle."

"What was your old master's name?"

"Desmit—Colonel Potem Desmit."

"I might have known that," said the clerk laughingly, "from the durned outlandish name. Well, Desmit is your surname, then, ain't it?"

"No 'taint, Mister. What right I got ter his name? He nebber gib it ter me no more'n he did ter you er Lugena h'yer."

"Pshaw, I can't stop to argue with you. Here's your certificate."

"Will you please read it, sah? I hain't got no larnin'. Ef you please, sah."

The clerk, knowing it to be the quickest way to get rid of them, read rapidly over the certificate that Nimbus and Lugena Desmit had been duly registered as husband and wife, under the provisions of an ordinance of the Convention ratified on the — day of —, 1865.

"So you's done put in dat name—Desmit?"

"Oh, I just had to, Nimbus. The fact is, a man can't be married according to law without two names."

"So hit appears; but ain't it quare dat I should hev ole Mahs'r's name widout his gibbin' it ter me, ner my axin' fer it, Mister?"

"It may be, but that's the way, you see."

"So hit seems. 'Pears like I'm boun' ter hev mo' names 'n I knows what ter do wid, jes' kase I's free. But de chillen—yer hain't sed nary word about dem, Mister."

"Oh, I've nothing to do with them."

"But, see h'yer, Mister, ain't de law a doin dis ter make dem lawful chillen?"

"Certainly."

"An' how's de law ter know which is de lawful chillen ef hit ain't on dat ar paper?"

"Sure enough," said the clerk, with amusement. "That would have been a good idea, but, you see, Nimbus, the law didn't go that far."

"Wal, hit ought ter hev gone dat fur. Now, Mister Clerk, couldn't you jes' put dat on dis yer paper, jes' ter 'commodate me, yer know."

"Perhaps so," good-naturedly, taking back the certificate; "what do you want me to write?"

"Wal, yer see, dese yer is our chillen. Dis yer boy Lone—Axylone, Marse Desmit called him, but we calls him Lone for short—he's gwine on fo'; dis yer gal Wicey, she's two past; and dis little brack cuss Lugena's a-holdin' on, we call Cap'n, kase he bosses all on us—he's nigh 'bout a year; an' dat's all."

The clerk entered the names and ages of the children on the back of the paper, with a short certificate that they were present, and were acknowledged as the children, and the only ones, of the parties named in the instrument.

And so the slave Nimbus was transformed, first into the "contraband" and mercenary soldier *George Nimbus,* and then by marriage into *Nimbus Desmit.*

CHAPTER VI.

THE TOGA VIRILIS.[7]

BUT THE TRANSFORMATIONS of the slave were not yet ended. The time came when he was permitted to become a citizen. For two years he had led an inchoate, nondescript sort of existence: free without power or right; neither slave nor freeman; neither property nor citizen. He had been, meanwhile, a bone of contention between the Provisional Governments of the States and the military power which controlled them. The so-called State Governments dragged him toward the whipping-post and the Black Codes and serfdom. They denied him his oath, fastened him to the land, compelled him to hire by the year, required the respectfulness of the old slave "Mahs'r" and "Missus," made his employer liable for his taxes, and allowed recoupment therefor; limited his avocations and restricted his opportunities. These would substitute serfdom for chattelism.[8]

On the other hand the Freedman's Bureau acted as his guardian and friend, looked after his interests in contracts, prohibited the law's barbarity, and insisted stubbornly that the freedman was a man, and must be treated as such. It needed only the robe of citizenship, it was thought, to enable him safely to dispense with the one of these agencies and defy the other. So the negro was transformed into a citizen, a voter, a political factor, by act of Congress, with the aid and assistance of the military power.[9]

A great crowd had gathered at the little town of Melton, which was one of the chief places of the county of Horsford, for the people had been duly notified by official advertisement that on this day the board of registration appointed by the commander of the military district in which Horsford County was situated would convene there, to take and record the names, and pass upon the qualifications, of all who desired to become voters of the new body politic which was to be erected therein, or of the old one which was to be reconstructed and rehabilitated out of the ruins which war had left.

The first provision of the law was that every member of such board of registration should be able to take what was known in those days as the "iron-clad oath," that is, an oath that he had never engaged in, aided, or abetted any rebellion against the Government of the United States. Men who could do this were exceedingly difficult to find in some sections. Of course there were abundance of colored men who could take this oath, but not one in a thousand of them could read or write. The military commander determined, however, to select in every registration district one of the most intelligent of this class, in order that he might look after the interests of his race, now for the first time to take part in any public or political movement. This would greatly increase the labors of the other members of the board, yet was thought not only just but necessary. As the labor of recording the voters of a county was no light one, especially as the lists had to be made out in triplicate, it was necessary to have some clerical ability on the board. These facts often made the composition of these boards somewhat heterogeneous and peculiar. The one which was to register the voters of Horsford consisted of a little old white man, who had not enough of stamina or character to have done or said anything in aid of rebellion, and who, if he had done the very best he knew, ought yet to have been held guiltless of evil accomplished. In his younger days he had been an overseer, but in his later years had risen to the dignity of a landowner and the possession of one or two slaves. He wrestled with the mysteries of the printed page with a sad seriousness which made one regret his inability to remember what was at the top until he had arrived at the bottom. Writing was a still more solemn business with him, but he was a brave man and would cheerfully undertake to transcribe a list of names, which he well knew that anything less than eternity would be too short to allow him to complete. He was a small, thin-haired, squeaky-voiced bachelor of fifty, and as full of good intentions as the road to perdition. If Tommy Glass ever did any evil it would not only be without intent but from sheer accident.

With Tommy was associated an old colored man, one of those known in that region as "old-issue free-niggers." Old Pharaoh Ray was a venerable man. He had learned to read before the Constitution of 1835 deprived the free-negro of his vote, and had read a little since. He wore an amazing pair of brass-mounted spectacles. His head was surmounted by a mass of snowy hair, and he was of erect and powerful figure despite the fact that he boasted a life of more than eighty years. He read about as fast and committed to memory more easily than his white associate, Glass. In writing they were about a match; Pharaoh wrote his name much more legibly than Glass could, but Glass accomplished the task in about three fourths of the time required by Pharaoh.

The third member of the board was Captain Theron Pardee, a young man who had served in the Federal army and afterward settled in an adjoining county. He was the chairman. He did the writing, questioning, and deciding, and as each voter had to be sworn he utilized his two associates by requiring them to administer the oaths and—look wise. The colored man in about two weeks learned these oaths so that he could repeat them. The white man did not commit the brief formulas in the four weeks they were on duty.

The good people of Melton were greatly outraged that this composite board should presume to come and pass upon the qualifications of its people as voters under the act of Congress, and indeed it was a most ludicrous affair. The more they contemplated the outrage that was being done to them, by decreeing that none should vote who had once taken an oath to support the Government of the United States and afterward aided the rebellion, the angrier they grew, until finally they declared that the registration should not be held. Then there were some sharp words between the ex-Federal soldier and the objectors. As no house could be procured for the purpose, he proposed to hold the registration on the porch of the hotel where he stopped, but the landlord objected. Then he proposed to hold it on the sidewalk under a big tree, but the town authorities declared against it. However, he was proceeding there, when an influential citizen kindly came forward and offered the use of certain property under his control. There was some clamor, but the gentleman did not flinch. Thither they adjourned, and the work went busily on. Among others who came to be enrolled as citizens was our old friend Nimbus.

"Where do you live?" asked the late Northern soldier sharply, as Nimbus came up in his turn in the long line of those waiting for the same purpose.

"Down ter Red Wing, sah?"

"Where's that?"

"Oh, right down h'yer on Hyco, sah."

"In this county?"

"Oh, bless yer, yes, Mister, should tink hit was. Hit's not above five or six miles out from h'yer."

"How old are you?"

"Wal, now, I don't know dat, not edzactly."

"How old do you think—twenty-one?"

"Oh, la, yes; more nor dat, Cap'."

"Born where?"

"Right h'yer in Horsford, sah."

"What is your name?"

"Nimbus."

"Nimbus what?" asked the officer, looking up.

"Nimbus nothin', sah; jes' straight along Nimbus."

"Well, but—" said the officer, looking puzzled, "you must have some sort of surname."

"No, sah, jes' one; nigger no use for two names."

"Yah! yah! yah!" echoed the dusky crowd behind him. "You's jes' right dah, you is! Niggah mighty little use fer heap o' names. Jes' like a mule—one name does him, an' mighty well off ef he's 'lowed ter keep dat."

"His name's Desmit," said a white man, the sheriff of the county, who stood leaning over the railing; "used to belong to old Potem Desmit, over to Louisburg. Mighty good nigger, too. I s'pec' ole man Desmit felt about as bad at losing him as ary one he had."

"Powerful good hand in terbacker," said Mr. Glass, who was himself an expert in "yaller leaf." "Ther' wasn't no better ennywhar' round."

"I knows all about him," said another. "Seed a man offer old Desmit eighteen hundred dollars for him afore the war—State money—but he wouldn't tech it. Reckon he wishes he had now."

"Yes," said the sheriff, "he's the best curer in the county. Commands almost any price in the season, but is powerful independent, and gittin' right sassy. Listen at him now?"

"They say your name is Desmit—Nimbus Desmit," said the officer; "is that so?"

"No, tain't."

"Wasn't that your old master's name?" asked the sheriff roughly.

"Co'se it war," was the reply.

"Well, then, ain't it yours too?"

"No, it ain't."

"Well, you just ask the gentleman if that ain't so," said the sheriff, motioning to the chairman of the board.

"Well," said that officer, with a peculiar smile, "I do not know that there is any law compelling a freedman to adopt his former master's name. He is without name in the law, a pure *nullius filius*—nobody's son. As a slave he had but one name. He *could* have no surname, because he had no family. He was arraigned, tried, and executed as 'Jim' or 'Bill' or 'Tom.' The volumes of the reports are full of such cases, as The State *vs.* 'Dick' or 'Sam.' The Roman custom was for the freedman to take the name of some friend, benefactor, or patron. I do not see why the American freedman has not a right to choose his own surname."

"That is not the custom here," said the sheriff, with some chagrin, he having begun the controversy.

"Very true," replied the chairman; "the custom—and a very proper and almost necessary one it seems—is to call the freedman by a former master's name. This distinguishes individuals. But when the freedman refuses to acknowledge the master's name as his, who can impose it on him? We are directed to register the names of parties, and while we might have the right to refuse one whom we found attempting to register under a false name, yet we have no power to make names for those applying. Indeed, if this man insists that he has but one name, we must, for what I can see, register him by that alone."

His associates looked wise, and nodded acquiescence in the views thus expressed.

"Den dat's what I chuse," said the would-be voter. "My name's Nimbus—noffin' mo'."

"But I should advise you to take another name to save trouble when you come to vote," said the chairman. His associates nodded solemnly again.

"Wal, now, Marse Cap'n, you jes' see h'yer. I don't want ter carry nobody's name widout his leave. S'pose I take ole Marse War's name ober dar?"

"You can take any one you choose. I shall write down the one you give me."

"Is you willin', Marse War'?"

"I've nothing to do with it, Nimbus," said Ware; "fix your own name."

"Wal sah," said Nimbus, "I reckon I'll take dat ef I must hev enny mo' name. Yer see he wuz my ole oberseer, Mahs'r, an' wuz powerful good ter me, tu. I'd a heap ruther hev his name than Marse Desmit's; but I don't *want* no name but Nimbus, nohow."

"All right," said the chairman, as he made the entry. "Ware it is then."

As there might be a poll held at Red Wing, where Nimbus lived, he was given a certificate showing that *Nimbus Ware* had been duly registered as an elector of the county of Horsford and for the precinct of Red Wing.

Then the newly-named Nimbus was solemnly sworn by the patriarchal Pharaoh to bear true faith and allegiance to the government of the United States, and to uphold its constitution and the laws passed in conformity therewith; and thereby the recent slave became a component factor of the national life, a full-fledged citizen of the American Republic.

As he passed out, the sheriff said to those about him, in a low tone,

"There'll be trouble with that nigger yet. He's too sassy. You'll see."

"How so?" asked the chairman. "I thought you said he was industrious, thrifty, and honest."

"Oh, yes," was the reply, "there ain't a nigger in the county got a better character for honesty and hard work than he, but he's too important—has got the big head, as we call it."

"I don't understand what you mean," said the chairman.

"Why he ain't respectful," said the other. "Talks as independent as if he was a white man."

"Well, he has as much right to talk independently as a white man. He is just as free," said the chairman sharply.

"Yes; but he ain't white," said the sheriff doggedly, "and our people won't stand a nigger's puttin' on such airs. Why, Captain," he continued in a tone which showed that he felt that the fact he was about to announce must carry conviction even to the incredulous heart of the Yankee officer. "You just ought to see his place down at Red Wing. Damned if he ain't better fixed up than lots of white men in the county. He's got a good house, and a terbacker-barn, and a church, and a nigger school-house, and stock, and one of the finest crops of terbacker in the county. Oh, I tell you, he's cutting a wide swath, he is."

"You don't tell me," said the chairman with interest. "I am glad to hear it.

There appears to be good stuff in the fellow. He seems to have his own ideas about things, too."

"Yes, that's the trouble," responded the sheriff. "Our people ain't used to that and won't stand it. He's putting on altogether too much style for a nigger."

"Pshaw," said the chairman, "if there were more like him it would be better for everybody. A man like him is worth something for an example. If all the race were of his stamp there would be more hope."

"The devil!" returned the sheriff, with a sneering laugh, "if they were all like him, a white man couldn't live in the country. They'd be so damned sassy and important that we'd have to kill the last one of 'em to have any peace."

"Fie, sheriff," laughed the chairman good-naturedly; "you seem to be vexed at the poor fellow for his thrift, and because he is doing well."

"I am a white man, sir; and I don't like to see niggers gittin' above us. Them's my sentiments," was the reply. "And that's the way our people feel."

There was a half-suppressed murmur of applause among the group of white men at this. The chairman responded,

"No doubt, and yet I believe you are wrong. Now, I can't help liking the fellow for his sturdy manhood. He may be a trifle too positive, but it is a good fault. I think he has the elements of a good citizen, and I can't understand why you feel so toward him."

There were some appreciative and good-natured cries of "Dar now," "Listen at him," "Now you're talkin'," from the colored men at this reply.

"Oh, that's because you're a Yankee," said the sheriff, with commiserating scorn. "You don't think, now, that it's any harm to talk that way before niggers and set them against the white people either, I suppose?"

The chairman burst into a hearty laugh, as he replied,

"No, indeed, I don't. If you call that setting the blacks against the whites, the sooner they are by the ears the better. If you are so thin-skinned that you can't allow a colored man to think, talk, act, and prosper like a man, the sooner you get over your squeamishness the better. For me, I am interested in this Nimbus. We have to go to Red Wing and report on it as a place for holding a poll and I am bound to see more of him."

"Oh, you'll see enough of him if you go there, never fear," was the reply.

There was a laugh from the white men about the sheriff, a sort of cheer from the colored men in waiting, and the business of the board went on without further reference to the new-made citizen.

The slave who had been transformed into a "contraband" and mustered as a soldier under one name, married under another, and now enfranchised under a third, returned to his home to meditate upon his transformations—as we found him doing in our first chapter.

The reason for these metamorphoses, and their consequences, might well puzzle a wiser head than that of the many-named but unlettered Nimbus.

CHAPTER VII.

DAMON AND PYTHIAS.[10]

AFTER HIS SOLILOQUY in regard to his numerous names, as given in our first chapter, Nimbus turned away from the gate near which he had been standing, crossed the yard in front of his house, and entered a small cabin which stood near it.

"Dar! 'Liab," he said, as he entered and handed the paper which he had been examining to the person addressed, "I reckon I'se free now. I feel ez ef I wuz 'bout half free, ennyhow. I wuz a sojer, an' fought fer freedom. I've got my house an' bit o' lan', wife, chillen, crap, an' stock, an' it's all mine. An' now I'se done been registered, an' when de 'lection comes off, kin vote jes' ez hard an' ez well an' ez often ez ole Marse Desmit. I hain't felt free afore—leastways I hain't felt right certain on't; but now I reckon I'se all right, fact an' truth. What you tinks on't, 'Liab?"

The person addressed was sitting on a low seat under the one window which was cut into the west side of the snugly-built log cabin. The heavy wooden shutter swung back over the bench. On the other side of the room was a low cot, and a single splint-bottomed chair stood against the open door. The house contained no other furniture.

The bench which he occupied was a queer compound of table, desk, and work-bench. It had the leathern seat of a shoemaker's bench, except that it was larger and wider. As the occupant sat with his back to the window, on his left were the shallow boxes of a shoemaker's bench, and along its edge the awls and other tools of that craft were stuck in leather loops secured by tacks, as is the custom of the crispin the world over. On the right was a table whose edge was several inches above the seat, and on which were some books, writing materials, a slate, a bundle of letters tied together with a piece of shoe-thread, and some newspapers and pamphlets scattered about in a manner which showed at a glance that the owner was unaccustomed to their care, but which is yet quite indescribable. On the wall above this table, but within easy reach of the sitter's hand, hung a couple of narrow hanging shelves, on which a few books were neatly arranged. One lay open on the table, with a shoemaker's last placed across it to prevent its closing.

Eliab was already busily engaged in reading the certificate which Nimbus had given him. The sun, now near its setting, shone in at the open door and fell upon him as he read. He was a man apparently about the age of Nimbus—younger rather than older—having a fine countenance, almost white, but with just enough of brown in its sallow paleness to suggest the idea of colored blood, in a region where all degrees of admixture were by no means rare. A splendid head of black hair waved above his broad, full forehead, and an intensely black silky beard and mustache framed the lower portion of his face most fittingly. His eyes were soft and womanly, though there was a patient boldness about their great brown pupils and a directness of gaze which suited well the bearded face beneath. The lines of suffering were deeply cut upon the thoughtful brow and around the liquid eyes, and showed in the mobile workings of the broad mouth, half shaded by the dark mustache. The face was not a handsome one, but there was a serious and earnest calmness about it which gave it an unmistakable nobility of expression and prompted one to look more closely at the man and his surroundings.

The shoulders were broad and square, the chest was full, the figure erect, and the head finely poised. He was dressed with unusual neatness for one of his race and surroundings, at the time of which we write. One comprehended at a glance that this worker and learner was also deformed. There was that in his surroundings which showed that he was not as other men. The individuality of weakness and suffering had left its indelible stamp upon the habitation which he occupied. Yet so erect and self-helping in appearance was the figure on the cobbler's bench that one for a moment failed to note in what the affliction consisted. Upon closer observation he saw that the lower limbs were sharply flexed and drawn to the leftward, so that the right foot rested on its side under the left thigh. This inclined the body somewhat to the right, so that the right arm rested naturally upon the table for support when not employed. These limbs, especially below the knees, were shrunken and distorted. The shoe of the right foot whose upturned sole rested on the left leg just above the ankle, was many sizes too small for a development harmonious with the trunk.

Nimbus sat down in the splint-bottomed chair by the door and fanned himself with his dingy hat while the other read.

"How is dis, Nimbus? What does dis mean? *Nimbus Ware?* Where did you get dat name?" he asked at length, raising his eyes and looking in pained surprise toward the new voter.

"Now, Bre'er 'Liab, don't talk dat 'ere way ter Nimbus, ef yo please. Don't do it now. Yer knows I can't help it. Ebberybody want ter call me by ole Mahs'r's name, an' dat I can't abide nohow; an' when I kicks 'bout it, dey jes gib me some odder one. Dey all seems ter tink I'se boun' ter hev two names, though I hain't got no manner o' right ter but one."

"But how did you come to have dis one—Ware?" persisted Eliab.

"Wal, you see, Bre'er 'Liab, de boss man at der registerin' he ax me fer my las' name, an' I tell him I hadn't got none, jes so. Den Sheriff Gleason, he put in his oar, jes ez he allus does, an' he say my name wuz *Desmit,* atter ole Mahs'r. Dat made me mad, an' I 'spute him, an' sez I, 'I won't hev no sech name'. Den de boss man, he shet up Marse Gleason purty smart like, and *he* sed I'd a right ter enny name I chose ter carry, kase nobody hadn't enny sort o' right ter fasten enny name at all on ter me 'cept myself. But he sed I'd better hev two, kase most other folks hed 'em. So I axed Marse Si War' ef he'd lend me his name jes fer de 'casion, yer know, an' he sed he hadn't no 'jection ter it. So I tole der boss man ter put it down, an' I reckon dar 'tis."

"Yes, here it is, sure 'nough, Nimbus; but didn't you promise me you wouldn't have so many names?"

"Co'se I did; an' I did try, but they all 'llowed I got ter have two names whe'er er no."

"Then why didn't you take your old mahs'r's name, like de rest, and not have all dis trouble?"

"Now, 'Liab, yer knows thet I won't nebber do dat."

"But why not, Nimbus?"

"Kase I ain't a-gwine ter brand my chillen wid no sech slave-mark! Nebber! You hear dat, 'Liab? I hain't got no ill-will gin Marse Desmit, not a mite—only 'bout dat ar lickin, an' dat ain't nuffin now; but I ain't gwine ter war his name ner giv it ter my chillen ter mind 'em dat der daddy wuz jes anudder man's critter one time. I tell you I can't do hit, nohow; an' I *won't,* Bre'er 'Liab. I don't hate Marse Desmit, but I does hate slavery—dat what made me his—worse'n a pilot hates a rattlesnake; an' I hate everyting dat 'minds me on't, I do!"

The black Samson had risen in his excitement and now sat down upon the bench by the other.

"I don't blame you for dat, Nimbus, but—"

"I don't want to heah no 'buts' 'bout it, an' I won't."

"But the chillen, Nimbus. You don't want dem to be different from others and have no surname?"

"Dat's a fac', 'Liab," said Nimbus, springing to his feet. "I nebber t'ought o' dat. Dey must hev a name, an' I mus' hev one ter gib 'em, but how's I gwine ter git one? Dar's nobody's got enny right ter gib me one, an' ef I choose one dis week what's ter hender my takin' ob anudder nex week?"

"Perhaps nothing," answered 'Liab, "but yourself. You must not do it."

"Pshaw, now," said Nimbus, "what sort o' way is dat ter hev things? I tell ye what orter been done, 'Liab; when de law married us all, jes out of han' like, it orter hev named us too. Hit mout hev been done, jes ez well's not. Dar's old Mahs'r now, he'd hev named all de niggas in de county in a week, easy. An' dey'd been good names, too."

"But you'd have bucked at it ef he had," said 'Liab, good-naturedly.

"No I wouldn't, 'Liab. I hain't got nuffin 'gin ole Mahrs'r. He war good enough ter me—good 'nuff. I only hate what *made* him 'Old Mahs'r,' an' dat I does hate. Oh, my God, how I does hate it, Liab! I hates de berry groun' dat a slave's wukked on! I do, I swar! When I wuz a-comin' home to-day an' seed de gullies 'long der way, hit jes made me cuss, kase dey wuz dar a-testifyin' ob de ole' time when a man war a critter—a dog—a nuffin!"

"Now you oughtn't to say dat, Nimbus. Just think of me. Warn't you better off as a slave than I am free?"

"No, I warn't. I'd ruther be a hundred times wuss off ner you, an' free, than ez strong as I am an' a slave."

"But think how much more freedom is worth to you. Here you are a voter, and I—"

"Bre'er 'Liab," exclaimed Nimbus, starting suddenly up, "what for you no speak 'bout dat afore. Swar to God I nebber tink on't—not a word, till dis bressed minit. Why didn't yer say nuffin' 'bout bein' registered yo'self, eh? Yer knowed I'd a tuk yer ef I hed ter tote ye on my back, which I wouldn't. I wouldn't gone a step widout yer ef I'd only a t'ought. Yer knows I wouldn't."

"Course I does, Nimbus, but I didn't want ter make ye no trouble, nor take the mule out of the crap," answered 'Liab apologetically.

"Damn de crap!" said Nimbus impetuously.

"Don't; don't swear, Nimbus, if you please."

"Can't help it, 'Liab, when you turn fool an' treat me dat 'ere way. I'd swar at ye ef yer wuz in de pulpit an' dat come ober me, jes at de fust. Yer knows Nimbus better ner dat. Now see heah, 'Liab Hill, yer's gwine ter go an' be registered termorrer, jes ez sure ez termorrer comes. Here we thick-headed dunces hez been up dar to-day a-takin' de oath an' makin' bleve we's full grown men, an' here's you, dat knows more nor a ten-acre lot full on us, a lyin' here an' habin' no chance at all."

"But you want to get de barn full, and can't afford to spend any more time," protested 'Liab.

"Nebber you min' 'bout de barn. Dat's Nimbus' business, an' he'll take keer on't. Let him alone fer dat. Yis, honey, I'se comin' d'reckly!" he shouted, as his wife called him from his own cabin.

"Now Bre'er 'Liab, yer comes ter supper wid us. Lugena's jes' a callin' on't."

"Oh, don't, Nimbus," said the other, shrinking away. "I can't! You jes send one of the chillen in with it, as usual."

"No yer don't," said Nimbus; "yer's been a scoldin' an' abusin' me all dis yer time, an' now I'se gwine ter hab my way fer a little while."

He went to the door and called:

"Gena! *Oh,* Gena!" and as his wife did not answer, he said to one of his children, "*Oh,* Axylone, jes run inter de kitchen, son, an' tell yer ma ter put on anudder plate, fer Bre'er 'Liab's comin' ober ter take a bite wid us."

Eliab kept on protesting, but it was in vain. Nimbus bent over him as tenderly as a mother over the cradle of her first-born, clasped his arms about him, and lifting him from the bench bore him away to his own house.

With an unconscious movement, which was evidently acquired by long experience, the afflicted man cast one arm over Nimbus' shoulder, put the other around him, and leaning across the stalwart breast of his friend so evenly distributed his weight that the other bore him with ease. Entering his own house, Nimbus placed his burden in the chair at the head of the table, while he himself took his seat on one of the wooden benches at the side.

"I jes brought Bre'er 'Liab in ter supper, honey," said he to his wife; "kase I see'd he war gettin' inter de dumps like, an' I 'llowed yer'd chirk him up a bit ef yer jes hed him over h'yer a while."

"Shan't do it," said the bright-eyed woman saucily.

"Kase why?" queried her husband.

"Kase Bre'er 'Liab don't come oftener. Dat's why."

"Dar, now, jes see what yer done git fer being so contrary-like, will yer?" said the master to his guest. "H'yer, you Axylone," he continued to his eldest born, "fo'd up yer han's while Bre'er 'Liab ax de blessin'. You, too, Capting," shaking his finger at a roll of animated blackness on the end of the seat opposite. "Now, Bre'er 'Liab."

The little black fingers were interlocked, the close-clipped, kinky heads were bowed upon them; the master of the house bent reverently over his plate; the plump young wife crossed her hands demurely on the bright handle of the big coffee-pot by which she stood, and "Bre'er 'Liab," clasping his slender fingers, uplifted his eyes and hands to heaven, and uttered a grace which grew into a prayer. His voice was full of thankfulness, and tears crept from under his trembling lids.

The setting sun, which looked in upon the peaceful scene, no doubt flickered and giggled with laughter as he sank to his evening couch with the thought, "How quick these 'sassy' free-niggers do put on airs like white folks!"

In the tobacco-field on the hillside back of his house, Nimbus and his wife, Lugena, wrought in the light of the full moon nearly all the night which followed, and early on the morrow Nimbus harnessed his mule into his canvas-covered wagon, in which, upon a bed of straw, reclined his friend Eliab Hill, and drove again to the place of registration. On arriving there he took his friend in his arms, carried him in and sat him on the railing before the Board. Clasping the blanket close about his deformed extremities the cripple leaned upon his friend's shoulder and answered the necessary questions with calmness and precision.

"There's a pair for you, captain," said Gleason, nodding good-naturedly toward Nimbus as he bore his helpless charge again to the wagon.

"Is he white?" asked the officer, with a puzzled look.

"White?" exclaimed Sheriff Gleason, with a laugh. "No, indeed! He's a nigger preacher who lives with Nimbus down at Red Wing. They're great cronies—always together. I expect he's at the bottom of all the black nigger's perversity, though he always seems as smooth and respectful as you please. He's a deep one. I 'llow he does all the scheming, and just makes Nimbus a cat's-paw to do his work. I don't know much about him, though. He hardly ever talks with anybody."

"He seems a very remarkable man," said the officer.

"Oh, he is," said the sheriff. "Even in slave times he was a very influential man among the niggers, and since freedom he and Nimbus together rule the whole settlement. I don't suppose there are ten white men in the county who could control, square out and out, as many votes as these two will have in hand when they once get to voting."

"Was he a slave? What is his history?"

"I don't exactly know," answered the sheriff. "He is quite a young man, and somehow I never happened to hear of him till some time during the war. Then he was a sort of prophet among them, and while he did a power of praying for you Yanks, he always counselled the colored people to be civil and patient, and not try to run away or go to cutting up, but just to wait till the end came. He was just right, too, and his course quieted the white folks down here on the river, where there was a big slave population, more than a little."

"I should like to know more of him," said the chairman.

"All right," said Gleason, looking around. "If Hesden Le Moyne is here, I'll get him to tell you all about him, at noon. If he is not here then, he will come in before night, I'm certain."

CHAPTER VIII.

A FRIENDLY PROLOGUE.

AS THEY WENT FROM the place of registration to their dinner at the hotel, the sheriff, walking beside the chairman, said: "I spoke to Le Moyne about that negro fellow, Eliab Hill, and he says he's very willing to tell you all he knows about him; but, as there are some private matters connected with the story, he prefers to come to your room after dinner, rather than speak of it more publicly."

"I am sure I shall be much obliged to him if he will do so," said Pardee.

"You will find him one of the very finest men you ever met, I'm thinking," continued Gleason. "His father, Casaubon Le Moyne, was very much of a gentleman. He came from Virginia, and was akin to the Le Moynes of South Carolina, one of the best of those old French families that brag so much of their Huguenot blood. I never believed in it myself, but they are a mighty elegant family; no doubt of that. I've got the notion that they were not as well off as they might be. Perhaps the family got too big for the estate. That would happen with these old families, you know; but they were as high-toned and honorable as if their forebears had been kings. Not proud, I don't mean—not a bit of that—but high-spirited and hot-tempered.

"His mother was a Richards—Hester Richards—the daughter of old man

Jeems Richards. The family was a mighty rich one; used to own all up and down the river on both sides, from Red Wing to Mulberry Hill, where Hesden now lives. Richards had a big family of boys and only one gal, who was the youngest. The boys was all rather tough customers, I've heard say, taking after their father, who was about as hard a man to get along with as was ever in this country. He came from up North somewhere about 1790, when everybody thought this pea-vine country was a sort of new Garden of Eden. He was a well educated and capable man, but had a terrible temper. He let the boys go to the devil their own way, just selling off a plantation now and then and paying their debts. He had so much land that it was a good thing for him to get rid of it. But he doted on the gal, and sent her off to school and travelled with her and give her every sort of advantage. She was a beauty, and as sweet and good as she was pretty. How she come to marry Casaubon Le Moyne nobody ever knew; but it's just my opinion that it was because they loved each other, and nothing else. They certainly were the best matched couple that I ever saw. They had but one child—this young man Hesden. His mother was always an invalid after his birth; in fact hasn't walked a step since that time. She was a very remarkable woman, though, and in spite of her sickness took charge of her son's education and fitted him for college all by herself. The boy grew up sorter quiet like, probably on account of being in his mother's sick room so much; but there wasn't anything soft about him, after all.

"The old man Casaubon was a Unioner—the strongest kind. Mighty few of them in this county, which was one of the largest slave-holding counties in the State. It never had anything but a big Democratic majority in it, in the old times. I think the old man Le Moyne, run for the Legislature here some seven times before he was elected, and then it was only on his personal popularity. That was the only time the county ever had a Whig representative even.[11] When the war came on, the old man was right down sick. I do believe he saw the end from the beginning. I've heard him tell things almost to a fraction jest as they came out afterward. Well, the young man Hesden, he had his father's notions, of course, but he was pluck. He couldn't have been a Le Moyne, or a Richards either, without that. I remember, not long after the war begun—perhaps in the second year, before the conscription came on, anyhow—he came into town riding of a black colt that he had raised. I don't think it had been backed more than a few times, and it was just as fine as a fiddle. I've had some fine horses myself, and believe I know what goes to make up a good nag, but I've never seen one that suited my notion as well as that black. Le Moyne had taken a heap of pains with him.

A lot of folks gathered 'round and was admiring the beast, and asking questions about his pedigree and the like, when all at once a big, lubberly fellow named Timlow—Jay Timlow—said it was a great pity that such a fine nag should belong to a Union man an' a traitor to his country. You know, captain, that's what we called Union men in them days. He hadn't more'n got the words out of his mouth afore Hesden hit him. I'd no idea he could strike such a blow. Timlow was forty pounds heavier than he, but it staggered him back four or five steps, and Le Moyne follered him up, hitting just about as fast as he could straighten his arm, till he dropped. The queerest thing about it was that the horse follered right along, and when Timlow come down with his face all battered up, and Le Moyne wheeled about and started over to the Court House, the horse kept on follerin' him up to the very steps. Le Moyne went into the Court House and stayed about ten minutes. Then he came out and walked straight across the square to where the crowd was around Timlow, who had been washing the blood off his face at the pump. Le Moyne was as white as a sheet, and Timlow was jest a-cussing his level best about what he would do when he sot eyes on him again. I thought there might be more trouble, and I told Timlow to hush his mouth—I was a deputy then—and then I told Le Moyne he mustn't come any nearer. He was only a few yards away, with a paper in his hand, and that horse just behind him. He stopped when I called him, and said:

"'You needn't fear my coming for any further difficulty, gentlemen. I merely want to say'—and he held up the paper—'that I have enlisted in the army of the Confederate States, and taken this horse to ride—given him to the Government. And I want to say further, that if Jay Timlow wants to do any fighting, and will go and enlist, I'll furnish him a horse, too.'

"With that he jumped on his horse and rode away, followed by a big cheer, while Jay Timlow stood on the pump platform sopping his head with his handkerchief, his eyes as big as saucers, as they say, from surprise. We were all surprised, for that matter. As soon as we got over that a little we began to rally Timlow over the outcome of his little fracas. There wasn't no such timber in him as in young Le Moyne, of course—a big beefy fellow—but he couldn't stand that, and almost before we had got well started he put on his hat, looked round at the crowd a minute, and said, 'Damned if I don't do it!' He marched straight over to the Court House and did it, too.

"Le Moyne stood up to his bargain, and they both went out in the same company a few days afterward. They became great friends, and they do say the Confederacy had mighty few better soldiers than those two boys. Le Moyne was offered promotion time and again, but he wouldn't take it. He said he didn't like war, didn't believe in it, and didn't want no responsibility only for himself. Just about the last fighting they had over about Appomattox—perhaps the very day before the Surrender—he lost that horse and his left arm a-fighting over that same Jay Timlow, who had got a ball in the leg, and Le Moyne was trying to keep him out of the hands of you Yanks.

"He got back after a while, and has been living with his mother on the old plantation ever since. He married a cousin just before he went into the service—more to have somebody to leave with his ma than because he wanted a wife, folks said. The old man, Colonel Casaubon, died during the war. He never seemed like himself after the boy went into the army. I saw him once or twice, and I never did see such a change in any man. Le Moyne's wife died, too. She left a little boy, who with Le Moyne and his ma are all that's left of the family. I don't reckon there ever was a man thought more of his mother, or had a mother more worth setting store by, than Hesden Le Moyne."

They had reached the hotel when this account was concluded, and after dinner the sheriff came to the captain's room and introduced a slender young man in neatly fitting jeans, with blue eyes, a dark brown beard, and an empty coat-sleeve, as Mr. Hesden Le Moyne.

He put his felt hat under the stump of his left arm and extended his right hand as he said simply:

"The sheriff said you wished to see me about Eliab Hill."

"I did," was the response; "but after what he has told me, I desired to see you much more for yourself."

The sheriff withdrew, leaving them alone together, and they fell to talking of army life at once, as old soldiers always will, each trying to locate the other in the strife which they had passed through on opposite sides.

CHAPTER IX.

A BRUISED REED.[12]

"ELIAB[13] HILL," said Le Moyne, when they came at length to the subject in relation to which the interview had been solicited, "was born the slave of Potem Desmit, on his plantation Knapp-of-Reeds, in the lower part of the county. His mother was a very likely woman, considerable darker than he, but still not more than a quadroon, I should say. She was brought from Colonel Desmit's home plantation to Knapp-of-Reeds some little time before her child was born. It was her first child, I believe, and her last one. She was a very slender woman, and though not especially unhealthy, yet never strong, being inclined to consumption, of which she finally died. Of course his paternity is unknown, though rumor has not been silent in regard to it. It is said that a stubborn refusal on his mother's part to reveal it led Colonel Desmit, in one of his whimsical moods, to give the boy the name he bears. However, he was as bright a child as ever frolicked about a plantation till he was some five or six years old. His mother had been a house-servant before she was sent to Knapp-of-Reeds, and being really a supernumerary there, my father hired her a year or two afterward as a nurse for my mother, who has long been an invalid, as you may be aware."

His listener nodded assent, and he went on:

"Her child was left at Knapp-of-Reeds, but Saturday nights it was brought over to stay the Sunday with her, usually by this boy Nimbus, who was two or three years older than he. The first I remember of his misfortune was one Saturday, when Nimbus brought him over in a gunny-sack, on his back. It was not a great way, hardly half a mile, but I remember thinking that it was a pretty smart tug for the little black rascal. I was not more than a year or two older than he, myself, and not nearly so strong.

"It seems that something had happened to the boy, I never knew exactly what—seems to me it was a cold resulting from some exposure, which settled in his legs, as they say, producing rheumatism or something of that kind—so that he could not walk or hardly stand up. The boy Nimbus had almost the sole charge of him during the week, and of course he lacked for intelligent treatment. In fact, I doubt if Desmit's overseer knew anything about it until it was too late to do any good. He was a bright, cheerful child, and Nimbus was the same dogged, quiet thing he is now. So it went on, until his mother, Moniloe, found that he had lost all use of his legs. They were curled up at one side, as you saw them, and while his body has developed well they have grown but little in comparison.

"Moniloe made a great outcry over the child, to whom she was much attached, and finally wrought upon my father and mother to buy herself and her crippled boy. Colonel Desmit, on whom the burden of his maintenance would fall, and who saw no method of making him self-supporting, was willing to sell the mother on very moderate terms if my father would take the child and guarantee his support. This was done, and they both became my father's property. Neither forgot to be grateful. The woman was my mother's faithful nurse until after the war, when she died, and I have never been able to fill her place completely, since. I think Eliab learned his letters, and perhaps to read a little, from me. He was almost always in my mother's room, being brought in and set down upon a sheepskin on one side the fireplace in the morning by his mammy. My mother had great sympathy with his misfortune, the more, I suppose, because of her own very similar affliction. She used to teach him to sew and knit, and finally, despite the law, began to encourage him to read. The neighbors, coming in and finding him with a book in his hands, began to complain of it, and my father, in order to silence all such murmurs, manumitted him square out and gave bonds for his support, as the law required.

"As he grew older he remained more and more in his mother's cabin, in one corner of which she had a little elevated platform made for him. He could crawl around the room by means of his hands, and had great skill in clambering about by their aid. When he was about fifteen a shoemaker came to the house to do our plantation work. Eliab watched him closely all the first day; on the second desired to help, and before the month had passed was as good a shoemaker as his teacher. From that time he worked steadily at the trade, and managed very greatly to reduce the cost of his support.

"He was a strange boy, and he and this fellow Nimbus were always together except when prevented by the latter's tasks. A thousand times I have known Nimbus to come over long after dark and leave before daylight, in order to stay with his friend over night. Not unfrequently he would carry him home upon his back and keep him for several days at Knapp-of-Reeds, where both were prime favorites, as they were with us also. As they grew older this attachment became stronger. Many's the time I have passed there and seen Nimbus working in the tobacco and Eliab with his hammers and lasts pounding away under a tree near by. Having learned to read, the man was anxious to know more. For a time he was indulged, but as the hot times just preceding the war came on, it became indiscreet for him to be seen with a book.

"While he was still very young he began to preach, and his ministrations were peculiarly prudent and sensible. His influence with his people, even before emancipation, was very great, and has been increased by his correct and manly conduct since. I regard him, sir, as one of the most useful men in the community.

"For some reason, I have never known exactly what, he became anxious to leave my house soon after Nimbus' return from the army, although I had offered him the free use of the little shop where he and his mother had lived, as long as he desired. He and Nimbus, by some hook or crook, managed to buy the place at Red Wing. It was a perfectly barren piney old-field then, and not thought of any account except for the timber there was on it. It happened to be at the crossing of two roads, and upon a high sandy ridge, which was thought to be too poor to raise peas on. The man who sold it to them—their old master Potem Desmit—no doubt thought he was getting two or three prices for it; but it has turned out one of the best tobacco farms in the county. It is between two very rich sections, and in a country having a very large colored population, perhaps the largest in the county, working the river plantations on one side and the creek bottoms on the other. I have heard that Nimbus takes great credit to himself for his sagacity in foreseeing the capabilities of Red Wing. If he really did detect its value at that time, it shows a very fine judgment and accounts for his prosperity since. Eliab Hill affirms this to be true, but most people think he does the planning for the whole settlement. Nimbus has done extremely well, however. He has sold off, I should judge, nearly half his land, in small parcels, has worked hard, and had excellent crops. I should not wonder, if his present crop comes off well and the market holds on, if before Christmas he were worth as many thousands as he had hundreds the day he bought that piney old-field. It don't take much tobacco at a dollar a pound, which his last crop brought, lugs and all, to make a man that does his own work and works his own land right well off. He's had good luck, has worked hard, and has either managed well or been well advised; it don't matter which.

"He has gathered a good crowd around him too, sober, hard-working men; and most of them have done well too. So that it has become quite a flourishing little settlement. I suppose there are some fifty or sixty families live there. They have a church, which they use for a school-house, and it is by a great deal the best school-house in the county too. Of course they got outside help, some from the Bureau, I reckon, and more perhaps from some charitable association. I should think the church or school-house must have cost fifteen hundred or two thousand dollars. They have a splendid school. Two ladies from the North are teaching there—real ladies, I should judge, too."

The listener smiled at this indorsement.

"I see," said Le Moyne, "it amuses you that I should qualify my words in that manner. It seems unneccessary to you."

"Entirely so."

"Well, it may be; but I assure you, sir, we find it hard to believe that any one who will come down here and teach niggers is of very much account at home."

"They are generally of the very cream of our Northern life," said the other. "I know at this very time the daughters of several prominent clergymen, of two college professors, of a wealthy merchant, of a leading manufacturer, and of several wealthy farmers, who are teaching in these schools. It is missionary work, you see—just as much as going to Siam or China. I have never known a more accomplished, devoted, or thoroughly worthy class of ladies, and do not doubt that these you speak of, well deserve your praise without qualification."

"Well, it may be," said the other dubiously; "but it is hard for us to understand, you know. Now, they live in a little old house, which they have fixed up with flowers and one thing and another till it is very attractive—on the outside, at least. I know nothing about the inside since their occupancy. It was a notable place in the old time, but had quite run down before they came. I don't suppose they see a white person once a month to speak to them, unless indeed some of the officers come over from the post at Boyleston, now and then. I am sure that no lady would think of visiting them or admitting them to her house. I know a few gentlemen who have visited the school just out of curiosity. Indeed, I have ridden over once myself, and I must say it is well worth seeing. I should say there were three or four hundred scholars, of all ages, sizes, and colors—black, brown, white apparently, and all shades of what we used to call 'ginger-cake.' These two ladies and the man Eliab teach them. It is perfectly wonderful how they do get on. You ought to see it."

"I certainly shall," said Pardee, "as a special duty calls me there. How would it do for a polling-place?"

"There ought to be one there, but I should be afraid of trouble," answered Le Moyne seriously.

"Name me one or two good men for poll-holders, and I will risk any disorder."

"Well, there is Eliab. He's a good man if there ever was one, and capable too."

"How about Nimbus?"

"He's a good man too, honest as the day is long, hard-headed and determined, but he can't read or write."

"That is strange."

"It *is* strange, but one of the teachers was telling me so when I was there. I think he has got so that he can sign his first name—his only one, he insists—but that is all, and he cannot read a word."

"I should have thought he would have been one of the first to learn that much at least."

"So should I. He is the best man of affairs among them all—has good judgment and sense, and is always trying to do something to get on. He says he is 'too busy to get larnin', an' leaves that and preachin' to Bre'er 'Liab.'"

"Do they keep up their former intimacy?"

"Keep it up? 'Liab lives in Nimbus' lot, has his meals from his table, and is toted about by Nimbus just the same as if they were still boys. Nimbus seems to think more of him than he would of a brother—than he does of his brothers, for he has two whom he seems to care nothing about. His wife and children are just as devoted to the cripple as Nimbus, and 'Liab, on his part, seems to think as much of them as if they were his own. They get along first-rate, and are prospering finely, but I am afraid they will have trouble yet."

"Why so?"

"Oh, well, I don't know; they are niggers, you see, and our people are not used to such things."

"I hope your apprehensions are groundless."

"Well, I hope so too."

The officer looked at his watch and remarked that he must return to his duty, and after thanking his companion for a pleasant hour, and being invited to call at Mulberry Hill whenever occasion might serve, the two men parted, each with pleasant impressions of the other.

CHAPTER X.

AN EXPRESS TRUST.

FORTUNATELY FOR NIMBUS, he had received scarcely anything of his pay while in the service, and none of the bounty-money[14] due him, until some months after the surrender, when he was discharged at a post near his old home. On the next day it happened that there was a sale of some of the transportation at this post, and through the co-operation of one of his officers he was enabled to buy a good mule with saddle and bridle for a song, and by means of these reached home on the day after. He was so proud of his new acquisition that he could not be induced to remain a single day with his former comrades. He had hardly more than assured himself of the safety of his wife and children before he went to visit his old friend and playmate, Eliab Hill. He found that worthy in a state of great depression.

"You see," he explained to his friend, "Mister Le Moyne" (with a slight emphasis on the title) "bery kindly offered me de use ob dis cabin 's long as I might want it, and has furnished me with nearly all I have had since the S'rrender. While my mother lived and he had her services and a well-stocked plantation and plenty ob hands, I didn't hab no fear o' being a burden to him. I knew he would get good pay fer my support, fer I did de shoemakin' fer his people, and made a good many clo'es fer dem too. Thanks to Miss Hester's care, I had learned to use my needle, as you know, an' could do common tailorin' as well as shoemakin'. I got very little fer my wuk but Confederate money and provisions, which my mother always insisted that Mr. Le Moyne should have the benefit on, as he had given me my freedom and was under bond for my support.

"Since de S'rrender, t'ough dere is plenty ob wuk nobody has any money. Mr. Le Moyne is just as bad off as anybody, an' has to go in debt fer his supplies. His slaves was freed, his wife is dead, he has nobody to wait on Miss Hester, only as he hires a nuss; his little boy is to take keer on, an' he with only one arm an' jest a bare plantation with scarcely any stock left to him. It comes hard fer me to eat his bread and owe him so much when I can't do nothin' fer him in return. I know he don't mind it, an' b'lieve he would feel hurt if he knew how I feel about it; but I can't help it, Nimbus—I can't, no way."

"Oh, yer mustn't feel that 'ere way, Bre'er 'Liab," said his friend. "Co'se it's hard fer you jes now, an' may be a little rough on Marse Moyne. But yer mus' member dat atter a little our folks 'll hev money. White folks got ter have wuk done; nebber do it theirselves; you know dat; an' ef we does it now we's boun' ter hev pay fer it. An' when we gits money, you gits wuk. Jes' let Marse Moyne wait till de crap comes off, an' den yer'll make it all squar wid him. I tell yer what, 'Liab, it's gwine ter be great times fer us niggers, now we's free. Yer sees dat mule out dar?" he asked, pointing to a sleek bay animal which he had tied to the rack in front of the house when he rode up.

"Yes, o' course I do," said the other, with very little interest in his voice.

"Likely critter, ain't it?" asked Nimbus, with a peculiar tone.

"Certain. Whose is it?"

"Wal, now, dat's jes edzackly de question I wuz gwine ter ax of you. Whose yer spose 'tis?"

"I'm sure I don't know. One o' Mr. Ware's?"

"I should tink not, honey; not edzackly now. Dat ar mule b'longs ter *me*—Nimbus! D'yer h'yer dat, 'Liab?"

"No! Yer don't tell me? Bless de Lord, Nimbus, yer's a fortunit man. Yer fortin's made, Nimbus. All yer's got ter do is ter wuk fer a livin' de rest of this year, an' then put in a crap of terbacker next year, an' keep gwine on a wukkin' an' savin', an' yer fortin's made. Ther ain't no reason why yer shouldn't be rich afore yer's fifty. Bless the Lord, Nimbus, I'se that glad for you dat I can't find no words fer it."

The cripple stretched out both hands to his stalwart friend, and the tears which ran down his cheeks attested the sincerity of his words. Nimbus took his outstretched hands, held them in his own a moment, then went to the door, looked carefully about, came back again, and with some embarrassment said,

"An' dat ain't all, Bre'er 'Liab. Jes' you look dar."

As he spoke Nimbus took an envelope from the inside pocket of his soldier jacket and laid it on the bench where the other sat. 'Liab looked up in surprise, but in obedience to a gesture from Nimbus opened it and counted the contents.

"Mos' five hundred dollars!" he said at length, in amazement. "Dis yours too, Bre'er Nimbus?"

"Co'se it is. Didn't I tell yer dar wuz a good time comin'?"

"Bre'er Nimbus," said Eliab solemnly, "you gib me your word you git all dis money honestly?"

"Co'se I did. Yer don't s'pose Nimbus am a-gwine ter turn thief at dis day, does yer?"

"How you get it?" asked Eliab sternly.

"How I git it?" answered the other indignantly. "You see dem clo'es? Hain't I been a-sojerin' nigh onter two year now? Hain't I hed pay an' bounty, an' rations too? One time I wuz cut off from de regiment, an' 'ported missin' nigh bout fo' months afo' I managed ter git over ter Port R'yal an' 'port fer duty, an' dey gib me money fer rations all dat time. Tell yer, 'Liab, it all counts up. I'se spent a heap 'sides dat."

Still Eliab looked incredulous.

"You see dat *dis*charge?" said Nimbus, pulling the document from his pocket. "You jes look at what de paymaster writ on dat, ef yer don't b'lieve

Nimbus hez hed any luck. 'Sides dat, I'se got de dockyments h'yer ter show jes whar an' how I got dat mule."

The care which had been exercised by his officer in providing Nimbus with the written evidence of his ownership of the mule was by no means needless. According to the common law, the possession of personal property is *prima facie* evidence of its ownership; but in those early days, before the nation undertook to spread the ægis of equality over him, such was not the rule in the case of the freedman. Those first legislatures, elected only by the high-minded land-owners of the South, who knew the African, his needs and wants, as no one else could know them, and who have always proclaimed themselves his truest friends, enacted with especial care that he should not "hold nor own nor have any rights of property in any horse, mule, hog, cow, steer, or other stock," unless the same was attested by a bill of sale or other instrument of writing executed by the former owner. It was well for Nimbus that he was armed with his "dockyments."

Eliab Hill took the papers handed him by Nimbus, and read, slowly and with evident difficulty; but as he mastered line after line the look of incredulity vanished, and a glow of solemn joy spread over his face. It was the first positive testimony of actual freedom—the first fruits of self-seeking, self-helping manhood on the part of his race which had come into the secluded country region and gladdened the heart of the stricken prophet and adviser.

With a sudden jerk he threw himself off his low bench, and burying his head upon it poured forth a prayer of gratitude for this evidence of prayer fulfilled. His voice was full of tears, and when he said "Amen," and Nimbus rose from his knees and put forth his hand to help him as he scrambled upon his bench, the cripple caught the hand and pressed it close, as he said:

"Bress God, Nimbus, I'se seen de time often an' often 'nough when I'se hed ter ax de Lor' ter keep me from a-envyin' an' grudgin' de white folks all de good chances dey hed in dis world; but now I'se got ter fight agin' covetin' anudder nigga's luck. Bress de Lor', Nimbus, I'se gladder, I do b'lieve, fer what's come ter you dan yer be yerself. It'll do you a power of good—you an' yours—but what good wud it do if a poor crippled feller like me hed it? Not a bit. Jes' git him bread an' meat, Nimbus, dat's all. Oh, de Lord knows what he's 'bout, Nimbus. Mind you dat. He didn't give you all dat money fer nothing, an' yer'll hev ter 'count fer it, dat you will; mighty close too, 'kase he keeps his books right. Yer must see ter dat, Bre'er Nimbus." The exhortation was earnestly given, and was enforced with tears and soft strokings of the dark strong hand which he still clasped in his soft and slender ones.

"Now don't you go ter sayin' nuffin' o' dat kind, ole feller. I'se been a-tinkin' ebber sence I got dat money dat it's jes ez much 'Liab's ez 'tis mine. Ef it hadn't been fer you I'd nebber knowed 'nough ter go ober to de Yanks, when ole Mahs'r send me down ter wuk on de fo'tifications, an' so I neber git it at all. So now, yer see, Bre'er 'Liab, *you's* gwine ter keep dat 'ere money. I don't feel half safe wid it nohow, till we find out jes what we wants ter do wid it. I 'lows dat we'd better buy a plantation somewheres. Den I kin wuk it, yer know, an' you kin hev a shop, an' so we kin go cahoots, an' git along right smart. Yer see, ef we do dat, we allers hez a livin', anyhow, an' der ain't no such thing ez spendin' an' losin' what we've got."

There was great demurrer on the part of the afflicted friend, but he finally consented to become his old crony's banker. He insisted, however, on giving him a very formal and peculiarly worded receipt for the money and papers which he received from him. Considering that they had to learn the very rudiments of business, Eliab Hill was altogether right in insisting upon a scrupulous observance of what he deemed "the form of sound words."

In speaking of the son of his former owner as "Mister," Eliab Hill meant to display nothing of arrogance or disrespect. The titles "Master" and "Missus," were the badges of slavery and inferiority. Against their use the mind of the freedman rebelled as instinctively as the dominant race insisted on its continuance. The "Black Codes" of 1865, the only legislative acts of the South since the war which were not affected in any way by national power or Northern sentiment, made it incumbent on the freedman, whom it sought to continue in serfdom, to use this form of address, and denounced its neglect as disrespectful to the "Master" or "Mistress." When these laws ceased to be operative, the custom of the white race generally was still to demand the observance of the form, and this demand tended to embitter the dislike of the freedmen for it. At first, almost the entire race refused. After a while the habit of generations began to assert itself. While the more intelligent and better educated of the original stock discarded its use entirely, the others, and the children who had grown up since emancipation, came to use it almost interchangeably with the ordinary form of address. Thus Eliab Hill, always nervously alive to the fact of freedom, never allowed the words to pass his lips after the Surrender, except when talking with Mrs. Le Moyne, to whose kindness he owed so much in early years. On the other hand, Nimbus, with an equal aversion to everything connected with slavery, but without the same mental activity, sometimes dropped into the old familiar habit. He would have died rather than use the word at another's dictation or as a badge of inferiority, but the habit was too strong for one of his grade of intellect to break away from at once. Since the success of the old slave-holding element of the South in subverting the governments based on the equality of political right and power, this form of address has become again almost universal except in the cities and large towns.

CHAPTER XI.

RED WING.

SITUATED ON THE SANDY, undulating chain of low, wooded hills which separated the waters of two tributaries of the Roanoke, at the point where the "big road" from the West crossed the country road which ran northward along the crest of the ridge, as if in search of dry footing between the rich valleys on either hand, was the place known as Red Wing. The "big road" had been a thoroughfare from the West in the old days before steam diverted the ways of traffic from the trails which the wild beasts had pursued. It led through the mountain gaps, by devious ways but by easy grades, along the banks of the water-courses and across the shallowest fords down to the rich lowlands of the East. It was said that the buffalo, in forgotten ages, had marked out this way to the ever-verdant reed-pastures of the then unwooded East; that afterward the Indians had followed his lead, and, as the season served, had fished upon the waters of Currituck or hunted amid the romantic ruggedness of the Blue Appalachians. It was known that the earlier settlers along the Smoky Range and on the Piedmont foothills had used this thoroughfare to take the stock and produce of their farms down to the great plantations of the East, where cotton was king, and to the turpentine orchards of the South Atlantic shore line.

At the crossing of these roads was situated a single house, which had been known for generations, far and near, as the Red Wing Ordinary. In the old colonial days it had no doubt been a house of entertainment for man and beast. Tradition, very well based and universally accepted, declared that along these roads had marched and countermarched the hostile forces of the Revolutionary period. Greene and Cornwallis had dragged their weary columns over the tenacious clay of this region, past the very door of the low-eaved house, built up of heavy logs at first and covered afterward with fat-pine siding, which had itself grown brown and dark with age. It was said that the British regulars had stacked their arms around the trunk of the monster white-oak that stretched its great arms out over the low dark house, which seemed to be creeping nearer and nearer to its mighty trunk for protection, until of late years the spreading branches had dropped their store of glossy acorns and embossed cups even on the farther slope of its mossy roof, a good twenty yards away from the scarred and rugged bole. "Two decks and a passage"—two moderate-sized rooms with a wide open passway between, and a low dark porch running along the front—constituted all that was left of a once well-known place of public refreshment. At each end a stone chimney, yellowish gray and of a massiveness now wonderful to behold, rose above the gable like a shattered tower above the salient of some old fortress. The windows still retained the little square panes and curious glazing of a century ago. Below it, fifty yards away to the eastward, a bold spring burst out of the granite rock, spread deep and still and cool over its white sandy bottom, in the stone-walled inclosure where it was confined (over half of which stood the ample milk-house), and then gurgling along the stony outlet ran away over the ripple-marked sands of its worn channel, to join the waters of the creek a mile away.

It was said that in the olden time there had been sheds and out-buildings, and perhaps some tributary houses for the use of lodgers, all of which belonged to and constituted a part of the Ordinary. Two things had deprived it of its former glory. The mart-way had changed even before the iron horse charged across the old routes, scorning their pretty curves and dashing in an almost direct line from mountain to sea. Increasing population had opened new routes, which diverted the traffic and were preferred to the old way by travelers. Besides this, there had been a feud between the owner of the Ordinary and the rich proprietor whose outspread acres encircled on every side the few thin roods which were attached to the hostel, and when the owner thereof died and the property, in the course of administration, was put upon the market, the rich neighbor bought it, despoiled it of all its accessories, and left only the one building of two rooms below and two above, a kitchen and a log stable, with crib attached, upon the site of the Ordinary which had vexed him so long. The others were all cleared away, and even the little opening around the Ordinary was turned out to grow up in pines and black-jacks all but an acre or two of garden-plot behind the house. The sign was removed, and the overseer of Colonel Walter Greer, the new owner, was installed in the house, which thenceforth lost entirely its character as an inn.

In the old days, before the use of artificial heat in the curing of tobacco, the heavy, coarse fibre which grew upon rich, loamy bottom lands or on dark clayey hillsides was chiefly prized by the grower and purchaser of that staple. The light sandy uplands, thin and gray, bearing only stunted pines or a light growth of chestnut and clustering chinquapins, interspersed with sourwood, while here and there a dogwood or a white-coated, white-hearted hickory grew, stubborn and lone, were not at all valued as tobacco lands. The light silky variety of that staple was entirely unknown, and even after its discovery was for a long time unprized, and its habitat and peculiar characteristics little understood. It is only since the war of Rebellion that its excellence has been fully appreciated and its superiority established. The timber on this land was of no value except as wood and for house-logs. Of the standard timber tree of the region, the oak, there was barely enough to fence it, should that ever be thought desirable. Corn, the great staple of the region next to tobacco, could hardly be "hired" to grow upon the "droughty" soil of the ridge, and its yield of the smaller grains, though much better, was not sufficient to tempt the owner of the rich lands adjacent to undertake its cultivation. This land itself, he thought, was only good "to hold the world together" or make a "wet-weather road" between the rich tracts on either hand. Indeed, it was a common saying in that region that it was "too poor even to raise a disturbance upon."

To the westward of the road running north and south there had once been an open field of some thirty or forty acres, where the wagoners were wont to camp and the drovers to picket their stock in the halcyon days of the old hostelry. It had been the muster-ground of the militia too, and there were men yet alive, at the time of which we write, whose fathers had mustered with the county forces on that ground. When it was "turned out," however, and the Ordinary ceased to be a place of entertainment, the pines shot up, almost as thick as grass-blades in a meadow, over its whole expanse. It is strange how they came there. Only black-jacks and the lighter decidua which cover such sandy ridges had grown there before, but after these were cleared away by the hand of man and the plow for a few years had tickled the thin soil, when nature again resumed her sway, she sent a countless army of evergreens, of mysterious origin, to take and hold this desecrated portion of her domain. They sprang up between the corn-rows before the stalks had disappeared from sight; they shot through the charred embers of the deserted camp-fire; everywhere, under the shade of each deciduous bush, protected by the shadow of the rank weeds which sprang up where the stock had fed, the young pines grew, and protected others, and shot slimly up, until their dense growth shut out the sunlight and choked the lately protecting shrubbery. Then they grew larger, and the weaker ones were overtopped by the stronger and shut out from the sunlight and starved to death, and their mouldering fragments mingled with the carpet of cones and needles which became thicker and thicker under their shade, until at the beginning of the war a solid, dark mass of pines fit for house-logs, and many even larger, stood upon the old muster-field, and constituted the chief value of the tract of two hundred acres which lay along the west side of the plantation of which it formed a part.

It was this tract that Nimbus selected as the most advantageous location for himself and his friend which he could find in that region. He rightly judged that the general estimate of its poverty would incline the owner to part with a considerable tract at a very moderate price, especially if he were in need of ready money, as Colonel Desmit was then reputed to be, on account of the losses he had sustained by the results of the war. His own idea of its value differed materially from this, and he was thoroughly convinced that, in the near future, it would be justified. He was cautious about stating the grounds of this belief even to Eliab, having the natural fear of one unaccustomed to business that some other person would get wind of his idea and step into his Bethesda while he, himself, waited for the troubling of the waters.[15]

He felt himself quite incompetent to conduct the purchase, even with Eliab's assistance, and in casting about for some white man whom they could trust to act as their agent, they could think of no one but Hesden Le Moyne. It was agreed, therefore, that Eliab should broach the matter to him, but he was expressly cautioned by Nimbus to give him no hint of the particular reasons which led them to prefer this particular tract or of their means of payment, until he had thoroughly sounded him in regard to the plan itself. This Eliab did, and that gentleman, while approving the plan of buying a plantation, if they were able, utterly condemned the idea of purchasing a tract so notoriously worthless, and refused to have anything to do with so wild a scheme. Eliab, greatly discouraged, reported this fact to his friend and urged the abandonment of the plan. Nimbus, however, was stubborn and declared that "if Marse Hesden would not act for him he would go to Louisburg and buy it of Marse Desmit himself."

"Dar ain't no use o' talkin', 'Liab," said he. "You an' Marse Hesden knows a heap more'n I does 'bout most things; dar ain't no doubt 'bout dat an' nobody knows it better'n I does. But what Nimbus knows, he *knows,* an' dat's de eend on't. Nobody don't know it any better. Now, I don't know nuffin' 'bout books an' de scripter an' sech-like, only what I gits second-hand—no more'n you does 'bout sojerin', fer instance. But I tell ye what, 'Liab, I does know 'bout terbacker, an' I knows *all* about it, too. I kin jes' gib you an' Marse Hesden, an' a heap mo' jes like you uns, odds on dat, an' beat ye all holler ebbery time. What I don't know 'bout dat ar' crap dar ain't no sort ob use a tryin' to tell me. I got what I knows de reg'lar ole-fashioned way, like small-pox, jes by 'sposure, an' I tell yer 'Liab, hit beats any sort ob 'noculation all ter rags. Now, I tell *you,* 'Liab Hill, dat ar' trac' ob lan' 'bout dat ole Or'nery is jes' de berry place we wants, an' I'm boun' ter hev it, ef it takes a leg. Now you heah dat, don't yer?"

Eliab saw that it was useless for him to combat this determination. He knew the ruggedness of his friend's character and had long ago learned that he could only be turned from a course, once fixed upon in his own mind, by presenting some view of the matter which had not occurred to him before. He had great confidence in Mr. Le Moyne's judgment—almost as much as in Nimbus', despite his admiration for his herculean comrade—so he induced his friend to promise that nothing more should be done about the matter until he could have an opportunity to examine the premises, with which he was not as familiar as he would like to be, before it was altogether decided. To this Nimbus readily consented, and soon afterwards he borrowed a wagon and took Eliab, one pleasant day in the early fall, to spy out their new Canaan. When they had driven around and seen as much of it as they could well examine from the vehicle, Nimbus drove to a point on the east-and-west road just opposite the western part of the pine growth, where a sandy hill sloped gradually to the northward and a little spring burst out of it and trickled across the road.

"Dar," he said, waving his hand toward the slope; "dar is whar I wants my house, right 'longside ob dat ar spring, wid a good terbacker barn up on de hill dar."

"Why, what do yer want ter lib dar fer?" asked the other in surprise, as he peered over the side of the wagon, in which he sat upon a thick bed of fodder which Nimbus had spread over the bottom for his comfort.

"Kase dat ar side-hill am twenty-five acres ob de best terbacker groun' in Ho'sford County."

"Yer don't say so, Nimbus?"

"Dat's jes what I do say, 'Liab, an' dat's de main reason what's made me so stubborn, 'bout buyin' dis berry track of lan'. Pears ter me it's jes made fer us. It's all good terbacker lan', most on't de berry best. It's easy clar'd off an' easy wukked. De 'backer growed on dis yer lan' an' cured wid coal made outen dem ar pines will be jes es yaller ez gold an' as fine ez silk, 'Liab. I knows; I'se been a watchin' right smart, an' long ago, when I used ter pass by here, when dey fust begun ter vally de yaller terbacker, I used ter wonder dat some pore white man like Marse War', dat knowed how ter raise an' cure terbacker, didn't buy de ole place an' wuk for demselves, 'stead ob overseein' fer somebody else. It's quar dey nebber t'ought on't. It allers seemed ter me dat I wouldn't ax fer nothin' better."

"But what yer gwine ter do wid de ole house?" asked Eliab.

"Wal, Bre'er Liab," said Nimbus with a queer grimace, "I kinder 'llowed dat I'd let you hab dat ar ter do wid jes 'bout ez yer like."

"Oh, Bre'er Nimbus, yer don't mean dat now?"

"Don't I? wal, you jes see ef I don't. I'se gwine ter lib right h'yer, an' ef yer don't occupy dat ole Red Wing Or'nery I'm durned ef it don't rot down. Yer heah dat man? Dar don't nobody else lib in it, shuah."

Eliab was very thoughtful and silent, listening to Nimbus' comments and plans until finally, as they sat on the porch of the old house eating their "snack," he said, "Nimbus, dar's a heap ob cullud folks libbin' jes one way an' anudder from dis yer Red Wing cross-roads."

"Co'se dey is, an' dat's de berry reason I'se sot my heart on yer habbin' a shop right h'yer. Yer shore ter git de wuk ob de whole country roun', an' der's mo' cullud folks right up an' down de creek an' de ribber h'yer dan ennywhar hereabouts dat I knows on."

"But, Nimbus—" said he, hesitatingly.

"Yis, 'Liab, I hears ye."

"Couldn't we hab a church here?"

"Now yer's *talkin'*," exclaimed Nimbus. "Swar ter God, it's quare I nebber tink ob dat, now. An' you de minister? Now yer *is* talkin', shuah! Why de debble I nebber tink ob dat afo'? Yer see dem big pines dar, straight ez a arrer an' nigh 'bout de same size from top ter bottom? What yer s'pose dem fer, 'Liab? Dunno? I should tink not. House logs fer de church, 'Liab. Make it jes ez big ez yer wants. Dar 'tis. Only gib me some few shingles an' a flo', an' dar yer hev jes ez good a church ez de 'postles ebber hed ter preach in."

"An' de school, Nimbus?" timidly.

"Shuah 'nough. Why I nebber tink ob dat afo'? An' you de teacher! Now you *is* talkin', 'Liab, *certain* shuah! Dat's jes de ting, jes what we wants an' hez got ter hev. Plenty o' scholars h'yer-abouts, an' de church fer a school-house an' Bre'er 'Liab fer de teacher! 'Clar fer it, Bre'er 'Liab, you hez got a head-piece, dat's a fac'. Now I nebber tink of all dat togedder. Mout hev come bimeby, little to a time, but not all to wonst like, as 'tis wid you. Lord, how plain I sees it all now! De church an' school-house up dar on de knoll; Nimbus' house jes about a hundred yards furder on, 'cross de road; an' on de side ob de hill de 'backer-barn; you a teachin' an' a preachin' an' Nimbus makin' terbacker, an' Gena a-takin' comfort on de porch, an' de young uns gittin' larnin'! Wh-o-o-p! Bre'er 'Liab, yer's a great man, shuah!"

Nimbus caught him in his strong arms and whirled him about in a frenzy of joy. When he sat him down Eliab said quietly:

"We must get somebody else to teach for a while. 'Liab don't know 'nough ter do dat ar. I'll go to school wid de chillen an' learn 'nough ter do it bimeby. P'raps dis what dey call de 'Bureau' mout start a school here ef you should ax 'em, Nimbus. Yer know dey'd be mighty willin' ter 'blige a soldier, who'd been a fightin' fer 'em, ez you hev."

"I don't a know about dat ar, Bre'er 'Liab, but leastaways we can't do no more'n make de trial, anyhow."

After this visit, Eliab withdrew all opposition, not without doubt, but hoping for the best, and trusting, prayerfully, that his friend's sanguine expectations might be justified by the result. So it was determined that Nimbus should make the purchase, if possible, and that the old Ordinary, which had been abandoned as a hostel on the highway to the Eastern market, be made a New Inn upon the road which the Freedman must now take, and which should lead to liberty and light.

CHAPTER XII.

ON THE WAY TO JERICHO.[16]

COLONEL DESMIT'S DEVOTION to the idea that slave property was more profitable than any other, and the system by which he had counted on almost limitless gain thereby, was not only overthrown by the universal emancipation which attended the issue of the war, but certain unlooked-for contingencies placed him upon the very verge of bankruptcy. The location of his interests in different places, which he had been accustomed, during the struggle, to look upon as a most fortunate prevision, resulted most disastrously. As the war progressed, it came about that those regions which were at first generally regarded as the most secure from hostile invasion became the scene of the most devastating operations.

The military foresight of the Confederate leaders long before led them to believe that the struggle would be concluded, or would at least reach its climax, in the Piedmont region. From the coast to the mountains the Confederacy spanned, at this point, only two hundred miles. The country was open, accessible from three points upon the coast, at which lodgment was early made or might have been obtained, and only one flank of the forces marching thence toward the heart of the Confederacy could be assailed. It was early apprehended by them that armies marching from the coast of North Carolina, one column along the course of the Cape Fear and another from Newberne, within fair supporting distance and converging toward the center of the State, would constitute the most dangerous movement that could be made against the Confederacy, since it would cut it in twain if successful; and, in order to defeat it, the Army of Virginia would have to be withdrawn from its field of operations and a force advancing in its track from the James would be enabled to co-operate with the columns previously mentioned. It is instructive to note that, upon the other side, the untrained instinct of President Lincoln was always turning in the same direction. In perusing the field of operations his finger would always stray to the eastern coast of North Carolina as the vital point, and no persuasions could induce him to give up the apparently useless foothold which we kept there for more than three years without material advantage. It was a matter of constant surprise to the Confederate military authorities that this course was not adopted, and the final result showed the wisdom of their premonition.

Among others, Colonel Desmit had obtained an inkling of this idea, and instead of concentrating all his destructible property in the region of his home, where, as it resulted, it would have been comparatively secure, he pitched upon the "piney-woods" region to the southeastward, as the place of greatest safety.

He had rightly estimated that cotton and naval stores would, on account of the rigorous blockade and their limited production in other countries, be the most valuable products to hold when the period of war should end. With these ideas he had invested largely in both, and in and about a great factory at the falls of a chief tributary of the Pedee, he had stored his cotton; and in the heart of that sombre-shadowed stretch of soughing pines which lies between the Cape Fear and the Yadkin he had hidden his vast accumulation of pitch, turpentine, and resin. Both were in the very track of Sherman's ruthless legions.[17] First the factory and the thousands of bales carefully placed in store near by were given to the flames. Potestatem Desmit had heard of their danger, and had ridden post-haste across the rugged region to the northward in the vain hope that his presence might somehow avert disaster. From the top of a rocky mountain twenty miles away he had witnessed the conflagration, and needed not to be told of his loss. Turning his horse's head to the eastward, at a country-crossing near at hand, he struck out with unabated resolution to reach the depot of his naval stores before the arrival of the troops, in order that he might interpose for their preservation. He had quite determined to risk the consequences of capture in their behalf, being now fully convinced of the downfall of the Confederacy.

During the ensuing night he arrived at his destination, where he found everything in confusion and affright. It was a vast collection of most valuable stores. For two years they had been accumulating. It was one of the sheet-anchors which the prudent and far-seeing Potestatem Desmit had thrown out to windward in anticipation of a coming storm. For half a mile along the bank of the little stream which was just wide enough to float a loaded batteau, the barrels of resin and pitch and turpentine were piled, tier upon tier, hundreds and thousands upon thousands of them. Potestatem Desmit looked at them and shuddered at the desolation which a single torch would produce in an instant. He felt that the chances were desperate, and he had half a mind to apply the torch himself and at least deprive the approaching horde of the savage pleasure of destroying his substance. But he had great confidence in himself, his own powers of persuasion and diplomacy. He would try them once more, and would not fail to make them serve for all they might be worth, to save this hoarded treasure.

It was barely daylight the next morning when he was awakened by the cry, "The Yanks are coming!" He had but a moment to question the frightened messenger, who pressed on, terror-stricken, in the very road which he might have known would be the path of the advancing enemy, instead of riding two miles into the heart of the boundless pine forest which stretched on either hand, where he would have been as safe from capture as if he had been in the center of the pyramid of Cheops.

Potestatem Desmit had his carriage geared up, and went coolly forth to meet the invaders. He had heard much of their savage ferocity, and was by no means ignorant of the danger which he ran in thus going voluntarily into their clutches. Nevertheless he did not falter. He had great reliance in his personal presence. So he dressed with care, and arrayed in clean linen and a suit of the finest broadcloth, then exceedingly rare in the Confederacy, and with his snowy hair and beard, his high hat, his hands crossed over a gold-headed cane, and gold-mounted glasses upon his nose, he set out upon his mission. The night before he had prudently removed from the place every drop of spirits except a small demijohn of old peach-brandy, which he put under the seat of his carriage, intending therewith to regale the highest official whom he should succeed in approaching, even though it should be the dreaded Sherman himself.

He had proceeded perhaps half a mile, when his carriage was all at once surrounded by a motley crew of curiously dressed but well-armed ruffians, whose very appearance disgusted and alarmed him. With oaths and threats the lumbering chariot, which represented in itself no little of respectability, was stopped. The appearance of such a vehicle upon the sandy road of the pine woods coming directly toward the advancing column struck the "bummers" with surprise. They made a thousand inquiries of the frightened driver, and were about to remove and appropriate the sleek span of carriage-horses when the occupant of the carriage, opening the window, thrust out his head, and with a face flaming with indignation ordered them to desist, bestowing upon them a volley of epithets, beginning with "rascals" and running as far into the language of abuse as his somewhat heated imagination could carry him.

"Hello, Bill," said the bummer who was unfastening the right-wheeler, as he looked back and saw the red face framed in a circlet of white hair and beard. "Just look at this old sunflower, will you? I guess the old bird must think he commands this brigade. Ha! ha! ha! I say, old fellow, when did you leave the ark?"

"And was Noah and his family well when you bid 'em good-by?" queried another.

This levity and ridicule were too much for Colonel P. Desmit to endure. He leaned out of the carriage window, and shaking his gold-headed cane at the mirthful marauders denounced them in language fearful in its impotent wrath.

"Take me to General Sherman, you rascals! I want to see the general!" he yelled over and over again.

"The hell you do! Well, now, mister, don't you know that the General is too nervous to see company today? He's just sent us on ahead a bit to say to strangers that he's compelled to refuse all visitors to-day. He gits that way sometimes, does 'Old Bill,' so ye mustn't think hard of him, at all."

"Take me to the general, you plundering pirates!" vociferated the enraged Colonel. "I'll see if a country gentleman travelling in his own carriage along the highway is to be robbed and abused in this manner!"

"Robbed, did he say?" queried one, with the unmistakable brogue of an Irishman. "Faith, it must be the gintleman has somethin' very important along wid him in the carriage, that he's gittin' so excited about; and its meself that'll not see the gintleman imposed upon, sure." This with a wink at his comrades. Then to the occupant of the carriage: "What did yer honor say might be yer name, now? It's very partickler the General is about insthructin' us ter ax the names of thim that's wantin' an' inthroduction to him, ye know?"

The solemnity of this address half deceived the irate Southron, and he answered with dignity, "Desmit—Colonel Potestatem Desmit, of Horsford County, sir."

"Ah, d'ye hear that, b'ys? Faith, it's a kurnel it is ye've been a shtoppin' here upon the highway! Shure it may be he's a goin' to the Gineral wid a flag of thruce, belike."

"I do wish to treat with the General," said Desmit, thinking he saw a chance to put in a favorable word.

"An' d'ye hear that, b'ys? Shure the gintleman wants to thrate the Gineral. Faith it'll be right glad the auld b'y'll be of a dhrap of somethin' good down here in the pine woods."

"Can I see the General, gentlemen?" asked Desmit, with a growing feeling that he had taken the wrong course to accomplish his end. The crowd of "bummers" constantly grew larger. They were mounted upon horses and mules, jacks and jennets, and one of them had put a "McClellan saddle" and a gag-bit upon one of the black polled cattle which abound in that region, and which ambled easily and briskly along with his rider's feet just brushing the low "poverty-pines" which grew by the roadside. They wore all sorts of clothing. The blue and the gray were already peacefully intermixed in the garments of most of them. The most grotesque variety prevailed especially in their head-gear, which culminated in the case of one who wore a long, barrel-shaped, slatted sun-bonnet made out of spotted calico. They were boisterous and even amusing, had they not been well armed and apparently without fear or reverence for any authority or individual. For the present, the Irishman was evidently in command, by virtue of his witty tongue.

"Can ye see the Gineral, Kurnel?" said he, with the utmost apparent deference; "av coorse ye can, sir, only it'll be necessary for you to lave your carriage an' the horses and the nagur here in the care of these gintlemen, while I takes ye to the Gineral mesilf."

"Why can I not drive on?"

"Why can't ye dhrive? Is it a Kurnel ye is, an' don't know that? Shure the cavalry an' the arthillery an' the caysons an' one thing an' another of that kind would soon crush a chayriot like that to flinders, ye know."

"I cannot leave my carriage," said Desmit.

"Mein Gott, shust hear him now!" said a voice on the other side, which caused Desmit to turn with a start. A bearded German, with a pair of myoptic glasses adding their glare to the peculiar intensity of the short-sighted gaze, had climbed upon the opposite wheel during his conversation with Pat, and leaning half through the window was scanning carefully the inside of the carriage. He had already one hand on the demijohn of peach-brandy upon which the owner's hopes so much depended. Potestatem Desmit was no coward, and his gold-headed cane made the acquaintance of the Dutchman's poll before he had time to utter a word of protestation.

It was all over in a minute, then. There was a rush and a scramble. The old man was dragged out of his carriage, fighting manfully but vainly. Twenty hands laid hold upon him. The gold-headed cane vanished; the gold-mounted glasses disappeared; his watch leaped from his pocket, and the chain was soon dangling at the fob of one of the still laughing marauders. Then one insisted that his hat was unbecoming for a colonel, and a battered and dirty infantry cap with a half-obliterated corps badge and regimental number was jammed down on his gray hairs; he was required to remove his coat, and then another took a fancy to his vest. The one who took his coat gave him in exchange a very ragged, greasy, and altogether disgusting cavalry jacket, much too short, and not large enough to button. The carriage was almost torn in pieces in the search for treasure. Swords and bayonets were thrust through the panelling; the cushions were ripped open, the cover torn off, and every possible hiding-place examined. Then thinking it must be about his person, they compelled him to take off his boots and stockings. In their stead a pair of almost soleless shoes were thrown him by one who appropriated the boots.

Meantime the Irishman had distributed the contents of the demijohn, after having filled his own canteen. Then there was great hilarity. The taste of the "colonel" was loudly applauded; his health was drunk, and it was finally decided to move on with him in charge. The "bummer" who rode the polled ox had, in the mean time, shifted his saddle to one of the carriage-horses, and kindly offered the steer to the "colonel." One who had come upon foot had already mounted the other horse. The driver performed a last service for his master, now pale, trembling, and tearful at the insults and atrocities he was called on to undergo, by spreading one of the carriage cushions over the animal's back and helping the queerly-habited potentate to mount his insignificant steed. It was better than marching through the hot sand on foot, however.

When they reached the little hamlet which had grown up around his collection of turpentine distilleries they saw a strange sight. The road which bore still further to the southward was full of blue-coated soldiers, who marched along with the peculiar swinging gait which marked the army that "went down to the sea." Beyond the low bridge, under a clump of pines which had been spared for shade, stood a group of horsemen, one of whom read a slip of paper, or rather shouted its contents to the soldiery as they passed, while he flourished the paper above his head. Instantly the column was in an uproar. Caps were thrown into the air, voices grew hoarse with shouting; frantic gesticulation, tearful eyes and laughter, yells, inane antics, queer combinations of sacrilegious oaths and absurd embraces were everywhere to be seen and heard.

"Who is that?" asked Desmit of the Irishman, near whom he had kept, pointing to the leading man of the group under the tree.

"Faith, Kurnel, that is Gineral —. Would ye like an inthroduction, Kurnel?"

"Yes, yes," said Desmit impatiently.

"Thin come wid me. Shure I'll give ye one, an' tell him ye sint him a dhrink of auld pache to cilebrate the good news with. Come along, thin!"

Just as they stepped upon the bridge Desmit heard a lank Hoosier ask,

"What is in them bar'ls?"

And some one answered,

"Turpentine."

"Hooray!" said the first. "A bonfire!"

"Hurry! hurry!" Desmit cried to his guide.

"Come on thin, auld gintleman. It's mesilf that'll not go back on a man that furnishes a good dhram for so joyful an occasion."

They dismounted, and, pressing their way through the surging mass on the bridge, approached the group under the pines.

"Gineral," said the Irishman, taking off the silk hat which Desmit had worn and waving it in the air; "Gineral, I have the honor to inthroduce to ye an' auld gintleman—one av the vera furst families—that's come out to mate ye, an' begs that ye'll taste jest a dhrap av the finest auld pache that ivver ran over yer tongue, jist ter cilebrate this vera joyful occasion."

He waved his hat toward Desmit, and handed up his canteen at once. The act was full of the audacity of his race, but the news had overthrown all sense of discipline. The officer even lifted the canteen to his lips, and no doubt finding Pat's assertion as to its quality to be true, allowed a reasonable quantity of its aromatic contents to glide down his throat, and then handed it to one of his companions.

"General! General!" shrieked Desmit in desperation, as he rushed forward.

"What do you want, sir?" said the officer sternly.

There was a rush, a crackle, and a still louder shout.

Both turned and saw a tongue of red flame with a black, sooty tip leap suddenly skyward. The great mass of naval stores was fired, and no power on earth could save a barrel of them now. Desmit staggered to the nearest tree, and faint and trembling watched the flame. How it raged! How the barrels burst and the liquid flame poured over the ground and into the river! Still it burned! The whole earth seemed aflame! How the black billows of heavy smoke poured upward, hiding the day! The wind shifted and swept the smoke-wave over above the crowding, hustling, shouting column. It began to rain, but under the mass of heavy smoke the group at the pines stood dry.

And still, out of the two openings in the dark pines upon the other side of the stream, poured the two blue-clad, steel-crowned columns! Still the staff officer shouted the glad tidings, "*Lee—surrendered—unconditionally!*"[18] Still waved aloft the dispatch! Still the boundless forests rang with shouts! Still the fierce flame raged, and from the column which had gone into the forest beyond came back the solemn chant, which sounded at that moment like the fateful voice of an avenging angel:

> "John Brown's body lies a-mouldering in the grave;
> His soul is marching on!"[19]

One who looked upon the scene thinks of it always when he reads of the last great day—the boundless flame—the fervent heat—the shouts—the thousands like the sands of the sea—all are not to be forgotten until the likeness merges into the dread reality!

The Irishman touched Desmit as he leaned against the pine.

"War that yours, misther?" he asked, not unkindly.

Desmit nodded affirmatively.

"Here," said the other, extending his canteen. "There's a drink left. Take it."

Desmit took it with a trembling hand, and drained it to the last drop.

"That's right," said the Irishman sympathetically. "I'm right sorry for ye, misther, that I am; but don't ye nivver give up heart. There's more turpentine where that come from, and this thing's over now. I couldn't find yer bull for ye, mister, but here's a mule. Ye'd better jest take him and git away from here before this row's over. Nobody'll miss ye now."

Two weeks afterward a queerly clad figure rode up to the elegant mansion of Colonel Potestatem Desmit, overlooking the pleasant town of Louisburg in the county of Horsford, and found a party of Federal officers lounging upon his wide porches and making merry after war's alarums!

CHAPTER XIII.

NEGOTIATING A TREATY.

NOT ONLY DID Colonel Desmit lose his cotton and naval stores; but the funds which he had invested, with cautious foresight, in the bonds of the State and the issues of its banks, were also made worthless by the result of the war. Contrary to the expectations of the most prudent and far-seeing, the bonds issued by the States in rebellion during the period of war, were declared to be attaint with treason, and by the supreme power of the land were forbidden to be paid. In addition to this he found himself what was properly termed "land-poor." The numerous small plantations which he had acquired in different parts of the country, in pursuance of his original and inherited design of acquiring wealth by slave-culture, though intrinsically very valuable, were just at this time in the highest degree unavailable. All lands had depreciated to a considerable extent, but the high price of cotton had tempted many Northern settlers and capitalists into that belt of country where this staple had been most successfully raised, and their purchases, as well as the continued high price of the staple, had kept up the prices of cotton-lands far beyond all others.

Then, too, the lack of ready money throughout the country and the general indebtedness made an absolute dearth of buyers. In the four years of war there had been no collections. The courts had been debarred from judgment and execution. The sheriff had been without process, the lawyer without fees, the creditor without his money. Few indeed had taken advantage of this state of affairs to pay debts. Money had been as plenty as the forest leaves in autumn, and almost as valueless. The creditor had not desired to realize on his securities, and few debtors had cared to relieve themselves. There had come to be a sort of general belief that when the war ended there would be a jubilee for all debtors—that each one would hold what he had, and that a promise to pay would no more trouble or make afraid even the most timid soul. So that when the courts came to be unchained and the torrent of judgments and executions poured forth under their seals, the whole country was flooded with bankruptcy. Almost nobody could pay. A few, by deft use of present advantgaes, gathered means to discharge their own liabilities and take advantage of the failure of others to do so. Yet they were few indeed. On every court-house the advertisements of sale covered the panels of the door and overflowed upon the walls. Thousands of homesteads, aye, hundreds of thousands of homes—millions of acres—were sold almost for a song—frequently less than a shilling an acre, generally less than a dollar.

Colonel Desmit had not been an exception to these rules. He had not paid the obligations maturing during the war simply because he knew he could not be compelled to do so. Instead of that, he had invested his surplus in lands, cotton, and naval stores. Now the evil day was not far off, as he knew, and he had little to meet it. Nevertheless he made a brave effort. The ruggedness of the disowned family of Smiths and the chicanery inherited from the gnarly-headed and subtle-minded old judge came to his rescue, and he determined not to fail without a fight. He shingled himself with deeds of trust and sales under fraudulent judgments or friendly liens, to delay if they did not avert calamity. Then he set himself at work to effect sales. He soon swallowed his wrath and appealed to the North—the enemy to whom he owed all his calamities, as he thought. He sent flaming circulars to bleak New England—health-exhibits to the smitten of consumption, painting the advantages of climate, soil, and society—did all in his power to induce immigrants to come and buy, in order that he might beat off poverty and failure and open disgrace. He made a brave fight, but it had never occurred to him to sell an acre to a colored man when he was accosted by Nimbus, who, still wearing some part of his uniform, came over to negotiate with him for the purchase of Red Wing.

All these untoward events had not made the master of Knapp-of-Reeds peculiarly amiable, or kindly disposed toward any whom he deemed in the remotest manner responsible for his loss. For two classes he could not find words sufficient to express his loathing—namely, Yankees and Secessionists. To the former directly and to the latter indirectly he attributed all his ills. The colored man he hated as a man, as bitterly as he had before highly prized him as a slave. At the outset of the war he had been openly blamed for his coolness toward the cause of the Confederacy. Then, for a time, he had acquiesced in what was done—had "gone with his State," as it was then expressed—and still later, when convinced of the hopelessness of the struggle, he had advocated peace measures; to save his property at all hazards, some said; because he was at heart a Unionist, others declared. So, he had come to regard himself as well disposed toward the Union, and even had convinced himself that he had suffered persecution for righteousness' sake, when, in truth, his "Unionism" was only an investment made to avoid loss.

These things, however, tended to embitter him all the more against all those persons and events in any manner connected with his misfortunes. It was in such a mood and under such circumstances, that word was brought to Mr. Desmit in his private library, that "a nigger" wanted to see him. The servant did not know his name, what he wanted, or where he came from. She could only say that he had ridden there on a "right peart mule" and was a "right smart-looking boy." She was ordered to bring him in, and Nimbus stood before his master for the first time since he had been sent down the country to work on fortifications intended to prevent the realization of his race's long-delayed vision of freedom. He came with his hat in his hand, saying respectfully,

"How d'ye, Marse Desmit?"

"Is that you, Nimbus? Get right out of here! I don't want any such grand rascal nigger in my house."

"But, Marse Desmit," began the colored man, greatly flurried by this rude greeting.

"I don't want any 'buts.' Damn you, I've had enough of all such cattle. What are you here for, anyhow? Why don't you go back to the Yankees that you ran away to? I suppose you want I should feed you, clothe you, support you, as I've been doing for your lazy wife and children ever since the surrender. I shan't do it a day longer—not a day! D'ye hear? Get off from my land before the sun goes down to-morrow or I'll have the overseer set his dogs on you."

"All right," said Nimbus coolly; "jes yer pay my wife what's due her and we'll leave ez soon ez yer please."

"Due her? You damned black rascal, do you stand there and tell me I owe her anything?"

Strangely enough, the colored man did not quail. His army life had taught him to stand his ground, even against a white man, and he had not yet learned how necessary it was to unlearn the lesson of liberty and assume again the role of the slave. The white man was astounded. Here was a "sassy nigger" indeed! This was what freedom did for them!

"Her papers dat you gib her at de hirin', Marse Potem," said Nimbus, "says dat yer shall pay her fo' dollars a month an' rations. She's hed de rations all reg'lar, Marse Desmit; dat's all right, but not a dollar ob de money."

"You lie, you black rascal!" said Desmit excitedly; "she's drawn every cent of it!"

"Wal," said Nimbus, "ef dat's what yer say, we'll hev ter let de 'Bureau' settle it."

"What, sir? You rascal, do you threaten me with the 'Bureau'?" shouted Desmit, starting toward him in a rage, and aiming a blow at him with the heavy walking-stick he carried.

"Don't do dat, Marse Desmit," cried the colored man; "don't do dat!"

There was a dangerous gleam in his eye, but the white man did not heed the warning. His blow fell not on the colored man's head, but on his up-raised arm, and the next moment the cane was wrested from his hands, and the recent slave stood over his former master as he lay upon the floor, where he had fallen or been thrown, and said:

"Don't yer try dat, Marse Desmit; I won't bar it—dat I won't, from no man, black ner white. I'se been a sojer sence I was a slave, an' ther don't no man hit me a lick jes cos I'm black enny mo'. Yer's an' ole man, Marse Desmit, an' yer wuz a good 'nough marster ter me in the ole times, but yer mustn't try ter beat a free man. I don't want ter hurt yer, but yer mustn't do dat!"

"Then get out of here instantly," said Desmit, rising and pointing toward the door.

"All right, Marse," said Nimbus, stooping for his hat; " 'tain't no use fer ye to be so mad, though. I jes come fer to make a trade wid ye."

"Get out of here, you damned, treacherous, ungrateful, black rascal. I wish every one of your whole race had the small-pox! Get out!"

As Nimbus turned to go, he continued:

"And get your damned lazy tribe off from my plantation before to-morrow night, if you don't want the dogs put on them, too!"

"I ain't afeard o' yer dogs," said Nimbus, as he went down the hall, and, mounting his mule, rode away.

With every step his wrath increased. It was well for Potestatem Desmit that he was not present to feel the anger of the black giant whom he had enraged. Once or twice he turned back, gesticulating fiercely and trembling with rage. Then he seemed to think better of it, and, turning his mule into the town a mile off his road, he lodged a complaint against his old master, with the officer of the "Bureau," and then rode quietly home, satisfied to "let de law take its course," as he said. He was glad that there was a law for him—a law that put him on the level with his old master—and meditated gratefully, as he rode home, on what the nation had wrought in his behalf since the time when "Marse Desmit" had sent him along that very road with an order to "Marse Ware" to give him "twenty lashes well laid on." The silly fellow thought that thenceforth he was going to have a "white man's chance in life." He did not know that in our free American Government, while the Federal power can lawfully and properly ordain and establish the theoretical rights of its citizens, it has no legal power to support and maintain those rights against the encroachment of any of the States, since in those matters the State is sovereign, and the part is greater than the whole.[20]

CHAPTER XIV.

BORN OF THE STORM.

PERHAPS THERE WAS NEVER any more galling and hated badge of defeat imposed upon a conquered people than the "Bureau of Freedmen, Refugees, and Abandoned Lands," a branch of the Federal executive power which grew out of the necessities of the struggle to put down rebellion, and to which, little by little, came to be referred very many of those matters which could by no means be neglected, but which did not properly fall within the purview of any other branch of military administration. It is known, in these latter days, simply as the Freedmen's Bureau, and thought to have been a terrible engine of oppression and terror and infamy, because of the denunciations which the former slave-owners heaped upon it, and the usually accepted idea that the mismanaged and malodorous Freedmen's Savings Bank[21] was, somehow or other, an outgrowth and exponent of this institution. The poor thing is dead now, and, like dead humanity, the good it did has been interred with its bones. It has been buried, with curses deep and bitter for its funeral obsequies. Its officers have been loaded with infamy. Even its wonderful results have been hidden from the sight of man, and its history blackened with shame and hate. It is one of the curious indices of public feeling that the North listened, at first, with good-natured indifference to the virulent diatribes of the recently conquered people in regard to this institution; after a time wonder succeeded to indifference; until finally, while it was still an active branch of the public service, wondering credulity succeeded, and its name became synonymous with disgrace; so that now there is hardly a corner of the land in which a man can be found brave enough to confess that he wore the uniform and performed the duties of an agent of the "Freedmen's Bureau." The thorough subserviency of Northern sentiment to the domination of that masterly will which characterized "the South" of the old regime was never better illustrated. "Curse me this people!" said the Southern Balak[22]—of the Abolitionist first, of the Bureau-Officer next, and then of the Carpet-Bagger. The Northern Balaam hemmed and paltered, and then—*cursed the children of his loins!*

Of the freedmen, our recent allies in war, the grateful and devoted friends of the nation which had opened for them the gateway of the future, not one of the whole four millions had a word to utter in reproach of this branch of the service, in which they were particularly interested. Strangely enough, too, none of those Union men of the South, who had been refugees during the war or friends of that Union after its close, joined in the complaints and denunciations which were visited on this institution and its agents. Neither did the teachers of colored schools, nor the officers and agents of those charitable and missionary associations of the North, whose especial work and purpose was the elevation and enlightenment of the colored man, see fit to unite in that torrent of detraction which swept over the country in regard to the "Bureau" and its agents. But then, it may be that none of these classes were able to judge truly and impartially of its character and works! They may have been prepossessed in its favor to an extent which prevented a fair and honest determination in regard to it.

Certain it is that those who stood upon the other side—those who instituted and carried on rebellion, or the greater part of them, and every one of those who opposed reconstruction, who fought to the last moment the enfranchisement of the black; every one who denied the right of the nation to emancipate the slave; every one who clamored for the payment of the State debts contracted during the war; all of those who proposed and imposed the famous "black codes,"—every one of these classes and every man of each class avowed himself unable to find words to express the infamy, corruption, and oppression which characterized the administration of that climacteric outrage upon a brave, generous, overwhelmed but unconquered —forgiving but not to be forgiven, people.

They felt themselves to have been in all things utterly innocent and guileless. The luck of war had been terribly against them, they considered, but the right remained with them. They were virtuous. Their opponents had not only been the aggressors at the outset, but had shown themselves little better than savages by the manner in which they had conducted the war; and, to crown the infamy of their character, had imposed upon "the South" at its close that most nefarious of all detestable forms of oppressive degradation, "the Bureau." Their orators grew magniloquent over its tyrannical oppression; the Southern press overflowed with that marvellous exuberance of diatribe of which they are the acknowledged masters—to all of which the complaisant North gave a ready and subservient concurrence, until the very name reeked in the public mind with infamous associations and degrading ideas.

A few men tried to stem the torrent. Some who had been in its service even dared to insist that they had not thereby rendered themselves infamous and unworthy. The nation listened for a time with kindly pity to their indignant protests, and then buried the troublesome and persistent clamorers in the silence of calm but considerate disbelief. They were quietly allowed to sink into the charitable grave of unquestioning oblivion. It was not any personal attaint which befouled their names and blasted their public prospects, but simply the fact that they had obeyed the nation's behest and done a work assigned to them by the country's rulers. Thus it came to pass that in one third of the country it was an ineffaceable brand of shame to have been at any time an agent or officer of this Bureau, and throughout the rest of the country it was accounted a fair ground for suspicion. In it all, the conquering element was simply the obedient indicator which recorded and proclaimed the sentiment and wish of the conquered. The words of the enemy were always regarded as being stamped with the mint-mark of truth and verity, while the declarations of our allies accounted so apparently false and spurious as to be unworthy of consideration, even when attested by sworn witnesses and written in blood upon a page of history tear-blotted and stained with savage deeds. All this was perfectly natural, however, and arose, almost unavoidably, from the circumstances under which the institution was created and the duties which it was called upon to discharge. It may not be amiss to consider again the circumstances under which it came to exist.

This is how this institution had its origin: As the war to put down rebellion progressed and our armies advanced farther and farther into the heart of the Confederacy, the most devoted and malignant adherents of the Confederate cause abandoned their homes and all that they could not easily take with them, and fled within the Confederate lines. Those white people who were adverse to the Confederate cause, or at least lukewarm in its support, spurred by the rigors of conscription and the dangers of proscription and imprisonment, took their lives in their hands, left their homes, and fled by every available road to the shelter of the Federal forces. Those who had no homes—the slaves—either deserted by their owners or fancying they saw in that direction a glimmer of possible freedom, swarmed in flank and rear of every blue-clad column which invaded the Confederacy, by thousands and tens of thousands. They fled as the Israelites did from the bondage of Egypt, with that sort of instinctive terror which has in all ages led individuals, peoples, and races to flee from the scene of oppression. The whites who came to us were called "refugees," and the blacks at first "contrabands," and after January 1, 1863, "freedmen." Of course they had to be taken care of. The "refugee" brought nothing with him; the freedman had nothing to bring. The abandoned lands of the Confederates were, in many cases, susceptible of being used to employ and supply these needy classes who came to us for aid and sustenance. It was to do this that the Freedmen's Bureau was created.

Its mission was twofold—to extend the helping hand to the needy who without such aid must have perished by disease and want, and to reduce the expenses of such charity by the cultivation and utilization of abandoned lands. It was both a business and a missionary enterprise. This was its work and mission until the war ended. Its "agents" were chosen from among the wounded veteran officers of our army, or were detached from active service by reason of their supposed fitness on account of character or attainments. Almost every one of them had won honor with the loss of limb or of health; all had the indorsement and earnest approval of men high in command of our armies, who had personal knowledge of their character and believed in their fitness. This renders it all the more remarkable that these men should so soon and so universally, as was stoutly alleged and weakly believed, have become thieves and vagabonds—corrupters of the blacks and oppressors of the whites. It only shows how altogether impossible it is to foresee the consequences of any important social or political movement upon the lives and characters of those exposed to its influences.

When the war ended there were four millions of men, women, and children without homes, houses, lands, money, food, knowledge, law, right, family, friends, or possibility for self-support. All these the Bureau adopted. They constituted a vast family of foundlings, whose care was a most difficult and delicate matter, but there was not one among them all who complained of the treatment they received.

It is somewhat strange, too, that the officers of this branch of the service should have all misbehaved in exactly the same manner. Their acts of oppression and outrage were always perpetrated in defence of some supposed right of a defenceless and friendless race, overwhelmed with poverty—the bondmen of ignorance—who had no money with which to corrupt, no art with which to beguile, and no power with which to overawe these representatives of authority. For the first time in the history of mankind, the corrupt and unprincipled agents of undefined power became the servants, friends, protectors, agents, and promoters of the poor and weak and the oppressors of the rich, the strong, the learned, and the astute.

It may be said that this view cannot be true; that thousands of men selected from the officers of our citizen-soldiery by the unanswerable certificate of disabling wounds and the added prestige of their commander's recommendation, a class of men in physical, intellectual and moral power and attainments far superior to the average of the American people—it may be said that such could not have become all at once infamously bad; and, if they did suffer such transformation, would have oppressed the blacks at the instigation of the whites, who were willing and able to pay well for such subversion of authority, and not the reverse. This would seem to be true, but we are not now dealing with speculations, but with facts! We know that they did become such a pest because at the South they were likened to the plagues of Egypt, and the North reiterated and affirmed this cry and condoled with the victims of the oppression with much show of penitence, and an unappeasable wrath toward the instruments of the iniquity. Thus the voice of the people—that voice which is but another form of the voice of God—proclaimed these facts to the world, so that they must thenceforth be held indisputable and true beyond the utmost temerity of scepticism. The *facts* remain. The puzzling *why*, let whosoever will endeavor to elucidate.

Perhaps the most outrageous and debasing of all the acts of the Bureau, in the eyes of those who love to term themselves "the South," was the fact that its officers and agents, first of all, allowed the colored man to be sworn in opposition to and in contradiction of the word of a white man.

That this should be exasperating and degrading to the Southern white man was most natural and reasonable. The very corner-stone of Southern legislation and jurisprudence for more than a hundred years was based upon this idea: the negro can have no rights, and can testify as to no rights or wrongs, as against a white man. So that the master might take his slave with him when he committed murder or did any other act in contravention of law or right, and that slave was like the mute eunuch of the seraglio, silent and voiceless before the law. Indeed, the law had done for the slave-owner, with infinitely more of mercy and kindness, what the mutilators of the upper Nile were wont to do for the keepers of the harems of Cairo and Constantinople —provided them with slaves who should see and hear and serve, but should never testify of what they saw and knew. To reverse this rule, grown ancient and venerable by the practice of generations, to open the mouths which had so long been sealed, was only less infamous and dangerous than to accord credence to the words they might utter. To do both was to "turn back the tide of time," indeed, and it passed the power of language to portray the anger, disgust, and degradation which it produced in the Southern mind. To be summoned before the officer of the Bureau, confronted with a negro who denied his most solemn averments, and was protected in doing so by the officer who, perhaps, showed the bias of the oppressor by believing the negro instead of the gentleman, was unquestionably, to the Southerner, the most degrading ordeal he could by any possibility be called upon to pass through.

From this it will be understood that Colonel Desmit passed a most uneasy night after Nimbus had left his house. He had been summoned before the Bureau! He had expected it. Hardly had he given way to his petulant anger when he recognized the folly of his course. The demeanor of the colored man had been so "sassy" and aggravating, however, that no one could have resisted his wrath, he was sure. Indeed, now that he came to look back at it, he wondered that he had been so considerate. He was amazed that he had not shot the impudent rascal on the spot instead of striking him with his walking-stick, which he was very confident was the worst that could be urged against him. However, that was enough, for he remembered with horror that, not long before, this same Bureau officer had actually imprisoned a most respectable and correct man for having whipped a "nigger" at work in his crop, who had been "too sassy" to be tolerated by any gentleman.

So it was with much trepidation that the old man went into the town the next morning, secured the services of a lawyer, and prepared for his trial before the "Bureau." Nimbus was intercepted as he came into town with his wife, and an attempt made to induce him to withdraw the prosecution, but that high-minded litigant would hear nothing of the proposed compromise. He had put his hand to the plow and would not look back. He had appealed to the law—"the Bureau" and only "the Bureau" should decide it. So Colonel Desmit and his lawyer asked a few hours' delay and prepared themselves to resist and disprove the charge of assault upon Nimbus. The lawyer once proposed to examine the papers in the case, but Desmit said that was useless—the boy was no liar, though they must make him out one if they could. So, at the time appointed, with his lawyer and train of witnesses, he went before "the Bureau," and there met Nimbus and his wife, Lugena.

"The Bureau" wore the uniform of a captain of United States infantry, and was a man about forty-five years of age, grave and serious of look, with an empty sleeve folded decorously over his breast. His calm blue eyes, pale, refined face, and serious air gave him the appearance of a minister rather than a ruthless oppressor, but his reputation for cruelty among certain people was as well established as that of Jeffreys.[23] He greeted Mr. Desmit and his attorney with somewhat constrained politeness, and when they were seated proceeded to read the complaint, which simply recited that Colonel Desmit, having employed Lugena, the wife of complainant, at a given rate per month, had failed to make payment, and had finally, without cause, ordered her off his premises.

"Is that all?" asked the lawyer.

"That is all," answered the officer.

"Has no other complaint been lodged against Colonel Desmit?"

"None."

"We cannot—that is—we did not expect this," said the attorney, and then after a whispered consultation with his client, he added, "We are quite willing to make this matter right. We had entirely misunderstood the nature of the complaint."

"Have you any further complaint to make against Colonel Desmit?" asked the officer, of Nimbus.

"No," said that worthy, doubtfully. "He was pretty brash wid me, an' 'llowed ter hit me wid a stick; but he didn't—at least not ter speak on—so I don't make no 'count ob dat. 'Twas jes dis matter ob Lugeny's wuk dat made me bring him h'yer—nuffin' else."

"When did this matter of the stick occur?" asked the officer.

"On'y jes yeste'day, sah."

"Where was it?"

"Up ter Marse Potem's, sah. In his house."

"How did it happen?"

"Wal, you see, sah, I went up dar ter see ef I could buy a track ob lan' from him, an'—"

"What!" exclaimed Desmit, in astonishment. "You didn't say a word to me about land."

"No more I didn't," answered Nimbus, "kase yer didn't gib me no chance ter say a word 'bout it. 'Peared like de fus sight on me made yer mad, an' den yer jes feathered away on me, spite ob all I could do er say. Yer see, sah," to the officer, "I'd made a bit ob money in de wah, an' wanted ter see ef I could buy a bit ob pore lan' ob Marse Desmit—a track jes good fer nothin on'y fer a nigga ter starve on—but afore I could git to dat Marse Desmit got so uproarous-like dat I clean fergot what 'twas I cum fer."

"There was evidently a misunderstanding," said the attorney.

"I should think so," said the officer, dryly. "You say you have no complaint to make about that affair?" he added to Nimbus.

"No," said he; " 'twan't a ting ob any 'count, nohow. I can't make out what 'twas made Marse Potem so fractious anyhow. I reckon, as he says, dar must hev ben some mistake about it. Ef he'll fix up dis matter wid Lugena, I hain't no mo' complaint, an' I'se mighty sorry 'bout dat, kase Marse Desmit hab allus been mighty kin' ter me—all 'cept dis time an' once afo'."

"There's the money for the woman," said the attorney, laying some bills on the officer's table; "and I may say that my client greatly regrets the unfortunate misunderstanding with one of the best of his old slaves. He desires me to say that the woman's services have been entirely satisfactory, and that she can keep right on under the contract, if she desires."

So that was settled. The officer discharged Colonel Desmit, commended Nimbus for the sensible view he had taken of the quarrel, and the parties gave way for other matters which awaited the officer's attention.

This would not seem to have been so very oppressive, but anything growing out of the war which had resulted so disastrously for him was hateful to Colonel Desmit, and we should not wonder if his grandchildren told over, with burning cheeks, the story of the affront which was offered to their ancestor in haling him before that infamous tribunal, "the Bureau," to answer a charge preferred by a "nigger."

CHAPTER XV.

TO HIM AND HIS HEIRS FOREVER.

AFTER LEAVING THE office of "the Bureau," the parties repaired to that of the lawyer, and the trade for the land which had been so inopportunely forestalled by Colonel Desmit's hasty temper was entered upon in earnest. That gentleman's financial condition was such as to render the three or four hundred dollars of ready money which Nimbus could pay by no means undesirable, while the property itself seemed of so little value as to be regarded almost as an incumbrance to the plantation of which it was a part. Such was its well-established reputation for poverty of soil that Desmit had no idea that the purchaser would ever be able to meet one of his notes for the balance of the purchase money, and he looked forward to resuming the control of the property at no distant day, somewhat improved by the betterments which occupancy and attempted use would compel the purchaser to make. He regarded the cash to be paid in hand as just so much money accidentally found in his pathway, for which, in no event, was he to render any *quid pro quo.* But of this he said nothing. It was not his business to look after the interests of a "sassy nigger." In fact, he felt that the money was in a sense due to him on account of the scurvy trick that Nimbus had played him, in deserting to the Yankees after agreeing to look after his "niggers" on the breastworks, although, as the event proved, his master would have gained nothing by his remaining. So the former master and slave met on the level of barter and sale, and gave and took in the conflict of trade.

Except the small tract just about the old hostel, which has already been mentioned, the plantation, which included Red Wing, was descended from an ancestor of the Richards family, who had come from the North about the close of the Revolution and "entered" an immense tract in this section. It had, however, passed out of the family by purchase, and about the beginning of the war of Rebellion a life estate therein was held by its occupant, while the reversion belonged to certain parties in Indiana by virtue of the will of a common ancestor. This life-tenant's necessities compelled him to relinquish his estate, which was bought by Colonel Desmit, during the second year of the war, together with the fee which he had acquired in the tract belonging to the old Ordinary, not because he wanted the land about Red Wing, but because the plantation to which it was attached was a good one, and he could buy it on reasonable terms for Confederate currency. He expected to treat with the Indiana heirs and obtain their respective interests in the fee, which no doubt he would have been able to acquire very cheaply but for the intervening accident of war, as the life-tenant was yet of middle age and the succession consequently of little probable value to living reversioners. This, however, he had not done; but as his deed from the life-tenant was in form an exclusive and unlimited conveyance, it had been quite forgotten that the will of his grandfather limited it to a life estate. So when Nimbus and his friend and counsellor, Eliab Hill, sought to negotiate the purchase of Red Wing, no mention was made of that fact; neither was it alluded to when they came again to conclude the purchase, nor when instructions were given to Colonel Desmit's lawyer to prepare the necessary papers.[24]

The trade was soon brought to an apparently happy conclusion. Nimbus bought two hundred acres at a price of eight hundred dollars, paying one half the price agreed upon in cash, and for the balance gave three notes of equal amounts, one maturing each year thereafter, and received from Colonel Desmit a bond for title to the whole tract, with full covenants of warranty and seizin. Colonel Desmit accounted the notes of little value; Nimbus prized the bond for title above any patent of nobility. Before the first note fell due all had been discharged, and the bond for title was exchanged for a deed in fee, duly executed. So the recent slave, who had but lately been the subject of barter and sale, was clothed with the rights of a proprietor.

According to the former law, the slave was a sort of chattel-real. Without being attached to the land, he was transferable from one owner to another only by deed or will. In some States he descended as realty, in others as personalty, while in others still, he constituted a separate kind of heritable estate, which was especially provided for in the canons of descent and statutes regulating administration. There was even then of record in the county of Horsford a deed of sale, bearing the hand and seal of P. Desmit, and executed little more than a year previously, conveying to one Peyton Winburn "all the right, title, and interest of said Desmit, in and to a certain runaway negro boy named Nimbus." The said Winburn was a speculator in slaves who had long been the agent of Desmit in marketing his human crop, and who, in the very last hours of the Confederacy, was willing to risk a few dollars on the result. As he well stated it to himself, it was only staking one form of loss against another. He paid Confederate money for a runaway negro. If the Confederacy failed, the negro would be free; but then, too, the money would be worthless. So with grim humor he said to himself that he was only changing the form of his risk and could not possibly lose by the result. Thus, by implication of law, the recent *subject* of transfer by deed was elevated to the dignity of being a *party* thereto. The very instrument of his bondage became thereby the sceptre of his power. It was only an incident of freedom, but the difference it measured was infinite.

No wonder the former slave trembled with elation as he received this emblem of autonomy, or that there was a look of gloom on the face of the former master as he delivered the carefully-enrolled deed, made complete by his hand and seal, and attested by his attorney. It was the first time the one had felt the dignity of proprietorship, or the other had known the shame of fraud. The one thought of the bright future which lay before his children, to whom he dedicated Red Wing at that moment in his heart, in terms more solemn than the legal phrases in which Potestatem Desmit had guaranteed to them the estate in fee therein. The other thought of the far-away Indiana reversioners, of whose rights none knew aught save himself—himself and Walter Greer, who had gone away to the wilds of Texas, and might never be heard of any more. It was the first time he had ever committed a deliberate fraud, and when he handed the freedman the deed and said sadly, "I never expected to come down to this," those who heard him thought he meant his low estate, and pitied his misfortunes. He smiled meaningly and turned hastily away, when Nimbus, forgetting his own elation, said, in tones of earnest feeling:

"I declar, Marse Desmit, I'se sorry fer you—I is dat; an' I hopes yer'll come outen dis yer trouble a heap better nor yer's lookin' for."

Then they separated—the one to treasure his apples of Sodom,[25] the other to nourish the memory of his shame.

CHAPTER XVI.

A CHILD OF THE HILLS.

"COME AT ONCE; Oscar very low."

This was the dispatch which an awkward telegraph messenger handed to the principal teacher of "No. 5," one soft September day of 1866. He waited upon the rough stone step, while she, standing in the doorway, read it again and again, or seemed to do so, as if she could not make out the import of the few simple words it contained.

"No. 5" was a school-house in one of the townships of Bankshire County, in the Commonwealth of Massachusetts. In it were taught the children, within school age, of one of those little hamlets which have crept up the valleys of the White Mountains, toled on and on, year after year, farther and farther up the little rivulets that dash down the mountain slopes, by the rumble and clatter of newly-erected machinery.

These mountain streams are the magic handiwork of the nymphs and fays who for ages have lain hidden in the springs that burst out into little lakes upon the birch-crowned summits, and come rushing and tumbling down the rocky defiles to join the waters of the Housatuck. School-house No. 5 was thriftily placed on a bit of refractory land just opposite the junction of two streams which had their rise in two lakelets miles away from each other—one lying under the shadow of Pixey Mountain, and the other hidden among the wooded hills of Birket. They were called "ponds," but are, in truth, great springs, in whose icy coldness the mountain trout delight.

Back of the school-house, which, indeed, was half built into it, was a sharp, rocky hillside; across the road which ran before it was a placid pond, bordered on the farther side by a dark fringe of evergreens that lay between it and the wide expanse of white-armed birches and flaming maples, now beginning to feel the autumn's breath, on the rugged mountain-side above. A little to the left was the narrow gorge through which one of the streams discharged, its bottom studded with ponds and mills, and its sharp sides flecked with the little white-painted homes of well-to-do operatives; to the right and left along the other branch and the course of the united streams, the rumble of water-wheels, the puff of laboring engines, and the groan of tortured machinery never ceased. Machine-shops and cotton-factories, bagging-mills and box-mills, and wrapping-mills, and print-mills, and fine-paper-mills, and even mills for the making of those filmy creations of marvellous texture and wonderful durability which become the representatives of value in the form of bank-notes, were crowded into the narrow gorges. The water was fouled with chemic combinations from source to mouth. For miles up and down one hardly got a breath of air untainted with the fumes of chemicals. Bales of rags, loads of straw, packages of woody pulp, boxes of ultramarine dye, pipes leading from the distant mountain springs, and, above all, the rumble and the groaning of the beating-engines told to every sense that this was one of the great hillside centres of paper-manufacture in New England. The elegant residences of the owners were romantically situated on some half-isolated promonotory around which the stream sweeps, embowered with maples and begirt with willows at its base; or nestled away in some nook, moss-lined and hemlock-shaded, which marks where some spring brook bubbles down its brief career to the larger stream; or in some plateau upon the other side, backed by a scraggly old orchard, and hidden among great groves of rock-maples which the careful husbandman spared a hundred years ago for a "sugar-bush," little dreaming that the nabobs of the rushing streams would build homesteads beneath their shade. And all along, here and there, wherever a house could find a foothold or the native ruggedness be forced to yield one lodgment, houses and shops and crowded tenements stood thick. It was a busy and a populous village, full of wealth and not barren of poverty, stretched along the rushing tributary for more than a mile, and then branching with its constituent forks up into the mountain gorges.

In the very centre of this busy whirl of life stood the little white two-story school-house, flanked on one side by the dwelling of a mill-owner, and on the other by a boarding-house; and just below it, across the street, a machine-shop, and a little cottage of cased logs, with minute-paned windows, and a stone chimney which was built before the Revolution by the first inhabitant of the little valley. A little to the left of the school-house was a great granite boulder, rising almost to its eaves, which had been loosened from the mountain-side two miles up the gorge when the dam at the mouth of the pond gave way years before in a freshet, and brought down and left by the respectful torrent almost at the threshold of the temple of knowledge.

Such was the scene the Indian summer sun looked down upon, while the teacher stood gazing fixedly at the message which she held. Curious faces peered out of the windows and through the door, which she left ajar when she came into the hall. She took no note of this infraction of discipline.

"Any answer, ma'am?" The messenger-boy shifts his weight awkwardly upon the other foot, as he asks, but receives no reply.

For two years Mollie Ainslie, with her assistants, had dispensed the sweets of knowledge at "No. 5," to the children of the little hamlet. The hazy morning light revealed a small, lithe figure, scarcely taller than the messenger-boy that stood before her; a fair, white face; calm, gray eyes; hair with a glint of golden brown, which waved and rippled about a low, broad brow, and was gathered in a great shining coil behind; and a mouth clear-cut and firm, but now drawn and quivering with deep emotion. The comely head was finely poised upon the slender neck, and in the whole figure there was an air of self-reliance and power that accorded well with the position which she held. A simple gray dress, with a bright ribbon at the throat and a bunch of autumn flowers carelessly tucked into the belt which circled the trim waist, completed the picture framed in the doorway of the white school-house. She stood, with eyes fastened on the paper which she held in one hand, while the other pressed a pencil-head against her cheek, unmindful of the curious glances that were fixed upon her from within, until the messenger-boy had twice repeated his customary question:

"Any answer, ma'am?"

She reached forth her hand, slowly and without reply. The boy looked up and saw that she was gazing far beyond him and had a strained, fixed look in her eyes.

"Want a blank?" he asked, in a tone of unconscious sympathy.

She did not answer, but as he put his pad of blanks into her outstretched hand she drew it back and wrote, in a slow and absent manner, a message in these words:

"TO CAPTAIN OSCAR AINSLIE, *Boyleston, Va.*

"Coming.

"MOLLIE."

"Collect?" asked the boy.

"No!"

She inquired, and paid the charges in the same unheeding way. The messenger departed with a wistful glance at the dry, pained eyes which heeded him not. With a look of dumb entreaty at the overhanging mountain and misty, Indian summer sky, and a half perceptible shiver of dread, Mollie Ainslie turned and entered again the school-room.

CHAPTER XVII.

GOOD-MORROW AND FAREWELL.

A WEEK AFTERWARD, Mollie Ainslie stood beside the bed of her only brother and watched the sharp, short struggle which he made with their hereditary enemy, consumption. Weakened by wounds and exposure, he was but ill-prepared to resist the advances of the insidious foe, and when she reached his side she saw that the hope, even of delay, was gone. So she took her place, and with ready hand, brave heart, and steady purpose, brightened his pathway to the tomb.

Oscar and Mollie Ainslie were the only children of a New England clergyman whose life had lasted long enough, and whose means had been sufficient, with the closest economy, to educate them both according to the rigorous standards of the region in which they were born. Until the son entered college they had studied together, and the sister was almost as well prepared for the university course as the brother when they were separated. Then she stepped out of the race, and determined, though scarcely more than a child, to become herself a bread-winner, in order that her father's meager salary might be able to meet the drain of her brother's college expenses. She did this not only without murmuring, but with actual pleasure. Her ambition, which was boundless, centered upon her brother. She identified herself with him, and cheerfully gave up every advantage, in order that his opportunities might be more complete. To Oscar these sacrifices on his sister's part were very galling. He felt the wisdom of the course pursued toward him by his family, and was compelled to accede in silence to prevent the disappointment which his refusal would bring. Yet it was the keenest trial for him to think of accepting his sister's earnings, and only the conviction that to do so was the quickest and surest way to relieve her of the burden of self-support, induced him to submit to such an arrangement.

Hardly had he entered upon his college course when the war of Rebellion came on, and Oscar Ainslie saw in the patriotic excitement and the promise of stirring events a way out of a situation whose fetters were too heavy for him to bear by reason of their very tenderness. He was among the first, therefore, to enlist, happy thereby to forestall his sister's determination to engage in teaching, for his sake. His father was grieved at the son's abandonment of his projected career, but his heart was too patriotic to object. So he gave the bright-eyed young soldier his blessing as he bade him good-by, standing there before him, strong and trim, in his close-fitting cavalry uniform. He knew that Oscar's heart beat high with hope, and he would not check it, though he felt sure that they looked into each other's eyes for the last time. When his own were glazing over with the ghastly grave-light, more than two years afterward, they were gladdened by the announcement which came throbbing along the wires and made bright the whole printed page from which he read: "Private Oscar Ainslie, promoted to a Captaincy for gallant conduct on the field of Gettysburg." Upon this he rallied his fading energies, and waited for a week upon the very brink of the chill river, that he might hear, before he crossed over, from the young soldier himself, how this honor was won. When he had learned this he fell asleep, and not long after, the faithful wife who had shared his toils and sacrifices heard the ceaseless cry of his lonely spirit, and was gathered again to his arms upon the shore where beauty fadeth not forever.

The little homestead upon the rocky hillside overlooking the village was all that was left to the brother and sister; but it was more than the latter could enjoy alone, so she fled away and entered upon the vocation in which we found her engaged. Meantime her brother had risen in rank, and at the close of the war had been transferred to the regular army as a reward of distinguished merit. Then his hereditary foe had laid siege to his weakened frame, and a brother officer had telegraphed to the sister in the Bankshire hills the first warning of the coming end.

It was a month after her arrival at Boyleston, when her brother, overcoming the infatuation which usually attends that disease, saw that the end was near and made provision respecting it.

"Sis," he said, calling her by the pet name of their childhood, "what day of the month is it?"

"The thirteenth, Oscar—your birthday," she replied briskly. "Don't you see that I have been out and gathered leaves and flowers to decorate your room, in honor of the event?"

Her lap was full of autumn leaves—maple and gum, flaming and variegated, brown oak of various shapes and shades, golden hickory, the open burrs of the chinquapin, pine cones, and the dun scraggly balls of the black-gum, some glowing bunches of the flame-bush, with their wealth of bursting red berries, and a full-laden branch of the black-haw.

The bright October sun shone through the open window upon her as she arranged them with deft fingers, contrasting the various hues with loving skill, and weaving ornaments for different points in the bare room of the little country hotel where her brother lay. He watched her awhile in silence, and then said sadly,

"Yes, my last birthday."

Her lips trembled, and her head drooped lower over her lap, but she would not let him see her agitation. So she simply said,

"Do not say that, Oscar."

"No," he replied, "I ought not to say so. I should have said, my last earthly birthday. Sit closer, Sis, where I can see you better. I want to talk to you."

"Do you know," he continued, as she came and sat upon his bedside, spreading her many-hued treasures over the white coverlet, "that I meant to have been at home to-day?"

"And are you not?" she asked cheerfully. "Am I not with you?"

"True, Sis, and you are my home now; but, after all, I did want to see the old New England hills once more. One yearns for familiar scenes after years of war. I meant to have gone back and brought you here, away from the cold winters that sting, and bite, and kill. I hoped that, after rest, I might recover strength, and that you might here escape the shadow which has fastened upon me."

"Have you seen my horse, Midnight?" he asked, after a fit of coughing, followed by a dreamy silence.

"Yes."

"How do you like him?"

"He is a magnificent creature."

"Would he let you approach him?"

"I had no trouble in doing so."

"None? He's very vicious, too. Everybody has had trouble with him. Do you think you could ride him?"

"I have ridden him every day for two weeks."

"Ah! that is how you have kept so fresh." Then, after a pause, "Do you know how I got him?"

"I heard that he was captured."

"Yes, in the very last fight before the surrender at Appomattox. I was with Sheridan, you know.[26] We were pursuing the retreating columns—had been pressing them hotly ever since the break at Petersburg—on the rear and on both flanks, fighting, worrying, and watching all the time. On the last day, when the retreat had become a rout, as it seemed, a stand was made by a body of cavalry just on the crest of a smoothly-sloping hill. Not anticipating serious resistance, we did not wait for the artillery to come up and dislodge them, but deploying a brigade we rode on, jesting and gay, expecting to see them disperse when we came within range and join the rabble beyond. We were mistaken. Just when we got within easy charging distance, down they came, pell-mell, as dashing a body of dirty veterans as I ever saw. The attack was so unexpected that for a time we were swept off our feet and fairly carried backward with surprise. Then we rallied, and there was a sharp, short struggle. The enemy retreated, and we pressed after them. The man that rode this horse seemed to have selected me as his mark. He rode straight at me from the first. He was a fine, manly-looking fellow, and our swords were about the last that were crossed in the struggle. We had a sharp tussle for a while. I think he must have been struck by a chance shot. At least he was unseated just about the time my own horse was shot under me. Looking around amid the confusion I saw this horse without a rider. I was in mortal terror of being trampled by the shifting squadrons and did not delay, but sprang into the saddle and gave him the spur. When the Confederate bugles sounded the retreat I had a terrible struggle to keep him from obeying orders and carrying me away into their lines. After that, however, I had no trouble with him. But he is not kind to strangers, as a rule. I meant to have taken him home to you," he added, sadly. "You will have him now, and will prize him for my sake, will you not, Sis?"

"You know, Oscar, that everything you have ever loved or used will be held sacred," she answered tearfully.

"Yes, I know," he rejoined. "Sis, I wish you would make me a promise."

"You know I will."

"Well, then, do not go back to our old home this winter, nor the next, nor—but I will not impose terms upon you. Stay as long as you can content yourself in this region. I am afraid for you. I know you are stronger and have less of the consumptive taint about you than I, but I am afraid. You would have worked for me when I was in college, and I have worked only for you, since that time. All that I have saved—and I have saved all I could, for I knew that my time was not long—is yours. I have some money on deposit, some bonds, and a few articles of personal property—among the latter, Midnight. All these are yours. It will leave you comfortable for a time at least. Now, dear, promise that I shall be buried and remain in the cemetery the Government is making for the soldiers who fell in those last battles.[27] Somehow, I think it will keep you here, in order that you may be near me, and save you from the disease which is devouring my life."

A week afterward his companions followed, with reversed arms, the funereally-caparisoned Midnight to the grounds of the National Cemetery, and fired a salute over a new-made grave.

Nimbus, taking with him his helpless friend, had appealed, soon after his purchase, to the officer of the Bureau for aid in erecting a school-house at Red Wing. By him he had been referred to one of those charitable associations, through whose benign agency the great-hearted North poured its free bounty into the South immediately upon the cessation of strife.

Perhaps there has been no grander thing in our history than the eager generosity with which the Christian men and women of the North gave and wrought, to bring the boon of knowledge to the recently-enslaved. As the North gave, willingly and freely, men and millions to save the nation from disruption, so, when peace came, it gave other brave men and braver women, and other unstinted millions to strengthen the hands which generations of slavery had left feeble and inept. Not only the colored, but the white also, were the recipients of this bounty. The Queen City of the Confederacy, the proud capital of the commonwealth of Virginia, saw the strange spectacle of her own white children gathered, for the first time, into free public schools which were supported by Northern charity, and taught by noble women with whom her high-bred Christian dames and dainty maidens would not deign to associate. The civilization of the North in the very hour of victory threw aside the cartridge-box, and appealed at once to the contribution-box to heal the ravages of war. At the door of every church throughout the North, the appeal was posted for aid to open the eyes of the blind whose limbs had just been unshackled; and the worshipper, as he gave thanks for his rescued land, brought also an offering to aid in curing the ignorance which slavery had produced.

It was the noblest spectacle that Christian civilization has ever witnessed—thousands of schools organized in the country of a vanquished foe, almost before the smoke of battle had cleared away, free to the poorest of her citizens, supported by the charity, and taught by kindly-hearted daughters of a quick-forgiving enemy. The instinct of our liberty-loving people taught them that light must go with liberty, knowledge with power, to give either permanence or value. Thousands of white-souled angels of peace, the tenderly-reared and highly-cultured daughters of many a Northern home, came into the smitten land to do good to its poorest and weakest. Even to this day, two score of schools and colleges remain, the glorious mementoes of this enlightened bounty and Christian magnanimity.[28]

And how did the white brothers and sisters of these messengers of a matchless benevolence receive them? Ah, God! how sad that history should be compelled to make up so dark a record—abuse, contumely, violence! Christian tongues befouled with calumny! Christian lips blistered with falsehood! Christian hearts overflowing with hate! Christian pens reeking with ridicule because other Christians sought to do their needy fellows good! No wonder that faith grew weak and unbelief ran riot through all the land when men looked upon the spectacle! The present may excuse, for charity is kind; but the future is inexorable and writes its judgments with a pen hard-nibbed! But let us not anticipate. In thousands of Northern homes still live to testify these devoted sisters and daughters, now grown matronly. They are scattered through every state, almost in every hamlet of the North, while other thousands have gone, with the sad truth carved deep upon their souls, to testify in that court where "the action lies in its true nature."

Nimbus found men even more ready to assist than he and his fellows were to be aided. He himself gave the land and the timbers; the benevolent association to whom he had appealed furnished the other materials required; the colored men gave the major part of the labor, and, in less than a year from the time the purchase was made, the house was ready for the school, and the old hostelry prepared for the teachers that had been promised.

So it was that, when Nimbus came to the officer in charge at Boyleston and begged that a teacher might be sent to Red Wing, and met the reply that because of the great demand they had none to send, Mollie Ainslie, hearing of the request, with her load of sorrow yet heavy on her lonely heart, said, "Here am I; take me." She thought it a holy work. It was, to her simple heart, a love-offering to the memory of him who had given his life to secure the freedom of the race she was asked to aid in lifting up. The gentle child felt called of God to do missionary work for a weak and struggling people. She thought she felt the divine commandment which rested on the Nazarene. She did not stop to consider of the "impropriety" of her course. She did not even know that there was any impropriety in it. She thought her heart had heard the trumpet-call of duty, and, like Joan of Arc, though it took her among camps and dangers, she would not flinch. So Nimbus returned happy; an officer was sent to examine the location and report. Mollie, mounted upon Midnight, accompanied him. Of course, this fact and her unbounded delight at the quaint beauty of Red Wing was no part of the reason why Lieutenant Hamilton made a most glowing report on the location; but it was owing to that report that the officer at the head of the "Bureau" in that district, the department-commander, and finally the head of the Bureau, General Howard himself, indorsed the scheme most warmly and aided it most liberally. So that soon afterward the building was furnished as a school-house, Mollie Ainslie, with Lucy Ellison, an old schoolmate, as her assistant, was installed at the old hostlery, and bore sway in the school of three hundred dusky pupils which assembled daily at Red Wing. Midnight was given royal quarters in the old log-stable, which had been recovered and almost rebuilt for his especial delectation, the great square stall, with its bed of dry oak leaves, in which he stood knee-deep, being sufficient to satisfy even Miss Mollie's fastidious demands for the comfort of her petted steed. After a time Eliab Hill, to whose suggestion the whole plan was due, became also an assistant instructor.

Mollie Ainslie did not at all realize the nature of the task she had undertaken, or the burden of infamy and shame which a Christian people would heap upon her because of this kindly-meant work done in their midst!

CHAPTER XVIII.

"PRIME WRAPPERS."

IT WAS MORE THAN a year afterward. Quite a little village had grown up around the church and school-house at Red Wing, inhabited by colored men who had been attracted thither by the novelty of one of their own members being a proprietor. Encouraged by his example, one and another had bought parcels of his domain, until its size was materially reduced though its value was proportionately enhanced. Those who settled here were mostly mechanics—carpenters and masons—who worked here and there as they could find employment, a black-smith who wrought for himself, and some farm laborers who dreaded the yearly system of hire as too nearly allied to the slave *régime*, and so worked by the day upon the neighboring plantations. One or two bought somewhat larger tracts, intending to imitate the course of Nimbus and raise the fine tobacco for which the locality was already celebrated. All had built cheap log-houses, but their lots were well fenced and their "truck-patches" clean and thrifty, and the little hamlet was far from being unattractive, set as it was in the midst of the green forests which belted it about. From the plantations on either side, the children flocked to the school. So that when the registering officer and the sheriff rode into the settlement, a few days after the registration at Melton, it presented a thriving and busy spectacle.

Upon the hillside, back of his house, Nimbus, his wife, and two men whom he had employed were engaged in cutting the tobacco which waved—crinkled and rank, with light yellowish spots showing here and there upon the great leaves—a billow of green in the autumn wind. The new-comers halted and watched the process for a moment as they rode up to the barn, while the sheriff explained to the unfamiliar Northman:

"This is the first cutting, as it is called. They only take out the ripest this time, and leave the rest for another cutting, a week or two later. You see, he goes through there," pointing to Nimbus, "and picks out the ripe, yellow-looking plants. Then he sets his knife in at the top of the stalk where it has been broken off to prevent its running up to seed, and splits it down almost to the ground; then he cuts the stalk off below the split, and it is ready to be hung on the thin narrow strips of oak, which you see stuck up here and there, where the cutting has been done. They generally put from seven to ten plants on a stick, according to the size of the plants, so that the number of sticks makes a very accurate measure of the size of the crop, and an experienced hand can tell within a few pounds the weight of any bulk of tobacco by simply counting the sticks."

They rode up to the barn and found it already half full of tobacco. Nimbus came and showed the officer how the sticks were laid upon beams placed at proper intervals, the split plants hanging tops downward, close together, but not touching each other. The upper portions of the barn were first filled and then the lower tiers, until the tobacco hung within two or three feet of the bottom. The barn itself was made of logs, the interstices closely chinked and daubed with clay, so as to make it almost air-tight. Around the building on the inside ran a large stone flue, like a chimney laid on the ground. Outside was a huge pile of wood and a liberal supply of charcoal. Nimbus thus described the process of curing:

"Yer see, Capting, we fills de barn chock full, an' then shets it up fer a day or two, 'cording ter de weather, sometimes wid a slow fire an' sometimes wid none, till it begins ter sweat—git moist, yer know. Den we knows it's in order ter begin de curin', an' we puts on mo' fire, an' mo', an' mo', till de whole house gits hot an' de leaves begins ter hev a ha'sh, rough feel about de edges, an' now an' den one begins ter yaller up. Den we raises de heat jes ez fast ez we kin an' not fire de barn. Some folks uses de flues alone an' some de coal alone, but I mostly 'pends on de flues wid a few heaps of coal jes here an' dar 'bout de flo', at sech a time, kase eberyting 'pends on a even reg'lar heat dat you kin manage good. Den you keeps watch on it mighty close an' don't let it git too hot nor yet fail ter be hot 'nough, but jes so ez ter keep it yallerin' up nicely. When de leaves is crisp an' light so dat dey rustles roun' in de drafts like dead leaves in the fall, yer know, it's cured; an' all yer's got ter du den is ter dry out de stems an' stalks. Dat's got ter be done, tho', kase ef yer leaves enny bit ob it green an' sappy-like, fust ting yer knows when it comes in order—dat is, gits damp an' soft—de green runs outen de stems down inter de leaves an' jes streaks 'em all ober, or p'raps it turns de fine yaller leaf a dull greenish brown.

So yer's got ter keep up yer fire till every stalk an' stem'll crack like a pipe-stem ez soon ez yer bends 'em up. Den yer lets de fire go down an' opens der do' fer it ter come in order, so't yer kin bulk it down."

"What do you mean by 'bulking it down'?"

"Put it in bulk, like dis yer," said he, pointing to a pile of sticks laid crosswise of each other with the plants still on them, and carefully covered to keep out the weather. "Yer see," he continued, "dis answers two pu'poses; fust yer gits yer barn empty an' uses it again. Den de weather don't git in ter signify, yer know, an' so it don't come inter order any more an' color up wid de wet; dat is, 'less yer leaves it too long or de wedder is mighty damp."

"Oh, he knows," said the sheriff, with a ring of pride in his voice. "Nimbus was raised in a tobacco-field, and knows as much as anybody about it. How did your first barn cure up, Nimbus?"

"Right bright and even, sah," answered the colored man, as he thrust his hand under the boards spread over the bulk near which he stood, and drew out a few leaves, which he smoothed out carefully and handed to his visitors. "I got it down in tol'able fa'r order, too, atter de rain t'odder evenin'. Dunno ez I ebber handled a barn thet, take it all round, 'haved better er come out fa'rer in my life—mighty good color an' desp'ut few lugs. Yer see, I got it cut jes de right time, an' de weather couldn't hev ben better ef I'd hed it made ter order."

The sheriff stretched a leaf to its utmost width, held it up to the sunshine, crumpled it between his great palms, held it to his face and drew a long breath through it, rubbed the edges between thumb and finger, pinched the stem with his thumb-nail till it broke in half a dozen places, and remarked with enthusiasm, to the Northern man, who stood rubbing and smelling of the sample he held, in awkward imitation of one whom he recognized as a connoisseur:

"That's prime terbacker, Captain. If it runs like that through the bulk and nothing happens to it before it gets to the warehouse, it'll bring a dollar a pound, easy. You don't often see such terbacker any year, much less such a one as this has been. Didn't it ripen mighty uneven, Nimbus?"

"Jest about ez it oughter—a little 'arlier on the hilltop an' dry places 'long de sides, an' den gradwally down ter de moister places. Dar wa'n't much ob dat pesky spotted ripenin' up—jes a plant h'yer an' anodder dar, all in 'mong de green, but jest about a good barn-full in tollable fa'r patches, an' den anodder comin' right on atter it. I'll hev it full agin an' fire up by to-morrer evenin'."

"Do you hang it right up after cutting?" asked the officer.

"Wal, we mout do so. Tain't no hurt ter do it dat er way, only it handles better ter let it hang on de sticks a while an' git sorter wilted—don't break de leaves off ner mash 'em up so much loadin' an' unloadin', yer know," answered Nimbus.

"How much have you got here?" asked the sheriff, casting his eye over the field; "forty thousand?"

"Wal," said Nimbus, "I made up sixty thousand hills, but I hed ter re-set some on 'em. I s'pose it'll run somewhere between fifty an' sixty thousand."

"A right good crop," said the sheriff. "I doubt if any man in the county has got a better, take it all 'round."

"I don't reckon ther's one wukked enny harder fer what he's got," said the colored man quietly.

"No, I'll guarantee ther hain't," said the other, laughing. "Nobody ever accused you of being lazy, Nimbus. They only fault you fer being too peart."

"All 'cause I wants my own, an' wuks fer it, an' axes nobody enny odds, but only a fa'r show—a white man's chance ter git along," responded Nimbus, with a touch of defiance in his tone.

"Well, well," said the sheriff good-naturedly, "I won't never fault ye for that, but they do say you're the only man, white er black, that ever got ahead of Potem Desmit in a trade yet. How's that, Nimbus?"

"I paid him all he axed," said the colored man, evidently flattered by this tribute to his judgment as to the value of Red Wing. "Kase white folks won't see good fine-terbacker lan' when dey walks ober it, tain't my fault, is it?"

"No more tain't, Nimbus; but don't yer s'pose yer Marse Potem's smartly worried over it?"

"La, no, I reckon not. He don't 'pear ter be, ennyhow. He war by here when I was curin' up dis barn, an' stopped in an' looked at it, an' axed a power ob questions, an' got Lugena ter bring him out some buttermilk an' a corn pone. Den he went up an' sot an hour in de school an' sed ez how he war mighty proud ter see one of his ole nigga's gittin' on dat er way."

"Wal, now, that was kind of him, wasn't it?"

"Dat it war, sah, an' hit done us all a power ob good, too. Hev you ebber ben ter de school, Mr. Sheriff? No? wal, yer oughter; an' you, too, Capting. Dar's a little Yankee woman, Miss Mollie Ainslie, a runnin' ob it, dat do beat all curration fer managin' tings. I'd nebber'd got long so h'yer, not by no means, ez I hez, but fer her advice—her'n an' 'Liab's, gentlemen. Dar she am now," he added, as a slight figure, mounted on a powerful black horse, and dressed in a dark riding-habit, with a black plume hanging from a low-crowned felt hat, came out of the woods below and cantered easily along the road a hundred yards away, toward the school-house. The visitors watched her curiously, and expressed a desire to visit the school. Nimbus said that if they would walk on slowly he would go by the house and get his coat and overtake them before they reached the school-house.

As they walked along the sheriff said,

"Did you notice the horse that Yankee schoolmarm rode?"

"I noticed that it was a very fine one," was the reply.

"I should think it was. I haven't seen a horse in an age that reminded me so much of the one I was telling you about that Hesden Le Moyne used to have. He is fuller and heavier, but if I was not afraid of making Hesden mad I would rig him about a nigger-teacher's riding his horse around the country. Of course it's not the same, but it would be a good joke, only Hesden Le Moyne is not exactly the man one wants to start a joke on."

When they arrived at the school-house they found that Mollie Ainslie had changed her habit and was now standing by the desk on the platform in the main room, clad in a neat half-mourning dress, well adapted to the work of the school-room, quiet and composed, tapping her bell to reduce to order the many-hued crowd of scholars of all ages and sizes who were settling into their places preparatory to the morning roll-call. Nimbus took his visitors up the broad aisle, through an avenue of staring eyes, and introduced them awkwardly, but proudly, to the self-collected little figure on the platform. She in turn presented to them her assistant, Miss Lucy Ellison, a blushing, peach-cheeked little Northern beauty, and Eliab Hill, now advanced to the dignity of an assistant also, who sat near her on the platform. The sheriff nodded awkwardly to the ladies, as if doubtful how much deference it would do to display, said, "How d'ye, 'Liab?" to the crippled colored man, laid his saddle-bags on the floor, and took the chair assigned to him. The Northern man greeted the young ladies with apparent pleasure and profound respect, shook hands with the colored man, calling him "Mister" Hill, and before sitting down looked out on the crowded school with evident surprise.

Before proceeding with the roll-call Miss Ainslie took the large Bible which lay upon her desk, and approaching the gentlemen said:

"It is our custom every morning to read a portion of the Scripture and offer prayer. We should be glad if either of you would conduct these exercises for us."

Both declined, the sheriff with some confusion, and the other remarking that he desired to see the school going on as if he were not present, in order that he might the better observe its exercises.

Miss Ainslie returned to her desk, called the roll of a portion of the scholars, and then each of her assistants called the names of those assigned to their charge. A selection from the Scripture was next read by the preceptress, a hymn sung under her lead with great spirit and correctness, and then Eliab Hill, clasping his hands, said, "Let us pray." The whole school knelt, the ladies bowed their heads upon the desk, and Eliab offered an appropriate prayer, in which the strangers were not forgotten, but were each kindly and fitly commended to the Divine care. Then there was an impromptu examination of the school. Each of the teachers heard a class recite, there was more singing, with other agreeable exercises, and it was noon before the visitors thought of departing. Then they were invited to dine with the lady teachers at the old Ordinary, and would have declined, on the ground that they must go on to the next precinct, but Nimbus, who had been absent for an hour, now appeared and brought word that the table was spread on the porch under the great oak, and their horses already cared for; so that excuse would evidently be useless. The sheriff was very uneasy, but the other seemed by no means displeased at the delay. However, the former recovered when he saw the abundant repast, and told many amusing stories of the old hostel. At length he said:

"That is a fine horse you rode this morning, Miss Ainslie. May I ask to whom it belongs?"

"To me, of course," replied the lady, in some surprise.

"I did not know," replied the sheriff, slightly confused. "Have you owned him long?"

"Nearly two years," she answered.

"Indeed? Somehow I can't get it out of my head that I have seen him before, while I am quite sure I never had the pleasure of meeting you until to-day."

"Quite likely," she answered; "Nimbus sometimes rides him into Melton for the mail."

"No," said he, shaking his head, "that is not it. But, no matter, he's a fine horse, and if you leave here or wish to sell him at any time, I hope you will remember and give me a first chance."

He was astonished at the result of his harmless proposal.

"Sir," said the little lady, her gray eyes filling and her voice choking with emotion, "that was my only brother's favorite horse. He rode him in the army, and gave him to me when he died. No money could buy him under any circumstances."

"Beg pardon," said the sheriff; "I had no idea—I—ah—"

To relieve his embarrassment the officer brought forward the special object of his visit by stating that it was thought desirable to establish a voting precinct at Red Wing for the coming election, if a suitable place to hold the election could be found, and asked if the school-house could be obtained for that purpose. A lively conversation ensued, in which both gentlemen set forth the advantages of the location to the voters of that section. Miss Ellison seemed to favor it, but the little lady who was in charge only asked questions and looked thoughtful. When at length her opinion was directly asked, she said:

"I had heard of this proposal through both Mr. Hill and Nimbus, and I must say I quite agree with the view taken by the former. If it were necessary in order to secure the exercise of their rights by the colored men I would not object; but I cannot see that it is. It would, of course, direct even more attention to our school, and I do not think the feeling toward us among our white neighbors is any too kindly now. We have received no serious ill-treatment, it is true, but this is the first time any white person has ventured into our house. I don't think that anything should be done to excite unnecessary antipathy which might interfere with what I must consider the most important element of the colored man's development, the opportunity for education."

"Why, they hold the League[29] meetings there, don't they?" asked the sheriff, with a twinkle which questioned her sincerity.

"Certainly," she answered calmly. "At least I gave them leave to do so, and have no doubt they do. I consider that necessary. The colored men should be encouraged to consider and discuss political affairs and decide in regard to them from their own standpoint. The League gives them this opportunity. It seems to be a quiet and orderly gathering. They are all colored men of the same way of thought, in the main, and it is carried on entirely by them; at least, such is the case here, and I consider the practice which it gives in the discussion of public affairs and the conduct of public assemblies as a most valuable training for the adults who will never have a chance to learn otherwise."

"I think Nimbus is in favor of having the election here," said Captain Pardee.

"No doubt," she replied. "So are they all, and they have been very pressing in their importunity—all except Mr. Hill. They are proud of their school and the building, which is the joint product of their own labor and the helpfulness of Northern friends, and are anxious for every opportunity to display their unexpected prosperity. It is very natural, but I think unwise."

"Nimbus owns the land, don't he?" asked the sheriff.

"No. He gave that for school and church purposes, and, except that they have a right to use it on the Sabbath, it is in my charge as the principal teacher here," she replied, with dignity.

"And you do not desire the election held here?" asked Captain Pardee.

"I am sorry to discommode the voters around here, white or black, but I would not balance a day's time or a day's walk against the more important interests of this school to the colored people. They can walk ten miles to vote, if need be, but no exertion of theirs could replace even the building and its furniture, let alone the school which it shelters."

"That is very true," said the officer, thoughtfully.

So the project was abandoned, and Melton remained the nearest polling-place to Red Wing.

As they rode away the two representatives of antipodal thought discussed the scenes they had witnessed that day, which were equally new to them both, and naturally enough drew from them entirely different conclusions. The Northern man enthusiastically prophesied the rapid rise and miraculous development of the colored race under the impetus of free schools and free thought. The Southern man only saw in it a prospect of more "sassy niggers," like Nimbus, who was "a good enough nigger, but mighty aggravating to the white folks."

With regard to the teachers, he ventured only this comment:

"Captain, it's a mighty pity them gals are teaching a nigger school. They're too likely for such work—too likely by half."

The man whom he addressed only gave a low, quiet laugh at this remark, which the other found it difficult to interpret.

CHAPTER XIX.

THE SHADOW OF THE FLAG.

AS SOON AS IT became known that the plan of having a polling-place at Red Wing had been abandoned, there was an almost universal expression of discontent among the colored people. Never before had the authority or wisdom of the teachers been questioned. The purity of their motives and the devotion they had displayed in advancing every interest of those to whom they had come as the missionaries of light and freedom, had hitherto protected them from all jealousy or suspicion on the part of the beneficiaries of their devotion. Mollie Ainslie had readily and naturally fallen into the habit of controlling and directing almost everything about her, simply because she had been accustomed to self-control and self-direction, and was by nature quick to decide and resolute to act. Conscious of her own rectitude, and fully realizing the dangers which might result from the experiment proposed, she had had no hesitation about withholding her consent, without which the school-house could not be used, and had not deemed it necessary to consult the general wish of the villagers in regard to it. Eliab Hill had approved her action, and she had briefly spoken of it to Nimbus—that was all.

Now, the people of Red Wing, with Nimbus at their head, had set their hearts upon having the election held there. The idea was flattering to their importance, a recognition of their manhood and political co-ordination which was naturally and peculiarly gratifying. So they murmured and growled, and the discontent grew louder and deeper until, on the second day thereafter, Nimbus, with two or three other denizens of Red Wing, came, with gloomy, sullen faces, to the school-house at the hour for dismissal, to hold an interview with Miss Ainslie on the subject. She knew their errand, and received them with that cool reserve which so well became her determined face and slight, erect figure. When they had stated their desire, and more than half indicated their determination to have the election held there at all hazards, she said briefly,

"I have not the slightest objection."

"Dar now," said Nimbus exultingly; "I 'llowed dar mus' be somethin' wrong 'bout it. They kep' tellin' me that you 'posed it, an' tole de Capting dat it couldn't never be held here wid your consent while you wuz in de school."

"So I did."

"You don't say? an' now yer's changed yer mind."

"I have not changed my mind at all."

"No? Den what made you say yer hadn't no 'jections, just now."

"Because I have not. It is a free country. You say you are determined to have the election here. I am fully convinced that it would do harm. Yet you have a right to provide a place, and hold it here, if you desire. That I do not question, and shall not attempt to prevent; only, the day that you determine to do so I shall pack up my trunk, ride over to Boyleston, deliver the keys to the superintendent, and let him do as he chooses about the matter."

"Yer don't mean ter say yer'd go an' leave us fer good, does yer, Miss Mollie?" asked Nimbus in surprise.

"Certainly," was the reply; "when the people have once lost confidence in me, and I am required to give up my own deliberate judgment to a whimsical desire for parade, I can do no more good here, and will leave at once."

"Sho, now, dat won't do at all—no more it won't," responded Nimbus. "Ef yer feel's dat er way 'bout it, der ain't no mo' use a-talkin'. Dere's gwine ter be nary 'lection h'yer ef it really troubles you ladies dat 'er way."

So it was decided, and once again there was peace.

To compensate themselves for this forbearance, however, it was suggested that the colored voters of Red Wing and vicinity should meet at the church on the morning of election and march in a body to the polls with music and banners, in order most appropriately and significantly to commemorate their first exercise of the electoral privilege. To this Miss Ainslie saw no serious objection, and in order fully to conciliate Nimbus, who might yet feel himself aggrieved by her previous decision, she tendered him the loan of her horse on the occasion, he having been elected marshal.

From that time until the day of the election there was considerable excitement. There were a number of political harangues made in the neighborhood; the League met several times; the colored men appeared anxious and important about the new charge committed to their care; the white people were angry, sullen, and depressed. The school at Red Wing went peaceably on, interrupted only by the excitement attendant upon the preparations making for the expected parade.

Almost every night, after work was over, the colored people would gather in the little hamlet and march to the music of a drum and fife, and under the command of Nimbus, whose service in the army had made him a tolerable proficient in such tactical movements as pertained to the "school of the company." Very often, until well past midnight the fife and drum, the words of command, and the rumble of marching feet could be heard in the little village. The white people in the country around about began to talk about "the niggers arming and drilling," saying that they intended to "seize the polls on election day;" "rise up and murder the whites;" "burn all the houses along the river;" and a thousand other absurd and incredible things which seemed to fill the air, to grow and multiply like baleful spores, without apparent cause. As a consequence of this there grew up a feeling of apprehension among the colored men also. They feared that these things were said simply to make a ready and convenient excuse for violence which was to be perpetrated upon them in order to prevent the exercise of their legal rights.

So there were whisperings and apprehension and high resolve upon both sides. The colored men, conscious of their own rectitude, were either unaware of the real light in which their innocent parade was regarded by their white neighbors, or else laughed at the feeling as insincere and groundless. The whites, having been for generations firm believers in the imminency of servile insurrections; devoutly crediting the tradition that the last words of George Washington, words of wisdom and warning, were, "Never trust a nigger with a gun;" and accustomed to chafe each other into a fever heat of excitement over any matter of public interest, were ready to give credence to any report—all the more easily because of its absurdity. On the other hand, the colored people, hearing these rumors, said to themselves that it was simply a device to prevent them from voting, or to give color and excuse for a conflict at the polls.

There is no doubt that both were partly right and partly wrong. While the parade was at first intended simply as a display, it came to be the occasion of preparation for an expected attack, and as the rumors grew more wild and absurd, so did each side grow more earnest and sincere. The colored men determined to exercise their rights openly and boldly, and the white men were as fully determined that at any exhibition of "impudence" on the part of the "niggers" they would teach them a lesson they would not soon forget.

None of this came to the ears of Mollie Ainslie. Nevertheless she had a sort of indefinite foreboding of evil to come out of it, and wished that she had exerted her influence to prevent the parade.

On the morning of the election day a motley crowd collected at an early hour at Red Wing. It was noticeable that every one carried a heavy stick, though there was no other show of arms among them. Some of them, no doubt, had pistols, but there were no guns in the crowd. They seemed excited and alarmed. A few notes from the fife, however, banished all irresolution, and before eight o'clock two hundred men gathered from the country round marched away toward Melton, with a national flag heading the column, in front of which rode Eliab Hill in the carryall belonging to Nimbus. With them went a crowd of women and children, numbering as many more, all anxious to witness the first exercise of elective power by their race, only just delivered from the bonds of slavery. The fife screeched, the drum rattled; laughter and jests and high cheer prevailed among them all. As they marched on, now and then a white man rode past them, silent and sullen, evidently enraged at the display which was being made by the new voters. As they drew nearer to the town it became evident that the air was surcharged with trouble. Nimbus sent back Miss Ainslie's horse, saying that he was afraid it might get hurt. The boy that took it innocently repeated this remark to his teacher.

Within the town there was great excitement. A young man who had passed Red Wing while the men were assembling had spurred into Melton and reported with great excitement that the "niggers" were collecting at the church and Nimbus was giving out arms and ammunition; that they were boasting of what they would do if any of their votes were refused; that they had all their plans laid to meet negroes from other localities at Melton, get up a row, kill all the white men, burn the town, and then ravish the white women. This formula of horrors is one so familiar to the Southern tongue that it runs off quite unconsciously whenever there is any excitement in the air about the "sassy niggers." It is the "form of sound words,"[30] which is never forgotten. Its effect upon the Southern white man is magical. It moves him as the red rag does a mad bull. It takes away all sense and leaves only an abiding desire to kill.

So this rumor awakened great excitement as it flew from lip to lip. Few questioned its verity, and most of those who heard felt bound in conscience to add somewhat to it as they passed it on to the next listener. Each one that came in afterward was questioned eagerly upon the hypothesis of a negro insurrection having already taken shape. "How many are there?" "Who is at the head of it?" "How are they armed?" "What did they say?" were some of the queries which overwhelmed every new comer. It never seemed to strike any one as strange that if the colored men had any hostile intent they should let these solitary horsemen pass them unmolested. The fever spread. Revolvers were flourished and shot-guns loaded; excited crowds gathered here and there, and nearly everybody in the town sauntered carelessly toward the bridge across which Nimbus' gayly-decked column must enter the town. A few young men rode out to reconnoitre, and every few minutes one would come dashing back upon a reeking steed, revolver in hand, his mouth full of strange oaths and his eyes flaming with excitement.

It was one of these that precipitated the result. The flag which waved over the head of the advancing column had been visible from the town for some time as now and then it passed over the successive ridges to the eastward.

The sound of fife and drum had become more and more distinct, and a great portion of the white male population, together with those who had come in to the election from the surrounding country, had gathered about the bridge spanning the swift river which flowed between Melton and the hosts of the barbarous and bloodthirsty "niggers" of the Red Wing country. Several of the young scouts had ridden close up to the column with tantalizing shouts and insulting gestures and then dashed back to recount their own audacity; until, just as the Stars and Stripes began to show over the last gullied hill, one of them, desirous of outdoing his comrades in bravado, drew his revolver, flourished it over his head, and cast a shower of insulting epithets upon the colored pilgrims to the shrine of ballatorial power. He was answered from the dusky crowd with words as foul as his own. Such insult was not to be endured. Instantly his pistol was raised, there was a flash, a puff of fleecy smoke, a shriek from amid the crowd.[31]

At once all was confusion. Oaths, cries, pistol-shots, and a shower of rocks filled the air as the young man turned and spurred back to the town. In a moment the long covered-bridge was manned by a well-armed crowd, while others were seen running toward it. The town was in an uproar.

The officers of election had left the polls, and in front of the bridge could be seen Hesden Le Moyne and the burly sheriff striving to keep back the angry crowd of white men. On the hill the colored men, for a moment struck with amazement, were now arming with stones, in dead earnest, uttering loud cries of vengeance for one of their number who, wounded and affrighted, lay groaning and writhing by the roadside. They outnumbered the whites very greatly, but the latter excelled them in arms, in training, and in position. Still, such was their exasperation at what seemed to them a wanton and unprovoked attack, that they were preparing to charge upon the bridge without delay. Nimbus especially was frantic with rage.

"It's the flag!" he shouted; "the damned rebels are firing on the flag!"

He strode back and forth, waving an old cavalry sabre which he had brought to mark his importance as marshal of the day, and calling on his followers to stand by him and they would "clean out the murderous crowd." A few pistol shots which were fired from about the bridge but fell far short, added to their excitement and desperation.

Just as they were about to rush down the hillside, Mollie Ainslie, with a white set face, mounted on her black horse, dashed in front of them, and cried,

"Halt!"

Eliab Hill had long been imploring them with upraised hands to be calm and listen to reason, but his voice was unheeded or unheard in the wild uproar. The sight of the woman, however, whom all of them regarded so highly, reining in her restive horse and commanding silence, arrested the action of all. But Nimbus, now raging like a mad lion, strode up to her, waving his sword and cursing fearfully in his wild wrath, and said hoarsely:

"You git out o' de way, Miss Mollie! We all tinks a heap ob you, but yer hain't got no place h'yer! De time's come for *men* now, an' dis is men's wuk, an' we's gwine ter du it, too! D'yer see dat man dar, a-bleedin' an' a-groanin'? Blood's been shed! We's been fired into kase we wuz gwine ter exercise our rights like men under de flag ob our kentry, peaceable, an' quiet, an' dis-turbin' nobody! 'Fore God, Miss Mollie, ef we's men an' fit ter hev enny rights, we won't stan' dat! We'll hev blood fer blood! Dat's what we means! You jes git outen de way!" he added imperiously. "We'll settle dis yer matter ourselves!" He reached out his hand as he spoke to take her horse by the bit.

"Stand back!" cried the brave girl. "Don't you touch him, sir!" She urged her horse forward, and Nimbus, awed by her intensity, slowly retreated before her, until she was but a pace or two in front of the line which stretched across the road. Then leaning forward, she said,

"Nimbus, give me your sword!"

"What you wants ob dat, Miss Mollie?" he asked in surprise.

"No matter; hand it to me!"

He took it by the blade, and held the heavy basket-hilt toward her. She clasped her small white fingers around the rough, shark-skin handle and raised it over her head as naturally as a veteran leader desiring to command attention, and said:

"Now, Nimbus, and the rest of you, you all know that I am your friend. My brother was a soldier, and fought for your liberty on this very horse. I have never advised you except for your good, and you know I never will. If it is right and best for you to fight now, I will not hinder you. Nay, I will say God-speed, and for aught I know fight with you. I am no coward, if I am a woman. You know what I have risked already for your good. Now tell me what has happened, and what this means."

There was a cheer at this, and fifty excited voices began the story.

"Stop! stop!" she cried. "Keep silent, all of you, and let Mr. Hill tell it alone. He was here in front and saw it all."

Thereupon she rode up beside the carry-all, which was now in the middle of the throng, and listened gravely while Eliab told the whole story of the march from Red Wing. There was a buzz when he had ended, which she stilled by a word and a wave of the hand, and then turning to Nimbus she said:

"Nimbus, I appoint you to keep order in this crowd until my return. Do not let any man, woman, or child move forward or back, whatever may occur. Do you understand?"

"Yes, ma'am, I hears; but whar you gwine, Miss Mollie?"

"Into the town."

"No yer don't, Miss Mollie," said he, stepping before her. "Dey'll kill you, shore."

"No matter. I am going. You provoked this affray by your foolish love of display, and it must be settled now, or it will be a matter of constant trouble hereafter."

"But, Miss Mollie—"

"Not a word! You have been a soldier and should obey orders. Here is your sword. Take it, and keep order here. Examine that poor fellow's wound, and I will go and get a doctor for him."

She handed Nimbus his sword and turned her horse toward the bridge. Then a wail of distress arose from the crowd. The women begged her not to go, with tears. She turned in her saddle, shook her head, and raised her hand to show her displeasure at this. Then she took a handkerchief from her pocket and half waving it as she proceeded, went toward the bridge.

"Well, I swear," said the sheriff; "if that are gal ain't coming in with a flag of truce. She's pluck, anyhow. You ought to give her three cheers, boys."

The scene which had been enacted on the hill had been closely watched from the bridge and the town, and Mollie's conduct had been pretty well interpreted though her words could not be heard. The nerve which she had exhibited had excited universal comment, and it needed no second invitation to bring off every hat and send up, in her honor, the shrill yell with which our soldiers became familiar during the war.

Recognizing this, her pale face became suffused with blushes, and she put her handkerchief to her lips to hide their tremulousness as she came nearer. She ran her eyes quickly along the line of strange faces, until they fell upon the sheriff, by whom stood Hesden Le Moyne. She rode straight to them and said,

"Oh, Mr. Sheriff—"

Then she broke down, and dropping the rein on her horse's neck, she pressed her handkerchief to her face and wept. Her slight frame shook with sobs. The men looked at her with surprise and pity. There was even a huskiness in the sheriff's voice as he said,

"Miss Ainslie—I—I beg your pardon, ma'am—but—"

She removed the handkerchief, but the tears were still running down her face as she said, glancing round the circle of sympathizing faces:

"Do stop this, gentlemen. It's all a mistake. I know it must be a mistake!"

"We couldn't help it, ma'am," said one impulsive youth, putting in before the elders had time to speak; "the niggers was marching on the town here. Did you suppose we was going to sit still and let them burn and ravage without opposition? Oh, we haven't got so low as that, if the Yankees did outnumber us. Not yet!"

There was a sneering tone in his voice which did more than sympathy could, to restore her equanimity. So she said, with a hint of a smile on her yet tearful face,

"The worst thing those poor fellows meant to do, gentlemen, was to make a parade over their new-found privileges—march up to the polls, vote, and march home again. They are just like a crowd of boys over a drum and fife, as you know. They carefully excluded from the line all who were not voters, and I had them arranged so that their names would come alphabetically, thinking it might be handier for the officers; though I don't know anything about how an election is conducted," she added, with an ingenuous blush.[32] "It's all my fault, gentlemen! I did not think any trouble could come of it, or I would not have allowed it for a moment. I thought it would be better for them to come in order, vote, and go home than to have them scattered about the town and perhaps getting into trouble."

"So 'twould," said the sheriff. "Been a first-rate thing if we'd all understood it—first-rate."

"Oh, I'm so sorry, gentlemen—so sorry, and I'm afraid one man is killed. Would one of you be kind enough to go for a doctor?"

"Here is one," said several voices, as a young man stepped forward and raised his hat respectfully.

"I will go and see him," he said.

He walked on up the hill alone.

"Well, ma'am," said the sheriff, "what do you think should be done now?"

"If you would only let these people come in and vote, gentlemen. They will return at once, and I would answer with my life for their good behavior. I think it was all a misunderstanding."

"Certainly—certainly, ma'am," said the sheriff. "No doubt about it."

She turned her horse and was about to ride back up the hill, but Hesden Le Moyne, taking off his hat, said:

"Gentlemen, I think we owe a great deal to the bravery of this young lady. I have no doubt but all she says is literally true. Yet we like to have got into trouble which might have been very serious in its consequences, nay, perhaps has already resulted seriously. But for her timely arrival, good sense, and courage there would have been more bloodshed; our town would have been disgraced, troops posted among us, and perhaps lives taken in retaliation. Now, considering all this, I move a vote of thanks to the lady, and that we all pledge ourselves to take no notice of these people, but let them come in and vote and go out, without interruption. All that are in favor of that say Aye!"

Every man waved his hat, there was a storm of "ayes," and then the old rebel yell again, as, bowing and blushing with pleasure, Mollie turned and rode up the hill.

There also matters had assumed a more cheerful aspect by reason of her cordial reception at the bridge, and the report of the surgeon that the man's wound, though quite troublesome, was by no means serious. She told in a few words what had occurred, explained the mistake, reminded them that such a display would naturally prove very exasperating to persons situated as the others were, counselled moderation and quietness of demeanor, and told them to re-form their ranks and go forward, quietly vote, and return. A rousing cheer greeted her words. Eliab Hill uttered a devout prayer of thankfulness. Nimbus blunderingly said it was all his fault, "though he didn't mean no harm," and then suggested that the flag and music should be left there in charge of some of the boys, which was approved. The wounded man was put into the carry-all by the side of Eliab, and they started down the hill. The sheriff, who was waiting at the bridge, called out for them to bring the flag along and have the music strike up.

So, with flying colors and rattling drum-beat, the voters of Red Wing marched to the polls; the people of Melton looked good-naturedly on; the young hot-bloods joked the dusky citizens, and bestowed extravagant encomiums on the plucky girl who had saved them from so much threatened trouble; and Mollie Ainslie rode home with a hot, flushed face, and was put to bed by her co-laborer, the victim of a raging headache.

"I declare, Mollie Ainslie," said Lucy, "you are the queerest girl I ever saw. I believe you would ride that horse into a den of lions, and then faint because you were not eaten up. I could never do what you have done—never in the world—but if did I wouldn't get sick because it was all over."

CHAPTER XX.

PHANTASMAGORIA.

THE DAY AFTER the election a colored lad rode up to the school-house, delivered a letter for Miss Ainslie to one of the scholars, and rode away. The letter was written in an even, delicate hand, which was yet full of feminine strength, and read as follows:

"MISS AINSLIE:

"My son Hesden has told me of your courage in preventing what must otherwise have resulted in a most terrible conflict yesterday, and I feel it to be my duty, in behalf of many ladies whose husbands and sons were present on that occasion, to express to you our gratitude. It is seldom that such opportunity presents itself to our sex, and still more seldom that we are able to improve it when presented. Your courage in exerting the power you have over the peculiar people toward whom you hold such important relations, commands my utmost admiration. It is a matter of the utmost congratulation to the good people of Horsford that one of such courage and prudence occupies the position which you hold. I am afraid that the people whom you are teaching can never be made to understand and appreciate the position into which they have been thrust by the terrible events of the past few years. I am sure, however, that you will do all in your power to secure that result, and most earnestly pray for your success. Could I leave my house I should do myself the pleasure to visit your school and express my gratitude in person. As it is, I can only send the good wishes of a weak old woman, who, though once a slave-mistress, was most sincerely rejoiced at the down-fall of a system she had always regarded with regret, despite the humiliation it brought to her countrymen.

"HESTER LE MOYNE."

This was the first word of commendation which had been received from any Southern white woman, and the two lonely teachers were greatly cheered by it. When we come to analyze its sentences there seems to be a sort of patronizing coolness in it, hardly calculated to awaken enthusiasm. The young girls who had given themselves to what they deemed a missionary work of peculiar urgency and sacredness, did not stop to read between the lines, however, but perused with tears of joy this first epistle from one of their own sex in that strange country where they had been treated as leprous outcasts by all the families who belonged to the race of which they were unconscious ornaments. They jumped to the conclusion that a new day was dawning, and that henceforth they would have that companionship and sympathy which they felt that they deserved from the Christian women by whom they were surrounded.

"What a dear, good old lady she must be!" exclaimed the pretty and gushing Lucy Ellison. "I should like to kiss her for that sweet letter."

So they took heart of grace, talked with the old "Mammy" who had charge of their household arrangements about the gentle invalid woman, whom she had served as a slave, and pronounced "jes de bestest woman in de worl', nex' to my young ladies," and then they went on with their work with renewed zeal.

Two other results followed this affair, which tended greatly to relieve the monotony of their lives. A good many gentlemen called in to see the school, most of them young men who were anxious for a sight of the brave lady who had it in charge, and others merely desirous to see the pretty Yankee "nigger teachers." Many would, no doubt, have become more intimate with them, but there was something in the terms of respectful equality on which they associated with their pupils, and especially with their co-worker, Eliab Hill, which they could not abide or understand. The fame of the adventure had extended even beyond the county, however, and raised them very greatly in the esteem of all the people.

Miss Ainslie soon noticed that the gentlemen she met in her rides, instead of passing her with a rude or impudent stare began to greet her with polite respect. Besides this, some of the officers of the post at Boyleston, hearing of the gallant conduct of their country-woman, rode over to pay their respects, and brought back such glowing reports of the beauty and refinement of the teachers at Red Wing that the distance could not prevent others of the garrison from following their example; and the old Ordinary thereafter witnessed many a pleasant gathering under the grand old oak which shaded it. Both of the teachers found admirers in the gallant company, and it soon became known that Lucy Ellison would leave her present situation erelong to brighten the life of a young lieutenant. It was rumored, too, that another uniform covered the sad heart of a cavalier who asked an exchange into a regiment on frontier duty, because Mollie Ainslie had failed to respond favorably to his passionate addresses.

So they taught, read, sang, wandered along the wood-paths in search of new beauties to charm their Northern eyes; rode together whenever Lucy could be persuaded to mount Nimbus' mule, which, despite its hybrid nature, was an excellent saddle-beast; entertained with unaffected pleasure the officers who came to cheer their loneliness; and under the care of their faithful old "Mammy" and the oversight of a kind-hearted, serious-faced Superintendent, who never missed Red Wing in his monthly rounds, they kept their oddly transformed home bright and cheerful, their hearts light and pure, and their faith clear, daily thanking God that they were permitted to do what they thought to be His will.

All of their experiences were not so pleasant. By their own sex they were still regarded with that calm, unobserving indifference with which the modern lady treats the sister who stands without the pale of reputable society. So far as the "ladies" of Horsford were concerned, the "nigger teachers" at Red Wing stood on the plane of the courtesan—they were *seen* but not *known.* The recognition which they received from the gentlemen of Southern birth had in it not a little of the shame-faced curiosity which characterizes the intercourse of men with women whose reputations have been questioned but not entirely destroyed. They were treated with apparent respect, in the school-room, upon the highway, or at the market, by men who would not think of recognizing them when in the company of their mothers, sisters, or wives. Such treatment would have been too galling to be borne had it not been that the spotless-minded girls were all too pure to realize its significance.

CHAPTER XXI.

A CHILD-MAN.

ELIAB HILL HAD from the first greatly interested the teachers at Red Wing. The necessities of the school and the desire of the charitable Board having it in charge, to accustom the colored people to see those of their own race trusted and advanced, had induced them to employ him as an assistant teacher, even before he was really competent for such service. It is true he was given charge of only the most rudimentary work, but that fact, while it inspired his ambition, showed him also the need of improvement and made him a most diligent student.

Lucy Ellison, as being the most expert in housewifely accomplishments, had naturally taken charge of the domestic arrangements at the Ordinary, and as a consequence had cast a larger share of the school duties upon her "superior officer," as she delighted to call Mollie Ainslie. This division of labor suited well the characteristics of both. To plan, direct, and manage the school came as naturally and easily to the stirring Yankee "school-marm" as did the ordering of their little household to the New York farmer's daughter. Among the extra duties thus devolved upon the former was the supervision and direction of the studies of Eliab Hill. As he could not consistently with the requisite discipline be included in any of the regular classes that had been formed, and his affliction prevented him from coming to them in the evening for private instruction, she arranged to teach him at the school-house after school hours. So that every day she remained after the school was dismissed to give him an hour's instruction. His careful attention and rapid progress amply repaid her for this sacrifice, and she looked forward with much pleasure to the time when, after her departure, he should be able to conduct the school with credit to himself and profit to his fellows.

Then, for the first time, she realized how great is the momentum which centuries of intelligence and freedom give to the mind of the learner—how unconscious is the acquisition of the great bulk of that knowledge which goes to make up the Caucasian manhood of the nineteenth century.

Eliab's desire to acquire was insatiable, his application was tireless, but what he achieved seemed always to lack a certain flavor of completeness. It was without that substratum of general intelligence[33] which the free white student has partly inherited and partly acquired by observation and experience, without the labor or the consciousness of study. The whole world of life, business, society, was a sealed book to him, which no other hand might open for him; while the field of literature was but a bright tangled thicket before him.

That unconscious familiarity with the past which is as the small change of daily thought to us was a strange currency to his mind. He had, indeed, the key to the value of each piece, and could, with difficulty, determine its power when used by another, but he did not give or receive the currency with instinctive readiness. Two things had made him clearly the intellectual superior of his fellows—the advantages of his early years by which he learned to read, and the habit of meditation which the solitude of his stricken life induced. This had made him a thinker, a philosopher far more profound than his general attainments would naturally produce. With the supersensitiveness which always characterizes the afflicted, also, he had become a most acute and subtle observer of the human countenance, and read its infinite variety of expression with ease and certainty. In two things he might be said to be profoundly versed—the spirit of the Scriptures, and the workings of the human heart. With regard to these his powers of expression were commensurate with his knowledge. The Psalms of David were more comprehensible to him than the simplest formulas of arithmetic.

Mollie Ainslie was not unfrequently amazed at this inequality of nature in her favorite pupil. On one side he seemed a full-grown man of grand proportions; on the other, a pigmy-child. She had heard him pour forth torrents of eloquence on the Sabbath, and felt the force of a nature exceptionally rich and strong in its conception of religious truths and human needs, only to find him on the morrow floundering hopelessly in the mire of rudimentary science, or getting, by repeated perusals, but an imperfect idea of some author's words, which it seemed to her he ought to have grasped at a glance.

He had always been a man of thought, and now for two years he had been studying after the manner of the schools, and his tasks were yet but rudimentary. It is true, he had read much and had learned not a little in a thousand directions which he did not appreciate, but yet he was discouraged and despondent, and it is no wonder that he was so. The mountain which stood in his pathway could not be climbed over nor passed by, but pebble by pebble and grain by grain must be removed, until a broad, smooth highway showed instead. And all this he must do before he could comprehend the works of those writers whose pages glow with light to *our* eyes from the very first. He read and re-read these, and groped his way to their meaning with doubt and difficulty.

Being a woman, Mollie Ainslie was not speculative. She could not solve this problem of strength and weakness. In power of thought, breadth of reasoning, and keenness of analysis she felt that he was her master; in knowledge—the power of acquiring and using scientific facts—she could but laugh at his weakness. It puzzled her. She wondered at it; but she had never sought to assign a reason for it. It remained for the learner himself to do this. One day, after weeks of despondency, he changed places with his teacher during the hour devoted to his lessons, and taught her why it was that he, Eliab Hill, with all his desire to learn and his ceaseless application to his tasks, yet made so little progress in the acquisition of knowledge.

"It ain't so much the words, Miss Mollie," he said, as he threw down a book in which he had asked her to explain some passage she had never read before, but the meaning of which came to her at a glance—"it ain't so much the words as it is the ideas that trouble me. These men who write seem to think and feel differently from those I have known. I can learn the words, but when I have them all right I am by no means sure that I know just what they mean."

"Why, you must," said the positive little Yankee woman; "when one has the words and knows the meaning of all of them, he cannot help knowing what the writer means."

"Perhaps I do not put it as I should," said he sadly. "What I want to say is, that there are thoughts and bearings that I can never gather from books alone. They come to you, Miss Ainslie, and to those like you, from those who were before you in the world, and from things about you. It is the part of knowledge that can't be put into books. Now I have none of that. My people cannot give it to me. I catch a sight of it here and there. Now and then, a conversation I heard years ago between some white men will come up and make plain something that I am puzzling over, but it is not easy for me to learn."

"I do not think I understand you," she replied; "but if I do, I am sure you are mistaken. How can you know the meanings of words, and yet not apprehend the thought conveyed?"

"I do not know *how,*" he replied. "I only know that while thought seems to come from the printed page to your mind like a flash of light, to mine it only comes with difficulty and after many readings, though I may know every word. For instance," he continued, taking up a volume of Tennyson which lay upon her table, "take any passage. Here is one: 'Tears, idle tears, I know not what they mean!'[34] I have no doubt that brings a distinct idea to your mind."

"Yes," she replied, hesitatingly; "I never thought of it before, but I think it does."

"Well, it does not to mine. I cannot make out what is meant by 'idle' tears, nor whether the author means to say that he does not know what 'tears' mean, or only 'idle' tears, or whether he does not understand such a display of grief because it *is* idle."

"Might he not have meant any or all of these?" she asked.

"That is it," he replied. "I want to know what he *did* mean. Of course, if I knew all about his life and ways, and the like, I could tell pretty fully his meaning. You know them because his thoughts are your thoughts, his life has been your life. You belong to the same race and class. I am cut off from this, and can only stumble slowly along the path of knowledge."

Thus the simple-minded colored man, taught to meditate by the solitude which his affliction enforced upon him, speculated in regard to the *leges non scriptæ*,[35] which control the action of the human mind and condition its progress.

"What has put you in this strange mood, Eliab?" asked the teacher wonderingly.

His face flushed, and the mobile mouth twitched with emotion as he glanced earnestly toward her, and then, with an air of sudden resolution, said:

"Well, you see, that matter of the election—you took it all in in a minute, when the horse came back. You knew the white folks would feel aggravated by that procession, and there would be trouble. Now, I never thought of that. I just thought it was nice to be free, and have our own music and march under that dear old flag to do the work of free men and citizens. That was all."

"But Nimbus thought of it, and that was why he sent back the horse," she answered.

"Not at all. He only thought they might pester the horse to plague him, and the horse might get away and be hurt. We didn't, none of us, think what the white folks would feel, because we didn't know. You did."

"But why should this affect you?"

"Just because it shows that education is something more than I had thought—something so large and difficult that one of my age, raised as I have been, can only get a taste of it at the best."

"Well, what then? You are not discouraged?"

"Not for myself—no. The pleasure of learning is reward enough to me. But my people, Miss Mollie, I must think of them. I am only a poor withered branch. They are the straight young tree. I must think of them and not of Eliab. You have taught me—this affair, everything, teaches me—that they can only be made free by knowledge. I begin to see that the law can only give us an opportunity to make ourselves freemen. Liberty must be earned; it cannot be given."

"That is very true," said the practical girl, whose mind recognized at once the fact which she had never formulated to herself. But as she looked into his face, working with intense feeling and so lighted with the glory of a noble purpose as to make her forget the stricken frame to which it was chained, she was puzzled at what seemed inconsequence in his words. So she added, wonderingly, "But I don't see why this should depress you. Only think how much you have done toward the end you have in view. Just think what you have accomplished—what strides you have made toward a full and complete manhood. You ought to be proud rather than discouraged."

"Ah!" said he, "that has been for myself, Miss Mollie, not for my people. What am I to my race? Aye," he continued, with a glance at his withered limbs, "to the least one of them not—not—"

He covered his face with his hands and bowed his head in the self-abasement which hopeless affliction so often brings.

"Eliab," said the teacher soothingly, as if her pupil were a child instead of a man older than herself, "you should not give way to such thoughts. You should rise above them, and by using the powers you have, become an honor to your race."

"No, Miss Mollie," he replied, with a sigh, as he raised his head and gazed into her face earnestly. "There ain't nothing in this world for me to look forward to only to help my people. I am only the dust on the Lord's chariot-wheels—only the dust, which must be brushed out of the way in order that their glory may shine forth. And that," he continued impetuously, paying no attention to her gesture of remonstrance, "is what I wanted to speak to you about this evening. It is hard to say, but I must say it—must say it now. I have been taking too much of your time and attention, Miss Mollie."

"I am sure, Mr. Hill—" she began, in some confusion.

"Yes, I have," he went on impetuously, while his face flushed hotly. "It is the young and strong only who can enter into the Canaan the Lord has put before our people. I thought for a while that we were just standing on the banks of Jordan—that the promised land was right over yon, and the waters piled up like a wall, so that even poor weak 'Liab might cross over. But I see plainer now. We're only just past the Red Sea, just coming into the wilderness, and if I can only get a glimpse from Horeb,[36] wid my old eyes by and by, 'Liab 'll be satisfied. It'll be enough, an' more'n enough, for him. He can only help the young ones—the lambs of the flock—a little, mighty little, p'raps, but it's all there is for him to do."

"Why, Eliab—" began the astonished teacher again.

"Don't! don't! Miss Mollie, if you please," he cried, with a look of pain. "I'se done tried—I hez, Miss Mollie. God only knows how I'se tried! But it ain't no use—no use," he continued, with a fierce gesture, and relapsing unconsciously into the rougher dialect that he had been training himself to avoid. "I can't do it, an' there's no use a-tryin'. There ain't nothin' good for me in this worl'—not in this worl'. It's hard to give it up, Miss Mollie—harder'n you'll ever dream; but I hain't blind. I knows the brand is on me. It's on my tongue now, that forgets all I've learned jes ez soon ez the time of trial comes."

He seemed wild with excitement as he leaned forward on the table toward her, and accompanied his words with that eloquence of gesticulation which only the hands that are tied to crippled forms acquire. He paused suddenly, bowed his head upon his crossed arms, and his frame shook with sobs. She rose, and would have come around the table to him. Raising his head quickly, he cried almost fiercely:

"Don't! don't! don't come nigh me, Miss Mollie! I'm going to do a hard thing, almost too hard for me. I'm going to get off the chariot-wheel—out of the light of the glory—out of the way of the young and the strong! Them that's got to fight the Lord's battles must have the training, and not them that's bound to fall in the wilderness. The time is precious—precious, and must not be wasted. You can't afford to spend so much of it on me! The Lord can't afford ter hev ye, Miss Mollie! I must step aside, an' I'se gwine ter do it now. If yer's enny time an' strength ter spar' more'n yer givin' day by day in the school, I want yer should give it to—to—Winnie an' 'Thusa—they're bright girls, that have studied hard, and are young and strong. It is through such as them that we must come up—our people, I mean. I want you to give them my hour, Miss Mollie—*my* hour! Don't say you won't do it!" he cried, seeing a gesture of dissent. "Don't say it! You *must* do it! Promise me, Miss Mollie—for my sake! for—promise me—now—quick! afore I gets too weak to ask it!"

"Why, certainly, Eliab," she said, in amazement, while she half shrank from him as if in terror. "I will do it if you desire it so much. But you should not get so excited. Calm yourself! I am sure I don't see why you should take such a course; but, as you say, they are two bright girls and will make good teachers, which are much needed."

"Thank God! thank God!" cried the cripple, as his head fell again upon his arms. After a moment he half raised it and said, weakly,

"Will you please call Nimbus, Miss Mollie? I must go home now. And please, Miss Mollie, don't think hard of 'Liab—don't, Miss Mollie," he said humbly.

"Why should I?" she asked in surprise. "You have acted nobly, though I cannot think you have done wisely. You are nervous now. You may think differently hereafter. If you do, you have only to say so. I will call Nimbus. Good-by!"

She took her hat and gloves and went down the aisle. Happening to turn near the door to replace a book her dress had brushed from a desk, she saw him gazing after her with a look that haunted her memory long afterward.

As the door closed behind her he slid from his chair and bowed his head upon it, crying out in a voice of tearful agony, "Thank God! thank God!" again and again, while his unfinished form shook with hysteric sobs.

"And *she* said I was not wise!" he half laughed, as the tears ran down his face and he resumed his invocation of thankfulness. Thus Nimbus found him and carried him home with his wonted tenderness, soothing him like a babe, and wondering what had occurred to discompose his usually sedate and cheerful friend.

"I declare, Lucy," said Mollie Ainslie that evening, to her co-worker, over their cosy tea, "I don't believe that I shall ever understand these people. There is that Eliab Hill, who was getting along so nicely, has concluded to give up his studies. I believe he is half crazy anyhow. He raved about it, and glared at me so that I was half frightened out of my wits. I wonder why it is that cripples are always so queer, anyhow?"

She would have been still more amazed if she had known that from that day Eliab Hill devoted himself to his studies with a redoubled energy, which more than made up for the loss of his teacher's aid. Had she herself been less a child she would have seen that he whom she had treated as such was, in truth, a man of rare strength.

CHAPTER XXII.

HOW THE FALLOW WAS SEEDED.

THE TIME HAD COME when the influences so long at work, the seed which the past had sown in the minds and hearts of races, must at length bear fruit. The period of actual reconstruction had passed, and independent, self-regulating States had taken the place of Military Districts and Provisional Governments. The people of the South began, little by little, to realize that they held their future in their own hands—that the supervising and restraining power of the General Government had been withdrawn. The colored race, yet dazed with the new light of liberty, were divided between exultation and fear. They were like a child taking his first steps—full of joy at the last accomplished, full of terror at the one which was before.

The state of mind of the Southern white man, with reference to the freedman and his exaltation to the privilege of citizenship is one which cannot be too frequently analyzed or too closely kept in mind by one who desires fully to apprehend the events which have since occurred, and the social and political structure of the South at this time.

As a rule, the Southern man had been a kind master to his slaves. Conscious cruelty was the exception. The real evils of the system were those which arose from its *un*-conscious barbarism—the natural and inevitable results of holding human beings as chattels, without right, the power of self-defence or protestation—dumb driven brutes, deprived of all volition or hope, subservient to another's will, and bereft of every motive for self-improvement as well as every opportunity to rise. The effect of this upon the dominant race was to fix in their minds, with the strength of an absorbing passion, the idea of their own innate and unimpeachable superiority, of the unalterable inferiority of the slave-race, of the infinite distance between the two, and of the depth of debasement implied by placing the two races, in any respect, on the same level. The Southern mind had no antipathy to the negro in a menial or servile relation. On the contrary, it was generally kind and considerate of him, as such. It regarded him almost precisely as other people look upon other species of animate property, except that it conceded to him the possession of human passions, appetites, and motives. As a farmer likes to turn a favorite horse into a fine pasture, watch his antics, and see him roll and feed and run; as he pats and caresses him when he takes him out, and delights himself in the enjoyment of the faithful beast—just so the slave-owner took pleasure in the slave's comfort, looked with approval upon his enjoyment of the domestic relation, and desired to see him sleek and hearty, and physically well content.

It was only *as a man* that the white regarded the black with aversion; and, in that point of view, the antipathy was all the more intensely bitter since he considered the claim to manhood an intrusion upon the sacred and exclusive rights of his own race. This feeling was greatly strengthened by the course of legislation and legal construction, both national and State. Many of the subtlest exertions of American intellect were those which traced and defined the line of demarcation, until there was built up between the races, *considered as men,* a wall of separation as high as heaven and as deep as hell.

It may not be amiss to cite some few examples of this, which will serve at once to illustrate the feeling itself, and to show the steps in its progress.

1 It was held by our highest judicial tribunal that the phrase "we the people," in the Declaration of Independence, did not include slaves, who were excluded from the inherent rights recited therein and accounted di-

vine and inalienable, embracing, of course, the right of self-government, which rested on the others as substantial premises.[37]

2 The right or privilege, whichever it may be, of intermarriage with the dominant race was prohibited to the African in all the States, both free and slave, and, for all legal purposes, that man was accounted "colored" who had one-sixteenth of African blood.

3 The common-law right of self-defence was gradually reduced by legal subtlety, in the slave States, until only the merest shred remained to the African, while the lightest word of disobedience or gesture of disrespect from him, justified an assault on the part of the white man.

4 Early in the present century it was made a crime in all the States of the South to teach a slave to read, the free blacks were disfranchised,[38] and the most stringent restraining statutes extended over them, including the prohibition of public assembly, even for divine worship, unless a white man were present.

5 Emancipation was not allowed except by decree of a court of record after tedious formality and the assumption of onerous responsibilities on the part of the master; and it was absolutely forbidden to be done by testament.

6 As indicative of the fact that this antipathy was directed against the colored man as a free agent, a man, solely, may be cited the well-known fact of the enormous admixture of the races by illicit commerce at the South, and the further fact that this was, in very large measure, consequent upon the conduct of the most refined and cultivated elements of Southern life. As a thing, an animal, a mere existence, or as the servant of his desire and instrument of his advancement, the Southern Caucasian had no antipathy to the colored race. As one to serve, to nurse, to minister to his will and pleasure, he appreciated and approved of the African to the utmost extent.

7 Every exercise of manly right, sentiment, or inclination, on the part of the negro, was rigorously repressed. To attempt to escape was a capital crime if repeated once or twice; to urge others to escape was also capitally punishable; to learn to read, to claim the rights of property, to speak insolently, to meet for prayer without the sanction of the white man's presence, were all offences against the law; and in this case, as in most others, the law was an index as well as the source of a public sentiment, which grew step by step with its progress in unconscious barbarity.

8 Perhaps the best possible indication of the force of this sentiment, in its ripened and intensest state, is afforded by the course of the Confederate Government in regard to the proposal that it should arm the slaves. In the

very crisis of the struggle, when the passions of the combatants were at fever heat, this proposition was made. There was no serious question as to the efficiency or faithfulness of the slaves. The masters did not doubt that, if armed, with the promise of freedom extended to them, they would prove most effective allies, and would secure to the Confederacy that autonomy which few thoughtful men at that time believed it possible to achieve by any other means. Such was the intensity of this sentiment, however, that it was admitted to be impossible to hold the Southern soldiery in the field should this measure be adopted. So that the Confederacy, rather than surrender a tithe of its prejudice against the negro *as a man,* rather than owe its life to him, serving in the capacity of a soldier, chose to suffer defeat and overthrow. The African might raise the food, build the breastworks, and do aught of menial service or mere manual labor required for the support of the Confederacy, without objection or demurrer on the part of any; but they would rather surrender all that they had fought so long and so bravely to secure, rather than admit, even by inference, his equal manhood or his fitness for the duty and the danger of a soldier's life. It was a grand stubborness, a magnificent adherence to an adopted and declared principle, which loses nothing of its grandeur from the fact that we may believe the principle to have been erroneous.

9 Another very striking and peculiar illustration of this sentiment is the fact that one of the most earnest advocates of the abolition of slavery, and a type of its Southern opponents, the author of "The Impending Crisis"[39] —a book which did more than any other to crystallize and confirm the sentiment awakened at the North by "Uncle Tom's Cabin"—was perhaps more bitterly averse to the freedom, citizenship, and coexistence of the African with the Caucasian than any man that has ever written on the subject. He differed from his slaveholding neighbors only in this: *they* approved the African as a menial, but abominated him as a self-controlling man; *he* abhorred him in both relations. With *them,* the prejudice of race made the negro hateful only when he trenched on the sacred domain of their superior and self-controlling manhood; with *him,* hatred of the race overleaped the conventional relation and included the African wherever found, however employed, or in whatsoever relation considered. His horror of the black far overtopped his ancient antipathy to the slave. The fact that he is an exception, and that the extravagant rhodomontades[40] of "Nojoque" are neither indorsed nor believed by any considerable number of the Southern people, confirms most powerfully this analysis of their temper toward the African.

10 Still another signal instance of its accuracy is the striking fact that one of the hottest political struggles since the war arose out of the proposition to give the colored man the right to testify, in courts of justice, against a white man. The objection was not bottomed on any desire to deprive the colored man of his legal rights, but had its root in the idea that it would be a degradation of the white man to allow the colored man to take the witness-stand and traverse the oath of a Caucasian.

Now, as it relates to our story:—That this most intense and vital sentiment should find expression whenever the repressive power of the conquering people was removed was most natural; that it would be fanned into a white heat by the freedman's enfranchisement was beyond cavil; and that Red Wing should escape such manifestations of the general abhorrence of the work of development there going on was not to be expected, even by its most sanguine friend.

Although the conduct of the teachers at Red Wing had been such as to awaken the respect of all, yet there were two things which made the place peculiarly odious. One was the influence of Eliab Hill with his people in all parts of the county, which had very greatly increased since he had ceased to be a pupil, in appearance, and had betaken himself more than ever to solitude and study. The other was the continued prosperity and rugged independence of Nimbus, who was regarded as a peculiarly "sassy nigger." To the malign influence of these two was attributed every difference of opinion between employer and employee, and every impropriety of conduct on the part of the freedmen of Horsford. Eliab was regarded as a wicked spirit who devised evil continually, and Nimbus as his willing familiar, who executed his purpose with ceaseless diligence. So Red Wing was looked upon with distrust, and its two leading characters, unconsciously to themselves, became marked men, upon whom rested the suspicion and aversion of a whole community.

CHAPTER XXIII.

AN OFFERING OF FIRST-FRUITS.

AN ELECTION WAS impending for members of the Legislature,[41] and there was great excitement in the county of Horsford. Of white Republicans there were not above a half dozen who were openly known as such. There were two or three others who were regarded with some suspicion by their neighbors, among whom was Hesden Le Moyne. Since he had acted as a judge of election at the time of the adoption of the Constitution,[42] he had never been heard to express any opinion upon political matters. He was known to have voted for that Constitution, and when questioned as to his reasons for such a course, had arrogantly answered,

"Simply because I saw fit to do so."

His interrogator had not seen fit to inquire further. Hesden Le Moyne was not a man with whom one wished to provoke a controversy. His unwillingness to submit to be catechised was generally accepted as a proof positive of his "Radical" views. He had been an adviser of Nimbus, his colored playmate, in the purchase of the Red Wing property, his interest in Eliab Hill had not slackened since that worthy cast in his lot with Nimbus, and he did not hesitate to commend the work of the school. He had several times attended the examinations there, had become known to the teachers, and took an active interest in the movement there going on. What his personal views were in regard to the very peculiar state of affairs by which he was surrounded he had never found it necessary to declare. He attended quietly to the work of his plantation, tenderly cared for his invalid mother, and watched the growth of his little son with the seemingly settled conviction that his care was due to them rather than to the public. His counsel and assistance were still freely sought in private matters by the inhabitants of the little village of Red Wing, and neither was ever refused where he saw that it might do good. He was accounted by them a friend, but not a partisan, and none of them had ever discussed any political questions with him, except Eliab Hill, who had more than once talked with him upon the important problem of the future of that race to which the unfortunate cripple was so slightly akin and yet so closely allied.

There was a large majority of colored men in the county, and one of the candidates for the Legislature was a colored man.[43] While elections were under the military control there had been no serious attempt to overcome this majority, but now it was decided that the county should be "redeemed," which is the favorite name in that section of the country for an unlawful subversion of a majority. So the battle was joined, and the conflict waged hot and fierce. That negroes—no matter how numerous they might be—should rule, should bear sway and control in the county of Horsford, was a thought not by any means to be endured. It was a blow on every white cheek—an insult to every Caucasian heart. Men cursed wildly when they thought of it.

Women taunted them with cowardice for permitting it. It was the one controlling and consuming thought of the hour.

On the other hand, the colored people felt that it was necessary for them to assert their newly-acquired rights if they expected to retain them. So that both parties were influenced by the strongest considerations which could possibly affect their action.

Red Wing was one of the points around which this contest raged the hottest. Although it had never become a polling precinct, and was a place of no mercantile importance, it was yet the center from which radiated the spirit that animated the colored men of the most populous district in the county. It was their place of meeting and conference. Accustomed to regard their race as peculiarly dependent upon the Divine aid because of the lowly position they had so long occupied, they had become habituated to associate political and religious interests. The helplessness of servitude left no room for hope except through the trustfulness of faith. The generation which saw slavery swept away, and they who have heard the tale of deliverance from the lips of those who had been slaves, will never cease to trace the hand of God visibly manifested in the events culminating in liberty, or to regard the future of the freed race as under the direct control of the Divine Being. For this reason the political and religious interests and emotions of this people are quite inseparable. Wherever they meet to worship, there they will meet to consult of their plans, hopes, and progress, as at once a distinct race and a part of the American people. Their religion is tinged with political thought, and their political thought shaped by religious conviction.

In this respect the colored race in America are the true children of the Covenanters and the Puritans. Their faith is of the same unquestioning type, which no disappointment or delay can daunt, and their view of personal duty and obligation in regard to it is not less intense than that which led men to sing psalms and utter praises on board the storm-bound "Mayflower." The most English of all English attributes has, by a strange transmutation, become the leading element in the character of the Africo-American. The same mixed motive of religious duty toward posterity and devotion to political liberty which peopled the bleak hills of New England and the fertile lands of Canaan with peoples fleeing from bondage and oppression, may yet cover the North with dusky fugitives from the spirit and the situs of slavery.

From time to time there had been political meetings held at the church or school-house, composed mainly of colored men, though now and then a little knot of white men would come in and watch their proceedings, sometimes from curiosity, and sometimes from spleen. Heretofore, however, there had been no more serious interruption than some sneering remarks and derisive laughter. The colored men felt that it was their own domain, and showed much more boldness than they would ever manifest on other occasions. During this campaign, however, it was determined to have a grand rally, speeches, and a barbecue at Red Wing. The colored inhabitants of that section were put upon their mettle. Several sheep and pigs were roasted, rude tables were spread under the trees, and all arrangements made for a great occasion.

At an early hour of the day when it was announced that the meeting would be held, groups of colored people of all ages and both sexes began to assemble. They were all talking earnestly as they came, for some matter of unusual interest seemed to have usurped for the moment their accustomed lightness and jollity of demeanor.

Nimbus, as the most prosperous and substantial colored man of the region, had always maintained a decided leadership among them, all the more from the fact that he had sought thereby to obtain no advantage for himself. Though a most ardent supporter of that party with which he deemed the interests of his race inseparably allied, he had never taken a very active part in politics, and had persistently refused to be put forward for any official position, although frequently urged to allow himself to be named a candidate.

"No," he would always say; "I hain't got no larnin' an' not much sense. Besides, I'se got all I kin manage, an' more too, a-takin' keer o' dis yer farm. Dat's what I'm good fer. I kin manage terbacker, an' I'd ruther hev a good plantation an' run it myself, than all the offices in the worl'. I'se jes fit fer dat, an' I ain't fit fer nuffin' else."

His success proved the justice of his estimate, and the more he prospered the stronger was his hold upon his people. Of course, there were some who envied him his good-fortune, but such was his good-nature and readiness to render all the assistance in his power that this dangerous leaven did not spread. "Bre'er Nimbus" was still the heart and life of the community which had its center at Red Wing. His impetuosity was well tempered by the subtle caution of Eliab Hill, without whose advice he seldom acted in any important matter.

The relations between these two men had continued singularly close, although of late Eliab had been more independent of his friend's assistance than formerly; for, at the suggestion of the teachers, his parishioners had contributed little sums—a dime, a quarter, and a few a half-dollar apiece—to get him one of those wheeled chairs which are worked by the hands, and by means of which the infirm are frequently enabled to move about without other aid. It was the first time they had ever given anything to a minister of their own, and it was hard for those who had to support families upon a pittance which in other parts of the country would mean starvation; yet so many had hastened to give, that the "go-cart," as it was generally called, proved a vehicle of marvelous luxury and finish to the unaccustomed eyes of these rude children of the plantation.

In this chair Eliab was able to transport himself to and from the school-room, and even considerable distances among his people. This had brought him into nearer relations with them, and it was largely owing to his influence that, after Northern benevolence began to restrict its gifts and to condition its benevolence upon the exercise of a self-help which should provide for a moiety of the expense, the school still continued full and prosperous, and the services of Miss Ainslie were retained for another year—the last she intended to give to the missionary work which accident had thrust upon her young life. Already her heart was pining for the brightness and kindly cheer of the green-clad hills from which she had been exiled so long, and the friends whose hearts and arms would welcome her again to her childhood's home.

On the morning of the barbecue Nimbus and his household were astir betimes. Upon him devolved the chief burden of the entertainment which was to be spread before his neighbors. There was an abundance of willing hands, but few who could do much toward providing the requisite material. His premises had undergone little change beyond the wide, cool, latticed walk which now led from his house to the kitchen, and thence to "Uncle 'Liab's" house, over which Virginia-creepers and honeysuckle were already clambering in the furious haste which that quick-growing clime inspires in vegetation. A porch had also been added to his own house, up the posts and along the eaves of which the wisteria was clambering, while its pendulous, lilac flower-stems hung thick below. A few fruit-trees were planted here and there, and the oaks, which he had topped and shortened back when he cut away the forest for his house-lot, had put out new and dense heads of dark-green foliage that gave to the humble home a look of dignity and repose hardly to be matched by more ornate and costly structures. Upon the north side the corn grew rank and thick up to the very walls of the mud-daubed gable, softening its rudeness and giving a charm even to the bare logs of which it was formed. Lugena had grown full and matronly, had added two to her brood of lusty children, and showed what even a brief period of happiness and prosperity would do for her race as she bustled about in neat apparel with a look of supreme content on her countenance.

Long before the first comers from the country around had made their appearance, the preparations were completed, the morning meal cleared away, the table set in the latticed passage for the dinner of the most honored guests, the children made tidy, and Nimbus, magnificently attired in clean shirt, white pants and vest, a black alpaca coat and a new Panama hat, was ready to welcome the expected arrivals.

Eliab, too, made tidy by the loving care of his friends, was early mounted in his hand-carriage, and propelling himself here and there to meet the first comers. The barbecue was roasting under the charge of an experienced cook; the tables were arranged, and the speakers' stand at the back of the school-house in the grove was in the hands of the decorators. All was mirth and happiness. The freedmen were about to offer oblations to liberty—a sacrifice of the first-fruits of freedom.

CHAPTER XXIV.

A BLACK DEMOCRITUS.[44]

"I SAY, BRE'ER Nimbus!" cried a voice from the midst of a group of those first arriving, "how yer do dis mornin'? Hope yer's well, Squar', you an' all de family."

The speaker was a slender, loose-jointed young man, somewhat shabbily attired, with a shapeless narrow-brimmed felt hat in his hand, who was bowing and scraping with a mock solemnity to the dignitary of Red Wing, while his eyes sparkled with fun and his comrades roared at his comic gestures.

"Is dat you, Berry?" said Nimbus, turning, with a smile. "How yer do, Berry? Glad ter see ye well," nodding familiarly to the others and extending his hand.

"Thank ye, sah. You do me proud," said the jester, sidling towards him and bowing to the crowd with serio-comic gravity. "Ladies an' gemmen, yer jes takes notice, ef yer please, dat I ain't stuck up—not a mite, I ain't, ef I *is* pore. I'se not ashamed ter shake hands wid Mr. Squar' Nimbus—Desmit—War'. I stan's by him whatever his name, an' no matter how many he's got, ef it's more'n he's got fingers an' toes." He bowed low with a solemn wave of his grimy hat, as he shook the proffered hand, amid the laughter of his audience, with whom he seemed to be a prime favorite.

"Glad ter know it, Berry," said Nimbus, shaking the other's hand warmly, while his face glowed with evident pleasure. "How's all gittin' on wid ye, ennyhow?"

"Gittin' on, Bre'er Nimbus?" replied Berry, striking an attitude. "Gittin' on, did yer say? Lor' bress yer soul, yer nebber seed de beat—nebber. Ef yer ebber pegs out h'yer at Red Wing, Bre'er Nimbus, all yer's got ter du is jes ter come up on de Kentry Line whar folks *libs.* Jes you look o' dar, will yer?" he continued, extending a slender arm ending in a skinny hand, the widely parted fingers of which seemed like talons, while the upturned palm was worn smooth and was of a yellowish, pallid white about the fingers' ends. "Jes see de 'fec's ob high libbin' on a nigger. Dar's muscle fer ye. All you needs, Bre'er Nimbus, is jest a few weeks ob good feed! Come up dar now an' wuk a farm on sheers, an' let Marse Sykes 'llowance ye, an' yer'll come out like me an' git some good clothes, too! Greatest place ter start up a run-down nigger yer ever seed. Jes' look at me, now. When I went dar I didn't hev a rag ter my back—nary a rag, an' now jes see how I'se covered wid 'em!"

There was a laugh from the crowd in which Berry joined heartily, rolling his eyes and contorting his limbs so as to show in the completest manner the striking contrast between his lank, stringy, meanly-clad frame and the full, round, well-clothed form of Nimbus.

When the laughter had subsided he struck in again, with the art of an accomplished tease, and sidling still closer to the magnate of Red Wing, he said, with a queer assumption of familiarity:

"An' how is yer good lady, Missus Lugena, an' all de babies, Squar'? They tell me you're gittin' on right smart an' think of settin' up yer kerridge putty soon. Jes' ez soon ez yer git it ready, Sally an' me's a-comin' over ter christen it. We's cousins, yer know, Squar', leastways, Sally an' Lugena's allus said ter be kin on the fayther's side—the white side ob de family, yer know. Yer wouldn't go back on yer relations, would yer, Nimbus? We ain't proud, not a bit proud, Bre'er Nimbus, an' yer ain't a gwine ter forgit us, is yer? Yah, yah, yah!"

There was a tinge of earnestness in this good-natured banter, but it was instantly dissipated by Nimbus's reply:

"Not a bit of it, cousin Berry. Lugena charged me dis berry mornin', jes ez soon ez I seed you an' Sally, ter invite ye ter help eat her big dinner to-day. Whar' is Sally?"

"Dar now," said Berry, "dat's jes what I done tole Sally, now. She's got a notion, kase you's rich yer's got stuck up, you an' Lugena. But I tole her, sez I, 'Nimbus ain't dat ar sort of a chile, Nimbus hain't. He's been a heap luckier nor de rest of us, but he ain't got de big-head, nary bit.' Dat's what I say, an' durn me ef I don't b'lieve it too, I does. We's been hevin' purty hard times, Sally an' me hez. Nebber did hev much luck, yer know—'cept for chillen. Yah, yah! An' jes' dar we's hed a trifle more'n we 'zackly keered about. Might hev spared a few an' got along jest ez well, 'cordin' ter my notion. Den de ole woman's been kinder peaked this summer, an' some two or free ob de babies hez been right poorly, an' Sal—wal, she got a leettle fretted, kase yer know we both wuks purty hard an' don't seem ter git ahead a morsel. So she got her back up, an' sez she ter me dis mornin': 'Berry,' sez she, 'I ain't a gwine ter go near cousin Nimbus', I ain't, kase I hain't got no fine clo'es, ner no chicken-fixing ter take ter de barbecue nuther.' So she's done stop up ter Bob Mosely's wid de baby, an' I t'ought I'd jes come down an' spy out de lan' an' see which on us wuz right. Dat's de fac' truf, Bre'er Nimbus, an' no lyin'. Yah, yah!"

"Sho, sho, Berry," replied Nimbus, reproachfully; "what makes Sally sech a big fool? She oughter be ashamed ter treat her ole fren's dat ar way."

"Now yer talkin', Bre'er Nimbus, dat you is! But la sakes! Bre'er Nimbus, dat ar gal hain't got no pride. Why yer wouldn't b'lieve hit, but she ain't even 'shamed of Berry—fac'! Yah, yah! What yer tinks ob dat now?"

"Why, co'se she ain't," said Nimbus. "Don't see how she could be. Yer always jes dat peart an' jolly dat nobody couldn't git put out wid yer."

"Tink so, Bre'er Nimbus? Wal, now, I 'shures ye dat yer couldn't be wuss mistaken ef yer'd tried. On'y jes' dis mornin' Marse Sykes got put out wid me jes de wus kind."

"How's dat, Berry?"

"Wal, yer se, I'se been a wukkin' fer him ebber sence de s'rrender jes de same ez afore, only dat he pays me an' I owes him. He pays me in sto' orders, an' it 'pears like I owes him mo' an' mo' ebbery time we settles up. Didn't use ter be so when we hed de Bureau, kase den Marse Sykes' 'count didn't use ter be so big; but dese las' two year sence de Bureau done gone, bress God, I gits nex' ter nuffin' ez we goes 'long, an' hez less 'n nuffin' atterwards."[45]

"What wages d'ye git?" asked Nimbus.

"Marse Sykes, he sez I gits eight dollahs a month, myself, an' Sally she gits fo'; an' den we hez tree pounds o'meat apiece an' a peck o'meal, each on us, ebbery week. We could git along right peart on dat—we an' de chillens, six on 'em—wid jes' a drop o' coffee now an' agin, yer know; but yer see, Sally, she's a leetle onsartin an' can't allus wuk, an' it 'pears like it takes all ob my wuk ter pay fer her rations when she don't wuk. I dunno how 'tis, but dat's de way Marse Sykes figgers it out."

"Yer mus' buy a heap ob fine clo'es," said one of the bystanders.

"Wall, ef I does, I leaves 'em ter home fer fear ob wearin' 'em out, don't I?" said Berry, glancing at his dilapidated costume. "Dat's what's de matter. I'se bad 'nough off, but yer jest orter see dem chillen! Dey war's brak ebbery day jes' like a minister, yer knows—not sto' clo'es dough, oh, no! home-made all de time! Mostly bar'-skins, yer know! Yah, yah!"

"An' yer don't drink, nuther," said one whose words and appearance clearly showed that he regarded it as a matter of surprise that any one should not.

" 'Ceptin' only de Christmas an' when some feller treats," responded Berry.

"P'raps he makes it outen de holidays," said a third. "Dar's whar my boss sloshes it on ter me. Clar ef I don't hev more holidays than dar is wuk-days, 'cordin 'ter his 'count."

"Holidays!" said Berry; "dat's what's de matter. Hain't hed but jes tree holidays 'cep' de Chris'mas weeks, in all dat time. So, I 'llowed I'd take one an' come ter dis yer meetin'. Wal, 'long de fust ob de week, I make bold ter tell him so, an' ebber sence dat 'pears like he's gwine ter hu't hisself, he's been so mad. I'se done tried not ter notice it, kase I'se dat solemn-like myself, yer knows, I couldn't 'ford ter take on no mo' ob dat kind; but every day or two he's been a lettin' slip somethin' 'bout niggas gaddin' roun', yer know."

"That was mean," said Nimbus, "kase ef yer is allus laughin' an' hollerin' roun', I'm boun' ter say dar ain't no stiddier han' in de county at enny sort ob wuk."

"Jes' so. Much obleeged ter ye, Squar', fer dat. Same ter yeself 'tu. Howsomever, *he* didn't make no sech remark, not ez I heerd on, an' dis mornin' bright an' airly, he comed roun' an' axes me didn't I want ter take de carry-all and go ter Lewyburg; an' when I 'llowed dat I didn't keer tu, not jes to-day, yer know, he axed me, was I comin' h'yer ter dis yer meetin', an' when I 'llowed I was, he jes' got up an' rar'd. Yah, yah! how he did make de turf fly, all by hissef, kase I wur a whistlin' 'Ole Jim Crow' an' some other nice psalm-tunes, jes' ter keep myself from larfin' in his face! Till finally he sez, sez he, 'Berry Lawson, ef yer goes ter dat er Radikil meetin', yer needn't never come back ter my plantation no mo'.[46] Yer can't stay h'yer no longer—' jes so. Den I made bold ter ax him how our little 'count stood, kase we's been livin' mighty close fer a while, in hopes ter git a mite ahead so's ter sen' de two oldes' chillen ter school h'yer, 'gin winter. An' den sez he, ''Count be damned!'—jes so; 'don't yer know hit's in de papers dat ef yer don't 'bey me an' wuk obedient ter my wishes, yer don't git nary cent, nohow at all?' I tole him I didn't know dat ar, and didn't reckon he did. Den he out wid de paper an' read it ober ter me, an' shure 'nough, dar 'tis, dough I'll swar I nebber heerd nothin' on't afo'. Nebber hed no sech ting in de papers when de Bureau man drawed 'em up, dat's shuah."

"How de debble yer come ter sign sech a paper, Berry?" said Nimbus.

"Dod burned ef I know, Cousin Nimbus. Jes kase I don' know no better, I s'pose. How I gwine ter know what's in dat paper, hey? Does you read all de papers yer signs, Squar' Nimbus? Not much, I reckons; but den you keeps de minister right h'yer ter han' tu read 'em for ye. Can't all ob us afford dat, Bre'er Nimbus."

"Yah, yah, dat's so!" "Good for *you,* Berry!" from the crowd.

"Wal, yer orter hev a guardian—all on us ought, for dat matter," said Nimbus; "but I don't s'pose dere's ary man in de country dat would sign sech a paper ef he know'd it, an' nobody but Granville Sykes that would hev thought of sech a dodge."

"It's jes so in mine," said one of the bystanders. "And in mine;" "an' mine," added one and another.

"And has any one else offered to turn men off for comin' here?" asked Nimbus.

To his surprise, he learned that two thirds the men in the crowd had been thus threatened.

"Jes let 'em try it!" he exclaimed, angrily. "Dey dassent do it, nohow. They'll find out dat a man can't be imposed on allus, ef he *is* pore an' black. Dat dey will! I'se only jes a pore man, but I hain't enny sech mean cuss ez to stan' roun' an' see my race an' kin put on in dat ar way, I hain't."

"All right, Cousin Nimbus, ef Marse Sykes turns me outen house an' home, I knows right whar I comes ter, now."

"Co'se yer do," said Nimbus, proudly. "Yer jes comes ter me an' I takes keer on ye. I needs anudder han' in de crap, ennyhow."

"Now, Cousin Nimbus, yer ain't in airnest, is yer? Yer don't mean dat, pop-suah, does yer now?" asked Berry anxiously.

"Dat I does, Cousin Berry! dat I does!" was the hearty response.

"Whoop, hurrah!" cried Berry, throwing up his hat, turning a handspring, and catching the hat as it came down. "Whar's dat Sally Ann? H'yeah, you fellers, clar away dar an' let me come at her. H'yer I goes now, I jes tole her dis yer bressed mornin' dat it tuk a fool fer luck. Hi-yah!" he cried, executing a sommersault, and diving through the crowd he ran away. As he started off, he saw his wife walking along the road toward Nimbus' house by the side of Eliab Hill in his rolling-chair. Berry dashed back into the circle where Nimbus was engaged in earnest conversation with the crowd in relation to the threats which had been made to them by their employers.

"H'yer, Cousin Nimbus," he cried, "I done fergot ter thank ye, I was dat dar' flustered by good luck, yer know. I'se a t'ousan' times obleeged ter ye, Bre'er Nimbus, jes' a t'ousan' times, an' h'yer's Sally Ann, right outside on de road h'yer, she'll be powerful glad ter hear on't. I'd jes ez lief wuk fer you as a white man, Bre'er Nimbus. I ain't proud, I ain't! Yah! yah!"

He dragged Nimbus through the crowd to intercept his wife, crying out as soon as they came near:

"H'yer, you Sally Ann, what yer tinks now? H'yer's Bre'er Nimbus sez dat ef dat ole cuss, Marse Sykes, should happen ter turn us off, he's jest a gwine ter take us in bag an' baggage, traps, chillen and calamities, an' gib us de bes' de house affo'ds, an' wuk in de crap besides. What yer say now, you Sally Ann, ain't yer 'shamed fer what yer sed 'bout Bre'er Nimbus only dis yere mornin'?"

"Dat I be, Cousin Nimbus," said Sally, turning a comely but careworn face toward Nimbus, and extending her hand with a smile. "Bre'er 'Liab was jest a-tellin' me what a fool I was ter ever feel so toward jes de bes' man in de kentry, ez he sez."

"An' I be damned ef he ain't right, too," chimed in Berry.

"Sho, you Berry. Ain't yer 'shamed now—usin' cuss-words afore de minister!" said Sally.

"Beg yer parding, Bre'er Hill," said Berry, taking off his hat, and bowing with mock solemnity to that worthy. "Hit's been sech a long time sence Sunday come ter our house dat I nigh 'bout forgot my 'ligion."

"An' yer manners too," said Sally briskly, turning from her conversation with Nimbus.

"Jes so, Bre'er Hill, but yer see I was dat ar flustered by my ole woman takin' on so 'bout dat ar sneakin' cuss ob a Marse Sykes a turnin' on us off, dat I hardly knowed which from todder, an' when Cousin Nimbus 'greed ter take me up jes de minnit he dropped me down, hit kinder tuk me off my whoopendickilar, yer know."

CHAPTER XXV.

A DOUBLE-HEADED ARGUMENT.

THE ATTEMPT TO prevent the attendance of voters at the meeting, showing as it did a preconcerted purpose and design on the part of the employers to use their power as such, to overcome their political opponents, was the cause of great indignation at the meeting, and gave occasion for some flights of oratory which would have fallen upon dull ears but for the potent truth on which they were based. Even the cool and cautious Eliab Hill could not restrain himself from an allusion to the sufferings of his people when he was raised upon the platform, still sitting in his rolling-chair, and with clasped hands and reverent face asked God's blessing upon the meeting about to be held.

Especially angry was our friend Nimbus about this attempt to deprive his race of the reasonable privileges of a citizen. Perhaps the fact that he was himself a proprietor and employer rendered him still more jealous of the rights of his less fortunate neighbors. The very immunity which he had from any such danger no doubt emboldened him to express his indignation more strongly, and after the regular speeches had been made he mounted the platform and made a vigorous harangue upon the necessity of maintaining the rights which had been conferred upon them by the chances of war.

"We's got ter take keer ob ourselves," said he. "De guv'ment hez been doin' a heap for us. It's gin us ourselves, our wives, our chillen, an' a chance ter du fer ourselves an' fer dem; an' now we's got ter du it. Ef we don't stan' togedder an' keep de white folks from a-takin' away what we's got, we nebber gits no mo'. In fac', we jes goes back'ards instead o' forrards till yer can't tell de difference twixt a free nigger an' a rale ole time slave. Dat's my 'pinion, an' I say now's de time ter begin—jes when dey begins. Ef a man turns off ary single one fer comin' ter dis meetin' evr'y han' dat is ter wuk for him oughter leave him to once an' nary colored man ought ter do a stroke ob wuk fer him till he takes 'em back."

Loud cheers greeted this announcement, but one old white-headed man arose and begged leave to ask him a question, which being granted, he said:

"Now, feller citizens, I'se been a listenin' ter all dat's been said here to-day, an' I'm jest ez good a 'Publikin ez enny ub de speakers. Yer all knows dat. But I can't fer de life ob me see how we's gwine ter carry out sech advice. Ef we leave one man, how's we gwine ter git wuk wid anodder? An' ef we does, ain't it jest a shiftin' ub han's? Does it make ary difference—at least enough ter speak on—whether a white man hez his wuk done by one nigger er another?"

"But," said Nimbus, hotly, "we oughtn't ter *none* on us wuk fer him."

"Then," said the old man, "what's we ter do fer a libbin'? Here's half er two thirds ob dis crowd likely ter be turned off afore to-morrer night. Now what's yer gwine ter do 'bout it? We's got ter lib an' so's our wives an' chillens? How's we gwine ter s'port dem widout home or wuk?"

"Let them git wuk wid somebody else, that's all," said Nimbus.

"Yes, Bre'er Nimbus, but who's a-gwine ter s'port 'em while we's waitin' fer de white folks ter back down, I wants ter know?"

"I will," said Nimbus, proudly.

"I hain't no manner ob doubt," said the other, "dat Bre'er Nimbus 'll do de berry bes' dat he can in sech a case, but he must 'member dat he's only one and we's a great many. He's been mighty fortinit an' I'se mighty glad ter know it; but jes s'pose ebbery man in de county dat hires a han' should turn him off kase he comes ter dis meetin' an' goes ter 'lection, what could Bre'er Nimbus du towards a feedin' on us? Ob co'se, dey's got ter hev wuk in de crop, but you mus' 'member dat when de 'lection comes off de crap's all laid by, an' der ain't no mo' pressin' need fer wuk fer months ter come. Now, how's we gwine ter lib during dat time? Whar's we gwine ter lib? De white folks kin stan' it—dey's got all dey wants—but we can't. Now, what's we gwine ter do? Jest ez long ez de guv'ment stood by us an' seed dat we hed a fa'r show, we could stan' by de guv'ment. I'se jest ez good a 'Publikin ez ennybody h'yer, yer all knows dat; but I hain't a gwine ter buck agin impossibles, I ain't. I'se got a sick wife an' five chillen. I ain't a gwine ter bring 'em nex' do' ter starvation 'less I sees some use in it. Now, I don't see no use in dis h'yer notion, not a bit. Ef de white folks hez made up der minds—an' hit seems ter me dey hez—dat cullu'd folks shan't vote 'less dey votes wid dem, we mout jest ez well gib up fust as las'!"

"Nebber! nebber, by God!" cried Nimbus, striding across the platform, his hands clenched and the veins showing full and round on neck and brow.

The cry was echoed by nearly all present. Shouts, and cheers, and groans, and hisses rose up in an indistinguishable roar.

"Put him out! Down wid him!" with other and fiercer cries, greeted the old man's ears.

Those around now began to jostle and crowd upon him. Already violent hands were upon him, when Eliab Hill dashed up the inclined plane which had been made for his convenience, and, whirling himself to the side of Nimbus, said, as he pointed with flaming face and imperious gesture to the hustling and boisterous crowd about the old man,

"Stop that!"

In an instant Nimbus was in the midst of the swaying crowd, his strong arms dashing right and left until he stood beside the now terrified remonstrant.

"Dar, dar, boys, no mo' ob dat," he cried, as he pushed the howling mass this way and that. "Jes you listen ter Bre'er 'Liab. Don't yer see he's a talkin' to yer?" he said, pointing to the platform where Eliab sat with upraised hand, demanding silence.

When silence was at last obtained he spoke with more earnestness and power than was his wont, pleading for moderation and thoughtfulness for each other, and a careful consideration of their surroundings.

"There is too much truth," he said, "in all that has been said here to-day. Brother Nimbus is right in saying that we must guard our rights and privileges most carefully, if we would not lose them. The other brother is right, too, in saying that but few of us can exercise those privileges if the white men stand together and refuse employment to those who persist in voting against them. It is a terrible question, fellow-citizens, and one that it is hard to deal with. Every man should do his duty and vote, and act as a citizen whenever called upon to do so, for the sake of his race in the future. We should not be weakly and easily driven from what has been gained for us. We may have to suffer—perhaps to fight and die; but our lives are nothing to the inheritance we may leave our children.

"At the same time we should not grow impatient with our brethren who cannot walk with us in this way. I believe that we shall win from this contest the supreme seal of our race's freedom. It may not come in our time, but it will be set on the foreheads of our children. At all events, we must work together, aid each other, comfort each other, stand by each other. God has taught us patience by generations of suffering and waiting, and by the light which came afterwards. We should not doubt Him now. Let us face our danger like men; overcome it if we may, and if not, bow to the force of the storm and gather strength, rooting ourselves deep and wide while it blows, in order that we may rise erect and free when it shall have passed.

"But above all things there must be no disagreement. The colored people must stand or fall together. Those who have been as fortunate as our Brother Nimbus may breast the tempest, and we must all struggle on and up to stand beside them. It will not do to weakly yield or rashly fight. Remember that our people are on trial, and more than mortal wisdom is required of us by those who have stood our friends. Let us show them that we are men, not only in courage to do and dare, but also to wait and suffer. Let the young and strong, and those who have few children, who have their own homes or a few months' provision, let them bid defiance to those who would oppress us; but let us not require those to join us who are not able or willing to take the worst that may come. Remember that while others have given us freedom, we must work and struggle and wait for liberty—that liberty which gives as well as receives, self-supporting, self-protecting, holding the present and looking to the future with confidence. We must be as free of the employer as we are of the master—free of the white people as they are of us. It will be a long, hard struggle, longer and harder than we have known perhaps; but as God lives, we shall triumph if we do but persevere with wisdom and patience, and trust in Him who brought us up out of the Egypt of bondage and set before our eyes the Canaan of liberty."

The effect of this address was the very opposite of what Eliab had intended. His impassioned references to their imperilled liberty, together with his evident apprehension of even greater danger than was then apparent, accorded so poorly with his halting counsel for moderation that it had the effect to arouse the minds of his hearers to resist such aggression even at every risk. So decided was this feeling that the man whom Nimbus had just rescued from the rudeness of those about him and who had been forgotten during the remarks of the minister, now broke forth and swinging his hat about his head, shouted:

"Three cheers for 'Liab Hill! an' I tells yer what, brudderin', dat ef dis yer is ter be a fight fer takin' keer ob de freedom we's got, I'se in fer it as fur ez ennybody. We must save the crap that's been made, ef we don't pitch ary other one in our day at all. Them's my notions, an' I'll stan' by 'em—er die by 'em ef wust comes ter wust."

Then there was a storm of applause, some ringing resolutions were adopted, and the meeting adjourned to discuss the barbecue and talk patriotism with each other.

There was much clamor and boasting. The candidates, in accordance with a time-honored custom in that region, had come prepared to treat, and knowing that no liquor could be bought at Red Wing, had brought a liberal supply, which was freely distributed among the voters.

On account of the large majority of colored voters in this country, no attempt had previously been made to influence them in this manner, so that they were greatly excited by this threat of coercion. Of course, they talked very loud, and many boasts were made, as to what they would do if the white people persisted in the course indicated. There was not one, however, who in his drunkest moment threatened aught against their white neighbors unless they were unjustly debarred the rights which the law conferred upon them. They wanted "a white man's chance." That was all.

There was no such resolution passed, but it was generally noised abroad that the meeting had resolved that any planter who discharged a hand for attending that meeting would have the privilege of cutting and curing his tobacco without help. As this was the chief crop of the region, and one admitting of no delay in its harvesting and curing, it was thought that this would prove a sufficient guaranty of fair treatment. However, a committee was appointed to look after this matter, and the day which had seemed to dawn so inauspiciously left the colored voters of that region more united and determined than they had ever been before.

CHAPTER XXVI.

TAKEN AT HIS WORD.

IT WAS PAST midnight of the day succeeding the meeting, when Nimbus was awakened by a call at his front gate. Opening the door he called out:

"Who's dar?"

"Nobody but jes we uns, Bre'er Nimbus," replied the unmistakable voice of Berry. "H'yer we is, bag an' baggage, traps an' calamities, jest ez I tole yer. Call off yer dogs, ef yer please, an' come an' 'scort us in as yer promised. H'yer we is—Sally an' me an' Bob an' Mariar an' Bill an' Jim an' Sally junior—an' fo' God I can't get fru de roll-call alone. Sally, you jest interduce Cousin Nimbus ter de rest ob dis family, will yer?"

Sure enough, on coming to the gate, Nimbus found Berry and Sally there with their numerous progeny, several bundles of clothing and a few household wares.

"Why, what does dis mean, Berry?" he asked.

"Mean? Yah, yah!" said the mercurial Berry. "Wal now, ain't dat cool? H'yer he axes me ter come ter his house jest ez soon ez ever Marse Granville routs us offen his plantation, an' ez soon's ever we comes he wants ter know what it means! How's dat fer cousinin', eh? Now don't yer cry, Sally Ann. Jes yer wait till I tell Cousin Nimbus de circumstanshuels an' see ef he don't ax us inside de gate."

"Oh, Cousin Nimbus," said Sally, weeping piteously, "don't yer go ter fault us now—don't please. Hit warn't our fault at all; leastways we didn't mean it so. I did tell Berry he'd better stay an' du what Marse Sykes wanted him ter, 'stead of comin' tu der meetin', an' my mind misgive me all day kase he didn't. But I didn't look for no sech bad luck as we've hed."

"Come in, come in, gal," said Nimbus, soothingly, as he opened the gate, "an' we'll talk it all ober in de mornin'."

"Oh, der ain't nuffin' mo' to be told, Squar'," said Berry, "on'y when we done got home we foun' dis yer truck outdoors in the road, an' de chillen at a neighbor's cryin' like de mischief. De house was locked up an' nailed up besides. I went down ter Marse Sykes' an' seed him, atter a gret while, but he jes sed he didn't know nothin' 'bout it, only he wanted the house fer somebody ez 'ud wuk when he tole 'em tu, instead ub gaddin' roun' ter p'litcal meetins; an' ez my little traps happened ter be in de way he'd jes sot 'em inter de big-road, so dey'd be handy when I come ter load 'em on ter take away. So we jes take de lightest on 'em an' de chillen an' comed on ter take up quarters wid you cordin' ter de 'rangement we made yesterday."

"Dat's all right; jes right," said Nimbus; "but I don't understand it quite. Do yer mean ter say dat Marse Sykes turn you uns offen his plantation while you'se all away, jes kase yer come ter de meetin' yesterday?"

"Nuffin' else in de libbin yairth. Jes put us out an' lock de do' an' nailed up de winders, an' lef' de tings in de big-road."

"But didn't yer leave the house locked when you came here?"

"Nary bit. Nebber lock de do' at all. Got no lock, ner key, ner nuffin' ter steal ub enny account ef enny body should want ter break in. So what I lock de do' fer? Jes lef de chillen wid one ob de neighbors, drawed de do' tu, an' comes on. Dat's all."

"An' he goes in an' takes de tings out? We'll hab de law ob him; dat we will, Berry. De law'll fotch him, pop sure. Dey can't treat a free man dat 'ere way no mo', specially sence de constooshunel 'mendments. Dat dey can't."

So Berry became an inmate of Castle Nimbus, and the next day that worthy proprietor went over to Louisburg to lay the matter before Captain Pardee, who was now a practising lawyer in that city. He returned at night and found Berry outside the gate with a banjo which he accounted among the most precious of his belongings, entertaining a numerous auditory with choice selections from an extensive repertory.

Berry was a consummate mimic as well as an excellent singer, and his fellows were never tired either of his drolleries or his songs. Few escaped his mimicry, and nothing was too sacred for his wit. When Nimbus first came in sight, he was convulsing his hearers by imitating a well-known colored minister of the county, giving out a hymn in the most pompous manner.

"De congregashun will now rise an' sing, ef yer please, the free hundred an' ferty-ferd *hime.*" Thereupon he began to sing:

"Sinner-mans will yer go
To de high lans' o' Hebben,
Whar de sto'ms nebber blow
An' de mild summer's gibben?
Will yer go? will yer go?
Will yer go, sinner-mans?
Oh, say, sinner-mans, will yer go?"

Then, seeing Nimbus approach, he changed at once to a political song.

"De brack man's gittin' awful rich
The people seems ter fear,
Alt'ough he 'pears to git in debt
A little ebbery year.
Ob co'se he gits de biggest kind
Ob wages ebbery day,
But when he comes to settle up
Dey dwindles all away.

"Den jes fork up de little tax
Dat's laid upon de poll.
It's jes de tax de state exac's
Fer habben ob a soul!"

Yer got no lan', yer got no cash,
Yer only got some debts;
Yer couldn't take de bankrupt law

'Cos ye hain't got no 'assets.'
De chillen dey mus' hev dere bread;
De mudder's gettin' ole,
So darkey, you mus' skirmish roun'
An' pay up on yer poll."

"Den jes fork up de little tax, etc.

"Yer know's yer's wuked dis many a year,
To buy de land for 'Marster,'
An' now yer orter pay de tax
So 't he kin hold it faster.
He wuks one acre 'n ebbery ten,
De odders idle stan';
So pay de tax upon *yo're* poll
An' take it off *his* lan'.

Den jes fork up de little tax, etc.

"Oh! dat's de song dat some folks sing!
Say, how d'y'e like de soun'?
Dey say de pore man orter pay
For walkin' on de groun'!
When cullud men was slaves, yer know',
'Twas dreffful hard to tax 'em;
But jes de minnit dat dey's free,
God save us! how dey wax 'em!

Den jes fork up de little tax, etc."[47]

"What you know 'bout poll-tax, Berry?" asked Nimbus, good-naturedly, when the song was ended. "Yer hain't turned politician, hez yer?"

"What I know 'bout poll-tax, Squar' Nimbus? Dat what yer ax? Gad! I knows all 'bout 'em, dat I do, from who tied de dog loose. Who'se a better right, I'd like ter know? I'se paid it, an' ole Marse Sykes hes paid it for me; an' den I'se hed ter pay him de tax an' half a dollah for 'tendin' ter de biznis for me. An' den, one time I'se been 'dicted for not payin' it, an' Marse Sykes tuk it up, an' I hed ter wuk out de tax an' de costs besides. Den I'se hed ter wuk de road ebbery yeah some eight er ten days, an' den wuk nigh 'bout ez many more fer my grub while I wuz at it. Oh, I knows 'bout poll-tax, *I* does! Dar can't nobody tell a nigger wid five er six chillen an' a sick wife, dat's a wukkin' by de yeah an' a gettin' his pay in ole clo'es an' sto' orders—dar can't nobody teach *him* nothin' 'bout poll-tax, honey!"

There was a laugh at this which showed that his listeners agreed fully with the views he had expressed.

The efforts to so arrange taxation as to impose as large a burden as possible upon the colored man, immediately after his emancipation, were very numerous and not unfrequently extremely subtle. The Black Codes, which were adopted by the legislatures first convened under what has gone into history as the "Johnsonian"[48] plan of reconstruction, were models of ingenious subterfuge. Among those which survived this period was the absurd notion of a somewhat onerous poll-tax. That a man who had been deprived of every benefit of government and of all means of self-support or acquisition, should at once be made the subject of taxation, and that a failure to list and pay such tax should be made an indictable offense, savored somewhat of the ludicrous. It seemed like taxing the privilege of poverty.

Indeed, the poor men of the South, including the recent slaves, were in effect compelled to pay a double poll-tax. The roads of that section are supported solely by the labor of those living along their course. The land is not taxed, as in other parts of the country, for the support of those highways the passability of which gives it value; but the poor man who travels over it only on foot must give as much of his labor as may be requisite to maintain it. This generally amounts to a period ranging from six to ten days of work per annum. In addition to this, he is required to pay a poll-tax, generally about two dollars a year, which is equivalent to at least one fourth of a month's pay. During both these periods he must board himself.

So it may safely be estimated that the average taxes paid by a colored man equals one half or two thirds of a month's wages, even when he has not a cent of property, and only maintains his family by a constant miracle of effort which would be impossible but for the harsh training which slavery gave and which is one of the beneficent results of that institution. If he refuses to work the road, or to pay or list the poll-tax, he may be indicted, fined, and his labor sold to the highest bidder, precisely as in the old slave-times, to discharge the fine and pay the tax and costs of prosecution. There is a grim humor about all this which did not fail to strike the colored man and induce him to remark its absurdity, even when he did not formulate its actual character.

A thousand things tend to enhance this absurdity and seeming oppression which the imagination of the thoughtful reader will readily supply. One is the self-evident advantage which this state of things gives to the land-owners. By it they are enabled to hold large tracts of land, only a small portion of which is cultivated or used in any manner. By refusing to sell on reasonable terms and in small parcels, they compel the freedmen to accept the alternative of enormous rents and oppressive terms, since starvation is the only other that remains to them.

The men who framed these laws were experts in legislation and adepts in political economy. It would perhaps be well for countries which are to-day wrestling with the question: "What shall we do with our poor?" to consider what was the answer the South made to this same inquiry. There were four millions of people who owned no property. They were not worth a dollar apiece. Of lands, tenements and hereditaments they had none. Life, muscle, time, and the clothes that conceal nakedness were their only estate. But they were rich in "days' works." They had been raised to work and liked it. They were accustomed to lose *all* their earnings, and could be relied on to endure being robbed of a part, and hardly know that they were the subject of a new experiment in governmental ways and means. So, the dominant class simply taxed the possibilities of the freedman's future, and lest he should by any means fail to recognize the soundness of this demand for tribute and neglect to regard it as a righteous exemplification of the Word, which declares that "from him that hath not shall be taken away even that which he hath,"[49] they frugally provided:

1 That the ignorant or inept citizen neglecting to list his poll for taxation should be liable to indictment and fine for such refusal or neglect.
2 That if unable to pay such tax and fine and the costs of prosecution, he should be imprisoned and his labor sold to the highest bidder until this claim of the State upon his poverty should be fully redeemed.
3 That the employer should be liable to pay the personal taxes of his employees, and might recoup himself from any wages due to said hirelings or to become due.
4 To add a further safeguard, in many instances they made the exercise of the elective franchise dependent upon the payment of such tax.

Should the effete monarchies of the Old World ever deign to glance at our civil polity, they will learn that taxation is the only sure and certain cure for pauperism, and we may soon look for their political economists to render thanks to the "friends" of the former slave for this discovery of a specific for the most ancient of governmental ills!

The song that has been given shows one of the views which a race having little knowledge of political economy took of this somewhat peculiar but perhaps necessary measure of governmental finance.

The group broke up soon after Nimbus arrived, and Berry, following him upon the porch said, as he laid his banjo in the window:

"Wal, an' what did de Cap'n say 'bout my case 'gin Marse Granville Sykes?"

"He said you could indict him, an' hev him fined by de court ef he turned yer off on 'count ob yer perlitical principles."

"Bully fer de Cap'n!" said Berry, "dat's what I'll do, straight away. Yah, yah! won't dat er be fun, jes makin' ole Mahs'r trot up ter de lick-log fer meanness ter a nigger? Whoop! h'yer she goes!" and spreading his hands he made "a cart-wheel" and rolled on his outstretched hands and feet half way to the gate, and then turned a handspring back again, to show his approval of the advice given by the attorney.

"An' he says," continued Nimbus, who had looked seriously on at his kinsman's antics, "dat yer can sue him an' git yer wages fer de whole year, ef yer kin show dat he put yer off widout good reason."

"Der ain't no mite ob trouble 'bout dat ar, nary mite," said Berry, confidently. "You knows what sort uv a wuk-hand I is in de crap, Bre'er Nimbus?"

"Yes, I knows dat," was the reply; "but de cap'n sez dat it mout take two or tree year ter git dese cases fru de court, an' dar must, of co'se, be a heap ob cost an' trouble 'bout 'em."

"An' he's right tu', Bre'er Nimbus," said Berry seriously.

"Dat's so, Berry," answered Nimbus, "an' on account ob dat, an' der fac' dat yer hain't got no money an' can't afford ter resk de wages dat yer family needs ter lib on, an' 'cause 'twould make smart ob feelin' an' yer don't stan' well fer a fa'r show afore de court an' jury, kase of yer color, *he* sez yer'd better jes thank de Lo'd fer gittin' off ez well ez yer hev, an' try ter look out fer breakers in de futur. He sez ez how it's all wrong an' hard an' mean an' all dat, but he sez, tu, dat yer ain't in no sort ob fix ter make a fight on't wid Marse Sykes. Now, what *you* think, Berry?"

The person addressed twirled his narrow-brimmed felt hat upon his finger for a time and then said, looking suddenly up at the other:

"Uncle Nimbus, Berry's right smart ob a fool, but damn me ef I don't b'lieve de Cap'n's in de right on't. What you say, now?"

Nimbus had seated himself and was looking toward the darkening west with a gloomy brow. After a moment's silence he said:

"I'se mighty feared yer both right, Bre'er Berry. But it certain ar' a mighty easy way ter git wuk fer nothin', jes ter wait till de crap's laid by an' den run a man off kase he happens ter go ter a political meetin'! 'Pears like tain't *much* more freedom dan we hed in ole slave-times."

"Did it ebber 'ccur ter you, Uncle Nimbus," said Berry, very thoughtfully, "dat dis yer ting *freedom* waz a durn curus affair fer we cullud people, ennyhow?"

"Did it ever? Wal, now, I should tink it hed, an' hit 'ccurs ter me now dat it's growin' quarer an' quarer ebbery day. Though I'se had less on't ter bear an' puzzle over than a-most enny on ye, dat I hez, I don't know whar it'll wuk out. 'Liab sez de Lord's a doin' His own wuk in His own way, which I 'specs is true; but hit's a big job, an' He's got a quare way ob gittin' at it, an' seems ter be a-takin' His own time fer it, tu. Dat's my notion."

It was no doubt childish for these two simple-minded colored men to take this gloomy view of their surroundings and their future. They should have realized that the fact that their privileges were insecure and their rights indefensible was their own misfortune, perhaps even their fault. They should have remembered that the susceptibilities of that race among whom their lot had been cast by the compulsion of a strange providence, were such as to be greatly irritated by anything like a manly and independent exercise of rights by those who had been so long accounted merely a superior sort of cattle. They should not have been at all surprised to find their race helpless and hopeless before the trained and organized power of the whites, controlled by the instinct of generations and animated by the sting of defeat.

All this should have been clear and plain to them, and they should have looked with philosophic calmness on the abstract rights which the Nation had conferred and solemnly guaranteed to them, instead of troubling themselves about the concrete wrongs they fancied they endured. Why should Berry Lawson care enough about attending a political meeting to risk provoking his employer's displeasure by so doing; or why, after being discharged, should he feel angry at the man who had merely enforced the words of his own contract? He was a free man; he signed the contract, and the courts were open to him as they were to others, if he was wronged. What reason was there for complaint or apprehension, on his part?

Yet many a wiser head than that of Berry Lawson, or even that of his more fortunate kinsman, the many-named Nimbus, has been sorely puzzled to understand how ignorance and poverty and inexperience should maintain the right, preserve and protect themselves against opposing wisdom, wealth and malicious skill, according to the spirit and tenor of the Reconstruction Acts. But it is a problem which ought to trouble no one, since it has been enacted and provided by the Nation that all such persons shall have all the rights and privileges of citizens. That should suffice.[50]

However, the master-key to the feeling which these colored men noted and probed in their quiet evening talk was proclaimed aloud by the county newspaper which, commenting on the meeting at Red Wing and the dismissal of a large number of colored people who attended it in opposition to the wish of their employers, said:

> "Our people are willing that the colored man should have all his rights of *person* and of *property;* we desire to promote his *material* welfare; but when he urges his claim to political right, he offers a flagrant insult to the white race. We have no sympathy to waste on negro-politicians or those who sympathize with and encourage them."*

The people of Horsford county had borne a great deal from negro-domination. New men had come into office by means of colored votes, and the old set to whom office had become a sort of perquisite were deprived thereby of this inherited right. The very presence of Nimbus and a few more who like him were prosperous, though in a less degree, had been a constant menace to the peace of a community which looked with peculiar jealousy upon the colored man in his new estate. This might have been endured with no evil results had their prosperity been attended with that humility which should characterize a race so lately lifted from servitude to liberty. It was the "impudent" assertion of their "rights" that so aggravated and enraged the people among whom they dwelt. It was not so much the fact of their having valuable possessions, and being entitled to pay for their labor, that was deemed such an outrage on the part of the colored race, but that they should openly and offensively use those possessions to assert those rights and continually hold language which only "white men" had a right to use. This was more than a community, educated as the Southerners had been, could be expected peaceably to endure.

As a farmer, a champion tobacco-grower and curer, as the most prosperous man of his race in that section, Horsford was not without a certain pride in Nimbus; but when he asserted the right of his people to attend a political meeting without let or hindrance, losing only from their wages as hirelings the price of the time thus absent, he was at once marked down as a "dangerous" man. And when it was noised abroad that he had proposed that

* Taken from the *Patriot-Democrat*, Clinton, La., Oct. 1876.

all the colored men of the county should band together to protect themselves against this evil, as he chose to regard it, he was at once branded not only as "dangerous" but as a "desperate" and "pestiferous" nigger, instead of being considered merely "sassy," as theretofore.

So this meeting and its results had the effect to make Nimbus far more active in political matters than he had ever been before, since he honestly believed that their rights could only be conserved by their political co-operation. To secure this, he travelled about the country all the time he could spare from his crop, visiting the different plantations and urging his political friends to stand firm and not be coaxed or driven away from the performance of their political duty. By this means he became very "obnoxious" to the "best people" of Horsford, and precipitated a catastrophe that might easily have been avoided had he been willing to enjoy his own good fortune, instead of clamoring about the collective rights of his race.[51]

CHAPTER XXVII.

MOTES IN THE SUNSHINE.

MOLLIE AINSLIE'S third year of teacher's life was drawing near its close. She had promised her brother to remain at the South during that time in order that she might escape the perils of their native climate. She was of vigorous constitution but of slight build, and he dreaded lest the inherited scourge should take an ineradicable hold upon her system. She had passed her school-girl life with safety; but he rightly judged that a few years in the genial climate where she then was would do very much toward enabling her to resist the approaches of disease.

The work in which she had been engaged had demanded all her energies and commanded all her devotion. Commencing with the simplest of rudimentary training she had carried some of her pupils along until a fair English education had been achieved. One of these pupils had already taken the place vacated a few months before by Lucy Ellison, since which time Mollie had occupied alone the north rooms of the old hostelry—a colored family who occupied the other portion serving as protectors, and bringing her meals to her own apartments. A friend had spent a portion of this time with her, a schoolmate whose failing health attested the wisdom of the condition her dying brother had imposed in regard to herself. As the warm weather approached this friend had returned to her New England home, and Mollie Ainslie found herself counting the days when she might also take her flight.

Her work had not grown uninteresting, nor had she lost any of her zeal for the unfortunate race she had striven to uplift; but her heart was sick of the terrible isolation that her position forced upon her. She had never once thought of making companions, in the ordinary sense, of those for whom she labored. They had been so entirely foreign to her early life that, while she labored unremittingly for their advancement and entertained for many of them the most affectionate regard, there was never any inclination to that friendly intimacy which would have been sure to arise if her pupils had been of the same race as herself. She recognized their right most fully to careful and polite consideration; she had striven to cultivate among them gentility of deportment; but she had longed with a hungry yearning for friendly white faces, and the warm hands and hearts of friendly associates.

Her chief recreation in this impalpable loneliness—this Chillon[52] of the heart in which she had been bound so long—was in daily rides upon her horse, Midnight. Even in her New England home she had been passionately fond of a horse, and while at school had been carefully trained in horsemanship, being a prime favorite with the old French riding-master who had charge of that branch of education in the seminary of her native town. Midnight, coming to her from the dying hand of her only brother, had been to her a sacred trust and a pet of priceless value. All her pride and care had centered upon him, and never had horse received more devoted attention. As a result, horse and rider had become very deeply attached to each other. Each knew and appreciated the other's good qualities and varying moods. For many months the petted animal had shown none of that savageness with which his owner had before been compelled occasionally to struggle. He had grown sleek and round, but had lost his viciousness, so far as she was concerned, and obeyed her lightest word and gesture with a readiness that had made him a subject of comment in the country around, where the "Yankee school-marm" and her black horse had become somewhat noted.

There was one road that had always been a favorite with the horse from the very first. Whenever he struck that he pressed steadily forward, turning neither to the right or left until he came to a rocky ford five miles below, which his rider had never permitted him to cross, but from which he was always turned back with difficulty—at first with a troublesome display of temper, and at the last, with evident reluctance.

It was in one of her most lonely moods, soon after the incidents we have just narrated, that Mollie Ainslie set out on one of her customary rides. In addition to the depression which was incident to her own situation, she was also not a little disturbed by the untoward occurrences affecting those for whom she had labored so long. She had never speculated much in regard to the future of the freedmen, because she had considered it as assured. Growing to womanhood in the glare of patriotic warfare, she had the utmost faith in her country's honor and power. To her undiscriminating mind the mere fact that this honor and power were pledged to the protection and elevation of the negro had been an all-sufficient guarantee of the accomplishment of that pledge. In fact, to her mind, it had taken on the reality and certainty of a fact already accomplished. She had looked forward to their prosperity as an event not to be doubted. In her view Nimbus and Eliab Hill were but feeble types of what the race would "in a few brief years" accomplish for itself. She believed that the prejudice that prevailed against the autonomy of the colored people would be suppressed, or prevented from harmful action by the national power, until the development of the blacks should have shown them to be of such value in the community that the old-time antipathy would find itself without food to exist upon longer.

She had looked always upon the rosy side, because to her the country for which her brother and his fellows had fought and died was the fairest and brightest thing upon earth. There might be spots upon the sun's face, but none were possible upon her country's escutcheon. So she had dreamed and had fondly pictured herself as doing both a patriot's and a Christian's duty in the work in which she had been engaged. She felt less of anger and apprehension with regard to the bitter and scornful whites than of pity and contempt for them, because they could not appreciate the beauty and grandeur of the Nation of which they were an unwilling part, and of the future that lay just before. She regarded all there had been of violence and hate as the mere puerile spitefulness of a subjugated people. She had never analyzed their condition or dreamed that they would ever be recognized as a power which might prove dangerous either to the freedman's rights or to the Nation itself.

The recent events had opened her eyes. She found that, unknown to herself, knowledge had forced itself upon her mind. As by a flash the fact stood revealed to her consciousness that the colored man stood alone. The Nation had withdrawn its arm. The flag still waved over him, but it was only as a symbol of sovereignty renounced—of power discarded. Naked privileges had been conferred, but the right to enforce their recognition had been abandoned. The weakness and poverty of the recent slave was pitted alone and unaided against the wealth and power and knowledge of the master. It was a revelation of her own thought to herself, and she was stunned and crushed by it.

She was no statesman, and did not comprehend anything of those grand policies whose requirements overbalance all considerations of individual right—in comparison with which races and nations are but sands upon the shore of Time. She little realized how grand a necessity lay at the back of that movement which seemed to her so heartless and inexcusable. She knew, of course, vaguely and weakly, that the Fathers made a Constitution on which our government was based. She did not quite understand its nature, which was very strange, since she had often heard it expounded, and as a matter of duty had read with care several of those books which tell us all about it.

She had heard it called by various names in her far New England home by men whom she loved and venerated, and whose wisdom and patriotism she could not doubt. They had called it "a matchless inspiration" and "a mass of compromises;" "the charter of liberty" and "a league with Hell;"[53] "the tocsin of liberty" and "the manacle of the slave." She felt quite sure that nobler-minded, braver-hearted men than those who used these words had never lived, yet she could not understand the thing of which they spoke so positively and so passionately. She did not question the wisdom or the patriotism of the Fathers who had propounded this enigma. She thought they did the best they knew, and knew the best that was at that time to be known.

She had never *quite* believed them to be inspired, and she was sure they had no models to work after. Greece and Rome were not republics in the sense of our day, and in their expanded growth did not profess to be, at any time; Switzerland and San Marino were too limited in extent to afford any valuable examples; Venice while professedly a republic had been as unique and inimitable as her own island home. Then there were a few experiments here and there, tentative movements barren of results, and that was all that the civilized world had to offer of practical knowledge of democracy at that time. Beyond this were the speculations of philosophers and the dreams of poets. Or perhaps the terms should be reversed, for the dreams were oft-times more real and consistent than the lucubrations. From these she did not doubt that our ancient sages took all the wisdom they could gather and commingled it with the riper knowledge of their own harsh experience.

But yet she could not worship the outcome. She knew that Franklin was a great man and had studied electricity very profoundly, for his day; but there are ten thousand unnoted operators to-day who know more of its properties, power and management than he ever dreamed of. She did not know but it might be so with regard to free government. The silly creature did not know that while the world moves in all things else, it stands still or goes backward in governmental affairs. She never once thought that while in science and religion humanity is making stupendous strides, in government as in art, it turns ever to the model of the antique and approves the wisdom only of the ancient.

So it was that she understood nothing of the sacredness of right which attaches to that impalpable and indestructible thing, a State of the American Union—that immortal product of mortal wisdom, that creature which is greater than its creator, that part which is more than the whole, that servant which is lord and master also.[54] If she had been given to metaphysical researches, she would have found much pleasure in tracing the queer involutions of that network of wisdom that our forefathers devised, which their sons have labored to explain, and of which the sword had already cut some of the more difficult knots. Not being a statesman or a philosopher, she could only wonder and grow sad in contemplating the future that she saw impending over those for whom she had labored so long.

CHAPTER XXVIII.

IN THE PATH OF THE STORM.

WHILE MOLLIE AINSLIE thought of these things with foreboding, her steed had turned down his favorite road, and was pressing onward with that persistency which characterizes an intelligent horse having a definite aim in view. The clouds were gathering behind her, but she did not notice them. The horse pressed on and on. Closer and closer came the storm. The road grew dark amid the clustering oaks which overhung its course. The thunder rolled in the distance and puffs of wind tossed the heavy-leafed branches as though the trees begged for mercy from the relentless blast. A blinding flash, a fierce, sharp peal, near at hand, awoke her from her reverie. The horse broke into a quick gallop, and glancing back she saw a wall of black cloud, flame-lighted and reverberant, and felt the cold breath of the summer storm come sweeping down upon her as she sped away.

She saw that it would be useless to turn back. Long before she could reach any shelter in that direction she would be drenched. She knew she was approaching the river, but remembering that she had noticed some fine-looking houses just on the other side, she decided that she would let the horse have his own way, and apply at one of these for shelter. She was sure that no one would deny her that in the face of such a tornado as was raging behind her. The horse flew along as if a winged thing. The spirit of the storm seemed to have entered into him, or else the thunder's voice awakened memories of the field of battle, and for once his rider found herself powerless to restrain his speed or direct his course. He laid back his ears, and with a short, sharp neigh dashed onward with a wild tremor of joy at the mad race with wind and storm. The swaying tree-tops waved them on with wild gesticulations. The lightning and the thunder added wings to the flying steed.

Just before reaching the river bank they had to pass through a stretch of tall pines, whose dark heads were swaying to and fro until they almost met above the narrow road, making it so dark below that the black horse grew dim in the shadow, while the gaunt trunks creaked and groaned and the leaves hissed and sobbed as the wind swept through them. The resinous fragrance mingled with the clayey breath of the pursuing storm. The ghost-like trunks stood out against the lightning flashes like bars before the path of flame. She no longer tried to control her horse. Between the flashes, his iron feet filled the rocky road with sparks of fire. He reached the ford and dashed knee-deep into the dark, swift stream, casting a cool spray around him before he checked his speed. Then he halted for an instant, tossed his head as if to give the breeze a chance to creep beneath his flowing mane, cast a quick glance back at his rider, and throwing out his muzzle uttered a long, loud neigh that seemed like a joyful hail, and pressed on with quick, careful steps, picking his way along the ledge of out-cropping granite which constituted the ford, as if traversing a well-remembered causeway.

The water grew deeper and darker; the rider reached down and gathered up her dark habit and drew her feet up close beneath her. The current grew swifter. The water climbed the horse's polished limbs. It touched his flanks and foamed and dashed about his rugged breast. Still he picked his way among the rocks with eager haste, neighing again and again, the joy-ringing neighs of the home-coming steed. The surging water rose about his massive shoulders and the rider drew herself still closer up on the saddle, clinging to bow and mane and giving him the rein, confident in his prowess and intelligence, wondering at his eagerness, yet anxious for his footing in the dashing current. The wind lifted the spray and dashed it about her. The black cloud above was fringed with forked lightning and resonant with swift-succeeding peals of thunder. The big drops began to fall hissing into the gurgling waters. Now and then they splashed on her hands and face and shot through her close-fitting habit like icy bolts. The brim of the low felt hat she wore and its dark plume were blown about her face. Casting a hurried glance backward, she saw the grayish-white storm-sheet come rushing over the sloping expanse of surging pines, and heard its dull heavy roar over the rattle of the aerial artillery which echoed and re-echoed above her.

And now the wind shifted, first to one point and then to another. Now it swept down the narrow valley through which the stream ran; now it dashed the water in her face, and anon it seemed about to toss her from her seat and hurl her over her horse's head. She knew that the fierce storm would strike her before she could reach any place of shelter. The wild excitement of a struggle with the elements flamed up in her face and lighted her eyes with joy. She might have been a viking's daughter as her fair hair blew over her flushed face, while she patted her good steed and laughed aloud for very glee at the thought of conflict with the wild masterful storm and the cool gurgling rapid which her horse breasted so gallantly.

There was a touch of fun, too, in the laugh, and in the arch gleaming of her eyes, as she thought of the odd figure which she made, perched thus upon the saddle in mid-river, blown and tossed by the wind, and fleeing from the storm. Her rides were the interludes of her isolated life, and this storm was a part of the fun. She enjoyed it as the vigorous pleasure-seeker always enjoys the simulation of danger.

The water shoaled rapidly as they neared the farther shore. The black horse mounted swiftly to the bank, still pressing on with unabated eagerness. She leaned over and caught up the stirrup, thrust her foot into it, regained her seat and seized the reins, as with a shake and a neigh he struck into a long easy gallop.

"Go!" she said, as she shook the reins. The horse flew swiftly along while she swayed lightly from side to side as he rose and fell with great sinewy strides. She felt him bound and quiver beneath her, but his steps were as though the black, corded limbs were springs of steel. Her pride in the noble animal she rode overcame her fear of the storm, which followed swifter than they fled. She looked eagerly for a by-path leading to some farm-house, but the swift-settling darkness of the summer night hid them from her eager glance, if any there were. Half a mile from the ford, and the storm overtook them—a wall of wind-driven rain, which dashed and roared about them, drenching the rider to the skin in an instant. In a moment the red-clay road became the bed of a murky torrent. The horse's hoofs, which an instant before echoed on the hard-beaten track, splashed now in the soft mud and threw the turbid drops over her dripping habit and into her storm-washed face. A quarter of a mile more, and the cold streams poured down her back and chilled her slight frame to the marrow. Her hands were numb and could scarce cling to the dripping reins. Tears came into her eyes despite herself. Still the wild cloud-burst hurled its swift torrents of icy rain upon them. She could scarcely see her horse's head, through the gray, chilly storm-sheet.

"Whoa! whoa, Midnight!" she cried, in tremulous tones through her chattering teeth and white, trembling lips. All her gay exultant courage had been drenched and chilled out of her. She tried to check his stride with a loose convulsive clutch at the reins as she peered about with blinded eyes for a place of shelter. The horse shook his head with angry impatience, neighed again, clasped the bit in his strong teeth, stretched his neck still further and covered the slippery ground with still swifter strides. A hundred yards more and he turned into a narrow lane at the right, between two swaying oaks, so quickly as almost to unseat his practiced rider, and with neigh after neigh dashed down to a great, rambling, old farm-house just visible under the trees at the foot of the lane, two hundred yards away. The way was rough and the descent sharp, but the horse did not slacken his speed. She knew it was useless to attempt to check him, and only clung to the saddle pale with fear as he neared the high gate which closed its course. As he rose with a grand lift to take the leap she closed her eyes in terror. Easy and swift as a bird's flight was the leap with which the strong-limbed horse cleared, the high palings and lighted on the soft springy turf within; another bound or two and she heard a sharp, strong voice which rang above the storm with a tone of command that betrayed no doubt of obedience:

"Whoa, Satan! Stand, sir!"

The fierce horse stopped instantly. Mollie Ainslie was thrown heavily forward, clasped by a strong arm and borne upon the piazza. When she opened her eyes she saw the torrents pouring from the eaves, the rain beating itself into spray upon the ground without, the black horse steaming and quivering at the steps of the porch, and Hesden Le Moyne gazing anxiously down into her face. The water dripped from her garments and ran across the porch. She shook as if in an ague-fit. She could not answer the earnest inquiries that fell from his lips. She felt him chafing her chill, numbed hands, and then the world was dark, and she knew no more of the kindly care which was bestowed upon her.

CHAPTER XXIX.

LIKE AND UNLIKE.

WHEN SHE AWOKE to consciousness she was lying on a bed in an apartment which was a strange compound of sitting- and sleeping-room. The bed stood in a capacious alcove which seemed to have been built on as an afterthought. The three sides were windows, in the outer of which were tastefully arranged numerous flowering plants, some of which had clambered up to the ceiling and hung in graceful festoons above the bed. The window-shades were so arranged as to be worked by cords, which hung within easy reach of one lying there. The night had not fully come, but a lamp was burning at the side of the bed yet beyond its head-board, so that its rays lit up the windows and the green trailing vines, but did not fall upon the bed. In an invalid's chair drawn near the bedside, a lady well past the middle age but with a face of singular sweetness and refinement was watching and directing the efforts which were being made for the resuscitation of the fainting girl by two servant women, who were busily engaged in chafing her hands and making warm applications to her chilled limbs.

As she opened her eyes they took in all these things, but she could not at once remember what had happened or where she was. This sweet vision of a home interior was so different from the low, heavy-beamed rooms and little diamond-paned windows of the Ordinary, even after all her attempts to make it cosy, that she seemed to have awakened in fairy land. She wondered dully why she had never trained ivies and Madeira vines over those dark beams, and blushed at the thought that so simple a device had never occurred to her. She lay motionless until she had recalled the incidents of the day. She had recognized Mr. Le Moyne at once, and she knew by instinct that the graceful lady who sat beside her was she who had written her the only word of sympathy or appreciation she had ever received from one of her own sex in the South. She was anxious for a better view and turned toward her.

"Ah, here are you, my dear!" said a soft, low voice, as the light fell upon her opened eyes. "Move me up a little, Maggie," to one of the servants. "We are glad to see you coming around again. Don't move, dear," she continued, as she laid her thin soft hand upon the plump one of the reclining girl. "You are among friends. The storm and the ride were too much for you, and you fainted for a little while. That is all. There is no trouble now. You weren't hurt, were you?" she asked anxiously.

"No," said the other, wonderingly.

"We are glad of that," was the reply. "You are exhausted, of course, but if you do not get cold you will soon be all right. Maggie," she continued, to the servant, "tell Mr. Hesden to bring in that hot toddy now. He had better put the juice of a lemon in it, too. Miss Ainslie may not be accustomed to taking it. I am Mrs. Le Moyne, I forgot to say," she added, turning to her unintended guest, "and Hesden, that is my son, tells me that you are Miss Ainslie, the brave young teacher at Red Wing whom I have long wished to see. I am really glad that chance, or Hesden's old war horse Satan, brought you here, or I am afraid I should never have had that pleasure. This is Hesden," she continued, nodding toward him as he entered with a small silver waiter on which was a steaming pitcher and a delicate glass. "He has been my nurse so long that he thinks no one can prepare a draught for a sick person so well as he, and I assure you that I quite agree with his notion. You have met before, I believe. Just take a good dose of this toddy and you will be better directly. You got a terrible drenching, and I was afraid you would have a congestive chill when they brought you in here as white as a sheet with your teeth chattering like castanets."

Hesden Le Moyne filled the glass with the steaming decoction and held the salver toward her. She took it and tried to drink.

"Hand me the waiter, Hesden," said his mother, reprovingly, "and raise her head. Don't you see that Miss Ainslie cannot drink lying there. I never saw you so stupid, my son. I shall have to grow worse again soon to keep you from getting out of practice entirely."

Thus reproached, Hesden Le Moyne put his arm hesitatingly beneath the pillow, raised the flushed face upon it and supported the young lady while she quaffed the hot drink. Then he laid her easily down, smoothed the pillow with a soft instinctive movement, poured out a glass of the toddy which he offered to his mother, and then, handing the waiter to the servant, leaned over his mother with a caressing movement and said:

"You must look out, little mother. Too much excitement will not do for you. You must not let Miss Ainslie's unexpected call disturb you."

"No indeed, Hesden," she said, as she looked up at him gratefully, "I feel really glad of any accident that could bring her under our roof, now that I am satisfied that she is to experience no harm from her stormy ride. She will be all right presently, and we will have supper served here as usual. You may tell Laura that she need be in no haste."

Having thus dismissed her son she turned to her guest and said:

"I have been an invalid so long that our household is all ordered with regard to that fact. I am seldom able to be taken out to dinner, and we have got into the habit of having a late supper here, just Hesden, his little boy, and I, and to-night we will have the table set by the bedside and you will join us."

The sudden faint was over; the toddy had sent the blood tingling through the young girl's veins. The *rôle* of the invalid was an unaccustomed one for her to play, and the thought of supping in bed was peculiarly distasteful to her self-helping Northern training. It was not long before she began to manifest impatience.

"Are you in pain, dear?" asked the good lady, noticing with the keen eye of the habitual invalid her restive movements.

"No, indeed," was the reply. "I am not at all sick. It was only a little faint. Really, Mrs. Le Moyne, I would rather get up than lie here."

"Oh, lie still," said the elder lady, cheerfully. "The room hardly looks natural unless the bed is occupied. Besides," she added with a light laugh, "you will afford me an excellent opportunity to study effects. You seem to me very like what I must have been when I was first compelled to abandon active life. You are very nearly the same size and of much the same complexion and cast of features. You will pardon an old lady for saying it, I am sure. Lest you should not, I shall be compelled to add that I was considered something of a beauty when I was young. Now, you shall give me an idea of how I have looked in all the long years that couch has been my home. I assure you I shall watch you very critically, for it has been my pride to make my invalid life as pleasant to myself and as little disagreeable to others as I could. Knowing that I could never be anything else, I devised every plan I could to make myself contented and to become at least endurable to my family."

"Everyone knows how well you have succeeded, Mrs. Le Moyne," said the young girl. "It must indeed have been a sad and burdened life, and it seems to me that you have contrived to make your sick room a perfect paradise."

"Yes, yes," said the other, sadly, "it is beautiful. Those who loved me have been very indulgent and very considerate, too. Not only every idea of my own has been carried into effect, but they have planned for me, too. That alcove was an idea of my husband's. I think that the sunlight pouring in at those windows has done more to prolong my life than anything else. I did not think, when thirty years ago I took to my bed, that I should have survived him so long—so long—almost eight years. He was considerably older than I, but I never looked to outlive him, never.

"That lamp-stand and little book-rack," she continued, with the garrulity of the invalid when discoursing of his own affairs, "were Hesden's notions, as were many other things in the room. The flowers I had brought in, one by one, to satisfy my hunger for the world without. In the winter I have many more. Hesden makes the room a perfect conservatory, then. They have come to be very dear to me, as you may well suppose. That ivy now, over the foot of the bed, I have watched it from a little slip not a finger high. It is twenty-seven years old."

So she would have run on, no one knows to what length, had not the servant entered to set the table for supper. Under her mistress' directions she was about to place it beside the bed, when the young girl sprang into a sitting posture and with flaming cheeks cried out:

"Please, Mrs. Le Moyne, I had rather not lie here. I am quite well—just as well as ever, and I wish you would let me get up."

"But how can you, dear?" was the reply. "Your clothes are drying in the kitchen. They were completely drenched."

"Sure enough," answered Miss Ainslie. "I had forgotten that."

She laid herself down resignedly as the invalid said:

"If Hesden's presence would annoy you, he shall not come. I only thought it might be pleasanter for you not to be confined to the conversation of a crippled old woman. Besides, it is his habit, and I hardly know what he would do if he had to eat his supper elsewhere."

"Oh, certainly, I would not wish to disturb your usual arrangement," answered Mollie, "but—" she began, and then stoppd with some signs of confusion.

"But what, my dear?" asked the elder lady, briskly. "Do you mean that you are not accustomed as I am to invalidism, and hardly like the notion of supping in bed as an introduction to strangers? Well, I dare say it would be annoying, and if you think you are quite well enough to sit up, I reckon something better may be arranged."

"I assure you, Mrs. Le Moyne," said the other, "that I am quite well, but pray do not let me make you any trouble."

"Oh, no trouble at all, dear; only you will have to wear one of my gowns now many years old. I thought they were very pretty then, I assure you. I should be very glad to see them worn again. There are few who could wear them at all; but I think they would both fit and suit you. You are like enough to me to be my daughter. Here, you Maggie!"

She called the servant, and gave some directions which resulted in her bringing in several dresses of an ancient pattern but exquisite texture, and laying them upon the bed.

"You will have to appear in full dress, my dear, for I have no other gowns that would be at all becoming," said Mrs. Le Moyne.

"How very beautiful!" said the girl sitting up in the bed, gazing at the dainty silks and examining their quaint patterns. "But really, Mrs. Le Moyne—"

"Now, please oblige me by making no more objections," interrupted that lady. "Indeed," she added, shaking her finger threateningly at her guest, "I will not listen to any more. The fit has seized me now to have you sit opposite me at the table. It will be like facing my own youth; for now that I look at you more closely, you seem wonderfully like me. Don't you think so, Maggie?"

"'Deed I do," said the servant, "an' dat's jes what Laura was a sayin' ter me when we done fotch de young lady in here in a faint. She sez ter me, sez she, 'Maggie, ebber you see anybody look so much like de Mistis made young again?' "

"Hush, Maggie," said her mistress, gaily; "don't you see how the young lady is blushing, while it is the poor, faded woman here in the chair who ought to blush at such a compliment?"

And indeed the bright flushed face with its crown of soft golden hair escaped from its customary bondage, tossing in sunny tendrils about the delicate brow and rippling in waves of light over her shoulders, was a picture which any woman past the middle life might well blush and sigh to recognize as the counterpart of her youth. The two women looked at each other and both laughed at the admiration each saw in the other's glance.

"Well," said Mollie, as she sank smilingly on her pillow, "I see I must submit. You will have your own way."

She raised her arm above her head and toyed with a leaf of the ivy which hung in graceful festoons about the head-board. As she did so the loose-sleeved wrapper which had been flung about her when her own drenched clothing was removed, fell down almost to her shoulder and revealed to the beauty-worshipping watcher by the bedside an arm of faultless outline, slender, pink-tinged, plump and soft. When she had toyed lazily for a moment with the ivy, she dropped her arm listlessly down upon the bed. It fell upon one of the dresses which lay beside her.

"Ah, thank you!" exclaimed Mrs. Le Moyne. "You have relieved me greatly. I was trying to decide which one I wanted you to wear, when your arm dropped across that pale, straw-colored silk, with the vine border around the corsage and the clambering roses running down the front. That is the one you must wear. I never wore it but once, and the occasion is one I shall always like to recall."

There was a gleeful time in the invalid's room while the fair girl was being habited in the garments of a bygone generation, and when Hesden Le Moyne and his boy Hildreth were admitted to the hearty evening meal, two women who seemed like counterparts sat opposite each other at the sparkling board—the one habited in black silk with short waist, a low, square bodice with a mass of tender lawn showing about the fair slender neck, puffed at the shoulders with straight, close sleeves reaching to the wrists, around which peeped some rows of soft white lace; the white hair combed in puffs beside the brow, clustering above its pinky softness and falling in a silvery cataract upon the neck. The style of the other's dress was the same, save that the shoulders were uncovered, and except for the narrow puff which seemed but a continuation on either side, of the daintily-edged bodice, the arm hung pink and fair over the amber satin, uncovered and unadorned save at the wrist, where a narrow circlet of gold clung light and close about it. Her hair was dressed in the same manner as the elder lady's, and differed only in its golden sheen. The customary lamp had been banished, and colored wax-candles, brought from some forgotten receptacle, burned in the quaint old candelabra with which the mantels of the house had long been decorated.

The one-armed veteran of thirty gazed in wonder at this unaccustomed brightness. If he needed to gaze long and earnestly at the fair creature who sat over against his mother, to determine the resemblances which had been noted between the permanent and the temporary invalid, who shall blame him for so doing?

Little Hildreth in his six-year-old wonderment was less judicial, or at least required less time and inquiry to decide, for he cried out even before an introduction could be given,

"Oh, papa, see, I've got a new, young grandma."

It was a gay party at that country supper-table, and four happier people could hardly have gone afterward into the parlor where the invalid allowed herself to be wheeled by her son in special honor of their unintended guest.

Miss Ainslie was soon seated at the piano which Hesden had kept in tune more for the pleasure of occasional guests than his own. It was three years since she had touched one, but the little organ, which some Northern benefactor had given to the church and school at Red Wing, had served to prevent her fingers from losing all their skill, and in a few minutes their wonted cunning returned. She had been carefully trained and had by nature rare musical gifts. The circumstances of the day had given a wonderful exhilaration to her mind and thought. She seemed to have taken a leaf out of Paradise and bound it among the dingy pages of her dull and monotonous life. Every thing about her was so quaint and rare, the clothes she wore so rich and fantastic, that she could not control her fancy. Every musical fantasy that had ever crept into her brain seemed to be trooping along its galleries in a mad gallop as her fair fingers flew over the time-stained keys. The little boy stood clinging to her skirt in silent wonder, his fair, sensitive face working, and his eyes distended, with delighted amazement.

The evening came to an end at last, and when the servant went with her in her quaint attire, lighting her up the winding stairway from the broad hall to the great airy room above, with its yawning fireplace cheery with the dying embers of a fire built hours ago to drive out the dampness, and its two high-posted beds standing there in lofty dignity, the little Yankee school marm could hardly realize what madcap freaks she had perpetrated since she bounded over the gate at the foot of the lane leading from the highway down to Mulberry Hill, the ancestral home of the Richards family.

As she sat smiling and blushing over the memory of what she had done and said in those delicious hours, a servant tapped at the door and announced that Master Hildreth, whom she bore in her arms and whose chubby fists were stuck into his eyes, was crying most disconsolately lest he should lose his "new grandma" while he slept. She had brought him, therefore, to inquire whether he might occupy one of the beds in the young lady's room. Mollie had not seen for so many years a child that she could fondle and caress, that it was with unbounded delight that she took the little fellow from his nurse's arms, laid him on the bed and coaxed his eyes to slumber.

CHAPTER XXX.

AN UNBIDDEN GUEST.

WHEN THE MORNING dawned the boy awoke with hot cheeks and bloodshot eyes, moaning and restless, and would only be quiet when pillowed in the arms of his new-found friend. A physician who was called pronounced his ailment to be scarlet-fever. He soon became delirious, and his fretful moans for his "new grandma" were so piteous that Miss Ainslie could not make up her mind to leave him. She stayed by his bedside all day, saying nothing of returning to Red Wing, until late in the afternoon a messenger came from there to inquire after her, having traced her by inquiry among several who had seen her during the storm, as well as by the report that had gone out from the servants of her presence at Mulberry Hill.

When Hesden Le Moyne came to inform her of the messenger's arrival, he found her sitting by his son's bedside, fanning his fevered brow, as she had done the entire day. He gazed at them both in silence a moment before making known his errand. Then he took the fan from her hand and informed her of the messenger's arrival. His voice sounded strangely, and as she looked up at him she saw his face working with emotion. She cast down her eyes quickly. She could not tell why. All at once she felt that this quiet, maimed veteran of a lost cause was not to her as other men. Perhaps her heart was made soft by the strange occurrences of the few hours she had passed beneath his mother's roof. However that may be, she was suddenly conscious of a feeling she had never known before. Her cheeks burned as she listened to his low, quiet tones. The tears seemed determined to force themselves beneath her downcast lids, but her heart bounded with a strange undefined joy.

She rose to go and see the messenger. The sick boy moaned and murmured her name. She stole a glance at the father, and saw his eyes filled with a look of mingled tenderness and pain. She walked to the door. As she opened it the restless sufferer called for her again. She went out and closed it quickly after her. At the head of the stairs she paused, and pressed her hand to her heart while she breathed quick and her face burned. She raised her other hand and pushed back a stray lock or two as if to cool her forehead. She stood a moment irresolute; glanced back at the door of the room she had left, with a half frightened look; placed a foot on the first stair, and paused again. Then she turned suddenly back with a scared resolute look in her gray eyes, opened the door and glided swiftly to the bedside. Hesden Le Moyne's face was buried in the pillow. She stood over him a moment, her bosom heaving with short, quick sighs. She reached out her hand as if she would touch him, but drew it quickly back. Then she spoke, quietly but with great effort, looking only at the little sufferer.

"Mr. Le Moyne?" He raised his head quickly and a flush of joy swept over his face. She did not see it, at least she was not looking at him, but she knew it. "Would you like me to—to stay—until—until this is over?"

He started, and the look of joy deepened in his face. He raised his hand but let it fall again upon the pillow, as he answered humbly and tenderly,

"If you please, Miss Ainslie."

She put her hand upon the bed, in order to seem more at ease, as she replied, with a face which she knew was all aflame,

"Very well. I will remain for—the present."

He bent his head and kissed her hand. She drew it quickly away and added in a tone of explanation:

"It would hardly be right to go back among so many children after such exposure." So quick is love to find excuse. She called it duty, nor ever thought of giving it a tenderer name.

He made no answer. So easy is it for the fond heart to be jealous of a new-found treasure.

She waited a moment, and then went out and wrote a note to Eliab Hill. Then she went into the room of the invalid mother. How sweet she looked, reclining on the bed in the pretty alcove, doing penance for her unwonted pleasure of the night before! The excited girl longed to throw her arms about her neck and weep. It seemed to her that she had never seen any one so lovely and loveable. She went to the bedside and took the slender hand extended toward her.

"So," said Mrs. Le Moyne, "I hear they have sent for you to go back to Red Wing. I am sorry, for you have given us great pleasure; but I am afraid you will have only sad memories of Mulberry Hill. It is too bad! Poor Hildreth had taken such a liking to you, too. I am sure I don't blame him, for I am as much in love with you as an invalid can be with any one but herself. Hesden will have a hard time alone in this great house with two sick people on his hands."

"I shall not go back to Red Wing to-day."

"Indeed?"

"No, I do not think it would be right to endanger so many by exposure to the disease."

"Oh," carelessly; "but I am afraid you may take it yourself."

"I hope not. I am very well and strong. Besides, Hildreth calls for me as soon as I leave him for a moment."

"Poor little fellow! It is pitiable to know that I can do nothing for him."

"I will do what I can, Mrs. Le Moyne."

"But you must not expose yourself in caring for a strange child, my dear. It will not do to be too unselfish."

"I cannot leave him, Mrs. Le Moyne."

She left the room quickly and returned to her place at the sufferer's bedside. Hesden Le Moyne rose as she approached. She took the fan from his hand and sat down in the chair he had occupied. He stood silent a moment, looking down upon her as she fanned the uneasy sleeper, and then quietly left the room.

"What a dear, tender-hearted thing she is!" said Mrs. Le Moyne to herself after she had gone. "So ladylike and refined too. How can such a girl think of associating with niggers and teaching a nigger school? Such a pity she is not one of our people. She would be just adorable then. Don't you think so, Hesden?" she said aloud as her son entered. Having been informed of the subject of her cogitations, Mr. Hesden Le Moyne replied, somewhat absently and irrelevantly, as she thought, yet very warmly,

"Miss Ainslie is a very remarkable woman."

He passed into the hall, and his mother, looking after him, said,

"Poor fellow! he has a heap of trouble." And then it struck her that her son's language was not only peculiar but amusing. "A remarkable woman!" She laughed to herself as she thought of it. A little, brown-haired, bright-eyed, fair-skinned chit, pretty and plucky, and accomplished no doubt, but not at all "remarkable." She had no style nor pride. Yankee women never had. And no family of course, or she would not teach a colored school. "Remarkable!" It was about the only thing Miss Ainslie was not and could not be. It was very kind of her to stay and nurse Hildreth, though she only did that out of consideration for the colored brats under her charge at Red Wing. Nevertheless she was glad and gratified that she did so. She was a very capable girl, no doubt of that, and she would feel much safer about Hildreth because of her care. It was just in her line. She was like all Yankee women—just a better class of housemaids. This one was very accomplished.

She had played the piano exquisitely and had acted the lady to perfection in last night's masquerade. But Hesden must be crazy to call her remarkable. She chuckled lightly as she determined to rally him upon it, when she saw him next. When that time came, the good lady had quite forgotten her resolve.

CHAPTER XXXI.

A LIFE FOR A LIFE.

IT WAS A TIME of struggle at Mulberry Hill. Love and death fought for the life of little Hildreth Le Moyne. The father and the "new grandma" watched over him most assiduously; the servants were untiring in their exertions; the physician's skill was not lacking, but yet none could foresee the result. The invalid below sent frequent inquiries. First one and then the other stole away to ask her some question or bring her tidings in regard to the lad in whose life was bound up the hope of two old families.

One morning, while the child was still very sick, when Miss Ainslie awoke after the brief sleep which had been all the rest she had allowed herself from her self-imposed task, her head seemed strangely light. There was a roaring in her ears as if a cataract were playing about them. Her limbs ached, and every movement seemed unusually difficult—almost painful. She walked across the room and looked dully into the mirror on her dressing-case, resting her hands on the top of the high old-fashioned furniture as she did so. She was only able to note that her eyes looked heavy and her face flushed and swollen, when a sharp pain shot through her frame, her sight grew dim, the room spun round and round. She could only crawl back and clamber with difficulty upon the high-posted bed, where the servant found her fevered and unconscious when she came an hour later to awaken her for breakfast. The struggle that had been waged around the bed of the young child was now renewed by that of his self-constituted nurse. Weeks passed away before it was over, and ere that time the music of little feet had ceased about the ancient mansion, and the stroke to pride and love had rendered the invalid grandmother still more an invalid.

The child had been her hope and pride as its mother had been her favorite. By a strange contrariety the sunny-faced little mother had set herself to accomplish her son's union with the tall, dark, and haughty cousin, who had expired in giving birth to little Hildreth. There was nothing of spontaneity and no display of conjugal affection on the part of the young husband or his wife; but during the absence of her son, the invalid was well cared for and entertained by the wife, whom she came to love with an intensity second only to that she lavished on her son. In the offspring of these two her heart had been wrapped up from the hour of his birth. She had dreamed out for him a life full of great actualities, and had even reproached Hesden for his apathy in regard to public affairs during the stirring scenes enacting around them, urging him to take part in them for his son's sake.

She was a woman of great ambition. At first this had centered in her son, and she had even rejoiced when he went into the army, though he was earnestly opposed to the war, in the hope that it might bring him rank and fame. When these did not come, and he returned to her a simple private, with a bitterer hate for war and a sturdier dislike for the causes which had culminated in the struggle than he had when it began, she had despaired of her dream ever being realized through him, but had fondly believed that the son of the daughter-in-law she had so admired and loved would unite his father's sterling qualities with his mother's pride and love of praise, and so fulfill her desire that the family name should be made famous by some one descended from herself. This hope was destroyed by the death of the fair, bright child whom she loved so intensely, and she felt a double grief in consequence. In her sorrow, she had entirely secluded herself, seeing no one but her nurse and, once or twice, her son. The sick girl in the room above was somehow unpleasantly connected with her grief, and received no real sympathy in her illness. There was even something of jealousy in the mind of the confirmed invalid, when she remembered the remarkable manner in which the child had been attracted toward the new-comer, as well as the fact that she had nursed him so faithfully that his last words were a moan for his "new grandma," while his real grandmother lay useless and forgotten in her dim-shadowed room below.

Besides, it was with a feeling of envy that she recognized the fact that, for the first time in his life, her son was more absorbed in another's welfare than in her own. The chronic ailment of the mother had no doubt become so much a thing of habit in his life that it failed to impress him as it should, while the illness of the young girl, having, as he believed, been incurred by her voluntary attendance upon his son inspired him with a feeling of responsibility that would not otherwise have existed. Something had occurred, too, which had aroused a feeling upon his part which is often very close akin to a tenderer one. As soon as he had learned of her illness, he had endeavored to induce some of his female relatives to come and attend her, but they had all flatly refused. They would come and care for the child, they said; they would even send the "Yankee school-marm" flowers, and make delicacies to tempt her appetite, but they would not demean themselves by waiting upon a sick "nigger teacher." They did not fear the contagion; indeed they would have come to take care of little Hildreth but that they did not care to meet his Yankee nurse. They even blamed Hesden for allowing her to come beneath his roof, and intimated that she had brought contagion with her.

He was angry at their injustice and prejudice. He had known of its existence, but it never before seemed so hateful. Somehow he could not rid himself of two thoughts: one was of the fairy creature whose song and laughter and bird-like grace and gaiety, as she masqueraded in the quaint dress of olden time, had made the dull old mansion bright as a dream of Paradise for a single night. It had seemed to him, then, that nothing so bright and pure had ever flitted through the somber apartments of the gray old mansion. He remembered the delight of his boy—that boy whom he loved more than he had ever loved any one, unless it were his invalid mother—and he could not forget the same slight form, with serious shadowed face and earnest eyes moving softly about the sick-room of the child, her eyes full of sorrowful anxiety as if the life she sought to save were part of her own being. He wondered that any one could think of her as a stranger. It was true she had come from the North and was engaged in a despised avocation, but even that she had glorified and exalted by her purity and courage until his fastidious lady mother herself had been compelled to utter words of praise. So his heart grew sore and his face flushed hot with wrath when his cousins sneered at this lily which had been blighted by the fevered breath of his son.

They tauntingly advised him to send to Red Wing and get some of her "nigger" pupils to attend upon her. Much to their surprise he did so, and two quiet, gentle, deft-handed watchers came, who by day and by night sat by her bedside, gladly endeavoring to repay the debt they owed to the faithful teacher. But this did not seem to relieve Mr. Le Moyne of anxiety. He came often and watched the flushed face, heard the labored breathing, and listened with pained heart to the unmeaning murmurs which fell from her lips—the echoes of that desert dreamland through which fever drags its unconscious victims. He heard his own name and that of the fast-failing sufferer in the adjoining room linked in sorrowful phrase by the stammering tongue. Even in the midst of his sorrow it brought him a thrill of joy. And when his fear became fact, and he mourned the young life no love could save, his visits to the sick-room of her who had been his co-watcher by his child's bedside became more frequent. He would not be denied the privilege until the crisis came, and reason resumed her sway. Then he came no more, but every day sent some token of remembrance.

Mrs. Le Moyne had noted this solicitude, and with the jealousy of the confirmed invalid grudged the sick girl the slightest of the thoughtful attentions that she alone had been accustomed to receive. She did not dream that her son, Hesden Le Moyne, cared anything for the little Yankee chit except upon broadly humanitarian grounds, or perhaps from gratitude for her kindly attention to his son; but even this fretted her. As time went on, she came more and more to dislike her and to wish that she had never come beneath their roof. So the days flew by, grew into weeks, and Mollie Ainslie was still at Mulberry Hill, while important events were happening at Red Wing.

CHAPTER XXXII.

A VOICE FROM THE DARKNESS.

IT WAS TWO WEEKS after Miss Ainslie's involuntary flight from Red Wing that Nimbus, when he arose one morning, found a large pine board hung across his gateway. It was perhaps six feet long and some eighteen or twenty inches wide in the widest part, smoothly planed upon one side and shaped like a coffin lid. A whole had been bored in either end, near the upper corner, and through each of these a stout cord had been passed and tied into a loop, which, being slipped over a paling, one on each side the gate, left the board swinging before it so as effectually to bar its opening unless the board were first removed.

The attention of Nimbus was first directed to it by a neighbor-woman who, stopping in front of the gate, called out to him in great excitement, as he sat with Berry Lawson on his porch waiting for his breakfast:

"Oh, Bre'er Nimbus, what in de libbin' yairth is dis h'yer on your gate? La sakes, but de Kluckers is atter you now, shore 'nough!"

"Why, what's de matter wid yer, Cynthy?" said Nimbus, cheerfully. "Yer hain't seen no ghosteses nor nuffin', hez ye?"

"Ghosteses, did yer say?" answered the excited woman. "Jes yer come an' look, an' ef yer don't say hit wuss ner ghosteses, yer may count Cynthy a fool. Dat's all."

Berry started down to the gate, Nimbus following him, carelessly.

"Why, hello, Bre'er Nimbus! Yer shore hez got a signboard cross de passway. Jes look a' dat now! What yer 'spect it mout be, cousin?" said Berry, stopping short and pointing to the board hung on the fence.

" 'Clar, I dunno," said Nimbus, as he strode forward and leaned over the fence to get a sight of the other side of the board. " 'Spec' it must be some of dem Ku Kluck's work, ez Cynthy says."

After examining it a moment, he directed Berry to lift up the other end, and together they carried it to the house of Eliab Hill, where its grotesque characters were interpreted, so far as he was able to translate them, as well as the purport of a warning letter fastened on the board by means of a large pocket-knife thrust through it, and left sticking in the soft wood.

Upon the head of the coffin-shaped board was roughly drawn, in black paint, a skull and cross-bones and, underneath them, the words "ELIAB HILL and NIMBUS DESMIT," and below these still, the mystic cabala, "K.K.K," a formulary at which, just at that time, a great part of the nation was laughing as a capital illustration of American humor. It was accounted simply a piece of grotesquerie intended to frighten the ignorant and superstitious negro.[55]

The old claim of the South, that the colored man could be controlled and induced to labor only by the lash or its equivalent, had many believers still, even among the most earnest opponents of slavery, and not a few of these even laughed good-naturedly at the grotesque pictures in illustrated journals of shadowy beings in horrible masks and terrified negroes cowering in the darkness with eyes distended, hair rising in kinky tufts upon their heads, and teeth showing white from ear to ear, evidently clattering like castanets. It was wonderfully funny to far-away readers, and it made uproarious mirth in the aristocratic homes of the South. From the banks of the Rio Grande to the waters of the Potomac, the lordly Southron laughed over his glass, laughed on the train, laughed in the street, and laughed under his black cowl of weirdly decorated muslin—not so much at the victims of the terrible Klan, as at the silly North which was shaking its sides at the mask he wore. It was an era of fun. Everybody laughed. The street gamins imitated the *Kluck,* which gave name to the Klan. It was one of the funniest things the world had ever known.

The Yankee—Brother Jonathan[56]—had long been noted as a droll. A grin was as much a part of his stock apparel as tow breeches or a palm-leaf hat. The negro, too, had from time immemorial been portrayed upon the stage and in fiction as an irrepressible and inimitably farcical fellow. But the "Southern gentleman" was a man of different kidney from either of these. A sardonic dignity hedged him about with peculiar sacredness. He was chivalrous and baronial in his instincts, surroundings, and characteristics. He was nervous, excitable, and bloodthirsty. He would "pluck up drowned honor by the locks"[57] and make a target of every one who laughed. He hunted, fought, gambled, made much of his ancestors, hated niggers, despised Yankees, and swore and swaggered on all occasions. That was the way he was pictured in the ancient days. He laughed—sometimes—not often, and then somewhat sarcastically—but he did not make himself ridiculous. His *amour propre*[58] was most intense. He appreciated fun, but did not care that it should be at his expense. He was grave, irritable and splenetic; but never comical. A braggart, a rough-rider, an aristocrat; but never a masquerader. That was the old-time idea.

Yet so had the war and the lapse of half a decade changed this people that in one State forty thousand men, in another thirty, in others more and in others less, banded together with solemn oaths and bloody ceremonies, just to go up and down the earth in the bright moonlight, and play upon the superstitious fears of the poor ignorant and undeveloped people around them. They became a race of jesters, moonlight masqueraders, personators of the dead. They instituted clubs and paraded by hundreds, the trained cavalry of a ghostly army organized into companies, battalions, divisions, departments, having at their head the "Grand Wizard of the Empire."[59] It was all in sport—a great jest, or at the worst designed only to induce the colored man to work somewhat more industriously from apprehension of ghostly displeasure. It was a funny thing—the gravest, most saturnine, and self-conscious people on the globe making themselves ridiculous, ghostly masqueraders by the hundred thousand! The world which had lately wept with sympathy for the misfortunes of the "Lost Cause," was suddenly convulsed with merriment at the midnight antics of its chivalric defenders. The most vaunted race of warriors seized the cap and bells and stole also the plaudits showered upon the fool. Grave statesmen, reverend divines, legislators, judges, lawyers, generals, merchants, planters, all who could muster a good horse, as it would seem, joined the jolly cavalcade and rollicked through the moonlight nights, merely to make fun for their conquerors by playing on the superstitious fear of the sable allies of the Northmen. Never before was such good-natured complaisance, such untiring effort to please. So the North laughed, the South chuckled, and the world wondered.

But the little knot of colored men and women who stood around Eliab Hill while he drew out the knife which was thrust through the paper into the coffin-shaped board laid across the front of his "go-cart," and with trembling lips read the message it contained—these silly creatures did *not* laugh. They did not even smile, and a joke which Berry attempted, fell flat as a jest made at a funeral.

There is something very aggravating about the tendency of this race to laugh at the wrong time, and to persist in being disconsolate when every one can see that they ought to dance. Generation after generation of these perverse creatures in the good old days of slavery would insist on going in search of the North Pole under the most discouraging circumstances. On foot and alone, without money or script or food or clothing; without guide or chart or compass; without arms or friends; in the teeth of the law and of nature, they gave themselves to the night, the frost, and all the dangers that beset their path, only to seek what they did not want!

We know there was never a happier, more contented, light-hearted, and exuberant people on the earth than the Africo-American slave! He had all that man could reasonably desire—and more too! Well-fed, well-clothed, luxuriously housed, protected from disease with watchful care, sharing the delights of an unrivalled climate, relieved of all anxiety as to the future of his offspring, without fear of want, defiant of poverty, undisturbed by the bickerings of society or heartburnings of politics, regardless of rank or station, wealth, kindred, or descent, it must be admitted that, from an earthly point of view, his estate was as near Elysian[60] as the mind can conceive. Besides all this, he had the Gospel preached unto him—for nothing; and the law kindly secured him against being misled by false doctrines, by providing that the Bread of Life should never be broken to him unless some reputable Caucasian were present to vouch for its quality and assume all responsibility as to its genuineness![61]

That a race thus carefully nourished, protected, and guarded from error as well as evil should be happy, was just as natural as that the sun should shine. That they were happy only lunatics could doubt. All their masters said so. They even raved when it was denied. The ministers of the Gospel—those grave and reverend men who ministered unto them in holy things, who led their careless souls, blindfolded and trustful, along the straight and narrow way—all declared before high Heaven that they were happy, almost too happy, for their spiritual good. Politicians, and parties, and newspapers; those who lived among them and those who went and learned all about them from the most intelligent and high-toned of their Caucasian fellow-beings—nigh about everybody, in fact—declared, affirmed, and swore that they were at the very utmost verge of human happiness! Yet even under these circumstances the perverse creatures *would* run away. Indeed, to run away seemed to be a characteristic of the race like their black skin and kinkling hair! It would have seemed, to an uninformed on-looker, that they actually desired to escape from the paternal institution which had thrown around their lives all these blissful and beatifying circumstances. But we know it was not so. It was only the inherent perversity of the race!

Again, when the war was ended and they were thrown upon the cold charity of an unfriendly world, naked, poor, nameless, and homeless, without the sheltering and protecting care of that master who had ever before been to them the incarnation of a kindly Providence—at that moment when, by all the rules which govern Caucasian human nature, their eyes should have been red with regretful tears, and their hearts overburdened with sorrow, these addled-pated children of Africa, moved and instigated by the perverse devil of inherent contrariness, were grinning from ear to ear with exasperating exultation, or bowed in still more exasperating devotion, were rendering thanks to God for the calamity that had befallen them!

So, too, when the best people of the whole South masqueraded for their special benefit, they stupidly or stubbornly failed and refused to reward their "best friends" for the entertainment provided for them, at infinite pains and regardless of expense, even with the poor meed of approving cachinnation.[62] They ought to have been amused; they no doubt were amused; indeed, it is morally impossible that they should not have been amused—but they would not laugh! Well may the Caucasian of the South say of the ebony brother whom he has so long befriended and striven to amuse: "I have piped unto you, and you have not danced!"[63]

So Eliab read, to a circle whose cheeks were gray with pallor, and whose eyes glanced quickly at each other with affright, these words:

"ELIAB HILL AND NIMBUS DESMIT: You've been warned twice, and it hain't done no good. This is your last chance. If you don't git up and git out of here inside of ten days, the buzzards will have a bait that's been right scarce since the war. The white folks is going to rule Horsford, and sassy niggers must look out. We're not going to have any such San Domingo[64] hole as Red Wing in it, neither. Now just sell off and pack up and git clear off and out of the country before we come again, which will be just as soon as the moon gits in the left quarter, and has three stars in her lower horn. If you're here then you'll both need coffins, and that boy Berry Lawson that you coaxed away from his employer will hang with you.

"Remember! *Remember!* REMEMBER!

"By order of the Grand Cyclops of the Den and his two Night Hawks, and in the presence of all the Ghouls,[65] on the fifth night of the sixth Dark Moon!

"K. K. K."

Hardly had he finished reading this when a letter was brought to him which had been found on the porch of the old Ordinary. It was addressed to "MISS MOLLIE AINSLIE, Nigger Teacher at Red Wing," but as it was indorsed "K. K. K." Eliab felt no compunctions in opening it in her absence. It read:

"MISS AINSLIE: We hain't got no spite against you and don't mean you no harm; but the white folks owns this country, and is going to rule it, and we can't stand no such nigger-equality schools as you are running at Red Wing. It's got to stop, and you'd better pick up and go back North where you come from, and that quick, if you want to keep out of trouble. Remember!

"By order of the Grand Cyclops of the Den and his Ghouls,

K. K. K."

"P.S. We don't mean to hurt you. We don't make no war on women and children as the Yankees did, but we mean what we say—git out! And don't come back here any more neither!"

The rumor of the mysterious Klan and its terrible doings had been in the air for many months. From other States, and even from adjoining counties, had come to their ears the wail of its victims. But so preponderating was the colored population of Horsford, and so dependent upon their labor was its prosperity, that they had entertained little fear of its coming among them. Two or three times before, Nimbus and Eliab had received warnings and had even taken some precautions in regard to defense; but they did not consider the matter of sufficient moment to require them to make it public. Indeed, they were inclined to think that as there had been no acts of violence in the county, these warnings were merely the acts of mischievous youngsters who desired to frighten them into a display of fear. This seemed to be a more serious demonstration, but they were not yet prepared to give full credence to the threat conveyed in so fantastic a manner.

CHAPTER XXXIII.

A DIFFERENCE OF OPINION.

"WAL, DEY MANAGE to fotch Berry inter it widout sending him a letter all to hissef, atter all," said that worthy, when Eliab, with pale lips, but a firm voice, had finished reading the paper. "Ben done 'spectin' dat, all de time sence I come h'yer, Cousin Nimbus. I'se been a-hearin' 'bout dese Ku Kluckers dis smart while now, ober yer in Pocatel and Hanson counties, an' I 'spected Marse Sykes 'd be a-puttin' 'em on ter me jest ez soon as dey got ober here. He hed no idear, yer know, but what I'd hev ter go back an' wuk fer jes what I could git; an sence I hain't he's mad about it, dat's all. What yer gwine ter do 'bout it, Nimbus?"

"I'se gwine ter stay right h'yer an' fight it out, I is," said Nimbus, doggedly. "I'se fout fer de right ter live in peace on my own lan' once, an' I kin fight for it agin. Ef de Ku Kluckers wants ter try an' whip Nimbus, jes let 'em come on," he said, bringing down his clenched right hand upon the board which was upheld by his left, with such force that it was split from end to end.

"Hi! you take keer dar, Cousin Nimbus," said Berry, hopping out of the way of the falling board with an antic gesture. "Fust you know, yer hurt yer han' actin' dat er way. What *you* gwine ter do 'bout dis yer matter, Uncle 'Liab?" he continued, turning to the preacher.

The man addressed was still gazing on the threatening letter. His left hand wandered over his dark beard, but his face was full of an unwavering light as he replied:

"The Lord called me to my work; He has opened many a door before me and taken me through many trials. He has written, 'I will be with thee alway, even unto the end.' Bless His holy Name! Hitherto, when evil has come I have waited on Him. I may not do a man's part like you, my brother," he continued, laying his hand on Nimbus' knotted arm and gazing admiringly upon his giant frame, "but I can stand and wait, right here, for the Lord's will to be done; and here I will stay—here with my people. Thank the Lord, if I am unable to fight I am also unable to fly. He knew what a poor, weak creature I was, and He has taken care of that. I shall stay, let others do as they may. What are you going to do, Brother Berry? You are in the same danger with Nimbus and me."

"Wal, Bre'er 'Liab," replied Berry, "I hab jes 'bout made up *my* min' ter run fer it. Yer see, I'se jes a bit differently sarcumstanced from what either o' you 'uns is. Dar's Nimbus now, he's been in de wah an' knows all 'bout de fightin' business; an' you's a preacher an' knows all der is ob de prayin' trade. But I never was wuth nothin' ob any account at either. It's de feet ez hez allers stood by me," he added, executing a double-shuffle on the plank walk where he stood; "an' I 'llows ter stan' by dem, an' light outen here, afore dem ar Kluckers comes roun' fer an answer ter dat ar letter. Dat's my notion, Bre'er 'Liab."

"Yer don't mean yer gwine ter run away on de 'count ob dese yer Ku Kluckers, does yer, Berry?" said Nimbus, angrily.

"Dat's jes 'zackly what I do mean, Cousin Nimbus—no mistake 'bout dat," answered Berry, bowing towards Nimbus with a great show of mock politeness. "What else did yer tink Berry mean, hey? Didn't my words 'spress demselves cl'ar? Yer know, cousin, dat I'se not one ob de fightin' kine. Nebber hed but one fight in my life, an' den dar wuz jes de wuss whipped nigger you ebber seed. Yer see dem sinners, eh?" rolling up his sleeve and showing a round, close-corded arm. "Oh, I'se some when I gits started, I is. All whip-cord an' chain-lightnin', whoop! I'll bet a harf dollar now, an borrer de money from Bre'er Nimbus h'yer ter pay it, dat I kin turn more han'-springs an' offener an' longer nor ary man in dis crowd. Oh, I'se some an' more too, I is, an' don't yer fergit it. 'Bout dat fight?" he continued to a questioner, "oh, yes, dat was one ob de mos' 'markable fights dar's ever been in Ho'sford county. Yer see 'twuz all along uv Ben Slade an' me. Lor' bress yer, how we did fight! 'Pears ter me dat it must hev been nigh 'bout harf a day we wuz at it."

"But you didn't lick Ben, did you, Berry?" asked one of the bystanders in surprise.

"Lick him? Yer jes' orter see de corn I wollered down 'long wid dat nigga'! Dar must hev been close on ter harf an acre on't."

"But he's a heap bigger'n you, Berry, ez stout ez a bull an' one ob de bes' fighters ebber on de hill at Louisburg. Yer jest romancin' now, Berry," said Nimbus, incredulously.

"Oh, but yer don't understan' it, cousin," said Berry. "Yer see I played fer de *under holt*—an' got it, dat I did. Lor'! how dat ar Ben did thrash de groun' wid me! Ole Mahs'r lost a heap ob corn on 'count dat ar fight! But I hung on ter him, an' nebber would hev let him go till now, ef—ef somebody hedn't pulled me out from under him!"

There was a roar of laughter at this, in which Berry joined heartily, and as it began to die out he continued:

"Dat's de only fight I ebber hed, an' I don't want no mo'. I'se a peaceable man, an' don't want ter hurt nobody. Ef de Kluckers wants ter come whar I is, an' gibs me sech a perlite notice ez dat ter quit, I'se gwine ter git out widout axin' no imper'ent questions 'bout who was dar fust. An' I'se gwine ter keep gittin' tu—jest' ez fur an' ez fast ez dey axes me ter move on, ez long ez de road's cut out an' I don't come ter no jumpin'-off place. Ef dey don't approve of Berry Lawson a stayin' roun' h'yer, he's jes' a gwine West ter grow up wid der kentry."

"I'd sooner be dead than be sech a limber-jinted coward!" said Nimbus. "I'm sorry I ebber tuk ye in atter Marse Sykes hed put yer out in de big road, dat I am." There was a murmur of approval, and he added: "An' ef yer hed enny place ter go ter, yer shouldn't stay in my house nary 'nother minit."

"Now, Cousin Nimbus," said Berry, soberly, "dar hain't nary bit ob use ob enny sech talk ter me. Berry arns his libbin' ef he does hab his joke now an' agin."

"Oh, no doubt o' dat," said Nimbus. "Ther ain't no better han' in enny crop dan Berry Lawson. I've said dat often an' over."

"Den yer jes take back dem hard words yer spoke 'bout Berry, won't yer now, Cousin Nimbus?" said Berry, sidling up to him and looking very much as if he intended to give the lie to his own account of his fighting proclivities.

"No, I won't," said Nimbus, positively. "I do say dat any man ez runs away kase de Ku Kluck tries ter scar him off is a damn coward, 'n I don't care who he calls his name neither."

"Wal, now, Cousin Nimbus," said Berry, his eyes flashing and his whole appearance falsifying his previous poltroonery, "dar's two sides ter dat ar question. I hain't nebber been a sojer like you, cousin, an' it's a fac' dat I don't keer ter be; but I du say ez how I'd be ez willin' ter stan' up an' fight fer de rights we's got ez enny man dat ebber's trod de sile ennywhere's 'bout Red Wing, ef I thought ez how 'twould do de least bit ob good. But I tell yer, gemmen, hit won't do enny good, not de least bit, an' I knows it. I'se seen de Ku Kluckers, gemmen, an' I knows who some on 'em is, an' I knows dat when sech men takes hold ob sech a matter wid only pore niggers on de udder side, dar ain't no chance fer de niggers. I'se seen 'em, an' I *knows.*"

"When?" "Whar?" "Tell us 'bout it, Berry!" came up from all sides in the crowd which had collected until now almost all the inhabitants of Red Wing and its vicinity were there.

"Oh, 'tain't nuffin'," said he, nonchalantly. "What Berry says ain't no 'count, nohow."

"Yes, tell us 'bout it," said Nimbus, in a conciliatory tone.

"Wal, ef *you* wants ter hear, I'll tell it," said Berry, condescendingly. "Yer mind some tree er fo' weeks ago I went ter Bre'er Rufe's, ober in Hanson county, on a Friday night, an' didn't git back till a Monday mornin'?"

"Sartin," said Nimbus, gravely.

"Wal, 'twas along o' dis yer business dat I went thar. I know'd yer'd got one er two warnin's sence I'd come yere wid yer, an' I 'llowed it were on account ob me, kase dem ar Sykeses is monstrous bad folks when dey gits mad, an' ole Marse Granville, he war powerful mad at me findin' a home here wid my own relations. So, I tole Sally Ann all 'bout it, an' I sez to her, 'Sally,' sez I, 'I don't want ter make Nimbus no sort o' trouble, I don't, kase he's stood up fer us like a man. Now, ef dey should take a notion ter trouble Bre'er Nimbus, hit mout do him a heap of harm, kase he's got so much truck 'round him here ter lose.' So we made it up dat I was ter go ter Bre'er Rufe Paterson's, ober in Hanson county an' see ef we couldn't find a place ter lib dar, so's not ter be baitin' de hawks on ter you, Cousin Nimbus."

"Now you, Berry," said Nimbus, extending his hand heartily, "what for yer no tell me dis afore?"

"Jes kase 'twas no use," answered Berry. "Wall, yer know, I left h'yer 'bout two hours ob de sun, an' I pushes on right peart, kase it's a smart step ober ter Rufe's, ennyhow, an' I wanted ter see him an' git back ter help Nimbus in de crap ob a Monday. Sally hed fixed me up a bite o' bread an' a piece o' meat, an' I 'llowed I'd jes stop in some piney ole-field when I got tired, eat my snack, go ter sleep, an' start fresh afo' daylight in de mornin' for de rest ob de way. I'd been a wukkin' right peart in de new-ground dat day, an' when I got ter dat pine thicket jes past de spring by de Brook's place, 'twixt de Haw Ribber an' Stony Fork, 'long 'bout nine o'clock I reckon, I wuz dat done out dat I jes takes a drink at de spring, eats a bite o' bread an' meat, hunts a close place under de pines, an' goes ter sleep right away.

"Yer knows dar's a smart open place dar, whar dey used ter hev de ole muster-ground. 'Twas de time ob de full moon, an' when I woke up a-hearin' somethin', an' kind o' peeped out under de pine bushes, I t'ought at fust dat it was de ghostesses ob de ole chaps dat hed come back ter muster dar, sure 'nough. Dey warn't more'n ten steps away from me, an' de boss man, he sot wid his back to me in dat rock place what dey calls de Lubber's Cheer. De hosses was tied all round ter de bushes, an' one ob 'em warn't more'n tree steps from me, nohow. I heard 'em talk jest ez plain ez you can hear me, an' I know'd right smart ob de voices, tu; but, la sakes! yer couldn't make out which from t'odder wid dem tings dey hed on, all ober der heads, an' way down to der feet."

"What did they say?" asked Eliab Hill.

"Wal, Bre'er 'Liab, dey sed a heap, but de upshot on't all was dat de white folks hed jes made up dar min's ter run dis kentry, spite ob ebbery ting. Dey sed dat dey wuz all fixed up in ebbery county from ole Virginny clean ter Texas, an' dey wuz gwine ter teach de niggers dere place agin, ef dey hed ter kill a few in each county an' hang 'em up fer scarecrows—jes dat 'ere way. Dey wa'n't no spring chickens, nuther. Dar wur Sheriff Gleason. He sed he'd comed over ter let 'em know how they was gittin' on in Ho'sford. He sed dat ebbery white man in de county 'cept about ten or twelve was inter it, an' dey wuz a gwine ter clean out nigger rule h'yer, *shore.* He sed de fust big thing they got on hand wuz ter break up dis buzzard-roost h'yer at Red Wing, an' he 'llowed dat wouldn't be no hard wuk kase dey'd got some pretty tough tings on Nimbus an' 'Liab both.

"Dey wuz all good men. I seed de hosses, when dey mounted ter go 'way. I tell ye dey wuz good 'uns! No pore-white trash dar; no lame hosses ner blind mules ner wukked-down crap-critters. Jes sleek gentlemen's hosses, all on 'em.

"Wal, dey went off atter an hour er two, an' I lay dar jes in a puffick lather o' sweat. I was dat dar skeered, I couldn't sleep no mo' dat ar night, an' I darsn't walk on afore day kase I wuz afeared o' meetin' some on 'em. So I lay, an' t'ought dis ting all ober, an' I tell ye, fellers, 'tain't no use. 'Spose all de white men in Ho'sford is agin us, what's we gwine ter do? We can't lib. Lots o' niggers can't lib a week widout wuk from some white man. 'Sides dat, dey's got de hosses an' de guns, an' de 'sperience; an' what we got? Jes nuffin'. Der ain't no mo' use o'fightin' dan ob tryin' ter butt down 'simmons off a foot-an'-a-half tree wid yer head. It don't make no sort o' matter 'bout our rights. Co'se we'se got a *right* ter vote, an' hold meetin's, an' be like white folks; but we can't do it ef dey's a mind ter stop us. An' dey *is*—dat berry ting!

"Nimbus sez he's gwine ter fight, an' 'Liab sez he's gwine ter pray. Dat's all right, but it won't do nobody else enny good nor them nuther. Dat's my notion. What good did fightin' er prayin' either used ter do in ole slave times? Nary bit. An' dey's got us jest about ez close ez dey hed us den, only de halter-chain's a leetle mite longer, dat's all. All dey's got ter do is jes ter shorten up on de rope an' it brings us in, all de same ez ever. Dat's my notion. So I'se gwine ter move on ebbery time dey axes me tu; kase why, I can't help it. Berry'll git enough ter eat most ennywhar, an' dat's 'bout all he 'spects in dis worl'. It's a leetle better dan de ole slave times, an' ef it keeps on a-growin' better 'n better, gineration atter gineration, p'raps some of Berry's kinfolks'll git ter hev a white man's chance some time."

Berry's experience was listened to with profound interest, but his conclusions were not received with favor. There seemed to be a general conviction that the colored race was to be put on trial, and that it must show its manhood by defending itself and maintaining its rights against all odds. His idea of running away was voted a cowardly and unworthy one, and the plan advocated by Nimbus and Eliab, to stay and fight it out or take whatever consequences might result, was accepted as the true one to be adopted by men having such responsibility as rested upon them, as the first generation of freemen in the American history of their race.

So, Nimbus and his friends made ready to fight by holding a meeting in the church, agreeing upon signals, taking account of their arms, and making provision to get ammunition. Berry prepared for his exodus by going again to his brother Rufus' house and engaging to work on a neighboring plantation, and some two weeks afterward he borrowed Nimbus' mule and carry-all and removed his family also. As a sort of safeguard on this last journey, he borrowed from Eliab Hill a repeating Spencer carbine, which a Federal soldier had left at the cabin of that worthy, soon after the downfall of the Confederacy. He was probably one of those men who determined to return home as soon as they were convinced that the fighting was over. Sherman's army, where desertion had been unknown during the war, lost thousands of men in this manner between the scene of Johnston's surrender and the Grand Review at Washington,[66] which ended the spectacular events of the war. Eliab had preserved this carbine very carefully, not regarding it as his own, but ready to surrender it to the owner or to any proper authority when demanded. It was useless without the proper ammunition, and as this seemed to be a peculiar emergency, he allowed Berry to take it on condition that he should stop at Boyleston and get a supply of cartridges. Eliab had never fired a gun in his life, but he believed in defending his rights, and thought it well to be ready to resist unlawful violence should it be offered.

CHAPTER XXXIV.

THE MAJESTY OF THE LAW.

A FEW DAYS after the events narrated in the last two chapters, the sheriff presented himself at Red Wing. There was a keen, shrewd look in the cold, gray eyes under the overhanging brows, as he tied his horse to the rack near the church, and taking his saddle-bags on his arm, crossed the road toward the residence of Nimbus and Eliab Hill.

Red Wing had always been a remarkably peaceful and quiet settlement. Acting under the advice of Miss Ainslie and Eliab, Nimbus had parted with none of his possessions except upon terms which prevented the sale of spirituous liquors there. This was not on account of any "fanatical" prejudice in favor of temperance, since the Squire of Red Wing was himself not exactly averse to an occasional dram; but he readily perceived that if such sale could be prohibited in the little village the chances for peace and order would be greatly improved. He recognized the fact that those characters that were most likely to assemble around a bar-room were not the most likely to be valuable residents of the settlement. Besides the condition in his own deeds, therefore, he had secured through the members of the Legislature from his county the passage of an act forever prohibiting the sale of spirituous liquors within one mile of the school-house at Red Wing. Just without this limit several little shanties had been erected where chivalric white men doled out liquor to the hard-working colored men of Red Wing. It was an easy and an honorable business and they did not feel degraded by contact with the freedmen across the bar. The superior race did not feel itself debased by selling bad whisky at an extravagant price to the poor, thirsty Africans who went by the "shebangs" to and from their daily toil. But Nimbus and the law would not allow the nearer approach of such influences.

By these means, with the active co-operation of the teachers, Red Wing had been kept so peaceful, that the officers of the law rarely had occasion to appear within its limits, save to collect the fiscal dues from its citizens.

It was with not a little surprise, therefore, that Nimbus saw the stalwart sheriff coming towards him where he was at work upon the hillside back of his house, "worming" and "topping" a field of tobacco which gave promise of a magnificent yield.

"Mornin', Nimbus," said the officer, as he drew near, and turning partially around glanced critically over the field and furtively at the little group of buildings below. "A fine stand of terbacker you've got—mighty even, good growth. Don't think I've seen quite as good-looking a crap this year. There's old man George Price up about Rouseville, he's got a mighty fine crap—always does have, you know. I saw it yesterday and didn't think anything could be better, but your's does beat it, that's sure. It's evener and brighter, and a trifle heavier growth, too. I told him that if anybody in the county could equal it you were the man; but I had no idea you could beat it. This is powerful good land for terbacker, certain."

" 'Tain't so much the land," said Nimbus, standing up to his arm-pits in the rank-leaved crop above which his bare black arms glistened in the hot summer sun, "as 'tis the keer on't. Powerful few folks is willin' ter give the keer it takes ter grow an' cure a fine crop o' terbacker. Ther ain't a minit from the time yer plant the seed-bed till ye sell the leaf, that ye kin take yer finger offen it widout resk ob losin' all yer wuk."

"That's so," responded the sheriff, "but the land has a heap to do with it, after all."

"Ob co'se," said Nimbus, as he broke a sucker into short pieces between his thumb and finger, "yer's got ter hab de sile; but ther's a heap mo' jes ez good terbacker lan' ez dis, ef people only hed the patience ter wuk it ez I do mine."

"Wal, now, there's not so much like this," said the sheriff, sharply, "and you don't think so, neither. You wouldn't take a big price for your two hundred acres here now." He watched the other's countenance sharply as he spoke, but the training of slavery made the face of the black Ajax[67] simply Sphinx-like in its inscrutability.

"Wal, I don't know," said Nimbus, slowly, "I mout and then again I moutn't, yer know. Ther'd be a good many pints ter think over besides the quality of the sile afore I'd want ter say 'yes' er 'no' to an offer ob dat kind."

"That's what I thought," said the sheriff. "You are nicely fixed here, and I don't blame you. I had some little business with you, and I'm glad I come today and caught ye in your terbacker. It's powerful fine."

"Business wid me?" asked Nimbus in surprise. "What is it?"

"Oh, I don't know," said the officer, lightly, as he put on his spectacles, opened his saddle-bags and took out some papers. "Some of these lawyers have got after you, I suppose, thinking you're getting along too peart. Let me see," he continued, shuffling over the papers in his hand. "Here's a summons in a civil action—the old man, Granville Sykes, against Nimbus Desmit and Eliab Hill. Where is 'Liab? I must see him, too. Here's your copy," he continued, handing Nimbus the paper and marking the date of service on the original in pencil with the careless promptitude of the well-trained official.

Nimbus looked at the paper which was handed him in undisguised astonishment.

"What is dis ting, anyhow, Marse Sheriff?" he asked.

"That? Why, that is a summons. Can't you read it? Here, let me take it."

He read over the legal formulary requiring Nimbus to be and appear at the court house in Louisburg on the sixth Monday after the second Monday in August, to answer the demand of the plaintiff against him, and concluding with the threat that in default of such appearance judgment would be entered up against him.

"You see, you've got to come and answer old man Granville's complaint, and after that you will have a trial. You'll have to get a lawyer, and I expect there'll be smart of fuss about it before it's over. But you can afford it; a man as well fixed as you, that makes such terbacker as this, can afford to pay a lawyer right smart. I've no doubt the old man will get tired of it before you do; but, after all, law is the most uncertain thing in the world."

"What does it mean? Has he sued me?" asked Nimbus.

"Sued you? I should rather think he had—for a thousand dollars damages too. That is you and 'Liab, between you."

"But what for? I don't owe him anythin' an' never did."

"Oh, that's nothing. He says you've damaged him. I've forgot what it's about. Let me see. Oh, yes, I remember now. He says you and 'Liab enticed away his servant—what's his name? that limber-jinted, whistlin' feller you've had working for you for a spell."

"What, Berry?"

"That's it, Berry—Berry Lawson. That's the very chap. Well, old Granville says you coaxed him to leave his employ, and he's after you under the statute."

"But it's a lie—every word on't! I nebber axed Berry ter leave him, an' hed no notion he was a gwine ter do it till Marse Sykes throwed him out in de big road."

"Wal, wal, I don't know nothing about that, I'm sure. He says you did, you say you didn't. I s'pose it'll take a court and jury to decide betwixt ye. It's none of my concern. Oh, yes," he continued, "I like to have forgot it, but here's a *capias*[68] for you, too—you and 'Liab again. It seems there's a bill of indictment against you. I presume it's the same matter. I must have a bond on this for your appearance, so you'd better come on down to 'Liab's house with me. I'll take you for him, and him for you, as sureties. I don't suppose 'Liab'll be apt to run away, eh, and you're worth enough for both."

"What's this all about?" asked Nimbus.

"Well, I suppose the old man Sykes got ye indicted under the statute making it a misdemeanor, punishable with fine and imprisonment, to coax, hire, or seduce away one's niggers after he's hired 'em.[69] Just the same question as the other, only this is an indictment and that's a civil action—an action under the code, as they call it, since you Radicals tinkered over the law. One is for the damage to old man Sykes, and the other because it's a crime to coax off or harbor any one's hirelings."

"Is dat de law, Mister Sheriff?"

"Oh, yes, that's the law, fast enough. No trouble about that. Didn't know it, did you? Thought you could go and take a man's "hands" right out from under his nose, and not get into trouble about it, didn't ye?"

"I t'ought dat when a man was free anudder could hire him widout axin' leave of his marster. Dat's what I t'ought freedom meant."

"Oh, not exactly; there's lots of freedom lyin' round loose, but it don't allow a man to hire another man's hands, nor give them aid and comfort by harboring and feeding them when they break their contracts and run away. I reckon the old man's got you, Nimbus. If one hook don't catch, the other will. You've been harborin' the cuss, if you didn't entice him away, and that's just the same."

"Ef you mean by harborin' that I tuk my wife's kinsman in when old Marse Sykes turned his family out in de big road like a damned ole rascal—"

"Hold on, Nimbus!" said the sheriff, with a dangerous light in his cold gray eyes; "you'd better not talk like that about a white gentleman."

"Whose ter hender my talkin', I'd like ter know? Hain't I jes' de same right ter talk ez you er Marse Sykes, an' wouldn't you call me a damn rascal ef I'd done ez he did? Ain't I ez free ez he is?"

"You ain't white!" hissed the sheriff.

"No, an' it seems I ain't free, nuther!" was the hot reply. "H'yer t'other night some damn scoundrels—I 'specs they wuz white, too, an' yer may tell 'em from me dat I called 'em jes what I did—come an' hung a board 'fore my gate threatening ter kill me an' 'Liab kase we's 'too sassy,' so they sed. Now, 'Liab Hill ner me nebber disturb nobody, an' nebber do nothin' only jes stan' up for our own rights, respectful and peaceable-like; but we hain't ter be run down in no sech way. I'se a free man, an' ef I think a man's a gran' rascal I'se gwine ter *say* so, whether he's black er white; an' ef enny on 'em comes ter Ku Klux me I'll put a bullet t'rough dem! I will, by God! Ef I breaks the law I'll take the consequences like a man, but I'll be damned ef ennybody shall Ku Kluck me without somebody's goin' 'long with me, when I drops outen dis world! Dat much I'se sot on!"

The sheriff did not answer, only to say, "Careful, careful! There's them that would give you a high limb[70] if they heard you talk like that."

They went together to the house. The required bonds were given, and the sheriff started off with a chuckle. He had hardly passed out of sight when he checked his horse, returned, and calling Nimbus to the gate, said to him in a low tone:

"See here, Nimbus, if you should ever get in the notion of selling this place, remember and let me have the first chance."

"All right, Marse Gleason."

"And see here, these little papers I've served to-day—you needn't have any trouble about them in that case. You understand," with a wink.

"Dunno ez I does, Marse Sheriff," stolidly.

"Oh, well, if you sell to me, I'll take care of them, that's all."

"An' ef I don't?"

"Oh, well, in that case, you must look out for yourself."

He wheeled his horse and rode off with a mocking laugh.

Nimbus returned to the porch of Eliab's house where the preacher sat thoughtfully scanning the summons and *capias*.

"What you tink ob dis ting, 'Liab?"

"It is part of a plan to break you up, Nimbus," was the reply.

"Dar ain't no sort ob doubt 'bout that, 'Liab," answered Nimbus, doggedly, "an' dat ole Sheriff Gleason's jes' at de bottom ob it, I do b'lieve. But I ain't ter be druv off wid law-suits ner Ku Kluckers. I'se jest a gwine ter git a lawyer an' fight it out, dat I am."

CHAPTER XXXV.

A PARTICULAR TENANCY LAPSES.

THE SECOND DAY after the visit of the sheriff, Nimbus was sitting on his porch after his day's work when there was a call at his gate.

"Who's dar?" he cried, starting up and gazing through an opening in the honeysuckle which clambered up to the eaves and shut in the porch with a wall of fragrant green. Seeing one of his white neighbors, he went out to the gate, and after the usual salutations was greeted with these words:

"I hear you's gwine to sell out an' leave, Nimbus?"

"How 'd ye hear dat?"

"Wal, Sheriff Gleason's a' been tellin' of it 'round, and ther ain't no other talk 'round the country only that."

"What 'ud I sell out an' leave for? Ain't I well 'nough off whar I is?"

"The sheriff says you an' 'Liab Hill has been gittin' into some trouble with the law, and that the Ku Klux has got after you too, so that if you don't leave you're likely to go to States prison or have a whippin' or hangin' bee at your house afore you know it."

"Jes let 'em come," said Nimbus, angrily—"Ku Kluckers or sheriffs, it don't make no difference which. I reckon it's all 'bout one an' de same ennyhow. It's a damn shame too. Dar, when de 'lection come las' time we put Marse Gleason in agin, kase we hadn't nary white man in de county dat was fitten for it an' could give de bond; an' of co'se dere couldn't no cullu'd man give it. An' jes kase we let him hev it an' he's feared we mout change our minds now, here he is a runnin' 'roun' ter Ku Klux meetin's an' a tryin' ter stir up de bery ole debble, jes ter keep us cullu'd people from hevin' our rights. He can't do it wid me, dat's shore. I hain't done nuffin' an' I won't run. Ef I'd a-done ennythin' I'd run, kase I don't b'lieve more'n ennybody else in a man's stayin' ter let de law git a holt on him; but when I hain't done nary ting, ther ain't nobody ez kin drive me outen my tracks."

"But the Ku Klux mout *lift*[71] ye outen 'em," said the other with a weak attempt at wit.

"Jes let 'em try it once!" said Nimbus, excitedly. "I'se purty well prepared for 'em now, an' atter tomorrer I'll be jes ready for 'em. I'se gwine ter Louisburg to-morrer, an' I 'llow that atter I come back they won't keer ter meddle wid Nimbus. Tell yer what, Mister Dossey, I bought dis place from ole Marse Desmit, an' paid for it, ebbery cent; an' I swar I ain't a gwine ter let no man drive me offen it—nary foot. An' ef de Ku Klux comes, I's jest a gwine ter kill de las' one I gits a chance at. Now, you min' what I say, Mister Dossey, kase I means ebbery word on't."

The white man cowered before the other's energy. He was of that class who were once denominated "poor whites." The war taught him that he was as good a man to stop bullets as one that was gentler bred, and during that struggle which the non-slaveholders fought at the beck and in the interest of the slaveholding aristocracy, he had learned more of manhood than he had ever known before. In the old days his father had been an overseer on a plantation adjoining Knapp-of-Reeds, and as a boy he had that acquaintance with Nimbus which every white boy had with the neighboring colored lads—they hunted and fished together and were as near cronies as their color would allow. Since the war he had bought a place and by steady work had accumulated some money. His plantation was on the river and abutted on the eastern side with the property of Nimbus. After a moment's silence he said:

"That reminds me of what I heard to-day. Your old Marse Potem is dead."

"Yer don't say, now!"

"Yes—died yesterday and will be buried to-morrow."

"La, sakes! An' how's he lef' ole Missus an' de gals, I wonder?"

"Mighty pore I'm afraid. They say he's been mighty bad off lately, an' what he's got won't more'n half pay his debts. I reckon the widder an' chillen'll hev ter 'homestead it' the rest of their lives."

"Yer don't tink so? Wal, I do declar', hit's too bad. Ez rich ez he was, an' now ter come down ter be ez pore ez Nimbus—p'raps poorer!"

"It's mighty hard, that's sure. It was all along of the wah that left everybody pore in this country, just as it made all the Yankees rich with bonds and sech-like."

"Sho'! what's de use ob bein' a fool? 'Twan't de wah dat made Marse Desmit pore. 'Twuz dat ar damn fool business ob slavery afo' de wah dat wound him up. Ef he'd never been a 'speculator' an' hadn't tried to grow rich a raisin' men an' wimmen for market he'd a been richer'n ever he was, when he died."

"Oh, you're mistaken 'bout that, Nimbus. The wah ruined us all."

"Ha! ha! ha!" roared Nimbus, derisively. "What de wah ebber take from you, Mister Dossey, only jes yer oberseer's whip? An' dat wur de berry best ting ebber happen ter ye, kase it sot yer to wuk an' put yer in de way ob makin' money for yerself. It was hard on sech ez ole Mahs'r, dat's a fac, even ef 'twas mostly his own fault; but it was worth a million ter sech ez you. You 'uns gained mo' by de outcome ob de wah, right away, dan we cullu'd folks'll ebber git, I'm afeared."

"Yer may be right," said Dawsey, laughing, and with a touch of pride in his tone. "I've done pretty well since the wah. An' that brings me back to what I come over for. I thought I'd ax, if ye should git in a notion of selling, what yer'd take fer yer place here?"

"I hain't no idea uv selling, Mister Dossey, an' hain't no notion uv hevin' any 'nuther. You an' ebberybody else mout jest ez well larn, fust ez las', dat I shan't never sell only jes ter make money. Ef I put a price on Red Wing it'll be a big one; kase it ain't done growing yet, an' I might jest ez well stay h'yr an' grow ez ter go West an' grow up wid de kentry, ez dat fool Berry Lawson's allers tellin' about."

"Wal, that's all right, only ef you ever want ter sell, reasonable-like, yer know who to come to for your money. Good-night!"

The man was gathering up his reins when Nimbus said:

"When did yer say ole Mahsr's funeral was gwine ter be?"

"To-morrow afternoon at four o'clock, I heerd."

"Thank ye. I'se 'bout made up my mind ter go ter Louisburg to-morrer, stay ter dat funeral, an' come back nex' day. Seems ter me ole Mahs'r'd be kind o' glad ter see Nimbus at his funeral, fer all I wan't no gret fav'rite o' his'n. He wa'nt sich a bad marster, an' atter I bought Red Wing he use ter come ober ebbery now an agin, an' gib me a heap ob advice 'bout fixin' on it up. I allus listened at him, tu, kase ef ennybody ever knowed nex' do' ter ebberyting, dat ar man wuz ole Marse Potem. I'se sorry he's dead, I is; an' I'se mighty sorry for ole Missus an' de gals. An' I'se a gwine ter go ter dat er funeral an' see him laid away, ef it do take anudder day outen de crap; dat I is, shore."

"An' that 'minds me," said the white man, "that I heard at the same time, that Walter Greer, who used to own the plantation afore yer Marse Desmit bought it, died sometime lately, 'way out in Texas. It's quare, ain't it, that they should both go nigh about the same time. Good-night."

The "poor-white" neighbor rode away, little dreaming that the colored man had estimated him aright, and accounted him only an emissary of his foes, nor did he comprehend the importance of the information he had given.

CHAPTER XXXVI.

THE BEACON-LIGHT OF LOVE.

MOLLIE AINSLIE had been absent from Red Wing more than a month. It was nearly midnight. The gibbous[72] moon hung over the western tree-tops. There was not a sound to be heard in the little hamlet, but strangely draped figures might have been seen moving about in the open glades of the piney woods which skirted Red Wing upon the west.

One after another they stole across the open space between the church and the pine grove, in its rear, until a half-dozen had collected in its shadow. One mounted on another's shoulders and tried one of the windows. It yielded to his touch and he raised it without difficulty. He entered and another after him. Then two or three strange-looking packages were handed up to them from the outside. There was a whispered discussion, and then the parties within were heard moving cautiously about and a strong benzoic odor came from the upraised window. Now and then a sharp metallic clang was heard from within. At length the two that had entered returned to the window. There was a whispered consultation with those upon the outside. One of these crept carefully to the corner and gave a long low whistle. It was answered after a moment's interval, first from one direction and then from another, until every part of the little hamlet resounded with short quick answers. Then the man at the corner of the church crept back and whispered,

"All right!"

One of the parties inside came out upon the window-sill and dropped lightly to the ground. The other mounted upon the window-sill, and turned round upon his knees; there was a gleam of light within the building, a flicker and a hiss, and then with a mighty roar the flame swept through it as if following the trail of some combustible. Here and there it surged, down the aisles and over the desks, white and clear, showing in sharpest silhouette every curve and angle of building and furniture. The group at the window stood gazing within for a moment, the light playing on their faces and making them seem ghastly and pale by the reflection; then they crept hastily back into the shadow of the wood—all but one, who, clad in the horribly grotesque habit of the Ku Klux Klan, stood at the detached bell-tower, and when the flames burst forth from the windows solemnly tolled the bell until driven from his post by the heat.

One had hardly time to think, before the massive structure of dried pitch-pine which northern charity had erected in the foolish hope of benefiting the freedmen, where the young teachers had labored with such devotion, and where so many of the despised race had laid the foundation of a knowledge that they vainly hoped might lift them up into the perfect light of freedom, was a solid spire of sheeted flame.

By its ghastly glare, in various parts of the village were to be seen groups and single armed sentries, clad in black gowns which fell to their very feet, spire-pointed caps, grotesquely marked and reaching far above the head, while from the base a flowing masque depended over the face and fell down upon the shoulders, hiding all the outlines of the figure.

The little village was taken completely by surprise. It had been agreed that the ringing of the church bell should be the signal for assembling at the church with such arms as they had to resist the Ku Klux. It had not been thought that the danger would be imminent until about the expiration of the time named in the notice; so that the watch which had been determined upon had not been strictly kept, and on this night had been especially lax on one of the roads leading into the little hamlet.

At the first stroke of the bell all the villagers were awake, and from half-opened doors and windows they took in the scene which the light of the moon and the glare of the crackling fire revealed. Then dusky-skinned forms stole hastily away into the shadows of the houses and fences, and through the rank-growing corn of the little truck-patches, to the woods and fields in the rear. There were some who since the warning had not slept at home at all, but had occupied little leafy shelters in the bush and half-hid burrows on the hillside. On the eyes of all these gleamed the blaze of the burning church, and each one felt, as he had never realized before, the strength of that mysterious band which was just putting forth its power to overturn and nullify a system of laws that sought to clothe an inferior and servile race with the rights and privileges theretofore exercised solely by the dominant one.

Among those who looked upon this scene was Eliab Hill. Sitting upon his bench he gazed through the low window of his little cottage, the flame lighting up his pale face and his eyes distended with terror. His clasped hands rested on the window-sill and his upturned eyes evidently sought for strength from heaven to enable him manfully to perform the part he had declared his determination to enact. What he saw was this:

A company of masked men seemed to spring out of the ground around the house of Nimbus, and, at a whistle from one of their number, began swiftly to close in upon it. There was a quick rush and the door was burst open. There were screams and blows, angry words, and protestations within. After a moment a light shot up and died quickly out again—one of the party had struck a match. Eliab heard the men cursing Lugena, and ordering her to make up a light on the hearth. Then there were more blows, and the light shone upon the window. There were rough inquiries for the owner, and Eliab thanked God that his faithful friend was far away from the danger and devastation of that night. He wondered, dully, what would be his thought when he should return on the morrow, and mark the destruction wrought in his absence, and tried to paint his rage.

While he thought of these things the neighboring house was ransacked from top to bottom. He heard the men cursing because their search was fruitless. They brought out the wife, Lugena, and two of her children, and coaxed and threatened them without avail. A few blows were struck, but the wife and children stoutly maintained that the husband and father was absent, attending his old master's funeral, at Louisburg. The yellow light of the blazing church shone on the house, and made fantastic shadows all around. The lurid glare lighted up their faces and pictured their terror. They were almost without clothing. Eliab noticed that the hand that clasped Lugena's black arm below the band of the chemise was white and delicate.

The wife and children were crying and moaning in terror and pain. Oaths and blows were intermingled with questions in disguised voices, and gasping broken answers. Blood was running down the face of the wife. The younger children were screaming in the house. Children and women were shrieking in every direction as they fled to the shelter of the surrounding woods. The flame roared and crackled as it licked the resin from the pine logs of the church and leaped aloft. It shone upon the glittering needles of the surrounding pines, lighted up the ripening tobacco on the hillside, sparkled in the dewy leaves of the honeysuckle which clambered over the freedman's house and hid the staring moon with its columns of black smoke.

The search for Nimbus proving unavailing—they scarcely seemed to expect to find him—they began to inquire of the terror-stricken woman the whereabouts of his friend.

"Where is 'Liab Hill?" asked the man who held her arm.

"What have you done with that snivelling hop-toad minister?" queried another.

"Speak, damn you! and see that you tell the truth," said a third, as he struck her over the bare shoulders with a stick.

"Oh! don't! don't!" shrieked the poor woman as she writhed in agony. "I'll tell! I will, gentlemens—I will—I will! Oh, my God! don't! *don't!*" she cried, as she leaped wildly about, tearing the one garment away in her efforts to avoid the blows which fell thick and fast on every part of her person, now fully exposed in the bright light.

"Speak, then!" said the man who held the goad. "Out with it! Tell where you've hid him!"

"He ain't—here, gentlemen! He—he—don't—stay here no mo'."

Again the blows came thick and fast. She fell upon the ground and rolled in the dust to avoid them. Her round black limbs glistened in the yellow light as she writhed from side to side.

"Here I am—here!" came a wild, shrill shriek from Eliab's cabin.

Casting a glance towards it, one of the men saw a blanched and pallid face pressed against the window and lighted by the blazing church—the face of him who was wont to minister there to the people who did not know their own "best friends!"

"There he is!"—"Bring the damn rascal out!"—"He's the one we want, anyhow!"

These and numerous other shouts of similar character, beat upon the ears of the terrified watcher, as the crowd of masked marauders rushed towards the little cabin which had been his home ever since Red Wing had passed into the possession of its present owner. It was the first building erected under the new proprietorship, and was substantially built of pine logs. The one low window and the door in front were the only openings cut through the solidly-framed logs. The door was fastened with a heavy wooden bar which reached across the entire shutter and was held in place by strong iron staples driven into the heavy door-posts. Above, it was strongly ceiled, but under the eaves were large openings made by the thick poles which had been used for rafters. If the owner had been capable of defense he could hardly have had a castle better adapted for a desperate and successful struggle than this.

Eliab Hill knew this, and for a moment his face flushed as he saw the crowd rush towards him, with the vain wish that he might fight for his life and for his race. He had fully made up his mind to die at his post. He was not a brave man in one sense of the word. A cripple never is. Compelled to acknowledge the physical superiority of others, year after year, he comes at length to regard his own inferiority as a matter of course, and never thinks of any movement which partakes of the aggressive. Eliab Hill had procured the strong bar and heavy staples for his door when first warned by the Klan, but he had never concocted any scheme of defense. He thought vaguely, as he saw them coming towards him in the bright moonlight and in the brighter glow of the burning sanctuary, that with a good repeating arm he might not only sell his life dearly, but even repel the attack. It would be a proud thing if he might do so. He was sorry he had not thought of it before. He remembered the Spencer carbine which he had given a few days before to Berry Lawson to clean and repair, and to obtain cartridges of the proper calibre, in order that it might be used by some one in the defense of Red Wing. Berry had not yet returned. He had never thought of using it himself, until that moment when he saw his enemies advancing upon him with wild cries, and heard the roar of the flaming church. He was not a hero. On the contrary, he believed himself a coward.

He was brave enough in suffering, but his courage was like that of a woman. He was able and willing to endure the most terrible evils, but he did not think of doing brave things or achieving great acts. His courage was not aggressive. He could be killed, but did not think of killing. Not that he was averse to taking life in self-defense, but he had been so long the creature of another's will in the matter of locomotion that it did not occur to him to do otherwise than say: "Do with me as thou wilt. I am bound hand and foot. I cannot fight, but I can die."

He shrank from acute pain with that peculiar terror which the confirmed invalid always exhibits, perhaps because he realizes its horror more than those who are usually exempt from its pangs.

As he pressed his face close to the flame-lighted pane, and watched the group of grotesquely disguised men rushing toward his door, his eyes were full of wild terror and his face twitched, while his lips trembled and grew pale under the dark mustache. There was a rush against the door, but it did not yield. Another and another; but the heavy bar and strong staples held it fast. Then his name was called, but he did not answer. Drawing his head quickly from the window, he closed the heavy wooden shutter, which fitted closely into the frame on the inside, and fastened it with a bar like that upon the door. Hardly had he done so when a blow shattered the window. Something was thrust in and passed around the opening, trying here and there to force open the shutter, but in vain. Then it was pressed against the bottom, just where the shutter rested on the window-sill. There was an instant's silence save that Eliab Hill heard a click which he thought was caused by the cocking of a revolver, and threw himself quickly down upon his bench. There was a sharp explosion, a jarring crash as the ball tore through the woodwork, and hurtling across the room buried itself in the opposite wall. Then there were several shots fired at the door. One man found a little hole in the chinking, between two of the logs, and putting his revolver through, fired again and again, sending spits of hot flame and sharp spiteful reverberations through the darkness of the cabin.

Eliab Hill watched all this with fixed, staring eyes and teeth set, but did not move or speak. He scrambled off the bench, and crawled, in his queer tripedal fashion, to the cot, crept into it, and with hands clasped, sat bolt upright on the pillow. He set his back against the wall, and, facing the door, waited for the end. He wished that some of the bullets that were fired might pierce his heart. He even prayed that his doom might come sharp and swift—that he might be saved from torture—might be spared the lash. He only feared lest his manhood should fail him in the presence of impending suffering.

There came a rush against the door with some heavy timber. He guessed that it was the log from the hitching rack in front of Nimbus' house. But the strong bar did not yield. They called out his name again, and assured him that if he did not undo the door they would fire the house. A strange look of relief, even of joy, passed over his face as he heard this declaration. He clasped his hands across his breast as he sat upon the bed, and his lips moved in prayer. He was not afraid to die, but he was afraid that he might not be strong enough to endure all the pain that might be caused by torture, without betraying his suffering or debasing his manhood. He felt very weak and was glad to know that fire and smoke would hide his groans and tears.

While he waited for the hissing of the flame the blows of an axe resounded on the door. It was wielded by stalwart hands, and ere long the glare from without shone through the double planking.

"Hello, 'Liab—'Liab Hill!" cried a voice at the opening which seemed to the quiet listener within strangely like that of Sheriff Gleason. "Damn me, boys, if I don't believe you've killed the nigger, shooting in there. Hadn't we better just set the cabin afire and let it burn?"

"Put in your hand and see if you can't lift the bar," said another. "I'd like to know whether the scoundrel is dead or alive. Besides that, I don't fancy this burning houses. I don't object to hanging a sassy nigger, or anything of that kind, but burning a house is a different matter. That's almost too mean for a white man to do. It's kind of a nigger business, to my notion."

"For instance!" said another, with a laugh, pointing to the blazing church.

"Oh, damn it!" said the former, "that's another thing. A damn nigger school-house ain't of no more account than a brush-pile, anyhow."

A hand was thrust through the opening and the bar lifted from one socket and drawn out of the other. Then the door flew open and a half dozen men rushed into the room. The foremost fell over the rolling chair which had been left near the door, and the others in turn fell over him.

"What the hell!" cried one. "Bring the light here. What is this thing, anyhow?"

The light was brought, and the voice continued: "Damned if it ain't the critter's go-cart. Here, kick the damn thing out—smash it up! Such things ain't made for niggers to ride on, anyhow. He won't need it any more—not after we have got through with him.

"That he won't!" said another, as the invalid's chair which had first given Eliab Hill power to move himself about was kicked out of the door and broken into pieces with blows of the axe.

Eliab Hill felt as if a part of his life was already destroyed. He groaned for the fate of this inseparable companion of all his independent existence. It had grown dearer to him than he knew. It hurt him, even then, to hear the coarse, grim jests which were uttered as its finely-wrought frame cracked beneath the blows of the axe, and its luxurious belongings were rent and torn by the hands that would soon rend and tear its owner. He had come to look upon the insensate machine with a passionate regard. While it seemed like tearing away his limbs to take it from him, yet there was a feeling of separate animate existence about it which one never feels towards his own members. He had petted and polished and cared for this strong, pretty, and easily worked combination of levers and springs and wheels that had served him so faithfully, until it seemed to his fancy like an old and valued friend.

CHAPTER XXXVII.

THE "BEST FRIENDS" REVEAL THEMSELVES.

"BRING A LIGHT!" shouted the leader. One of the men rushed into the house of Nimbus, and snatched a flaming brand from the hearth. As he ran with it out of the front door, he did not see a giant form which leaped from the waving corn and sprang into the back door. The black foot was bare and made no sound as it fell upon the threshold. He did not see the black, furious face or the right arm, bared above the elbow, which snatched a saber from the top of a cupboard. He did not see the glaring, murderous eyes that peered through the vine-leaves as he rushed, with his flaming brand aloft, out of the house to the hut of Eliab. As he reached the door the light fell upon the preacher, who sat upon the bed. The fear of death had passed away—even the fear of suffering was gone. His lips moved in prayer, the forgiving words mingling with the curses of his assailants: "O God, my help and my shield!"[73] ("*Here he is, God damn him!*") "Forgive them, Father—" ("*I've got him!*") "They know not—a—h!"

A long, shrill shriek—the voice of a man overborne by mortal agony—sounded above the clamor of curses, and above the roar of the blazing church. There was a fall upon the cabin floor—the grating sound of a body swiftly drawn along its surface—and one of the masked marauders rushed out dragging by the foot the preacher of the Gospel of Peace. The withered leg was straightened. The weakened sinews were torn asunder, and as his captor dragged him out into the light and flung the burden away, the limb dropped, lax and nerveless, to the ground. Then there were blows and kicks and curses from the crowd, which rushed upon him. In the midst, one held aloft a blazing brand. Groans and fragments of prayer came up through the din.*

All at once there was a roar as of a desert lion bursting from its lair. They looked and saw a huge black form leap from the porch of the other house and bound toward them. He was on them in an instant. There was the swish of a saber swung by a practiced hand, and the high-peaked mask of the leader bent over the hissing blade, and was stripped away, leaving a pale, affrighted face glaring stupidly at the ebon angel of wrath in the lurid fire-light. A fearful oath came through the white, strong teeth, which showed hard-set below the moustache. Again the saber whistled round the head of the avenger. There was a shriek of mortal agony, and one of the masquer-aders fell. The others shrunk back. One fired a shot. The man with the torch stood for the moment as though transfixed, with the glaring light still held aloft. Then, with his revolver, he aimed a close, sure shot at the dusky giant whom he watched.

Suddenly he saw a woman's naked figure, that seemed to rise from the ground. There was a gleam of steel, and then down through mask and flesh and bone crashed the axe[74] which had fallen by the door step, and the blood spurted upon Lugena's unclothed form and into the face of the prostrate Eliab, as the holder of the torch fell beside him. Then the others gave way, and the two black forms pursued. There were some wild shots fired back, as they fled toward the wood beyond the road.

* Those who are interested in such matters may find some curiously exact parallels of the characters and incidents of this chapter testified to under oath in the "Report of the Committee on Ku-Klux Outrages in the Southern States." The facts are of no special interest, however, except as illustrations of the underlying spirit and cause of this strange epidemic of violence.[75]

Then from its depths came a flash and a roar. A ball went shrieking by them and flew away into the darkness beyond. Another, and another and another! It was not the sharp, short crack of the revolver, but the fierce angry challenge of the rifle. They had heard it before upon the battle-field, and terror lent them wings as they fled. The hurtling missiles flew here and there, wherever a masked form could be seen, and pursued their fleeing shadows into the wood, glancing from tree to tree, cutting through spine and branch and splintering bole, until the last echo of their footsteps had died away.

Then all was still, except the roar of the burning church and the solemn soughing of the pines, as the rising west wind rustled their branches.

Nimbus and his wife stood listening in the shade of a low oak, between the scene of conflict and the highway. No sound of the flying enemy could be heard.

"Nimbus! *Oh,* Nimbus!" the words came in a strained, low whisper from the unclad figure at his side.

"Wal, 'Gena?"

"Is you hurt, honey?"

"Nary bit. How should I be? They run away ez quick ez I come. Did they 'buse you, 'Gena?"

"None of enny 'count," she answered, cautiously, for fear of raising his anger to a point beyond control—"only jest a tryin' ter make me tell whar you was—you an' 'Liab."

"Whar's yer clo'es, honey?"

"In de house, dar, only what I tore, getting away from 'em."

"An' de chillen?"

"Dey's run out an' hid somewheres. Dey scattered like young pa'tridges."

"Dey's been hunted like 'em too!"

He lays his hand in caution upon the bare shoulder next him, and they both crouch closer in the shadow and listen. All is quiet, except groans and stertorous[76] breathing near the cabin.

"It's one of them damned villains. Let me settle him!" said Nimbus.

"Don't, don't!" cried Lugena, as she threw her arms about his neck. "Please don't, honey!"

"P'raps it's Bre'er 'Liab! Let me go!" he said, hastily.

Cautiously they started back through the strip of yellow light which lay between them and the cabin of Eliab. They could not believe that their persecutors were indeed gone. Nimbus's hand still clutched the saber, and Lugena had picked up the axe which she had dropped.

The groaning came indeed from Eliab. He had partially recovered from the unconsciousness which had come over him while undergoing torture, and with returning animation had come the sense of acute suffering from the injuries he had received.

"Bre'er 'Liab!" whispered Nimbus, bending over him.

"Is that you, Nimbus?" asked the stricken man in surprise. "How do you come to be here?"

"Jes tuk it inter my head ter come home atter de funeril, an' done got here jest in time ter take a han' in what was gwine on."

"Is the church all burned down, Nimbus?"

"De ruf hez all fell in. De sides 'll burn a long while yet. Dey'se logs, yer know."

"Did 'Gena get away, Nimbus?"

"Here I is, Bre'er 'Liab."

"Is anybody hurt?"

"Not ez we knows on, 'cept two dat's lyin' on de groun' right h'yer by ye," said Nimbus.

"Dead?" asked 'Liab, with a shudder. He tried to raise himself up but sank back with a groan.

"Oh, Bre'er 'Liab! Bre'er 'Liab!" cried Nimbus, his distress overcoming his fear, "is you hurt bad? My God!" he continued, as he raised his friend's head and saw that he had lapsed again into insensibility, "my God! 'Gena, he's dead!"

He withdrew the hand he had placed under the shoulders of the prostrate man. It was covered with blood.

"Sh—sh! You hear dat, Nimbus?" asked Lugena, in a choked whisper, as she started up and peered toward the road. "Oh, Nimbus, run! run! Do, honey, do! Dar dey comes! Dey'll kill you, shore!"

She caught her husband by the arm, and endeavored to drag him into the shadow of the cabin.

"I can't leave Bre'er 'Liab," said Nimbus, doggedly.

"Yer can't help him. Yer'll jes stay an' be killed ye'self! Dar now, listen at dat!" cried the trembling woman.

The sound to which she referred was that of hurried footfalls in the road beyond their house. Nimbus heard it, and stooping over his insensible friend, raised him in his arms and dashed around the cabin into the rank-growing corn beyond. His wife followed for a few steps, still carrying the axe. Then she turned and peered through the corn-rows, determined to cover her husband's retreat should danger threaten him from that direction. After waiting awhile and hearing nothing more, she concluded to go to the house, get some clothing, and endeavor to rally her scattered brood.

Stealing softly up to the back door—the fire had died out upon the hearth—she entered cautiously, and after glancing through the shaded porch began to dress. She had donned her clothing and taken up her shoes preparatory to going back to the shelter of the cornfield, when she thought she heard a stealthy footstep on the porch. Her heart stood still with terror. She listened breathlessly. It came again. There was no doubt of it now—a slow, stealthy step! A board creaked, and then all was still. Again! Thank God it was a *bare* foot! Her heart took hope. She stole to the open door and peeped out. There, in the half shadow of the flame-lit porch, she saw Berry Lawson stealing toward her. She almost screamed for joy. Stepping into the doorway she whispered,

"Berry!"

"Is dat you, 'Gena?" whispered that worthy, tiptoeing hastily forward and stepping into the shadow within the room. "How'd yer manage ter live t'rough dis yer night, 'Gena? An' whar's Nimbus an' de chillen?"

These questions being hastily answered, Lugena began to inquire in regard to his presence there.

"Whar I come from? Jes got back from Bre'er Rufe's house. Druv at night jes ter save de mornin' ter walk back in. Lef' Sally an' de chillen dar all right. When I come putty nigh ter Red Wing I sees de light o' de fire, an' presently I sez to myself, sez I, 'Berry, dat ain't no common fire, now. Ain't many houses in the kentry roun' make sech a fire ez dat. Dat mus' be de church, Berry.' Den I members 'bout de Ku Kluckers, an' I sez ter myself agin, sez I, 'Berry, dem rascals hez come ter Red Wing an' is raisin' de debble dar now, jes dere own way.' Den I runs de mule and de carryall inter de woods, 'bout a mile down de road, an' I takes out Bre'er 'Liab's gun, dat I'd borrered fer company, yer know, an' hed got some cattridges fer, ober at Lewyburg, an' I comes on ter take a han' in—ef dar wa'n't no danger, yer know, honey.

"When I gits ober in de woods, dar, I heah de wust sort ob hullabaloo ober h'yer 'bout whar Bre'er 'Liab's house was—hollerin' an' screamin' an' cussin' an' fightin'. I couldn't make it all out, but I 'llowed dat Nimbus wuz a-habbin' a hell ob a time, an' ef I wuz gwine ter do anyting, dat wuz about de right time fer me ter put in. So I rested dis yer ole gal," patting the carbine in his hand, "agin a tree an' jes slung a bullet squar ober dere heads. Ye see, I dassent shoot too low, fer fear ob hurtin' some of my fren's. 'D'ye heah dat shot, 'Gena? Lord! how de ole gal did holler. 'Pears like I nebber hear a cannon sound so big. De Ku Kluckers 'peared ter hear it too, fer dey comed squar outen h'yer inter de big road. Den I opened up an' let her bark at 'em ez long ez I could see a shadder ter pull trigger on. Wonder ef I hurt enny on 'em. D'yer know, 'Gena, wuz enny on 'em killed?"

"Dar's two on 'em a layin' out dar by 'Liab's house," said the woman.

"Yer don't say so!" said Berry with a start. "La, sakes! what's dat?" he continued, breathlessly, as a strange sound was heard in the direction indicated. They stole out upon the porch, and as they peered through the clustering vine-leaves a ghastly spectacle presented itself to their eyes.

One of the prostrate forms had risen and was groping around on its hands and knees, uttering a strange moaning sound. Presently it staggered to its feet, and after some vain efforts seized the mask, the long flowing cape attached to which fell down upon the shoulders, and tore it away. The pale, distorted face with a bloody channel down the middle was turned inquiringly this way and that. The man put his hand to his forehead as if to collect his thoughts. Then he tried to utter a cry; the jaw moved, but only unintelligible sounds were heard.

Lugena heard the click of the gun-lock, and turning, laid her hand on Berry, as she said,

"Don't shoot! 'Tain't no use!"

"Yer right, it ain't," said Berry with chattering teeth. "Who ebber seed a man walkin' 'roun' wid his head split wide open afo'?"

The figure staggered on, looked a moment at the house, turned toward the burning church, and then, seeming to recall what had happened, at once assumed a stealthy demeanor, and, still staggering as it went, crept off toward the gate, out of which it passed and went unsteadily off down the road.

"Dar ain't no sort of use o' his dodgin' 'round," said Berry, as the footsteps died away. "De berry debble 'd gib him de road, enny time."

As he spoke, a whistle sounded down the road. Berry and Lugena instantly sought shelter in the corn. Crouching low between the rows, they saw four men come cautiously into the yard, examine the prostrate man that remained, and bear him off between them, using for a stretcher the pieces of the coffin-shaped board which had been hung upon the gate two weeks before.

CHAPTER XXXVIII.

"THE ROSE ABOVE THE MOULD."[77]

THE CONVALESCENCE OF Mollie Ainslie was very rapid, and a few days after the crisis of her disease her attendants were able to return to their homes at Red Wing. Great was the rejoicing there over the recovery of their favorite teacher. The school had been greatly crippled by her absence and showed, even in that brief period, how much was due to her ability and skill. Everybody was clamorous for her immediate return—everybody except Eliab Hill, who after an almost sleepless night sent a letter begging her not to return for a considerable time.

It was a strangely earnest letter for one of its apparent import. The writer dwelt at considerable length upon the insidious and treacherous character of the disease from which she was recovering. He grew eloquent as he detailed all that the people of Red Wing owed to her exertions in their behalf, and told how, year after year, without any vacation, she had labored for them. He showed that this must have been a strain upon her vital energies, and pointed out the danger of relapse should she resume her duties before she had fully recovered. He begged her, therefore, to remain at Mulberry Hill at least a month longer; and, to support his request, informed her that with the advice and consent of the Superintendent he had dismissed the school until that time. He took especial pains, too, to prevent the report of the threatened difficulty from coming to her ears. This was the more easily accomplished from the fact that those who had apprehended trouble were afraid of being deemed cowardly if they acknowledged their belief. So, while the greater number of the men in the little hamlet were accustomed to sleep in the neighboring thickets, in order to be out of harm's way should the Ku Klux come to make good their decree, very little was said, even among themselves, about the threatened attack.

In utter unconsciousness, therefore, of the fate that brooded over those in whom she took so deep an interest, Mollie abandoned herself to the restful delights of convalescence. She soon found herself able to visit the room of the confirmed invalid below, and though she seemed to detect a sort of coolness in her manner she did not dream of associating the change with herself. She attributed it entirely to the sore affliction which had fallen upon the household since her arrival, and which, she charitably reasoned, her own recovery must revive in their minds in full force. So she pardoned the fair, frail invalid who, reclining languidly upon the couch, asked as to her health and congratulated her in cool, set phrases upon her recovery.

Such was not the case, however, with her host. There were tears in his eyes when he met her on the landing for the first time after she left her sick-bed. She knew they were for the little Hildreth whom she had nursed and whom her presence recalled. And yet there was a gleam in his eyes which was not altogether of sorrow. She, too, mourned for the sweet child whom she had learned to love, and her eyes responded to the tender challenge with copious tears. Yet her own feelings were not entirely sad. She did not know why. She did not stop to analyze or reason. She only gave him her hand—how thin and white it was compared with the first time he had seen her and had noted its soft plumpness!

Their lips quivered so that they could not speak. He held her hand and assisted the servant in leading her into the parlor. She was still so weak that they had to lay her on the sofa. Hesden Le Moyne bent over her for a little while, and then hurried away. He had not said a word, and both had wept; yet, as she closed her eyes after he had gone she was vaguely conscious that she had never been so happy before in her life. So the days wore on, quietly and swiftly, full of a tender sorrow tempered with an undefined joy. Day by day she grew stronger and brighter, needing less of assistance but receiving even more of attention from the stricken father of her late charge.

"You have not asked about Satan," said Mr. Le Moyne suddenly one day.

"Why should I?" she replied, with an arch look. "If that personage will be equally forgetful of me I am sure I shall be very glad."

"Oh, I mean your horse—Midnight, as you call him," laughed Hesden.

"So I supposed," she replied. "I have a dim notion that you applied that epithet to him on the night of my arrival. Your mother, too, said something about 'Satan,' that night, which I remember puzzled me very greatly at the moment, but I was too much flustered to ask about it just then. Thinking of it afterward, I concluded that she intended to refer to my black-skinned pet. But why do you give him that name?"

"Because that was the first name he ever knew," answered Hesden, with an amused smile.

"The first name he ever knew? I don't understand you," she replied. "My brother captured him at Appomattox, or near there, and named him Midnight, and Midnight he has been ever since."

"Very true," said Hesden, "but he was Satan before that, and very well earned this name, in his young days."

"In his young days?" she asked, turning towards him in surprise. "Did you know him then?"

"Very well, indeed," he replied, smiling at her eagerness. "He was raised on this plantation and never knew any other master than me until that day at Rouse's Bridge."

"Why, that is the very place my brother captured him. I remember the name now that you mention it!" she exclaimed.

"Is it anything surprising," said he, "that the day I lost him should be the day he captured him?"

"No—not exactly—but then"—she paused in confusion as she glanced at the empty sleeve which was pinned across his breast.

"Yes," said he, noticing her look, "I lost that there," pointing to the empty sleeve as he spoke; "and though it was a sore loss to a young man who prided himself somewhat on his physical activity, I believe I mourned the horse more than I did the arm."

"But my brother—" she began with a frightened look into his face.

"Well, he must have been in my immediate vicinity, for Satan was the best-trained horse in the squadron. Even after I was dismounted, he would not have failed to keep his place in the ranks when the retreat was sounded, unless an unusually good horseman were on his back."

"My brother said he had as hard a struggle with him then as he had with his rider before," she said, looking shyly up.

"Indeed! I am obliged to him," he responded with a smile. "The commendation of an enemy is always pleasant to a soldier."

"Oh, he said you were terribly bloodthirsty and rode at him as if nothing would satisfy you but his life," she said, with great eagerness.

"Very likely," he answered, lightly. "I have some reputation for directness of purpose, and that was a moment of desperation. We did not know whether we should come back or not, and did not care. We knew that the end was very near, and few of us wished to outlive it. Not that we cared so much—many of us at least—for the cause we fought for; but we dreaded the humiliation of surrender and the stigma of defeat. We felt the disgrace to our people with a keenness that no one can appreciate who has not been in like circumstances. I was opposed to the war myself, but I would rather have died than have lived to see the surrender."

"It must have been hard," she said, softly.

"Hard!" he exclaimed. "I should think it was! But then," he added, his brow suddenly clearing, "next to the fact of surrender I dreaded the loss of my horse. I even contemplated shooting him to prevent his falling into the hands of the enemy."

"My brother thought you were rather anxious to throw away your own life," she said, musingly.

"No," he answered, "just indifferent. I wonder if I saw him at all."

"Oh, you must, for you—" she began eagerly, but stopped in confusion.

"Well, what did I do? Nothing very bad, I hope?" he asked.

"Well, you left an ugly scar on a very smooth forehead, if you call that bad, sir," she said, archly.

"Indeed! Of course I do," was the reply, but his tone indicated that he was thinking less of the atrocity which she had laid to his charge than of the events of that last day of battle. "Let me see," said he, musingly. "I had a sharp turn with a fellow on a gray horse. He was a slender, fair-haired man"—looking down at the figure on the sofa behind which he stood as if to note if there were any resemblance. "He was tall, as tall as I am, I should say, and I thought—I was of the impression—that he was of higher rank than a captain. He was somewhat in advance of his line and right in my path. I remember thinking, as I crossed swords with him that if—if we were both killed, the odds would be in favor of our side. He must have been a colonel at least, or I was mistaken in his shoulder-straps."

"My brother was a colonel of volunteers," she said, quietly. "He was only a captain, however, after his transfer to the regular army."

"Indeed!" said he with new interest. "What was he like?"

For answer Mollie put her hand to her throat, and opening a gold locket which she wore, held up the case so far as the chain would allow while Hesden bent over to look at it. His face was very near her own, and she noted the eagerness with which he scanned the picture.

"Yes, that is the man!" he said at length, with something like a sigh. "I hope I did not injure him seriously."

"Only his beauty," she replied, pleasantly.

"Of which, judging from what I see," he said saucily, letting his eyes wander from the miniature to her face, "he could afford to lose a good deal and yet not suffer by comparison with others."

It was a bold, blunt compliment, yet it was uttered with evident sincerity; but she had turned the locket so that she could see the likeness and did not catch the double meaning of his words. So she only answered calmly and earnestly,

"He was a good brother."

A shadow passed over his face as he noticed her inattention to his compliment, but he added heartily,

"And a gallant one. I am glad that my horse fell into his hands."

She looked at him and said,

"You were very fond of your horse?"

"Yes, indeed!" he answered. "He was a great pet before we went into the service, and my constant companion for nearly three years of that struggle. But come out on the porch, and let me show you some of the tricks I taught him, and you will not only understand how I prized him, but will appreciate his sagacity more than you do now."

He assisted her to a rocking-chair upon the porch, and, bidding a servant to bring out the horse, said:

"You must remember that I have but one arm and have not seen him, until lately, at least, for five years. "Poor old fellow!" he added, as he went down the steps of the porch, and told the servant to turn him loose. He called him up with a snap of his thumb and finger as he entered the yard and patted his head which was stretched out to receive the caress. "Poor fellow! he is not so young as he was then, though he has had good care. The gray hairs are beginning to show on his muzzle, and I can detect, though no one else might notice them, the wrinkles coming about his eyes. Let me see, you are only nine years old, though,—nine past. But it's the war that tells—tells on horses just as well as men. You ought to be credited with about five years for what you went through then, old fellow. And a man—Do you know, Miss Mollie," he said, breaking suddenly off—"that a man who was in that war, even if he did not get a shot, discounted his life about ten years? It was the wear and tear of the struggle. We are different from other nations. We have no professional soldiers—at least none to speak of. To such, war is merely a business and peace an interlude. There is no mental strain in their case. But in our war we were all volunteers. Every man, on both sides, went into the army with the fate of a nation resting on his shoulders, and because he felt the burden of responsibility. It was that which killed—killed and weakened —more than shot and shell and frost and heat together. And then—what came afterward?"

He turned towards her as he spoke, his hand still resting on the neck of the horse which was rubbing against him and playfully nipping at him with his teeth, in manifestation of his delight.

Her face had settled into firm, hard lines. She seemed to be looking beyond him, and the gray coldness which we saw about her face when she read the telegram in the far-away Bankshire hills, settled on cheek and brow again, as she slowly repeated, as though unconscious of their meaning, the lines:

> "In the world's broad field of battle,
> In the bivouac of Life,
> Be not like dumb, driven cattle!
> Be a hero in the strife!"[78]

Hesden Le Moyne gazed at her a moment in confused wonder. Then he turned to the horse and made him perform various tricks at his bidding. He made him back away from him as far as he chose by the motion of his hand, and then, by reversing the gesture, brought him bounding back again. The horse lifted either foot at his instance, lay down, rolled over, stood upon his hind feet, and finally knelt upon the edge of the porch in obeisance to his mistress, who sat looking, although in a preoccupied manner, at all that was done. Hesden Le Moyne was surprised and somewhat disappointed at her lack of enthusiasm over what he thought would give her so much pleasure. She thanked him absently when it was over, and retired to her own room.

CHAPTER XXXIX.

WHAT THE MIST HID.

THE DARKNESS WAS already giving way to the gray light of a misty morning following the attack on Red Wing. The mocking-birds, one after another, were responding to each other's calls, at first sleepily and unwillingly, as though the imprisoned melody compelled expression, and then, thoroughly aroused and perched upon the highest dew-laden branches swaying and tossing beneath them, they poured forth their rival orisons. Other sounds of rising day were coming through the mist that still hung over the land, shutting out the brightness which was marching from the eastward. The crowing of cocks, the neighing of horses, and the lowing of cattle resounded from hill to hill across the wide bottom-lands and up and down the river upon either hand. Nature was waking from slumber—not to the full, boisterous wakefulness which greets the broad day, but the half-consciousness with which the sluggard turns himself for the light, sweet sleep of the summer morning.

There was a tap at the open window that stood at the head of Hesden Le Moyne's bed. His room was across the hall from his mother's, and upon the same floor. It had been his room from childhood. The window opened upon the wide, low porch which ran along three sides of the great rambling house. Hesden heard the tap, but it only served to send his half-awakened fancy on a fantastic trip through dreamland. Again came the low, inquiring tap, this time upon the headboard of the old mahogany bedstead. He thought it was one of the servants coming for orders about the day's labors. He wondered, vaguely and dully, what could be wanted. Perhaps they would go away if he did not move. Again it came, cautious and low, but firm and imperative, made by the nail of one finger struck sharply and regularly against the polished headboard. It was a summons and a command for silence at once. Hesden raised himself quickly and looked toward the window. The outline of a human figure showed dimly against the gray darkness beyond.

"Who's there?"—in a low, quiet voice, as though caution had been distinctly enjoined.

"Marse Hesden!"—a low whisper, full of suppressed excitement.

"You, Nimbus?" said Le Moyne, as he stepped quickly out of bed and approached the window. "What's the matter?"

"Marse Hesden," whispered the colored man, laying a hand trembling with excitement on his shoulder as he came near, "is yer a friend ter 'Liab Hill?"

"Of course I am; you know that"—in an impatient undertone.

"Sh—sh! Marse Hesden, don't make no noise, please," whispered Nimbus. "I don't mean ter ax ef yer's jes got nothin' agin' him, but is yer that kind ob a friend ez 'll stan' by him in trouble?"

"What do you mean, Nimbus?" asked Hesden in surprise.

"Will yer come wid me, Marse Hesden—slip on yer clo'es an' come wid me, jist a minnit?"

Hesden did not think of denying this request. It was evident that something of grave importance had occurred. Hardly a moment had elapsed before he stepped cautiously out upon the porch and followed Nimbus. The latter led the way quickly toward a spring which burst out of the hillside fifty yards away from the house, at the foot of a giant oak. Lying in the shadow of this tree and reclining against its base, lay Eliab Hill, his pallid face showing through the darkness like the face of the dead.

A few words served to tell Hesden Le Moyne what the reader already knows.

"I brought him here, Marse Hesden, kase ther ain't no place else dat he'd be safe whar he could be tuk keer on. Dem ar Kluckers is bound ter kill him ef dey kin. He's got ter be hid an' tuk keer on till he's well—ef he ever gits well at all."

"Why, you don't think he's hurt—not seriously, do you?"

"Hurt, man!" said Nimbus, impatiently. "Dar ain't much difference atwixt him an' a dead man, now."

"Good God! Nimbus, you don't mean that. He seems to sleep well," said Hesden, bending over the prostrate form.

"Sleep! Marse Hesden, I'se kerried him tree miles sence he's been a-sleepin' like dat; an' de blood's been a runnin' down on my hans an' a-breakin' my holt ebbery now an' den, tu!"

"Why, Nimbus, what is this you tell me? Was any one else hurt?"

"Wal, dar's a couple o' white men a-layin' mighty quiet dar, afo' 'Liab's house."

Hesden shuddered. The time he had dreaded had come! The smouldering passion of the South had burst forth at last! For years—ever since the war—prejudice and passion, the sense of insult and oppression had been growing thicker and blacker all over the South. Thunders had rolled over the land. Lightnings had fringed its edges. The country had heard, but had not heeded. The nation had looked on with smiling face, and declared the sunshine undimmed. It had taken no note of exasperation and prejudice. It had unconsciously trampled under foot the passionate pride of a conquered people. It had scorned and despised a sentiment more deeply inwrought than that of caste in the Hindoo breast.

The South believed, honestly believed, in its innate superiority over all other races and peoples. It did not doubt, has never doubted, that, man for man, it was braver, stronger, better than the North. Its men were "gentlemen"—grander, nobler beings than the North ever knew. Their women were "ladies"—gentle, refined, ethereal beings, passion and devotion wrapped in forms of ethereal mould, and surrounded by an impalpable effulgence which distinguished them from all others of the sex throughout the world. Whatever was of the South was superlative. To be Southern-born was to be *prima facie*[79] better than other men. So the self-love of every man was enlisted in this sentiment. To praise the South was to praise himself; to boast of its valor was to advertise his own intrepidity; to extol its women was to enhance the glory of his own achievements in the lists of love; to vaunt its chivalry was to avouch his own honor; to laud its greatness was to extol himself. He measured himself with his Northern compeer, and decided without hesitation in his own favor.

The South, he felt, was unquestionably greater than the North in all those things which were most excellent, and was only overtopped by it in those things which were the mere result of numbers. Outnumbered on the field of battle, the South had been degraded and insulted by a sordid and low-minded conqueror, in the very hour of victory. Outnumbered at the ballot-box, it had still dictated the policy of the Nation. The Southern white man naturally compared himself with his Northern brother. For comparison between himself and the African—the recent slave, the scarcely human anthropoid—he found no ground. Only contrast was possible there. To have these made co-equal rulers with him, seated beside him on the throne of popular sovereignty, merely, as he honestly thought, for the gratification of an unmanly spite against a fallen foe, aroused every feeling of exasperation and revenge which a people always restive of restraint could feel.

It was not from hatred to the negro, but to destroy his political power and restore again their own insulted and debased supremacy that such things were done as have been related. It was to show the conqueror that the bonds in which the sleeping Samson[80] had been bound were green withes which he scornfully snapped asunder in his first waking moment. Pride the most overweening, and a prejudice of caste the most intense and ineradicable, stimulated by the chagrin of defeat and inflamed by the sense of injustice and oppression—both these lay at the bottom of the acts by which the rule of the majorities established by reconstructionary legislation were overthrown. It was these things that so blinded the eyes of a whole people that they called this bloody masquerading, this midnight warfare upon the weak, this era of unutterable horror, "redeeming the South!"

There was no good man, no honest man, no Christian man of the South who for an instant claimed that it was right to kill, maim, beat, wound and ill-treat the black man, either in his old or his new estate. He did not regard these acts as done to another *man,* a compeer, but only as acts of cruelty to an inferior so infinitely removed from himself as to forbid any comparison of rights or feelings. It was not right to do evil to a "nigger;" but it was infinitely less wrong than to do it unto one of their own color. These men did not consider such acts as right in themselves, but only as right in view of their comparative importance and necessity, and the unspeakable inferiority of their victims.

For generations the South had regarded the uprising of the black, the assertion of his manhood and autonomy, as the *ultima thule*[81] of possible evil. San Domingo and hell were twin horrors in their minds, with the odds, however, in favor of San Domingo. To prevent negro domination anything was justifiable. It was a choice of evils, where on one side was placed an evil which they had been taught to believe, and did believe, infinitely outweighed and overmatched all other evils in enormity. Anything, said these men in their hearts; anything, they said to each other; anything, they cried aloud to the world, was better, is better, must be better, than negro rule, than African domination.

Now, by negro rule *they* meant the exercise of authority by a majority of citizens of African descent, or a majority of which they constituted any considerable factor. The white man who acted with the negro in any relation of political co-ordination was deemed even worse than the African himself. If he became a leader, he was anathematized for self-seeking. If he only co-operated with his ballot, he was denounced as a coward. In any event he was certain to be deemed a betrayer of his race, a renegade and an outcast.

Hesden Le Moyne was a Southern white man. All that has just been written was essential truth to him. It was a part of his nature. He was as proud as the proudest of his fellows. The sting of defeat still rankled in his heart. The sense of infinite distance between his race and that unfortunate race whom he pitied so sincerely, to whose future he looked forward with so much apprehension, was as distinct and palpable to him as to any one of his compeers. The thousandth part of a drop of the blood of the despised race degraded, in his mind, the unfortunate possessor.

He had inherited a dread of the ultimate results of slavery. He wished—it had been accounted sensible in his family to wish—that slavery had never existed. Having existed, they never thought of favoring its extinction. They thought it corrupting and demoralizing to the white race. They felt that it was separating them, year by year, farther and farther from that independent self-relying manhood, which had built up American institutions and American prosperity. They feared the fruit of this demoralization. *For the sake of the white man,* they wished that the black had never been enslaved. As to the blacks—they did not question the righteousness of their enslavement. They did not care whether it were right or wrong. They simply did not consider them at all. When the war left them free, they simply said, "Poor fellows!" as they would of a dog without a master. When the blacks were entrusted with the ballot, they said again, "Poor fellows!" regarding them as the blameless instrument by which a bigoted and revengeful North sought to degrade and humiliate a foe overwhelmed only by the accident of numbers; the colored race being to these Northern people like the cat with whose paw the monkey dragged his chestnuts from the fire. Hesden had only wondered what the effect of these things would be upon "the South;" meaning by "the South" that regnant class to which his family belonged—a part of which, by a queer synecdoche, stood for the whole.

His love for his old battle-steed, and his curious interest in its new possessor, had led him to consider the experiment at Red Wing with some care. His pride and interest in Eliab as a former slave of his family had still further fixed his attention and awakened his thought. And, finally, his acquaintance with Mollie Ainslie had led him unconsciously to sympathize with the object of her constant care and devotion.

So, while he stood there beside the stricken man, whose breath came stertorous and slow, he was in that condition of mind of all others most perilous to the Southern man—he had begun to *doubt*: to doubt the infallibility of his hereditary notions; to doubt the super-excellence of Southern manhood, and the infinite superiority of Southern womanhood; to doubt the incapacity of the negro for self-maintenance and civilization; to doubt, in short, all those dogmas which constitute the differential characteristics of "the Southern man." He had gone so far—a terrible distance to one of his origin—as to admit the possibility of error. He had begun to question—God forgive him, if it seemed like sacrilege—he had begun to question whether the South might not have been wrong—might not still be wrong—wrong in the principle and practice of slavery, wrong in the theory and fact of secession and rebellion, wrong in the hypothesis of hate on the part of the conquerors, wrong in the assumption of exceptional and unapproachable excellence.

The future was as misty as the gray morning.

CHAPTER XL.

DAWNING.

HESDEN LE MOYNE stood with Nimbus under the great low-branching oak, in the chill morning, and listened to the labored breathing of the man for the sake of whose humanity his father had braved public opinion in the old slave-era, which already seemed centuries away in the dim past. The training of his life, the conditions of his growth, bore fruit in that moment.

He pitied the outraged victim, he was shocked at the barbarity of his fellows; but there was no sense of injustice, no feeling of sacred rights trampled on and ignored in the person of the sufferer. He remembered when he had played with Eliab beside his mother's hearth; when he had varied the monotony of study by teaching the crippled slave-boy the tasks he himself was required to perform. The tenderness of old associations sprang up in his mind and he felt himself affronted in the person of the protege of his family. He disliked cruelty; he hated cowardice; and he felt that Eliab Hill had been the victim of a cruel and cowardly assault. He remembered how faithfully this man's mother had nursed his own. Above all, the sentiment of comradeship awoke. This man who had been his playfellow had been brutally treated because of his weakness. He would not see him bullied. He would stand by him to the death.

"The cowards!" he hissed through his teeth. "Bring him in, Nimbus, quick! They needn't expect me to countenance such brutality as this!"

"Marse Hesden," said the black Samson who had stood, silently watching the white playmate of his boyhood, while the latter recovered himself from the sort of stupor into which the revelation he had heard had thrown him, "God bress yer fer dem words! I 'llowed yer'd stan' by 'Liab. Dat's why I fotched him h'yer."

"Of course I would, and by you too, Nimbus."

"No, Marse Hesden, dat wouldn't do no sort o' good. Nimbus hez jes got ter cut an' run fer it. I 'specs them ar dat's a lyin' dar in front ob 'Liab's do' ain't like ter do no mo' troublin'; an' yer knows, Marse Hesden, 'twouldn't nebber be safe fer a cullu'd man dat's done dat ar ter try an' lib h'yerabouts no mo'!"

"But you did it in defense of life. You had a right to do it, Nimbus."

"Dar ain't no doubt o' dat, Marse Hesden, but I'se larned dat de right ter du a ting an' de doin' on't is two mighty diff'rent tings, when it's a cullu'd man ez does it. I hed a right ter buy a plantation an' raise terbacker; an' 'Liab hed a right ter teach an' preach; an' we both hed a right ter vote for ennybody we had a mind ter choose. An' so we did; an' dat's all we done, tu. An' now h'yer's what's come on't, Marse Hesden."

Nimbus pointed to the bruised creature before them as he spoke, and his tones sounded like an arraignment.

"I am afraid you are right, Nimbus," said the white man, with a sense of self-abasement he had never thought to feel before one of the inferior race. "But bring him in, we must not waste time here."

"Dat's a fac'," said Nimbus, with a glance at the East. "'Tain't more'n 'bout a hour till sun-up, an' I mustn't be seen hereabouts atter dat. Dey'll be a lookin' atter me, an' 'twon't be safe fer Nimbus ter be no whar 'cept in de mos' lonesome places. But whar's ye gwine ter put 'Liab, Marse Hesden?"

"In the house—anywhere, only be quick about it. Don't let him die here!" said Hesden, bending over the prostrate man and passing a hand over his forehead with a shudder.

"But whar'bouts in de house yer gwine ter put him, Marse Hesden?"

"Anywhere, man—in my room, if nowhere else. Come, take hold here!" was Hesden's impatient rejoinder as he put his one hand under Eliab's head and strove to raise him up.

"Dat won't do, Marse Hesden," said Nimbus solemnly. 'Liab had a heap better go back ter de woods an' chance it wid Nimbus, dan be in your room."

"Why so?"

"Why? Kase yer knows dat de men what done dis ting ain't a-gwine ter let him lib ef dey once knows whar he's ter be found. He's de one dey wuz atter, jest ez much ez Nimbus, an' p'raps a leetle more, dough yer knows ther ain't a mite o' harm in him, an' nebber was. But dat don't matter. Dey tinks dat he keeps de cullu'd folks togedder, an' makes 'em stan' up for dere rights, an' dat's why dey went fer him. 'Sides dat, ef he didn't hurt none on 'em dey know he seed an' heerd 'em, an' so'll be afeared ter let up on him on dat account."

"I'd like to see the men that would take him out of my house!" said Le Moyne, indignantly.

"Dar 'd jes be two men killed instead ob one, ef yer should," said the other, dryly.

"Perhaps you're right," said Le Moyne, thoughtfully. "The men who did this will do anything. But where *shall* we put him? He can't lie here."

"Marse Hesden, does yer mind de loft ober de ole dinin'-room, whar we all used ter play ob a Sunday?"

"Of course, I've got my tobacco bulked down there now," was the answer.

"Dat's de place, Marse Hesden!"

"But there's no way to get in there except by a ladder," said Hesden.

"So much de better. You gits de ladder, an' I brings 'Liab."

In a few minutes Eliab was lying on some blankets, hastily thrown over a bulk of leaf tobacco, in the loft over the old dining-room at Mulberry Hill, and Hesden Le Moyne was busy bathing his face, examining his wounds, and endeavoring to restore him to consciousness.

Nimbus waited only to hear his report that the wounds, though numerous and severe, were not such as would be likely to prove fatal. There were several cuts and bruises about the head; a shot had struck the arm, which had caused the loss of blood; and the weakened tendons of the cramped and unused legs had been torn asunder. These were all the injuries Le Moyne could find. Nimbus dropped upon his knees, and threw his arms about the neck of his friend at this report, and burst into tears.

"God bress yer, 'Liab! God bress yer!" he sobbed. "Nimbus can't do no mo' fer ye, an' don't 'llow he'll nebber see ye no mo'—no mo' in dis world! Good-by, 'Liab, good-by! Yer don't know Nimbus's gwine away, does yer? God bress yer, p'raps it's better so—better so!"

He kissed again and again the pale forehead, from which the dark hair had been brushed back by repeated bathings. Then rising and turning away his head, he extended his hand to Le Moyne and said:

"Good-bye, Marse Hesden! God bress yer! Take good keer o' 'Liab, Mahs'r, an'—an'—ef he gits round agin, don't let him try ter stay h'yrabouts—don't, please! 'Tain't no use! See ef yer can't git him ter go ter de Norf, er somewhar. Oh, my God!" he exclaimed, suddenly, as the memory of his care of the stricken friend came suddenly upon him, "my God! what'll he ebber do widout Nimbus ter keer fer him?"

His voice was drowned in sobs and his grip on the hand of the white man was like the clasp of a vice.

"Don't go, Nimbus, don't!" pleaded Hesden.

"I must, Marse Hesden," said he, repressing his sobs. "I'se got ter see what's come o' 'Gena an' de rest, an' it's best fer both. Good-by! God bress yer! Ef he comes tu, ax him sometimes ter pray for Nimbus. But 'tain't no use—no use—fer he'll do it without axin'. Good-by!"

He opened the wooden shutter, ran down the ladder, and disappeared, as the misty morning gave way to the full and perfect day.

CHAPTER XLI.

Q. E. D.[82]

AS MOLLIE AINSLIE grew stronger day by day, her kind host had done all in his power to aid her convalescence by offering pleasing attentions and cheerful surroundings. As soon as she was able to ride, she had been lifted carefully into the saddle, and under his watchful supervision had made, each day, longer and longer rides, until, for some days preceding the events of the last few chapters, her strength had so fully returned that they had ridden several miles. The flush of health had returned to her cheeks, and the sleep that followed her exercise was restful and refreshing.

Already she talked of returning to Red Wing, and, but for the thoughtfulness of Eliab Hill in dismissing the school for a month during her illness, would have been present at the terrible scenes enacted there. She only lingered because she was not quite recovered, and because there was a charm about the old plantation, which she had never found elsewhere. A new light had come into her life. She loved Hesden Le Moyne, and Hesden Le Moyne loved the Yankee school-marm. No word of love had been spoken. No caress had been offered. A pall hung over the household, in the gloom of which the lips might not utter words of endearment. But the eyes spoke; and they greeted each other with kisses of liquid light when their glances met. Flushed cheeks and tones spoke more than words. She waited for his coming anxiously. He was restive and uneasy when away. The peace which each one brought to the other's heart was the sure witness of well-grounded love. She had never asked herself where was the beginning or what would be the end. She had never said to herself, "I love him;" but his presence brought peace, and in her innocence she rested there as in an undisturbed haven.

As for him—he saw and trembled. He could not shut his eyes to her love or his own. He did not wish to do so. And yet, brave man as he was, he trembled at the thought. Hesden Le Moyne was proud. He knew that Mollie Ainslie was as proud as himself. He had the prejudices of his people and class, and he knew also that she had the convictions of that part of the country where she had been reared. He knew that she would never share his prejudices; he had no idea that he would ever share her convictions. He wished that she had never taught a "nigger school"—not for his own sake, he said to himself, with a flush of shame, but for hers. How could she face sneers? How could he endure insults upon his love? How could he ask her to come where sneers and insults awaited her?

Love had set himself a hard task. He had set before him this problem: "New England Puritanism and Southern Prejudice; how shall they be reconciled?" For the solution of this question, there were given on one side a maiden who would have plucked out her heart and trampled it under her feet, rather than surrender one tenet in her creed of righteousness; and on the other side a man who had fought for a cause he did not approve rather than be taunted with having espoused one of the fundamental principles of her belief. To laugh at locksmiths was an easy thing compared with the reading of this riddle!

On the morning when Eliab was brought to Mulberry Hill, Mrs. Le Moyne and Mollie breakfasted together alone in the room of the former. Both were troubled at the absence of the master of the house.

"I cannot see why he does not come," said Mrs. Le Moyne. "He is the soul of punctuality, and is never absent from a meal when about home. He sent in word by Laura early this morning that he would not be at breakfast, and that we should not wait for him, but gave no sort of reason. I don't understand it."

"I hope he is not sick. You don't think he has the fever, do you?" said Mollie, with evident anxiety.

The elder woman glanced keenly at her as she replied in a careless tone:

"Oh, no indeed. You have no occasion for anxiety. I told Laura to take him a cup of coffee and a roll in his room, but she says he is not there. I suppose something about the plantation requires his attention. It is very kind of you, I am sure; but I have no doubt he is quite well."

There was something in the tone as well as the words which cut the young girl to the heart. She could not tell what it was. She did not dream that it was aimed at herself. She only knew that it sounded harsh and cold, and unkind. Her heart was very tender. Sickness and love had thrown her off her guard against sneers and hardness. It did not once occur to her that the keen-sighted invalid, whose life was bound up in her son's life, had looked into the heart which had never yet syllabled the love which filled it, and hated what she saw. She did not deem it possible that there should be aught but kindly feeling for her in the household she had all but died to serve. Moreover, she had loved the delicate invalid ever since she had received a letter from her hand. She had always been accustomed to that unconscious equality of common right and mutual courtesy that prevails so widely at the North, and had never thought of construing the letter as one of patronizing approval. She had counted it a friendly commendation, not only of herself, but of her work. This woman she had long pictured to herself as one that rose above the prejudice by which she was surrounded. She who, in the old times, had bravely taught Eliab Hill to read in defiance of the law, would surely approve of a work like hers.

So thought the silly girl, not knowing that the gentle invalid had taught Eliab Hill the little that he knew before emancipation more to show her defiance of meddling objectors, than for the good of the boy. In fact, she had had no idea of benefiting him, other than by furnishing him a means of amusement in the enforced solitude of his affliction. Mollie did not consider that Hester Le Moyne was a Southern woman, and as such, while she might admire courage and accomplishments in a woman of Northern birth, always did so with a mental reservation in favor of her own class. When, however, one came from the North to teach the negroes, in order that they might overpower and rule the whites, which she devoutly believed to be the sole purpose of the colored educational movement, no matter under what specious guise of charity it might be done, she could not go even so far as that.

Yet, if such a one came to her, overwhelmed by stress of weather, she would give her shelter; if she were ill she would minister unto her; for these were Christian duties. If she were fair and bright, and brave, she would delight to entertain her; for that was a part of the hospitality of which the South boasted. There was something enjoyable, too, in parading the riches of a well-stocked wardrobe and the lavish splendors of an old Southern home to one who, she believed, had never seen such magnificence before; for the belief that poverty and poor fare are the common lot of the country folks at the North is one of the fallacies commonly held by all classes at the South. As slavery, which was the universal criterion of wealth and culture at the South, did not prevail at all at the North, they unconsciously and naturally came to associate self-help with degradation, and likened the Northern farmer to the poor white "cropper." Where social rank was measured by the length of the serving train, it was not strange that the Northern self-helper should be despised and his complacent assumption of equal gentility scorned.

So Mrs. Le Moyne had admired the courage of Mollie Ainslie before she saw her; she had been charmed with her beauty and artless grace on the first night of her stay at Mulberry Hill, and had felt obliged to her for her care of the little Hildreth; but she had not once thought of considering her the peer of the Richardses and the Le Moynes, or as standing upon the same social plane as herself. She was, no doubt, good and honest and brave, very well educated and accomplished, but by no means a lady in *her* sense of the word. Mrs. Le Moyne's feeling toward the Northern school-teacher was very like that which the English gentry express when they use the word "person." There is no discredit in the term. The individual referred to may be the incarnation of every grace and virtue, only he is of a lower degree in the social scale. He is of another grade.

Entertaining such feelings toward Mollie, it was no wonder that Mrs. Le Moyne was not pleased to see the anxious interest that young lady freely exhibited in the health of her son.

On the other hand, the young New England girl never suspected the existence of such sentiments. Conscious of intellectual and moral equality with her hostess, she did not imagine that there could be anything of patronage, or anything less than friendly sympathy and approval, in the welcome she had received at Mulberry Hill. This house had seemed to her like a new home. The exile which she had undergone at Red Wing had unfitted her for the close analysis of such pleasing associations. Therefore, the undertone in Mrs. Le Moyne's remarks came upon her like a blow from an unseen hand. She felt hurt and humbled, but she could not exactly tell why. Her heart grew suddenly heavy. Her eyes filled with tears. She dallied a little while with coffee and toast, declined the dainties pressed upon her with scrupulous courtesy, and presently, excusing her lack of appetite, fled away to her room and wept.

"I must be nervous this morning," she said to herself smilingly, as she dried her eyes and prepared for her customary morning ride. On going down stairs she found a servant in waiting with her horse ready saddled, who said: "Mornin', Miss Mollie. Marse Hesden said ez how I was ter tell yer dat he was dat busy dis mornin' dat he couldn't go ter ride wid yer to-day, nohow. I wuz ter gib yer his compliments, all de same, an' say he hopes yer'll hev a pleasant ride, an' he wants ter see yer when yer gits back. He's powerful sorry he can't go."

"Tell Mr. Le Moyne it is not a matter of any consequence at all, Charley," she answered pleasantly.

"Yer couldn't never make Marse Hesden b'lieve dat ar, no way in de world," said Charles, with deft flattery, as he lifted her into the saddle. Then, glancing quickly around, he said in a low, earnest voice: "Hez ye heerd from Red Wing lately, Miss Mollie?"

"Not for a day or two. Why?" she asked, glancing quickly down at him.

"Oh, nuffin', only I wuz afeared dar'd been somethin' bad a gwine on dar, right lately."

"What do you mean, Charles?" she asked, bending down and speaking anxiously.

"Don't say nuffin' 'bout it, Miss Mollie—dey don't know nuffin' 'bout it in h'yer," nodding toward the house, "but de Ku Kluckers was dar las' night."

"You don't mean it, Charles?"

"Dat's what I hear," he answered doggedly.

"Anybody hurt?" she asked anxiously.

"I don't know dat, Miss Mollie. Dat's all I hear—jes dat dey'd been dar."

CHAPTER XLII.

THROUGH A CLOUD-RIFT.

IT WAS WITH a heavy heart that Mollie Ainslie passed out of the gate and rode along the lane toward the highway. The autumn sun shone bright, and the trees were just beginning to put on the gay trappings in which they are wont to welcome wintry death. Yet, somehow, everything seemed suddenly to have grown dark and dull. Her poor weak brain was overwhelmed and dazed by the incongruity of the life she was leaving with that to which she was going back—for she had no hesitation in deciding as to the course she ought to pursue.

She did not need to question as to what had been done or suffered. If there was any trouble, actual or impending, affecting those she had served, her place was with them. They would look to her for guidance and counsel. She would not fail them. She did not once think of danger, nor did she dream that by doing as she proposed she was severing herself entirely from the pleasant life at the fine old country seat which had been so eventful.

She did, indeed, think of Hesden. She always thought of him of late. Everything, whether of joy or of sorrow, seemed somehow connected with him. She thought of him—not as going away from him, or as putting him out of her life, but as deserving his approval by her act. "He will miss me when he finds that I do not return. Perhaps he will be alarmed," she said to herself, as she cantered easily toward the ford. "But then, if he hears what has happened, he will know where I have gone and will approve my going. Perhaps he will be afraid for me, and then he will—" Her heart seemed to stop beating! All its bright current flew into her face. The boundless beatitude of love burst on her all at once. She had obeyed its dictates and tasted its bliss for days and weeks, quite unconscious of the rapture which filled her soul. Now, it came like a great wave of light that overspread the earth and covered with a halo all that was in it.

How bright upon the instant was everything! The sunshine was a beating, pulsing ether animated with love! The trees, the fields, the yellow-breasted lark, pouring forth his autumn lay, the swallows, glancing in the golden sunshine and weaving in and out on billowy wing the endless dance with which they hie them southward ere the winter comes—everything she saw or heard was eloquent with look and tones of love! The grand old horse that carried her so easily, how strange and how delightful was this double ownership, which yet was only one! Hers? Hesden's? Hesden's because hers, for—ah, glowing cheek! ah, bounding heart! how sweet the dear confession, breathed—nay told unspokenly—to autumn sky and air, to field and wood and bird and beast, to nature's boundless heart—*she* was but Hesden's! The altar and the idol of his love! Oh, how its incense thrilled her soul and intoxicated every sense! There was no doubt, no fear, no breath of shame! He would come and ask, and she—would give? No! no! no! She could not give, but she would tell, with word and look and swift embrace, how she *had* given—ah! given all—and knew it not! Oh, fairer than the opened heaven is earth illumined with love!

As she dreamed, her horse's swift feet consumed the way. She reached the river—a silver billow between emerald banks, to-day! Almost unheedingly she crossed the ford, just smiling, rapt in her vision, as memory brought back the darkness of her former crossing! Then she swept on, through the dark, over-arching pines, their odor mingling with the incense of love which filled her heart. She had forgotten Red Wing and all that pertained to it. The new song her lips had been taught to sing had made thin and weak every melody of the past. Shall care cumber the heart of the bride? She knew vaguely that she was going to Red Wing. She recognized the road, but it seemed glorified since she travelled it before. Once, she thought she heard her name called. The tone was full of beseeching. She smiled, for she thought that love had cheated her, and syllabled the cry of that heart which would not be still until she came again. She did not see the dark, pleading face which gazed after her as her horse bore her swiftly beyond his ken.

On and on, easily, softly! She knows she is approaching her journey's end, but the glamour of love enthralls her senses yet. The last valley is passed. She ascends the last hill. Before her is Red Wing, bright and peaceful as Paradise before the spoiler came. She has forgotten the story which the hostler told. The sight of the little village but heightens her rapture. She almost greets it with a shout, as she gives her horse the rein and dashes down the little street. How her face glows! The wind toys with stray tresses of her hair! How dull and amazed the people seem whom she greets so gayly! Still on! Around the angle of the wood she turns—and comes upon the smouldering church!

Ah, how the visions melt! What a cry of agony goes up from her white lips! How pale her cheeks grow as she drops the rein from her nerveless fingers! The observant horse needs no words to check his swift career. The scene of desolation stops him in an instant. He stretches out his head and looks with staring eyes upon the ruin. He snuffs with distended nostrils the smoke that rises from the burning.

The villagers gather around. She answers every inquiry with low moans. Gently they lead her horse under the shadow of the great oak before the old Ordinary. Very tenderly she is lifted down and borne to the large-armed rocker on the porch, which the weeping, trembling old "mammy" has loaded with pillows to receive her.

All day long she heard the timid tread of dusky feet and listened to the tale of woe and fear. Old and young, those whom she had counselled, and those whom she had taught, alike sought her presence and advice. Lugena came, and showed her scarred form; brought her beaten children, and told her tale of sorrow. The past was black enough, but the shadow of a greater fear hung over the little hamlet. They feared for themselves and also for her. They begged her to go back to Mr. Le Moyne's. She smiled and shook her head with a soft light in her eyes. She would not go back until the king came and entreated her. But she knew that would be very soon. So she roused herself to comfort and advise, and when the sun went down, she was once more the little Mollie Ainslie of the Bankshire hills, only fairer and ruddier and sweeter than ever before, as she sat upon the porch and watched with dewy, love-lit eyes the road which led to Mulberry Hill.

The shadows came. The night fell; the stars came out; the moon arose—he came not. Stealthy footsteps came and went. Faithful hearts whispered words of warning with trembling lips. She did not fear. Her heart was sick. She had not once dreamed that Hesden would fail to seek her out, or that he would allow her to pass one hour of darkness in this scene of horror. She almost began to wish the night might be a counterpart of that which had gone before. She took out her brother's heavy revolver, loaded every chamber, laid it on the table beside her chair, and sat, sleepless but dry-eyed, until the morning.

The days went by. Hesden did not come, and sent no word. He was but five miles away; he knew how she loved him; yet the grave was not more voiceless! She hoped—a little—even after that first night. She pictured possibilities which she hoped might be true. Then the tones of the mother's voice came back to her—the unexplained absence—the unfulfilled engagement—and doubt was changed to certainty! She did not weep or moan or pine. The Yankee girl had no base metal in her make-up. She folded away her vision of love and laid it aside, embalmed in the fragrance of her own purity, in the inmost recess of her heart of hearts. The rack could not have wrung from her a whisper of that one day in Paradise. She was simply Mollie Ainslie, the teacher of the colored school at Red Wing, once more; quiet, cool, and practical, giving herself day by day, with increased devotion, to the people whom she had served so faithfully before her brief translation.

CHAPTER XLIII.

A GLAD GOOD-BY.

A FEW DAYS after her departure from Mulberry Hill, Mollie Ainslie wrote to Mrs. Le Moyne:

"MY DEAR MADAM: You have no doubt heard of the terrible events which have occurred at Red Wing. I had an intimation of trouble just as I set out on my ride, but had no idea of the horror which awaited me upon my arrival here, made all the more fearful by contrast with your pleasant home.

"I cannot at such a time leave the people with whom I have labored so long, especially as their only other trusted adviser, the preacher, Eliab Hill, is missing. With the utmost exertion we have been able to learn nothing of him or of Nimbus since the night of the fire. There is no doubt that they are dead. Of course, there is great excitement, and I have had a very anxious time. I am glad to say, however, that my health continues to improve. I left some articles scattered about in the room I occupied, which I would be pleased if you would have a servant collect and give to the bearer.

"With the best wishes for the happiness of yourself and Mr. Hesden, and with pleasant memories of your delightful home, I remain,

"Yours very truly,

"MOLLIE AINSLIE."

To this she received the following reply:

"MISS MOLLIE AINSLIE: I very much regret the unfortunate events which occasioned your hasty departure from Mulberry Hill. It is greatly to be hoped that all occasion for such violence will soon pass away. It is a great calamity that the colored people cannot be made to see that their old masters and mistresses are their best friends, and induced to follow their advice and leadership, instead of going after strangers and ignorant persons of their own color, or low-down white men, who only wish to use them for their own advantage. I am very sorry for Eliab and the others, but I must say I think they have brought it all on themselves. I am told they have been mighty impudent and obstreperous, until really the people in the neighborhood did not feel safe, expecting every day that their houses or barns would be burned down, or their wives or daughters insulted, or perhaps worse, by the lazy, saucy crowd they had gathered about them.

"Eliab was a good boy, but I never did like that fellow Nimbus. He was that stubborn and headstrong, even in his young days, that I can believe anything of him. Then he was in the Yankee army during the war, you know, and I have no doubt that he is a desperate character. I learn he has been indicted once or twice, and the general belief is that he set the church on fire, and, with a crowd of his understrappers, fixed up to represent Ku Klux, attacked his own house, abused his wife and took Eliab off and killed him, in order to make the North believe that the people of Horsford are only a set of savages, and so get the Government to send soldiers here to carry the election, in order that a filthy negro and a low-down, dirty, no-account poor-white man may *mis*represent this grand old county in the Legislature again.

"I declare, Miss Ainslie, I don't see how you endure such things. You seemed while here very much of a lady, for one in your sphere of life, and I cannot understand how you can reconcile it with your conscience to encourage and live with such a terrible gang.

"My son has been very busy since you left. He did not find time to inquire for you yesterday, and seemed annoyed that you had not apprised him of your intention to leave. I suppose he is afraid that his old horse might be injured if there should be more trouble at Red Wing.

"Yours truly,

"HESTER RICHARDS LE MOYNE."

"P.S.—I understand that they are going to hunt the fellow Nimbus with dogs to-morrow. I hope they will catch him and hang him to the nearest tree. I have no doubt he killed poor Eliab, and did all the rest of the bad things laid to his charge. He is a desperate negro, and I don't see how you can stand up for him. I hope you will let the people of the North know the truth of this affair, and make them understand that Southern gentlemen are not such savages and brutes as they are represented."

The letter was full of arrows designed to pierce her breast; but Mollie Ainslie did not feel one of them. After what she had suffered, no ungenerous flings from such a source could cause her any pain. On the contrary, it was an object of interest to her, in that it disclosed how deep down in the heart of the highest and best, as well as the lowest and meanest, was that prejudice which had originally instigated such acts as had been perpetrated at Red Wing. The credulous animosity displayed by this woman to whom she had looked for sympathy and encouragement in what she deemed a holy work, revealed to her for the first time how deep and impassable was the channel which time had cut between the people of the North and those of the South.

She did not lose her respect or regard for Mrs. Le Moyne. She did not even see that any word which had been written was intended to stab her, as a woman. She only saw that the prejudice-blinded eyes had led a good, kind heart to endorse and excuse cruelty and outrage. The letter saddened but did not enrage her. She saw and pitied the pride of the sick lady whom she had learned to love in fancy too well to regard with anger on account of what was but the natural result of her life and training.

CHAPTER XLIV.

PUTTING THIS AND THAT TOGETHER.

AFTER MOLLIE HAD read the letter of Mrs. Le Moyne, it struck her as a curious thing that she should write to her of the hunt which was to be made after Nimbus, and the great excitement which there was in regard to him. Knowing that Mrs. Le Moyne and Hesden were both kindly disposed toward Eliab, and the latter, as she believed, toward Nimbus also, it occurred to her that this might be intended as a warning, given on the hypothesis that those parties were in hiding and not dead.

At the same time, also, it flashed upon her mind that Lugena had not seemed so utterly cast down as might naturally be expected of a widow so suddenly and sadly bereaved. She knew something of the secretive powers of the colored race. She knew that in the old slave times one of the men now living in the little village had remained a hidden runaway for months, within five miles of his master's house, only his wife knowing his hiding-place. She knew how thousands of these people had been faithful to our soldiers escaping from Confederate prisons during the war, and she felt that a secret affecting their own liberty, or the liberty of one acting or suffering in their behalf, might be given into the keeping of the whole race without danger of revelation. She remembered that amid all the clamorous grief of others, while Lugena had mourned and wept over the burning of the church and the scenes of blood and horror, she had exhibited little of that poignant and overwhelming grief or unappeasable anger which she would have expected, under the circumstances, from one of her temperament. She concluded, therefore, that the woman might have some knowledge in regard to the fate of her husband, Eliab, and Berry, which she had not deemed it prudent to reveal. With this thought in mind, she sent for Lugena and asked if she had heard that they were going to hunt for her husband with dogs.

"Yes, Miss Mollie, I'se heerd on't," was the reply, "but nebber you mind. Ef Nimbus is alive, dey'll nebber git him in no sech way ez dat, an' dey knows it. 'Sides dat, it's tree days ago, an' Nimbus ain't no sech fool ez ter stay round dat long, jes ter be cotched now. I'se glad ter hear it, dough, kase it shows ter me dat dey hain't killed him, but wants ter skeer him off, an' git him outen de kentry. De sheriff—not de high-sheriff, but one ob his understrappers—wuz up ter our house to-day, a-purtendin' ter hunt atter Nimbus. I didn't put no reliance in dat, but somehow I can't make out cla'r how dey could hev got away with him an' Berry an' 'Liab, all on 'em, atter de fight h'yer, an' not left no trace nor sign on 'em nowhar.

"Now, I tell yer what's my notion, Miss Mollie," she added, approaching closer, and speaking in a whisper; "I'se done a heap o' tinkin' on dis yer matter, an' dis is de way I'se done figgered it out. I don't keer ter let on 'bout it, an' mebbe you kin see furder inter it nor I kin, but I'se jes made up my min' dat Nimbus is all right somewhars. I don't know whar, but it's somewhar not fur from 'Liab—dat yer may be shore on, honey. Now, yer see, Miss Mollie, dar's two or tree tings makes me tink so. In de fus' place, yer know, I see dat feller, Berry, atter all dis ting wuz ober, an' talked wid him an' told him dat Nimbus lef' all right, an' dat he tuk 'Liab wid him, an' dat' Bre'er 'Liab wuz mighty bad hurt. Wal, atter I told him dat, an' he'd helped me hunt up de chillens dat wuz scattered in de co'n, an' 'bout one place an' anudder, Berry he 'llows dat he'll go an' try ter fin' Nimbus an' 'Liab. So he goes off fru de co'n wid dat ar won'ful gun dat jes keeps on a-shootin' widout ary load.

"Atter a while I heahs him ober in de woods a-whistlin' an' a-carryin' on like a mockin'-bird, ez you'se heerd de quar critter du many a time." Mollie nodded affirmatively, and Lugena went on: "I couldn't help but laugh den, dough I wuz nigh about skeered ter death, ter tink what a mighty cute trick it wuz. I knowed he wuz a callin' Nimbus an' dat Nimbus 'ud know it, tu, jest ez soon ez he heerd it; but yer know ennybody dat hadn't heerd it over an offen, wouldn't nebber tink dat it warn't a mocker waked up by de light, or jes mockin' a cat-bird an' rain-crow, an' de like, in his dreams, ez dey say dey does when de moon shines, yer know."

Mollie smiled at the quaint conceit, so well justified by the fact she had herself often observed. Lugena continued:

"I tell yer, Miss Mollie, dat ar Berry's a right cute nigga, fer all dey say 'bout him. He ain't stiddy, like Nimbus, yer know, ner pious like 'Liab—dat is not ter hurt, yer know—but he sartin hab got a heap ob sense, fer all dat."

"It was certainly a very shrewd thing, but I don't see what it has to do with the fate of Nimbus," said Mollie. "I don't wish to seem to discourage you, but I am quite certain, myself, that we shall never see Nimbus or Eliab again."

"Oh, yer can't discourage *me,* Miss Mollie," answered the colored woman bravely. "I jes knows, er ez good ez knows, dat Nimbus is all right yit awhile. Now I tells yer, honey, what dis yer's got ter du wid it. Yer see, it must ha' been nigh about a half-hour atter Nimbus left afore Berry went off; jes dat er way I tole yer 'bout."

"Well?" said Mollie, inquiringly.

"Wal," continued Lugena, "don't yer see? Dar hain't been nary word heard from neither one o' dem boys sence."

"Well?" said Mollie, knitting her brows in perplexity.

"*Don't* yer see, Miss Mollie," said the woman impatiently, "dat dey couldn't hab got 'em bofe togedder, 'cept Berry had found Nimbus fust?"

"Well?"

"*Wal!* Don't yer see dar would hev been a—a—*terrible* fight afore dem two niggas would hev gin up Bre'er 'Liab, let alone derselves? Yer must 'member dat dey had dat ar gun. Sakes-a-massy! Miss Mollie, yer orter hev heern it dat night. 'Peared ter me yer could hab heard it clar' roun' de yairth, ef it *is* round, ez yer say 'tis. Now, somebody—some cullu'd body—would have been shore ter heah dat gun ef dar'd been a fight."

"I had not thought of that, Lugena," said Mollie.

"Co'se yer hadn't, honey; an' dere's sunthin' else yer didn't tink ob, nuther, kase yer didn't know it," said Lugena. "Yer min' dat boy Berry, he'd done borrered our mule, jest afo' dat, ter take Sally an' de chillen an' what few duds dey hez down inter Hanson County, whar his brudder Rufe libs, an' whar dey's gwine ter libbin' tu. Dar didn't nobody 'spect him ter git back till de nex' day, any more'n Nimbus; an' it war jes kinder accidental-like dat either on 'em got h'yer dat night. Now, Miss Mollie, what yer s'pose hez come ob dat ar mule an' carryall? Dat's de question."

"I'm sure I don't know, 'Gena," said Mollie thoughtfully.

"Ner I don't know, nuther," was the response; "but it's jes my notion dat whar dey is, right dar yer'll fin' Nimbus an' Berry, an' not fur off from dem yer'll find Bre'er 'Liab."

"You may be right," said her listener, musingly.

"I'se pretty shore on't, honey. Yer see when dat ar under-sheriff come ter day an' had look all 'round fer Nimbus, he sed, finally, sez he, 'I'se got a 'tachment'—dat's what he call it, Miss Mollie—a 'tachment 'gin de property, or sunthin' o' dat kine. I didn't know nary ting 'bout it, but I spunked up an' tole him ebbery ting in de house dar was mine. He argyfied 'bout it a right smart while, an' finally sed dar wan't nuffin' dar ob no 'count, ennyhow. Den he inquired 'bout de mule an' de carryall, an' atter dat he went out an' levelled on de crap."

"Did what?" asked Mollie.

"Levelled on de crap, Miss, dat's what he said, least-a-ways. Den he called fer de key ob de 'backer-barn, an' I tole him 'twan't nowheres 'bout de house—good reason too, kase Nimbus allus do carry dat key in his breeches pocket, 'long wid his money an' terbacker. So he takes de axe an' goes up ter de barn, an' I goes 'long wid him ter see what he's gwine ter du. Den he breaks de staple an' opens de do'. Now, Miss Mollie, 'twan't but a week er two ago, of a Sunday atternoon, Nimbus an' I wuz in dar lookin' roun', an' dar wuz a right smart bulk o' fine terbacker dar—some two er tree hundred poun's on't. Now when de sheriff went in, dar wa'n't more'n four or five han's ob 'backer scattered 'long 'twixt whar de pile had been an' de do'. Yah! yah! I couldn't help laughin' right out, though I wuz dat mad dat I couldn't hardly see, kase I knowed ter once how 'twas. D'yer see *now,* Miss Mollie?"

"I confess I do not," answered the teacher.

"No? Wal, whar yer 'spose dat 'backer gone ter, hey?"

"I'm sure I don't know. Where do you think?"

"What I tink become ob dat 'backer? Wal, Miss Mollie, I tink Nimbus an' Berry put dat 'backer in dat carryall, an' den put Bre'er 'Liab in on dat 'backer, an' jes druv off somewhar—'Gena don't know whar, but dat 'backer'll take 'em a long way wid dat ar mule an' carryall. It's all right, Miss Mollie, it's all right wid Nimbus. 'Gena ain't feared. She knows her ole man too well fer dat!

"Yer know he runned away once afo' in de ole slave times. He didn't say nary word ter me 'bout gwine ober ter de Yanks, an' de folks all tole me dat I nebber'd see him no mo'. But I knowed Nimbus, an' shore 'nough, atter 'bout two year, back he come! An' dat's de way it'll be dis time—atter de trouble's ober, he'll come back. But dat ain't what worries me now, Miss Mollie," continued Lugena. "Co'se I'd like ter know jes whar Nimbus is, but I know he's all right. I'se a heap fearder 'bout Bre'er 'Liab, fer I 'llow it's jes which an' t'other ef we ever sees him again. But what troubles me now, Miss Mollie, is 'bout myseff."

"About yourself?" asked Mollie, in surprise.

"'Bout me an' my chillens, Miss Mollie," was the reply.

"Why, how is that, 'Gena?"

"Wal yer see, dar's dat ar 'tachment matter. I don't understan' it, nohow."

"Nor I either," said Mollie.

"P'raps yer could make out sunthin' 'bout it from dese yer," said the colored woman, drawing a mass of crumpled papers from her pocket.

Mollie smoothed them out upon the table beside her, and began her examination by reading the endorsements. The first was entitled, "*Peyton Winburn* v. *Nimbus Desmit,* et al. *Action for the recovery of real estate. Summons.*" The next was endorsed, "*Copy of Complaint,*" and another, "*Affidavit and Order of Attachment against Non-Resident or Absconding Debtor.*"

"What's dat, Miss Mollie?" asked Lugena, eagerly, as the last title was read. "Dat's what dat ar sheriff man said my Nimbus was—a non—*non*—what, Miss Mollie? I tole him 'twan't no sech ting; but la sakes! I didn't know nothing in de worl' 'bout it. I jes 'llowed dat 'twas sunthin' mighty mean, an' I knowed dat I couldn't be very fur wrong nohow, ef I jes contraried ebbery word what he said. What does it mean, Miss Mollie?"

"It just means," said Mollie, "that Nimbus owes somebody—this Mr. Winburn, I judge, and—"

"It's a lie! A clar, straight-out lie!" interrupted Lugena. "Nimbus don't owe nobody nary cent—not nary cent, Miss Mollie! Tole me dat hisself jest a little time ago."

"Yes, but this man *claims* he owes him—swears so, in fact; and that he has run away or hidden to keep from paying it," said Mollie. "He swears he is a non-resident—don't live here, you know; lives out of the State somewhere."

"An' Peyton Winburn swars ter dat?" asked the woman, eagerly.

"Yes, certainly."

"Didn't I tell yer dat Nimbus was safe, Miss Mollie?" she cried, springing from her chair. "Don't yer see how dey cotch derselves? Ef der's ennybody on de green yairth dat knows all 'bout dis Ku Kluckin' it's Peyton Winburn, and dat ar Sheriff Gleason. Now, don't yer know dat ef he was dead dey wouldn't be a suin' on him an' a swearin' he'd run away?"

"I'm sure I don't know, but it would seem so," responded Mollie.

"Seem so! it's boun' ter *be* so, honey," said the colored woman, positively.

"I don't know, I'm sure," said Mollie. "It's a matter I don't understand. I think I had better take these papers over to Captain Pardee, and see what ought to be done about them. I am afraid there is an attempt to rob you of all your husband has acquired, while he is away."

"Dat's what I'se afeared on," said the other. "An' it wuz what Nimbus 'spected from de fust ob dis h'yer Ku Kluck matter. Dear me, what ebber will I do, I dunno—I dunno!" The poor woman threw her apron over her head and began to weep.

"Don't be discouraged, 'Gena," said Mollie, soothingly. "I'll stand by you and get Mr. Pardee to look after the matter for you."

"T'ank ye, Miss Mollie, t'ank ye. But I'se afeared it won't do no good. Dey's boun' ter break us up, an' dey'll do it, sooner or later! It's all of a piece—a Ku Kluckin' by night, and a-suin' by day. 'Tain't no use, t'ain't no use! Dey'll hab dere will fust er last, one way er anudder, shore!"

Without uncovering her head, the sobbing woman turned and walked out of the room, across the porch and down the path to the gate.

"Not if I can help it!" said the little Yankee woman, as she smoothed down her hair, shut her mouth close, and turned to make a more thorough perusal of the papers Lugena had left with her. Hardly had she finished when she was astonished by Lugena's rushing into the room and exclaiming, as she threw herself on her knees:

"Oh, Miss Mollie, I done forgot—I was dat ar flustered 'bout de 'tachment an' de like, dat I done forgot what I want ter tell yer most ob all. Yer know, Miss Mollie, dem men dat got hurt dat ar night—de Ku Kluckers, two on 'em, one I 'llow, killed out-an'-out, an' de todder dat bad cut—oh, my God!" she cried with a shudder, "I nebber see de likes—no nebber, Miss Mollie. All down his face—from his forehead ter his chin, an' dat too—yes, an' his breast-bone, too—looked like dat wuz all split open an' a-bleedin'! Oh, it war horrible, horrible, Miss Mollie!"

The woman buried her face in the teacher's lap as if she would shut out the fearful spectacle.

"There, there," said Mollie, soothingly, as she placed a hand upon her head. "You must not think of it. You must try and forget the horrors of that night."

"Don't yer know, Miss Mollie, dat dem Ku Kluckers ain't a-gwine ter let de one ez done dat lib roun' h'yer, ner ennywhar else, ef dey can come at 'em, world widout end?"

"Well, I thought you were sure that Nimbus was safe?"

"Nimbus?" said the woman in surprise, uncovering her face and looking up. "Nimbus? 'Twan't him, Miss Mollie, 'twan't him. I 'llows it mout hev been him dat hurt de one dat 'peared ter hev been killed straight out; but it was *me* dat cut de odder one, Miss Mollie."

"You?" cried Mollie, in surprise, instinctively drawing back. "You?"

"Yes'm," said Lugena, humbly, recognizing the repulse. "Me—wid de axe! I hope yer don't fault me fer it, Miss Mollie."

"Blame you? no indeed, 'Gena!" was the reply. "Only it startled me to hear you say so. You did entirely right to defend yourself and Nimbus. You should not let that trouble you for a moment."

"No, Miss Mollie, but don't yer know dat de Ku Kluckers ain't a-gwine ter fergit it?"

"Heavens!" said the Yankee girl, springing up from her chair in uncontrollable excitement. "You don't think they would hurt you—a woman?"

"Dat didn't save me from bein' stripped an' beat, did it?"

"Too true, too true!" moaned the teacher, as she walked back and forth wringing her hands. "Poor child! What can you do?—what can you do?"

"Dat's what I want ter know, Miss Mollie," said the woman. "I dassent sleep ter home at night, an' don't feel safe ary hour in de day. Dem folks won't fergit, an' 'Gena won't nebber be safe ennywhar dat dey kin come, night ner day. What will I do, Miss Mollie, what will I do? Yer knows Nimbus 'll 'llow fer 'Gena ter take keer ob herself an' de chillen an' de plantation, till he comes back, er sends fer me, an' I dassent stay, not 'nudder day, Miss Mollie! What'll I do? What'll I do?"

There was silence in the little room for a few moments, as the young teacher walked back and forth across the floor, and the colored woman sat and gazed in stupid hopelessness up into her face. Presently she stopped, and, looking down upon Lugena, said with impetuous fervor:

"You shall not stay, Lugena! You shall not stay! Can you stand it a few nights more?"

"Oh, yes, I kin stan' it, 'cause I'se got ter. I'se been sleepin' in de woods ebber sence, an' kin keep on at it; but I knows whar it'll end, an' so der you, Miss Mollie."

"No, it shall not, 'Gena. You are right. It is not safe for you to stay. Just hide yourself a few nights more, till I can look after things for you here, and I will take you away to the North, where there are no Ku Klux!"

"Yer don't mean it, Miss Mollie!"

"Indeed I do."

"An' de chillen?"

"They shall go too."

"God bress yer, Miss Mollie! God bress yer!"

With moans and sobs, the torrent of her tears burst forth, as the poor woman fell prone upon the floor, and catching the hem of the teacher's robe, kissed it again and again, in a transport of joy.

CHAPTER XLV.

ANOTHER OX GORED.

THERE WAS A caller who begged to see Mr. Le Moyne for a few minutes. Descending to the sitting-room, Hesden found there Mr. Jordan Jackson, who was the white candidate for the Legislature upon the same ticket with a colored man who had left the county in fright immediately after the raid upon Red Wing. Hesden was somewhat surprised at this call, for although he had known Mr. Jackson from boyhood, yet there had never been more than a passing acquaintance between them. It is true, Mr. Jackson was a neighbor, living only two or three miles from Mulberry Hill; but he belonged to such an entirely different class of society that their knowledge of each other had never ripened into anything like familiarity.

Mr. Jackson was what used to be termed a poor man. He and his father before him, as Hesden knew, had lived on a little, poor plantation, surrounded by wealthy neighbors. They owned no slaves, and lived scantily on the products of the farm worked by themselves. The present occupant was about Hesden's own age. There being no free schools in that county, and his father having been unable, perhaps not even desiring, to educate him otherwise, he had grown up almost entirely illiterate. He had learned to sign his name, and only by strenuous exertions, after his arrival at manhood, had become able, with difficulty, to spell out words from the printed page and to write an ordinary letter in strangely-tangled hieroglyphics, in a spelling which would do credit to a phonetic reformer. He had entered the army, probably because he could not do otherwise, and being of stalwart build, and having great endurance and native courage, before the struggle was over had risen, despite his disadvantages of birth and education, to a lieutenancy.

This experience had been of advantage to him in more ways than one. Chief among these had been the opening of his eyes to the fact that he himself, although a poor man, and the scion of a poor family, was, in all the manly requisites that go to make up a soldier, always the equal, and very often the superior, of his aristocratic neighbors. Little by little, the self-respect which had been ground out of him and his family by generations of that condition of inferiority which the common-liver, the self-helper of the South, was forced to endure under the old slave *régime,* began to grow up in his heart. He began to feel himself a man, and prized the rank-marks on his collar as the certificate and endorsement of his manhood. As this feeling developed, he began to consider the relations between himself, his family, and others like them, and the rich neighbors by whom they were surrounded and looked down upon. And more and more, as he did so, the feeling grew upon him that he and his class had been wronged, cheated—"put upon," he phrased it—in all the past. They had been the "chinking" between the "mud" of slavery and the "house-logs" of aristocracy in the social structure of the South—a little better than the mud because of the same grain and nature as the logs; but useless and nameless except as in relation to both. He felt the bitter truth of that stinging aphorism which was current among the privates of the Confederate army, which characterized the war of Rebellion as "the rich man's war and the poor man's fight."

So, when the war was over, Lieutenant Jordan Jackson did not return easily and contentedly to the niche in the social life of his native region to which he had been born and bred. He found the habit of leadership and command very pleasant, and he determined that he would rise in the scale of Horsford society as he had risen in the army, simply because he was brave and strong. He knew that to do this he must acquire wealth, and looking about, he saw opportunities open before him which others had not noticed. Almost before the smoke of battle had cleared away, Jordan Jackson had opened trade with the invaders, and had made himself a prime favorite in the Federal camps. He coined money in those days of transition. Fortunately, he had been too poor to be in debt when the war broke out. He was independently poor, because beyond the range of credit. He had lost nothing, for he had nothing but the few poor acres of his homestead to lose.

So he started fair, and before the period of reconstruction began he had by thrifty management accumulated quite a competency. He had bought several plantations whose aristocratic owners could no longer keep their grip upon half-worked lands, had opened a little store, and monopolized a considerable trade. Looking at affairs as they stood at that time, Jordan Jackson said to himself that the opportunity for him and his class had come. He had a profound respect for the power and authority of the Government of the United States, *because* it had put down the Rebellion. He had been two or three times at the North, and was astounded at its collective greatness. He said that the colored man and the poor-whites of the South ought to put themselves on the side of this great, busy North, which had opened the way of liberty and progress before them, and establish free schools and free thought and free labor in the fair, crippled, South-land. He thought he saw a great and fair future looming up before his country. He freely gave expression to these ideas, and, as he traded very largely with the colored people, soon came to be regarded by them as a leader, and by "the good people of Horsford" as a low-down white nigger, for whom no epithet was too vile.

Nevertheless, he grew in wealth, for he attended to his business himself, early and late. He answered raillery with raillery, curses with cursing, and abuse with defiance. He was elected to conventions and Legislatures, where he did many foolish, some bad, and a few wise things in the way of legislation. He knew what he wanted—it was light, liberty, education, and a "fair hack" for all men. How to get it he did not know. He had been warned a thousand times that he must abandon this way of life. The natural rulers of the county felt that if they could neutralize his influence and that which went out from Red Wing, they could prevent the exercise of ballatorial power by a considerable portion of the majority, and by that means "redeem" the county.

They did not wish to hurt Jordan Jackson. He was a good enough man. His father had been an honest man, and an old citizen. Nobody knew a word against his wife or her family, except that they had been poor. The people who had given their hearts to the Confederate cause, remembered too, at first, his gallant service; but that had all been wiped out from their minds by his subsequent "treachery." Even after the attack on Red Wing, he had been warned by his friends to desist.

One morning, he had found on the door of his store a paper containing the following words, written inside a little sketch of a coffin:

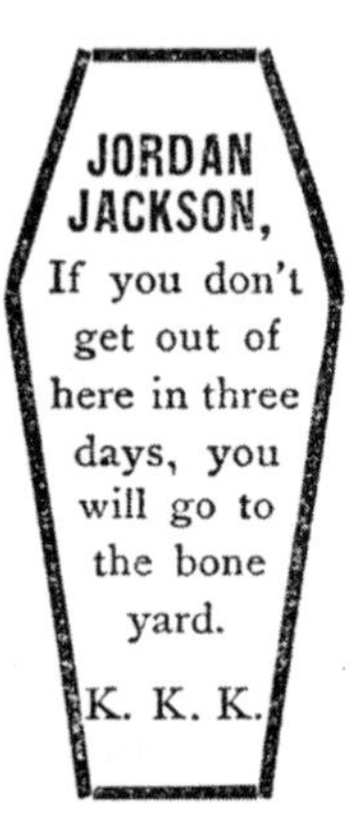

He had answered this by a defiant, ill-spelled notice, pasted just beside it, in which he announced himself as always ready to meet any crowd of "cowards and villains who were ashamed of their own faces, at any time, night or day." His card was English prose of a most vigorous type, interspersed with so much of illiterate profanity as to satisfy any good citizen that the best people of Horsford were quite right in regarding him as a most desperate and dangerous man—one of those whose influence upon the colored people was to array them against the whites, and unless promptly put down, bring about a war of races—which the white people were determined never to have in Horsford, if they had to kill every Radical in the county in order to live in peace with their former slaves, whom they had always nourished with paternal affection and still regarded with a most tender care.

This man met Hesden as the latter came out upon the porch, and with a flushed face and a peculiar twitching about his mouth, asked if he could see him in private for a moment.

Hesden led the way to his own room. Jackson then, having first shut the door, cautiously said:

"You know me, Mr. Le Moyne?"

"Certainly, Jackson."

"An' you knew my father before me?"

"Of course. I knew old man Billy Jackson very well in my young days."

"Did you ever know anything mean or disreputable about him?"

"No, certainly not; he was a very correct man, so far as I ever heard."

"Poor but honest?"—with a sneer.

"Well, yes; a poor man, but a very correct man."

"Well, did you ever know anything disreputable about *me?*" keenly.

"Well—why—Mr. Jackson—you—" stammered Hesden, much confused.

"Out with it!" angrily. "I'm a Radical?"

"Yes—and—you know, your political course has rendered you very unpopular."

"Of course! A man has no right to his own political opinions."

"Well, but you know, Mr. Jackson, yours have been so peculiar and so obnoxious to our best people. Besides, you have expressed them so boldly and defiantly. I do not think our people have any ill-feeling against you, personally; but you cannot wonder that so great a change as we have had should excite many of them very greatly. You should not be so violent, Mr. Jackson."

"Violent—Hell! You'd better go and preach peace to Eliab Hill. Poor fellow! I don't reckon the man lives who ever heard him say a harsh thing to any one. He was always that mild I used to wonder the Lord didn't take him long ago. Nigger as he was, and cripple as he was, I'd ruther had his religion than that of all the mean, hypocritical, murdering aristocrats in Horsford."

"But, Mr. Jackson, you should not speak in that way of our best citizens."

"Oh, the devil! I know—but that is no matter, Mr. Le Moyne. I didn't come to argue with you. Did you ever hear anything agin' me outside of my politics?"

"I don't know that I ever did."

"If you were in a tight place, would you have confidence in Jordan Jackson as a friend?"

"You know I have reason to remember that," said Hesden, with feeling. "You helped me when I could not help myself. It's not every man that would care about his horse carrying double when he was running away from the Yanks."

"Ah! you remember that, then?" with a touch of pride in his voice.

"Yes, indeed! Jackson," said Hesden, warmly.

"Well, would you do me a good turn to pay for that?"

"Certainly—anything that—" hesitating.

"Oh, damn it, man, don't strain yourself! I didn't ask any questions when I helped you!"

"Mr. Jackson," said Hesden, with dignity, "I merely wished to say that I do not care at this time to embroil myself in politics. You know I have an old mother who is very feeble. I have long regretted that affairs are in the condition that they are in, and have wondered if something could not be done. Theoretically, you are right and those who are with you. Practically, the matter is very embarrassing. But I do not hesitate to say, Mr. Jackson, that those who commit such outrages as that perpetrated at Red Wing disgrace the name of gentleman, the county, and State, the age we live in, and the religion we profess. That I *will* say."

"And that's quite enough, Mr. Le Moyne. All I wanted was to ask you to act as my trustee."

"Your trustee in what?"

"There is a deed I have just executed conveying everything I have to you, and I want you to sell it off and dispose of it the best you can, and send me the money."

"*Send* it to you?"

"Yes, I'm going away."

"Going away? Why? You are not in debt?"

"I don't owe a hundred dollars."

"Then why are you doing this? I don't understand."

"Mr. Le Moyne," said Jackson, coming close to him and speaking in a low intense tone, "I was *whipped* last night!"

"Whipped!"

"Yes."

"By whom?"

"By my own neighbors, in the sight of my wife and daughter!"

"By the Ku Klux?"

"That's what they call themselves."

"My God, it cannot be!"

"Cannot?" The man's face twitched nervously, as, dropping his hat, he threw off his light coat and, opening his shirt-collar and turning away his head, showed his shoulder covered with wales, still raw and bleeding.

"My God!" cried Hesden, as he put up his hand and started back in horror. "And you a white man?"

"Yes, Mr. Le Moyne," said Jackson, turning his face, burning with shame and indignation, toward his high-bred neighbor, "and the only reason this was done—the only thing agin me—is that I was honestly in favor of giving to the colored man the rights which the law of the land says he shall have, like other men. When the war was over, Mr. Le Moyne, I didn't 'give up,' as all you rich folks talked about doing, and try to put up with what was to come afterward. I hadn't lost nothing by the war, but, on the contrary, had gained what I had no chance to git in any other way. So I jest looked things square in the face and made up my mind that it was a good thing for me, and all such as me, that the damned old Confederacy was dead. And the more I thought on't the more I couldn't help seein' and believin' that it was right and fair to free the niggers and let them have a fair show and a white man's chance—votin' and all. That's what I call a fair hack, and I swear, Mr. Le Moyne, I don't know how it may seem to you, but to my mind any man that ain't willing to let any other man have that, is a damn coward! I'm as white as anybody, and hain't no more reason to stand up for niggers than any of the rest of the white people—no, nor half as much as most of 'em, for, as fur as I know, I hain't got no relations among 'em. But I do say that if the white folks of the South can't stand up to a fair fight with the niggers at the polls, without cuttin', and murderin', and burnin', and shootin', and whippin', and Ku Kluxin', and cheatin', and swindlin', they are a damned no-'count people, and don't deserve no sort of show in the world—no more than a mean, sneakin', venomous moccasin-snake—there!"

"But you don't think—" Hesden began.

"Think? Damn it, I *know!*" broke in Jackson. "They said if I would quit standin' up for the niggers, they'd let me off, even after they'd got me stripped and hung up. I wouldn't do it! I didn't believe then they'd cut me up this way; but they did! An' now I'm goin'. I'd stay an' fight, but 'tain't no use; an' I couldn't look a man in the eye who I thought tuk a hand in that whippin' without killin' him. I've got to go, Le Moyne," he said with clenched fists, "or I shall commit murder before the sun goes down."

"Where are you going?"

"God knows! Somewhere where the world's free and the earth's fresh, and where it's no crime to have been born poor or to uphold and maintain the laws of the land."

"I'm sorry, Jackson, but I don't blame you. You can't live here in peace, and you are wise to go," said Hesden, extending his hand.

"Will you be my trustee?"

"Yes."

"God bless you!"

The angry, crushed, and outraged man broke into tears as he shook the hand he held.

There was an hour or two of close consultation, and then Hesden Le Moyne looked thoughtfully after this earnest and well-meaning man, who was compelled to flee from the land for which he had fought, simply because he had adopted the policy and principles which the conquering power had thrust into the fundamental law, and endeavored to carry them out in good faith. Like the fugitive from slavery in the olden time, he had started toward the North Pole on the quest for liberty.

CHAPTER XLVI.

BACKWARD AND FORWARD.

THE TASK WHICH Hesden Le Moyne undertook when he assumed the care and protection of Eliab Hill, was no trivial one, as he well understood.

He realized as fully as did Nimbus the necessity of absolute concealment, for he was well aware that the blaze of excitement which would sweep over Horsford, when the events that had occurred at Red Wing should become known, would spare no one who should harbor or conceal any of the recognized leaders of the colored men. He knew that not only that organization which had just shown its existence in the county, but the vast majority of all the white inhabitants as well, would look upon this affair as indubitable evidence of the irrepressible conflict of races, in which they all believed most devoutly.

He had looked forward to this time with great apprehension. Although he had scrupulously refrained from active participation in political life, it was not from any lack of interest in the political situation of the country. He had not only the ordinary instinct of the educated Southern man for political thought—an instinct which makes every man in that section first of all things a partisan, and constitutes politics the first and most important business of life—but besides this general interest in public affairs he had also an inherited bias of hostility to the right of secession, as well as to its policy. His father had been what was termed a "Douglas Democrat,"[83] and the son had absorbed his views. With that belief in a father's infallibility which is so general in that part of the country, Hesden, despite his own part in the war and the chagrin which defeat had brought, had looked only for evil results to come out of the present struggle, which he believed to have been uselessly precipitated.

It was in this state of mind that he had watched the new phase of the "irrepressible conflict"[84] which supervened upon the downfall of the Rebellion. In so doing, he had arrived at the following conclusions:

1 That it was a most fortunate and providential thing that the Confederacy had failed. He had begun to realize the wisdom of Washington when he referred to the dogma of "State rights" as "that bantling—I like to have said *that monster.*"[85]
2 That the emancipation of the slaves would ultimately prove advantageous to the white man.
3 That it was the part of honorable men fairly and honestly to carry out and give effect to all the conditions, expressed and implied, on which power, representation, and autonomy were restored to the recently rebellious States. This he believed to be a personal duty, and a failure so to do he regarded as a disgrace to every man in any way contributing to it, especially if he had been a soldier and had shared the defeat of which these conditions were a consequence.
4 He did not regard either the war or the legislation known as reconstructionary as having in any manner affected the natural relation of the races. In the old times he had never felt or believed that the slave was inherently endowed with the same rights as the master; and he did not see how the results of war could enhance his natural rights. He did not believe that the colored man had an inherent right to freedom or to self-government. Whatever right of that kind he might now have was simply by the free grace of the conqueror. He had a right to the fruit of his own labor, to the care, protection, and service of his own children, to the society and comfort of his wife, to the protection of his own person, to marriage, the ballot, possessory capacity, and all those things which distinguish the citizen from the chattel—not because of his manhood, nor because of inherent coequality of right with the white man; but simply because the national legislation gave it to him as a condition precedent of statal rehabilitation.

These may seem to the Northern reader very narrow views; and so they are, as compared with those that underlay the spirit of resistance to rebellion, and the fever heat for human rights, which was the animating principle in the hearts of the people when they endorsed and approved those amendments which were the basis of reconstructionary legislation. It should be remembered, however, that even these views were infinitely in advance of the ideas generally entertained by his white fellow-citizens of the South. Nearly all of them regarded these matters in a very different light; and most naturally, too, as any one may understand who will remember what had gone before, and will keep in mind that defeat does not mean a new birth, and that warfare leaves *men* unchanged by its results, whatever may be its effects on nations and societies.

They regretted the downfall of the Confederacy as the triumph of a lower and baser civilization—the ascendency of a false idea and an act of unrighteous and unjustifiable subversion. To their minds it was a forcible denial of their rights, and, to a large portion of them, a dishonorable violation of that contract or treaty upon which the Federal Union was based, and by which the right for which they fought had, according to their construction, been assured. As viewed by them, the result of the war had not changed these facts, nor justified the infraction of the rights of the South.

In the popular phrase of that day, they "accepted the situation"—which to *their* minds simply meant that they would not fight any more for independent existence. The North understood it to mean that they would accept cheerfully and in good faith any terms and conditions which might be imposed upon them as a condition of rehabilitation.

The masses of the Southern whites regarded the emancipation of the negro simply as an arbitrary exercise of power, intended as a punishment for the act of attempted secession—which act, while many believed it to have been impolitic, few believed to be in conflict with the true theory of our government. They considered the freeing of the slave merely a piece of wanton spite, inspired, in great measure, by sheer envy of Southern superiority, in part by angry hate because of the troubles, perils, and losses of the war, and, in a very small degree, by honest though absurd fanaticism. They did not believe that it was done for the sake of the slave, to secure his liberty or to establish his rights; but they believed most devoutly that it was done solely and purposely to injure the master, to punish the rebel, and to still further cripple and impoverish the South. It was, to them, an unwarrantable measure of unrighteous retribution inspired by the lowest and basest motives.

But if, to the mass of Southern white men, emancipation was a measure born of malicious spite in the breast of the North, what should they say of that which followed—the *enfranchisement* of the black? It was a gratuitous insult—a causeless infamy! It was intended to humiliate, without even the mean motive of advantage to be derived. They did not for a moment believe —they do not believe to-day—that the negro was enfranchised for his own sake, or because the North believed that he was entitled to self-government, or was fit for self-government; but simply and solely because it was hoped thereby to degrade, overawe, and render powerless the white element of the

Southern populations. They thought it a fraud in itself, by which the North pretended to give back to the South her place in the nation; but instead, gave her only a debased and degraded co-ordination with a race despised beyond the power of words to express.

This anger seemed—and still seems to the Northern mind—useless, absurd, and ridiculous. It appears to us as groundless and almost as laughable as the frantic and impotent rage of the Chinaman who has lost his sacred queue by the hand of the Christian spoiler.[86] To the Northern mind the cause is entirely incommensurate with the anger displayed. One is inclined to ask, with a laugh, "Well, what of it?" Perhaps there is not a single Northern resident of the South who has not more than once offended some personal friend by smiling in his face while he raged, with white lips and glaring eyes, about this culminating ignominy. Yet it was sadly real to them. In comparison with this, all other evils seemed light and trivial, and whatever tended to prevent it, was deemed fair and just. For this reason, the Southerners felt themselves not only justified, but imperatively called upon, in every way and manner, to resist and annul all legislation having this end in view. Regarding it as inherently fraudulent, malicious, and violent, they felt no compunctions in defeating its operation by counter-fraud and violence.

It was thus that the elements of reconstruction affected the hearts and heads of most of the Southern whites. To admit that they were honest in holding such views as they did is only to give them the benefit of a presumption which, when applied to the acts and motives of whole peoples, becomes irrefutable. A mob may be wrong-headed, but it is always right-hearted. What it does may be infamous, but underlying its acts is always the sting of a great evil or the hope of a great good.

Thus it was, too, that to the subtler mind and less selfish heart of Hesden Le Moyne, every attempt to nullify the effect or evade the operation of the Reconstruction laws was tinged with the idea of personal dishonor. To his understanding, the terms of surrender were, not merely that he would not again fight for a separate governmental existence, but, also, that he would submit to such changes in the national polity as the conquering majority might deem necessary and desirable as conditions precedent to restored power; and would honestly and fairly, as an honorable man and a brave soldier, carry out those laws either to successful fruition or to fair and legitimate repeal.

He was not animated by any thought of advantage to himself or to his class to arise from such ideas. Unlike Jordan Jackson, and men of his type, there was nothing which his class could gain thereby, except a share in the ultimate glory and success of an enlarged and solidified nation. The self-abnegation which he had learned from three years of duty as a private soldier and almost a lifetime of patient attendance upon a loved but exacting invalid, inclined him to study the movements of society and the world, without especial reference to himself, or the narrow circle of his family or class. To his mind, *honor*—that honor which he accounted the dearest birthright his native South had given—required that from and after the day of his surrender he should seek and desire, not the gratification of revenge nor the display of prejudice, but the success and glory of the great republic. He felt that the American Nation had become greater and more glorious by the very act of overcoming rebellion. He recognized that the initial right or wrong of that struggle, whatever it might have been, should be subordinated in all minds to the result—an individual Nation. It was a greater and a grander thing to be an American than to have been a Confederate! It was more honorable and knightly to be true in letter and in spirit to every law of his reunited land than to make the woes of the past an excuse for the wrongs of the present. He felt all the more scrupulous in regard to this, because those measures were not altogether such as he would have adopted, nor such as he could yet believe would prove immediately successful. He thought that every Southern man should see to it especially that, if any element of reconstruction failed, it should not be on account of any lack of honest, sincere and hearty co-operation on his part.

It was for this reason that he had taken such interest in the experiment that was going on at Red Wing in educating the colored people. He did not at first believe at all in the capacity of the negro for culture, progress, self-support, or self-government; but he believed that the experiment, having been determined on by the nation, should be fairly and honestly carried out and its success or failure completely demonstrated. He admitted frankly that, if they had such capacity, they undoubtedly had the right to use it; because he believed the right inherent and inalienable with any race or people having the capacity. He considered that it was only the lack of co-ordinate capacity that made the Africans unfit to exercise co-ordinate power with individuals of the white race.

He thought they should be encouraged by every means to develop what was in them, and readily admitted that, should the experiment succeed and all distinction of civil right and political power be successfully abolished, the strength and glory of the nation would be wonderfully enhanced. His partiality for the two chief promoters of the experiment at Red Wing had greatly increased his interest in the result, which had by no means been diminished by his acquaintance with Mollie Ainslie.

It was not, however, until he bent over his unconscious charge in the stillness of the morning, made an examination of the wounds of his old playmate by the flickering light of the lamp, and undertook the process of resuscitation and cure, that he began to realize how his ancient prejudice was giving way before the light of what he could not but regard as truth. The application of some simple remedies soon restored Eliab to consciousness, but he found that the other injuries were so serious as to demand immediate surgical attendance, and would require considerable time for their cure.

His first idea had been to keep Eliab's presence at his house entirely concealed; but as soon as he realized the extent of his injuries, he saw that this would be impossible, and concluded that the safer way would be to entrust the secret to those servants who were employed "about the lot," which includes, upon a Southern plantation, all who are not regularly engaged in the crop. He felt the more willing to do this because of the attachment felt for the sweet-tempered but deformed minister at Red Wing by all of his race in the county. He carefully impressed upon the two women and Charles, the stable-boy, the necessity of the utmost caution in regard to the matter, and arranged with them to care for his patient by turns, so as never to leave him alone. He sent to the post at Boyleston for a surgeon, whose coming chanced not to be noticed by the neighbors, as he arrived just after dark and went away before daylight to return to his duty. A comfortable cot was arranged for the wounded man, and, to make the care of him less onerous, as well as to avoid the remark which continual use of the ladder would be sure to excite, Charles was directed to cut a doorway through the other gable of the old house into one of the rooms in a newer part. Charles was one of those men found on almost every plantation, who can "turn a hand to almost anything." In a short time he had arranged a door from the chamber above "Marse Hesden's room," and the task of nursing the stricken man back to life and such health as he might thereafter have, was carried on by the faithful band of watchers in the dim light of the old attic and amid the spicy odor of the "bulks" of tobacco, which was stored there awaiting a favorable market.

Hesden was so occupied with this care that it was not until the next day that he became aware of Mollie's absence. As she had gone without preparation or farewell, he rightly judged that it was her intention to return. At first, he thought he would go at once to Red Wing and assure himself of her safety, but a moment's consideration showed him not only that this was probably unnecessary, but also that to do so would attract attention, and perhaps reveal the hiding-place of Eliab. Besides, he felt confident that she would not be molested, and thought it quite as well that she should not be at Mulberry Hill for a few days, until the excitement had somewhat worn away.

On the next day, Eliab inquired so pitifully for both Miss Mollie and Nimbus, that Hesden, although he knew it was a half-delirious anxiety, had sent Charles on an errand to a plantation in that vicinity, with directions to learn all he could of affairs there, if possible without communicating directly with Miss Ainslie.

This he did, and reported everything quiet—Nimbus and Berry not heard from; Eliab supposed to have been killed; the colored people greatly alarmed; and "Miss Mollie a-comfortin' an encouragin' on 'em night an' day."

Together with this anxiety came the trust confided to Hesden by Jordan Jackson, and the new, and at first somewhat arduous, duties imposed thereby. In the discharge of these he was brought into communication with a great many of the best people of the county, and did not hesitate to express his opinion freely as to the outrage at Red Wing. He was several times warned to be prudent, but he answered all warnings so firmly, and yet with so much feeling, that he was undisturbed. He stood so high, and had led so pure a life, that he could even be allowed to entertain obnoxious sentiments without personal danger, so long as he did not attempt to reduce them to practice or attempt to secure for colored people the rights to which he thought them entitled. However, a great deal of remark was occasioned by the fact of his having become trustee for the fugitive Radical, and he was freely charged with having disgraced and degraded himself and his family by taking the part of a "renegade, Radical white nigger," like Jackson. This duty took him from home during the day in a direction away from Red Wing, and a part of each night he sat by the bedside of Eliab. So that more than a week had passed, during which he had found opportunity to take but three meals with his mother, and had not yet been able to visit Red Wing.

CHAPTER XLVII.

BREASTING THE TORRENT.

TO MAKE UP for the sudden loss of society occasioned by the simultaneous departure of Mollie and the unusual engrossment of Hesden in business matters of pressing moment, as he had informed her, Mrs. Le Moyne had sent for one of the sisters of her son's deceased wife, Miss Hetty Lomax, to come and visit her. It was to this young lady that Hesden had appealed when the young teacher was suddenly stricken down in his house, and who had so rudely refused. Learning that the object of her antipathy was no longer there, Miss Hetty came and made herself very entertaining to the invalid by detailing to her all the horrors, real and imagined, of the past few days. Day by day she was in the invalid's room, and it was from her that Mrs. Le Moyne had learned all that was contained in her letter to Mollie concerning the public feeling and excitement. A week had elapsed, when Miss Hetty one day appeared with a most interesting budget of news, the recital of which seemed greatly to excite Mrs. Le Moyne. At first she listened with incredulity and resentment; then conviction seemed to force itself upon her mind, and anger succeeded to astonishment. Calling her serving woman, she asked impetuously:

"Maggie, is your Master Hesden about the house?"

"Really now mistis," said the girl in some confusion, "I can't edsackly tell. He war, de las' time I seed him; but then he mout hev gone out sence dat, yer know."

"Where was he then?"

"He war in his room, ma'am, wid a strange gemmen."

"Yes," added the mistress, in a significant tone, "he seems to have a great deal of strange company lately."

The girl glanced at her quickly as she arranged the bed-clothing, and the young lady who sat in the easy chair chuckled knowingly.

So the woman answered artfully, but with seeming innocence:

"La, mistis, it certain am quare how you finds out t'ings. 'Pears like a mouse can't stir 'bout de house, but you hears it quicker nor de cat."

It was deft flattery, and the pleased mistress swallowed the bait with a smile.

"I always try to know what is going on in my own house," she responded, complacently.

"Should t'ink yer did," said the colored woman, gazing at her in admiring wonder. "I don't 'llow dar's ennybody come inter dis yer house in one while, dat yer didn't know all 'bout 'em widout settin' eyes on 'em. I wouldn't be at all s'prised, dat I wouldn't," said she to the young lady, "ter find dat she knows whose h'yer now, an' whose been h'yer ebbery day sence Marse Hesden's been so busy. La! she's a woman—she's got a head-piece, she hab!"

"Yes," said the invalid; "I know that that odious scallawag, Jordan Jackson, has been here and has been shut up with my son, consulting and planning the Lord knows what, here in this very house of mine. Pretty business for a Le Moyne and a Richards to be in! You all thought you'd keep it from me; but you couldn't."

"La, sakes!" said the girl, with a look of relief, "yer mustn't say *me. I* didn't never try ter keep it. I know'd yer'd find it out."

"When do you say you saw him?"

"I jes disremembers now what time it war. Some time dis mornin' though. It mout hev been some two—free hours ago."

"Who was the gentleman with him—I hope he was a *gentleman?*"

"Oh la, ma'am, dat he war—right smart ob one, I should jedge, though I nebber seen his face afo' in my born days."

"And don't know his name?"

"Not de fust letter ob it, mistis."

Maggie might well say that, since none of the letters of the alphabet were known to her; but when she conveyed the idea that she did not know the name of the visitor, it was certainly a stretch of the truth; but then she did not know as "Marse Hesden" would care about his mother knowing the name of his visitor, and she had no idea of betraying anything which concerned him against his wish. So in order to be perfectly safe, she deemed it best to deceive her mistress.

"Tell your Master Hesden I wish to see him immediately, Maggie," said Mrs. Le Moyne, imperiously.

"Yes'm," said the girl, as she left the room to perform her errand.

There was a broad grin upon her face as she crossed the passage and knocked at the door of Hesden's room, thinking how she had flattered her mistress into a revelation of her own ignorance. She was demure enough, however, when Hesden himself opened the door and inquired what she wished.

"Please, sah, de mistis tole me ter ax yer ter come inter her room, right away."

"Anything the matter, Maggie?"

"Nuffin', only jes she wants ter talk wid yer 'bout sunthin', I reckon."

"Who is with her?"

"Miss Hetty."

"Yes"—musingly.

"An' de mistis 'pears powerfully put out 'bout sunthin' or udder," volunteered the girl.

"Yes," repeated Hesden, absently. "Well, Maggie, say to my mother that I am very closely engaged, and I hope she will please excuse me for a few hours."

The girl returned and delivered her message.

"What!" exclaimed the sick woman, in amazement. "He must have turned Radical sure enough, to send me such an answer as that! Maggie," she continued, with severe dignity, "you must be mistaken. Return and tell my son that I am sure you are mistaken."

"Oh, dar ain't no mistake 'bout it, mistis. Dem's de berry words Marse Hesden said, shore."

"Do as I bade you, Maggie," said the mistress, quietly.

"Oh, certain, mistis, certain—only dar ain't no mistake," said the woman, as she returned with the message she was charged to deliver.

"Did you ever see such a change?" asked Mrs. Le Moyne of her companion as soon as the door was closed upon the servant. "There never was a time before when Hesden did not come the instant I called, no matter upon what he might be engaged."

"Yes," said the other, laughingly, "I used to tell Julia that it would make me awfully jealous to have a husband jump up and leave me to go and pet his mother before the honeymoon was over."

"Poor Julia!" sighed the invalid. "Hesden never appreciated her—never. He didn't feel her loss as I did."

"I should think not," replied the sister-in-law, sharply. "But he might at least have had regard enough for her memory not to have flirted so outrageously with that Yankee school-marm."

"What do you mean, Hetty!" said Mrs. Le Moyne, severely. "Please remember that it is my son of whom you are speaking."

"Oh, yes," said Miss Hetty, sharply, "we have been speaking of him all along, and—"

The door from the hall was opened quickly, and Hesden looking in, said pleasantly,

"I hope you are not suffering, mother?"

"Not more than usual, Hesden," said Mrs. Le Moyne, "but I wish to see you very particularly, my son."

"I am very busy, mother, on a most important matter; but you know I will always make everything give way for you."

So saying, he stepped into the room and stood awaiting his mother's pleasure, after bowing somewhat formally to the younger lady.

"What are these reports I hear about you, Hesden?" asked his mother, with some show of anger.

"I beg your pardon, little mother," said Hesden smiling; "but was it to make this inquiry you called me from my business?"

"Yes, indeed," was the reply; "I should like to know what there could be of more importance to you than such slanderous reports as Cousin Hetty tells me are being circulated about you."

"I have no doubt they are interesting if Cousin Hetty brings them," said Hesden; "but you will please excuse me now, as I have matters of more importance to attend to."

He bowed, and would have passed out, but the good lady cried out almost with a shriek,

"But Hesden! Hesden! Hetty says that—that—that they say—you—are a—a Radical!"

She started from her pillows, and leaned forward with one white hand uplifted, as she waited his reply.

He turned back instantly, stepped quickly to the bedside, and put his one arm caressingly about her as he said earnestly, "I am afraid, mother, if one speaks of things which have occurred in Horsford during the past few days as a man of honor ought, he must expect to be called bad names."

"But Hesden—you are not—do tell me, my son," said his mother, in a tone of entreaty, "that you are *not* one of those horrid Radicals!"

"There, there; do not excite yourself, mother. I will explain everything to you this evening," said he, soothingly.

"But you are not a Radical?" she cried, catching his hand.

"I am a man of honor, always," he replied, proudly.

"Then you cannot be a Radical," she said, with a happy smile.

"But he is—he is!" exclaimed the younger lady, starting forward with flushed cheeks and pointing a trembling finger at his face, as if she had detected a guilty culprit. "He is!" she repeated. "Deny it if you dare, Hesden Le Moyne!"

"Indeed, Miss Hetty," said Hesden, turning upon her with dignified severity. "May I inquire who constituted you either my judge or my accuser."

"Oh fie! Hesden," said his mother. "Isn't Hetty one of the family?"

"And has every Richards and Le Moyne on the planet a right to challenge my opinions?" asked Hesden.

"Certainly!" said his mother, with much energy, while her pale face flushed, and her upraised hand trembled—"certainly they have, my son, if they think you are about to disgrace those names. But do deny it! Do tell me you are not a Radical!" she pleaded.

"But suppose I were?" he asked, thoughtfully.

"I would disown you! I would disinherit you!" shrieked the excited woman, shrinking away from his arm as if there were contagion in the touch. "Remember, sir," she continued threateningly, "that Mulberry Hill is still mine, and it shall never go to a Radical—never!"

"There, there, mother; do not excite yourself unnecessarily," said Hesden. "It is quite possible that both these matters are beyond either your control or mine."

"Why, what do you mean?"

"I simply mean that circumstances over which we have no control have formed my opinions, and others over which we have as little control may affect the ownership of this plantation."

"Why—what in the world! Hesden, are you mad? You know that it is mine by the will of my father! Who or what could interfere with my right?"

"I sincerely hope that no one may," answered Hesden; "but I shall be able to tell you more about these matters after dinner, when I promise that you shall know all that I fear, without reservation."

There had been a calm, almost sorrowful, demeanor about Hesden during this conversation, which had held the excited women unconsciously in check. They were so astonished at the coolness of his manner and the matter-of-fact sincerity of his tones that they were quite unable to express the indignation and abhorrence they both felt that his language merited. Now, however, as he moved toward the door, the younger lady was no longer able to restrain herself.

"I knew it was so!" she said. "That miserable nigger-teacher wasn't here for nothing! The mean, low hussy! I should think he would have been ashamed to bring her here anyhow—under his mother's very nose!"

Hesden had almost reached the door of the room when these words fell upon his ear. He turned and strode across the room until he stood face to face with his mother once more. There was no lack of excitement about him now. His face was pale as death, his eyes blazed, and his voice trembled.

"Mother," said he, "I have often told you that I would never bring to you a wife whom you did not approve. I hope never to do so; but I wish to say one thing: Miss Ainslie is a pure and lovely woman. None of us have ever known her superior. She is worthy of any man's devotion. I would not have said this but for what has been spoken here. But now I say, that if I ever hear that any one having a single drop of our blood in her veins has spoken ill of her—ay, or if her name is linked with mine in any slighting manner, even by the breath of public rumor—I will make her my wife if she will accept my hand, whatever your wishes. And further, if any one speaks slightingly of her, I will resent it as if she were my wife, so help me God!"

He turned upon his heel, and strode out of the room.

He had not once looked at or spoken to her whose words had given the offense. The mother and cousin were overwhelmed with astonishment at the intensity of the usually quiet and complaisant Hesden. Miss Hetty soon made excuse for returning to her home, and Mrs. Le Moyne waited in dull wonder for the revelation which the evening was to bring. It seemed to her as if the world had lost its bearings and everything must be afloat, now that Hesden had been so transformed as to speak thus harshly to the mother for whom his devotion had become proverbial in all the country around.

CHAPTER XLVIII.

THE PRICE OF HONOR.

WHEN HESDEN CAME to his mother's room that night, his countenance wore an unusually sad and thoughtful expression. His mother had not yet recovered from the shock of the morning's interview. The more she thought of it, the less she could understand either his language or his manner. That he would once think of allying himself in political thought with those who were trying to degrade and humiliate their people by putting them upon a level with the negro, she did not for a moment believe, despite what he had said. Neither did she imagine, even then, that he had any feeling for Mollie Ainslie other than mere gratitude for the service she had rendered, but supposed that his outburst was owing merely to anger at the slighting language used toward her by Cousin Hetty. Yet she felt a dim premonition of something dreadful about to happen, and was ill at ease during the evening meal. When it was over, the table cleared, and the servant had retired, Hesden sat quiet for a long time, and then said, slowly and tenderly:

"Mother, I am very sorry that all these sad things should come up at this time—so soon after our loss. I know your heart, as well as mine, is sore, and I wish you to be sure that I have not, and cannot have, one unkind thought of you. Do not cry," he added, as he saw the tears pouring down her face, which was turned to him with a look of helpless woe upon it—"do not cry, little mother, for we shall both of us have need of all our strength."

"Oh, Hesden," she moaned, "if you only would not—"

"Please do not interrupt me," he said, checking her with a motion of his hand; "I have a long story to tell, and after that we will speak of what now troubles you. But first, I wish to ask you some questions. Did you ever hear of such a person as Edna Richards?"

"Edna Richards—Edna Richards?" said Mrs. Le Moyne, wiping away her tears and speaking between her sobs. "It seems as if I had, but—I—I can't remember, my son. I am so weak and nervous."

"Calm yourself, little mother; perhaps it will come to your mind if I ask you some other questions. Our grandfather, James Richards, came here from Pennsylvania, did he not?"

"Certainly, from about Lancaster. He always promised to take me to see our relatives there, but he never did. You know, son, I was his youngest child, and he was well past fifty when I was born. So he was an old man when I was grown up, and could not travel very much. He took me to the North twice, but each time, before we got around to our Pennsylvania friends, he was so tired out that he had to come straight home."

"Did you ever know anything about his family there?"

"Not much—nothing except what he told me in his last days. He used to talk about them a great deal then, but there was something that seemed to grieve and trouble him so much that I always did all I could to draw his mind away from the subject. Especially was this the case after the boys, your uncles, died. They led rough lives, and it hurt him terribly."

"Do you know whether he ever corresponded with any of our relatives at the North?"

"I think not. I am sure he did not after I was grown. He often spoke of it, but I am afraid there was some family trouble or disagreement which kept him from doing so. I remember in his last years he used frequently to speak of a cousin to whom he seemed to have been very much attached. He had the same name as father, who used to call him 'Red Jim.'"

"Was he then alive?"

"I suppose so—at least when father last heard from him. I think he lived in Massachusetts. Let me see, what was the name of the town. I don't remember," after a pause.

"Was it Marblehead?" asked the son, with some eagerness.

"That's it, dear—Marblehead. How funny that you should strike upon the very name?"

"You think he never wrote?"

"Oh, I am sure not. He mourned about it, every now and then, to the very last."

"Was my grandfather a bachelor when he came here?"

"Of course, and quite an old bachelor, too. I think he was about thirty when he married your grandmother in 1794."

"She was a Lomax—Margaret Lomax, I believe?"

"Yes; that's how we come to be akin to all the Lomax connection."

"Just so. You are sure he had never married before?"

"Sure? Why, yes, certainly. How could he? Why, Hesden, what *do* you mean? Why do you ask all these questions? You do not—you cannot—Oh, Hesden!" she exclaimed, leaning forward and trembling with apprehension.

"Be calm, mother. I am not asking these questions without good cause," he answered, very gravely.

After a moment, when she had recovered herself a little, he continued, holding toward her a slip of paper, as he asked:

"Did you ever see that signature before?"

His mother took the paper, and, having wiped her glasses, adjusted them carefully and glanced at the paper. As she did so a cry burst from her lips, and she said,

"Oh, Hesden, Hesden, where did you get it? Oh, dear! oh, dear!"

"Why, mother, what is it?" cried Hesden in alarm, springing up and going quickly to her side.

"That—that horrid thing, Hesden! Where *did* you get it? Do you know it was that which made that terrible quarrel between your grandfather and Uncle John, when he struck him that—that last night, before John's body was found in the river. He was drowned crossing the ford, you know. I don't know what it was all about; but there was a terrible quarrel, and John wrote that on a sheet of paper and held it before your grandfather's face and said something to him—I don't know what. I was only a little girl then, but, ah me! I remember it as if it was but yesterday. And then father struck him with his cane. John fell as if he were dead. I was looking in at the window, not thinking any harm, and saw it all. I thought he had killed John, and ran away, determined not to tell. I never breathed a lisp of it before, son, and nobody ever knew of that quarrel, only your grandfather and me. I know it troubled him greatly after John died. Oh, I can see that awful paper, as John held it up to the light, as plain as this one in my hand now."

The slip of paper which she held contained only the following apparently unintelligible scrawl:[87]

"And you never saw it but once?" asked Hesden, thoughtfully.

"Never but once before to-night, dear."

"It was not Uncle John's usual signature, then?"

"No, indeed. Is it a signature? She glanced curiously at the paper while Hesden pointed out the letters,

"That is what I take it to be, at least," he said. "Sure enough," said Mrs. Le Moyne, "and that might stand for John Richards or James Richards. It might be Uncle John or your grandfather, either, child."

"True, but grandfather always wrote his name plainly, J. RICHARDS. I have seen a thousand of his signatures, I reckon. Besides, Uncle John was not alive in 1790."

"Of course not. But what has that to do with the matter? What does it all mean anyhow? There must be some horrid secret about it, I am sure."

"I do not know what it means, mother, but I am determined to find out. That is what I have been at all day, and I will not stop until I know all about it."

"But how did you come to find it? What makes you think there is anything to be known about it?"

"This is the way it occurred, mother. The other day it became necessary to cut a door from the chamber over my room into the attic of the old kitchen, where I have been storing the tobacco. You know the part containing the dining-room was the original house, and was at first built of hewed logs. It was, in fact, two houses, with a double chimney in the middle. Afterward, the two parts were made into one, the rude stairs torn away, and the whole thing ceiled within and covered with thick pine siding without. In cutting through this, Charles found between two of the old logs and next to the chinking put in on each side to keep the wall flush and smooth, a pocket-book, carefully tied up in a piece of coarse linen, and containing a yellow, dingy paper, which, although creased and soiled, was still clearly legible. The writing was of that heavy round character which marked the legal hand of the old time, and the ink, though its color had somewhat changed by time, seemed to show by contrast with the dull hue of the page even more clearly than it could have done when first written. The paper proved to be a will, drawn up in legal form and signed with the peculiar scrawl of which you hold a tracing. It purported to have been made and published in December, 1789, at Lancaster, in the State of Pennsylvania, and to have been witnessed by James Adiger and Johan Welliker of that town."

"How very strange!" exclaimed Mrs. Le Moyne. "I suppose it must have been the will of your grandfather's father."

"That was what first occurred to me," answered Hesden, "but on closer inspection it proved to be the will of James Richards, as stated in the caption, of Marblehead, in the State of Massachusetts, giving and bequeathing all of his estate, both real and personal, after some slight bequests, to his beloved wife Edna, except—"

"Stop, my son," said Mrs. Le Moyne, quickly, "I remember now. Edna was the name of the wife of father's cousin James—"Red Jim,"[88] he called him. It was about writing to *her* he was always talking toward the last. So I suppose her husband must have been dead."

"I had come to much the same conclusion," said Hesden, "though I never heard that grandfather had a cousin James until to-night. I should never have thought any more of the document, however, except as an old relic, if it had not gone on to bequeath particularly 'my estate in Carolina to my beloved daughter, Alice E., when she shall arrive at the age of eighteen years,' and to provide for the succession in case of her death prior to that time."

"That is strange," said Mrs. Le Moyne. "I never knew that we had any relatives in the State upon that side."

"That is what I thought," said the son. "I wondered where the estate was which had belonged to this James Richards, who was not our ancestor, and, looking further, I found it described with considerable particularity. It was called Stillwater, and was said to be located on the waters of the Hyco, in Williams County."

"But the Hyco is not in Williams County," said his listener.

"No, mother, but it was then," he replied. "You know that county has been many times subdivided."

"Yes, I had forgotten that," she said. "But what then?"

"It went on," continued Hesden, "to say that he held this land by virtue of a grant from the State which was recorded in the Registry of Deeds in Williams County, in Book A, page 391."

"It is an easy matter to find where it was, then, I suppose," said the mother.

"I have already done that," he replied, "and that is the strange and unpleasant part of what I have to tell you."

"I do hope," she said, smiling, "that you have not made us out cousins of any low-down family."

"As to that I cannot tell, mother; but I am afraid I have found something discreditable in our own family history."

"Oh, I hope not, Hesden," she said, plaintively. "It is so unpleasant to look back upon one's ancestors and not feel that they were strictly honorable. Don't tell me, please. I had rather not hear it."

"I wish you might not," said he; "but the fact which you referred to today—that you are, under the will of my grandfather, the owner of Mulberry Hill, makes it necessary that you should."

"Please, Hesden, don't mention that. I was angry then. Please forget it. What can that have to do with this horrid matter?"

"It has this to do with it, mother," he replied. "The boundaries of that grant, as shown by the record, are identical with the record of the grant under which our grandfather claimed the estate of which this is a part, and which is one of the first entered upon the records of Horsford County."

"What do you mean, Hesden? I don't understand you," said his mother, anxiously.

"Simply that the land bequeathed in this will of J. Richards, is the same as that afterward claimed and held by my grandfather, James Richards, and in part now belonging to you."

"It cannot be, Hesden, it cannot be! There must be some mistake!" she exclaimed, impatiently.

"I wish there were," he answered, "but I fear there is not. The will names as executor, 'my beloved cousin James Richards, of the borough of Lancaster, in the State of Pennsylvania.' I presume this to have been my grandfather. I have had the records of both counties searched and find no record of any administration upon this will."

"You do not think a Richards could have been so dishonorable as to rob his cousin's orphans?"

"Alas! mother, I only know that we have always claimed title under that very grant. The grant itself is among your papers in my desk, and is dated in 1789. I have always understood that grandfather married soon after coming here."

"Oh, yes, dear," was the reply, "I have heard mother tell of it a hundred times."

"And that was in 1794?"

"Yes, yes; but he might have been here before, child."

"That is true, and I hope it may all turn out to have been only a strange mistake."

"But if it does not, Hesden?" said his mother, after a moment's thought. "What do you mean to do?"

"I mean first to go to the bottom of this matter and discover the truth."

"And then—if—if there was—anything wrong?"

"Then the wrong must be righted."

"But that—why, Hesden, it might turn us out of doors! It might make us beggars!"

"We should at least be honest ones."

"But Hesden, think of me—think—" she began.

"So I will, little mother, of you and for you till the last hour of your life or of mine. But mother, I would rather you should leave all and suffer all, and that we should both die of starvation, than that we should live bounteously on the fruit of another's wrong." He bent over her and kissed her tenderly again and again. "Never fear, mother," he said, "we may lose all else by the acts of others, but we can only lose honor by our own. I would give my life for you or to save your honor."

She looked proudly upon him, and reached up her thin white hand to caress his face, as she said with overflowing eyes:

"You are right, my son! If others of our name have done wrong, there is all the more need that we should do right and atone for it."

CHAPTER XLIX.

HIGHLY RESOLVED.

MOLLIE AINSLIE HAD made all her preparations to leave Red Wing. She had investigated the grounds of the suit brought by Winburn against Nimbus and others. Indeed, she found herself named among the "others," as well as all those who had purchased from Nimbus or were living on the tract by virtue of license from him. Captain Pardee had soon informed her that the title of Nimbus was, in fact, only a life-estate, which had fallen in by the death of the life tenant, while Winburn claimed to have bought up the interests of the reversioners. He intimated that it was possible that Winburn had done this while acting as the agent of Colonel Desmit, but this was probably not susceptible of proof, on account of the death of Desmit. He only stated it as a conjecture at best.

At the same time, he informed her that the small tract about the old ordinary, which had come to Nimbus by purchase, and which was all that she occupied, was not included in the life-estate, but was held in fee by Walter Greer. She had therefore instructed him to defend for her upon Nimbus's title, more for the sake of asserting his right than on account of the value of the premises. The suit was for possession and damages for detention and injury of the property, and an attachment had been taken out against Nimbus's property, on the claim for damages, as a non-resident debtor. As there seemed to be no good ground for defense on the part of those who had purchased under Nimbus, the attorney advised that resistance to the suit would be useless. Thus they lost at once the labor of their whole life of freedom, and were compelled to begin again where slavery had left them. This, taken in connection with the burning of the church, the breaking up of the school, and the absence of Eliab and Nimbus, had made the once happy and busy little village most desolate and forlorn.

The days which Mollie Ainslie had passed in the old hostel since she left Mulberry Hill had been days of sorrow. Tears and moans and tales of anxious fear had been in her ears continually. All over the county, the process of "redemption" was being carried on. The very air was full of horrors. Men with bleeding backs, women with scarred and mutilated forms, came to her to seek advice and consolation. Night after night, devoted men, who did not dare to sleep in their own homes, kept watch around her, in order that her slumbers might be undisturbed. It seemed as if all law had been forgotten, and only a secret Klan had power in the land. She did not dare, brave as she was, to ride alone outside of the little village. She did not really think she would be harmed, yet she trembled when the night came, and every crackling twig sent her heart into her mouth in fear lest the chivalric masqueraders should come to fulfil their vague threats against herself. But her heart bled for the people she had served, and whom she saw bowed down under the burden of a terrible, haunting fear.

If she failed to make due allowance for that savageness of nature which generations of slavery are sure to beget in the master, let us not blame her.

She was only a woman, and saw only what was before her. She did not see how the past injected itself into the present, and gave it tone and color. She reasoned only from what met her sight. It is not strange that she felt bitterly toward those who had committed such seemingly vandal acts. No wonder she spoke bitterly, wrote hard things to her Northern friends, and denied the civilization and Christianity of those who could harry, oppress, and destroy the poor, the ignorant, and the weak. It is not surprising that she sneered at the "Southern Gentleman," or that she wrote him down in very black characters in the book and volume of her memory. She was not a philosopher nor a politician, and she had never speculated on the question as to how near of kin virtue and vice may be. She had never considered how narrow a space it is that very often divides the hero from the criminal, the patriot from the assassin, the gentleman from the ruffian, the Christian saint from the red-handed savage. Her heart was hot with wrath and her tongue was tipped with bitterness.

For the first time she blushed at the thought of her native land. That the great, free, unmatched Republic should permit these things, should shut its eyes and turn its back upon its helpless allies in their hour of peril, was a most astounding and benumbing fact to her mind. What she had loved with all that tenacity of devotion which every Northern heart has for the flag and the country, was covered with ignominy by these late events. She blushed with shame as she thought of the weak, vacillating nation which had given the promise of freedom to the ears of four millions of weak but trustful allies, and broken it to their hearts. She knew that the country had appealed to them in its hour of mortal agony, and they had answered with their blood. She knew that again it had appealed to them for aid to write the golden words of Freedom in its Constitution, words before unwritten, in order that they might not be continued in slavery, and they had heard and answered by their votes;[89] and then, while the world still echoed with boastings of these achievements, it had taken away the protecting hand and said to those whose hearts were full of hate, "Stay not thine hand."

She thought, too, that the men who did these things—the midnight masqueraders—were rebels still in their hearts. She called them so in hers at least—enemies of the country, striving dishonorably to subvert its laws. She did not keep in mind that to every Southern man and woman, save those whom the national act brought forth to civil life, the Nation is a thing remote and secondary. To them the State is first, and always so far first as to make the country a dim, distant cloud, to be watched with suspicion or aversion as a something hostile to their State or section. The Northern man thinks of the Nation first. His love of country centers there. His pride in his native State is as a part of the whole. As a *Northerner,* he has no feeling at all. He never speaks of his section except awkwardly, and when reference to it is made absolutely necessary by circumstances. He may be from the East or the West or the Middle, from Maine or Minnesota, but he is first of all things an American. Mollie thought that the result of the war—defeat and destruction—ought to have made the white people of the South just such Americans. In fact it never occurred to her simple heart that they had not always been such. She could not understand how they could have been otherwise. She had never dreamed that there were any Americans with whom it was not the first and ever-present thought that they *were* Americans.

She might have known, if she had thought so far, that in that mystically-bounded region known as "the South," the people were first of all "Southerners;" next "Georgians," or "Virginians," or whatever it might be; and last and lowest in the scale of political being, "Americans." She might have known this had she but noted how the word "Southern" leaps into prominence as soon as the old "Mason and Dixon's line" is crossed. There are "Southern" hotels and "Southern" railroads, "Southern" steamboats, "Southern" stage-coaches, "Southern" express companies, "Southern" books, "Southern" newspapers, "Southern" patent-medicines, "Southern" churches, "Southern" manners, "Southern" gentlemen, "Southern" ladies, "Southern" restaurants, "Southern" bar-rooms, "Southern" whisky, "Southern" gambling-hells, "Southern" principles, "Southern" *everything!* Big or little, good or bad, everything that courts popularity, patronage or applause, makes haste to brand itself as distinctively and specifically "Southern."

Then she might have remembered that in all the North—the great, busy, bustling, over-confident, giantly Great-heart of the continent—there is not to be found a single "Northern" hotel, steamer, railway, stage-coach, bar-room, restaurant, school, university, school-book, or any other "Northern" institution. The word "Northern" is no master-key to patronage or approval. There is no "Northern" clannishness, and no distinctive "Northern" sentiment that prides itself on being such. The "Northern" man may be "Eastern" or "Western." He may be "Knickerbocker," "Pennamite," "Buck-eye," or "Hoosier;"[90] but above all things, and first of all things in his allegiance and his citizenship, he is an American. The "Southern" man is proud of the Nation chiefly because it contains his section and State; the "Northern" man is proud of his section or State chiefly because it is a part of the Nation.

But Mollie Ainslie did not stop to think of these differences, or of the bias which habit gives to the noblest mind; and so her heart was full of wrath and much bitterness. She had forgiven coldness, neglect, and aspersion of herself, but she could not forgive brutality and violence toward the weak and helpless. She saw the futility of any hope of aid from the Nation that had deserted its allies. She felt, on the other hand, the folly of expecting any change in a people steeped in intolerance and gloating in the triumph of lawless violence over obnoxious law. She thought she saw that there was but little hope for that people for whom she had toiled so faithfully to grow to the full stature of the free man in the region where they had been slaves. She was short-sighted and impatient, but she was earnest and intense. She had done much thinking in the sorrowful days just past, and had made up her mind that whatsoever others might do, she, Mollie Ainslie, would do her duty.

The path seemed plain to her. She had been, as it seemed to her, mysteriously led, step by step, along the way of life, always with blindfolded eyes and feet that sought not to go in the way they were constrained to take. Her father and mother dead, her brother's illness brought her to the South; there his wish detained her; a seeming chance brought her to Red Wing; duties and cares had multiplied with her capacity; the cup of love, after one sweet draught, had been dashed from her lips; desolation and destruction had come upon the scene of her labors, impoverishment and woe upon those with whom she had been associated, and a hopeless fate upon all the race to which they belonged in the land wherein they were born.

She did not propose to change these things. She did not aspire to set on foot any great movement or do any great deed, but she felt that she was able to succor a few of the oppressed race. Those who most needed help and best deserved it, among the denizens of Red Wing, she determined to aid in going to a region where thought at least was free. It seemed to her altogether providential that at this time she had still, altogether untouched, the few thousands which Oscar had given her of his army earnings, and also the little homestead on the Massachusetts hills, toward which a little town had been rapidly growing during the years of unwonted prosperity succeeding the war, until now its value was greatly increased from what it was but a few years before. She found she was quite an heiress when she came to take an inventory of her estate, and made up her mind that she would use this estate to carry out her new idea. She did not yet know the how or the where, but she had got it into her simple brain that somewhere and somehow this money might be invested so as to afford a harbor of refuge for these poor colored people, and still not leave herself unprovided for. She had not arranged the method, but she had fully determined on the undertaking.

This was the thought of Mollie Ainslie as she sat in her room at the old ordinary, one afternoon, nearly two weeks after her departure from the Le Moyne mansion. She had quite given up all thought of seeing Hesden again. She did not rave or moan over her disappointment. It had been a sharp and bitter experience when she waked out of the one sweet dream of her life. She saw that it *was* but a dream, foolish and wild; but she had no idea of dying of a broken heart. Indeed, she did not know that her heart *was* broken. She had loved a man whom she had fancied as brave and gentle as she could desire her other self to be. She had neither proffered her love to him nor concealed it. She was not ashamed that she loved nor ashamed that he should know it, as she believed he did. She thought he must have known it, even though she did not herself realize it at the time. If he had been that ideal man whom she loved, he would have come—have claimed her love, and declared his own. That man could never have let her go alone into desolation and danger without following at once to inquire after her. It was not that she needed his protection, but she had desired—nay, expected as a certainty—that he would come and proffer it. The ideal of her love would have done so. If Hesden Le Moyne had come then, she would have given her life into his keeping forever after, without the reservation of a thought. That he did not come only showed that he was not her ideal, not the one she had loved, but only the dim likeness of that one. It was so much the worse for Mr. Hesden Le Moyne, but none the worse for Mollie Ainslie. She still loved her ideal, but knew now that it was only an ideal.

Thus she mused, although less explicitly, as the autumn afternoon drew to its close. She watched the sun sinking to his rest, and reflected that she would see him set but once more over the pines that skirted Red Wing. There was but little more to be done—a few things to pack up, a few sad farewells to be said, and then she would turn her face towards the new life she had set her heart upon.

There was a step upon the path. She heard her own name spoken and heard the reply of the colored woman, who was sitting on the porch. Her heart stopped beating as the footsteps approached her door. She thought her face flushed burning red, but in reality it was of a hard, pallid gray as she looked up and saw Hesden Le Moyne standing in the doorway.

CHAPTER L.

FACE ANSWERETH TO FACE.

"HOW DO YOU do, Miss Mollie?"

She caught her breath as she heard his ringing tone and noted his expectant air. Oh, if he had only come before! If he had not left her to face alone—he knew not what peril! But he had done so, and she could not forget it. So she went forward, and, extending her hand, took his without a throb as she said, demurely,

"I am very well, Mr. Le Moyne. How are you, and how have you left all at home?"

She led the way back to the table and pointed to a chair opposite her own as she spoke.

Hesden Le Moyne had grown to love Mollie Ainslie almost as unconsciously as she had given her heart to him. The loss of his son had been a sore affliction. While he had known no passionate love for his cousin-wife, he yet had had the utmost respect for her, and had never dreamed that there were in his heart deeper depths of love still unexplored. After her death, his mother and his child seemed easily and naturally to fill his heart. He had admired Mollie Ainslie from the first. His attention had been first particularly directed to her accomplishments and attractions by the casual conversation with Pardee in reference to her, and by the fact that the horse she rode was his old favorite. He had watched her at first critically, then admiringly, and finally with an unconscious yearning which he did not define.

The incident of the storm and the bright picture she made in his somewhat somber home had opened his eyes as to his real feelings. At the same time had come the knowledge that there was a wide gulf between them, but he would have bridged it long before now had it not been for his affliction, which, while it drew him nearer to the object of his devotion than he had ever been before, also raised an imperative barrier against words of love. Then the time of trial came. He found himself likely to be stripped of all hope of wealth, and he had been goaded into declaring to others his love for Mollie, although he had never whispered a word of it to her. Since that time, however, despite his somewhat dismal prospects, he had allowed his fancy greater play. He had permitted himself to dream that some time and somehow he might be permitted to call Mollie Ainslie his wife. She seemed so near to him! There was such a calm in her presence!

He had never doubted that his passion was reciprocated. He thought that he had looked down into her heart through the soft, gray eyes, and seen himself. She had never manifested any consciousness of love, but in those dear days at the Hill she had seemed to come so close to him that he thought of her love as a matter of course, as much so as if it had been already plighted. He felt too that her instinct had been as keen as his own, and that she must have discovered the love he had taken no pains to conceal. But the events which had occurred since she went to Red Wing had to his mind forbidden any further expression of this feeling. For her sake as well as for his own honor it must be put aside. He had no wish to conceal or deny it. The fact that he must give her up was the hardest element of the sacrifice which the newly discovered will might require at his hands.

So he had come to tell her all, and he hoped that she would see where honor led him, and would hold him excused from saying, "I love you. Will you be my wife?" He believed that she would, and that they would part without distrust and with unabated esteem for each other. Never, until this moment, had he thought otherwise. Perhaps he was not without hope still, but it was not such as could be allowed to control his action. He could not say now why it was; he could not tell what was lacking, but somehow there seemed to have been a change. She was so far away—so intangible. It was the same lithe form, the same bright face, the same pleasant voice; but the life, the soul, seemed to have gone out of the familiar presence.

He sat and watched her keenly, wonderingly, as they chatted for a moment of his mother. Then he said:

"We have had strange happenings at Mulberry Hill since you left us, Miss Mollie."

"You don't tell me!" she said laughingly. "I cannot conceive such a thing possible. Dear me! How strange to think of anything out of the common happening there!"

The tone and the laugh hurt him.

"Indeed," said he, gravely, "except for that I should have made my appearance here long ago."

"You are very kind. And I assure you, I am grateful that you did not entirely forget me." Her tone was mocking, but her look was so guileless as almost to make him disbelieve his ears.

"I assure you, Miss Mollie," said he, earnestly, "you do me injustice. I was so closely engaged that I was not even aware of your departure until the second day afterward."

He meant this to show how serious were the matters which claimed his attention. To him it was the strongest possible proof of their urgency. But she remembered her exultant ride to Red Wing, and said to herself, "And he did not think of me for two whole days!" As she listened to his voice, her heart had been growing soft despite her; but it was hard enough now. So she smiled artlessly, and said:

"Only two days? Why, Mr. Le Moyne, I thought it was two weeks. That was how I excused you. Charles said you were too busy to ride with me; your mother wrote that you were too busy to ask after me; and I supposed you had been too busy to think of me, ever since."

"Now, Miss Mollie," said he, in a tone of earnest remonstrance, "please do not speak in that way. Things of the utmost importance have occurred, and I came over this evening to tell you of them. You, perhaps, think that I have been neglectful."

"I had no right to demand anything from Mr. Le Moyne."

"Yes, you had, Miss Ainslie," said he, rising and going around the table until he stood close beside her. "You know that only the most pressing necessity could excuse me for allowing you to leave my house unattended."

"That is the way I went there," she interrupted, as she looked up at him, laughing saucily.

"But that was before you had, at my request, risked your life in behalf of my child. Let us not hide the truth, Miss Ainslie. We can never go back to the relation of mere acquaintanceship we held before that night. If you had gone away the next morning it might have been different, but every hour afterward increased my obligations to you. I came here to tell you why I had seemed to neglect them. Will you allow me to do so?"

"It is quite needless, because there is no obligation—none in the least—unless it be to you for generous hospitality and care and a pleasant respite from tedious duty."

"Why do you say that? You cannot think it is so," he said, impetuously. "You know it was my duty to have attended you hither, to have offered my services in that trying time, and by my presence and counsel saved you such annoyance as I might. You know that I could not have been unaware of this duty, and you dare not deny that you expected me to follow you very speedily after your departure."

"Mr. Le Moyne," she said, rising, with flushed cheeks and flashing eyes, "you have no right to address such language to me! It was bad enough to leave me to face danger and trouble and horror alone; but not so bad as to come here and say such things. But I am not ashamed to let you know that you are right. I *did* expect you, Hesden Le Moyne. As I came along the road and thought of the terrors which the night might bring, I said to myself that before the sun went down you would be here, and would counsel and protect the girl who had not shrunk from danger when you asked her to face it, and who had come to look upon you as the type of chivalry. Because I thought you better and braver and nobler than you are, I am not ashamed to confess what I expected. I know it was foolish. I might have known better. I might have known that the man who would fight for a cause he hated rather than be sneered at by his neighbors, would not care to face public scorn for the sake of a 'nigger-teacher'—no matter what his obligations to her."

She stood before him with quivering nostrils and flashing eyes. He staggered back, raising his hand to check the torrent of her wrath.

"Don't, Miss Ainslie, don't!" he said, in confused surprise.

"Oh, yes!" she continued bitterly, "you no doubt feel very much surprised that a 'Yankee nigger-teacher' should dare to resent such conduct. You thought you could come to me, now that the danger and excitement have subsided, and resume the relations we held before. I know you and despise you, Hesden Le Moyne! I have more respect for one of those who made Red Wing a scene of horror and destruction than for you. Is that enough, sir? Do you understand me now?"

"Oh, entirely, Miss Ainslie," said Hesden, in a quick, husky tone, taking his hat from the table as he spoke. "But in justice to myself I must be allowed to state some facts which, though perhaps not sufficient, in your opinion, to justify my conduct, will I hope show you that you have misjudged me in part. Will you hear me?"

"Oh, yes, I will hear anything," she said, as she sat down. "Though nothing can be said that will restore the past."

"Unfortunately, I am aware of that. There is one thing, however, that I prize even more than that, and that is my honor. Do not take the trouble to sneer. Say, what I *call* my honor, if it pleases you better. I will not leave a stain upon that, even in your mind, if I can help it."

"Yes, I hear," she said, as he paused a moment. "Your *honor,* I believe you said."

"Yes, Miss Ainslie," he replied with dignity; "my honor requires that I should say to you now what I had felt forbidden to say before—that, however exalted the opinion you may have formed of me, it could not have equalled that which I cherished for you—not for what you did, but for what you were—and this feeling, whatever you may think, is still unchanged."

Mollie started with amazement. Her face, which had been pale, was all aflame as she glanced up at Hesden with a frightened look, while he went on.

"I do not believe that you would intentionally be unjust. So, if you will permit me, I will ask you one question. If you knew that on the day of your departure, and for several succeeding days, a human life was absolutely dependent upon my care and watchfulness, would you consider me excusable for failure to learn of your unannounced departure, or for not immediately following you hither on learning that fact?" He paused, evidently expecting a reply.

"Surely, Mr. Le Moyne," she said, looking up at him in wide-eyed wonder, "you know I would."

"And would you believe my word if I assured you that this was the fact?"

"Of course I would."

"I am very glad. Such was the case; and that alone prevented my following you and insisting on your immediate return."

"I did not know your mother had been so ill," she said, with some contrition in her voice.

"It was not my mother. I am sorry, but I cannot tell you now who it was. You will know all about it some time. And more than that," he continued, "on the fourth day after you had gone, one who had saved my life in battle came and asked me to requite my debt by performing an important service for him, which has required nearly all my time since that."

"Oh, Mr. Le Moyne!" she said, as the tears came into her eyes, "please forgive my anger and injustice."

"I have nothing to forgive," he said. "You were not unjust—only ignorant of the facts, and your anger was but natural."

"Yet I should have known better. I should have trusted you more," said she, sobbing.

"Well, do not mind it," he said, soothingly. "But if my explanation is thus far sufficient, will you allow me to sit down while I tell you the rest? The story is a somewhat long one."

"Oh, pray do, Mr. Le Moyne. Excuse my rudeness as well as my anger. Please be seated and let me take your hat."

She took the hat and laid it on a table at the side of the room, and then returned and listened to his story. He told her all that he had told his mother the night before, explaining such things as he thought she might not fully understand. Then he showed her the pocket-book and the will, which he had brought with him for that purpose.

At first she listened to what he said with a constrained and embarrassed air. He had not proceeded far, however, before she began to manifest a lively interest in his words. She leaned forward and gazed into his face with an absorbed earnestness that awakened his surprise. Two or three times she reached out her hand, and her lips moved, as though she would interrupt him. He stopped; but, without speaking, she nodded for him to go on. When he handed her the pocket-book and the will, she took them with a trembling hand and examined them with the utmost care. The student-lamp had been lighted before his story was ended. Her face was in the soft light which came through the porcelain shade, but her hands were in the circle of bright light that escaped beneath it. He noticed that they trembled so that they could scarcely hold the paper she was trying to read. He asked if he should not read it for her. She handed him the will, but kept the pocket-book tightly clasped in both hands, with the rude scrawl,

MARBLEHEAD, MASS.,

in full view. She listened nervously to the reading, never once looking up. When he had finished, she said,

"And you say the land mentioned there is the plantation you now occupy?"

"It embraces my mother's plantation and much more. Indeed, this very plantation of Red Wing, except the little tract around the house here, is a part of it. The Red Wing Ordinary tract is mentioned as one of those which adjoins it upon the west. This is the west line, and the house at Mulberry Hill is very near the eastern edge. It is a narrow tract, running down on this side the river until it comes to the big bend near the ford, which it crosses, and keeps on to the eastward.[91]

"It is a large belt, though I do not suppose it was then of any great value—perhaps not worth more than a shilling an acre. It is almost impossible to realize how cheap land was in this region at that time. A man of moderate wealth might have secured almost a county. Especially was that the case with men who bought up what was termed "Land Scrip" at depreciated rates, and then entered lands and paid for them with it at par."

"Was that the way this was bought?" she asked.

"I cannot tell," he replied. "I immediately employed Mr. Pardee to look the matter up, and it seems from the records that an entry had been made some time before, by one Paul Cresson, which was by him assigned to James Richards. I am inclined to think that it was a part of the Crown grant to Lord Granville,[92] which had not been alienated before the Revolution, and of which the State claimed the fee afterward by reason of his adhesion to the Crown. The question of the right of such alien enemies to hold under Crown grants was not then determined, and I suppose the lands were rated very low by reason of this uncertainty in the title."

"Do you think—that—that this will is genuine?" she asked, with her white fingers knotted about the brown old pocket-book.

"I have no doubt about its proving to be genuine. That is evident upon its face. I hope there may be something to show that my grandfather did not act dishonorably," he replied.

"But suppose—suppose there should not be; what would be the effect?"

"Legally, Mr. Pardee says, there is little chance that any valid claim can be set up under it. The probabilities are, he says, that the lapse of time will bar any such claim. He also says that it is quite possible that the devisee may have died before coming of age to take under the will, and the widow, also, before that time; in which case, under the terms of the will, it would have fallen to my grandfather."

"You are not likely to lose by it then, in any event?"

"If it should prove that there are living heirs whose claims are not barred by time, then, of course, they will hold, not only our plantation, but also the whole tract. In that case, I shall make it the business of my life to acquire enough to reimburse those who have purchased of my grandfather, and who will lose by this discovery."

"But you are not bound to do that?" she asked, in surprise.

"Not legally. Neither are we bound to give up the plantation if the heir is legally estopped.[93] But I think, and my mother agrees with me, that if heirs are found who cannot recover the land by reason of the lapse of time, even then, honor requires the surrender of what we hold."

"And you would give up your home?"

"I should gladly do so, if I might thereby right a wrong committed by an ancestor."

"But your mother, Hesden, what of her?"

"She would rather die than do a dishonorable thing."

"Yes—yes; but—you know—"

"Yes, I know that she is old and an invalid, and that I am young and—and unfortunate; but I will find a way to maintain her without keeping what we had never any right to hold."

"You have never known the hardship of self-support!" she said.

"I shall soon learn," he answered, with a shrug.

She sprang up and walked quickly across the room. Her hands were clasped in front of her, the backs upward and the nails digging into the white flesh. Hesden wondered a little at her excitement.

"Thank God! thank God!" she exclaimed at last, as she sank again into her chair, and pressed her clasped hands over her eyes.

"Why do you say that?" he asked, curiously.

"Because you—because I—I hardly know," she stammered.

She looked at him a moment, her face flushing and paling by turns, and stretching out her hand to him suddenly across the table, she said, looking him squarely in the face:

"Hesden Le Moyne, you are a brave man!"

He took the hand in his own and pressed it to his lips, which trembled as they touched it.

"Miss Mollie," he said, tenderly, "will you forgive my not coming before?"

"If you will pardon my lack of faith in you."

"You see," he said, "that my duty for the present is to my mother and the name I bear."

"And mine," she answered, "is to the poor people whose wrongs I have witnessed."

"What do you mean?" he asked.

"I mean that I will give myself to the task of finding a refuge for those who have suffered such terrible evils as we have witnessed here at Red Wing."

"You will leave here, then?"

"In a day or two."

"To return—when?"

"Never."

Their hands were still clasped across the narrow table. He looked into her eyes, and saw only calm, unflinching resolution. It piqued his self-love that she should be so unmoved. Warmly as he really loved her, self-sacrificing as he felt himself to be in giving her up, he could not yet rid himself of the thought of her Northern birth, and felt annoyed that she should excel him in the gentle quality of self-control. He had no idea that he would ever meet her again. He had made up his mind to leave her out of his life forever, though he could not cast her out of his heart. And yet, although he had no right to expect it, he somehow felt disappointed that she showed no more regret. He had not quite looked for her to be so calm, and he was almost annoyed by it; so dropping her hand, he said, weakly,

"Shall I never see you again?"

"Perhaps"—quietly.

"When?"

"When you are willing to acknowledge yourself proud of me because of the work in which I have been engaged! Hesden Le Moyne," she continued, rising, and standing before him, "you are a brave man and a proud one. You are so brave that you would not hesitate to acknowledge your regard for me, despite the fact that I am a 'nigger-teacher.' It is a noble act, and I honor you for it. But I am as proud as you, and have good reason to be, as you will know some day; and I say to you that I would not prize any man's esteem which coupled itself with an apology for the work in which I have been engaged. I count that work my highest honor, and am more jealous of its renown than of even my own good name. When you can say to me, 'I am as proud of your work as of my own honor—so proud that I wish it to be known of all men, and that all men should know that I approve,' then you may come to me. Till then, farewell!"

She held out her hand. He pressed it an instant, took his hat from the table, and went out into the night, dazed and blinded by the brightness he had left behind.

CHAPTER LI.

HOW SLEEP THE BRAVE?

TWO DAYS AFTERWARD, Mollie Ainslie took the train for the North, accompanied by Lugena and her children. At the same time went Captain Pardee, under instructions from Hesden Le Moyne to verify the will, discover who the testator really was, and then ascertain whether he had any living heirs.

To Mollie Ainslie the departure was a sad farewell to a life which she had entered upon so full of abounding hope and charity, so full of love for God and man, that she could not believe that all her bright hopes had withered and only ashes remained. The way was dark. The path was hedged up. The South was "redeemed."

The poor, ignorant white man had been unable to perceive that liberty for the slave meant elevation to him also. The poor, ignorant colored man had shown himself, as might well have been anticipated, unable to cope with intelligence, wealth, and the subtle power of the best trained political intellects of the nation; and it was not strange. They were all alone, and their allies were either as poor and weak as themselves, or were handicapped with the brand of Northern birth. These were their allies—not from choice, but from necessity. Few, indeed, were there of the highest and the best of those who had fought the nation in war as they had fought against the tide of liberty before the war began—who would accept the terms on which the nation gave re-established and greatly-increased power to the States of the South.

So there were ignorance and poverty and a hated race upon one side, and, upon the other, intelligence, wealth, and pride. The former *outnumbered* the latter; but the latter, as compared with the former, were a Grecian phalanx matched against a scattered horde of Scythian bowmen.[94] The Nation gave the jewel of liberty into the hands of the former, armed them with the weapons of self-government, and said: "Ye are many; protect what ye have received." Then it took away its hand, turned away its eyes, closed its ears to every cry of protest or of agony, and said: "We will not aid you nor protect you. Though you are ignorant, from you will we demand the works of wisdom. Though you are weak, great things shall be required at your hands." Like the ancient taskmaster, the Nation said: "*There shall no straw be given you, yet shall ye deliver the tale of bricks.*"[95]

But, alas! they were weak and inept. The weapon they had received was two-edged. Sometimes they cut themselves; again they caught it by the blade, and those with whom they fought seized the hilt and made terrible slaughter. Then, too, they were not always wise—which was a sore fault, but not their own. Nor were they always brave, or true—which was another grievous fault; but was it to be believed that one hour of liberty would efface the scars of generations of slavery? Ah! well might they cry unto the Nation, as did Israel unto Pharaoh: "There is no straw given unto thy servants, and they say to us, 'Make brick': and behold thy servants are beaten; but the fault is in thine own people."[96] They had simply demonstrated that in the years of Grace of the nineteenth century liberty could not be maintained nor prosperity achieved by ignorance and poverty, any more than in the days of Moses adobe bricks could be made without straw. The Nation gave the power of the South into the hands of ignorance and poverty and inexperience, and then demanded of them the fruit of intelligence, the strength of riches, and the skill of experience. It put before a keen-eyed and unscrupulous minority—a minority proud, aggressive, turbulent, arrogant, and scornful of all things save their own will and pleasure—the temptation to enhance their power by seizing that held by the trembling hands of simple-minded and unskilled guardians. What wonder that it was ravished[97] from their care?

Mollie Ainslie thought of these things with some bitterness. She did not doubt the outcome. Her faith in truth and liberty, and her proud confidence in the ultimate destiny of the grand Nation whose past she had worshiped from childhood, were too strong to permit that. She believed that some time in the future light would come out of the darkness; but between then and the present was a great gulf, whose depth of horror no man knew, in which the people to serve whom she had given herself must sink and suffer—she could not tell how long. For them there was no hope.

She did not, indeed, look for a continuance of the horrors which then prevailed. She knew that when the incentive was removed the acts would cease. There would be peace, because there would no longer be any need for violence. But she was sure there would be no real freedom, no equality of right, no certainty of justice. She did not care who ruled, but she knew that this people—she felt almost like calling them *her* people—needed the incentive of liberty, the inspiriting rivalry of open and fair competition, to enable them to rise. Ay, to prevent them from sinking lower and lower. She greatly feared that the words of a journal which gloried in all that had been done toward abbreviating and annulling the powers, rights, and opportunities of the recent slaves might yet become verities if these people were deprived of such incentives. She remembered how deeply-rooted in the Southern mind was the idea that slavery was a social necessity. She did not believe, as so many had insisted, that it was founded merely in greed. She believed that it was with sincere conviction that a leading journal had declared: "The evils of free society are insufferable. Free society must fail and give way to a *class society*—a social system old as the world, universal as man."[98]

She knew that the leader of a would-be nation had declared: "A thousand must die as slaves or paupers in order that one gentleman may live. Yet they are cheap to any nation, even at that price."[99]

So she feared that the victors in the *post-bellum* strife which was raging around her would succeed, for a time at least, in establishing this ideal "class society." While the Nation slumbered in indifference, she feared that these men, still full of the spirit of slavery, in the very name of law and order, under the pretense of decency and justice, would re-bind those whose feet had just begun to tread the path of liberty with shackles only less onerous than those which had been dashed from their limbs by red-handed war. As she thought of these things she read the following words from the pen of one who had carefully watched the process of "redemption," and had noted its results and tendency—not bitterly and angrily, as she had done, but coolly and approvingly:

"We would like to engrave a prophecy on stone, to be read of generations in the future. The Negro, in these [the Southern] States, will be slave again or cease to be. His sole refuge from extinction will be in slavery to the white man."*

She remembered to have heard a great man say, on a memorable occasion, that "the forms of law have always been the graves of buried liberties." She feared that, under the "forms" of *subverted* laws, the liberties of a helpless people would indeed be buried. She had little care for the Nation. It was of those she had served and whose future she regarded with such engrossing interest that she thought. She did not dream of remedying the evil. That was beyond her power. She only thought she might save some from its scath. To that she devoted herself.

The day before, she had visited the cemetery where her brother's ashes reposed. She had long ago put a neat monument over his grave, and had herself supplemented the national appropriation for its care. It was a beautiful inclosure, walled with stone, verdant with soft turf, and ornamented with rare shrubbery. Across it ran a little stream, with green banks sloping either way. A single great elm drooped over its bubbling waters. A pleasant drive ran with easy grade and graceful curves down one low hill and up another. The iron gate opened upon a dusty highway. Beside it stood the keeper's neat brick lodge. In front, and a little to the right, lay a sleepy Southern town half hidden in embowering trees. Across the little ravine within the cemetery, upon the level plateau, were the graves, marked, in some cases, by little

* Out of the numerous declarations of this conviction which have been made by the Southern press every year since the war, I have selected one from the *Meridian (Miss.) Mercury* of July 31st, 1880. I have done this simply to show that the sentiment is not yet dead.

square white monuments of polished marble, on which was but the single word, "Unknown." A few bore the names of those who slept below. But on one side there were five long mounds, stretching away, side by side, as wide as the graves were long, and as long as four score graves. Smoothly rounded from end to end, without a break or a sign, they seemed a fit emblem of silence. Where they began, a granite pillar rose high, decked with symbols of glory interspersed with emblems of mourning. Cannon, battered and grim, the worn-out dogs of war, gaped with silent jaws up at the silent sky. No name was carved on base or capital, nor on the marble shield upon the shaft. Only, "Sacred to the memory of the unknown heroes who died—."

How quick the memory fills out the rest! There had been a military prison of the Confederacy just over the hill yonder, where the corn now grew so rank and thick. Twelve thousand men died there and were thrown into those long trenches where are now heaped-up mounds that look like giants' graves—not buried one by one, with coffin, shroud, and funeral rite, but one upon another heaped and piled, until the yawning pit would hold no more. No name was kept, no grave was marked, but in each trench was heaped one undistinguishable mass of dead humanity![100]

Mollie Ainslie, when she had bidden farewell to her brother's grave, looked on these piled-up trenches, scanned the silent shaft, and going into the keeper's office just at hand, read for herself the mournful record:

Known.	94
Unknown	12,032
Total	12,126
Died in—Prison	11,700

As she wandered back to the town, she gleaned from what she had seen a lesson of charity for the people toward whom her heart had been full of hardness.

"It was thus," she said to herself, "that they treated brave foemen of their own race and people, who died, not on the battle-field, but of lingering disease in crowded prison pens, in the midst of pleasant homes and within hearing of the Sabbath chimes. None cared enough to give to each a grave, put up a simple board to mark the spot where love might come and weep—nay, not enough even to make entry of the name of the dead some heart must mourn. And if they did this to their dead foemen and kinsmen, their equals, why should we wonder that they manifest equal barbarity toward the living freedman—their recent slave, now suddenly exalted. *It is the lesson and the fruitage of slavery!*"

And so she made excuse both for the barbarity of war and the savagery which followed it by tracing both to their origin. She did not believe that human nature changed in an hour, but that centuries past bore fruit in centuries to come. She thought that the former master must be healed by the slow medicament of time before he could be able to recognize in all men the sanctity of manhood, as well as that the freedman must be taught to know and to defend his rights.

When she left the cemetery, she mounted Midnight for a farewell ride. The next morning, before he arose, Hesden Le Moyne heard the neigh of his old war-horse, and, springing from his bed, he ran out and found him hitched at his gate. A note was tied with a blue ribbon to his jetty forelock. He removed it, and read:

"I return your noble horse with many thanks for the long loan. May I hope that he will be known henceforth only as Midnight?

"MOLLIE."

He thought he recognized the ribbon as one which he had often seen encircling the neck of the writer, and foolishly treasured it upon his heart as a keepsake.

The train bore away the teacher, and with her the wife and children who fled, not knowing their father's fate, and the lawyer who sought an owner for an estate whose heir was too honorable to hold it wrongfully.

CHAPTER LII.

REDEEMED OUT OF THE HOUSE OF BONDAGE.

THREE MONTHS PASSED peacefully away in Horsford. In the "redeemed" county its "natural rulers" bore sway once more. The crops which Nimbus had cultivated were harvested by a Receiver of the Court. The families that dwelt at Red Wing awaited in sullen silence the outcome of the suits which had been instituted. Of Nimbus and Eliab not a word had been heard. Some thought they had been killed; others that they had fled. The family of Berry Lawson had disappeared from the new home which he had made near "Bre'er Rufe Patterson's," in Hanson County. Some said that they had gone South; others that they had gone East. "Bre'er Rufe" declared that he did not know where they had gone. All he knew was that he was "ober dar ob a Saturday night, an' dar dey was, Sally an' de chillen; an' den he went dar agin ob a Monday mornin' arly, an' dar dey wasn't, nary one ob 'em."

The excitement with regard to the will, and her fear that Hesden was infected with the horrible virus of "Radicalism," had most alarmingly prostrated the invalid of Mulberry Hill. For a long time it was feared that her life of suffering was near its end. Hesden did not leave home at all, except once or twice to attend to some business as the trustee for the fugitive Jackson. Cousin Hetty had become a regular inmate of the house. All the invalid's affection for her dead daughter-in-law seemed to have been transferred to Hetty Lomax. No one could serve her so well. Even Hesden's attentions were less grateful. She spoke freely of the time when she should see Hetty in her sister's place, the mistress of Mulberry Hill. She had given up all fear of the property being claimed by others, since she had heard how small were the chances of discovering an heir whose claims were not barred; and though she had consented to forego her legal rights, she trusted that a way would be found to satisfy any who might be discovered. At any rate, she was sure that her promise would not bind her successor, and, with the usual stubbornness of the chronic invalid, she determined that the estate should not pass out of the family. In any event, she did not expect to live until the finding of an heir, should there chance to be one.

One of the good citizens of the county began to show himself in public for the first time since the raid on Red Wing. An ugly scar stretched from his forehead down along his nose and across his lips and chin. At the least excitement it became red and angry, and gave him at all times a ghastly and malevolent appearance. He was a great hero with the best citizens; was *fêted,* admired, and praised; and was at once made a deputy sheriff under the new *régime.*[101] Another most worthy citizen, the superintendent of a Sabbath-school, and altogether one of the most estimable citizens of the county, had been so seriously affected with a malignant brain-fever since that bloody night that he had not yet left his bed.

The colored men, most of whom from a foolish apprehension had slept in the woods until the election, now began to perceive that the nights were wholesome, and remained in their cabins. They seemed sullen and discontented, and sometimes whispered among themselves of ill-usage and unfair treatment; but they were not noisy and clamorous, as they had been before the work of "redemption." It was especially noted that they were much more respectful and complaisant to their superiors than they had been at any time since the Surrender. The old time "Marse" was now almost universally used, and few "niggers" presumed to speak to a white man in the country districts without removing their hats. In the towns the improvement was not so perceptible. The "sassy" ones seemed to take courage from their numbers, and there they were still sometimes "boisterous" and "obstreperous." On the whole, however, the result seemed eminently satisfactory, with a prospect of growing better every day. Labor was more manageable, and there were much fewer appeals to the law by lazy, impudent, and dissatisfied laborers. The master's word was rarely disputed upon the day of settlement, and there was every prospect of reviving hope and continued prosperity on the part of men who worked their plantations by proxy, and who had been previously very greatly annoyed and discouraged by the persistent clamor of their "hands" for payment.

There had been some ill-natured criticism of the course of Hesden Le Moyne. It was said that he had made some very imprudent remarks, both in regard to the treatment of Jordan Jackson and the affair at Red Wing. There were some, indeed, who openly declared that he had upheld and encouraged the niggers at Red Wing in their insolent and outrageous course, and had used language unworthy of a "Southern gentleman" concerning those patriotic men who had felt called upon, for the protection of their homes and property, to administer the somewhat severe lesson which had no doubt nipped disorder in the bud, saved them from the war of races which had imminently impended, and brought "redemption" to the county. Several of Hesden's personal friends called upon him and remonstrated with him upon his course. Many thought he should be "visited," and "Radicalism in the county stamped out" at once, root and branch. He received warning from the Klan to the effect that he was considered a dangerous character, and must change his tone and take heed to his footsteps. As, however, his inclination to the dangerous doctrines was generally attributed in a great measure to his unfortunate infatuation for the little "nigger-teacher," it was hoped that her absence would effect a cure. Especially was this opinion entertained when it became known that his mother was bitterly opposed to his course, and was fully determined to root the seeds of "Radicalism" from his mind. His attachment for her was well known, and it was generally believed that she might be trusted to turn him from the error of his ways, particularly as she was the owner of Red Wing, and had freely declared her intention not to leave him a foot of it unless he abandoned his absurd and vicious notions. Hesden himself, though he went abroad but little, saw that his friends had grown cool and that his enemies had greatly multiplied.

This was the situation of affairs in the good County of Horsford when, one bright morning in December—the morning of "that day whereon our Saviour's birth is celebrate"—Hesden Le Moyne rode to the depot nearest to his home, purchased two tickets to a Northern city, and, when the morning train came in, assisted his "boy" Charles to lift from a covered wagon which stood near by, the weak and pallid form of the long-lost "nigger preacher," Eliab Hill, and place him upon the train. It was noticed by the loungers about the depot that Hesden carried but half concealed a navy revolver which seemed to have seen service. There was some excitement in the little crowd over the reappearance of Eliab Hill, but he was not interfered with. In fact, the cars moved off so quickly after he was first seen that there was no time to recover from the surprise produced by the unexpected apparition. It was not until the smoke of the engine had disappeared in the distance that the wrath of the bystanders clothed itself in words.

Then the air reeked with expletives. What ought to have been done was discussed with great freedom. An excited crowd gathered around Charles as he was preparing to return home, and plied him with questions. His ignorance was phenomenal, but the look of stupefied wonder with which he regarded his questioners confirmed his words. It was not until he had proceeded a mile on his homeward way, with Midnight in leading behind the tail-board, that, having satisfied himself that there was no one within hearing, by peeping from beneath the canvas covering of the wagon, both before and behind, he tied the reins to one of the bows which upheld the cover, abandoned the mule to his own guidance, and throwing himself upon the mattress on which Eliab had lain, gave vent to roars of laughter.

"Yah, yah, yah!" he cried, as the tears rolled down his black face. "It du take Marse Hesden to wax dem fellers! Dar he war, jest ez cool an' keerless ez yer please, a'standin' roun' an' waitin' fer de train an' payin' no 'tention at all ter me an' de wagon by de platform, dar. Swar, but I war skeered nigh 'bout ter death, till I got dar an' seed him so quiet and keerless; an' Bre'er 'Liab, he war jest a-prayin' all de time—but dat's no wonder. Den, when de train whistle, Marse Hesden turn quick an' sharp an' I seed him gib dat ole pistol a jerk roun' in front, an' he come back an' sed, jest ez cool an' quiet, 'Now, Charles!' I declar' it stiddied me up jes ter hear him, an' den up comes Bre'er 'Liab in my arms. Marse Hesden helps a bit an' goes fru de crowd wid his mouf shet like a steel trap. We takes him on de cars. All aboard! *Whoo-*

oop—puff, puff! Off she goes! an' dat crowd stan's dar a-cussin' all curration an' demselves to boot! Yah, yah, yah! 'Rah for Marse Hesden!"

CHAPTER LIII.

IN THE CYCLONE.

THEN THE STORM burst. Every possible story was set afloat. The more absurd it seemed the more generally was it credited. Men talked and women chattered of nothing but Hesden Le Moyne, his infamous "negro-loving Radicalism," his infatuation with the "Yankee school-marm," the anger of his mother, his ill-treatment of his cousin, Hetty Lomax; his hiding of the "nigger preacher" in the loft of the dining-room, his alliance with the Red Wing desperadoes to "burn every white house on that side of the river"—in short, his treachery, his hypocrisy, his infamy.

On the street, in the stores, at the churches—wherever men met—this was the one unfailing theme of conversation. None but those who have seen a Southern community excited over one subject or one man can imagine how much can be said about a little matter. The newspapers of that and the adjoining counties were full of it. Colored men were catechized in regard to it. His friends vied with his enemies in vituperation, lest they should be suspected of a like offense. He was accounted a monster by many, and an enemy by all who had been his former associates, and, strangely enough, was at once looked upon as a friend and ally by every colored man, and by the few white men of the county who secretly or silently held with the "Radicals." It was the baptism of fire which every Southern man must face who presumes to differ from his fellows upon political questions.

Nothing that he had previously done or said or been could excuse or palliate his conduct. The fact that he was of a good family only rendered his alliance with "niggers" against his own race and class the more infamous. The fact that he was a man of substantial means, and had sought no office or aggrandizement by the votes of colored men, made his offence the more heinous, because he could not even plead the poor excuse of self-interest. The fact that he had served the Confederacy well, and bore on his person the indubitable proof of gallant conduct on the field of battle, was a still further aggravation of his act, because it marked him as a renegade and a traitor to the cause for which he had fought. Compared with a Northern Republican he was accounted far more infamous, because of his desertion of his family, friends, comrades, and "the cause of the South"—a vague something which no man can define, but which "fires the Southern heart" with wonderful facility. Comparison with the negro was still more to his disadvantage, since he had "sinned against light and knowledge," while they did not even know their own "best friends." And so the tide of detraction ebbed and flowed while Hesden was absent, his destination unknown, his return a matter of conjecture, and his purpose a mystery.

The most generally-accepted theory was that he had gone to Washington for the purpose of maliciously misrepresenting and maligning the good people of Horsford, in order to secure the stationing of soldiers in that vicinity, and their aid in arresting and bringing to trial, for various offences against the peace and persons of the colored people, some of the leading citizens of the county.[102] In support of this they cited his intimate relations with Jordan Jackson, as well as with Nimbus and Eliab. It was soon reported that Jackson had met him at Washington; that Nimbus Desmit had also arrived there; that the whole party had been closeted with this and that leading "Radical"; and that the poor, stricken, down-trodden South—the land fairest and richest and poorest and most peaceful and most chivalric, the most submissive and the most defiant; in short, the most contradictory in its self-conferred superlatives—that this land of antipodal excellences must now look for new forms of tyranny and new measures of oppression.

The secrecy which had been preserved for three months in regard to Eliab's place of concealment made a most profound impression upon Hesden's neighbors of the County of Horsford. They spoke of it in low, horrified tones, which showed that they felt deeply in regard to it. It was ascertained that no one in his family knew of the presence of Eliab until the morning of his removal. Miss Hetty made haste to declare that in her two months and more of attendance upon the invalid she had never dreamed of such a thing. The servants stoutly denied all knowledge of it, except Charles, who could not get out of having cut the door through into the other room. It was believed that Hesden had himself taken all the care of the injured man, whose condition was not at all understood. How badly he had been hurt, or in what manner, none could tell. Many visited the house to view the place of concealment. Only the closed doors could be seen, for Hesden had taken the key with him. Some suggested that Nimbus was still concealed there, and several advised Mrs. Le Moyne to get some one to go into the room. However, as no one volunteered to go, nothing came of this advice. It was rumored, too, that Hesden had brought into the county several detectives, who had stolen into the hearts of the unsuspecting people of Horsford, and had gone Northward loaded down with information that would make trouble for some of the "best men."

It was generally believed that the old attic over the dining-room had long been a place where "Radicals" had been wont to meet in solemn conclave to "plot against the whites." A thousand things were remembered which confirmed this view. It was here that Hesden had harbored the detectives, as Rahab[103] had hidden the spies. It was quite evident that he had for a long time been an emissary of the Government at Washington, and no one could guess what tales of outrage he might not fabricate in order to glut his appetite for inhuman revenge. The Southern man is always self-conscious. He thinks the world has him in its eye, and that he about fills the eye. This does not result from comparative depreciation of others so much as from a habit of magnifying his own image. He always poses for effect. He walks, talks, and acts "as if he felt the eyes of Europe on his tail,"[104] almost as much as the peacock.

There are times, however, when even he does not care to be seen, and it was observed that about this time there were a goodly number of the citizens of Horsford who modestly retired from the public gaze, some of them even going into remote States with some precipitation and an apparent desire to remain for a time unknown.[105] It was even rumored that Hesden was with Nimbus, disguised as a negro, in the attack made on the Klan during the raid on Red Wing, and that, by means of the detectives, he had discovered every man engaged in that patriotic affair, as well as those concerned in others of like character. The disappearance of these men was, of course, in no way connected with this rumor. Since the "Southern people" have become the great jesters of the world, their conduct is not at all to be judged by the ordinary rules of cause and effect as applied to human action. It might have been mere buffoonery, quite as well as modesty, that possessed some of the "best citizens of Horsford" with an irrepressible desire to view the Falls of Niagara from the Canadian side in mid-winter. There is no accounting for the acts of a nation of masqueraders!

But perhaps the most generally-accepted version of Hesden's journey was that he had run away to espouse Mollie Ainslie. To her was traced his whole bias toward the colored population and "Radical" principles. Nothing evil was said of her character. She was admitted to be as good as anybody of her class could be—intelligent, bigoted, plucky, pretty, and malicious. It was a great pity that a man belonging to a good family should become infatuated by one in her station. He could never bring her home, and she would never give up her "nigger-equality notions." She had already dragged him down to what he was. Such a man as he, it was strenuously asserted, would not degrade himself to stand up for such a man as Jordan Jackson or to associate with "niggers," without some powerful extraneous influence. That influence was Mollie Ainslie, who, having inveigled him into "Radicalism," had now drawn him after her into the North and matrimony.

But nowhere did the conduct of Hesden cause more intense or conflicting feelings than at Mulberry Hill. His achievement in succoring, hiding, and finally rescuing Eliab Hill was a source of never-ending wonder, applause, and mirth in the kitchen. But Miss Hetty could not find words to express her anger and chagrin. Without being at all forward or immodest, she had desired to succeed her dead sister in the good graces of Hesden Le Moyne, as well as in the position of mistress of the Hill. It was a very natural and proper feeling. They were cousins, had always been neighbors, and Hesden's mother had encouraged the idea, almost from the time of his first wife's death. It was no wonder that she was jealous of the Yankee school-marm. Love is keen-eyed, and she really loved her cousin. She had become satisfied, during her stay at the Hill, that he was deeply attached to Mollie Ainslie, and knew him too well to hope that he would change. Such a conviction was, of course, not pleasant to her vanity. But when she was convinced that he had degraded himself and her by espousing "Radicalism" and associating with "niggers," her wrath knew no bounds. It seemed an especial insult to her that the man whom she had honored with her affection should have so demeaned himself.

Mrs. Le Moyne was at first astonished, then grieved, and finally angry. She especially sympathized with Hetty, the wreck of whose hope she saw in this revelation. If Mollie Ainslie had been "one of our people," instead of "a Northern nigger school-teacher," there would have been nothing so very bad about it. He had never professed any especial regard or tenderness for Miss Hetty, and had never given her any reason to expect a nearer relation than she had always sustained toward him. Mollie was good enough in her way, bright and pretty and—but faugh! the idea! She would not believe it! Hesden was not and could not be a "Radical." He might have sheltered Eliab—ought to have done so; that she *would* say. He had been a slave of the family, and had a right to look to her son for protection. But to be a

"Radical!" She would not believe it. There was no use of talking to her. She remained stubbornly silent after she had gotten to the conclusive denial: "He could not do it!"

Nevertheless, she thought it well to use her power while she had any. If he was indeed a "Radical," she would never forgive him—never! So she determined to make her will. A man learned in the law was brought to the Hill, and Hester Le Moyne, in due form, by her last will and testament devised the plantation to her beloved son Hesden Le Moyne, and her affectionate cousin Hetty Lomax, jointly, and to their heirs forever, on condition that the said devisees should intermarry with each other within one year from the death of the devisor; and in case either of the said devisees should refuse to intermarry with the other, then the part of such devisee was to go to the other, who should thereafter hold the fee in severalty, free of all claim from the other.

The New York and Boston papers contained, day after day, this "personal:"

> "The heirs of James Richards, deceased, formerly of Marblehead, Massachusetts, will learn something to their advantage by addressing Theron Pardee, care of James & Jones, Attorneys, at No.—Broadway, N. Y."

Mrs. Le Moyne was well aware of this, and also remembered her promise to surrender the estate, should an heir be found. But that promise had been made under the influence of Hesden's ardent zeal for the right, and she found by indirection many excuses for avoiding its performance. "Of course," she said to herself, "if heirs should be found in my lifetime, I would revoke this testament; but it is not right that I should bind those who come after me for all time to yield to his Quixotic notions. Besides, why should I be juster than the law? This property has been in the family for a long time, and ought to remain there."

Her anger at Hesden burned very fiercely, and she even talked of refusing to see him, should he return, as she had no real doubt he would. The excitement, however, prostrated her as usual, and her anger turned into querulous complainings as she grew weaker.

The return of Hesden, hardly a week after his departure, brought him to face this tide of vituperation at its flood. All that had been said and written and done in regard to himself came forthwith to his knowledge. He was amazed, astounded for a time, at the revelation. He had not expected it. He had expected anger, and was prepared to meet it with forbearance and gentleness; but he was not prepared for detraction and calumny and insult.

He had not been so very much surprised at the odium which had been heaped upon Jordan Jackson. He belonged to that class of white people at the South to whom the better class owed little duty or regard. It was not so strange that they should slander that man. He could understand, too, how it was that they attributed to the colored people such incredible depravity, such capacity for evil, such impossible designs, as well as the reason why they invented for every Northern man that came among them with ideas different from their own a fictitious past, reeking with infamy.

He could sympathize in some degree with all of this. He had not thought, himself, that it was altogether the proper thing for the illiterate "poor-white" man, Jordan Jackson, to lead the negroes of the county in political hostility to the whites. He had felt naturally the distrust of the man of Northern birth which a century of hostility and suspicion had bred in the air of the South. He had grown up in it. He had been taught to regard the "Yankees" (which meant all Northerners) as a distinct people—sometimes generous and brave, but normally envious, mean, low-spirited, treacherous, and malignant. He admitted the exceptions, but they only proved the rule. As a class he considered them cold, calculating, selfish, greedy of power and wealth, and regardless of the means by which these were acquired. Above all things, he had been taught to regard them as animated by hatred of the South. Knowing that this had been his own bias, he could readily excuse his neighbors for the same.

But in his own case it was different. *He* was one of themselves. They knew him to be brave, honorable, of good family, of conservative instincts, fond of justice and fair play, and governed in his actions only by the sincerest conviction. That they should accuse him of every mean and low impossibility of act and motive, and befoul his holiest purposes and thoughts, was to him a most horrible thing. His anger grew hotter and hotter, as he listened to each new tale of infamy which a week had sufficed to set afloat. Then he heard his mother's reproaches, and saw that even her love was not proof against a mere change of political sentiment on his part. These things set him to thinking as he had never thought before. The scales fell from his eyes, and from the kindly gentle Southern man of knightly instincts and gallant achievements was born—the "pestiferous Radical." He did not hesitate to avow his conviction, and from that moment there was around him a wall of fire. He had lost his rank, degraded his caste, and fallen from his high estate. From and after that moment he was held unworthy to wear the proud appellation, "A Southern Gentleman."

However, as he took no active part in political life, and depended in no degree upon the patronage or good will of his neighbors for a livelihood, he felt the force of this feeling only in his social relations. Unaware, as yet, of the disherison[106] which his mother had visited upon him in his absence, he continued to manage the plantation and conduct all the business pertaining to it in his own name, as he had done ever since the close of the war. At first he entertained a hope that the feeling against him would die out. But as time rolled on, and it continued still potent and virulent, he came to analyze it more closely, judging his fellows by himself, and saw that it was the natural fruit of that intolerance which slavery made necessary—which was essential to its existence. Then he no longer wondered at them, but at himself. It did not seem strange that they should feel as they did, but rather that he should so soon have escaped from the tyrannical bias of mental habit. He saw that the struggle against it must be long and bitter, and he determined not to yield his convictions to the prejudices of others.

It was a strange thing. In one part of the country—and that the greater in numbers, in wealth, in enterprise and vigor, in average intelligence and intellectual achievements—the sentiments he had espoused were professed and believed by a great party which prided itself upon its intelligence, purity, respectability, and devotion to principle. In two thirds of the country his sentiments were held to be honorable, wise, and patriotic. Every act he had performed, every principle he had reluctantly avowed, would there have been applauded of all men. Nay, the people of that portion of the country were unable to believe that any one could seriously deny those principles. Yet in the other portion, where he lived, they were esteemed an ineffaceable brand of shame, which no merit of a spotless life could hide.

The *Southern Clarion,* a newspaper of the County of Horsford, in referring to his conduct, said:

> "Of all such an example should be made. Inaugurate social ostracism against every white man who gives any support to the Radical Party. Every true Southern man or woman should refuse to recognize as a gentleman any man belonging to that party, or having any dealings with it. Hesden Le Moyne has chosen to degrade an honored name. He has elected to go with niggers, nigger teachers, and nigger preachers; but let him forever be an outcast among the respectable and high-minded white people of Horsford, whom he has betrayed and disgraced!"

A week later, it contained another paragraph:

"We understand that the purpose of Hesden Le Moyne in going to the North was not entirely to stir up Northern prejudice and hostility against our people. At least, that is what he claims. He only went, we are informed he says, to take the half-monkey negro preacher who calls himself Eliab Hill to a so-called college in the North to complete his education. We shall no doubt soon have this misshapen, malicious hypocrite paraded through the North as an evidence of Southern barbarity.

"The truth is, as we are credibly informed, that the injuries he received on the night of the raid upon Red Wing were purely accidental. There were some in the company, it seems, who were disappointed at not finding the black desperado, Nimbus Desmit, who was organizing his depraved followers to burn, kill, and ravish, and proposed to administer a moderate whipping to the fellow Eliab, who was really supposed to be at the bottom of all the other's rascality. These few hot-heads burst in the door of his cabin, but one of the oldest and coolest of the crowd rushed in and, at the imminent risk of his own life, rescued him from them. In order to bring him out into the light where he could be protected, he caught the baboon-like creature by his foot, and he was somewhat injured thereby. He is said to have been shot also, but we are assured that not a shot was fired, except by some person with a repeating rifle, who fired upon the company of white men from the woods beyond the school-house. It is probable that some of these shots struck the preacher, and it is generally believed that they were fired by Hesden Le Moyne. Several who were there have expressed the opinion that, from the manner in which the shooting was done, it must have been by a man with one arm. However, Eliab will make a good Radical show, and we shall have another dose of Puritanical, hypocritical cant about Southern barbarity. Well, we can bear it. We have got the power in Horsford, and we mean to hold it. Niggers and nigger-worshippers must take care of themselves. This is a white man's country, and white men are going to rule it, no matter whether the North whines or not."

The report given in this account of the purpose of Hesden's journey to the North was the correct one. In the three months in which the deformed man had been under his care, he had learned that a noble soul and a rare mind were shut up in that crippled form, and had determined to atone for his former coolness and doubt, as well as mark his approval of the course of this hunted victim, by giving him an opportunity to develop his powers. He accordingly placed him in a Northern college, and became responsible for the expenses of his education.

CHAPTER LIV.

A BOLT OUT OF THE CLOUD.

A YEAR HAD passed, and there had been no important change in the relations of the personages of our story. The teacher and her "obstreperous" pupils had disappeared from Horsford and had been almost forgotten. Hesden, his mother, and Cousin Hetty still led their accustomed life at The Hill. Detraction had worn itself out upon the former, for want of a new occasion. He was still made to feel, in the little society which he saw, that he was a black sheep in an otherwise spotless fold. He did not complain. He did not account himself "ostracized," nor wonder at this treatment. He saw how natural it was, how consistent with the training and development his neighbors had received. He simply said to himself, and to the few friends who still met him kindly, "I can do without the society of others as long as they can do without mine. I can wait. This thing must end some time—if not in my day, then afterward. Our people must come out of it and rise above it. They must learn that to be Americans is better than to be 'Southern.' Then they will see that the interests and safety of the whole nation demand the freedom and political co-equality of all."

These same friends comforted him much as did those who argued with the man of Uz.[107]

Mrs. Le Moyne's life had gone back to its old channel. Shut out from the world, she saw only the fringes of the feeling that had set so strongly against her son. Indeed, she received perhaps more attention than usual in the way of calls and short visits, since she was understood to have manifested a proper spirit of resentment at his conduct. Hesden himself was almost the only one who did not know of her will. It was thought, of course, that she was holding it over him *in terrorem.*

Yet he was just as tender and considerate of her as formerly, and she was apparently just as fond of him. She had not yet given up her plan of a matrimonial alliance for him with Cousin Hetty, but that young lady herself had quite abandoned the notion. In the year she had been at Mulberry Hill she had come to know Hesden better, and to esteem him more highly than ever before. She knew that he regarded her with none of the feeling his mother desired to see between them, but they had become good friends, and after a short time she was almost the only one of his relatives that had not allowed his political views to sunder their social relations. Living in the same house, it was of course impossible to maintain a constant state of siege; but she had gone farther, and had held out a flag of truce, and declared her conviction of the honesty of his views and the honorableness of his *intention.* She did not think as he did, but she had finally become willing to let him think for himself. People said she was in love with Hesden, and that with his mother's aid she would yet conquer his indifference. She did not think so. She sighed when she confessed the fact to herself. She did indeed hope that he had forgotten Mollie Ainslie. She could never live to see her mistress at the dear old Hill!

The term of the court was coming on at which the suits that had been brought by Winburn against the occupants of Red Wing must be tried. Many had left the place, and it was noticed that from all who desired to leave, Theron Pardee had purchased, at the full value, the titles which they held under Nimbus, and that they had all gone off somewhere out West. Others had elected to remain, with a sort of blind faith that all would come out right after a while, or from mere disinclination to leave familiar scenes—that feeling which is always so strong in the African race.

It was at this time that Pardee came one day to Mulberry Hill and announced his readiness to make report in the matter intrusted to his charge concerning the will of J. Richards.

"Well," said Hesden, "have you found the heirs?"

"I beg your pardon, Mr. Le Moyne," said Pardee; "I have assumed a somewhat complicated relation to this matter, acting under the spirit of my instructions, which makes it desirable, perhaps almost necessary, that I should confer directly with the present owner of this plantation, and that is—?"

"My mother," said Hesden, as he paused. "I suppose it will be mine some time," he continued laughing, "but I have no present interest in it."

"Yes," said the lawyer. "And is Mrs. Le Moyne's health such as to permit her considering this matter now?"

"Oh, I think so," said Hesden. "I will see her and ascertain.

In a short time the attorney was ushered into the invalid's room, where Mrs. Le Moyne, reclining on her beautifully decorated couch, received him pleasantly, exclaiming,

"You will see how badly off I am for company, Captain Pardee, when I assure you that I am glad to see even a lawyer with such a bundle of papers as you have brought. I have literally nobody but these two children," glancing at Hesden and Hetty, "and I declare I believe I am younger and more cheerful than either of them."

"Your cheerfulness, madam," replied Pardee, "is an object of universal remark and wonder. I sincerely trust that nothing in these papers will at all affect your equanimity."

"But what have you in that bundle, Captain?" she asked. "I assure you that I am dying to know why you should insist on assailing a sick woman with such a formidable array of documents."

"Before proceeding to satisfy your very natural curiosity, madam," answered Pardee, with a glance at Miss Hetty, "permit me to say that my communication is of great moment to you as the owner of this plantation, and to your son as your heir, and is of such a character that you might desire to consider it carefully before it should come to the knowledge of other parties."

"Oh, never mind Cousin Hetty," said Mrs. Le Moyne quickly. "She has just as much interest in the matter as any one."

The lawyer glanced at Hesden, who hastened to say,

"I am sure there can be nothing of interest to me which I would not be willing that my cousin should know."

The young lady rose to go, but both Hesden and Mrs. Le Moyne insisted on her remaining.

"Certainly," said Pardee, "there can be no objection on my part. I merely called your attention to the fact as a part of my duty as your legal adviser."

So Miss Hetty remained sitting upon the side of the bed, holding one of the invalid's hands. Pardee seated himself at a small table near the bed, and, having arranged his papers so that they would be convenient for reference, began:

"You will recollect, madam, that the task intrusted to me was twofold; first, to verify this will found by your son and ascertain whose testament it was, its validity or invalidity; and, in case it was valid, its effect and force. Secondly, I was directed to make all reasonable effort, in case of its validity being established, to ascertain the existence of any one entitled to take under its provisions. In this book," said he, holding up a small volume, "I have kept a diary of all that I have done in regard to the matter, with dates and places. It will give you in detail what I shall now state briefly.

"I went to Lancaster, where the will purports to have been executed, and ascertained its genuineness by proving the signatures of the attesting witnesses, and established also the fact of their death. These affidavits"—holding up a bundle of papers—"show that I also inquired as to the testator's identity; but I could learn nothing except that the descendants of one of the witnesses who had bought your ancestor's farm, upon his removal to the South, still had his deed in possession. I copied it, and took a tracing of the signature, which is identical with that which he subsequently used—James Richards, written in a heavy and somewhat sloping hand, for that time. I could learn nothing more in regard to him or his family.

"Proceeding then to Marblehead, I learned these facts. There were two parties named James Richards. They were cousins; and in order to distinguish them from each other they were called by the family and neighbors, 'Red Jim' and 'Black Jim' respectively—the one having red hair and blue eyes, and the other dark hair and black eyes."

"Yes," interrupted Mrs. Le Moyne, "I was the only blonde in my family, and I have often heard my father say that I got it from some ancestral strain, perhaps the Whidbys, and resembled his cousins."

"Yes," answered Pardee, "a Whidby was a common ancestress of your father and his cousin, 'Red Jim.' It is strange how family traits reproduce themselves in widely-separated strains of blood."

"Well," said Hesden, "did you connect him with this will?"

"Most conclusively," was the reply. "In the first place, his wife's name was Edna—Edna Goddard—before marriage, and he left an only daughter, Alice. He was older than his cousin, 'Black Jim,' to whom he was greatly attached. The latter removed to Lancaster, when about twenty-five years of age, having inherited a considerable estate in that vicinity. I had not thought of examining the record of wills while in Lancaster, but on my return I went to the Prothonotary's office, and verified this also. So there is no doubt about the 'Black Jim' of the Marblehead family being your ancestor."

"Stop! stop! Captain Pardee!" interrupted Mrs. Le Moyne quickly. "Isn't Marblehead near Cape Cod?"

"Yes, madam."

"And Buzzard's Bay?"

"Certainly."

"No wonder," said she, laughing, "that you wanted Hetty to leave before you opened your budget. Do pray run away, child, before you hear any more to our discredit. Hesden, do please escort your cousin out of the room," she added, in assumed distress.

"No indeed," laughed Miss Hetty; "I am getting interested, and as you would not let me go when I wished to, I have now determined to stay till the last horror is revealed."

"It is too late, mother," said Hesden ruefully; "fortunately, Cousin Hetty is not attainted, except collaterally, thus far."

"Well, go on, Captain," said Mrs. Le Moyne gayly. "What else? Pray what was the family occupation—'calling' I believe they say in New England. I suppose they had some calling, as they never have any 'gentlemen' in that country."

Pardee's face flushed hotly. He was born among the New Hampshire hills himself. However, he answered calmly, but with a slight emphasis,

"They were seafaring men, madam."

"Oh, my!" cried the invalid, clapping her hands. "Codfish! codfish! I knew it, Hetty! I knew it! Why didn't you go out of the room when I begged you to? Do you hear it, Hesden? That is where you get your Radicalism from. My! my!" she laughed, almost hysterically, "what a family! Codfish at one end and Radical at the other! 'And the last state of that man was worse than the first!' What would not the newspapers give to know that of you, Hesden?"

She laughed until the tears came, and her auditors laughed with her. Yet, despite her mirth, it was easy to detect the evidence of strong feeling in her manner. She carried it off bravely, however, and said,

"But, perhaps, Captain Pardee, you can relieve us a little. Perhaps they were not cod-fishers but mackerelers. I remember a song I have heard my father sing, beginning,

> "When Jake came home from mack'reling,
> He sought his Sary Ann,
> And found that she, the heartless thing,
> Had found another man!"

"Do please say that they were mackerelers!"

"I am sorry I cannot relieve your anxiety on that point," said Pardee, "but I can assure you they were a very respectable family."

"No doubt, as families *go* there," she answered, with some bitterness. "They doubtless sold good fish, and gave a hundred pounds for a quintal, or whatever it is they sell the filthy truck by."

"They were very successful and somewhat noted privateers during the Revolution," said Pardee.

"Worse and worse!" said Mrs. Le Moyne. "Better they were fishermen than pirates! I wonder if they didn't bring over niggers too?"

"I should not be at all surprised," answered Pardee coolly. "This 'Red Jim' was master and owner of a vessel of some kind, and was on his way back from Charleston, where it seems he had sold both his vessel and cargo, when he executed this will."

"But how do you know that it *is* his will?" asked Hesden.

"Oh, there is no doubt," said Pardee. "Being a shipmaster, his signature was necessarily affixed to many papers. I have found not less than twenty of these, all identical with the signature of the will."

"That would certainly seem to be conclusive," said Hesden.

"Taken with other things, it is," answered Pardee. "Among other things is a letter from your grandfather, which was found pasted inside the cover of a Bible that belonged to Mrs. Edna Richards, in regard to the death of her husband. In it he says that his cousin visited him on his way home; went from there to Philadelphia, and was taken sick; your grandfather was notified and went on, but death had taken place before he arrived. The letter states that he had but little money and no valuable papers except such as he sent. Out of the money he had paid the funeral expenses, and would remit the balance as soon as he could make an opportunity. The tradition in 'Red Jim's' family is that he died of yellow fever in Philadelphia, on his way home with the proceeds of his sale, and was robbed of his money before the arrival of his cousin. No suspicion seems ever to have fallen on 'Black Jim.'"[108]

"Thank God for that!" ejaculated Hesden fervently.

"I suppose you took care to awaken none," said Mrs. Le Moyne.

"I spoke of it to but one person, to whom it became absolutely necessary to reveal it. However, it is perfectly safe, and will go no farther."

"Well, did you find any descendants of this 'Red Jim' living?" asked Mrs. Le Moyne.

"One," answered Pardee.

"Only one?" said she. "I declare, Hesden, the Richards family is not numerous if it is strong."

"Why do you say 'strong,' mother?"

"Oh, codfish and Radicals, you know!"

"Now, mother—"

"Oh, if you hate to hear about it, why don't you quit the dirty crowd and be a gentleman again. Or is it your new-found cousin you feel so bad for? By the way, Captain, is it a boy or girl, and is it old or young?"

"It is a lady, madam, some twenty years of age or thereabout."

"A lady? Well, I suppose that it what they call them there. Married or single?"

"Single."

"What a pity you are getting so old, Hesden! You might make a match and settle her claim in that way. Though I don't suppose she has any in law."

"On the contrary, madam," said Pardee, "her title is perfect. She can recover not only this plantation but every rood of the original tract."

"You don't say!" exclaimed the invalid. "It would make her one of the richest women in the State!"

"Undoubtedly."

"Oh, it cannot be, Captain Pardee!" exclaimed Miss Hetty. "It cannot be!"

"There can be no doubt about it," said Pardee. "She is the great-granddaughter of 'Red Jim,' and his only lineal descendant. His daughter Alice, to whom this is bequeathed, married before arriving at the age of eighteen, and died in wedlock, leaving an only daughter, who also married before she became of age, and also died in wedlock, leaving a son and daughter surviving. The son died without heirs of his body, and only the daughter is left. There has never been an hour when the action of the statute was not barred."[109]

"Have you seen her?" asked Mrs. Le Moyne.

"Yes."

"Does she know her good luck?"

"She is fully informed of her rights."

"Indeed? You told her, I suppose?"

"I found her already aware of them."

"Why, how could that be?"

"I am sure I do not know," said Pardee, glancing sharply at Hesden.

"What," said Hesden, with a start; "what did you say is the name of the heir?"

"I did not say," said Pardee coolly. Hesden sprang to his feet, and going across the room stood gazing out of the window.

"Why don't you tell us the name of the heir, Captain? You must know we are dying to hear all about our new cousin," said Mrs. Le Moyne bitterly. "Is she long or short, fat or lean, dark or fair? Do tell us all about her?"

"In appearance, madam," said Pardee carelessly, "I should say she much resembled yourself at her age."

"Oh, Captain, you flatter me, I'm sure," she answered, with just a hint of a sneer. "Well, what is her name, and when does she wish to take possession?"

"Her name, madam, you must excuse me if I withhold for the present. I am the bearer of a proposition of compromise from her, which, if accepted, will, I hope, avoid all trouble. If not accepted, I shall find myself under the necessity of asking to be relieved from further responsibility in this matter."

"Come here, Hesden," said his mother, "and hear what terms your new cousin wants for Mulberry Hill. I hope we won't have to move out till spring. It would be mighty bad to be out of doors all winter. Go on, Captain Pardee, Hesden is ready now. This is what comes of your silly idea about doing justice to some low-down Yankee. It's a pity you hadn't sense enough to burn the will up. It would have been better all round. The wealth will turn the girl's head, and the loss of my home will kill me," she continued fiercely to her son.

"As to the young lady, you need have no fear," said Pardee. "She is not one of the kind that lose their heads.

"Ah, you seem to be quite an admirer of her?"

"I am, madam."

"If we do not accept her proposal, you will no doubt become her attorney?"

"I am such already."

"You don't say so? Well, you are making good speed. I should think you might have waited till you had dropped us before picking her up. But then, it will be a good thing to be the attorney of such an heiress, and we shall be poor indeed after she gets her own—as you say it is."

"Madam," said Pardee seriously, "I shall expect you to apologize both to me and to my client when you have heard her proposition."

"I shall be very likely to, Mr. Pardee," she said, with a dry laugh. "I come of an apologetic race. Old Jim Richards was full of apologies. He liked to have died of them, numberless times. But what is your proposal?"

"As I said," remarked Pardee, "my client—I beg pardon—the great-granddaughter of 'Red Jim' Richards, instructs me to say that she does not desire to stain her family name or injure your feelings by exposing the fraud of your ancestor, 'Black Jim' Richards.

"What, sir!" said Mrs. Le Moyne sharply. "Fraud! You had better measure your words, sir, when you speak of my father. Do you hear that, Hesden? Have you lost all spirit since you became a Radical?" she continued, while her eyes flashed angrily.

"I am sorry to say that I do not see what milder term could be used," said Hesden calmly. "Go on with your proposition, sir."

"Well, as I said," continued the lawyer, "this young lady, desiring to save the family name and your feelings from the shock of exposure, has instructed me to say: First, that she does not wish to disturb any of those rights which have been obtained by purchase from your ancestor; and second, that she understands that there is a dispute in regard to the title of a portion of it—the tract generally known as Red Wing—neither of the parties claiming which have any title as against her. She understands that the title held by Winburn is technically good against that of the colored man, Nimbus Desmit, providing hers is not set up.

"Now she proposes that if you will satisfy Winburn and obtain a quit-claim[110] from him to Desmit, she will make a deed in fee[111] to Mrs. Le Moyne of the whole tract; and as you hold by inheritance from one who purported to convey the fee, the title will thereafter be estopped,[112] and all rights held under the deeds of 'Black Jim' Richards will be confirmed."

"Well, what else?" asked Mrs. Le Moyne breathlessly, as he paused.

"There is nothing more."

"Nothing more! Why, does the girl propose to give away all this magnificent property for nothing?" she asked in astonishment.

"Absolutely nothing to her own comfort or advantage," answered the attorney.

"Well, now, that is kind—that *is* kind!" said the invalid. "I *am* sorry for what I have said of her, Captain Pardee."

"I thought you would be, madam," he replied.

"You must attend to that Red Wing matter immediately, Hesden," she said, thoughtfully.

"You accept the proposal then?" asked Pardee.

"Accept, man? Of course we do!" said Mrs. Le Moyne.

"Stop, mother!" said Hesden. "You may accept for yourself, but not for me. Is this woman able to give away such a fortune?" he asked of Pardee.

"She is not rich. She has been a teacher, and has some property—enough, she insists, for comfort," was the answer.

"If she had offered to sell, I would have bought at any possible price, but I cannot take such a gift!"

"Do you accept the terms?" asked Pardee of Mrs. Le Moyne.

"I do," she answered doggedly, but with a face flushing with shame.

"Then, madam, let me say that I have already shown the proofs in confidence to Winburn's attorney. He agrees that they have no chance, and is willing to sell the interest he represents for five hundred dollars. That I have already paid, and have taken a quit-claim to Desmit. Upon the payment of that, and my bill for services, I stand ready to deliver to you the title."

The whole amount was soon ascertained and a check given to Pardee for the sum. Thereupon he handed over to Mrs. Le Moyne a deed in fee-simple, duly executed, covering the entire tract, except that about Red Wing, which was conveyed to Nimbus in a deed directly to him. Mrs. Le Moyne unfolded the deed, and turning quickly to the last page read the name of the donor:

"MOLLIE AINSLIE!"

"What!" she exclaimed, "not the little nigger teacher at Red Wing?"

"The same, madam," said Pardee, with a smile and a bow.

The announcement was too much for the long-excited invalid. She fell back fainting upon her pillow, and while Cousin Hetty devoted herself to restoring her relative to consciousness, Pardee gathered up his papers and withdrew. Hesden followed him, presently, and asked where Miss Ainslie was.

"I am directed," said Pardee, "not to disclose her residence, but will at any time forward any communication you may desire to make."

CHAPTER LV.

AN UNCONDITIONAL SURRENDER.

THE NEXT DAY Mr. Pardee received a note from Mrs. Le Moyne, requesting him to come to Mulberry Hill at his earliest convenience. Being at the time disengaged, he returned with the messenger. Upon being ushered again into the invalid's room, he found Miss Hetty Lomax with a flushed face standing by the bedside. Both the ladies greeted him with some appearance of embarrassment.

"Cousin Hetty," said the invalid, "will you ask Hesden to come here for a moment?"

Miss Hetty left the room, and returned a moment afterward in company with Hesden.

"Hesden," said Mrs. Le Moyne, "were you in earnest in what you said yesterday in regard to receiving any benefits under this deed?"

"Certainly, mother," replied Hesden; "I could never consent to do so."

"Very well, my son," said the invalid; "you are perhaps right; but I wish you to know that I had heretofore made my will, giving to you and Cousin Hetty a joint interest in my estate. You know the feeling which induced me to do so. I am in the confessional to-day, and may as well admit that I was hasty and perhaps unjust in so doing. In justice to Cousin Hetty I wish also to say—"

"Oh, please, Mrs. Le Moyne," interrupted Hetty, blushing deeply.

"Hush, my child," said the invalid tenderly; "I must be just to you as well as to others. Hetty," she continued, turning her eyes upon Hesden, who stood looking in wonder from one to the other, "has long tried to persuade me to revoke that instrument. I have at length determined to cancel and destroy it, and shall proceed to make a new one, which I desire that both of you shall witness when it has been drawn."

Being thus dismissed, Hesden and his cousin withdrew, while Pardee seated himself at the little table by the bedside, on which writing materials had already been placed, and proceeded to receive instructions and prepare the will as she directed. When it had been completed and read over to her, she said, wearily,

"That is right."

The attorney called Hesden and his cousin, who, having witnessed the will by her request, again withdrew.

"Now Mr. Pardee," said Mrs. Le Moyne sadly, "I believe that I have done my duty as well as Hesden has done his. It is hard, very hard, for me to give up projects which I have cherished so long. As I have constituted you my executor, I desire that you will keep this will, and allow no person to know its contents unless directed by me to do so, until my death."

"Your wishes shall be strictly complied with, madam," said Pardee, as he folded the instrument and placed it in his pocket.

"I have still another favor to request of you, Mr. Pardee," she said. "I have written this note to Miss Ainslie, which I wish you to read and then transmit to her. No, no," she continued, as she saw him about to seal the letter which she had given him, without reading it; "you must read it. You know something of what it has cost me to write it, and will be a better judge than I as to whether it contains all that I should say."

Thus adjured, Pardee opened the letter and read:

"Mulberry Hill, Saturday, Oct. 8, 1871.

"MY DEAR MISS AINSLIE:

"Captain Pardee informed us yesterday of your nobly disinterested action in regard to the estate rightfully belonging to you. Words cannot express my gratitude for the consideration you have shown to our feelings in thus shielding the memory of the dead. Mr. Pardee will transmit to you with this the papers, showing that we have complied with your request. Pardon me if

I do not write as warmly as I ought. One as old and proud as I cannot easily adapt herself to so new and strange a rôle. I hope that time will enable me to think more calmly and speak more freely of this matter.

"Hoping you will forgive my constraint, and believe that it arises from no lack of appreciation of your magnanimity, but only springs from my own weakness; and asking your pardon for all unkindness of thought, word, or act in the past, I remain,

"Yours gratefully,
"HESTER RICHARDS LE MOYNE."

"My dear Mrs. Le Moyne," said Pardee, as he extended his hand and grasped that of the suffering woman, "I am sure Miss Ainslie would never require any such painful acknowledgment at your hands."

"I know she would not," was the reply; "it is not she that requires it, but myself—my honor, Mr. Pardee. You must not suppose, nor must she believe, that the wife of a Le Moyne can forget the obligations of justice, though her father may have unfortunately done so."

"But I am sure it will cause her pain," said Pardee.

"Would it cause her less were I to refuse what she has so delicately given?"

"No, indeed," said the attorney.

"Then I see no other way."

"Perhaps there is none," said Pardee thoughtfully.

"You think I have said enough?" she asked.

"You could not say more," was the reply. After a moment's pause he continued, "Are you willing that I should give Miss Ainslie any statement I may choose of this matter?"

"I should prefer," she answered, "that nothing more be said; unless," she added, with a smile, "you conceive that your duty imperatively demands it."

"And Hesden?" he began.

"Pardon me, sir," she said, with dignity; "I will not conceal from you that my son's course has given me great pain; indeed, you are already aware of that fact. Since yesterday, I have for the first time admitted to myself that in abandoning the cause of the Southern people he has acted from a sense of duty. My own inclination, after sober second thought," she added, as a slight flush overspread her pale face, "would have been to refuse, as he has done, this bounty from the hands of a stranger; more particularly from one in the position which Miss Ainslie has occupied; but I feel also that her unexpected delicacy demands the fullest recognition at our hands. Hesden will take such course as his own sense of honor may dictate."

"Am I at liberty to inform him of the nature of the testament which you have made?"

"I prefer not."

"Well," said Pardee, "if there is nothing more to be done I will bid you good-evening, hoping that time may yet bring a pleasant result out of these painful circumstances."

After the lawyer had retired, Mrs. Le Moyne summoned her son to her bedside and said,

"I hope you will forgive me, Hesden, for all—"

"Stop, mother," said he, playfully laying his hand over her mouth; "I can listen to no such language from you. When I was a boy you used to stop my confessions of wrong-doing with a kiss; how much more ought silence to be sufficient between us now."

He knelt by her side and pressed his lips to hers.

"Oh, my son, my son!" said the weeping woman, as she pushed back the hair above his forehead and looked into his eyes; "only give your mother time—you know it is so hard—so hard. I am trying, Hesden; and you must be very kind to me, very gentle. It will not be for long, but we must be alone—all alone—as we were before all these things came about. Only," she added sobbingly, "only little Hildreth is not here now."

"Believe me, mother," said he, and the tears fell upon the gentle face over which he bent, "I will do nothing to cause you pain. My opinions I cannot renounce, because I believe them right."

"I know, I know, my son," she said; "but it is so hard—so hard—to think that we must lose the place which we have always held in the esteem of—all those about us."

There was silence for a time, and then she continued,

"Hetty thinks it is best—that—that she—should—not remain here longer at this time. She is perhaps right, my son. You must not blame her for anything that has occurred; indeed—indeed she is not at fault. In fact," she added, "she has done much toward showing me my duty. Of course it is hard for her, as it is for me, to be under obligations to—to—such a one as Miss Ainslie. It is very hard to believe that she could have done as she has without some—some unworthy motive."

"Mother!" said Hesden earnestly, raising his head and gazing reproachfully at her.

"Don't—don't, my son! I am trying—believe me, I am trying; but it is so hard. Why should she give up all this for our sakes?"

"Not for ours mother—not for ours alone; for her own as well."

"Oh, my son, what does she know of family pride?"

"Mother," said he gravely, "she is prouder than we ever were. Oh, I *know* it,"—seeing the look of incredulity upon her face;—"prouder than any Richards or Le Moyne that ever lived; only it is a different kind of pride. She would *starve,* mother," he continued impetuously; "she would work her fingers to the bone rather than touch one penny of that estate."

"Oh, why—why, Hesden, should she do that? Just to shield my father's name?"

"Not alone for that," said Hesden. "Partly to show that she can give you pride for pride, mother."

"Do you think so, Hesden?"

"I am sure of it."

"Will you promise me one thing?"

"Whatever you shall ask."

"Do not write to her, nor in any way communicate with her, except at my request."

"As you wish."

CHAPTER LVI.

SOME OLD LETTERS.

I.

"Red Wing, Saturday, Feb. 15, 1873.

"MISS MOLLIE AINSLIE:

"I avail myself of your kind permission to address you a letter through Captain Pardee, to whom I will forward this to-morrow. I would have written to you before, because I knew you must be anxious to learn how things are at this place, where you labored so long; but I was very busy—and, to tell you the truth, I felt somewhat hurt that you should withhold from me for so long a time the knowledge even of where you were. It is true, I have known that you were somewhere in Kansas; but I could see no reason why you should not wish it to be known exactly where; nor can I now. I was so foolish as to think, at first, that it was because you did not wish the people where you now live to know that you had ever been a teacher in a colored school.

"When I returned here, however, and learned something of your kindness to our people—how you had saved the property of my dear lost brother Nimbus, and provided for his wife and children, and the wife and children of poor Berry, and so many others of those who once lived at Red Wing; and when I heard Captain Pardee read one of your letters to our people, saying that you had not forgotten us, I was ashamed that I had ever had such a thought. I know that you must have some good reason, and will never seek to know more than you may choose to tell me in regard to it. You may think it strange that I should have had this feeling at all; but you must remember that people afflicted as I am become very sensitive—morbid, perhaps—and are very apt to be influenced by mere imagination rather than by reason.

"After completing my course at the college, for which I can never be sufficiently grateful to Mr. Hesden, I thought at first that I would write to you and see if I could not obtain work among some of my people in the West. Before I concluded to do so, however, the President of the college showed me a letter asking him to recommend some one for a colored school in one of the Northern States. He said he would be willing to recommend me for that position. Of course I felt very grateful to him, and very proud of the confidence he showed in my poor ability. Before I had accepted, however, I received a letter from Mr. Hesden, saying that he had rebuilt the school-house at Red Wing, that the same kind people who furnished it before had furnished it again, and that he wished the school to be re-opened, and desired me to come back and teach here. At first I thought I could not come; for the memory of that terrible night—the last night that I was here—came before me whenever I thought of it; and I was so weak as to think I could not ever come here again. Then I thought of Mr. Hesden, and all that he had done for me, and felt that I would be making a very bad return for his kindness should I refuse any request he might make. So I came, and am very glad that I did.

"It does not seem like the old Red Wing, Miss Mollie. There are not near so many people here, and the school is small in comparison with what it used to be. Somehow the life and hope seem to have gone out of our people, and they do not look forward to the future with that confident expectation which they used to have. It reminds me very much of the dull, plodding hopelessness of the old slave time. It is true, they are no longer subject to the terrible cruelties which were for a while visited upon them; but they feel, as they did in the old time, that their rights are withheld from them, and they see no hope of regaining them. With their own poverty and ignorance and the prejudices of the white people to contend with, it does indeed seem a hopeless task for them to attempt to be anything more, or anything better, than they are now. I am even surprised that they do not go backward instead of forward under the difficulties they have to encounter.

"I am learning to be more charitable than I used to be, Miss Mollie, or ever would have been had I not returned here. It seems to me now that the white people are not so much to be blamed for what has been done and suffered since the war, as pitied for that prejudice which has made them unconsciously almost as much *slaves* as my people were before the war. I see, too, that these things cannot be remedied at once. It will be a long, sad time of waiting, which I fear our people will not endure as well as they did the tiresome waiting for freedom. I used to think that the law could give us our rights and make us free. I now see, more clearly than ever before, that we must not only make *ourselves* free, but must overcome all that prejudice which slavery created against our race in the hearts of the white people. It is a long way to look ahead, and I don't wonder that so many despair of its ever being accomplished. I know it can only be done through the attainment of knowledge and the power which that gives.

"I do not blame for giving way to despair those who are laboring for a mere pittance, and perhaps not receiving that; who have wives and children to support, and see their children growing up as poor and ignorant as themselves. If I were one of those, Miss Mollie, and whole and sound, I wouldn't stay in this country another day. I would go somewhere where my children would have a chance to learn what it is to be free, whatever hardship I might have to face in doing so, for their sake. But I know that they cannot go—at least not all of them, nor many of them; and I think the Lord has dealt with me as he has in order that I might be willing to stay here and help them, and share with them the blessed knowledge which kind friends have given to me.

"Mr. Hesden comes over to see the school very often, and is very much interested in it. I have been over to Mulberry Hill once, and saw the dear old 'Mistress.' She has failed a great deal, Miss Mollie, and it does seem as if her life of pain was drawing to an end. She was very kind to me, asked all about my studies, how I was getting on, and inquired very kindly of you. She seemed very much surprised when I told her that I did not know where you were, only that you were in the West. It is no wonder that she looks worn and troubled, for Mr. Hesden has certainly had a hard time. I do not think it is as bad now as it has been, and some of the white people, even, say that he has been badly treated. But, Miss Mollie, you can't imagine the abuse he has had to suffer because he befriended me, and is what they call a 'Radical.'

"There is one thing that I cannot understand. I can see why the white people of the South should be so angry about colored people being allowed to vote. I can understand, too, why they should abuse Mr. Hesden, and the few like him, because they wish to see the colored people have their rights and become capable of exercising them. It is because they have always believed that we are an inferior race, and think that the attempt to elevate us is intended to drag them down. But I cannot see why the people of the *North* should think so ill of such men as Mr. Hesden. It would be a disgrace for any man there to say that he was opposed to the colored man having the rights of a citizen, or having a fair show in any manner. But they seem to think that if a man living at the South advocates those rights, or says a word in our favor, he is a low-down, mean man. If we had a few men like Mr. Hesden in every county, I think it would soon be better; but if it takes as long to get each one as it has to get him, I am afraid a good many generations will live and die before that good time will come.

"I meant to have said more about the school, Miss Mollie; but I have written so much that I will wait until the next time for that. Hoping that you will have time to write to me, I remain

"Your very grateful pupil,

"ELIAB HILL."

II.

"Mulberry Hill, Wednesday, March 5, 1873.

"MISS MOLLIE AINSLIE:

"Through the kindness of our good friend, Captain Pardee, I send you this letter, together with an instrument, the date of which you will observe is the same as that of my former letter. You will see that I have regarded myself only as a trustee and a beneficiary, during life, of your self-denying generosity. The day after I received your gift, I gave the plantation back to you, reserving only the pleasing privilege of holding it as my own while I lived. The opportunity which I then hoped might some time come has now arrived. I can write to you now without constraint or bitterness. My pride has not gone; but I am proud of you, as a relative proud as myself, and far braver and more resolute than I have ever been.

"My end is near, and I am anxious to see you once more. The dear old plantation is just putting on its spring garment of beauty. Will you not come and look upon your gift in its glory, and gladden the heart of an old woman whose eyes long to look upon your face before they see the brightness of the upper world?

"Come, and let me say to the people of Horsford that you are one of us—a Richards worthier than the worthiest they have known!

"Yours, with sincerest love,

"HESTER RICHARDS LE MOYNE.

"P. S.—I ought to say that, although Hesden is one of the witnesses to my will, he knows nothing of its contents. He does not know that I have written to you, but I am sure he will be glad to see you.

"H. R. LE M."

III.

Mrs. Le Moyne received the following letter in reply:

"*March 15, 1873.*

"MY DEAR MRS. LE MOYNE:

"Your letter gave me far greater pleasure than you can imagine. But you give me much more credit for doing what I did than I have any right to receive. While I know that I would do the same now, to give you pleasure and save you pain, as readily as I did it then from a worse motive, I must confess to you that I did it, almost solely I fear, to show you that a Yankee girl, even though a teacher of a colored school, could be as proud as a Southern lady. I did it to humiliate *you.* Please forgive me; but it is true, and I cannot bear to receive your praise for what really deserves censure. I have been ashamed of myself very many times for this unworthy motive for an act which was in itself a good one, but which I am glad to have done, even so unworthily.

"I thank you for your love, which I hope I may better deserve hereafter. I inclose the paper which you sent me, and hope you will destroy it at once. I could not take the property you have so kindly devised to me, and you can readily see what trouble I should have in bestowing it where it should descend as an inheritance.

"Do not think that I need it at all. I had a few thousands which I invested in the great West when I left the South, three years ago, in order to aid those poor colored people at Red Wing, whose sufferings appealed so strongly to my sympathies. By good fortune a railroad has come near me, a town has been built up near by and grown into a city, as in a moment, so that my venture has been blessed; and though I have given away some, the remainder has increased in value until I feel myself almost rich. My life has been very pleasant, and I hope not altogether useless to others.

"I am sorry that I cannot do as you wish. I know that you will believe that I do not now act from any unworthy motive, or from any lack of appreciation of your kindness, or doubt of your sincerity. Thanking you again for your kind words and hearty though undeserved praises, I remain,

"Yours very truly,

"MOLLIE AINSLIE."

"Hesden," said Mrs. Le Moyne to her son, as he sat by her bedside while she read this letter, "will you not write to Miss Ainslie?"

"What!" said he, looking up from his book in surprise. "Do you mean it?"

"Indeed I do, my son," she answered, with a glance of tenderness. "I tried to prepare you a surprise, and wrote for her to come and visit us; but she will not come at my request. I am afraid you are the only one who can overcome her stubbornness.

"I fear that I should have no better success," he answered.

Nevertheless, he went to his desk, and, laying out some paper, he placed upon it, to hold it in place while he wrote, a great black hoof with a silver shoe, bearing on the band about its crown the word "Midnight." After many attempts he wrote as follows:

"MISS MOLLIE AINSLIE:

"Will you permit me to come and see you, upon the conditions imposed when I saw you last?

"HESDEN LE MOYNE."

IV.

While Hesden waited for an answer to this letter, which had been forwarded through Captain Pardee, he received one from Jordan Jackson. It was somewhat badly spelled, but he made it out to be as follows:

"Eupolia, Kansas, Sunday, March 23, 1873.

"MY DEAR LE MOYNE:

"I have been intending to write to you for a long time, but have been too busy. You never saw such a busy country as this. It just took me off my legs when I first came out here. I thought I knew what it meant to 'git up and git.' Nobody ever counted me hard to start or slow to move, down in that country; but here—God bless you, Le Moyne, I found I wasn't half awake! Work? Lord! Lord! how these folks do work and tear around! It don't seem so very hard either, because when they have anything to do they don't do nothing else, and when have nothing to do they make a business of that, too.

"Then, they use all sorts of machinery, and never do anything by hand-power that a horse can be made to do, in any possible way. The horses do all the ploughing, sowing, hoeing, harvesting, and, in fact, pretty much all the farm-work; while the man sits up on a sulky-seat and fans himself with a palm-leaf hat. So that, according to my reckoning, one man here counts for about as much as four in our country.

"I have moved from where I first settled, which was in a county adjoining this. I found that my notion of just getting a plantation to settle down on, where I could make a living and be out of harm's way, wasn't the thing for this country, nohow. A man who comes here must pitch in and count for all he's worth. It's a regular ground-scuffle, open to all, and everybody choosing his own hold. Morning, noon, and night the world is awake and alive; and if a man isn't awake too, it tramps on right over him and wipes him out, just as a stampeded buffalo herd goes over a hunter's camp.

"Everybody is good-natured and in dead earnest. Every one that comes is welcome, and no questions asked. Kin and kin-in-law don't count worth a cuss. Nobody stops to ask where you come from, what's your politics, or whether you've got any religion. They don't care, if you only mean 'business.' They don't make no fuss over nobody. There ain't much of what we call 'hospitality' at the South, making a grand flourish and a big lay-out over anybody; but they just take it, as a matter of course, that you are all right and square and honest, and as good as anybody till you show up different. There ain't any big folks nor any little ones. Of course, there are rich folks and poor ones, but the poor are just as respectable as the rich, feel just as big, and take up just as much of the road. There ain't any crawling nor cringing here. Everybody stands up straight, and don't give nor take any sass from anybody else. The West takes right hold of every one that comes into it and makes him a part of itself, instead of keeping him outside in the cold to all eternity, as the South does the strangers who go there.

"I don't know as you'd like it; but if any one who has been kept down and put on, as poor men are at the South, can muster pluck enough to get away and come here, he'll think he's been born over again, or I'm mistaken. Nobody asks your politics. I don't reckon anybody knew mine for a year. The fact is, we're all too busy to fuss with our neighbors or cuss them about their opinions. I've heard more politics in a country store in Horsford in a day than I've heard here in Eupolia in a year—and we've got ten thousand people here, too. I moved here last year, and am doing well. I wouldn't go back and live in that d—d hornet's nest that I felt so bad about leaving—not for the whole State, with a slice of the next one throwed in.

"I've meant to tell you, a half dozen times, about that little Yankee gal that used to be at Red Wing; but I've been half afraid to, for fear you would get mad about it. My wife said that when she came away there was a heap of talk about you being sorter 'sweet' on the 'nigger-school-marm.' I knew that she was sick at your house when I was there, and so, putting the two together, I 'llowed that for once there might be some truth in a Horsford rumor. I reckon it must have been a lie, though; or else she 'kicked' you, which she wouldn't stand a speck about doing, even if you were the President, if you didn't come up to her notion. It's a mighty high notion, too, let me tell you; and the man that gits up to it 'll have to climb. Bet your life on that!

"But that's all no matter. I reckon you'll be glad to know how she's gettin' on out here, anyhow. She come here not a great while after I did; but, bless your stars, she wasn't as green as I, not by any manner of means. She didn't want to hide out in a quiet part of the country, where the world didn't turn around but once in two days. No, sir! She was keen—just as keen as a razor-blade. She run her eye over the map and got inside the railroad projects somehow, blessed if I know how; and then she just went off fifty miles out of the track others was taking, and bought up all the land she could pay for, and got trusted for all the credit that that brought her; and here she is now, with Eupolia building right up on her land, and just a-busting up her quarter-sections into city lots, day after day, till you can't rest.

"Just think on't, Moyne! It's only three years ago and she was teaching a nigger school, there in Red Wing; and now, God bless you, here she is, just a queen in a city that wasn't nowhere then. I tell you, she's a team! Just as proud as Lucifer, and as wide-awake as a hornet in July. She beats anything I ever did see. She's given away enough to make two or three, and I'll be hanged if it don't seem to me that every cent she gives just brings her in a dollar. The people here just worship her, as they have a good right to; but she ain't a bit stuck up. She's got a whole lot of them Red Wing niggers here, and has settled them down and put them to work, and made them get on past all expectation. She just tells right out about her having taught a nigger school down in Horsford, and nobody seems to think a word on't. In fact, I b'lieve they rather like her better for it.

"I heard about her soon after she came here, but, to tell the truth, I thought I was a little better than a 'nigger-teacher,' if I was in Kansas. So I didn't mind anything about her till Eupolia began to grow, and I came to think about going into trading again. Then I came over, just to look around, you know. I went to see the little lady, feeling mighty 'shamed, you may bet, and more than half of the notion that she wouldn't care about owning that she'd ever seen me before. But, Lord love you! I needn't have had any fear about that. Nobody ever had a heartier welcome than she gave me, until she found that I had been living only fifty miles away for a year and hadn't let her know. Then she come down on me—Whew! I thought there was going to be a blizzard, sure enough.

"'Jordan Jackson,' said she, 'you just go home and bring that wife and them children here, where they can see something and have a rest.'

"I had to do it, and they just took to staying in Eupolia here nigh about all the time. So I thought I might as well come too; and here I am, doing right well, and would be mighty glad to see an old friend if you could make up your mind to come this way. We are all well, and remember you as the kindest of all old friends in our time of need.

"I never wrote as long a letter as this before, and never 'llow to do it again.

"Your true friend,

"JORDAN JACKSON."

V.

In due time there came to Hesden Le Moyne an envelope, containing only a quaintly-shaped card, which looked as if it had been cut from the bark of a brown-birch tree. On one side was printed, in delicate script characters,

"Miss Mollie Ainslie,
Eupolia,
Kansas."

On the other was written one word: "Come."

A bride came to Mulberry Hill with the May roses, and when Mrs. Le Moyne had kissed her who knelt beside her chair for a maternal benison, she placed a hand on either burning cheek, and, holding the face at arm's length, said, with that archness which never forsook her, "What am I to do about the old plantation? Hesden refuses to be my heir, and you refuse to be my devisee; must I give it to the poor?"

The summer bloomed and fruited; the autumn glowed and faded; and peace and happiness dwelt at Red Wing. But when the Christmas came, wreaths of *immortelles* lay upon a coffin in "Mother's Room," and Hesden and Mollie dropped their tears upon the sweet, pale face within.

So Hesden and Mollie dwelt at Red Wing. The heirs of "Red Jim" had their own, and the children of "Black Jim" were not dispossessed.

CHAPTER LVII.

A SWEET AND BITTER FRUITAGE.

THE CHARMS OF the soft, luxurious climate were peculiarly grateful to Mollie after the harshness of the Kansas winter and the sultry summer winds that swept over the heated plains. There was something, too, very pleasant in renewing her associations with that region in a relation so different from that under which she had formerly known it. As the teacher at Red Wing, her life had not been wholly unpleasant; but that which had made it pleasant had proceeded from herself and not from others. The associations which she then formed had been those of kindly charity—the affection which one has for the objects of sympathetic care. So far as the world in which she now lived was concerned—the white world and white people of Horsford—she had known nothing of them, nor they of her, but as each had regarded the other as a curious study. Their life had been shut out from her, and her life had been a matter that did not interest them. She had wondered that they did not think and feel as she did with regard to the colored people; and they, that any one having a white skin and the form of woman should come a thousand miles to become a servant of servants. The most charitable among them had deemed her a fool; the less charitable, a monster.

In the few points of contact which she had with them personally, she had found them pleasant. In the few relations which they held toward the colored people, and toward her as their friend, she had found them brutal and hateful beyond her power to conceive. Then, her life had been with those for whom she labored, so far as it was in or of the South at all. They had been the objects of her thought, her interest, and her care. Their wrongs had entered into her life, and had been the motive of her removal to the West. Out of these conditions, by a curious evolution, had grown a new life, which she vainly tried to graft upon the old without apparent disjointure.

Now, by kinship and by marriage, she belonged to one of the most respectable families of the region. It was true that Hesden had sullied his family name by becoming a Radical; but as he had never sought official position, nor taken any active part in enforcing or promulgating the opinions which he held; had, in fact, identified himself with the party of odious principles only for the protection of the victims of persecution or the assertion of the rights of the weak—he was regarded with much more toleration and forbearance than would otherwise have been displayed toward him.

In addition to this, extravagant rumors came into the good county of Horsford respecting the wealth which Mollie Ainslie had acquired, and of the pluck and enterprise which she had displayed in the far West. It was thought very characteristic of the brave young teacher of Red Wing, only her courage was displayed there in a different manner. So they took a sort of pride in her, as if she had been one of themselves; and as they told to each other the story of her success, they said, "Ah, I knew she would make her mark! Any girl that had her pluck was too good to remain a nigger-teacher long. It was lucky for Hesden, though. By George! he made his Radicalism pay, didn't he? Well, well; as long as he don't trouble anybody, I don't see why we should not be friends with him—if he *is* a Radical." So they determined that they would patronize and encourage Hesden Le Moyne and his wife, in the hope that he might be won back to his original excellence, and that she might be charmed with the attractions of Southern society and forget the bias of her Yankee origin.

The occupants of Mulberry Hill, therefore, received much attention, and before the death of Hesden's mother had become prime favorites in the society of Horsford. It is true that now and then they met with some exhibition of the spirit which had existed before, but in the main their social life was pleasant; and, for a considerable time, Hesden felt that he had quite regained his original status as a "Southern gentleman," while Mollie wondered if it were possible that the people whom she now met upon such pleasant terms were those who had, by their acts of violence, painted upon her memory such horrible and vivid pictures. She began to feel as if she had done them wrong, and sought by every means in her power to identify herself with their pleasures and their interests.

At the same time, she did not forget those for whom she had before labored, and who had shown for her such true and devoted friendship. The school at Red Wing was an especial object of her care and attention. Rarely did a week pass that her carriage did not show itself in the little hamlet, and her bright face and cheerful tones brought encouragement and hope to all that dwelt there. Having learned from Hesden and Eliab the facts with regard to the disappearance of Nimbus, she for a long time shared Lugena's faith in regard to her husband, and had not yet given up hope that he was alive. Indeed, she had taken measures to discover his whereabouts; but all these had failed. Still, she would not abandon the hope that he would some time reappear, knowing how difficult it was to trace one altogether unnoted by any except his own race, who were not accustomed to be careful or inquisitive with regard to the previous life of their fellows.

Acting as his trustee, not by any specific authority, but through mere good-will, Hesden had managed the property, since the conclusion of the Winburn suit, so as to yield a revenue, which Lugena had carefully applied to secure a home in the West, in anticipation of her husband's return. This had necessarily brought him into close relations with the people of Red Wing, who had welcomed Mollie with an interest half proprietary in its character. Was she not *their* Miss Mollie? Had she not lived in the old "Or'nary," taught in their school, advised, encouraged, and helped them? They flocked around her, each reminding her of his identity by recalling some scene or incident of her past life, or saying, with evident pride, "Miss Mollie, I was one of your scholars—I was."

She did not repel their approaches, nor deny their claim to her attention. She recognized it as a duty that she should still minister to their wants, and do what she could for their elevation. And, strangely enough, the good people of Horsford did not rebel nor cast her off for so doing. The rich wife of Hesden Le Moyne, the queen of the growing Kansas town, driving in her carriage to the colored school-house, and sitting as lady patroness upon the platform, was an entirely different personage, in their eyes, from the Yankee girl who rode Midnight up and down the narrow streets, and who wielded the pedagogic sceptre in the log school-house that Nimbus had built. She could be allowed to patronize the colored school; indeed, they rather admired her for doing so, and a few of them now and then went with her, especially on occasions of public interest, and wondered at the progress that had been made by that race whose capacity they had always denied.

Every autumn Hesden and Mollie went to visit her Kansas home, to look after her interests there, help and advise her colored protégés, breathe the free air, and gather into their lives something of the busy, bustling spirit of the great North. The contrast did them good. Hesden's ideas were made broader and fuller; her heart was reinvigorated; and both returned to their Southern home full of hope and aspiration for its future.

So time wore on, and they almost forgot that they held their places in the life which was about them by sufferance and not of right; that they were allowed the privilege of associating with the "best people of Horsford," not because they were of them, or entitled to such privilege, but solely upon condition that they should submit themselves willingly to its views, and do nothing or attempt nothing to subvert its prejudices.

Since the county had been "redeemed" it had been at peace. The vast colored majority, once overcome, had been easily held in subjection. There was no longer any violence, and little show of coercion, so far as their political rights were concerned. At first it was thought necessary to discourage the eagerness with which they sought to exercise the elective franchise, by frequent reference to the evils which had already resulted therefrom. Now and then, when some ambitious colored man had endeavored to organize his people and to secure political advancement through their suffrages, he had been politely cautioned in regard to the danger, and the fate which had overwhelmed others was gently recalled to his memory. For a while, too, employers thought it necessary to exercise the power which their relations with dependent laborers gave them, to prevent the neglect of agricultural interests for the pursuit of political knowledge, and especially to prevent absence from the plantation upon the day of election. After a time, however, it was found that such care was unnecessary. The laws of the State, carefully revised by legislators wisely chosen for that purpose, had taken the power from the irresponsible hands of the masses, and placed it in the hands of the few, who had been wont to exercise it in the olden time.

That vicious idea which had first grown up on the inclement shores of Massachusetts Bay, and had been nourished and protected and spread abroad throughout the North and West as the richest heritage which sterile New England could give to the states her sons had planted; that outgrowth of absurd and fanatical ideas which had made the North free, and whose absence had enabled the South to remain "slave"—the township system, with its free discussion of all matters, even of the most trivial interest to the inhabitants; that nursery of political virtue and individual independence of character, comporting, as it did, very badly with the social and political ideas of the South—this system was swept away, or, if retained in name, was deprived of all its characteristic elements.[113]

In the foolish fever of the reconstruction era this system had been spread over the South as the safeguard of the new ideas and new institutions then introduced. It was foolishly believed that it would produce upon the soil of the South the same beneficent results as had crowned its career at the North.

So the counties were subdivided into small self-governing communities, every resident in which was entitled to a voice in the management of its domestic interests. Trustees and school commissioners and justices of the peace and constables were elected in these townships by the vote of the inhabitants. The roads and bridges and other matters of municipal finance were put directly under the control of the inhabitants of these miniature boroughs.[114] Massachusetts was superimposed upon South Carolina. That system which had contributed more than all else to the prosperity, freedom, and intelligence of the Northern community was invoked by the political theorists of the reconstruction era as a means of like improvement there. It did not seem a dangerous experiment. One would naturally expect similar results from the same system in different sections, even though it had not been specifically calculated for both latitudes. Especially did this view seem natural, when it was remembered that wherever the township system had existed in any fullness or perfection, there slavery had withered and died without the scath of war; that wherever in all our bright land the township system had obtained a foothold and reached mature development, there intelligence and prosperity grew side by side; and that wherever this system had not prevailed, slavery had grown rank and luxuriant, ignorance had settled upon the people, and poverty had brought its gaunt hand to crush the spirit of free men and establish the dominion of class.

The astute politicians of the South saw at once the insane folly of this project. They knew that the system adapted to New England, the mainspring of Western prosperity, the safeguard of intelligence and freedom at the North, could not be adapted to the social and political elements of the South. They knew that the South had grown up a peculiar people; that for its government, in the changed state of affairs, must be devised a new and untried system of political organization, assimilated in every possible respect to the institutions which had formerly existed. It is true, those institutions and that form of government had been designed especially to promote and protect the interests of slavery and the power of caste. But they believed that the mere fact of emancipation did not at all change the necessary and essential relations between the various classes of her population, so far as her future development and prosperity were concerned.

Therefore, immediately upon the "redemption" of these states from the enforced and sporadic political ideas of the reconstruction era, they set themselves earnestly at work to root out and destroy all the pernicious elements of the township system, and to restore that organization by which the South had formerly achieved power and control in the national councils, had suppressed free thought and free speech, had degraded labor, encouraged ignorance, and established aristocracy. The first step in this measure of counter-revolution and reform was to take from the inhabitants of the township the power of electing the officers, and to greatly curtail, where they did not destroy, the power of such officers. It had been observed by these sagacious statesmen that in not a few instances incapable men had been chosen to administer the laws, as justices of the peace and as trustees of the various townships. Very often, no doubt, it happened that there was no one of sufficient capacity who would consent to act in such positions as the representatives of the majority. Sometimes, perhaps, incompetent and corrupt men had sought these places for their own advantage. School commissioners may have been chosen who were themselves unable to read. There may have been township trustees who had never yet shown sufficient enterprise to become the owners of land, and legislators whose knowledge of law had been chiefly gained by frequent occupancy of the prisoner's dock.

Such evils were not to be endured by a proud people, accustomed not only to self-control, but to the control of others. They did not stop to inquire whether there was more than one remedy for these evils. The system itself was attainted with the odor of Puritanism. It was communistic in its character, and struck at the very deepest roots of the social and political organization which had previously prevailed at the South.

So it was changed. From and after that date it was solemnly enacted that either the Governor of the State or the prevailing party in the Legislature should appoint all the justices of the peace in and for the various counties; that these in turn should appoint in each of the subdivisions which had once been denominated townships, or which had been clothed with the power of townships, school commissioners and trustees, judges of election and registrars of voters; and that in the various counties these chosen few, or the State Executive in their stead, should appoint the boards of commissioners, who were to control the county finances and have direction of all municipal affairs.

Of course, in this counter-revolution there was not any idea of propagating or confirming the power of the political party instituting it! It was done simply to protect the State against incompetent officials! The people were not wise enough to govern themselves, and could only become so by being wisely and beneficently governed by others, as in the ante-bellum era. From it, however, by a *curious accident,* resulted that complete control of the ballot and the ballot-box by a dominant minority so frequently observed in those states. Observe that the Legislature or the Executive appointed the justices of the peace; they in turn met in solemn conclave, a body of electors, taken wholly or in a great majority from the same party, and chose the commissioners of the county. These, again, a still more select body of electors, chose with the utmost care the trustees of the townships, the judges of election, and the registrars of voters. So that the utmost care was taken to secure entire harmony throughout the state. It mattered not how great the majority of the opposition in this county or in that; its governing officers were invariably chosen from the body of the minority.

By these means a *peculiar safeguard* was also extended to the ballot. All the inspectors throughout the state being appointed by the same political power, were carefully chosen to secure the results of good government. Either all or a majority of every board were of the same political complexion, and, if need be, the remaining members, placed there in order that there should be no just ground of complaint upon the part of the opposition, were unfitted by nature or education for the performance of their duty. If not blind, they were usually profound strangers to the Cadmean mystery.[115] Thus the registration of voters and the elections were carefully devised to secure for all time the beneficent results of "redemption." It was found to be a very easy matter to allow the freedman to indulge, without let or hindrance, his wonderful eagerness for the exercise of ballotorial power, without injury to the public good. From and after that time elections became simply a harmless amusement. There was no longer any need of violence. The peaceful paths of legislation were found much more pleasant and agreeable, as well as less obnoxious to the moral feelings of that portion of mankind who were so unfortunate as to dwell without the boundaries of these states.

In order, however, to secure entire immunity from trouble or complaint, it was in many instances provided that the ballots should be destroyed as soon as counted, and the inspectors were sworn to execute this law. In other instances, it was provided, with tender care for the rights of the citizen, that if by any chance there should be found within the ballot-box at the close of an election any excess of votes over and above the number the tally-sheet should show to have exercised that privilege at that precinct, instead of the whole result being corrupted, and the voice of the people thereby stifled, one member of the board of inspectors should be blindfolded, and in that condition should draw from the box so many ballots as were in excess of the number of voters, and that the result, whatever it might be, should be regarded and held as the voice of the people. By this means formal fraud was avoided, and the voice of the people declared free from all legal objection. It is true that when the ticket was printed upon very thin paper, in very small characters, and was very closely folded and the box duly shaken, the smaller ballots found their way to the bottom, while the larger ones remained upon the top; so that the blindfolded inspector very naturally removed these and allowed the tissue ballots to remain and be counted. It is true, also, that the actual will of the majority thus voting was thus not unfrequently overwhelmingly negatived. Yet this was the course prescribed by the law, and the inspectors of elections were necessarily guiltless of fraud.

So it had been in Horsford. The colored majority had voted when they chose. The ballots had been carefully counted and the result scrupulously ascertained and declared. Strangely enough, it was found that, whatever the number of votes cast, the majorities were quite different from those which the same voters had given in the days before the "redemption," while there did not seem to have been any great change in political sentiment. Perhaps half a dozen colored voters in the county professed allegiance to the party which they had formerly opposed; but in the main the same line still separated the races. It was all, without question, the result of wise and patriotic legislation!

CHAPTER LVIII.

COMING TO THE FRONT.

IN AN EVIL hour Hesden Le Moyne yielded to the solicitations of those whom he had befriended, and whose rights he honestly believed had been unlawfully subverted, and became a candidate in his county. It had been so long since he had experienced the bitterness of persecution on account of his political proclivities, and the social relations of his family had been so pleasant, that he had almost forgotten what he had once passed through; or rather, he had come to believe that the time had gone by when such weapons would be employed against one of his social grade.

The years of silence which had been imposed on him by a desire to avoid unnecessarily distressing his mother, had been years of thought, perhaps the richer and riper from the fact that he had refrained from active participation in political life. Like all his class at the South, he was, if not a politician by instinct, at least familiar from early boyhood with the subtle discussion of political subjects which is ever heard at the table and the fireside of the Southern gentleman. He had regarded the experiment of reconstruction, as he believed, with calm, unprejudiced sincerity; he had buried the past, and looked only to the future. It was not for his own sake or interest that he became a candidate; he was content always to be what he was—a quiet country gentleman. He loved his home and his plantation; he thoroughly enjoyed the pursuits of agriculture, and had no desire to be or do any great thing. His mother's long illness had given him a love for a quiet life, his books and his fireside; and it was only because he thought that he could do something to reconcile the jarring factions and bring harmony out of discord, and lead his people to see that The Nation was greater and better than The South; that its interests and prosperity were also their interest, their prosperity, and their hope—that Hesden Le Moyne consented to forego the pleasant life which he was leading and undertake a brief voyage upon the stormy sea of politics.

He did not expect that all would agree with him, but he believed that they would listen to him without prejudice and without anger. And he so fully believed in the conclusions he had arrived at that he thought no reasonable man could resist their force or avoid reaching a like result. His platform, as he called it, when he came to announce himself as a candidate at the Court House on the second day of the term of court, in accordance with immemorial custom in that county, was simply one of plain common-sense. He was not an office-holder or a politician. He did not come of an office-holding family, nor did he seek position or emolument. He offered himself for the suffrages of his fellow-citizens simply because no other man among them seemed willing to stand forth and advocate those principles which he believed to be right, expedient, and patriotic.

He was a white man, he said, and had the prejudices and feelings that were common to the white people of the South. He had not believed in the right or the policy of secession, in which he differed from some of his neighbors; but when it came to the decision of that question by force of arms he had yielded his conviction and stood side by side upon the field of battle with the fiercest fire-eaters of the land. No man could accuse him of being remiss in any duty which he owed his State or section. But all that he insisted was past. There was no longer any distinct sectional interest or principle to be maintained. The sword had decided that, whether right or wrong as an abstraction, the doctrine of secession should never be practically asserted in the government. The result of the struggle had been to establish, beyond a peradventure, what had before been an unsettled question: that the Nation had the power and the will to protect itself against any disintegrating movement. It might not have decided what was the meaning of the Constitution, and so not determined upon which side of this question lay the better reasoning; but it had settled the practical fact. This decision he accepted; he believed that they all accepted it—with only this difference, perhaps, that he believed it rendered necessary a change in many of the previous convictions of the Southern people. They had been accustomed to call themselves Southern men; after that, Americans. Hereafter it became their duty and their interest to be no longer Southern men, but Americans only.

"Having these views," he continued, "it is my sincere conviction that we ought to accept, in spirit as well as in form, the results of this struggle; not in part, but fully." The first result had been the freeing in the slave. In the main he believed that had been accepted, if not cheerfully, at least finally. The next had been the enfranchisement of the colored man. This he insisted had not been honestly accepted by the mass of the white people of the South. Every means, lawful and unlawful, had been resorted to to prevent the due operation of these laws. He did not speak of this in anger or to blame. Knowing their prejudices and feelings, he could well excuse what had been done; but he insisted that it was not, and could not be, the part of an honest, brave and intelligent people to nullify or evade any portion of the law of the land. He did not mean that it was the duty of any man to submit without opposition to a law which he believed to be wrong; but that opposition should never be manifested by unlawful violence, unmanly evasion, or cowardly fraud.

He realized that, at first, anger might over-bear both patriotism and honor, under the sting of what was regarded as unparalleled wrong, insult, and outrage; but there had been time enough for anger to cool, and for his people to look with calmness to the future that lay before, and let its hopes and duties overbalance the disappointments of the past. He freely admitted that had the question of reconstruction been submitted to him for determination, he would not have adopted the plan which had prevailed; but since it had been adopted and become an integral part of the law of the land, he believed that whoever sought to evade its fair and unhindered operation placed himself in the position of a law-breaker. They had the right, undoubtedly, by fair and open opposition to defeat any party, and to secure the amendment or repeal of any law or system of laws. But they had no right to resist law with violence, or to evade law by fraud.

The right of the colored man to exercise freely and openly his elective franchise, without threat, intimidation, or fear, was the same as that of the whitest man he addressed; and the violation of that right, or the deprivation of that privilege, was, really an assault upon the right and liberty of the white voter also. No rights were safe unless the people had that regard for law which would secure to the weakest and the humblest citizen the free and untrammeled enjoyment and exercise of every privilege which the law conferred. He characterized the laws that had been enacted in regard to the conduct of elections and the selection of local officers as unmanly and shuffling—an assertion of the right to nullify national law by fraud, which the South had failed to maintain by the sword, and had by her surrender virtually acknowledged herself in honor bound to abandon.

He did not believe, he would not believe, that his countrymen of the South, his white fellow-citizens of the good old county of Horsford, had fairly and honestly considered the position in which recent events and legislation had placed them, not only before the eyes of the country, but of the civilized world. It had always been claimed, he said, that a white man is by nature, and not merely by the adventitious circumstances of the past, innately and inherently, and he would almost add infinitely, the superior of the colored man. In intellectual culture, experience, habits of self-government and command, this was unquestionably true. Whether it were true as a natural and scientific fact was, perhaps, yet to be decided. But could it be possible that a people, a race priding itself upon its superiority, should be unwilling or afraid to see the experiment fairly tried? "Have we," he asked, "so little confidence in our moral and intellectual superiority that we dare not give the colored man an equal right with us to exercise the privilege which the Nation has conferred upon him? Are the white people of the South so poor in intellectual resources that they must resort to fraud or open violence to defeat the ignorant and weak colored man of even the least of his law-given rights?[116]

"We claim," he continued, "that he is ignorant. It is true. Are we afraid that he will grow wiser than we? We claim that he has not the capacity to acquire or receive a like intellectual development with ourselves. Are we afraid to give him a chance to do so? Could no intelligence cope with ignorance without fraud? Boasting that we could outrun our adversary, would we hamstring him at the starting-post? It was accounted by all men, in all ages, an unmanly thing to steal, and a yet more unmanly thing to steal from the weak; so that it has passed into a proverb, 'Only a dog would steal the blind man's dinner.' And yet," he said, "we are willing to steal the vote of the ignorant, the blind, the helpless colored man!"

It was not for the sake of the colored man, he said in conclusion, that he appealed to them to pause and think. It was because the honor, the nobility, the intelligence of the white man was being degraded by the course which passion and resentment, and not reason or patriotism, had dictated. He appealed to his hearers as *white men,* not so much to give to the colored man the right to express his sentiments at the ballot-box, as to regard that right as sacred because it rested upon the law, which constituted the foundation and safeguard of their own rights. He would not appeal to them as Southern men, for he hoped the day was at hand when there would no more be any such distinction. But he would appeal to them as men—honest men, honorable men—and as American citizens, to honor the law and thereby honor themselves.

It had been said that the best and surest way to secure the repeal of a bad law was first to secure its unhindered operation. Especially was this true of a people who had boasted of unparalleled devotion to principle, of unbounded honor, and of the highest chivalry. How one of them, or all of them, could claim any of these attributes of which they had so long boasted, and yet be privy to depriving even a single colored man of the right which the Nation had given him, or to making the exercise of that right a mockery, he could not conceive; and he would not believe that they would do it when once the scales of prejudice and resentment had fallen from their eyes. If they had been wronged and outraged as a people, their only fit revenge was to display a manhood and a magnanimity which should attest the superiority upon which they prided themselves.

This address was received by his white hearers with surprised silence; by the colored men with half-appreciative cheers. They recognized that the speaker was their friend, and in favor of their being allowed the free exercise of the rights of citizenship. His white auditors saw that he was assailing with some bitterness and earnest indignation both their conduct and what they had been accustomed to term their principles. There was no immediate display of hostility or anger; and Hesden Le Moyne returned to his home full of hope that the time was at hand for which he had so long yearned, when the people of his native South should abandon the career of prejudice and violence into which they had been betrayed by resentment and passion.

Early the next morning some of his friends waited upon him and adjured him, for his own sake, for the sake of his family and friends, to withdraw from the canvass. This he refused to do. He said that what he advocated was the result of earnest conviction, and he should always despise himself should he abandon the course he had calmly decided to take. Whatever the result, he would continue to the end. Then they cautiously intimated to him that his course was fraught with personal danger. "What!" he cried, "do you expect me to flinch at the thought of danger? I offered my life and gave an arm for a cause in which I did not believe; shall I not brave as much in the endeavor to serve my country in a manner which my mind and conscience approve? I seek for difficulty with no one; but it may as well be understood that Hesden Le Moyne does not turn in his tracks because of any man's anger. I say to you plainly that I shall neither offer personal insult nor submit to it in this canvass."

His friends left him with heavy hearts, for they foreboded ill. It was not many days before he found that the storm of detraction and contumely through which he had once passed was but a gentle shower compared with the tornado which now came down upon his head. The newspapers overflowed with threat, denunciation, and abuse.[117] One of them declared:

> "The man who thinks that he can lead an opposition against the organized Democracy of Horsford County is not only very presumptuous, but extremely bold. Such a man will require a bodyguard of Democrats in his canvass and a Gibraltar in his rear on the day of the election."

Another said:

> "The Radical candidate would do well to take advice. The white men of the State desire a peaceful summer and autumn. They are wearied of heated political strife. If they are forced to vigorous action it will be exceedingly vigorous, perhaps unpleasantly so. Those who cause the trouble will suffer most from it. Bear that in mind, persons colored and white-skinned. We reiterate our advice to the reflective and argumentative Radical leader, to be careful how he goes, and not stir up the animals too freely; they have teeth and claws."

Still another said:

> "Will our people suffer a covert danger to rankle in their midst until it gains strength to burst into an open enemy? Will they tamely submit while Hesden Le Moyne rallies the colored men to his standard and

hands over Horsford to the enemy? Will they stand idly and supinely, and witness the consummation of such an infamous conspiracy? No! a thousand times, No! Awake! stir up your clubs; let the shout go up; put on your red shirts[118] and let the ride begin. Let the young men take the van, or we shall be sold into political slavery."

Another sounded the key-note of hostility in these words:

"Every white man who dares to avow himself a Radical should be promptly branded as the bitter and malignant enemy of the South; every man who presumes to aspire to office through Republican votes should be saturated with stench. As for the negroes, let them amuse themselves, if they will, by voting the Radical ticket. We have the count. We have a thousand good and true men in Horsford whose brave ballots will be found equal to those of five thousand vile Radicals."

One of his opponents, in a most virulent speech, called attention to the example of a celebrated Confederate general.[119] "He, too," said the impassioned orator, "served the Confederacy as bravely as Hesden Le Moyne, and far more ably. But he became impregnated with the virus of Radicalism; he abandoned and betrayed the cause for which he fought; he deserted the Southern people in the hour of need and joined their enemies. He was begged and implored not to persevere in his course, but he drifted on and on, and floundered deeper and deeper into the mire, until he landed fast in the slough where he sticks to-day. And what has he gained? Scorn, ostracism, odium, ill-will—worse than all, the contempt of the men who stood by him in the shower of death and destruction. Let Hesden Le Moyne take warning by his example."

And so it went on, day after day. Personal affront was studiously avoided, but in general terms he was held up to the scorn and contempt of all honest men as a renegade and a traitor. Those who had seemed his friends fell away from him; the home which had been crowded with pleasant associates was desolate, or frequented only by those who came to remonstrate or to threaten. He saw his mistake, but he knew that anger was worse than useless. He did not seek to enrage, but to convince. Failing in this, he simply performed the duty which he had undertaken, as he said he would do it—fearlessly, openly, and faithfully.

The election came, and the result—was what he should have been wise enough to foresee. Nevertheless, it was a great and grievous disappointment to Hesden Le Moyne. Not that he cared about a seat in the Legislature; but it was a demonstration to him that in his estimate of the people of whom he had been so proud he had erred upon the side of charity. He had believed them better than they had shown themselves. The fair future which he had hoped was so near at hand seemed more remote than ever. His hope for his people and his State was crushed, and apprehension of unspeakable evil in the future forced itself upon his heart.

CHAPTER LIX.

THE SHUTTLECOCK OF FATE.

"MARSE HESDEN, Marse Hesden!" There was a timorous rap upon the window of Hesden Le Moyne's sleeping-room in the middle of the night, and, waking, he heard his name called in a low, cautious voice.

"Who is there?" he asked.

"Sh—sh! Don't talk so loud, Marse Hesden. Please come out h'yer a minnit, won't yer?"

The voice was evidently that of a colored man, and Hesden had no apprehension or hesitancy in complying with the request. In fact, his position as a recognized friend of the colored race had made such appeals to his kindness and protection by no means unusual. He rose at once, and stepped out upon the porch. He was absent for a little while, and when he returned his voice was full of emotion as he said to his wife,

"Mollie, there is a man here who is hungry and weary. I do not wish the servants to know of his presence. Can you get him something to eat without making any stir?"

"Why, what—" began Mollie.

"It will be best not to stop for any questions," said Hesden hurriedly, as he lighted a lamp and, pouring some liquor into a glass, started to return. "Get whatever you can at once, and bring it to the room above. I will go and make up a fire."

Mollie rose, and, throwing on a wrapper, proceeded to comply with her husband's request. But a few moments had elapsed when she went up the stairs bearing a well-laden tray. Her slippered feet made no noise, and when she reached the chamber-door she saw her husband kneeling before the fire, which was just beginning to burn brightly. The light shone also upon a colored man of powerful frame who sat upon a chair a little way back, his hat upon the floor beside him, his gray head inclined upon his breast, and his whole attitude indicating exhaustion.

"Here it is, Hesden," she said quietly, as she stepped into the room.

The colored man raised his head wearily as she spoke, and turned toward her a gaunt face half hidden by a gray, scraggly beard. No sooner did his eyes rest upon her than they opened wide in amazement. He sprang from his chair, put his hand to his head, as if to assure himself that he was not dreaming, and said,

"What!—yer ain't—'fore God it must be—Miss Mollie!"

"Oh, Nimbus!" cried Mollie, with a shriek. Her face was pale as ashes, and she would have fallen had not Hesden sprang to her side and supported her with his arm, while he said,

"Hush! hush! You must not speak so loud. I did not expect you so soon or I would have told you."

The colored man fell upon his knees, and gazed in wonder on the scene.

"Oh, Marse Hesden!" he cried, "is it—can it be our Miss Mollie, or has Nimbus gone clean crazy wid de rest ob his misfortins?"

"No, indeed!" said Hesden. "It is really Miss Mollie, only I have stolen her away from her old friends and made her mine."

"There is no mistake about it, Nimbus," said Mollie, as she extended her hand, which the colored man clasped in both his own and covered with tears and kisses, while he said, between his sobs,

"T'ank God! T'ank God! Nimbus don't keer now! He ain't afeared ob nuffin' no mo', now he's seen de little angel dat use ter watch ober him, an' dat he's been a-dreamin' on all dese yeahs! Bress God, she's alive! Dar ain't no need ter ax fer 'Gena ner de little ones now; I knows dey's all right! Miss Mollie's done tuk keer o' dem, else she wouldn't be h'yer now. Bress de Lord, I sees de deah little lamb once mo'."

"There, there!" said Mollie gently. "You must not talk any more now. I have brought you something to eat. You are tired and hungry. You must eat now. Everything is all right. 'Gena and the children are well, and have been looking for you every day since you went away."

"Bress God! Bress God! I don't want nuffin' mo'!" said Nimbus. He would have gone on, in a wild rhapsody of delight, but both Hesden and Mollie interposed and compelled him to desist and eat. Ah! it was a royal meal that the poor fugitive had spread before him. Mollie brought some milk. A coffee-pot was placed upon the fire, and while he ate they told him of some of the changes that had taken place. When at length Hesden took him into the room where Eliab had remained concealed so long, and closed the door and locked it upon him, they could still hear the low tones of thankful prayer coming from within. Hesden knocked upon the door to enjoin silence, and they returned to their room, wondering at the Providence which had justified the faith of the long-widowed colored wife.

The next day Hesden went to the Court House to ascertain what charges there were against Nimbus. He found there were none. The old prosecution for seducing the laborers of Mr. Sykes had long ago been discontinued. Strangely enough, no others had been instituted against him. For some reason the law had not been appealed to to avenge the injuries of the marauders who had devastated Red Wing. On his return, Hesden came by way of Red Wing and brought Eliab home with him.

The meeting between the two old friends was very affecting. Since the disappearance of Nimbus, Eliab had grown more self-reliant. His two years and more of attendance at a Northern school had widened and deepened his manhood as well as increased his knowledge, and the charge of the school at Red Wing had completed the work there begun. His self-consciousness had diminished, and it no longer required the spur of intense excitement to make him forget his affliction. His last injuries had made him even more helpless, when separated from his rolling-chair, but his life had been too full to enable him to dwell upon his weakness so constantly as formerly.

In Nimbus there was a change even more apparent. Gray hairs, a bowed form, a furrowed face, and that sort of furtive wildness which characterizes the man long hunted by his enemies, had taken the place of his former unfearing, bull-fronted ruggedness. His spirit was broken. He no longer looked to the future with abounding hope, careless of its dangers.

"Yer's growed away from me, Bre'er 'Liab," he said at length, when they had held each other's hands and looked into each other's faces for a long time. "Yer wouldn't know how ter take a holt o' Nimbus ter hev him tote yer roun', now. Yer's growed away from him—clean away," he added sadly.

"You, too, have changed, Brother Nimbus," said Eliab soothingly.

"Yes, I'se changed, ob co'se; but not as you hez, Bre'er 'Liab. Dis h'yer ole shell hez changed. Nimbus couldn't tote yer roun' like he used. I'se hed a hard time—a hard time, 'Liab, an' I ain't nuffin' like de man I used ter be; but I hain't changed inside like you hez. I'se jes de same ole Nimbus dat I allus wuz—jes de same, only kinder broke down in sperrit, Bre'er 'Liab. I hain't growed ez you hev. I hain't no mo' man dan I was den—not so much, in fac'.

I don't keer now no mo' 'bout what's a-gwine ter be. I'se an' ole man, 'Liab—an' ole man, ef I is young."

That night he told his story to a breathless auditory.

"Yes, Bre'er 'Liab, dar's a heap o' t'ings happened sence dat ar mornin' I lef' you h'yer wid Marse Hesden. Yer see, I went back fust whar I'd lef' Berry, an' we tuk an' druv de mule an' carry-all inter a big pine thicket, down by de ribber, an' dar we stays all day mighty close; only once, when I went out by de road an' sees Miss Mollie ridin' by. I calls out to her jest ez loud ez I dared to; but, la sakes! she didn't h'year me."

"Was that you, Nimbus?" asked Mollie, turning from a bright-eyed successor to little Hildreth, whom she had been proudly caressing. "I thought I heard some one call me, but did not think of its being you. I am so sorry! I stopped and looked, but could see nothing."

"No, you didn't see me, Miss Mollie, but it done me a power o' good ter see *you*. I knowed yer was gwine ter Red Wing, an' yer'd take keer on an' advise dem ez wuz left dar. Wal, dat night we went back an' got the 'backer out o' de barn. I tuk a look roun' de house, an' went ter de smoke-house, an' got a ham of meat an' some other t'ings. I 'llowed dat 'Gena'd know I'd been dar, but didn't dare ter say nuffin' ter nobody, fer fear de sheriff's folks mout be a watchin' roun'. I 'llowed dey'd hev out a warrant for me, an' p'raps fer Berry too, on account o' what we'd done de night afo'."

"They never did," said Hesden.

"Yer don't tell me!" exclaimed Nimbus, in surprise.

"No. There has never been any criminal process against you, except for enticing Berry away from old Granville Sykes," said Hesden.

"Wal," responded Nimbus, "t'was all de same. I t'ought dey would. De udder wuz 'nough, dough. Ef dey could once cotch me on dat, I reckon dey could hev hung me fer nuffin', fer dat matter."

"It was a very wise thing in you to leave the country," said Hesden. "There is no doubt of that."

"T'ank ye, Marse Hesden, t'ank ye," said Nimbus. "I'se glad ter know I hain't been a fool allus, ef I is now. But now I t'inks on't, Marse Hesden, I'd like ter know what come of dem men dat 'Gena an' me put our marks on dat night."

"One of them died a year or two afterward—was never well after that night—and the other is here, alive and well, with a queer seam down the middle of his face," said Hesden.

"Died, yer say?" said Nimbus. "Wal, I'se right sorry, but he lived a heap longer nor Bre'er 'Liab would, ef I hadn't come in jest about dat time."

"Yes, indeed," said Eliab, as he extended his hand to his old friend.

"Wal," continued Nimbus, "we went on ter Wellsboro, an' dar we sold de 'backer. Den we kinder divided up. I tuk most o' de money an' went on South, an' Berry tuk de mule an' carry-all an' started fer his home in Hanson County. I tuk de cars an' went on, a-stoppin' at one place an' anodder, an' a wukkin' a little h'yer an' dar, but jest a-'spectin' ebbery minnit ter be gobbled up by a officer an' brought back h'yer. I'd heard dat Texas wuz a good place fer dem ter go ter dat didn't want nobody ter find 'em; so I sot out ter go dar. When I got ez fur ez Fairfax, in Louisiana, I was tuk down wid de fever, an' fer nigh 'bout six month I wa'ant ob no account whatebber. An' who yer tink tuk keer ob me den, Marse Hesden?"

"I am sure I don't know," was the reply.

"No, yer wouldn't nebber guess," said Nimbus; "but twa'n't nobody else but my old mammy, Lorency."

"You don't say! Well, that was strange," said Hesden.

"It was quare, Marse Hesden. She was gittin' on to be a old woman den. She's dead sence. Yer see, she knowed me by my name, an' she tuk keer on me, else I'd nebber been here ter tell on't. Atter I got better like, she sorter persuaded me ter stay dar. I wuz powerful homesick, an' wanted ter h'year from 'Gena an' de chillen, an' ef I'd hed money 'nough left, I'd a come straight back h'yer; but what with travellin' an' doctors' bills, an' de like, I hadn't nary cent. Den I couldn't leave my ole mammy, nuther. She'd hed a hard time sence de wah, a-wukkin' fer herself all alone, an' I wuz boun' ter help her all I could. I got a man to write ter Miss Mollie; but de letter come back sayin' she wa'n't h'yer no mo'. Den I got him to write ter whar she'd been afo' she come South; but that come back too."

"Why did you not write to me?" said Hesden.

"Wal," said Nimbus, with some confusion, "I wuz afeared ter do it, Marse Hesden. I wuz afeared yer mout hev turned agin me. I dunno why 'twuz, but I wuz mighty skeered ob enny white folks, 'ceptin' Miss Mollie h'yer. So I made it up wid mammy, dat we should wuk on till we'd got 'nough ter come back; an' den we'd come, an' I'd stop at some place whar I wa'n't knowed, an' let her come h'yer an' see how t'ings wuz.

"I'd jest about got ter dat pint, when I hed anodder pull-back. Yer see, dar wuz two men, both claimed ter be sheriff o' dat parish. Dat was—let me see, dat was jes de tenth yeah atter de S'render, fo' years atter I left h'yer.[120] One on 'em, ez near ez I could make out, was app'inted by de Guv'ner, an' t'odder by a man dat claimed ter be Guv'ner. De fust one called on de cullu'd men ter help him hold de Court House an' keep t'ings a-gwine on right; an' de t'odder, he raised a little army an' come agin' us. I'd been a sojer, yer know, an' I t'ought I wuz bound ter stan' up fer de guv'ment. So I went in ter fight wid de rest. We t'rew up some bres'wuks, an' when dey druv us outen dem we fell back inter de Court House. Den dar come a boat load o' white folks down from Sweevepo't, an' we hed a hard time a-fightin' on 'em. Lots ob us got killed, an' some o' dem. We hadn't many guns ner much ammunition. It war powerful hot, an' water wuz skeerce.

"So, atter a while, we sent a flag o' truce, an' 'greed ter s'render ebberyting, on condition dat dey wouldn't hurt us no mo'. Jest ez quick ez we gib up dey tuk us all pris'ners. Dar was twenty-sebben in de squad I wuz wid. 'Long a while atter dark, dey tuk us out an' marched us off, wid a guard on each side. We hadn't gone more'n two or t'ree hundred yards afo' de guard begun ter shoot at us. Dey hit me in t'ree places, an' I fell down an' rolled inter a ditch by de roadside, kinder under de weeds like. Atter a while I sorter come ter myself an' crawled off fru de weeds ter de bushes. Nex' day I got a chance ter send word ter mammy, an' she come an' nussed me till we managed ter slip away from dar."

"Poor Nimbus!" said Mollie, weeping. "You have had a hard time indeed!"

"Not so bad as de odders," was the reply. "Dar wuz only two on us dat got away at all. The rest wuz all killed."

"Yes," said Hesden, "I remember that affair. It was a horrible thing. When will our Southern people learn wisdom!"

"I dunno dat, Marse Hesden," said Nimbus, "but I do know dat de cullu'd folks is larnin' enough ter git outen dat. You jes mark my words, ef dese t'ings keep a-gwine on, niggers'll be skeerce in dis kentry purty soon. We can't be worse off, go whar we will, an' I jes count a cullu'd man a fool dat don't pole out an' git away jest ez soon ez he finds a road cut out dat he kin trabbel on."

"But that was three years ago, Nimbus," said Hesden. "Where have you been since?"

"Wal, yer see, atter dat," said Nimbus, "we wuz afeared ter stay dar any mo'. So we went ober inter Miss'ippi, mammy an' me, an' went ter wuk agin. I wasn't berry strong, but we wukked hard an' libbed hard ter git money ter come back wid. Mammy wuz powerful anxious ter git back h'yer afo' she died. We got along tollable-like, till de cotting wuz about all picked, an' hadn't drawed no wages at all, to speak on. Den, one day, de boss man on de plantation, he picked a quarrel wid mammy 'bout de wuk, an' presently hit her ober her old gray head wid his cane. I couldn't stan' dat, nohow, so I struck him, an' we hed a fight. I warn't nuffin' ter what I war once, but dar war a power o' strength in me yet, ez he found out.

"Dey tuk me up an' carried me ter jail, an' when de court come on, my ole mammy wuz dead; so I couldn't prove she war my mammy, an' I don't 'llow 'twould hev made enny difference ef I had. The jury said I war guilty, an' de judge fined me a hundred dollars an' de costs, an' sed I wuz ter be hired out at auction ter pay de fine, an' costs, an' sech like. So I wuz auctioned off, an' brought twenty-five cents a day.[121] 'Cordin' ter de law, I hed ter wuk two days ter make up my keep fer ebbery one I lost. I war sick an' low-sperrited, an' hadn't no heart ter wuk, so I lost a heap o' days. Den I run away once or twice, but dey cotch me, an' brought me back. So I kep' losin' time, an' didn't git clean away till 'bout four months ago. Sence den I'se been wukkin' my way back, jes dat skeery dat I dassent hardly walk de roads fer fear I'd be tuk up agin. But I felt jes like my ole mammy dat wanted ter come back h'yer ter die."

"But you are not going to die," said Mollie, smiling through her tears. "Your plantation is all right. We will send for 'Gena and the children, and you and Eliab can live again at Red Wing and be happy."

"I don't want ter lib dar, Miss Mollie," said Nimbus. "I ain't a-gwine ter die, ez you say; but I don't want ter lib h'yer, ner don't want my chillen ter. I want 'em ter lib whar dey kin be free, an' hev 'bout half a white man's chance, ennyhow."

"But what about Red Wing?" asked Hesden.

"I'd like ter see it once mo'," said the broken-hearted man, while the tears ran down his face. "I 'llowed once that I'd hab a heap o' comfort dar in my ole days. But dat's all passed an' gone, now—passed an' gone! I'll tell yer what, Marse Hesden, I allus 'llowed fer Bre'er 'Liab ter hev half o' dat plantation. Now yer jes makes out de papers an' let him hev de whole on't, an' I goes ter Kansas wid 'Gena."

"No, no, Nimbus," said Eliab; "I could not consent—"

"Yes yer kin, 'Liab," said Nimbus quickly, with some of his old-time arrogance. "Yer kin an' yer will. You kin use dat er trac' o' lan' an' make it wuth sunthin' ter our people, an' I can't. So, yer sees, I'll jes be a-doin' my sheer, an' I'll allus t'ink, when I hears how yer's gittin' along an' a-doin' good, dat I'se a pardner wid ye in de wuk o' gibbin' light ter our people, so dat dey'll know how ter be free an' keep free forebber an' ebber. Amen!"

The listeners echoed his "amen," and Eliab, flinging himself into the arms of Nimbus, by whom he had been sitting, and whose hand he had held during the entire narrative, buried his face upon his breast and wept.

CHAPTER LX.

THE EXODIAN.

HESDEN AND MOLLIE were on their way homeward from Eupolia, where they had inspected their property and had seen Nimbus united with his family and settled for a new and more hopeful start in life. They had reached that wonderful young city of seventy-seven hills which faces toward free Kansas and reluctantly bears the ban which slavery put upon Missouri.[122] While they waited for their train in the crowded depot in which the great ever-welcoming far West meets and first shakes hands with ever-swarming East, they strolled about among the shifting crowd.

Soon they came upon a dusky group whose bags and bundles, variegated attire, and unmistakable speech showed that they were a party of those misguided creatures who were abandoning the delights of the South for the untried horrors of a life upon the plains of Kansas. These were of all ages, from the infant in arms to the decrepit patriarch, and of every shade of color, from Saxon fairness with blue eyes and brown hair to ebon blackness. They were telling their stories to a circle of curious listeners. There was no lack of variety of incident, but a wonderful similarity of motive assigned for the exodus they had undertaken.[123]

There were ninety-four of them, and they came from five different States —Alabama, Georgia, Mississippi, Louisiana, and Texas. They had started without preconcert, and were unacquainted with each other until they had collected into one body as the lines of travel converged on the route to Kansas. A few of the younger ones said that they had come because they had heard that Kansas was a country where there was plenty of work and good wages, and where a colored man could get pay for what he did. Others told strange tales of injustice and privation. Some, in explanation of their evident poverty, showed the contracts under which they had labored. Some told of personal outrage, of rights withheld, and of law curiously diverted from the ends of justice to the promotion of wrong. By far the greater number of them, however, declared their purpose to be to find a place where their children could grow up free, receive education, and have "a white man's chance" in the struggle of life. They did not expect ease or affluence themselves, but for their offspring they craved liberty, knowledge, and a fair start.

While Hesden and Mollie stood watching this group, with the interest one always feels in that which reminds him of home, seeing in these people the forerunners of a movement which promised to assume astounding proportions in the near future, they were startled by an exclamation from one of the party:

"Wall, I declar'! Ef dar ain't Miss Mollie—an' 'fore God, Marse Hesden, too!" Stumbling over the scattered bundles in his way, and pushing aside those who stood around, Berry Lawson scrambled into the presence of the travelers, bowing and scraping, and chuckling with delight; a battered wool hat in one hand, a shocking assortment of dilapidated clothing upon his person, but his face glowing with honest good-nature, and his tones resonant of fun, as if care and he had always been strangers.

"How d'ye, Miss Mollie—sah'vent, Marse Hesden. I 'llow I must be gittin' putty nigh ter de promised lan' when I sees you once mo'. Yah, yah! Yer hain't done forgot Berry, I s'pose? Kase ef yer hez, I'll jes hev ter whistle a chune ter call myself ter mind. Jes, fer instance now, like dis h'yer."

Then raising his hands and swaying his body in easy accompaniment, he began to imitate the mocking-bird in his mimicry of his feathered companions. He was very proud of this accomplishment, and his performance soon drew attention from all parts of the crowded depot. Noticing this, Hesden said,

"There, there Berry; that will do. There is no doubt as to your identity. We both believe that nobody but Berry Lawson could do that, and are very glad to see you." Mollie smiled assent.

"T'ank ye, sah. Much obleeged fer de compliment. Hope I see yer well, an' Miss Mollie de same. Yer do me proud, both on yer," said Berry, bowing and scraping again, making a ball of his old hat, sidling restlessly back and forth, and displaying all the limpsy litheness of his figure, in his embarrassed attempts to show his enjoyment. "'Pears like yer's trabblin' in company," he added, with a glance at Mollie's hand resting on Hesden's arm.

"Yes," said Hesden good-naturedly; "Miss Mollie is Mrs. Le Moyne now."

"Yer don't say!" said Berry, in surprise. "Der Lo'd an' der nation, what will happen next? Miss Mollie an' Marse Hesden done married an' a-meetin' up wid Berry out h'yer on de berry edge o' de kingdom! Jest ez soon hab expected to a' seen de vanguard o' de resurrection. Yer orter be mighty proud, Marse Hesden. We used ter t'ink, 'bout Red Wing, dat dar wa'n't nary man dat ebber cast a shadder good 'nough fer Miss Mollie."

"And so there isn't," said Hesden, laughing. "But we can't stand here and talk all day. Where are you from?"

"Whar's I frum? Ebbery place on de green yairth, Marse Hesden, 'ceptin' dis one, whar dey hez ter shoe de goats fer ter help 'em climb de bluffs; an' please de Lo'd I'll be from h'yer jest es soon ez de train come's 'long dat's 'boun' fer de happy land of Canaan.'"

"We shall have to stop over, dear," said Hesden to his wife. "There's no doing anything with Berry in the time we have between the trains. Have you any baggage?" he asked of Berry.

"Baggage? Dat I hab—a whole handkercher full o' clean clo'es—jest ez soon ez dey's been washed, yer know. Yah, yah!"

"Where are you going?"

"Whar's I gwine? Gwine West, ter grow up wid de kentry, Marse Hesden."

"There, there, take your bundle and come along."

"All right, Marse Hesden. Jest ez soon wuk fer you ez ennybody. Good-by, folkses," said he, waving his hat to his late traveling companions. "I'se mighty sorry to leave yer, but biz is biz, yer know, an' I'se got a job. Wish yer good luck, all on yer. Jes let 'em know I'm on der way, will yer?

> Ef yo' gits dar afo' I do,
> Jes tell 'em I'se a-comin' too,"[124]

he sang, as he followed Hesden and Mollie out of the depot, amid the laughter of the crowd which had gathered about them. Their baggage was soon removed from the platform, and, with Berry on the seat with the driver, they went to the hotel. Then, taking him down the busy street that winds around between the sharp hills as though it had crawled up, inch by inch, from the river-bottom below, Hesden procured him some new clothes and a valise, which Berry persisted in calling a "have'em-bag," and took him back to the hotel as his servant. As Hesden started to his room, the rejuvenated fugitive inquired,

"Please, Marse Hesden, does yer know ennyt'ing what's a come ob—ob my Sally an' de chillen. It's been a powerful time sence I seed 'em, Marse Hesden. I 'llow ter send fer 'em jest ez quick ez I find whar dey is, an' gits de money, yer know."

"They are all right, Berry. You may come to my room in half an hour, and we will tell you all about them," answered Hesden.

Hardly had he reached his room when he heard the footsteps of Berry without. Going to the door he was met by Berry with the explanation,

"Beg parding, Marse Hesden. I knowed 'twa'n't de time fer me ter come yit, but somehow I 'llowed it would git on pearter ef I wuz somewhar nigh you an' Miss Mollie. I'se half afeared I'se jes been dreamin' ennyhow."

"Well, come in," said Hesden. Berry entered the room, and sat in unwonted silence while Mollie and her husband told him what the reader already knows about his family and friends. The poor fellow's tears flowed freely, but he did not interrupt, save to ask now and then a question. When they had concluded, he sat a while in silence, and then said,

"Bress de Lo'd! Berry won't nebber hab no mo' doubt 'bout de Lo'd takin' keer ob ebberybody—speshully niggas an' fools. H'yer I'se been a-feelin' mighty hard kase de Ole Marster 'llowed Berry ter be boxed roun', h'yer an' dar, fus dis way an' now dat, an' let him be run off from his wife an' chillen dat he t'ought der couldn't nobody take keer on but hissef; an' h'yer all de time de good Lo'd hez been a-lookin' atter 'em an' a-nussin' 'em like little lambs, widout my knowin' ennyt'ing about it, er even axin' fer him ter do it. Berry!" he continued, speaking to himself, "yer's jest a gran' rascal, an' desarve ter be whacked roun' an' go hungry fer—"

"Berry," interrupted Mollie, "have you had your breakfast?"

"Brekfas', Miss Mollie?" said Berry, "what Berry want ob any brekfas'? Ain't what yer's been a-tellin' on him brekfas' an' dinner an' supper ter him? Brekfas' don't matter ter him now. He's jes dat full o' good t'ings dat he won't need no mo' for a week at de berry least."

"Tell the truth, Berry; when did you eat last?"

"Wal, I 'clar, Miss Mollie, ef Berry don't make no mistake, he hed a squar meal night afo' las', afo' we leave Saint Lewy. De yemergrant train runs mighty slow, an' Berry wa'n't patronizin' none o' dem cheap shops 'long de way—not much; yah, yah!"

Hesden soon arranged to relieve his discomfort, and that night he told them where he had been and what had befallen him in the mean time.

BERRY'S STORY.

"Yer see, atter I lef' Bre'er Nimbus, I went back down inter Hanson County; but I wuz jes dat bad skeered dat I darn't show myse'f in de daytime at all. So I jes' tuk Sally an' de chillen in de carry-all dat Nimbus lent me wid de mule, an' started on furder down east. 'Clar, I jes hev ter pay Nimbus fer dat mule an' carry-all, de berry fus' money I gits out h'yer in Kansas. It certain war a gret help ter Berry. Jest as long ez I hed dat ter trabbel wid, I knowed I war safe; kase nobody wouldn't nebber 'spect I was runnin' away in dat sort ob style. Wal, I went way down east, an' de nex' spring went ter crappin' on sheers on a cotting plantation. Sally 'n' me we jes made up our minds dat we wouldn't draw no rations from de boss man, ner ax him fer ary cent ob money de whole yeah, an' den, yer know, dar wouldn't be nary 'count agin us when de year wuz ober. So Sally, she 'llowed dat she'd wuk fer de bread an' meat an' take keer ob de chillen, wid de few days' help I might spar' outen de crap. De boss man, he war boun' by de writin's ter feed de mule. Dat's de way we sot in.

"We got 'long mighty peart like till some time atter de crap wuz laid by, 'long bout roastin'-ear-time. Den Sally tuk sick, an' de fus' dat I knowed we wuz out o' meat. Sally wuz powerful sot agin my goin' ter de boss man fer enny orders on de store, kase we knowed how dat wukked afo'. Den I sez, 'See h'yer, Sally, I'se done got it. Dar's dat piece ob corn dar, below de house, is jest a-gittin' good fer roastin yeahs. Now, we'll jes pick offen de outside rows, an' I'll be dod-dinged ef we can't git 'long wid dat till de crap comes off; an' I'll jes tell Marse Hooper—dat wuz de name o' de man what owned de plantation—dat I'll take dem rows inter my sheer.' So it went on fer a week er two, an' I t'ought I wuz jes gittin' on like a quarter hoss. Sally wuz nigh 'bout well, an' 'llowed she'd be ready ter go ter wuk de nex' week; when one mo'nin' I tuk the basket an' went down ter pick some corn. Jest ez I'd got de basket nigh 'bout full, who should start up dar, outen de bushes, on'y jes Marse Hooper; an' he sez, mighty brisk-like, 'So? I 'llowed I'd cotch yer 'fore I got fru! Stealin' corn, is yer?'

"Den I jes larfed right out, an' sez I, 'Dat's de fus' time I ebber heerd ob ennybody a-stealin' corn out ob his own field! Yah! yah!' Jes so-like. 'Ain't dis yer my crap, Marse Hooper? Didn't I make it, jest a-payin' ter you one third on't for de rent?' T'ought I hed him, yer know. But, law sakes, he didn't hev no sech notion, not much. So he sez, sez he:

"'No yer don't! Dat mout a' done once, when de Radikils wuz in power, but de legislatur las' winter dey made a diff'rent sort ob a law, slightually. Dey sed dat ef a renter tuk away enny 'o de crap afo' it wuz all harvested an' diwided, widout de leave o' de owner, got afo'hand, he was guilty o' stealin' '—larsininy,' he called it, but its all de same. An' he sed, sez he, 'Dar ain't no use now, Berry Lawson. Yer's jes got yer choice. Yer kin jes git up an' git, er else I hez yer 'dicted an' sent ter State prison fer not less ner one year nor more'n twenty—dat's 'cordin' ter de law."

"Den I begun ter be skeered-like, an' I sez, sez I, 'Arn't yer gwine ter let me stay an' gether my crap?'

"'Damn de crap,' sez he (axin' yer parding, Miss Mollie, fer usin' cuss-words), 'I'll take keer o' de crap; don't yer be afeared o' dat. Yer t'ought yer was damn smart, didn't yer, not takin' enny store orders, an' a-tryin' to fo'ce me ter pay yer cash in de lump? But now I'se got yer. Dis Lan'lo'd an' Tenant Act[125] war made fer jes sech cussed smart niggers ez you is.'

"'Marse Hooper,' sez I, 'is dat de law?'

"'Sartin,' sez he, 'jes you come long wid me ober ter Squar Tice's, an' ef he don't say so I'll quit—dat's all.'

"So we went ober ter Squar Tice's, an' he sed Marse Hooper war right—dat it war stealin' all de same, even ef it war my own crap. Den I seed dat Marse Hooper hed me close, an' I begun ter beg off, kase I knowed it war a heap easier ter feed him soft corn dan ter fight him in de law, when I wuz boun' ter git whipped. De Squar war a good sort ob man, an' he kinder 'suaded Marse Hooper ter 'comp' de matter wid me; an' dat's what we did finally. He gin me twenty dollahs an' I signed away all my right ter de crap. Den he turned in an' wanted ter hire me fer de nex yeah; but de Squar, he tuk me out an' sed I'd better git away from dar, kase ennybody could bring de matter up agin me an' git me put in de penitentiary fer it, atter all dat hed been sed an' done. So we geared up, an' moved on. Sally felt mighty bad, an' it did seem hard; but I tried ter chirk her up, yer know, an' tole her dat, rough ez it war, it war better nor we'd ebber done afo', kase we hed twenty dollahs an' didn't owe nuffin'.

"I 'llowed we'd git clean away dat time, an' we didn't stop till we'd got inter anodder State."

"Wal, dar I sot in ter wuk a cotting crap agin. Dis time I 'llowed I'd jes take de odder way; an' so I tuk up all de orders on de sto' dat de boss man would let me hev, kase I 'llowed ter git what I could ez I went 'long, yer know. So, atter de cotting wuz all picked, an' de 'counts all settled up, dar warn't only jest one little bag ob lint a comin' ter Berry. I tuk dat inter de town one Saturday in de ebenin', an' went roun' h'yer an' dar, a-tryin' ter git de biggest price 'mong de buyers dat I could.

It happened dat I done forgot al 'bout it's comin' on late, an' jest a little atter sun-down, I struck on a man dat offered me 'bout a cent a poun' more'n ennybody else hed done, an' I traded wid him. Den I druv de mule roun', an' hed jes got de cotting out ob de carry-all an' inter de sto', when, fust I knowed, 'long come a p'liceman an' tuk me up for selling cotting atter sun-down. I tole him dat it was my own cotting, what I'd done raised myself, but he sed ez how it didn't make no sort of diff'rence at all. He 'clared dat de law sed ez how ennybody ez sold er offered fer sale any cotting atter sundown an' afore sun-up, should be sent ter jail jes de same ez ef he'd done stole it.[126] Den I axed de man dat bought de cotting ter gib it back ter me, but he wouldn't do dat, nohow, nor de money for it nuther. So dey jes' toted me off ter jail.

I knowed der warn't no use in sayin' nuffin' den. So when Sally come in I tole her ter jes take dat ar mule an' carry-all an' sell 'em off jest ez quick ez she could, so dat nobody wouldn't git hold ob dem. But when she tried ter do it, de boss man stopped her from it, kase he hed a mortgage on 'em fer de contract; an' he sed ez how I hedn't kep' my bargain kase I'd gone an' got put in jail afo' de yeah was out. So she couldn't git no money ter pay a lawyer, an' I don't s'pose 'twould hev done enny good ef she hed. I tole her not ter mind no mo' 'bout me, but jes ter come back ter Red Wing an' see ef Miss Mollie couldn't help her out enny. Yer see I was jes shore dey'd put me in de chain-gang, an' I didn't want her ner de chillen ter be whar dey'd see me a totin' 'roun' a ball an' chain.

Shore 'nough, when de court come on, dey tried me an' fotch me in guilty o' sellin' cotting atter sundown. De jedge, he lectured me powerful fer a while, an' den he ax me what I'd got ter say 'bout it. Dat's de way I understood him ter say, ennyhow. So, ez he wuz dat kind ez ter ax me ter speak in meetin', I 'llowed twa'n't no mo' dan polite fer me ter say a few words, yer know. I told him squar out dat I t'ought 'twas a mighty quare law an' a mighty mean one, too, dat put a man in de chain-gang jes kase he sold his own cotting atter sundown, when dey let ennybody buy it an' not pay fer it at all. I tole him dat dey let 'em sell whisky an' terbacker an' calico and sto' clo'es an' ebbery t'ing dat a nigger hed ter buy, jest all times o' day an' night;[127] an' I jest bleeved dat de whole t'ing war jest a white man's trick ter git niggas in de chain-gang. Den de jedge he tried ter set down on me an' tole me ter stop, but I wuz dat mad dat when I got a-gwine dar warn't no stoppin' me till de sheriff he jes grabbed me by de scruff o' de neck, an' sot me down jest ennyway—all in a heap, yer know. Den de jedge passed sentence, yer know, an' he sed dat he gib me one year fer de stealin' an' one year fer sassin' de Court.

"So dey tuk me back ter jail, but, Lor' bress ye, dey didn't git me inter de chain-gang, nohow. 'Fore de mo'nin' come I'd jes bid good-by ter dat jail an' was a pintin' outen dat kentry, in my weak way, ez de ministers say, jest ez fast ez I could git ober de groun'.

"Den I jes clean gib up. I couldn't take my back trac nowhar, fer fear I'd be tuk up. I t'ought it all ober while I wuz a trabblin' 'long; an' I swar ter God, Marse Hesden, I jes did peg out ob all hope. I couldn't go back ter Sallie an' de chillen, ner couldn't do 'em enny good ef I did; ner I couldn't send fer dem ter come ter me, kase I hedn't nuffin' ter fotch 'em wid. So I jes kinder gin out, an' went a-sloshin' roun', not a-keerin' what I done er what was ter come on me. I kep' a'sendin' letters ter Sally h'yer an' dar, but, bress yer soul, I nebber heard nuffin' on 'em atterwards. Den I t'ought I'd try an' git money ter go an' hunt 'em up, but it was jes' ez it was afo'. I dunno how, but de harder I wuk de porer I got, till finally I jes started off afoot an' alone ter go ter Kansas; an' h'yer I is, ready ter grow up wid de kentry, Marse Hesden, jest ez soon ez I gits ter Sally an' de chillen."

"I'm glad you have not had any political trouble," said Hesden.

"P'litical trouble?" said Berry. "Wal, Marse Hesden, yer knows dat Berry is jes too good-natered ter do ennyt'ing but wuk an' larf, an' do a little whistlin' an banjo-pickin' by way ob a change; but I be dinged ef it don't 'pear ter me dat it's all p'litical trouble. Who's Berry ebber hurt? What's he ebber done, I'd like ter know, ter be debbled roun' dis yer way? I use ter vote, ob co'se. T'ought I hed a right ter, an' dat it war my duty ter de kentry dat hed gib me so much. But I don't do dat no mo'. Two year ago I quit dat sort o' foolishness. What's de use? I see'd 'em count de votes, Marse Hesden, an' den I knowed dar warn't no mo' use ob votin' gin dat. Yer know, dey 'pints all de jedges ob de 'lection derselves, an' so count de votes jest ez dey wants 'em. Dar in our precinct war two right good white men, but dey 'pinted nary one o' dem ter count de votes. Oh no, not ter speak on! Dey puts on de Board a good-'nough old cullu'd man dat didn't know 'B' from a bull's foot. Wal, our white men 'ranges de t'ing so dat dey counts our men ez dey goes up ter de box an' dey gibs out de tickets dereselves. Now, dar wuz six hundred an' odd ob our tickets went inter dat box. Dat's shore. But dar wa'n't t'ree hundred come out. I pertended ter be drunk, an' laid down by de chimbly whar dar was a peep-hole inter dat room, an' seed dat countin' done. When dey fust opened de box one on 'em sez, sez he,

" 'Lord God! what a lot o' votes!' Den dey all look an' 'llowed dar war a heap mo 'votes than dey'd got names. So they all turned in ter count de votes. Dar wuz two kinds on 'em. One wuz little bits ob slick, shiny fellers, and de odders jes common big ones. When dey'd got 'em all counted they done some figurin,' an' sed dey'd hev ter draw out 'bout t'ree hundred an' fifty votes. So dey put 'em all back in de box, all folded up jest ez dey wuz at de start, an' den dey shuck it an' shuck it an' shuck it, till it seemed ter me 'em little fellers wuz boun' ter slip fru de bottom. Den one on 'em wuz blindfolded, an' he drew outen de box till he got out de right number—mostly all on 'em de big tickets, mind ye, kase dey wuz on top, yer know. Den dey count de rest an' make up de papers, an' burns all de tickets.

"Now what's de use o' votin' agin dat? I can't see what fer dey put de tickets in de box at all. 'Tain't half ez fa'r ez a lottery I seed one time in Melton; kase dar dey kep turnin' ober de wheel, an' all de tickets hed a fa'r show. No, Marse Hesden, I nebber does no mo' votin' till I t'inks dar's a leetle chance o' habbin' my vote counted jest ez I drops it inter de box, 'long wid de rest. I don't see no use in it."

"You are quite right, Berry," said Hesden; "but what do *you* say is the reason you have come away from the South?"

"Jest kase a poor man dat hain't got no larnin' is wuss off dar dan a cat in hell wid out claws; he can't fight ner he can't climb. I'se wukked hard an' been honest ebber sence de S'render an' I hed ter walk an' beg my rations ter git h'yer.* Dat's de reason!" said Berry, springing to his feet and speaking excitedly.

"Yes, Berry, you have been unfortunate, but I know all are not so badly off."

"T'ank God fer dat!" said Berry. "Yer see I'd a' got 'long well 'nough ef I'd hed a fa'r shake an' hed knowd' all 'bout de law, er ef de law hadn't been made ter cotch jes sech ez me. I didn't ebber 'spect nuffin' but jest a tollable libbin', only a bit ob larnin, fer my chillen. I tried mighty hard, an' dis is jes what's come on't. I don't pertend ter say what's de matter, but sunthin' is wrong, or else sunthin' *hez been* wrong, an' dis that we hez now is jest de fruits on't—I dunno which. I can't understand it, nohow. I don't hate nobody, an' I don't know ez dar's enny way out, but only jes ter wait an' wait ez we did in slave times fer de good time ter come. I wuz jes dat tuckered out a-tryin,' dat I t'ought I'd come out h'yer an' wait an' see ef I couldn't grow up wid de kentry, yer know. Yah, yah!"

The next morning the light-hearted exodian departed, with a ticket for Eupolia and a note to his white fellow-fugitive from the evils which a dark past has bequeathed to the South—Jordan Jackson, now the agent of Hesden and Mollie in the management of their interests at that place. Hesden and Mollie continued their homeward journey, stopping for a few days in Washington on their way.

* The actual words used by a colored man well-known to the writer in giving his reason for joining the "exodus," in a conversation in the depot at Kansas City, in February last.

CHAPTER LXI.

WHAT SHALL THE END BE?

TWO MEN SAT upon one of the benches in the shade of a spreading elm in the shadow of the National Capitol, as the sun declined toward his setting. They had been walking and talking as only earnest, thoughtful men are wont to talk. They had forgotten each other and themselves in the endeavor to forecast the future of the country after a consideration of its past.

One was tall, broad, and of full habit, with a clear blue eye, high, noble forehead, and brown beard and hair just beginning to be flecked with gray, and of a light complexion inclining to floridness. He was a magnificent type of the Northern man. He had been the shaper of his own destiny, and had risen to high position, with the aid only of that self-reliant manhood which constitutes the life and glory of the great free North. He was the child of the North-west, but his ancestral roots struck deep into the rugged hills of New England. The West had made him broader and fuller and freer than the stock from which he sprang, without impairing his earnestness of purpose or intensity of conviction.

The other, more slender, dark, with something of sallowness in his sedate features, with hair and beard of dark brown clinging close to the finely-chiseled head and face, with an empty sleeve pinned across his breast, showed more of litheness and subtlety, and scarcely less of strength, than the one on whom he gazed, and was an equally perfect type of the Southern-born American. The one was the Honorable Washington Goodspeed, M.C., and the other was Hesden Le Moyne.

"Well, Mr. Le Moyne," said the former, after a long and thoughtful pause, "is there any remedy for these things? Can the South and the North ever be made one people in thought, spirit, and purpose? It is evident that they have not been in the past; can they become so in the future? Wisdom and patriotism have thus far developed no cure for this evil; they seem, indeed, to have proved inadequate to the elucidation of the problem. Have you any solution to offer?"

"I think," replied Le Moyne, speaking slowly and thoughtfully, "that there is a solution lying just at our hand, the very simplicity of which, perhaps, has hitherto prevented us from fully appreciating its effectiveness."

"Ah!" said Goodspeed, with some eagerness, "and what may that be?"

"Education!" was the reply.

"Oh, yes," said the other, with a smile. "You have adopted, then, the Fourth of July remedy for all national ills?"

"If you mean by 'Fourth of July remedy,'" replied Hesden with some tartness, "that it is an idea born of patriotic feeling alone, I can most sincerely answer, Yes. You will please to recollect that every bias of my mind and life has been toward the Southern view of all things. I doubt if any man of the North can appreciate the full force and effect of that bias upon the minds and hearts of those exposed to its operation. When the war ended I had no reason or motive for considering the question of rebuilding the national prosperity and power upon a firmer and broader basis than before. That was left entirely to you gentlemen of the North. It was not until you, the representatives of the national power, had acted—ay, it was not until your action had resulted in apparent failure—that I began to consider this question at all. I did so without any selfish bias or hope, beyond that which every man ought to have in behalf of the Nation [of] which he is a part, and in which he expects his children to remain. So that I think I may safely say that my idea of the remedy does spring from a patriotism as deep and earnest as ever finds expression upon the national holiday."

"Oh, I did not mean that," was the half-apologetic rejoinder; "I did not mean to question your sincerity at all; but the truth is, there has been so much impracticable theorizing upon this subject that one who looks for results can scarcely restrain an expression of impatience when that answer is dogmatically given to such an inquiry."

"Without entirely indorsing your view as to the impracticality of what has been said and written upon this subject," answered Le Moyne, "I must confess that I have never yet seen it formulated in a manner entirely satisfactory to myself. For my part, I am thoroughly satisfied that it is not only practicable, but is also the sole practicable method of curing the ills of which we have been speaking. It seems to me also perfectly apparent why the remedy has not previously been applied—why the patriotism and wisdom of the past has failed to hit upon this simple remedy."

"Well, why was it?"

"The difference between the North and the South before the war," said Le Moyne, "was twofold; both the political and the social organizations of the South were utterly different from those of the North, and could not be harmonized with them. The characteristics of the *social* organization you, in common with the intelligent masses of the North, no doubt comprehend as fully and clearly as is possible for one who has not personally investigated its phenomena. Your Northern social system was builded upon the idea of inherent equality—that is, of equality and opportunity; so that the only inequality which could exist was that which resulted from the accident of wealth or difference of capacity in the individual.

"The social system of the South was opposed to this in its very elements. At the very outset it was based upon a wide distinction, never overlooked or forgotten for a single moment. Under no circumstances could a colored man, of whatever rank or grade of intellectual power, in any respect, for a single instant overstep the gulf which separated him from the Caucasian, however humble, impoverished, or degraded the latter might be. This rendered easy and natural the establishment of other social grades and ideas, which tended to separate still farther the Northern from the Southern social system. The very fact of the African being thus degraded led, by natural association, to the degradation of those forms of labor most frequently delegated to the slave. By this means free labor became gradually to be considered more and more disreputable, and self-support to be considered less and less honorable. The necessities of slavery, as well as the constantly growing pride of class, tended very rapidly toward the subversion of free thought and free speech; so that, even with the white man of any and every class, the right to hold and express opinions different from those entertained by the bulk of the master-class with reference to all those subjects related to the social system of the South soon came to be questioned, and eventually utterly denied. All these facts the North—that is, the Northern people, Northern statesmen, Northern thinkers—have comprehended *as* facts. Their influence and bearings, I may be allowed to say, they have little understood, because they have not sufficiently realized their influence upon the minds of those subjected, generation after generation, to their sway.

"On the other hand, the wide difference between the *political* systems of the North and the South seems never to have affected the Northern mind at all. The Northern statesmen and political writers seem always to have proceeded upon the assumption that the removal of slavery, the changing of the legal status of the African, resulting in the withdrawal of one of the props which supported the *social* system of the South, would of itself overthrow not only that system, but the political system which had grown up along with it, and which was skillfully designed for its maintenance and support. Of the absolute difference between the political systems of the South and the North, and of the fact that the social and political systems stood to each other in the mutual relation of cause and effect, the North seems ever to have been profoundly ignorant."

"Well," said Mr. Goodspeed, "I must confess that I cannot understand what difference there is, except what arose out of slavery."

"The question is not," said Le Moyne, "whether it *arose* out of slavery, but whether it would of necessity fall with the extinction of slavery *as a legal status.* It is, perhaps, impossible for any one to say exactly how much of the political system of the South grew out of slavery, and how much of slavery and its consequences were due to the Southern political system."

"I do not catch your meaning," said Goodspeed. "Except for the system of slavery and the exclusion of the blacks from the exercise and enjoyment of political rights and privileges, I cannot see that the political system of the South differed materially from that of the North."

"Precisely so," said Le Moyne. "Your inability to perceive my meaning very clearly illustrates to my mind the fact which I am endeavoring to impress upon you. If you will consider for a moment the history of the country, you will observe that a system prevailed in the non-slaveholding States which was unknown, either in name or essential attributes, throughout the slaveholding part of the country."

"Yes?" said the other inquiringly. "What may that have been?"

"In one word," said Le Moyne—"the 'township' system."

"Oh, yes," laughed the Congressman lightly; "the Yankee town-meeting."

"Exactly," responded Le Moyne; "yet I venture to say that the presence and absence of the town-meeting—the township system or its equivalent—in the North and in the South, constituted a difference not less vital and important than that of slavery itself. In fact, sir, I sincerely believe that it is to the township system that the North owes the fact that it is not to-day as much slave territory as the South was before the war."[128]

"What!" said the Northerner, with surprise, "you do not mean to say that the North owes its freedom, its prosperity, and its intelligence—the three things in which it differs from the South most materially—entirely to the Yankee town-meeting?"

"Perhaps not entirely," said Le Moyne; "but in the main I think it does. And there are certain facts connected with our history which I think, when you consider them carefully, will incline you to the same belief."

"Indeed; I should be glad to know them."

"The first of these," continued Le Moyne, "is the fact that in every state in which the township system really prevailed, slavery was abolished without recourse to arms, without civil discord or perceptible evil results. The next is that in the states in which the township system did not prevail in fact as well as name, the public school system did not exist, or had only a nominal existence; and the proportion of illiteracy in those states as a consequence was, *among the whites alone,* something like four times as great as in those states in which the township system flourished. And this, too, notwithstanding almost the entire bulk of the ignorant immigration from the old world entered into the composition of the Northern populations. And, thirdly, there resulted a difference which I admit to be composite in its causes—that is, the difference in average wealth. Leaving out of consideration the capital invested in slaves, the *per capita* valuation of the states having the township system was something more than three times the average in those where it was unknown."

"But what reason can you give for this belief?" said Goodspeed. "How do you connect with the consequences, which cannot be doubted, the cause you assign? The differences between the South and the North have hitherto been attributed entirely to slavery; why do you say that they are in so great a measure due to differences of political organization?"

"I can very well see," was the reply, "that one reared as you were should fail to understand at once the potency of the system which has always been to you as much a matter of course as the atmosphere by which you are surrounded. It was not until Harvey's time—indeed, it was not until a much later period—that we knew in what way and manner animal life was maintained by the inhalation of atmospheric air. The fact of its necessity was apparent to every child, but how it operated was unknown. I do not now profess to be able to give all of those particulars which have made the township system, or its equivalent, an essential concomitant of political equality, and, as I think, the vital element of American liberty. But I can illustrate it so that you will get the drift of my thought."

"I should be glad if you would," said Goodspeed.

"The township system," continued Le Moyne, "may, for the present purpose, be defined to be the division of the entire territory of the state into small municipalities, the inhabitants of which control and manage for themselves, directly and immediately, their own local affairs. Each township is in itself a miniature republic, every citizen of which exercises in its affairs equal power with every other citizen. Each of these miniature republics becomes a constituent element of the higher representative republic—

namely, a county, which is itself a component of the still larger representative republic, the State. It is patterned upon and no doubt grew out of the less perfect borough systems of Europe, and those inchoate communes of our Saxon forefathers which were denominated '*Hundreds.*' It is the slow growth of centuries of political experience; the ripe fruit of ages of liberty-seeking thought.

"The township is the shield and nursery of individual freedom of thought and action. The young citizen who has never dreamed of a political career becomes interested in some local question affecting his individual interests. A bridge is out of repair; a roadmaster has failed to perform his duty; a constable has been remiss in his office; a justice of the peace has failed to hold the scales with even balance between rich and poor; a school has not been properly cared for; the funds of the township have been squandered; or the assumption of a liability is proposed by the township trustees, the policy of which he doubts. He has the remedy in his own hands. He goes to the township meeting, or he appears at the town-house upon election day, and appeals to his own neighbors—those having like interests with himself. He engages in the struggle, hand to hand and foot to foot with his equals; he learns confidence in himself; he begins to measure his own power, and fits himself for the higher duties and responsibilities of statesmanship."

"Well, well," laughed Goodspeed, "there is something in that. I remember that my first political experience was in trying to defeat a supervisor who did not properly work the roads of his district; but I had never thought that in so doing I was illustrating such a doctrine as you have put forth."

"No; the doctrine is not mine," said Le Moyne. "Others, and especially that noted French political philosopher who so calmly and faithfully investigated our political system—the author of 'Democracy in America'—clearly pointed out, many years ago, the exceptional value of this institution, and attributed to it the superior intelligence and prosperity of the North."[129]

"Then," was the good-natured reply, "your prescription for the political regeneration of the South is the same as that which we all laughed at as coming from Horace Greeley[130] immediately upon the downfall of the Confederacy—that the Government should send an army of surveyors to the South to lay off the land in sections and quarter-sections, establish parallel roads, and enforce topographic uniformity upon the nation?"

"Not at all," said Le Moyne. "I think that the use of the term 'township' in a *double* sense has misled our political thinkers in estimating its value. It is by no means necessary that the township of the United States survey should be arbitrarily established in every state. In fact, the township system really finds its fullest development where such a land division does not prevail, as in New England, Pennsylvania, and other states. It is the *people* that require to be laid off in townships, not the land. Arkansas, Missouri, Alabama, all have their lands laid off in the parallelograms prescribed by the laws regulating United States surveys; but their *people* are not organized into self-governing communes."

"But was there no equivalent system of local self-government in those states?"

"No; and there is not to-day. In some cases there are lame approaches to it; but in none of the former slave States were the counties made up of self-governing subdivisions. The South is to-day and always has been a stranger to local self-government. In many of those states every justice of the peace, every school committeeman, every inspector of elections is appointed by some central power in the county, which is in turn itself appointed either by the Chief Executive of the State or by the dominant party in the Legislature. There may be the *form* of townships, but the differential characteristic is lacking—the self-governing element of the township."

"I don't know that I fully comprehend you," said Goodspeed. "Please illustrate."

"Well, take one state for an example, where the constitution adopted during the reconstruction period introduced the township system, and authorized the electors of each township to choose their justices of the peace, constables, school-committeemen, and other local officials. It permitted the people of the county to choose a board of commissioners, who should administer the financial matters of the county, and, in some instances, exercise a limited judicial authority. But now they have, in effect, returned to the old system.[131] The dominant party in the Legislature appoints every justice of the peace in the state. The justices of the peace of each county elect from their number the county commissioners; the county commissioners appoint the school-committeemen, the roadmasters, the registrars of election and the judges of election; so that every local interest throughout the entire state is placed under the immediate power and control of the dominant party, although not a tenth part of the voters of any particular township or county may belong to that party. In another state all this power, and even more, is exercised by the Chief Executive; and in all of them you will find that the county—or its equivalent, the parish—is the smallest political unit having a municipal character."

CHAPTER LXII.

HOW?

THERE WAS A moment of silence, after which the Northern man said thoughtfully,

"I think I understand your views, Mr. Le Moyne, and must admit that both the facts and the deductions which you make from them are very interesting, full of food for earnest reflection, and, for aught I know, may fully bear out your view of their effects. Still, I cannot see that your remedy for this state of affairs differs materially in its practicability from that of the departed philosopher of Chappaqua.[132] He prescribed a division of the lands, while, if I understand you, you would have the Government in some way prescribe and control the municipal organizations of the people of the various states. I cannot see what power the National Government has, or any branch of it, which could effectuate that result."

"It can only be done as it was done at the North," said Le Moyne quietly.

"Well, I declare!" said Goodspeed, with an outburst of laughter, "your riddle grows worse and worse—more and more insoluble to my mind. How, pray, was it done at the North? I always thought we got it from colonial times. I am sure the New England town-meeting came over in the Mayflower."

"So it did!" responded Hesden, springing to his feet; "so it did; it came over in the hearts of men who demanded, and were willing to give up everything else to secure the right of local self-government. The little colony upon the Mayflower was a township, and every man of its passengers carried the seed of the ideal township system in his heart."

"Admitted, admitted, Mr. Le Moyne," said the other, smiling at his earnestness. "But how shall we repeat the experiment? Would you import men into every township of the South, in order that they might carry the seeds of civil liberty with them, and build up the township system there?"

"By no means. I would make the men on the spot. I would so mold the minds of every class of the Southern people that all should be indoctrinated with the spirit of local self-government."

"But how would you do it?"

"With spelling-books!"[133] answered Hesden sententiously.

"There we are," laughed the other, "at the very point we started from. Like the poet of the Western barroom, you may well say, my friend, 'And so I end as I did begin.' "

"Yes," said Le Moyne, "we have considered the *desirability* of education, and you have continually cried, with good-natured incredulity, 'How shall it be done?' Are you not making that inquiry too soon?"

"Not at all," said the Congressman earnestly; "I see how desirable is the result, and I am willing to do anything in my power to attain it, if there is any means by which it can be accomplished."

"That is it," said Le Moyne; "you are *willing;* you recognize that it would be a good thing; you wish it might be done; you have no desire to stand in the way of its accomplishment. That is not the spirit which achieves results. Nothing is accomplished by mere assent. The American people must first be thoroughly satisfied that it is a necessity. The French may shout over a red cap, and overturn existing systems for a vague idea; but American conservatism consists in doing nothing until it is absolutely necessary. We never move until the fifty-ninth minute of the eleventh hour.

"Only think of it! You fought a rebellion, based professedly upon slavery as a corner-stone, for almost two years before you could bring yourselves to disturb that corner-stone. You knew the structure would fall if that were done; but the American people waited and waited until every man was fully satisfied that there was no other possible road to success. It is just so in this matter. I feel its necessity. You do not.'

"There I think you do me injustice," said Goodspeed, "I feel the necessity of educating every citizen of the Republic, as well as you."

"No doubt, in a certain vague way," was the reply; "but you do not feel it as the only safety to the Republic to-day; and I do."

"I confess I do not see, as you seem to, the immediate advantage, or the immediate danger, more than that which has always threatened us," answered the Congressman.

"This, after all, is the real danger, I think," said Le Moyne. "The states containing only one third of the population of this Union contain also more than two thirds of its entire illiteracy. Twenty-five out of every hundred—one out of every four—of the *white voters* of the former slave states cannot read the ballots which they cast; forty-five per cent of the entire voting strength of those sixteen states are unable to read or write."[134]

"Well?" said the other calmly, seeing Le Moyne look at him as though expecting him to show surprise.

"*Well!*" said Le Moyne. "I declare your Northern phlegm is past my comprehension. 'Well,' indeed! it seems to me as bad as bad can be. Only think of it—only six per cent of intelligence united with this illiterate vote makes a majority."

"Well?" was the response again, still inquiringly.

"And that majority," continued Le Moyne, "would choose seventy-two per cent of the electoral votes necessary to name a President of the United States!"

"Well," said the other, with grim humor, "they are not very likely to do it at present, anyhow."

"That is true," replied Le Moyne. "But there is still the other danger, and the greater evil. That same forty-five per cent are of course easily made the subjects of fraud or violence, and we face this dilemma: they may either use their power wrongfully, or be wrongfully deprived of the exercise of their ballotorial rights. Either alternative is alike dangerous. If we suppose the illiterate voter to be either misled or intimidated, or prevented from exercising his judgment and his equality of right with others in the control of our government, then we have the voice of this forty-five per cent silenced—whether by intimidation or by fraud matters not. Then a majority of the remaining fifty-four per cent, or, say, twenty-eight per cent of one third of the population of the Nation in a little more than one third of the States, might exercise seventy-two per cent of the electoral power necessary to choose a President, and a like proportion of the legislative power necessary to enact laws. Will the time ever come, my friend, when it will be safe to put in the way of any party such a temptation as is presented by this opportunity to acquire power?"

"No, no, no," said the Northern man, with impatience. "But what can you do? Education will not make men honest, or patriotic, or moral."

"True enough," was the reply. "Nor will the knowledge of toxicology prevent the physician from being a poisoner, or skill in handwriting keep a man from becoming a forger. But the study of toxicology will enable the physician to save life, and the study of handwriting is a valuable means of preventing the results of wrongful acts. So, while education does not make the voter honest, it enables him to protect himself against the frauds of others, and not only increases his power but inspires him to resist violence. So that, in the aggregate, you Northerners are right in the boast which you make that intelligence makes a people stronger and braver and freer."

"So your remedy is—" began the other.

"Not *my* remedy, but the *only* remedy, is to educate the people until they shall be wise enough to know what they ought to do, and brave enough and strong enough to do it."

"Oh, that is all well enough, if it could be done," said Goodspeed.

"Therefore it is," returned Hesden, "that it *must* be done."

"But *how?*" said the other querulously. "You know that the Constitution gives the control of such matters entirely to the States. The Nation cannot interfere with it. It is the duty of the States to educate their citizens—a clear and imperative duty; but if they will not do it the Nation cannot compel them."

"Yes," said Hesden, "I know. For almost a century you said that about slavery; and you have been trying to hunt a way of escape from your enforced denial of it ever since. But as a matter of fact, when you came to the last ditch and found no bridge across, you simply made one. When it became an unavoidable question whether the Union or slavery should live, you chose the Union. The choice may come between the Union and ignorance; and if it does, I have no fear as to which the people will choose. The doctrine of State Rights is a beautiful thing to expatiate upon, but it has been the root of nearly all the evil the country has suffered. However, I believe that this remedy can at once be applied without serious inconvenience from that source."

"How?" asked the other; "that is what I want to know."

"Understand me," said Le Moyne; "I do not consider the means so important as the end. When the necessity is fully realized the means will be discovered; but I believe that we hold the clue even now in our hands."

"Well, what is it?" was the impatient inquiry.

"A fund of about a million dollars," said Le Moyne, "has already been distributed to free public schools in the South, upon a system which does not seriously interfere with the jealously-guarded rights of those states."

"You mean the Peabody Fund?"[135]

"Yes; I do refer to that act of unparalleled beneficence and wisdom."

"But that was not the act of the Nation."

"Very true; but why should not the Nation distribute a like bounty upon the same system? It is admitted, beyond serious controversy, that the Nation may raise and appropriate funds for such purposes among the different states, provided it be not for the exclusive benefit of any in particular. It is perhaps past controversy that the Government might distribute a fund to the different states *in the proportion of illiteracy.*[136] This, it is true, would give greater amounts to certain states than to others, but only greater in proportion to the evil to be remedied."

"Yes," said the other; "but the experience of the Nation in distributing lands and funds for educational purposes has not been encouraging. The results have hardly been commensurate with the investment."

"That is true," said Hesden, "and this is why I instance the Peabody Fund. That is not given into the hands of the officers of the various states, but when a school is organized and fulfills the requirements laid down for the distribution of that fund, in regard to numbers and average attendance—in other words, is shown to be an efficient institution of learning—then the managers of the fund give to it a sum sufficient to defray a certain proportion of its expenses."

"And you think such a system might be applied to a Government appropriation?"

"Certainly. The amount to which the county, township, or school district would be entitled might be easily ascertained, and upon the organization and maintenance of a school complying with the reasonable requirements of a well-drawn statute in regard to attendance and instruction, such amount might be paid over."

"Yes," was the reply, after a thoughtful pause; "but would not that necessitate a National supervision of State schools?"

"To a certain extent, yes. Yet there would be nothing compulsory about it. It would only be such inspection as would be necessary to determine whether the applicant had entitled himself to share the Nation's bounty. Surely the Nation may condition its own bounty."

"But suppose these states should refuse to submit to such inspection, or accept such appropriation?"

"That is the point, exactly, to which I desire to bring your attention," said Le Moyne. "Ignorance, unless biased by religious bigotry, always clamors for knowledge. You could well count upon the forty-five per cent of ignorant voters insisting upon the reception of that bounty. The number of those that recognize the necessity of instructing the ignorant voter, even in those states, is hourly increasing, and but a brief time would elapse until no party would dare to risk opposition to such a course. I doubt whether any party would venture upon it, even now."

"But are not its results too remote, Mr. Le Moyne, to make such a measure of present interest in the cure of present evils?"

"Not at all," answered Hesden. "By such a measure you bring the purest men of the South into close and intimate relations with the Government. You cut off the sap which nourishes the yet living root of the State Rights dogma. You bring every man to feel as you feel, that there is something greater and grander than his State and section. Besides that, you draw the poison from the sting which rankles deeper than you think. The Southern white man feels, and justly feels, that the burden of educating the colored man ought not to be laid upon the South alone. He says truly, 'The Nation fostered and encouraged slavery; it gave it greater protection and threw greater safeguards around it than any other kind of property; it encouraged my ancestors and myself to invest the proceeds of generations of care and skill and growth in slaves. When the war ended it not only at one stroke dissipated all these accumulations, but it also gave to these men the ballot, and would now drive me, for my own protection, to provide for their education. This is unjust and oppressive. I will not do it, nor consent that it shall be done by my people or by our section alone.' To such a man—and there are many thousands of them—such a measure would come as an act of justice. It would be a grateful balm to his outraged feelings, and would incline him to forget, much more readily than he otherwise would, what he regards to be the injustice of emancipation. It will lead him to consider whether he has not been wrong in supposing that the emancipation and enfranchisement of the blacks proceeded from a feeling of resentment, and was intended as a punishment merely. It will incline him to consider whether the people of the North, the controlling power of the Government at that time, did not act from a better motive than he has given them credit for. But even if this plan should meet with disapproval, instead of approval, from the white voters of the South, it would still be the true and wise policy for the Nation to pursue."

"So you really think," said the Northerner dubiously, "that such a measure would produce good results even in the present generation?"

"Unquestionably," was the reply. "Perhaps the chief incentive to the acts which have disgraced our civilization—which have made the white people of the South almost a unit in opposing by every means, lawful and unlawful, the course of the Government in reconstruction, has been a deep and bitter conviction that hatred, envy, and resentment against them on the part of the North, were the motives which prompted those acts. Such a measure, planned upon a liberal scale, would be a vindication of the manhood of the North; an assertion of its sense of right as well as its determination to develop at the South the same intelligence, the same freedom of thought and action, the same equality of individual right, that have made the North prosperous and free and strong, while the lack of them has made the South poor and ignorant and weak."

"Well, well," said the Congressman seriously, "you may be right. I had never thought of it *quite* in that light before. It is worth thinking about, my friend; it is worth thinking about."

"That it is!" said Le Moyne, joyfully extending his hand. "Think! If you will only *think*—if the free people of the North will only think of this matter, I have no fears but a solution will be found. Mine may not be the right one. That is no matter. As I said, the question of method is entirely subordinate to the result. But let the people think, and they will think rightly. Don't think of it as a politician in the little sense of that word, but in the great one. Don't try to compel the Nation to accept your view or mine; but spur the national thought by every possible means to consider the evil, to demand its cure, and to devise a remedy."

So, day by day, the "irrepressible conflict"[137] is renewed. The Past bequeaths to the Present its wondrous legacy of good and ill. Names are changed, but truths remain. The soil which slavery claimed, baptized with blood becomes the Promised Land of the freedman and poor white. The late master wonders at the mockery of Fate. Ignorance marvels at the power of Knowledge. Love overleaps the barriers of prejudice, and Faith laughs at the Impossible.

"The world goes up and the world goes down,
The sunshine follows the rain;
And yesterday's sneer and yesterday's frown
Can never come over again."[138]

On the trestle-board of the Present, Liberty forever sets before the Future some new query. The Wise-man sweats drops of blood. The Greatheart abides in his strength. The King makes commandment. The Fool laughs.[139]

ANNOTATIONS

1 "Tri-nominate": Thrice-named.

2 "left-handed kinship with the Brutons": A child "by the left hand" is illegitimate; the name Bruton connotes brutishness and brutality.

3 "Junonian Rite": The goddess Juno, wife of Jupiter, king of the Roman gods, presided over marriage; the title comments ironically on slavery's desecration of a sacred rite.

4 "contraband": In May 1861 General Benjamin Butler declared that slaves seeking refuge in Union army camps should be regarded as "contraband of war"—goods confiscated from the enemy for military purposes—hence, that they should not be returned to their masters, as Lincoln's policy had initially decreed, unless those masters were loyal to the Union. Thereafter, fugitive slaves within Union army lines were called "contrabands."

5 "Nunc Pro Tunc": Latin, "now for then," a legal phrase used to denote that an act is performed at one time which ought to have been performed at another; in this case the act is the legal recognition of marriage.

6 "color-blinded": Color-blindness was one of Tourgée's favorite metaphors for the principle that the law and the system of justice should accord equal treatment to all human beings regardless of skin color, status, or other physical or social distinctions (see the introduction, 18, for his use of this metaphor as a Superior Court judge). Here he uses the term "color-blinded" to mean that the law, instead of being "color blind," was blinded by color into treating blacks and whites unequally. For perceptive analyses of the different ways in which Tourgée used the metaphor of color-blindness, see Brook Thomas, ed., *Plessy v. Ferguson: A Brief History with Documents* (Boston: Bedford/St. Martin's, 1997), 176; and Mark Elliott, *Color-Blind Justice: Albion Tourgée and the Quest for Racial Equality from the Civil War to Plessy v. Ferguson* (New York: Oxford University Press, 2006), chaps. 1, 9, 10.

7 "Toga Virilis": The toga was a loose outer garment worn in public by citizens of ancient Rome; at age 15 Roman boys put on the white toga of manhood,

signifying that they were now recognized as men and citizens. Tourgée refers in the second paragraph to "the robe of citizenship."

8 "substitute serfdom for chattelism": Tourgée is summing up the history of the period from 1865 to 1867 known as Presidential Reconstruction. The Provisional Governments were those formed by governors named by President Johnson while the former Confederate states were under military rule. They became state governments after holding elections and outlawing slavery in their constitutions. Tourgée refers to them as "so-called" because the U.S. Congress refused to recognize them after they passed Black Codes that perpetuated slavery under another guise. The Black Codes "denied [the freedman] his oath" by not allowing a black person to testify in court against a white. The system of forcing freedpeople to "hire by the year" prevented them from leaving abusive or exploitive employers, on pain of forfeiting the wages they had already earned and risking arrest. North Carolina's Black Code was less oppressive than those of Mississippi, South Carolina, and Louisiana, which tied the freedpeople to the land by restricting them to farming and domestic service and requiring passes for leaving the plantation.

9 "negro was transformed into a citizen": The Reconstruction Act of 1867 transformed "the negro . . . into a citizen, a voter," while the former Confederate states were under military rule.

10 "Damon and Pythias": Damon and Pythias, Pythagorean philosophers in ancient Syracuse, were famous for their devoted friendship. When one was condemned to death for allegedly plotting against King Dionysius, the other offered to die in his place, which so impressed the king that he let both go free.

11 "Whig representative even": In chap. 46, the narrator describes Hesden's father as a Douglas Democrat rather than a Whig. Both groups were strongly pro-Union and against secession in the late 1850s. Among Tourgée's white southern Unionist allies, the closest analogue to Hesden Le Moyne is state Supreme Court Judge Thomas Settle Jr., whose father was a Whig with free soil leanings.

12 "A Bruised Reed": See Isaiah 42:1, 3: "Behold my servant, whom I uphold; mine elect, in whom my soul delighteth; I have put my spirit upon him: he shall bring forth judgment to the Gentiles. . . . A bruised reed shall he not break . . . ; he shall bring forth judgment unto truth."

13 "Eliab": The name Eliab means "God is father," in keeping with both Eliab's calling as a preacher and his unknown paternity.

14 "bounty-money": During the war black soldiers in many regiments refused pay in protest against the U.S. government's allocation of lower pay to blacks than to whites; the protests finally forced Congress to enact an equal pay law on 15 June 1864, retroactive to 1 January 1864. The bounty was cash paid to a man for volunteering.

15 "troubling of the waters": John 5:2–4 describes the pool of Bethesda in Jerusalem, where an angel periodically "troubled the water," and whoever

first stepped into the troubled water was "made whole of whatsoever disease he had."

16 "On the Way to Jericho": The title evokes both the fall of the city of Jericho to the Israelites (Joshua 6), symbolizing the fall of the Confederacy, and the story of the man who "went down from Jerusalem to Jericho, and fell among thieves, which stripped him of his raiment, and wounded him, and departed, leaving him half dead" and who was finally rescued by the Good Samaritan (Luke 10:30–36).

17 "Sherman's ruthless legions": Civil War General William Tecumseh Sherman (1820–91) cut the Confederacy in half and left a trail of devastation behind as his troops marched through Georgia, South Carolina, and North Carolina. As Tourgée explains in the history of his regiment, *The Story of a Thousand*, Sherman's foraging soldiers, "termed 'bummers,' were a most important part of this campaign, not only as a means of support for the army, but also from the effect they had in disheartening the enemy and preventing the country through which the army passed from furnishing men and supplies to continue the war." Tourgée condemns the policy for sullying the reputation of the Union army and provoking "implacable" hatred of northerners (354–55).

18 "*Lee–surrendered–unconditionally!*": Confederate General Robert E. Lee surrendered to Union General Ulysses S. Grant at Appomattox Court House, Virginia, on 9 April 1865.

19 "His soul is marching on!" This was one of the Union soldiers' most popular marching songs; its lyrics expressed the soldiers' identification with Brown as a liberator fighting against slavery.

20 "greater than the whole": Tourgée is protesting against the doctrine of states' rights, which prevented the federal government from interfering in the internal affairs of the states and thus from implementing federal laws that mandated the equal protection of all American citizens. He believed that the defeat of the Confederacy, which had justified secession on the grounds of states' rights, should have discredited this doctrine and established the supremacy of federal over state sovereignty.

21 "Freedmen's Savings Bank": The Freedman's Savings and Trust Company, chartered in 1865, sought to inculcate habits of thrift in the freedpeople by encouraging them to deposit their savings. Thousands of freedpeople did so and lost everything they had invested when the company went bankrupt in the Panic of 1873, as a result of the directors' irresponsible financial speculation.

22 "Southern Balak": Balak, king of Moab, tried to induce the soothsayer's son Balaam to curse the people of Israel, who were about to invade Moab. Instead, Balaam heeded the warning of the angel of the Lord and blessed Israel (Numbers 22:2–24:25). Tourgée's point is that the "Northern Balaam" not only fails to heed the angel but curses his own progeny rather than a foreign invader.

23 "Jeffreys": George Jeffreys (1648–89) was a British judge notorious for his harsh sentences of the king's enemies in several dubious and vindictive trials.

24 "prepare the necessary papers": The owner from whom Desmit had bought the property held title to it only during his lifetime, after which the property was supposed to go to heirs in Indiana. Desmit's failure to pay off the Indiana heirs meant that they still had the title to the land and could claim it after the death of the owner from whom he bought it. Hence, in selling to Nimbus without clearing the title, Desmit is committing a deliberate fraud.

25 "apples of Sodom": Apples of Sodom looked beautiful on the outside but inside were nothing but ashes.

26 "Sheridan": Civil War General Philip Henry Sheridan (1831–88) is best known for his conquest of the Shenandoah Valley, which he was instructed to reduce to a "barren waste." Sheridan coordinated the assault that broke the long siege of Petersburg and led to the conquest of Richmond in the last week of the war.

27 "those last battles": Salisbury National Cemetery, in Salisbury, North Carolina. Originating as a burial site for Union prisoners of war who died at Salisbury Confederate Prison, it was officially named a national cemetery after the Civil War. In chapter 51 Mollie visits her brother's grave there.

28 "Christian magnanimity": Freedmen's Aid Societies began proliferating in the North well before the end of the war. Two main umbrella organizations, the secular American Freedmen's Union Commission (AFUC) and the evangelical American Missionary Association (AMA) predominated, but denominational organizations were also active. The Freedmen's Bureau coordinated and supervised freedmen's education until June 1872, when it ceased operations, its funding having already been drastically reduced by 1869. Most of the emphasis fell on teaching basic literacy, but institutions of higher learning were also founded to train teachers and professionals. Among those still extant are Fisk, Howard, Dillard, Clark Atlanta, and Hampton Universities. Historians consider education to have been the most successful aspect of the Reconstruction program.

29 "League": White supremacists considered the Union League a dangerous subversive organization and accused its members of criminal activities; historians have found no evidence to support these charges.

30 "form of sound words": In 2 Timothy 1:13, St. Paul exhorts believers: "Hold fast the form of sound words, which thou hast heard of me. . . ." The phrase can be translated in this context as "gospel truth."

31 "a shriek from amid the crowd": As detailed in the introduction (39–40), this incident is based on the massacre of black participants in an election rally in Camilla, Georgia, in September 1868.

32 "with an ingenuous blush": Women were not allowed to vote until ratification of the Nineteenth Amendment in 1920, although members of the women's rights movement were vigorously agitating for suffrage during the Reconstruction era. Tourgée supported woman suffrage.

33 "intelligence": Nineteenth-century writers often used the word "intelligence" to mean "knowledge" or "education," rather than "innate intellect."

34 " 'Tears, idle tears, I know not what they mean!' ": From "The Princess" (1847) by the British poet laureate Alfred, Lord Tennyson (1809–92). Tourgée is commenting on the problem of imposing an educational curriculum that most ex-slaves found culturally alien. The abolitionist Lydia Maria Child had tried to address this problem by publishing a school reader for ex-slaves made up of selections by or about people of color, *The Freedmen's Book* (1865).

35 "*leges non scriptæ*": Unwritten laws or customs.

36 "Horeb": On Mt. Horeb Moses uses his rod to smite a rock and thus bring water out of it (Exodus 17:5–6). This occurs shortly after the crossing of the Red Sea, described in Exodus 14:16–30. Eliab may be conflating Mt. Horeb with Mt. Pisgah, from which Moses views the Promised Land just before his death (Deuteronomy 34:1–4).

37 "substantial premises": In the Dred Scott decision of 1857 the Supreme Court held that neither the Declaration of Independence nor the Constitution acknowledged African slaves or their descendants as "a part of the people, nor intended to be included" in the statement "all men are created equal." The phrase "we the people of the United States" comes from the Preamble to the Constitution, not the Declaration of Independence, but Tourgée may have confused the two because the Dred Scott decision quotes from both documents.

38 "free blacks were disfranchised": During the era of the Revolution, free blacks enjoyed the right to vote except in Virginia, South Carolina, and Georgia. Beginning in 1799, many states that had previously allowed blacks to vote disfranchised them. By 1860 only five New England states allowed blacks to vote on the same basis as whites; New York raised property qualifications for black voters at the same time that it eliminated them for white voters.

39 "The Impending Crisis": In *The Impending Crisis of the South: How to Meet It* (1857), Hinton Rowan Helper (1829–1909) indicted slavery from the perspective of non-slaveholding whites. His book made a strong impression on both Tourgée and Emma when it appeared. In *Nojoque* ("No Joke" [1867]) he argued that God had destined the dark races for extermination, and he advocated accelerating the process by denying African Americans all rights and separating them completely from whites.

40 "rhodomontades": Rants.

41 "members of the Legislature": This may be the election of 1870, in which Conservatives recaptured control of the legislature by terrorizing Republican voters.

42 "adoption of the Constitution": North Carolina's new state constitution was ratified by the voters in the election of April 1868; for details, see the introduction (16–18).

43 "one of the candidates for the Legislature was a colored man": This may be Wilson Carey of Caswell County, which had a black population of more than 50 percent and was the site of greatest Klan violence during the 1870 electoral campaign; little is known about Carey, except that his electoral victory was

overthrown by the Conservative legislature. See Elizabeth Balanoff, "Negro Legislators in the North Carolina General Assembly, July, 1868–February, 1872," *North Carolina Historical Review* 49 (Jan. 1972): 22–55.

44 "Democritus": Democritus (b. ca. 460 BCE) was known as the "laughing philosopher" because he was constantly laughing at human follies.

45 "nuffin' atterwards": Berry is describing the system of sharecropping and debt peonage that replaced slavery throughout the South. Rather than work for wages under white supervision, landless freedpeople preferred to rent plots of land from the planters, who advanced them seed and supplies in return for a portion of the crop ranging from one third to two thirds. Without the protection of the Freedmen's Bureau, which discontinued its supervision of work relations between employers and freedpeople in North Carolina by the end of 1868 and in the rest of the South not long afterward, illiterate sharecroppers fell prey to fraud by planters who charged exorbitant rates for supplies, docked them for days lost through illness, and withheld more than their share of the harvest. Through such tactics, sharecroppers ended up indebted to the planters from year to year, obliging them to remain on the land—a condition known as debt peonage (which still prevails in many developing countries).

46 "my plantation no mo'": As early as 11 April 1868, the North Carolina *Daily Standard* reported that Conservative politicians had "advised land-owners to discharge every colored man who votes the Republican ticket" and that "colored families have already been turned off on account of their opinions." Such tactics intensified after the Freedmen's Bureau withdrew and the Conservatives won control of the state legislature.

47 "'de little tax, etc.'" Tourgée first published this song, which he said was "being sung by the colored men of this vicinity with much gusto," in the *National Anti-Slavery Standard* of 9 November 1867, under the title "Poll Tax. A Song of North Carolina Freedmen." Here a few words have been altered, more words have been rendered in dialect, and the last stanza has been cut:

Now haint we got a'most enuff
  Ob taxin on de polls,
When poor man hab to scrabble hard
  To keep alive der souls?
Den let de poor man use his vote
  An use it for himself,
And lay de little poll-tax up
  Upon de corner shelf.

In a letter to the North Carolina *Daily Standard* of 19 July 1870, AWTP (Albion W. Tourgée Papers) #1321, Tourgée recalls that it was later "published in slip [leaflet] form and circulated and sung in [Guilford] county." He also recalls that he had used his "utmost exertions" to abolish the poll tax during the 1868 constitutional convention, but "to its lasting disgrace," the convention had "refused to discard" it. Tourgée's unsuccessful battle against the poll tax is recorded in the North Carolina *Daily Standard* of 5 March 1868.

48 "'Johnsonian' plan": President Andrew Johnson's plan of Reconstruction, announced in two proclamations he issued on 29 May 1865, involved conferring amnesty and pardon on all who pledged loyalty to the Union and support for emancipation; appointing provisional governors of the former Confederate states and instructing them to call conventions to write slavery out of the state constitutions; and readmitting these states to the Union as soon as they ratified the Thirteenth Amendment and repudiated the Confederate debt. It left the states' racial and class hierarchies intact and kept blacks outside the political system. See also n. 8.

49 "'that which he hath'": Matthew 25:29: "For unto every one that hath shall be given, and he shall have abundance: but from him that hath not shall be taken away even that which he hath."

50 "That should suffice": Cf. the Wise Man Tourgée quotes in *A Fool's Errand*: "The government has done all it can be expected to do,—all it had power to do, in fact. It has given the colored man the ballot, armed him with the weapon of the freeman, and now he must show himself worthy to use it."

51 "rights of his race": By the 1890s Tourgée recognized that African Americans were as likely to be lynched for achieving individual prosperity as for "clamoring about the collective rights of [their] race." In a "Bystander" column of 25 June 1892, he wrote that the purpose of terrorist attacks on African Americans was "to drive [the black man] out of business, compel him to accept such wages as the 'superior race' may choose to give, and cease to assert in any way his own manhood."

52 "Chillon": The famous poem by Lord Byron (1788–1824), "The Prisoner of Chillon" (1816), made the dungeon of this thirteenth-century castle on an islet of Lake Geneva in Switzerland a powerful symbol of solitary confinement.

53 "a league with Hell": The abolitionist William Lloyd Garrison denounced the Constitution as a "covenant with death and an agreement with hell" because it protected slavery. Abolitionists were frequently misquoted as having called it a "league with hell." The other quotations remain unidentified.

54 "lord and master also": Tourgée is again attacking the doctrine of states' rights, which subordinates the power of the federal government to that of the states.

55 "superstitious negro": Democratic Party newspapers in the North as well as the South spread the myth that superstitious blacks were taken in by the claim of masked nightriders to be ghosts of Confederate soldiers; to prove their claim, nightriders would pretend to drink entire buckets full of water, saying they had not had a drop since dying in battle. This myth served both to trivialize Klan terrorism and to reinforce the white supremacist belief in black inferiority. The testimony of surviving black Klan victims indicates that few, if any, of them mistook the nightriders for ghosts.

56 "Brother Jonathan": A fictional character created during the era of the American Revolution to represent the archetypal American, Brother Jonathan ap-

pears frequently as an embodiment of the Union in Thomas Nast's Civil War cartoons for *Harper's Weekly*.

57 "pluck up drowned honor by the locks": From Shakespeare's *Henry IV, Part 1*, I.iii. 202.

58 "*amour propre*": Self-esteem.

59 " 'Grand Wizard of the Empire' ": The Klan was known as the Invisible Empire. The Grand Wizard heading it was Civil War General Nathan Bedford Forrest (also responsible for the cold-blooded massacre of African American troops at Fort Pillow in 1864).

60 "Elysian": Heavenly; Elysium was the heaven of ancient Greek mythology.

61 "its genuineness": Tourgée is referring ironically to the antebellum slave laws prohibiting blacks from holding religious services unless a white observer was present.

62 "cachinnation": Laughter.

63 " 'not danced' ": Matt. 11:16–17: "But whereunto shall I liken this generation? It is like unto children sitting in the markets, and calling unto their fellows, And saying, We have piped unto you and ye have not danced. . . ."

64 "San Domingo": Slaves in the French colony of St. Domingue, usually referred to by Americans as San Domingo, revolted in 1791 and founded the Republic of Haiti in 1804. Among white supremacists San Domingo conjured up the specter of black insurrection.

65 "Ghouls": Klan chapters, called dens, were each headed by a Grand Cyclops, assisted by two Night-Hawks. Rank-and-file Klan members were called Ghouls.

66 "Johnston's surrender and the Grand Review at Washington": Confederate General Joseph E. Johnston (1807–91) surrendered to Union General William Tecumseh Sherman on 26 April 1865. On 23–24 May, 200,000 Union troops marched down Pennsylvania Avenue in Washington in a grand review.

67 "black Ajax": The Greek warrior Ajax appears in Homer's *Iliad*, which describes him as brave, skillful, and colossal in height and build; the only warrior who does not receive help from the gods in his battles, he personifies hard work and perseverance—qualities that Nimbus also exemplifies.

68 "*capias*": Warrant for arrest.

69 "after he's hired 'em": The bill "to prevent enticing servants from fulfilling their contracts, or harboring" those who left their employers was a provision of the Black Code passed by the North Carolina General Assembly in 1866. Tourgée implies here that these laws were revived as soon as planters were no longer subject to oversight by the Freedmen's Bureau.

70 "high limb": Lynching; Tourgée may be conjuring up the lynching of Wyatt Outlaw on a tree limb pointing to the Alamance County courthouse.

71 "Ku Klux mout *lift*": Lynch by hanging.

72 "gibbous": Seen with more than half but not all of the apparent disk illuminated.

73 " 'my shield' ": Psalm 33:20: "Our soul waiteth for the Lord: he is our help and

our shield." Eliab also echoes Jesus' words on the cross: "Father, forgive them; for they know not what they do" (Luke 23:34).

74 "crashed the axe": The case on which Tourgée based this incident was extensively covered in the North Carolina *Daily Standard* of March-April 1869 and was also included in the *Senate Report* of 10 March 1871. See the introduction (42) for further details.

75 "epidemic of violence": The case of Elias Hill can be found in the 1872 *Report of the Joint Select Committee Appointed to Inquire into the Condition of Affairs in the Late Insurrectionary States*, 1:44–47, 1406–8. See the introduction (41–42) for further details.

76 "stertorous": Characterized by a gasping sound.

77 "'The Rose above the Mould'": From "Stanzas" by Thomas Hood (1799–1845). The line "I smell the rose above the mould" refers to a near death, followed by a convalescence.

78 "'Be a hero in the strife!'": From "A Psalm of Life" (1838) by Henry Wadsworth Longfellow (1807–82).

79 "*prima facie*": Self-evidently.

80 "sleeping Samson": In Judges 16:7–8, Samson's Philistine mistress Delilah asks him to tell her the secret of his strength. He at first lies, claiming that he will lose his strength if bound by "seven green withes" (slender, flexible branches), but when she tries that while he is sleeping, he easily snaps them on waking.

81 "*ultima thule*": Literally beyond the borders of the known world; in this context the worst thing imaginable. The 1791 uprising of the slaves of San Domingo led to the founding of the Republic of Haiti in 1804.

82 "Q.E.D.": Abbreviation for *quod erat demonstrandum*, "which was to be demonstrated."

83 "Douglas Democrat": Stephen A. Douglas (1813–61), Democratic senator from Illinois and a staunch Unionist, authored the Kansas-Nebraska Act (1854), which repealed the prohibition against introducing slavery into territories north of the 36 degree 30 minute latitude and allowed settlers in all remaining territories to vote on whether to enter the Union as slave or free states. The compromise satisfied neither Northerners nor Southerners, and the Democratic Party later split into northern and southern wings. As the northern Democrats' presidential candidate in the 1860 election, Douglas carried only the border state of Missouri, despite winning a significant minority of the popular vote in all parts of the country. In chap. 8, Sheriff Gleason describes Hesden's father as a Whig Unionist rather than a Douglas Democrat (124). Tourgée's white Unionist ally Thomas Settle Jr., on whom Hesden is partially modeled, was a Douglas Democrat and campaigned enthusiastically for Douglas, his cousin by marriage, in the 1860 election. Settle's father was a Whig Unionist.

84 "irrepressible conflict": The title of a famous speech given in 1858 by New York Senator William H. Seward (1801–72), predicting that the systems of slavery

and "free labor" would eventually collide, until the United States became "either entirely a slaveholding nation, or entirely a free-labor nation."

85 "'bantling—I like to have said *that monster*'": Tourgée is probably quoting from memory; in a letter of 10 March 1787 to John Jay, Washington refers to "the bantling—I had like to have said monster—sovereignty, which have taken such fast hold of the States." A bantling is a very young child.

86 "Chinaman who has lost his sacred queue by the hand of the Christian spoiler": Chinese men shaved their foreheads and wore the rest of their hair in a long braided queue or pigtail. Originally imposed by the Manchus who conquered China in the seventeenth century, this hairstyle had become a badge of Chinese identity by the nineteenth century, and attempts by Western missionaries to cut off the queue met with strong resistance.

87 cursive letters after "unintelligible scrawl": Tourgée's pocket calendar for 1872, item #1784 in the Albion W. Tourgée papers, transcribes this signature, which he found on a deed executed in 1804, the first recorded in Caswell County.

88 "'Red Jim'": Tourgée's pocket calendar for 1872 notes a similar family dispute in Caswell county between cousins named "'Red' George" and "'Black' George." This notation occurs just above the signature of Richards. The implication of the story Hesden pieces together from his mother's memories and his own investigation is that James Richards, Hesden's grandfather, killed his brother John Richards, Hesden's great uncle, and threw the body into the river, after John confronted James for having seized for himself the property rightfully belonging to his cousin, "Red Jim." James then concealed the will in which "Red Jim" had bequeathed the property to his own wife and daughter.

89 "their votes": The votes of African Americans in the former Confederate states were as decisive in ratifying the Fourteenth and Fifteenth Amendments as the Civil War service of African Americans was in winning the Union's victory, Tourgée implies. He puts military service and voting on the same level because African Americans had to brave threats of violence and economic reprisal to vote.

90 "'Hoosier'": Knickerbocker, a New Yorker; Pennamite, a Pennsylvanian; Buckeye, a native or resident of Ohio; Hoosier, a native or resident of Indiana.

91 "to the eastward": See the descriptions of Desmit's Knapp-of-Reeds plantation in chap. 2 and of the Red Wing property in chap. 11.

92 "Lord Granville": John Carteret, Earl of Granville (1696–1763), one of the eight Lords Proprietors of North Carolina, kept his landholdings after the other seven ceded theirs to the Crown. As a Loyalist, Carteret's son Robert forfeited his property rights to the state of North Carolina after the Revolution.

93 "estopped": Barred by estoppel, a doctrine that protects a party who would suffer detriment if she or he had relied on an expectation induced by another party.

94 "Scythian bowmen": A phalanx was a body of heavily armed infantry in ancient Greece formed in close, deep ranks; Scythians were an ancient nomadic people from the central Asian steppes.

95 "'*tale of bricks*'": Exodus 5:18. After Moses conveys God's message to Pharaoh, "Let my people go," Pharaoh orders his taskmasters to have the enslaved Israelites produce the same quantity of bricks without straw as they used to produce with straw.

96 "'thine own people'": Exodus 5:16.

97 "ravished": Seized and taken away by violence.

98 "universal as man": This quotation was attributed to the *Richmond Inquirer* by the British abolitionist Newman Hall and to the *Richmond Examiner* by the British abolitionist John Bright in speeches advocating that Britain support the Union. I have not located the original. Tourgée has changed "slave society" to "class society."

99 "even at that price": The "would-be nation" is the Confederacy, whose two main leaders were President Jefferson Davis and Vice President Alexander H. Stephens. The quotation remains unidentified.

100 "mass of dead humanity": Salisbury Confederate Prison; the figure Tourgée cites on deaths in prison comes from an 1871 U.S. government report, but a modern study puts the figure at five thousand.

101 "deputy sheriff under the new *régime*": According to the testimony cited in the 10 March 1871 *Senate Report* on North Carolina, this Klansman, named Joseph R. Steele, "fled the country as soon as he got well enough" and settled in Texas (33, 43).

102 "leading citizens of the county": This was the charge leveled at Tourgée, who did in fact go to Washington for that purpose.

103 "Rahab": Joshua 2:1–15 tells of how the harlot Rahab hides the Israelite spies from the officers of the king of Jericho.

104 "'eyes of Europe on his tail'": From "Ode to Rae Wilson, Esquire" by Thomas Hood (1799–1845):

> To picture that cold pride so harsh and hard,
> Fancy a peacock in a poultry yard,
> Behold him in conceited circles sail,
> Strutting and dancing, and now planted stiff,
> In all his pomp of pageantry, as if
> He felt "the eyes of Europe" on his tail!

105 "remain for a time unknown": After passage of the 1871 Ku Klux Klan Act, as Tourgée and other judges collected incriminating evidence from participants in Klan atrocities, many Klan members fled the country or went into hiding.

106 "disherison": Disinheritance.

107 "man of Uz": Job, whose friends try to comfort him for his undeserved tribulations by insisting that he must have done something to deserve God's punishment.

108 "No suspicion seems ever to have fallen on 'Black Jim'": Instead of fulfilling his duty as executor of his cousin's estate, "Black Jim" seized the property of "Red Jim" for himself, hid the will, and told the widow he had found neither money nor documents among her dead husband's effects. See note 88.

109 "statute was not barred": In accordance with the basic legal principle that no rights or benefits can ever be passed on by fraud, the defrauded heir would always take precedence over the heir of whoever committed the fraud. In this case, because the will was proved valid and an uninterrupted line of legitimate heirs existed, rights of inheritance that would arise by statute in the absence of a valid will or legitimate heirs are "barred."

110 "quit-claim": A legal document by which a person "quits" or renounces any claim she or he may have had to a property.

111 "deed in fee": Giving absolute title to the land, free of any other claims against the title, which one can sell or pass to another by will or inheritance.

112 "title will thereafter be estopped": The title will be protected against claims by others.

113 "all its characteristic elements": In *Democracy in America* (1835), the French traveler and social theorist Alexis de Tocqueville (1805–59) described the New England township system, which originated before 1650, as the fountainhead of American democracy: "The independence of the township was the nucleus round which the local interests, passions, rights, and duties collected and clung. It gave scope to the activity of a real political life, thoroughly democratic and republican. . . . The towns named their own magistrates of every kind, assessed themselves, and levied their own taxes. . . . [T]he affairs of the community were discussed, as at Athens, in the marketplace, by a general assembly of the citizens" (vol. 1, chap. 2). The North Carolina constitutional convention of 1875 abolished the township system introduced in the 1868 Constitution.

114 "miniature boroughs": Tourgée was responsible for introducing these provisions into the new constitution North Carolina ratified in April 1868; for details, see the introduction (17).

115 "Cadmean mystery": Cadmus, the legendary founder of Thebes, is said to have introduced into Greece the letters of the alphabet, which had been invented by the Phoenicians; hence, the Cadmean mystery is literacy.

116 "law-given rights": Hesden's speech closely parallels that of Tourgée's friend Thomas Settle Jr., in his 1876 campaign for the governorship of North Carolina. Settle argued that "forty millions of the great Anglo-Saxon race should . . . be willing to give to four millions of poor, ignorant, slave-ridden Africans an equal and fair race in the contest of life," and he appealed to whites to respect the Constitutional amendments and give African Americans "protection before the law, and the exercise of the ballot as citizens" (qtd. in Crow, "Thomas Settle Jr.," 721, cited in introduction, n. 121).

117 "threat, denunciation, and abuse": Tourgée's biographers, especially Olsen, have quoted many similar examples of vituperation and slander directed at him in the white supremacist press.

118 "red shirts": White supremacist supporters of former Confederate General Wade Hampton wore red shirts in the 1876 South Carolina gubernatorial election; the Red Shirts perpetrated numerous atrocities in that election, besides systematically disrupting Republican gatherings.

119 "celebrated Confederate general": Confederate General James Longstreet of Georgia (1821–1904) won many battles but was attacked as a traitor to the South after the war because he became a Republican and publicly advocated accepting black suffrage and submitting to federal authority.

120 "fo' years atter I left h'yer": Nimbus's description of the event corresponds closely to details of the April 1873 Colfax massacre in Louisiana, "the bloodiest single instance of racial carnage in the Reconstruction era" (Foner, *Reconstruction*, 437).

121 "twenty-five cents a day": All of the 1865–66 Black Codes had had similar provisions; once back in power, white supremacists revived these laws, but framed them in race-neutral language to conform to the Fourteenth Amendment.

122 "that wonderful young city of seventy-seven hills which faces toward free Kansas": Kansas City, Missouri; in the mid-1850s, "Bleeding Kansas" became the terrain of a civil war between antislavery and proslavery settlers. After the defeat of an attempt by a pro-southern convention to force a proslavery constitution on the territory without submitting it to a popular vote, Kansas was finally admitted into the Union as a free state on the eve of the Civil War.

123 "exodus they had undertaken": In 1879–80, 20,000 to 40,000 African Americans left the Deep South for Kansas in what became known as the Exodus. The mass migration of "Exodusters" received extensive coverage in the newspapers, and a Senate investigating committee held hearings on it in 1880. Blacks would purchase more than twenty thousand acres in Kansas and form a number of self-governing all-black communities.

124 "'Jes tell 'em I'se a-comin' too'": Verses from the slave spiritual "Wade in the Water": "If you get there before I do / God's gonna trouble the water / Tell all of my friends I'm coming too / God's gonna trouble the water."

125 "Lan'lo'd an' Tenant Act": "North Carolina's notorious Landlord and Tenant Act of 1877 placed the entire crop in the planter's hands until rent had been paid and allowed him full power to decide when a tenant's obligation had been fulfilled" (Foner, *Reconstruction*, 594).

126 "same ez ef he'd done stole it": In testimony before the Senate Committee on the Agricultural Labor Force of the South (1880), James T. Rapier cited a similar law among the oppressive conditions that were prompting African Americans to emigrate from his home state of Alabama: "Any person who shall buy, sell, receive, barter, or dispose of any cotton, corn, wheat, oats, pease, or potatoes after the hour of sunset and before the hour of sunrise of the next succeeding day . . . shall be guilty of a misdemeanor, and, on conviction, shall be fined not less than ten nor more [than] five hundred dollars, and may also be imprisoned in the county jail, or put to hard labor for the county, for not more than twelve months." The purpose of the law, Rapier explained, was to force the sharecropper or tenant to sell to the landlord, rather than seek the best price for his product.

127 "jest all times o' day an' night": The Alabama law cited in note 126 expressly exempted plantation owners selling to their laborers.

128 "as much slave territory as the South was before the war": See n. 113.

129 "superior intelligence and prosperity of the North." See n. 113 for the passage to which Tourgée refers.

130 "Horace Greeley": Horace Greeley (1811–72), influential editor of the New York *Tribune* and a founder of the Republican party. Diligent search through Greeley's postwar editorials has not turned up this proposal.

131 "old system": North Carolina's 1875 constitutional convention eliminated the township system introduced in the 1868 constitution.

132 "philosopher of Chappaqua": Horace Greeley, who arrived in Chappaqua, New York, in 1853, was known as the "philosopher of Chappaqua." As editor of the New York *Tribune*, Greeley promoted the Fourierite socialist movement in the 1840s, which sought to solve the problems of poverty and inequality by founding utopian communities. Later Greeley campaigned for land reform and for a homestead bill that would provide free land to settlers in the West.

133 "With spelling-books!": At the end of *A Fool's Errand* Tourgée had urged: "Make the spelling-book the scepter of national power" (346).

134 "unable to read or write": Tourgée develops this theme at length in *An Appeal to Caesar* (1884).

135 "Peabody Fund": Established in 1867, the Peabody Fund provided money for school construction, teacher salaries, and scholarships for the newly emancipated slaves. Tourgée admired the Peabody Fund's fostering of self-help through challenge grants to local communities.

136 "*proportion of illiteracy*": Tourgée devised this criterion to prevent southern states from directing the bulk of funds toward white schools; because the proportion of illiteracy was greater among African Americans than among whites, African American schools would receive more funding under his plan, which would not challenge school segregation but would counteract its worst effects. When in 1890 Tourgée's efforts to win passage of an education bill incorporating this provision failed, he worked to defeat the alternative bill proposed by Senator Henry W. Blair of New Hampshire, which would have allowed the states to control disbursement of federal funds. This uncompromising stand ironically put him on the same side as the white Southerners and northern Mugwumps who opposed federal aid to education; it also alienated many African Americans, who preferred half a loaf to none at all.

137 "irrepressible conflict": See n. 84 for the famous speech given by Senator William H. Seward.

138 "'Can never come over again'": From "Dolcino to Margaret" (1851) by Charles Kingsley (1819–74).

139 "In Hoc Signo Vinces" (motto ending *Bricks Without Straw*): Latin, "In this sign thou shalt conquer," the motto that the Roman Emperor Constantine was said to adopt after his vision of a cross in the sky just before a decisive battle.

INDEX

ALBION W. TOURGÉE's other important books include *Toinette. A Novel* (1874), first published under the pseudonym Henry Churton, then reissued under Tourgée's name without the last four chapters and retitled *A Royal Gentleman* (1881); *A Fool's Errand. By One of the Fools* (1879), first published anonymously; *The Invisible Empire* (1880), published as an appendix to the second edition of *A Fool's Errand*, under Tourgée's name; *An Appeal to Caesar* (1884); *The Veteran and His Pipe* (1886); *Letters to a King* (1888); *Pactolus Prime* (1890); and *Murvale Eastman, Christian Socialist* (1890).

CAROLYN L. KARCHER is a professor emerita of English, American Studies, and Women's Studies at Temple University. She is the author of *The First Woman in the Republic: A Cultural Biography of Lydia Maria Child* (1994); *Shadow over the Promised Land: Slavery, Race, and Violence in Melville's America* (1980). Her edited works include *Hope Leslie; or, Early Times in Massachusetts* by Catharine Maria Sedgwick (1998); *A Lydia Maria Child Reader* (1997); *An Appeal in Favor of That Class of Americans Called Africans* by Lydia Maria Child (1996); *Hobomok and Other Writings on Indians* by Lydia Maria Child (1986).

Library of Congress Cataloging-in-Publication Data

Tourgée, Albion Winegar, 1838–1905.
Bricks without straw : a novel / Albion W. Tourgée;
edited with a new introduction by Carolyn L. Karcher.
p. cm.
Includes bibliographical references and index.
ISBN 978-0-8223-4395-0 (cloth : alk. paper)
ISBN 978-0-8223-4413-1 (pbk. : alk. paper)
1 Reconstruction (U.S. history, 1865–1877)—Fiction.
2 Freedmen—Southern States—Fiction.
3 African Americans—Southern States—Fiction.
4 Southern States—Fiction.
I Karcher, Carolyn L.
II Title.
PS3087B75 2009
813′.4—dc22 2009001663